"A FASCINATING PORTRAYAL OF THE HISTORY OF OUR PEOPLE . . . A STORY OF SUFFERING AND HOPE, LONGING AND WANDERING, STRUGGLE AND ACHIEVEMENT."

—*Shimon Peres, former Prime Minister of Israel*

THE STUNNING BEST SELLER THAT HAS BEEN COMPARED TO *ROOTS, WAR AND PEACE,* AND THE WORKS OF JAMES MICHENER . . . BUT IS SO MUCH MORE. . . .

The Book of
Abraham

MAREK HALTER

"BREATHTAKINGLY BIBLICAL. . . . Only an imagination as learned and as indomitable as Mr. Halter's could have even conceived *The Book of Abraham.*"

—*The New York Times Book Review*

"A MAJESTIC HISTORICAL EPIC."

—*The Atlanta Journal and Constitution*

"A GREAT BOOK."   —*François Mitterand, President of France*

"WHAT A BOOK!"   —*Time*

"A MARVELOUS AND REFLECTIVE SAGA OF THE ENTIRE JEWISH PEOPLE AS TOLD THROUGH THE LIVES OF ONE FAMILY."

—*UPI*

"THERE IS . . . AN ELEMENT OF PASSION TO THIS BOOK, A STRONG MORAL DIMENSION THAT LIFTS IT ABOVE THE USUAL QUICK-READ ENCYCLOPEDIC HISTORICAL NOVEL. . . . It is the tenacity and grandeur of memory that this book is all about . . . a memory book about the principles that a people has lived for and, all too often, been forced to die for. It is a fascinating book by an admirable man and will amply reward readers who seek in a novel the worthy elements of moral passion, commitment, a good story, and a principled way of engaging the world."

—Chaim Potok, *The Wall Street Journal*

"AN EPIC OF PAIN AND SUFFERING—AND THAT MOST RARE AND PRECIOUS COMMODITY, HOPE."

—*The Grand Rapids Press*

"A MOVING ACCOUNT."

—*Library Journal*

The Book of
Abraham

MAREK HALTER

Translated by Lowell Bair

A DELL BOOK

Published by
Dell Publishing Co., Inc.
1 Dag Hammarskjold Plaza
New York, New York 10017

IN HONOR OF MY PARENTS:

Perl Halter, my mother, a Yiddish poet; Salomon Halter, my father, a printer, son of a printer, grandson of a printer, and so on for generations,

for having kept Abraham's memory alive in me

Originally published in France under the title *La Mémoire d'Abraham.*

Dell ® TM 681510, Dell Publishing Co., Inc.

ISBN: 0-440-10841-1

Reprinted by arrangement with Henry Holt and Company

Printed in the United States of America

September 1987

10 9 8 7 6 5 4 3 2 1

WFH

Contents

Part One

Part One

1

JERUSALEM

The Paths of Exile

AS USUAL, Abraham the scribe woke up all at once and lay still on his bed with his eyes wide open, waiting for daylight. In Jerusalem, dawn was a promise that filled the heart. Each morning Abraham vaguely looked to it for a sign that the things of heaven and earth were in order.

It always began with a powerful stirring in the night that hung over the wilderness east of the city. The stars suddenly dimmed, and then everything happened rapidly. Light rose like an incoming tide, wave after wave, laying down deposits of delicate colors and the glitter of quartz, setting ablaze the ocher of the ramparts, the silvery blue of olive trees, the white of terraces. Donkeys brayed, roosters crowed, and flies gathered in the shadows of houses, while in the courtyard of the Temple twenty Levites opened the Nicanor Gate, turning its two heavy bronze sections on their enormous hinges until they struck the wall with a booming sound that reverberated through the city a long time. Only then did Abraham the scribe get up, happy as if he had just prayed.

But on this day, the ninth of the month of Av in the year 3830 (August 31, A.D. 70) after the creation of the world by the Almighty, blessed be He, Abraham the scribe would not hear the opening of the Nicanor Gate: after three months of siege, Roman

11

legions had taken the Antonia, the fortress that commanded access to the Temple from the north. Nor would he hear the roosters and donkeys, because they had long since been eaten by the starving population of the besieged city.

Abraham did not move. As long as he had not yet plunged back into the stream of life, he could still believe that hunger, fear, and war were parts of a lingering dream, like those yellow dogs that lurked at the edges of villages in the morning and then retreated into the wilderness as soon as the day's activities began.

But dawn came, and the usual trumpet calls were sounded in the Roman camp. Soon the great catapults would resume their assault on the ramparts, the legionaries would hurl their iron-headed battering rams against the gates, there would be the shouting of soldiers, the clang of metal. . . . How much longer could the few remaining able-bodied Jews hold out against the best legions of the empire? Would the Romans take the city today?

Abraham's wife Judith lay beside him. When he heard a change in the rhythm of her light breathing, he cleared away what remained of the feelings that the night had left in his heart.

"Judith," he said, "we'll leave Jerusalem today, if it's not already too late."

"May God help us!" she replied.

"Amen!"

He got up, feeling weak from hunger, and pushed back the curtain that divided the room in two. His sons Elijah and Gamaliel were asleep; he thanked God, blessed be His name, for giving children that armor of innocence.

He went out into the little courtyard. The glare of the morning sunlight made him squint his eyes when he looked toward the Temple; the sharp points of pure gold on its roof seemed to pierce the sky. Abraham was a tall young man with dark skin and a thick beard. Like his father and grandfather before him, he was a Temple scribe.

After making sure he was alone, he bent down and pulled a loose stone out of the wall. This was where fear of bandits or people driven to theft by starvation had made him hide his treasure: a cloth bag that still contained a few handfuls of barley. He took it and went to give it to Judith. The children were still asleep.

He washed his hands over the stone slab in the window recess, put on his prayer shawl, strapped his phylacteries to his left arm and his forehead, and slowly recited the *shaharith,* the morning prayer: "My God, the soul You have placed in me is pure. You created it, You formed it, You breathed it into me, You preserve it within me. It is You who will take it from me, and restore it to me one day. . . . Blessed be You, O Lord, who restores souls to corpses. . . ."

Abraham was beseeching God not to forsake His city again, the ancient city of prophets and kings, when his spiritual concentration was broken by shouts.

"The Temple is burning! Abraham! The Temple is burning!"

It was his neighbors Samuel and Jonah, the potters. They stopped in the doorway, overwhelmed with despair. Abraham quickly took off his phylacteries.

Judith rushed toward him.

"Don't go there!" she said.

"But Judith, it's the Temple!" He saw her distraught face. "Don't be afraid. By the Almighty, don't be afraid! Keep the children in the house."

The three men went outside. Across the street they saw old Joseph of Galilee, his head covered with ashes, vigorously rocking backward and forward as he prayed on his terrace. He stopped abruptly.

"Fire, flames! Divine punishment!" he cried out with savage vehemence. Then he slowly raised his eyes to the heavens and recited, "Jerusalem sinned grievously, therefore she has become filthy."

"God bless you, Joseph," said Abraham the scribe.

"He would do better to save the city!" the old man replied, and began praying again.

The streets were filling with people on their way to the Temple, an eerie throng of gray-faced ghosts with swollen bellies. Many of them were villagers who, after coming to celebrate Passover in the Holy City, had been forced by the Zealots to stay and help defend it. They had been the first to suffer from hunger. Now that they had devoured all the dogs, leaves, and roots they could find, they fought for the leather handle of a shield, or the thong of a sandal. It was even said that a woman had eaten her child.

Since religious law forbade burying the dead within the walls of Jerusalem, there were decomposing bodies in the streets, alleys, and ravines. The living were afflicted and obsessed by the smell, and never became used to it; some of those who lay rotting there were relatives or friends.

Violently swirling smoke was rising from the Temple. The crowd

13

of Jews crossed the bridge over the Tyropoeon in a dense, jostling mass and, roaring with anger, pressed against the lead-sheathed gate of the Court of the Gentiles. Shrill voices wailed in anguish: "The Temple is burning! The Temple is burning!"

The heavy gates suddenly gave way. Abraham the scribe was separated from his friends the potters and propelled into the court. Despite the pressure of the crowd, he veered to his left, away from the triple avenue of the Royal Portico, and moved toward the gate of the Court of the Jews. He had gone through it every day, before the Antonia was taken, but Roman soldiers with drawn swords now stood at the top of the steps to bar access to the enclosure that pagans were forbidden to enter; a Greek inscription at its entrance warned that "anyone caught will have only himself to blame for his death." Today, the order of the world was reversed: pagans were preventing Jews from going to the Temple! Above the walls, the smoke spiraling into the almost white sky was fed by irreplaceable scrolls, sacred curtains, and precious woodwork.

The Jews were so distressed that they surged forward, swept aside the Roman guards, and rushed into the inner court, facing the sacrificial altar, which had also been deserted since the Romans stormed the Antonia. A thick cordon of legionaries surrounded the buildings of the Sanctuary and the Holy of Holies, protecting soldiers busily engaged in pulling down the clusters of golden grapes that hung from the cedar beams of the entrance hall, the symbol of Israel! The four gold-covered sections of the door of the Sanctuary, measuring ten by twenty cubits,* had already been torn from their hinges. It was better not to think of what those heathens —may their bones be ground to dust!—had done to the golden seven-branched candelabrum, or the way they were treating the shewbread table.

The Jews at the front of the crowd were driven forward till they touched the points of the soldiers' swords. Abraham the scribe struggled against the current to reach the women's court. He even exchanged a few blows with a group of Zealots who had lost their leader and were blocking the passage without knowing exactly why. Confusion, uproar, a smell of burning flesh, the crackling of high flames . . . Abraham wept with rage and pity.

Yet he had taken part in the first riot, set off four years earlier when Gessius Florus, the Roman procurator, took gold from the

---

* About seventeen feet by thirty-three feet.

Temple treasury. And after the Romans retaliated by slaughtering three thousand Jews in the streets of Jerusalem, Abraham had felt that the people were justified in rebelling, capturing the Antonia, and killing the guards. In the war that followed, the Jews had organized their defenses and beaten the Roman general, Cestius Gallus, while Eleazar and his Zealots took possession of the fortress of Masada, on the Dead Sea. Abraham remembered the triumphant elation shared by all Jews at that time. He was not a warrior in his heart, but he regarded the seizure of Jerusalem by the Romans as an offense against the Almighty, blessed be His name.

Nero had then sent Vespasian and his son Titus, who subdued Galilee and prepared for the siege of Jerusalem. Soon afterward, Nero had died and Vespasian had been proclaimed emperor by the army of Syria.

During that miraculous respite, the Jews had spent their time splitting into factions. As a result, when Titus resumed the siege of Jerusalem three groups were quarreling among themselves for control of the city. Abraham the scribe had applauded when the priests refused to sacrifice the three lambs and the ox that Caesar offered each day to the Temple, and he had danced for joy before the fire into which the Zealots threw the Romans' official records, destroying lists of taxpayers and poor people's written acknowledgments of debt. But he had been astonished to see that his teacher, Rabbi Yochanan ben Zakkai, did not share the enthusiasm of the populace. He clearly recalled the controversy that had taken place between the old rabbi and the fanatical Eleazar, son of Simon, on the porch of the Temple.

"You're fighting for stones, sand, and incense," the old man had declared. "When the Torah has deserted it, the Temple will collapse like an abandoned house!"

"We're fighting for the Torah, rabbi! We want to save it. That's why we resist the Romans, their gods, and their laws."

"If you had read the Prophets, you would know that the Torah is strengthened by charity, and not by sacrifice. It's not necessary to kill or be killed in order to obey its commandments."

"But, rabbi, how are we to defend the Torah other than by force of arms, when the high priests themselves are appointed by Rome and their holy garments are in the keeping of soldiers? Those people hate and despise us, their idols have invaded the city. . . . How can we commemorate the name of Israel in such circumstances? How can we celebrate the great deeds of the Almighty? Where can we honor the Torah?"

"The Torah, Eleazar, was given to us in the wilderness. Where it reigns, there stands the Temple."

"Even in a foreign land?"

"Even in a foreign land."

"But how will you take it with you among the nations? How will you preserve it in the midst of slaves who will dream only of sharing their masters' meat and bread?"

"By study, Eleazar, son of Simon. By teaching."

The dialogue was punctuated by murmurs from those listening to it. Swayed by each argument put forward, they wavered between the two opposing sides, as they did when men learned in the Law engaged each other in lofty debate for the pleasure and edification of all. But this time the arguments concerned matters of urgent importance.

"The Romans have authorized me to establish a school at Yabneh," said the old rabbi.

"Yabneh? That peasant village? What a fine home you've found, rabbi, for the Almighty, His Torah, and His people!" The Zealot raised his dagger. "Leave if you want to, rabbi. Go to Yabneh. But after you, no one will leave Jerusalem except the dead!"

This was at the beginning of the siege. Rabbi Yochanan ben Zakkai had left the city in a coffin carried by his disciples. After hesitating briefly, Abraham the scribe had decided to stay. He could not really believe that disaster would strike the Holy City; furthermore, someone had to keep a record of what happened during those days, and that was his task on earth.

So he had stayed, covering scrolls with his accounts of events as he knew them.

Titus had placed the bulk of his army on Mount Scopus while the Tenth Legion, having come from Jericho, camped on the Mount of Olives. He had had all trees cut down north of the city, and built engines of war: ballistae and helipoles. But the Jews had defended the city so fiercely that Titus had put up a wall around it to starve them into surrender. Less than two months later he had taken the Antonia, and the priests had ceased offering ritual sacrifices to the Almighty. Then, when another month had passed, a Roman soldier had set fire to the Temple.

Now the whole complex of buildings was burning. Stone blocks burst, pillars suddenly toppled, blazing beams fell into the terrified crowd. Finally the roofs began opening or slowly collapsing, like sinking ships, and the Jews who had climbed up on them to escape from the Roman soldiers plunged into the flames.

Those who were able to reach the open spaces of the courtyards fell to their knees, tearing their clothes and beating their breasts to beg forgiveness of the Almighty. Roman archers began sending a dense rain of arrows into their midst. The crowd rapidly spread outward, like molten metal spilled on the ground. Then its scattered members regrouped, as though they felt it was important to stay together in order to show that weapons could never overcome the spirit. The number of dead bodies strewn over the flagstones was steadily increasing. Finally the people of Israel, red with their own blood, exhausted, haggard, constantly threatened by those clouds of death, vanquished at last, began moving toward the gates. The Roman trumpeters raised their instruments to their lips.

Corpses, ruins. Abraham stared in bewilderment at what had been the second Temple. God has abandoned us, he thought. God has abandoned us. Beside him, a young man was weeping softly. Abraham took him by the arm, forced him to turn away, and led him to the main gate. He crossed the Xystus Bridge with him, then left him and went to the Upper Market, which was, strangely, deserted.

When he reached the Street of Potters, the sun was already sinking. With his clothes torn and dirty, his eyebrows singed, his face darkened by a layer of dust and soot mixed with tears, and his throat sore from having shouted so much, he went into his house.

It was cooler inside. When his eyes had adjusted to the dim light, he saw the motionless figures of his wife and sons.

"God . . ." he began. He had been about to say that God had abandoned His people, but he caught himself, not wanting to alarm the children. "God is putting His people to the test. The Temple is burning."

"You're all dirty," said Elijah, the older of his two sons. "Are we leaving?"

"We'll leave as soon as it's dark."

Abraham suddenly felt the weight of his fatigue and weakness. He sat down heavily on the stone bench.

"And when will it be dark?" Elijah insisted.

"In summer," said Abraham, "the days are longer. . . ."

"Why are the days longer in summer?"

Judith opened her mouth to intervene, but Abraham answered, "Because the Creator willed it to be so."

"Why did the Creator will it to be so?"

"We must not try to fathom what is hidden, Elijah."

Judith brought Abraham a meager portion of boiled barley in a bowl. While he ate, she stood beside him with a jug of water in her hand.

When he had finished eating, Abraham looked around the room, with its whitewashed walls. Giving up that house where he had always lived was going to be like leaving his life behind him. He stood up and went to the sycamore shelves that held his papyrus scrolls. He took one at random and unrolled it. It was a speech that Agrippa, the king of Judea appointed by Rome, had given a few years earlier to the people assembled at the Xystus. "Only you," Abraham read, "are indignant at being the slaves of those who hold dominion over the entire world. But how will you fight? With what army? With what weapons? Where is the money that will pay for your warfare?"

Abraham the scribe remembered Agrippa's sister Berenice, who was Titus's mistress. To attend the ceremony, she had dressed in Jewish style, wearing a turban and a long crimson tunic. Facing her were the people, their eyes shining as they felt anger rising inside them.

It's true, thought Abraham, that we were only a makeshift army, a band of villagers armed with daggers and slings. But for four years we held out against the invincible power of the Roman Empire, its generals, its proud legions, its engines of war. . . . Four years . . . He sat down again. He had just realized that his people were entering into a time of misery and affliction.

When it was finally dark, he overcame his weakness.

"With God's help," he said, "we'll leave now."

It was a blue, moonless night. The light of the stars was bright enough for Abraham and his family to find their way as they walked hand in hand. He carried his scrolls in a cloth bag slung over his shoulder. Judith had gathered their belongings in a square piece of cloth tied at the corners.

The sky above the Temple was still red. Gusts of wind deposited on people and things the precious ashes of what had been. Shadowy figures moved furtively along the narrow streets. Probably Jews like us, thought Abraham, who have decided to leave Jerusalem. He had chosen to go out through the Potsherd Gate because it was usually not guarded.

The four of them—Abraham in front, Judith behind—walked through little streets that took them southward, toward the royal rampart. They came to a large, dark square from which a staircase with several landings descended to the foot of the rampart. There they stopped a moment to listen to the night. Little Gamaliel, frightened, began crying. Judith took him in her arms to soothe and comfort him. Elijah showed that he was a big boy; he reminded his little brother of the story of the whale and the fox.

"We'll come back, Gamaliel, you know we will."

"On a white donkey?"

Abraham interrupted the conversation between the two boys.

"Let's go," he said.

"May God help us!" murmured Judith.

"Amen."

So that she could walk more freely, the young woman fastened the hem of her tunic to her belt, as men did.

After going through the Potsherd Gate they huddled in the shadow of the wall until their eyes adjusted to the darkness and they were able to find the path. It was a narrow goat trail, with a surface of rocks in some places and clay in others, that was sometimes used by herdsmen. It led to the Tyropoeon, the ravine that cut across the city and, further down, joined the Hinnom and Kidron valleys, then continued on to the Dead Sea beyond the Judean wilderness.

They seemed to see shadows and dangers everywhere, but they had to keep moving forward. Abraham tested the ground in front of him with each step. He felt Elijah's hand clutch his. It's Jerusalem, and not me, that God is punishing for its sins, he thought. I've never offended His name. Finally they came to the bottom of the ravine. Abraham embraced his wife and joyfully stroked his sons' hair. The hardest part was over.

"Praise be to You, O Lord our God and God of our fathers," he recited.

They set off again. As they continued on their way, they discovered the immensity of the ravine. Dark, ominous figures seemed to be carved into its sides. Abraham was now carrying Gamaliel on his shoulders and he felt the child falling asleep. He was so tired that his body was becoming numb, but he told himself that fatigue was a small price to pay for reaching safety. Now and then he looked back. The farther they moved away from Jerusalem, the redder the sky seemed above the city.

It turned cold just before morning but he knew they must not stop. Elijah had fallen asleep as he walked, like an old donkey. At dawn they came to the road that led to Hebron. Only then did they stop for a short rest. Gamaliel woke up, crying, and asked for something to eat. Judith took a few grains of barley from her treasures and divided them among her husband and children.

Abraham was so exhausted that he was caught off guard when a Roman patrol came around a bend in the road up ahead. Should they run away? Wait? Hide in the bushes? It was already too late. The legionaries were steadily coming closer. Their helmets and breastplates made them seem implacable. Abraham stood up. There was no escape.

The patrol stopped a few paces in front of him. Its leader, a decurion, stepped forward.

"Who are you?" he asked.

He spoke in Hebrew and Abraham answered in the same language.

"I'm Abraham, son of Solomon, with my wife and sons."

"Where are you going?"

"To Beth-Zachariah."

"And where are you coming from?"

"Galilee."

The decurion, a tall man with a pockmarked face and a harsh voice, looked at Abraham's cloth bag.

"What are you carrying?"

"Scrolls. I'm a scribe. Writing is my work."

"Give me that bag."

"But . . ."

The thought of losing his scrolls was unbearable to Abraham. He remained motionless. One of the Roman soldiers said something and the others laughed.

"Did you hear?" asked the decurion. "They say that if you don't want to part with your bag, they'll be satisfied with your wife."

Abraham, petrified, felt as if he were living a horrible nightmare. He heard the decurion's voice, seeming to come from a great distance:

"Seize him!"

The soldiers smelled of leather and heavy sweat. Abraham tried to defend himself but he was soon battered into unconsciousness.

When he regained his senses and opened his eyes he saw the tearful faces of Gamaliel and Elijah above him, blurred, as if he were seeing them through rain. He tried to get to his feet. A sharp pain at the base of his neck made him fall back. There was a taste of blood in his throat. He rolled over on his side, raised himself on all fours, and then succeeded in standing up. The decurion approached him.

"You Jews are strange people," he said.

"Where's my wife?" Abraham asked in a voice he did not recognize as his own.

"Here's your writing, scribe," said the officer, dropping the bag of scrolls at Abraham's feet. "Your wife is dead, but we didn't kill her. She killed herself. Ask your children, they'll tell you."

The soldiers were standing behind him, looking crestfallen and disappointed.

"Soldiers of Caesar, forward march!" ordered the decurion.

As he was about to rejoin his men, he turned to Abraham and said, "We're at war, Jew, we're at war!" Then he handed two biscuits to Elijah and strode away.

Abraham staggered toward the bushes beside the road, where he saw the white shape of a body on the ground. Judith lay among the stones and weeds, with her belly bare and her throat cut.

"Rebono shel olam!" [Master of the world!] murmured Abraham. "Why?"

He fell to his knees beside Judith, closed her eyes, and pulled down her tunic.

The bright golden sun was rising in the sky. Off in the distance, smoke still hung over Jerusalem.

Abraham turned to his children. They looked at him, holding each other by the hand. Elijah had put down the Roman's biscuits on the papyrus scrolls.

"We're going to bury her," Abraham said softly.

Despite his weakness, he picked up his dead wife and carried her a little farther on, to where there was a cleft in a large rock. He laid her in the cleft, covered her with his prayer shawl, dug a handfull of yellow earth, and dropped it on the tomb. Then he and the children placed stones on the body of the woman who had been part of them, until the cleft was entirely filled; Judith would at least be protected from wild animals.

"Do you remember the psalm I taught you when Grandfather died?" Abraham asked Gamaliel.

"Has she gone to be with Grandfather?" asked Elijah.

"My sons, your mother has gone to *sheol,* the home of the dead. It's a place of silence and darkness where not even divine wrath can reach her."

"He who dwells in the shelter of the Most High, who abides in the shadow of the Almighty . . ." they recited together, and Abraham the scribe, unable to restrain himself any longer, burst out sobbing.

When he had recovered his self-control he wiped his eyes, straightened his bloodstained tunic, and abruptly tore it at the shoulder as a sign of mourning. He gave each of his children one of the biscuits that the Roman had left them, but took no part of them for himself. The morning was already well along. The air was shimmering above the Judean hills. The wilderness, with its golden stones standing out in sharp relief, appeared as a vast temple, immovable and indestructible, like the God of Israel.

They set off along the road. Each step took them farther away from both Judith and Jerusalem, and pained their hearts. Abraham soon had to carry little Gamaliel on his shoulders again, while Elijah carried the papyrus scrolls. At midday they joined a group of refugees—women, children, old men—coming from Galilee. During a stop in the shade of an acacia tree, they were asked where they had come from.

"Jerusalem," replied Abraham.

The weary faces, gaunt from hunger, turned toward him.

"Is Jerusalem still holding out?" asked an old man.

"Yes."

"And the Temple?"

"It's been burned."

"Curses on the Romans!"

"You're in mourning?" asked a hard-faced woman who was nursing her baby.

"My wife," said Abraham, and his voice broke.

"The Romans?"

"Yes."

"Curses on them!"

The woman's tunic, covered with red dust, was stuck to her body by sweat. Her white breast seemed almost blue. She spat on the ground three times.

"Where are you going?" asked Abraham.

"Wherever we can," answered the old man. "There must be a country that will take us in. . . . Egypt, maybe."

The woman nursing her baby laughed bitterly.

"We left Egypt and we're going back there! Slaves!"

Abraham had an uncle, his father's brother, in Egypt. His name was Ezra and he lived in Alexandria, a city where it was said there were as many Jews as in Jerusalem.

As they were setting off again, hoping to find a well before evening, a patrol on horseback approached in a cloud of dust and the officer ordered his men to halt.

"Where are you going, Jews?" he asked, inspecting the refugees one by one.

No one answered. He stopped in front of Abraham and looked him up and down.

"What are you doing among these old men? Is this boy your son? What's he carrying in that bag?"

"I'm a scribe," replied Abraham. "Those are scrolls on which I've written an account of recent events."

"Are you sure they're not messages calling for war against the Romans?"

"Read them for yourself."

"I speak your language a little," said the officer, "but I can't read it. You'll come with us."

Elijah and Gamaliel were lifted onto horses and Abraham had to walk to the legionaries' camp. By the time they reached it that evening, he was so overwhelmed with fatigue and despair that he felt ready to die; only his children kept him from abandoning life. In the camp he was given water and then, a little later, some biscuits that he shared with his sons. His scrolls had been taken away from him.

It was not yet dark when he fell asleep on the ground with his two sons huddled beside him, thinking of his wife Judith. It was hard for him to believe she had died only that morning.

As in Jerusalem, he awoke before dawn. The smell of the camp reminded him of where he was and what had happened the day before. What have I done to God to make Him abandon me? he thought. He felt as if his heart had turned to ashes. He looked in the direction of Jerusalem, trying to see the red glow of the fire, but the sky was empty.

Soon after the soldiers got up—curses, men calling out to each other, sounds of metal striking metal, distribution of thin branches for the morning fires—Abraham was given some watery bean soup. He considered the straight rows of tents, the tethered horses, the sentries posted all around the camp, and wondered how the Jews of Jerusalem could have believed they were capable of defeating that empire and its army.What lunatics they had been!

Later in the morning he was taken to the enormous tent of General Placidus, who for the moment was joking with several young men dressed in short tunics that left their knees and one shoulder bare.

Abraham, holding Elijah and Gamaliel by the hand, was announced to the general. Placidus examined them attentively and called for his interpreter.

"Your older son hates me," he said to Abraham, through the interpreter. "If his eyes could kill me . . ."

"Roman soldiers raped and killed his mother yesterday," replied Abraham, and again his voice broke.

"Then you must hate me too."

"I have no hatred in my heart, only pity."

"Pity?"

"How could I not feel pity for men who are crueler than wild animals, and kill without the animals' excuse of hunger?"

"Then you forgive them?"

"Only God forgives, when the time comes."

"By all the gods, Jew, I like you! My interpreter has read your chronicles. He says you observe accurately and write well. Our legion needs a scribe to write descriptions of its battles and victories. From now on, you'll be the scribe of the most valiant legion of the empire!"

"With your permission," Abraham said quickly, "I'd rather continue on my way."

When the interpreter had translated this reply, there was an outburst of exclamations from the circle of young men. Placidus silenced them and spoke to Abraham.

"Where do you intend to go?"

"To Alexandria, God willing."

The Roman looked at Abraham and his two sons.

"Listen to me, Jew," he said. "Before long, a ship will leave from Joppa for Alexandria. You can take it if you wish. But bear in mind that if you stay, General Placidus will be glad to have you with him! Think it over, scribe."

24

LESS THAN TWO weeks later, Abraham, Elijah, and Gamaliel put to sea aboard a trireme laden with slaves and gifts for Tiberius Alexander, Caesar's companion and governor of Egypt. Abraham had been forced to leave all his scrolls with General Placidus. When he set foot on the dusty wharf at Alexandria he realized, for the first time in his life, what it meant to be in exile.

•   •   •

ACROSS NINETEEN CENTURIES and eighty generations, Abraham the scribe is my ancestor, and his story is my story.

It was when my mother died, I believe, that I began collecting the elements of that story, probably as a way of making myself feel less alone on this earth.

It seems to me that I traveled nearly all over the world on the trail of Abraham and his descendants. I drew up lists and classified names, dates, and events; wherever my ancestors had lived, I gathered landscapes, colors of stones and skies, smells, faces, music, accents; I recorded adventure stories and legends; I listened to silences—and spent a great deal of time daydreaming.

Then I began writing. But in spite of all my file cards and references, there was still something lacking, something that I confusedly felt to be essential. I decided to go back to Jerusalem, where everything had begun. This was in the winter of 1977. Having nothing specific to look for, I wandered at random for several days, questioning myself once again about the mystery of that city. In the sky, television antennas had replaced the thousands of gold needles that had bristled on the roof of the Temple to prevent birds from alighting on it and soiling it, but there was still a strange feeling of permanence, and even of eternity.

Also eternal were those silhouettes, those calling voices, those black goats on bare hillsides. There was no need to go very far from the highway to Tel Aviv to find the smell of wool grease and sour milk that permeates Bedouin camps.

One afternoon a sudden downpour caught me outside in the Old City. I took shelter in a doorway. An old man joined me there a moment later. He had long sidelocks and a white beard, and wore a black caftan and a shtramel. *He briefly shook himself.*

"The harder it rains, the sooner it stops," he said to me in Yiddish. "Come inside where it's dry."

I followed him down a hall that led to a large room furnished with a long pine table and narrow benches: a religious school, a Talmud Torah.

"Have a seat," said the old man.

I pulled up a bench. He sat down facing me.

"Where do you come from?" he asked.

"Paris."

"And before?"

"Warsaw."

"I came from there too, but it was a very long time ago! What's your name?"

"Halter."

"And your father?"

"Salomon."

"Is he still alive?"

"No."

"May God keep his soul! What did he do in Poland?"

"He was a printer."

"And your grandfather?"

"He was a printer and publisher."

"And your great-grandfather?"

"Also a printer and publisher."

"An excellent family! What was the name of the publishing house?"

"It was named for my great-grandfather, Meir-Ikhiel Halter."

The old man repeated the name several times: "Halter, Halter. . . ." Then he asked me to excuse him and left the room.

A low ceiling, a light bulb hanging by a wire, a varnished cabinet in which prayer books were stacked. On the wall, behind flyspecked glass, a framed picture of Jerusalem. What was I doing there?

The old man came back after a rather long time. He seemed annoyed.

"I'm sure I have a book published by Halter," he said. "I'll find it. You must come back and see me."

I told him I was leaving for Paris the next day.

"Then you'll come another time," he said.

His name was Rab Chaim. I had met so many others like him that I forgot him and took the plane to Paris. I had found nothing new. But maybe there was nothing to find and I was only inventing reasons to escape from that book in the process of being born.

Nevertheless, I began working again.

26

2

ALEXANDRIA

The Great Revolt

UNCLE EZRA owned a warehouse on the Alexandria waterfront where he bought and sold grain, oils, or perfumes, depending on the state of the market.

He was a plump, elderly, white-haired man who made sweeping gestures when he talked. Like nearly everyone in Alexandria, he dressed in Roman style. He welcomed Abraham and his two sons, thanking heaven for this chance to be generous, and took them into his big house at the edge of the Delta quarter.

Through Ezra's connections, Abraham soon began working as a scribe for the Alexandria sanhedrin and his older son Elijah was enrolled in the *beth ha-midrash* (house of study) of Rabbi Shabtai, a man renowned for his knowledge of the Law.

But Alexandria—a prosperous, cosmopolitan city whose parallel avenues, running from Canopus to the Nile delta, were intersected by streets that descended from the desert to the sea—remained for Abraham an alien place in which he could not feel at home. He did not understand those Jews, half the population of Alexandria, who passively accepted all sorts of prohibitions and taxes.

"But how," he asked Ezra one day, "can all of you go on living, doing business, and laughing, when Jerusalem has been destroyed?"

"We don't forget," replied Ezra, "but the Jews don't have only violence to oppose to violence. . . ."

The white-haired old man then gave him a glass of sweet wine and spoke of the Torah.

But Abraham the scribe remained inconsolable. His children now spoke Greek and Latin more confidently than Hebrew, and to him this was like another betrayal. When Gamaliel had learned enough to work in the warehouse with Uncle Ezra, Abraham felt that he no longer had any reason to live. He suddenly weakened. The doctors brought to his bedside by Ezra were unable to identify his mysterious illness. They did not understand that he was dying of sorrow.

He left his sons only an inkpot, several carefully sharpened reed pens, and a scroll of fine papyrus on which, for the first anniversary of the destruction of the Temple, he had written:

> Praise be to You, O Lord our God, God of our fathers. You have turned away from us because of our sins. You have abandoned us. The world You made for us still exists, and we, for whom You made it, are disappearing. But we are still Your people. Our memory is the abode of Your Law. By the letter and the word, by prayer and fasting, we will maintain love and respect for Your commandments. So that no one of my lineage will repudiate Your name in the suffering of exile, and so that none will be forgotten on the day of forgiveness, I inscribe the names of my sons on this scroll. I hope and desire that it will be preserved after my death and continued by my descendants from generation to generation, until the day of Your reconciliation.
>
> On this ninth day of the month of Av, a year after the fall of Jerusalem, I tear my garment as a sign of mourning. Until the day when the stones of the Temple are rejoined, after being disjoined like the edges of this cloth, may the names that I have written on this scroll, and the names that others will write on it after me, be spoken aloud to rend the silence. Holy, holy, holy, You are the Almighty. Amen.

When he had ceased to live, there was no weeping or wailing; the truth was that Abraham the scribe had died on the day when he lost Jerusalem and his beloved Judith.

Time passed. At fifteen, Gamaliel married his cousin Sarah, a pretty, buxom girl who gave him fifteen children. Four of them, thanks to the Almighty, lived through childhood and grew up in the affection of their parents. Gamaliel named his first daughter Judith.

Among the multitude of Jews who came from Judea after the fall of Jerusalem, many had settled in small towns and villages along the Nile, between Thebais and the delta; they lived modestly, cultivated gardens, fished, tried to be as inconspicuous as possible, and never spoke of a return to Judea. The others had preferred to settle in Alexandria, a powerful and militant center of Judaism. Their arrival rekindled the old hostility of the Greeks, who asked Rome to take steps to reduce the number of Jews in the city and abolish the freedom of religion that they had long enjoyed by imperial favor. But Emperor Trajan had no desire to revive the Judean war that had kept his best legions occupied for several years. He limited his efforts to imposing a kind of balance between the two communities, whose antagonism stemmed from a mixture of admiration, contempt, and fear. They found countless pretexts for confrontations, and sometimes fought bloody battles in the dark streets.

Gamaliel took part in all the fights. He was an impatient man who feared no one. The memory of his mother's violent death still gave him a fierce hatred of the Romans, which he vented on the Greeks of Alexandria: it was easy for him to hate them, with their arrogance and their way of appealing to the empire for help. Since Ezra's death, Gamaliel had managed the warehouse alone, but the added work and responsibility had not made him more peaceful; neither had the entreaties of his wife, Sarah, his duties as a father, or even the advance of age. He continued to foment plots against Rome and volunteer for all attacks on the Greeks. He was completely intransigent.

In the year 3874 (114) after the creation of the world by the Almighty, blessed be His name, forty-four years after the destruction of the Temple, Gamaliel, son of Abraham the scribe, arranged a marriage for his youngest son, Absalom. Absalom was also his favorite son and resembled him in body, face, and character, though he had a tendency to lapse into a dreamy silence that he had inherited from his mother. He married Aurelia, a young woman with loving eyes. The wedding took place in midsummer and was a joyously happy occasion. Toward the end of the seventh and last day of the festivities, when shadows were beginning to

29

lengthen, the guests were in the garden, lethargic from the effects of heat and wine, some of them dozing in the trellised arbor or in the shade of the palm trees. The blue, crimson, and saffron yellow of their summer clothes stood out sharply in the white light. Several big black-and-white ibises solemnly paced around the banquet tables, looking for scraps of food with their little round eyes. The women chatted beside the bread oven, happy as they always were at each new wedding and already scheming to bring about the next one.

Gamaliel rejoined the guests. They stood up heavily to give him the customary good wishes once again.

"Mazel tov, Gamaliel! Joy and happiness to you and all the House of Israel! May the voice of gladness, and the voices of young brides and grooms, soon be heard in the towns of Judea and the streets of Jerusalem!"

Gamaliel gently pushed the guests aside and went to the newly-weds, Absalom and Aurelia. He gravely contemplated them for a moment, then placed the palms of his hands on their heads and blessed them, saying, "Gladden this loving couple, O Lord our God, as You gladdened the first creature in the garden of Eden at the beginning of the world. Praise be to You, O Lord, who gladden the young bride and groom."

Aurelia, wearing the turban of a married woman, lowered her eyes. Absalom kissed his father's hand. The guests applauded. Gamaliel signaled to the musicians that they could begin playing, then he went into the house, where several men lay on divans, talking and drinking wine seasoned with honey and pepper, which slaves served to them in cups made from water-lily leaves. He was looking for his brother Elijah when Esri, his old Nubian servant, came in to announce a visitor.

"Where is he?" asked Gamaliel.

Esri, used to his master's plotting, had learned to recognize clandestine visitors, and had taken this one to an outbuilding so that the guests would not see him.

Gamaliel went there. A tall, burly man of about forty, with red hair and laughing eyes, came toward him and embraced him.

"Jonathan!" exclaimed Gamaliel.

"Mazel tov! I've just learned about your son's wedding."

Jonathan took off his loose, black-striped yellow toga and dropped it on the floor. His suntanned skin, the dust on his sandals, and a certain freedom in his movements showed that he had spent a long time on the road.

"Where have you come from this time?" asked Gamaliel.

Jonathan stepped closer to him.

"From Cyrene," he answered, lowering his voice.

"Cyrene? How are our friends?"

"They're worried, Gamaliel. We're not yet ready for the insurrection, but the people are becoming impatient. In Cyrene, a man has announced himself as the Messiah—still another one, can you believe it? His name is Lucuas. He's a fanatic who goes all over the city proclaiming that the time is approaching when Jerusalem will rise again. That madman may set off a riot at any moment."

"Well, what if he does? We'll take advantage of it!"

"You know it's too soon, Gamaliel."

"It's never too soon! If your Lucuas can help us, we'll use him."

"Gamaliel . . ." Jonathan said with a sigh. "You'll never change!"

It was an old debate between the two men, the firebrand and the organizer. They heard lute music from the garden.

Gamaliel pressed his friend's arm.

"I must go back to my guests now," he said, "but we'll talk about all this again. We'll have a meeting at the new moon, with representatives from the communities of Memphis, Elephantine, Athribis, Faiyum, and even Cyprus. Tell me where I can find you and I'll take you to the meeting."

"You'll find me with the whores behind Pompey's temple."

"Save your strength, Jonathan, we need you!"

They laughed together and embraced again.

As he was coming back from accompanying Jonathan away from the house, Gamaliel nearly collided with his brother Elijah.

"I've been looking for you," he said. "Do you have the scroll?"

Elijah wore an elegant tunic with gold threads. His black hair, curled in the Greek fashion, framed the delicate features of his face, in which the first wrinkles had already begun to appear. But Gamaliel had noticed that behind the self-assurance of the Hellenized Jew, the inexhaustible melancholy of the exile was becoming more evident from day to day.

"Who's that man who just left?" asked Elijah, without answering his brother's question.

"What man?"

"That stranger with a red beard. Gamaliel, it's time you stopped plotting."

Gamaliel was furious.

"Is your friend the prefect interested in my modest affairs?"

Since the death of Abraham the scribe, the two brothers had moved in radically different directions. Studious and reflective, Elijah had been the favorite pupil of Rabbi Shabtai, who liked his disquieting ability to discern injustice where he, the old teacher, would have preferred to see only the normal course of events and the effect of the divine will. Elijah's questions and answers prevented the rabbi from sinking into routine and complacency, and he was grateful to him for it.

One day, feeling as nervous as if it were the opening day of his school, Rabbi Shabtai had come to see Elijah in his room near the *beth din* to offer him his only daughter, Miriam, in marriage. Elijah had accepted the offer, and the wedding had taken place a few months later. The newlyweds had moved into a house outside the Jewish quarter, in Neapolis.

Soon afterward, Elijah became a scribe in the great synagogue of Alexandria, a huge building with gardens and vaulted galleries—so huge that, in the prayer room, worshipers who remained near the door could not hear the *chazzan*'s voice, and the *shammash,* perched on a raised platform, waved a flag each time the congregation was expected to say "Amen."

Elijah devoted most of his time to study. His advice was requested more and more often and he was always invited to take part in great debates among the Jews on such questions as whether or not they should reply to an anti-Jewish text written by the poet Juvenal. Rabbi Shabtai believed it was inadvisable to have a discussion with enemies of the Jews because, he said, it would not make them change their minds, and furthermore the attention attracted by the discussion might help them to propagate their views. Elijah did not agree. He felt that discussion should never be refused, since words had a power that had to be taken into account.

"Besides," he had added, "to speak is also to bear witness, and isn't that our duty as scholars and scribes?"

"Our only duty," Rabbi Shabtai had replied, "is to bear witness before the Almighty."

"But it's precisely for the Almighty, blessed be He, and for His laws, that we must bear witness before men!"

Someone had applauded and, for the first time, the old man had shown irritation.

"To what do you want to bear witness? Do you want to describe for posterity our disputes with our enemies? Do you want to tell about our bodily illnesses, the weather, the outer appearance of the Alexandria synagogue?"

His listeners had laughed and sided with him, but Elijah had replied very seriously, "I hadn't thought of it, rabbi, but you're right: someone should take the trouble to describe our synagogue. That would also be a way of bearing witness."

"Then you're afraid our synagogue will disappear?"

"Even the Temple was destroyed!"

That evening, at home, Elijah had taken a scroll of fine papyrus, dissolved a tablet of ink, and begun writing: "The children of Israel went to Alexandria, in Egypt, and settled there. They built a synagogue, the like of which has not been seen since Israel was exiled among the nations. . . ."

His view of the exile was totally opposed to Gamaliel's. He had no sense of betrayal when he accepted invitations to the house of the Roman prefect, Marcus Ritulius Lupus, where poetry and philosophy were the usual topics of conversation—and where he had more than once learned information that Gamaliel later put to use.

" 'My friend the prefect,' as you call him," he said to Gamaliel, "could already have arrested you a dozen times if he'd wanted to."

"Why hasn't he done it?"

"Probably because he thinks it's better to know where his enemies are."

Gamaliel suddenly became calm. He had played this scene so many times before that it no longer amused him. He leaned toward Elijah.

"Have you found out anything?"

"Nothing new, my dear brother."

"Come, we're going to assemble the family."

The evening breeze was rising, stirring up the smell of grass and the fragrance of flowers and fruit. The air was pleasantly warm; everyone at the wedding celebration had a feeling of well-being and wishes of happiness were still being exchanged, yet people and things all seemed to be suffused with a kind of melancholy.

In the large balconied room on the third floor, Gamaliel and Elijah opened a box and took out the scroll that their father Abraham had begun, with the stipulation that it was to be continued by his descendants. The glow of the sputtering castor-oil lamps made strange reflections on the distinctive glassware and funerary urns, produced only by the craftsmen of Alexandria, that Elijah collected. Through the balcony window a light could be seen appearing and disappearing at regular intervals, high above the sea: it came from the Third Wonder of the World, the colossal lighthouse of gray and pink granite that rose to a height of four hundred feet.

When his family and friends had arrived, Gamaliel covered his head with a prayer shawl and leaned over the papyrus with the devoutness of a sage studying the Torah. "Praise be to You, O Lord our God," he read intently, "God of our fathers. . . ."

Following the lines with his finger, he continued reading what could be regarded as the testament of Abraham the scribe. Elijah had scrupulously added the names of the new family members:

"Abraham, son of Solomon the Levite, lived in Jerusalem and the name of his wife was Judith. Elijah, his first son, became a scribe like his father. Gamaliel was the second son.

"Elijah begat Simon, Thermutorion, and Ezra. The name of his wife was Miriam. They lived in Alexandria, in exile.

"Gamaliel begat Theodoros, Judith, Rachel, and Absalom. The name of his wife was Sarah. They lived in Alexandria, in exile."

Then came the names of the daughters-in-law, sons-in-law, and grandchildren, who included more Abrahams, Judiths, and Absaloms. Gamaliel recited them as if he were praying, and in fact they did form a kind of prayer. When he had finished, after announcing in a fervent tone that Absalom had married Aurelia, the bell of a faraway ship was heard in the silence. Gamaliel's words were like the signals of the Alexandria lighthouse: a safeguard against becoming lost in the darkness of the world.

THAT MONTH, the new moon coincided with a *shabbat* evening. With the appearance of the first star in the sky, Jews in the various quarters of Alexandria left their homes and began walking toward one or another of the city's many synagogues. Washed and perfumed, wearing their best tunics and carrying their prayer shawls, they moved in a steady stream through streets where porters, mule drivers, and water bearers were still at work.

"Those Jews must be rich," one man said as he watched them pass, "since they can rest before we do!"

"Their slaves are also resting now," said another.

"Yahweh is the god of slaves!"

34

But it was *shabbat* and the Jews refrained from answering.

Gamaliel always went to the great synagogue, not only because Elijah was a scribe there, but also because it was a meeting place for everyone who had news to announce: travelers who were passing through the city or had just returned to it. Following the accepted protocol, the crowd was divided into occupational groups arranged in a hexagon around the rostrum. The seventy old men of the upper tribunal sat on seats adorned with gold, facing the Holy Ark, the cabinet in which the scrolls of the Law were kept.

Prayers were said in Greek, in accordance with the translation by the Septuaginta, seventy Jewish scholars who, having been enclosed two-by-two in separate cells on the island of Pharos, had produced thirty-five Greek versions of the Hebrew text of the Torah that were absolutely—and miraculously—identical, word for word. Gamaliel, however, refused to attribute any sacred character to that translation: the Torah in Greek was not the Torah. This was another subject on which he and Elijah had often clashed. Elijah regarded Judaism as a philosophy, and the Torah as the expression of a morality that was valid for adherents of all religions. "I won't listen to that kind of talk!" Gamaliel had once said to him indignantly. "The Torah is the Torah, the Law given by the Almighty to His chosen people! Anyone who wants to be united with Him must honor it in its entirety, and in the language of God, which is the Hebrew of our fathers!"

He therefore took part grudgingly in the congregation's recitations in Greek: "For out of Zion shall go forth the Law, and the word of the Lord from Jerusalem." In any case, his mind was not on prayer that day. Immediately after leaving the synagogue, he would go to a meeting of conspirators in the marshes. His son Absalom would go with him, and Jonathan, to whom he had sent word of the meeting, would be waiting for them on the shore of the lake.

The *shammash* waved his flag one last time and the congregation said "Amen." The synagogue became animated, like a forest after rain. In a hubbub of conversation, laughter, feet scraping on the floor, and benches being pushed back, the members of the congregation stood up and, with their hats askew under their prayer shawls, hurried toward one another in great disorder to exchange greetings and congratulate each other on that new moon, that new month, and that new week which God, in His goodness, had granted to them and all of Israel.

Gamaliel and Absalom discreetly left the merchants' bench and moved through the crowd to the room where Elijah worked. From there, they would cross the sycamore garden and reach the road to Canopus and the lake. Elijah embraced his brother and nephew, looking worried. He told them, making sure he could not be overheard by his colleagues, that earlier in the day he had seen a traveler who had just come from Rome with important news: Emperor Trajan dreamed of equaling Alexander the Great and was preparing to go off and conquer an empire.

"Much good may it do him!" said Gamaliel. "At least he'll leave us alone!"

"No, he won't. Since he doesn't want to have to worry about what's happening behind his back, he's ordered his prefects to crush all plots and rebellions without mercy, whether they're serious or not."

Gamaliel put his hand on Elijah's arm.

"Why are you telling me this?"

The two brothers smiled at each other; they were completely different, at opposite poles, but they were still brothers. Gamaliel and Absalom left the synagogue.

On the outskirts of the city, eight stadia from the sea, between the ramparts and the fertile land of the delta, a vast basin received part of the water of the Nile and formed a lake bordered by marshes in which currents pushed their way through exuberant aquatic vegetation. This was the exclusive domain of Alexandria's bandits. Most of them lived there in flimsy huts perched on absurdly small islands, but the richest of them had large, comfortable cabins. The police never ventured into that tangled mass of reeds and water lilies: it was said that the dark water of the lake quickly closed over anyone who showed too much curiosity.

Gamaliel and Absalom walked along a slippery path. For a time they had been feeling that someone was watching them. They decided to stop.

"Who goes there?" asked a harsh voice in the night.

"Friends!" replied Gamaliel.

A dark form appeared and lifted a lantern that revealed a frightening face. The man examined Gamaliel and Absalom from close up, then said, "May the Almighty protect you."

"Amen."

"Follow me. Be careful not to slip. Your friend Jonathan is already here."

They plunged into the watery terrain. In front of them, ghostly birds flew up in alarm, then came down a little farther on. Devoured by mosquitoes, sickened by the powerful stench of rotting vegetation, starting each time a frog abruptly hopped away from him, Gamaliel was relieved when he saw that they were approaching a makeshift landing stage with a boat beside it. Jonathan was there. Gamaliel stepped into the boat and it tilted dangerously when he tried to embrace his friend. That world of water and mud suddenly seemed even more repugnant to him.

"Peace be with us," he said.

"Amen," replied Jonathan.

The man who had accompanied them—a fisherman? a bandit?—took a long pole, pushed the boat away from the landing stage, and began guiding it along one of the many passages between walls of vegetation that sometimes closed overhead, forming a tunnel. Gamaliel had difficulty breathing. When they came to a place where light was able to penetrate from the sky, he was surprised to see that his son Absalom was as calm and relaxed as if he were thoroughly used to those marshes.

Finally the boat reached a little island with a cabin on it and stopped beside a landing stage.

Inside the cabin a group of men sat in a circle on the beaten-earth floor, around a shaded lantern and a pot containing burning herbs whose odor repelled insects. In the dim light, their faces were marked by deep shadows. The group included Artemion, head of the Cyprus conspirators; Julianus, leader of the revolt in Judea; Eleazar, from Nisibis, in Mesopotamia, representing the Parthian communities; Ruben, from Arsinoë, in Cyrenaica; Ezra Alexander, from Nyassa, in Cappadocia; old Simon of Memphis; Azaria, son of Zadok, from the distant, almost independent Jewish kingdom of Nehardea, in Babylonia; Rabbi Joseph, son of Anias, from Tarsus, in Cilicia; the valiant Gamalielus, from Syria; and Jacob Domitian, from Clysma, on the Red Sea.

All these men knew each other from other meetings of the same kind, here and there. They stood up when Gamaliel, Absalom, and Jonathan came in. There was an exchange of greetings and embraces that warmed Gamaliel's heart. Since they were in Alexandria, he would now be the one to lead the discussion.

"Praise be to You, Everlasting God, King of the World, who has given us life, maintained us in health, and enabled us to reach this time."

37

"Amen," said the others.

They sat down on the floor. A man wearing a fisherman's tunic brought a tray of fruit to the middle of the circle and withdrew.

"My friends," said Gamaliel, "let each of us speak in turn."

Artemion, the man who had come from Cyprus, raised his arm, then stood up. His brown hood fell over his eyes and he pushed it back with a hand on which he wore many rings.

"May the Almighty, Master of the world, guide our thoughts and our steps," he said. "This is the third time we've met, my brothers, and it's time something came of our meetings. Words can't replace action!"

A murmur of approval rose from the group.

"Emperor Trajan is in the north," Artemion continued, "at Antioch. He wants to open the way to India through Armenia and Parthia. He'll take his best generals with him, and his best legions are already marching to join him. Behind him, the field is clear. Let's take advantage of it!"

Another murmur, even more fervent.

"In Cyprus," said Artemion, again pushing back his hood, "we're ready. We've formed militias, and pirates devoted to our cause have stopped two Roman ships loaded with weapons." He proudly waited for the enthusiastic exclamations to die down, then concluded, "My brothers, there's a time for peace and a time for war. The time for war has come. With the help of the Almighty, we must decide when to begin the insurrection."

He sat down on the floor again, took a date from the tray, spat out the pit, and wiped his fingers on his beard.

Gamaliel pointed to a young man who was showing signs of great impatience.

"Speak, Eleazar."

"I've just come from Antioch," said Eleazar, standing up. "The Romans have turned the city into a fortified camp and are preparing to go into winter quarters there. Legions are coming in from everywhere. I passed several of them myself."

"And the Jews?" asked Gamaliel.

"In Nisibis and Babylonia we've formed armed militias. But the old men of the Antioch sanhedrin are collaborating with the Romans."

Eleazar's body seemed to tighten and relax, according to the news he announced.

"Is that all?" asked Gamaliel.

"I've been instructed to tell you that if you don't launch simultaneous insurrections in Judea, Egypt, Cyrenaica, and Cyprus, we won't be able to hold out very long against the united Roman armies. We're counting on you to make the Romans withdraw troops from the north."

A man with blond hair raised his fist, his eyes glowing with fierce passion.

"By Elohim, the God of vengeance, that's what we've come here to plan!" he said in the rough voice of someone used to public speaking in the open air.

He was a Judean whose father, a hero of the war in Judea, had been taken to Rome among Titus's trophies and crucified at the triumphal ceremony. His name was Julianus and he had been organizing the coming rebellion in Judea. Gamaliel liked his violence and the way he spoke—as if he were striking blows. Jonathan, however, mistrusted him. "A bow that's bent too far will break," he said.

Julianus stood up.

"No more speeches! No more incantations to the new moon, prayer meetings, burning incense! No more waiting! The time for the insurrection is now!"

He knew the inflammatory power of his voice and his words; he would soon have his listeners ready to take up arms without any further thought.

"The work of our hands," he continued, "will bring life back to the desert around the hills of Jerusalem. The Temple in ruins cries out for vengeance! Stop lamenting over the injustices of Rome: they're only natural. Give up the illusion that a Jew can live in freedom among pagans. You won't be respected anywhere until the kingdom of Judea regains its rights, until the Temple is restored to its glory and rebuilt for eternity!"

He himself was becoming inflamed. Jonathan, who knew him well, made a gesture of impatience. Julianus turned to him dramatically.

"Do you want to say something, Jonathan?"

"Yes. I want to say that words are only the shadow of action."

Julianus called the others to witness.

"Listen to him! For him, it's always too soon: we have to wait, and when we've waited we have to wait some more! And now he's talking to us about action!"

"Calm yourself, Julianus," said Jonathan.

"A quarrel is always a bad adviser," Gamaliel intervened. "Go on, Julianus."

"I'd like to ask Jonathan," said Julianus, "if he doesn't think we should strike now, without delay, when the Romans aren't expecting it."

"I think that, for a revolt like ours, we must make long preparations to avoid being crushed once and for all."

"You can't walk on glowing embers without burning your feet!"

"I'm not afraid of burning my feet, but it's too soon. We're not ready."

"Too soon, too soon! You talk like a Greek mourner!"

Jonathan leapt to his feet, stepped over the tray of fruit, and gripped Julianus by the front of his tunic.

"I ought to break your neck, you desert dog! You have the heart of a pagan! In the time of the real prophets, arrogant braggarts like you were stoned to death!"

Gamaliel came between the two men.

"Calm yourself, Jonathan, calm yourself."

But Jonathan was beside himself with rage.

"I'm the only one who's fought against the Romans, the only one who's been condemned to death, and you call me a Greek mourner!"

The others had stood up and were all talking at once. It took Gamaliel a long time to restore order. Jonathan and Julianus still seemed ready to attack each other. Then Jonathan suddenly burst out laughing.

"I'm sorry," he said.

"So am I," replied Julianus. "Especially about my tunic!"

The two men embraced and everyone sat down again. Gamaliel drew a lesson from the incident.

"Among us," he said, "there are Jews who want to take up arms immediately, and other Jews who consider it more sensible to wait till we're better prepared. This time the war of the Jews against the Romans mustn't be coupled, as it was before the destruction of the Temple, with a war of Jews against Jews!"

Everyone expressed agreement. The atmosphere was now more relaxed, and the tray of fruit was passed around.

"Julianus," Gamaliel went on, "is right to say that until the Temple has been rebuilt we'll always be aliens, wherever we are. But he's wrong to think that Rome isn't wary of us. My brother Elijah told me this evening that the prefects have been ordered to repress all attempts at rebellion. But we won't let that stop us. Even if the humiliations inflicted on our people aren't unbearable, we must fight. What's important now is to work out our strategy and decide on a date. . . . We'll probably have to wait till spring."

"So late!" exclaimed Julianus.

"But," said old Simon of Memphis, "if the legions are already in the north, now is the time to—"

More exclamations, followed by a tumultuous discussion. Absalom looked at the square of dark blue night framed by the window. He was seated at the back of the room, behind the others. He knew this cabin: he had sometimes come to it with a young Egyptian woman named Nefer, sister of the man who supplied his uncle Elijah with papyrus. They had shared a kind of innocent love, a violent tenderness that had no future, since they could not marry. Nefer was at home in those marshes, and sometimes, when they were together, Absalom had felt that he was holding in his arms one of the alluring creatures described in fishermen's legends.

He watched his father gesticulating in the shadowy light and thought of Nefer. The debate seemed far away to him, so far that he could scarcely hear the sound of voices. When someone asked him for his opinion, he was taken by surprise and mumbled confusedly that he did not know.

It seemed to him that those men were wasting a great deal of time in talking, but he realized that the revolt was their passion, the burning center of their lives—all those meetings, all that traveling, all those doubts, dangers, and suspicions, all those hopes constantly placed in question. . . . He had a desire for Jerusalem that was all the more obsessive because he had been born in exile, but as he looked at his father he wondered how that handful of Jews could defeat the legions of Rome. He was unable to evaluate the army that could be formed by the Jews scattered all over the earth. Probably there was no other feasible plan than the one advocated by Gamaliel: to preach resistance, patiently amass weapons, train clandestine militias, create stronger links among Jewish communities separated by distances that in some cases were very great, watch for favorable signs and wait for the best time to attack, then attack all together, seize the enemy by the throat, and hang on. But, by the Almighty, what a long road it was to travel!

The square of the window was becoming tinged with purple. "We must attack the legions one by one," a voice was saying, "before they can regroup at Antioch." "It's high time we humbled the pride of the Greeks," said another, "and crushed the contempt of the Egyptians." Julianus's rough voice quoted Joshua and called for the destruction of all pagan temples. Someone suggested that the insurrection be made to break out all across the empire on the anniversary of the destruction of the Temple, so that it would be a day of vengeance for all eternity. Jonathan maintained that they could not be ready in less than a year and Julianus retorted that they could not wait more than a month.

It was nearly daylight when they finally reached agreement: the great revolt of the Jews would be launched all over the Roman Empire on the twenty-seventh day of the month of Adar, between Purim and Passover, in the year 3876 (April 2, 116) after the creation of the world by the Almighty, blessed be He. They decided that there would be no need for another general meeting like this one.

When they separated, they embraced more warmly than usual. This time, the processes that would decide their fate were about to be set in motion.

Absalom returned to the shore of the lake with his father and Jonathan. But when the boat stopped beside the little landing stage he said abruptly, "I won't go back with you." He turned to his father. "Tell Aurelia I'll be late."

Gamaliel raised his gray eyebrows but asked no questions. Jonathan laughed.

"Be careful," Jonathan said, "not to covet a woman in your heart for her beauty!"

He gave Absalom a good-natured shove on the shoulder. Absalom waited till they had disappeared beneath the vault of reeds, then walked off in a different direction.

A little hut, made of earth, branches, and all sorts of leaves and aquatic plants, was hidden behind a tamarisk hedge. Absalom saw its reflection in the calm morning water. As he walked toward it, his heartbeat quickened.

Nefer was kneeling on a bed covered with yellow linen, combing her hair, when Absalom came through the doorway. He stopped in silence, as if he were afraid that a gesture, a word, or the sound of his heart might destroy the miraculous harmony of what he saw: the slow, precise movements and dark, smooth skin of that young body, the gentle stirring of the reeds, the golden light of morning. . . .

Nefer looked at him as though she had been expecting him.

"My beloved," she said.

Absalom stepped toward her. The Scriptures condemned adultery and there was no pardon for a man who lusted after a foreign woman. But ever since he had met Nefer and come to know the feel of her soft skin, he had always succumbed to that desire which was celebrated in song and poetry by the Greeks and regarded as sinful by the Jews. This was the first time he had seen Nefer since marrying Aurelia, and only now did he realize how much he had missed her.

"My beloved," she repeated.

They clasped each other in their arms.

"My love, my life . . ." he murmured.

"I pray Anubis to prolong this day."

But the morning passed quickly. A flock of cranes flew over the marsh, calling out to each other, and Absalom said, "I must go."

"Why? Because of your wife? Or are you busy planning the revolt of the Jews?"

"Who told you about the revolt?"

"Everyone knows about it," she said. "Be careful, my beloved. I hope your wife is making you happy."

"I'll come here again before long."

It was late afternoon when Absalom returned to the city. A festival in honor of the gods was just ending; the last processions were breaking up and the streets were filled with the sound of drunken laughter. Here and there, disheveled Greeks, wine-besotted musicians, and dancers wearing crude masks cavorted around floats adorned with flowers, while half-wild dogs snarled and fought over the remains of animals sacrificed to idols.

Absalom detested those pagan festivals, those hordes of incestuous gods sullied by crimes, those idols placed everywhere: at street corners, in public squares, at the doors of temples, on the thresholds of houses. At least the Jews could be glad that they were not required to bow to them, thought Absalom. Greeks turned to look at him as he hurried past, because he seemed happy.

When he was going through the Neapolis quarter, he saw coming toward him a flowered float bearing a representation of an immense, triumphant phallus with a gold star on its tip. He slipped into a side street, crossed the spice market, and, a little farther on, saw slaves loading carts with cages of guinea hens, pheasants, peacocks, and monkeys.

43

On the Canopus road he encountered his uncle Elijah, who asked him, "Are you going to the warehouse?"

"Yes. Have you just come from there?"

"No. I'm on my way to the palace. Give your father my best regards."

"The prefect is having a celebration?"

"Yes, and I'm invited."

"Peace be with you, uncle. But be careful: remember what may happen to a mouse that makes friends with a cat!"

Elijah watched Absalom walk away. He liked him, but never felt entirely at ease with him. Whenever they were together, Elijah always had an impulse to justify his relations with the Romans, and Absalom, with the cruelty of his age, lightheartedly made fun of him.

At the palace, after being received with the respect owed to a distinguished guest, Elijah was taken to a broad path bordered by old cedars. Prefect Marcus Ritulius Lupus was there, enjoying the coolness of evening on the silver bed that had been brought for him. He beckoned to Elijah as soon as he saw him.

"Ah, here you are at last! I was beginning to be bored."

Marcus Ritulius Lupus was a tall, bulky man of about fifty. His movements were slow but he had a sharp, quick mind. On becoming prefect of Egypt and Alexandria, he had tried to establish good relations with the main communities, but he regarded the Greeks as unworthy of their ancestors, the Egyptians as barbarians, the Arabs as deceitful and cruel, and the Jews as a people of fanatics and rebels. Yet it seemed to him that in the Jews he recognized some of the virtues that had once animated the Romans and enabled them to conquer the world. Wondering if they still had the sense of austere righteousness taught to them by their forefathers—peasants, priests, and warriors who lived only for the love of God—he had one day summoned ten of the most illustrious members of the Gerusia, the supreme council of the Jewish community. The ten old men had come to the palace with studied smiles and deliberately expressionless eyes. To all the prefect's questions on their religion and history, they had taken great care to give meaningless answers: to them, the Romans were the enemy, the people who had destroyed the Temple. Marcus Ritulius Lupus had soon tired of his fruitless questioning and sent them away.

Since then, he had been learning about Jewish matters from Elijah. He liked that Jew who was able to appreciate the art and

44

culture of the pagans while still remaining faithful to his God and the wisdom of his people. Elijah was as different from the rich, obsequious, and hypocritical merchants of the city as he was from those hostile old men whose stubborn silence was an omen of war.

The prefect was particularly glad to see Elijah that evening. He was tired: he had gotten up at dawn to go to the temple of Serapis for the sacrificial ceremony; he had then attended a theatrical performance dedicated to the glory of Emperor Trajan, and the endless procession of the gods of Alexandria, followed by gladiatorial combats, had exhausted him. He expected Elijah to provide him with the mental jousting that was his favorite diversion; he had prepared a trap for him, and was looking forward to seeing how Elijah would extricate himself from it.

"Did you go to the procession?" he asked.

"You know I didn't," replied Elijah.

The prefect half closed his eyes—from pleasure.

"How arrogant you Jews are, to consider the Parthenon unworthy of receiving Yahweh!"

The courtiers moved closer, as though to watch a gladiatorial combat whose winner they knew in advance. Surprised by the aggressive way in which the prefect had opened their conversation, Elijah tried to avoid a clash.

"Are you tired, O Marcus Ritulius Lupus, that you seek a quarrel with me?"

"Seneca!" cried the prefect, happy as a child at having recognized the quotation. The courtiers bowed and he addressed them, "My friend Elijah is the only Jew, from the Pillars of Hercules to the frontiers of the Arsacids, who knows our Latin poets by heart!"

He seemed as proud as if he himself were responsible for Elijah's erudition.

"You're too kind, Marcus Ritulius Lupus," said Elijah. "Assuming that I really do know them by heart, I'm surely not the only one." According to the unspoken rules of their game, it was now his turn to provoke an exchange. "But do you know the Jews?" he asked.

The prefect sat up on his bed and a slave raised the cushions behind his back.

"A good official," he said, "must try to know the people under his administration." He invited Elijah to sit on the foot of the silver bed and continued, "I know the Jews and their ideas, and I must say, with all due respect, that their ideas scarcely seem new to me.

You preach fasting, abstinence, and charity, but those same things are also preached by the Greek Cynics. Like you, the Stoics extol virtue. Our philosophers teach what was written by your prophets; our gods proclaim the laws of Yahweh. Tell me, Elijah, why do your people persist in their isolation?"

He had spoken with self-assurance, and loudly enough to be heard by everyone around him. The courtiers expressed approval. A Corinthian musician stopped playing her harp. Since darkness had begun to fall, slaves were walking back and forth with torches, so that insects would burn themselves in the flames.

"I know," the prefect went on, "you're going to tell me about your Messiah. . . . But what do you think of the Christians, who believe that the Messiah has already come? You may say that their Messiah isn't yours, yet Jesus was a Jew, wasn't he?"

"I believe," said Elijah, "that the Messiah won't come until mankind is worthy of his presence."

"Think for a moment! There would be no need for his presence if mankind were worthy of it!"

"You don't understand, Marcus Ritulius," Elijah replied sharply. "The Commandments serve to measure good and evil, but the Messiah will lead us to innocence: the innocence lost in the garden of Eden."

With a gesture, the prefect ordered a slave to serve wine. He suddenly seemed apprehensive.

"What of those Jews all over the empire who are becoming more and more agitated, who talk of defeating Rome and rebuilding Jerusalem in all its glory—do you think they're preparing for the coming of their Messiah?"

A small group of men was approaching along the tree-lined path. Among them was a centurion carrying his helmet on his arm. An officer of the palace guard introduced him.

"This is Marcellus Venitius, an imperial messenger who has just come from Antioch."

The centurion raised his right arm.

"Salutations and honor to the noble prefect of Egypt and Alexandria!"

The prefect turned to Elijah and said, "I'm sorry, but I must leave you now. Come back when you can; our conversations always stimulate my mind." He leaned close to him. "I expect the Jews to do nothing to hasten the coming of their Messiah . . . May the gods be with you!"

Elijah lingered awhile in the gardens, where the prefect's guests slowly strolled to and fro as they chatted with each other. Some of them occasionally stopped for a time in a small torchlit amphitheater ringed by statues, to watch masked actors miming the story of a deceived husband. Elijah wondered if the prefect had given him a message intended for Gamaliel, and finally concluded that he probably had.

When he returned home, Elijah lit an oil lamp, placed it in front of his inkstand, prepared a scroll, and dissolved a tablet of ink.

"Dear brother," he wrote, "I know nothing about your secrets, nor do I want to know anything about them, but I have just come from a visit to the prefect and I must warn you to be careful. He has an excellent system for gathering information and he is in contact with the emperor. . . ."

And he reported what Marcus Ritulius Lupus had said. When he had finished, he sealed the papyrus with red wax and immediately had it taken to Gamaliel by his faithful servant.

FOR GAMALIEL, the winter seemed endless. Filled with warm rain that veiled the horizon and made the ground muddy underfoot, it kept people at home. Gamaliel's business affairs had been prospering. He spent most of his time at the warehouse, where he put things in order during the lull in the activity of the port. He had carried out new transactions and expected to receive large amounts of merchandise in the spring. He believed that the ships and caravans bringing the goods he had ordered would turn the prefect's suspicion away from him: no real merchant would, for the sake of an uncertain revolt, take the risk of having his bags of spices go stale or his bales of Indian silk be spoiled by mildew.

Travelers regularly brought him information on preparations for the insurrection. In Cyrene, Jonathan had persuaded "King Lucuas" to delay his plans for raising an army of poor people to march on Jerusalem. Jonathan was supposedly in Rome now, trying to obtain the support of the Jewish community, and Gamaliel impatiently waited for the sea to become calm enough to allow the *Isis,* the ship that plied between Rome and Alexandria, to bring his friend back to him. Meanwhile, he prepared cargoes that would be sent to the Danube, the Rhine, or the Bosporus—and carefully counted the weapons hidden among blocks of granite from Upper Egypt or behind cases of gum arabic. Other weapons were stored in workshops in different quarters of Alexandria: the Delta, Edfu, and Rhakotis, near the temple of Isis in the heart of the city.

The best news of the winter was the announcement of an earthquake in Antioch: half the city destroyed, Emperor Trajan seriously injured. This could only be interpreted as a sign sent by the Almighty to His people, especially since the Roman legions were immobilized by the siege of Hatra and Generals Hadrian and Quietus were wasting precious time in quarreling with each other over the possible succession of the emperor.

Jonathan finally returned from Rome. He had been greatly impressed by the affluence and prestige of the Jewish community there: divided into eleven congregations, the Roman Jews carried on their activities even in the center of the city; they maintained good relations with the pagans; Jewish scholars worked in the service of senators, Jewish physicians treated the imperial family. . . .

"But will they help us?" Gamaliel asked abruptly.

"They're not like us, Gamaliel. We're impulsive and emotional; the Roman Jews are sober and deliberate in everything they do. They admire the maneuverability of light boats, but they send their merchandise only in big, sturdy ships."

"You haven't answered me. Will they help us?"

"I'm afraid not, my friend. Except that they might take in the survivors if we should fail—God forbid!"

"Yes, God forbid! Jonathan, are you beginning to have doubts?"

"Doubts can sometimes be as useful as faith!"

"Spring will soon be here, Jonathan, there's no more time for doubt. You must go to Syene, because the Jews there want to form a militia. And I'm about to become a grandfather again: Absalom and Aurelia. That's a good sign."

The Hebrew Scriptures use one word to mean both "history" and "childbirth." The time, like Aurelia, was heavy with an immense promise.

Jonathan went off to the south. In Alexandria, a rumor began to spread that the Jews were getting ready for some sort of uprising against the Romans. Less out of self-interest than to divert suspicion, Gamaliel began working even harder at the warehouse. His mind was focused on preparations for the revolt, but his business affairs made insistent demands on his attention because the first caravans of spring were beginning to arrive.

Appolonios, a rich shipowner from Cyprus with whom Gamaliel

had been doing business for twenty years, announced that a mime performance was going to be given, at his expense, in the old theater on the Bruchium hill. Gamaliel could not refuse Appolonios's invitation to attend it.

The tiered seats were packed with fifteen thousand people impatiently waiting in an acrid smell of sweat, perfume, and grease, calling out to each other, clashing in brief fights for possession of the better seats or simply for the pleasure of shouting loudly and hitting hard. Gamaliel and Absalom tried to make themselves as inconspicuous as possible because they realized that in the open, funnel-shaped theater, swept by the wind and heated by the white sun, any incident could degenerate into a large brawl and bring on action by the soldiers charged with keeping order. The spectators were divided according to guilds. Regarded as a guild in themselves, the Jews had their seats on the west side of the theater, which meant that they faced their quarter, the Delta, and had no view of the sea.

Finally the musicians took their places and tuned the citharas to the pitch of the lutes. Next came the priests of the various temples. The spectators knew them and greeted them with upraised arms. Behind them came jewel-bedecked courtesans who were loudly cheered as they made their way to the lower tiers to join the dignitaries in gold-embroidered cloaks. Then Prefect Marcus Ritulius Lupus made his entrance, announced by trumpets that sounded again when he took his place on the ebony seat reserved for him at the level of the stage. He was followed by a swarm of officials, some dressed in Roman style, others in Greek style, who went to their seats on the tiers. Now the performance could begin.

At the first shrill, piercing sounds from the musicians, the mimes bounded onto the stage. They acted with their whole bodies, using all the resources of their art to evoke the deeds of heroes and gods. The spectators applauded happily and exchanged comments.

When the sun was low on the horizon, the actors added spice to their performance. This was traditional and the spectators had been expecting it. With increasingly obscene gestures, the actors mimed Achilles, disguised as a woman, frolicking with Lycomedes's daughters, and Pasiphae offering herself to penetration by the bull. The crowd was tense with excitement. Gamaliel looked away from the stage: for a pious Jew, love was consummated in darkness and silence.

Suddenly an actor with a black-striped white shawl on his head pointed to his genitals and, with his hand, imitated the movement of a pair of scissors. Laughter burst from the spectators. "Circumcised!" someone shouted. "Circumcised! Circumcised!" the crowd echoed delightedly. A voice behind Gamaliel and Absalom called out, "Here they are! Here are the Jews!"

Absalom put his hand on his father's arm and said, "Ignore them. Don't move."

"Circumcised! Enemies of the gods! Enemies of the human race! Yahweh is the god of pigs!"

No one was laughing now. Everyone had turned toward the row of Jews. The actors made frantic efforts to regain the spectators' attention.

"Put the Jews on the stage!" cried a voice that was immediately joined by thousands of others.

Absalom felt his father's arm stiffen under his hand.

Gamaliel suddenly stood up.

"Pagans!" he shouted at the top of his lungs. "Curses on you!"

Hisses, insults. The first stones were thrown from the highest tiers. The Jews gathered into a small, tight group. They had to be ready to an assault from any direction.

Absalom was hit on the back of the neck. He counterattacked blindly. A tall, massive man swung his club and staggered Gamaliel with a blow on the shoulder. Gamaliel groaned, but quickly recovered. With a savage cry, he seized the man, lifted him as if he weighed nothing, threw him to the ground, and began pounding his face with his fists. Then a stone struck him on the temple. He collapsed onto his adversary. Gamaliel would never see the great revolt of the Jews.

"Father! Father!"

Absalom tried in vain to reach Gamaliel. Hands gripped him, tore his tunic, clawed his skin.

Suddenly trumpets sounded. The crowd froze. A detachment of soldiers strode into the theater, their swords gleaming in the light of the setting sun.

"The Romans have come to protect the Jews! Death to the Jews!"

The crowd was now roaring dangerously. The primitive urge to kill grew stronger with each passing second. It took all the cool-headed determination of the Roman soldiers to isolate the Jews and guard them as they left the theater, carrying Gamaliel's body and several wounded men.

That evening thousands of young Jews invaded the streets of the city. Armed with clubs, they pursued terrified pagans, smashed idols, and pillaged temples. During the night they set fire to the temple of Nemesis and several other buildings between the Gate of the Sun and the Gate of the Moon.

The Alexandrians were frightened: they had never before seen the Jews angry. Some barricaded themselves in their homes, others took refuge in public buildings under the protection of the prefect's guards and the municipal militia, still others left the city for the villages and towns of the delta.

The leaders of the main Jewish guilds gathered in Gamaliel's house that night while his body lay in the balcony room on the third floor, surrounded by his family and the rabbi. Professional mourners lamented on the stairs and in the torchlit garden.

"What shall we do?" asked Sabatius the sailor.

They were sitting in a small room on the ground floor, around three oil lamps.

"We must take out our stocks of weapons and arm our militias," Alfia Soteris the weaver said calmly.

"By the Almighty!" exclaimed Tobi the farmer. "Don't you realize that we'd be jeopardizing the great insurrection?"

"Tobi is right," said Jeroboam the baker. "We're still three weeks away from the date we agreed on. We'd be alone against the Romans and the Greeks. We'd have no chance to win!"

"If we don't take the city before dawn," Alfia Soteris declared harshly, "tomorrow the pagans will slaughter the Jews."

They all turned to Absalom. He was young, but his father's death gave weight to his opinion. He agreed with Alfia Soteris. The Jews now held the streets only because they had the advantage of darkness. When daylight came, the Greek militias would no doubt be called up, and then the hunt for Jews would begin. . . . Absalom wondered what his father would have said. My father is dead, he thought, and images of his life ran through his mind: Gamaliel reading the family scroll, Aurelia giving birth to a boy, Nefer kneeling, smooth and brown, on her bed covered with yellow linen. . . .

They heard shouting in the distance. Through the window they saw high red flames in the direction of the sea.

"It's the temple of Poseidon," said Absalom. He turned to one of his friends, Akiba, a thin young man with calm eyes beneath a

51

helmet of black hair. "Akiba, go and see what's happening, and come back quickly."

When Akiba had left, the others were silent for a time, then one of them suggested that they go up to the balcony.

There was constant movement between the garden and the room where Gamaliel's body lay. People came into the room, stood in contemplative silence for a few moments, then told extraordinary stories: the Roman fleet had been sunk in the harbor, the Jewish cemetery had been desecrated by the Greeks, the great synagogue was on fire, the elders of the Gerusia had been flogged in the agora. . . . After making these incendiary reports, they left, puffed up with their own importance.

The Delta quarter, as animated as in broad daylight, could be seen from the balcony. Excited voices cried out names in the night. Torches burned in windows. Absalom thought of both his son and his father. Death, life; a mysterious balance.

Finally Akiba returned. He had tucked up the bottom of his tunic and was breathing heavily.

"Well?" Absalom asked him urgently.

"God be praised! The city is in our hands!"

Despite the presence of Gamaliel's body—but how happy Gamaliel would have been!—this announcement was greeted with joyous exclamations. The men fervently embraced each other.

"Tell us about it!"

"When I left here," said Akiba, "I took the Canopus road. It seemed that all the Jews of Alexandria were outside. Near the Gymnasium, I saw the bodies of Greek policemen who had been killed with sticks and stones. I went on as fast as I could to the temple of Serapis. Part of the roof had fallen on some of the pagan worshipers. I went to the Museum. Young men had thrown the busts of the caesars onto the pavement. Farther on, I met Joseph the lame. He says the Romans have been routed everywhere."

"And the theater?" asked Alfia Soteris.

"Jews are there, burning the Roman banners."

"And the prefect?"

"Joseph the lame says he's retreated into his palace with two cohorts of legionaries."

"And the synagogue?"

"I just came from there. I went to it by way of the sycamore wood—"

"It's not burning?"

52

"I told you I just came from there. No, it's not burning. Jews are pouring into it to ask for weapons."

Absalom thought of his father.

"It's my opinion," he said, "that we should hand out the weapons."

The others expressed their agreement one by one; what was done was done, and they had already gone too far to turn back. Alfia Soteris, Tobi, and Jeroboam volunteered to open the stocks of weapons that had long been hidden in workshops and warehouses. Sabatius would distribute the javelins, slings, bows, arrows, and shields that Gamaliel had stored at the back of his warehouse.

When the others had all left, Absalom, his family, and the rabbi set off for the catacombs of Canopus to bury Gamaliel, son of Abraham.

The city was in the grip of a terrible frenzy. When the sun rose, the Jews looked at each other in astonishment, filled with wonder and pride. On that day in the year 3876 after the creation of the world by the Almighty, blessed be His name, the sons of Israel went to war for the second time against Rome.

•　　　•　　　•

AT THIS POINT in my story, I should have described the taking of Alexandria by the Jews. The reader would have seen Jewish sailors attacking the waterfront, Jewish butchers besieging the Gymnasium, Jewish bakers assaulting the prefect's palace; in short, the armed Jewish population of the city rising up against the awesome power of Rome. My mind was full of images: the Roman guards disarmed and imprisoned, the Greek militias put to flight, public buildings taken one by one—"The Gymnasium is in our hands!" a messenger might have announced, foreshadowing the words of the Israeli general Motta Gur when he arrived at the Wailing Wall in 1967: "Har habait beyadenu!" ("The Temple Mount is in our hands!")

Assaults, slaughter. The insurgents attacked on all fronts at once, impassioned, ferocious, and tireless. And I, a man of peace caught up in that throng of implacable fighters, was seized with an obscure fervor. I understood how, at such moments, it was possible to laugh and weep at the same time, and make war a kind of celebration. I understood it, but I was unable to write it.

The fact remains that Alexandria was conquered in three days. Drunken young Jews then amused themselves by making Greek and

Roman prisoners fight each other in the amphitheater. On the fourth day, from the direction of Lake Mareotis, the Roman Third Legion arrived, followed by five cohorts in good order and countless auxiliary troops—thousands and thousands of men with glittering weapons and armor, whose columns formed a terrifying snake that coiled in the vast basin of sunbaked clay facing the Karmuz catacombs.

The Roman legionaries, aided by the Greeks of the city, overwhelmed the Jews' fierce defense in a few days. The Edfu quarter was ravaged, the Delta quarter was partially destroyed, and the great synagogue was burned. Prefect Marcus Ritulius Lupus assembled the surviving Jews in the ruins of their quarter and had a security force assigned to them, consisting of the hundred twenty horsemen and six hundred foot soldiers of a cohort.

NEVERTHELESS, THE GREAT REVOLT of the Jews against the Romans was ignited all across the Roman East. Two weeks after Passover, Jonathan, at the head of a large army, captured Thebes, in the southern part of the Nile valley, then moved up the fluvial plain and took Parapolis, Hermapolis, and Memphis. At the same time, in Cyrenaica, "King Lucuas" took Ptolemais, Cyrene, and Barca, freed all the Jewish slaves, and set off toward Judea. In Cyprus, Artemion burned the capital, seized the ports of Amatus and Paphos, and had them fortified. Despite the proximity of imperial troops, disturbances broke out all over the Euphrates valley, and the city of Nisibis, in Babylonia, displayed the colors of the insurgents. A little later, Julianus and his Judeans defeated a Roman army on the plain of Jezreel.

The insurgents massacred Greeks and Romans everywhere, sometimes with the complicity of the local populations. Travelers reported horrible details: the Jews, they said, ate the flesh of their victims, made belts of their intestines, rubbed themselves with their blood, covered themselves with their skins. . . .

The Jews believed that the prophecies of Ezra and Baruch were coming true before their eyes. The synagogues resounded with fervent readings: "Soon you will see the downfall of your enemies, and you will put your feet upon their necks." "The world that rejoiced at the fall of Jerusalem will be grieved by its own devastation." "The Messiah will come when the wicked burn in a fire in which no one takes pity on them." And so that everything would be fulfilled, the Jews took no pity on those who had destroyed Jerusalem and dismantled their state.

Emperor Trajan, incredulous at first, then furious, had to delay setting off to follow in the footsteps of Alexander the Great. He ordered General Lucius Quietus, a cruel and ambitious Moor, to exterminate all the Jews of Babylonia and Mesopotamia. He summoned the prestigious General Marcius Turbo from Britain and placed him in command of the campaign to pacify Cyrenaica and Egypt.

The Jews went on fighting for more than a year, at sea and in the Libyan desert, harrying the massive Roman units, but were finally defeated, after which great numbers of them were slaughtered. Jonathan and Lucuas were chained and exhibited in an iron cage before being crucified on the Bruchium hill in Alexandria, in front of the theater. "God is one!" Jonathan said as he died. In Cyprus the leader of the revolt, Artemion, was beheaded, then his body was cut into small pieces and thrown to the sharks. A law banished Jews from the island forever and forbade them to set foot on its shore even if they were shipwrecked.

Emperor Trajan, ill, embittered, disheartened at having realized that he would never equal Alexander the Great, died in Cilicia, in the midst of plots and underhanded maneuvers, on the twenty-first day of the month of Kislev in the year 3878 (118). The Jews rejoiced over his death, proclaimed that day Yom Trianus (Trajan's Day), and made it a semi-holiday.

The new emperor, Publius Aelius Hadrianus, decreed the end of the Judean war. To win over the Jews, he authorized them to rebuild the Temple on its former site and pardoned Julianus, leader of the insurrection in Judea.

In Alexandria, Marcus Ritulius Lupus, regarded by the Greeks as being too favorable to the Jews, was replaced by a certain Quintus Ramnius Martialis, who deported a number of Jewish families.

THE GREAT REVOLT was over and Jewish armed resistance was a thing of the past, with rare exceptions. From then on the Jews took up arms, here and there, only when their situation was beyond all hope.

The convictions of Yochanan ben Zakkai the Pharisee had prevailed: the Book became the sole weapon of the people of Israel. To triumph is to endure.

3

ROME

Arsinoë Is Dead

ABSALOM HAD stayed in Alexandria until the time limit set by the prefect: the new moon of the month of Tevet, 3879 (119). He had then gone to Rome, where the new prefect had assigned forced residence to several Alexandrian Jewish families.

He did not like the Roman capital, with its long, rainy winters, its ceaseless noise, and the stench of the narrow little streets where excrement was allowed to accumulate. Rome was said to be the largest city in the world. About fifteen thousand Jews lived there, organized into eleven congregations, each with its own school, synagogue, and community services. Five of the synagogues were in Transtiberinus, a former wasteland on the right bank of the Tiber that, two centuries earlier, had been made the fourteenth district of Rome by Emperor Augustus, after he had emptied it of its prostitutes and robbers.

This was where the Alexandrian congregation settled. They went on speaking Greek, living and praying in acccordance with the customs and rites of the East, and reverently maintaining their memories of the faraway white city that smelled of the desert and the sea.

How often they had relived their great revolt!

After piously burying his father, Absalom had returned home

for *shiva*, the prescribed seven-day period of mourning. Sitting on the floor of the balcony room where Gamaliel had spent so much of his time, he had tried to pray, but instead he had listened to the clamor rising from the royal gardens, his heart pounding with excitement—for Gamaliel the indomitable rebel, this was the best prayer of all.

Elijah had come to sit beside Absalom. His eyes were red and he had a two-day beard. He sadly looked through the window at the two columns of black smoke that were like pillars holding up the sky. He seemed exhausted.

"Listen!" said Absalom. "The Jews will have taken the city by this evening!"

"They're mad!" murmured Elijah the scribe. He turned to Absalom. "When the Almighty wants to punish one of His creatures, He takes away his common sense. . . . Are you ready to face the Roman legionaries?"

"We'll face the whole Roman Empire, if we have to."

"Are you determined to die?"

"No, uncle, but I'm not afraid. It's said that the Almighty destroyed Jerusalem by fire and will restore it by fire. If He wills it so, we'll defeat the Romans."

"Don't you think you may be confusing Jerusalem with this Greek city?"

"This Greek city is my city, since I was born here. But Jerusalem is also my city, because I'm a Jew. Must we always choose between the father and the mother?"

Just then, Akiba came to tell Absalom that he was needed. Elijah stood up and took his nephew by the sleeve.

"You're not going to leave the house, are you? *Shiva* isn't over yet!"

"I know, but the Law allows us to interrupt it to save human lives."

"Save human lives? You'll get yourselves killed!"

"Some of us will die, uncle, but with the help of the Almighty we'll see to it that as few die as possible."

In the street, Absalom followed tradition by putting sand in his sandals, so that his body would remain in contact with the earth in which his father lay. He then went off with Akiba.

Three days of combat, elation, and turbulent emotions, three days that left memories as indelible as scars.

Absalom asked his Egyptian friend Pasis, Nefer's brother, to shelter his wife and their newborn son, Adar. Knowing they were safe, he felt freer to fight, and in the fever of those days he was sometimes carried away to the point where he forgot everything but the consuming joy of victory.

Then the Romans arrived. The Jews' courage and enthusiasm were no match for the experience, equipment, and methodical skill of those professional soldiers. Absalom had to acknowledge that this was the law of war and that the time had evidently not come for God to send His Messiah to mankind and overthrow His enemies. Even so, the vengeance of the Greeks, who ravaged and pillaged the Edfu and Delta quarters, seemed so unjust to him that it filled him with bitterness and despair. Armed with knives, axes, and clubs, the Greeks seized women, children, and old men and amused themselves by tying ropes to their ankles and dragging them through the streets, wearing away their skin, lacerating their flesh, annihilating their lives. . . . Akiba said that the Jews should have known it was the Greeks, rather than the Romans, who were their real enemies.

Akiba himself was killed later, when he and Absalom were trying to reach the Egyptian quarter after spending the night in a catacomb to escape from Roman patrols. They had crawled through a clump of terebinth trees, crossed the sycamore wood, and come to the Square of the Gods, at the intersection of Canopus Street and the Street of Columns. It was there that they were spotted by a group of young Greeks around the fountain, among the immense statues of Athena, Demeter, Elpis, and Harpocrates.

"Jews!" one of them cried out.

Absalom and Akiba ran away, but an accurately thrown javelin caught up with Akiba. . . .

Since then, Absalom had never been at peace in his soul: it was he who had insisted that they leave their hiding place in the catacomb.

IN ROME, his wife Aurelia had given birth to two children: a daughter, Arsinoë, and another son, Amnon. He had had to work hard, especially after Aurelia died of a pernicious fever. He had been a carter, a litter bearer, and a watchman. Then finally an important Jewish merchant, who had known Gamaliel, had made him the overseer of his warehouses in Ostia, and later placed him in charge of distributing his merchandise in the markets of Rome.

And so the years had passed. Absalom now worked near the

river port, opposite the Trigemina Gate, in a three-storied house. Like the rich Romans, he lived on the ground floor, which was equipped with running water and toilets. Adar was eighteen, Arsinoë was fifteen, and Amnon was fourteen. They spoke Greek and Latin and seemed insensitive to their father's nostalgia. Arsinoë was a beautiful girl with fair skin, black hair, and yellowish-green eyes. Strongly attached to her, Absalom was in no hurry to find a husband for her.

A week before Passover he came back from Ostia in a boat laden with melons. As it moved along the sun-drenched banks of the Tiber, he watched slaves resting in the shade of bushes. Suddenly he saw his son Adar in the distance, running toward him and gesturing for him to come quickly.

Absalom ordered the oarsmen to head for the riverbank. Adar leapt into the boat, out of breath.

"What's the matter, Adar?"

"Arsinoë . . ."

"Go on."

"She's with the Christians, father."

Adar bowed his head. He felt ashamed, as if he were responsible.

He told his father that Arsinoë had become friendly with a boatman named Claudius who was suspected of belonging to the sect of the Christians. She had disappeared two days earlier and, as Adar had verified, so had Claudius.

Absalom questioned Arsinoë's friends Simplicia, daughter of the *archisynagogos,* and Miriam; they knew nothing. He and Adar then set off for the house of Claudius the boatman. They crossed the Siblicius, one of the five bridges over the Tiber, and plunged into the steep, narrow streets on the Velia hill. Now that the overwhelming heat of the day had passed, life was beginning to stir again. Merchants were opening their stalls and crying their wares.

At Claudius's house, Absalom and Adar found only a crafty, one-eyed old man who pretended deafness to avoid answering their questions and kept saying, "Louder! Talk louder!"

They returned home and found Archisynagogos Julianus, Simplicia's father, waiting for them there.

"May the Almighty protect you, Absalom," he said.

He was a tall, hefty man with a thick gray beard. He opened his long sleeveless cloak, sat down on a divan as if he were in his own home, and, with a movement of his hand, invited Absalom to follow his example.

"If it rains on one of us, the rest of us have wet feet," he said without preliminaries. "Your daughter has disappeared. Some say she's gone off to become a Christian. To know if that's true, we must find her. Then it will be time either to punish her or comfort her." He tugged at his beard and gave Absalom a stern look. "In this barbaric city, the police are too closely linked with crime to hunt down criminals. The council of the synagogue has appointed ten men to help you."

"But, rabbi—"

Julianus stood up and made a gesture that could have been interpreted as meaning that there was no need to thank him.

"What is useful to the bee," he said, "is also useful to the hive, my son." He walked to the door, then stopped and added, "Man's heart seeks to choose the path he must follow, but his steps are guided by the Almighty. We'll be expecting you tomorrow evening, at the *shabbat* service."

One of the sons of Abbas the blacksmith had reported hearing, in the Tavern of the Four Sisters, near the Circus Maximus, that there was going to be a gathering of Christians in the catacombs on that same *shabbat* evening.

The *archisynagogos* gave Absalom and Adar permission to try to enter the catacombs with the Christians, but asked them not to do anything that might harm the community. When the first star appeared in the sky, young men would go to lurk outside the catacombs and try to discover the right entrance or overhear the password.

This plan was carried out. When Absalom and Adar left home that evening it was already dark. They wore loose hooded Gallic cloaks and each of them carried a knife. Adar led the way, holding a lantern. They went along the Via Appia, through the ancient Porta Capena and past the ruins of the Servius Tullius wall, then they reached the gate that led to hills covered with sandpits and wild fig trees.

Absalom suddenly remembered the day when he had gone to the theater with his father in Alexandria—the day when Gamaliel had been killed by the Greeks. Now *he* was the father, and he wondered if his son would come back alone from their nocturnal expedition. Ahead of him, in the light of the lantern, he saw Adar's broad shoulders, but for once he felt no pride at the sight of his son, because the doubt aroused in him by Arsinoë was cruelly gnawing at his heart.

As they were nearing the Jewish cemetery of Vigna Ramdanini, a shadowy figure approached them. It was the son of Joseph the litter bearer.

"Things are going well," he whispered. "We have the password. Follow me to the entrance."

"But what *is* the password?" Absalom asked impatiently.

"The question is 'Who are you?' and the answer is 'I am your brother.' "

"Did you hear that yourself?"

"No, Abner heard it. But I've tried it."

Absalom was comforted by a sense of brotherhood as he looked at the young man's eyes shining in the darkness.

They went to the entrance of the catacombs and waited for someone to come. Adar had extinguished his lantern. The night air was heavy with the fragrance of flowers and grass. Finally three silhouettes appeared. Absalom touched his son's arm. They followed the newcomers through a cemetery flanked by two rows of cypress trees that were like high black flames in the blue of the night, then they stopped in front of a doorway so narrow that only one person could go through it at a time.

Two men were standing there, in the faint glow of a shaded lantern. It was impossible to avoid them.

"Who are you?" one of them asked Absalom softly.

"I am your brother," replied Absalom.

The man gave his arm a friendly squeeze and let him pass.

"Who are you?" the other man asked Adar.

Adar was dying of fear. He had an impulse to turn away, run home, shut himself up in his room, and go to sleep.

"Who are you?" repeated the voice, more insistently this time.

"I'm his son," said Adar, pointing to Absalom's back.

"You don't know the password?"

Adar tried to collect his wits. The password?

"I am your brother," he said.

He was allowed to go in behind Absalom. They walked along a passageway lighted by smoking torches thrust into the wall at distant intervals. Burial chambers had been dug into the soft rock on either side of the passageway, and they went through rooms containing rows of sarcophagi and tombstones.

They heard the gathering before they saw it. It was being held in a room larger than the others, and more brightly lighted. There were about a hundred people present: men, women, and children.

61

The walls were decorated with vivid paintings that showed a man undergoing martyrdom or a lamb in front of a cross. One sign, the image of a fish, was repeated so often that Absalom wondered if it was the emblem of the sect.

A man in a white robe stood facing the gathering.

"Do you renounce sin?" he asked.

"I renounce it," the gathering replied in unison.

"Do you renounce that which leads to evil?"

"I renounce it."

"Do you believe in the Almighty Father, creator of heaven and earth?"

"I believe."

"Do you believe in Jesus Christ, His only Son, our Lord, who suffered the Passion, was buried, arose from the dead, and sits at the right hand of the Father?"

"I believe."

"Do you believe in the forgiveness of sin, the resurrection of the flesh, and eternal life?"

"I believe."

Absalom tried to recognize his daughter among the worshipers and distinguish her voice among those that resounded beneath the vaulted stone ceiling.

Bread and wine were brought in. The congregation stood up.

The man in white said loudly. "On the night of His betrayal, when He was about to enter freely into His Passion, Jesus took bread, gave thanks for it, broke it, and gave it to His disciples, saying, 'Take this and eat; it is my body, which is broken for you.' At the end of the meal He took a cup, and again He gave thanks. He gave the cup to His disciples and said, 'Take this and drink of it, all of you; this is my blood, the blood of the new and eternal covenant, which will be poured out for you and the multitude, for the remission of sin. Do this in remembrance of me.' "

The bread and wine were served to the congregation. Absalom was sensitive to the fervor and solemnity of the moment but he was filled with horror at the thought that his daughter might be practicing this rite.

The man in white now said, "By Him, with Him, and in Him, to You, God the Father Almighty in the unity of the Holy Spirit, all honor and glory, world without end."

"Amen," replied the congregation.

Adar tugged at his father's arm and discreetly pointed to the corner of the room where those distributing the bread and wine had just arrived. Faces were being raised, and hands outstretched.

"Arsinoë!" Absalom suddenly cried out. "Arsinoë! It's I, your father!"

Everyone turned to him. He quickly found himself surrounded by several determined-looking men. Should he fight? He remembered how he and his father had fought against the Greeks in the theater in Alexandria.

"I'm that girl's father," he said. "I've come to take her away." And he called her again: "Arsinoë!"

The man in white, who was evidently the leader of the congregation, came over to Absalom. He had deep-set eyes, and two furrows on each side of his mouth.

"Arsinoë is dead, Jew. Mary has been born. We have baptized her and she has received the new life of the children of God."

Absalom and Adar were pushed outside without having been able to approach Arsinoë.

When he returned home, Absalom began the rite of *shiva,* as if his daugther actually were dead. After seven days of mourning he resumed his work, but he was never the same again. He spoke little, spent more time in the synagogue than he had done before, and often sent Amnon, his younger son, to replace him at the river port. He had made Amnon come back from Ostia, where he had been studying with the famous Rabbi Eleazar.

Absalom seemed to have lost interest in everything. Even the news of another Jewish revolt in Judea left him indifferent.

Despite the promises made at the beginning of his reign, Emperor Aelius Hadrianus had forbidden the Jews to rebuild the Temple and Jerusalem had become a Roman city named Aelia Capitolina. Again there was a Jew who rose up against betrayal and deceit: Simeon ben Kosiba. Akiba ben Joseph, an influential rabbi, hailed him as the Messiah and gave him the name Bar Kokhba, "Son of a Star," for it was written in the Torah, "A star shall come forth out of Jacob, and a scepter shall rise out of Israel." He reportedly demanded that those who joined his forces cut off one of their own fingers to prove their courage.

In answer to Bar Kokhba's call, tens of thousands of men rebelled against Rome once again. Their daring and faith enabled them to rout all the Roman armies in the East. At the end of the year 3892 (132) after the creation of the world, they were victorious in Judea, Samaria, and Galilee, where they soon gained total control and restored the Jewish state.

In Rome, there were increasingly frequent demonstrations of hostility against the Jews They left their homes only when necessary, and in the synagogues they prayed for the salvation of Israel. Amnon wanted to join Bar Kokhba's army but his father Absalom forbade it, without giving him an explanation.

One day Archisynagogos Julianus said to Absalom, "You've changed. Your son is less affected by your refusal to let him leave than by your silence. Be careful, Absalom: the soul is shaped by habits, and we finally come to think as we live."

But Absalom maintained his refusal. He did not speak of it until Bar Kokhba had been defeated by a new Roman army. The Jewish state had lasted less than three years. In the month of Av in the year 3895—sixty-five years, to the month, after the destruction of the Temple by Titus—Betar, the last Jewish stronghold, fell into the hands of Emperor Hadrian.

When the news reached Rome, Absalom wept. He invited his son Amnon to take a walk with him. They strolled along the Tiber, to the shipyards. Now and then he leaned on Amnon's shoulder. For a time they watched the workmen building hulls in a smell of tar and mud, then Absalom said abruptly, "My son, it's better not to have taken part in the revolt than to be one of those men who have suffered defeat in war."

"But if no one ever fights . . ."

"Listen to me, Amnon. Defeated men often lose hope, and from now on we Jews will be kept alive by hope."

Amnon was surprised by his father's solemnity. He understood the reason for it that evening when Absalom sent for his two sons —Adar, a scribe at the synagogue, was now married and a father himself—and announced to them that he was going to Alexandria.

"You no longer need me," he said. "Follow the precepts of the Torah without weakness and bring up your children in fear of the Almighty. Remember that a tree that doesn't yield good fruit is cut down and thrown into the fire."

"Father," asked Adar, "are you thinking of our sister?"

"I don't know who you're talking about."

Absalom took nothing with him when he left Rome. Even his heart was empty.

Judea, it was said, had been turned into a desert. Sand was ruining the Plain of Jezreel and wild animals reigned in Samaria.

To the survivors of the war, Emperor Hadrian had forbidden circumcision, observance of the sabbath, and study of the Law. Being a Jew in the land of the Jews was punished by death! And, in his fury, Hadrian went so far as to change the name of Judea to Palestine, from the name of a people who had once occupied the environs of Ashkelon: the Philistines.

When Hadrian died in the month of Tammuz in the year 3898, it was a deliverance for all Jews. From then on, whenever they spoke his name they accompanied it with this curse: "May God reduce his bones to dust!"

ON THE FIRST MORNING of Passover in the year 3913 (153), a wine merchant from Alexandria who had come to Rome on business delivered to Adar a long wooden box painted black and decorated with carved birds and cattle, images dear to the Egyptians. Inside it, Adar found two scrolls of fine papyrus. One of them was a long letter from his father Absalom:

To my sons Adar and Amnon. May the Almighty keep you in His holy protection.

My body is beginning to forget me. I am old and tired. Man is as light as a cloud; when a breeze touches him, he disappears. I do not know how much more time on this earth has been allotted to me by Him who knows the real meaning of things, but I could not resign myself to joining the guardian of *sheol*, with my soul at peace, without blessing you one last time.

I must tell you that Uncle Elijah—may his soul rest in peace—with whom I had so many discussions in the past, has been called to the Almighty. My brother Theodoros, who is as vain as ever, lives with his five grown children in the house of our father, Gamaliel—God keep his soul—in the Delta quarter. The white, luminous, gracious city of Alexandria is still dear to my heart, but unfortunately I had to leave it because I was denounced to the Romans. I went to live in Memphis. Nefer, sister of my Egyptian friend Pasis, joined me here. During the terrible days of the great revolt, she and Pasis sheltered your mother—may her soul rest in peace—and you, Adar, when you were still in your cradle. Like Ruth the Moabite, Nefer converted to our faith. We married and had a son,

65

Abraham. If one day the Master of the world places him on your path, love him: he is your brother.

Last year I set foot in the land of our fathers. Fifteen years after the revolt, the country still seems to have been plunged forever into grief and dereliction. Jews are permitted to go to Jerusalem only once a year, on the ninth of Av, anniversary of the destruction of the Temple. I was able to take advantage of that permission last year. With a multitude of men and women from all parts of the empire, I climbed the abandoned hills of Judea, singing.

And as I was weeping with them before the only wall of the sanctuary that is still standing, I wondered if our revolts—that of my grandfather Abraham, that of my father Gamaliel and myself, that of Bar Kokhba—are the best path to deliverance. Perhaps our defeats mean that the Almighty will not restore the covenant unless His people again consent to revere His Law.

After Rab Akiba was martyred, his pupils settled in Usha, a village in Galilee, to continue studying the Law of charity, justice, and love, and to gather and comment on the teachings of tradition handed down from father to son.

I spent two moons there, listening to those Tanaim, and that time was among the happiest of my life. I heard Rabbi Meir, Rabbi Simeon bar Yochai, Rabbi Judah ben Ilai, Rabbi Yoseh ben Chalafta, Rabbi Eliezer ben Jacob, Rabbi Yochanan of Alexandria, and Rabbi Nehemiah. Those seven men are the greatest of the great. The stronghold they have built can never be destroyed, neither by pagan armies nor by the lies of the Christians. Who could destroy an invisible Temple?

When this letter reaches you, my sons, I may no longer be of this world. Do not weep for me. I ask only that you gather around the scroll that I am sending you in this same box. It is the story of our family, written in accordance with the wishes of my grandfather, Abraham. Elijah, my uncle, continued it until his death, but his two sons, who are arrogant men puffed up with wind, may God forgive them, prefer to interest themselves in the vanities of this world. Read it aloud, complete it, and at the end of the time allotted to you by the Almighty, God of Abraham, Isaac, and Jacob, hand it on to your children.

With a lump in his throat, Adar had to stop reading for a few moments before continuing:

> Of the thirty-two thousand sesterces that I possess at this time, earned entirely by my own work, I bequeath twelve thousand to the synagogue of Memphis for the benefit of the poor, and ten thousand to my wife Nefer and our son Abraham. The remaining ten thousand will be sent to you. Use that money to good advantage, without forgetting to share your gains with the needy. The world subsists only by study of the Torah and by charity. May the Almighty guide your steps. Holy, holy, holy is His name. Amen.

4

ALEXANDRIA

Ezra's House

"... MAY THE names that I have written on this scroll, and the names that others will write on it after me, be spoken aloud to rend the silence. Holy, holy, holy, You are the almighty. Amen."

A hundred years had passed since Adar, Absalom's older son, had brought up to date and continued what was now known in the family as the Scroll of Abraham. It was the year 4013 (253) after the creation of the world by the Almighty, blessed be His name. With his family standing around him, Gadias was solemnly reading the names of those who had preceded him in this world, and from whom he was descended. Abraham . . . Esther . . . Theodoros . . . Words floated through the semidarkness, bearing inexpressible messages, and slowly sank into the memories of children with big, serious eyes.

Gadias, patriarch of the descendants of Abraham the scribe, had just decided to leave Rome. The family had grown and prospered from generation to generation, despite epidemics and sporadic persecutions, but the Christians were becoming more and more intrusive, thousands of Goths had just been enrolled in the militia, and Rome had lost some of its ancient splendor. These reasons would not have been sufficient, however, if Gadias, having reached the evening of his life, had not felt that it was his duty, a mission

68

entrusted to him personally, to put an end to that Roman exile which he regarded as senseless.

Since Jerusalem was still forbidden to Jews, except for one day a year, he would take his family back to Alexandria. He reverently put the Scroll of Abraham back into the black wooden box and gave it to his oldest son Joseph, known as Joseph the lame because he had one leg shorter than the other.

IN ALEXANDRIA, the family occupied "Ezra's house," as it was called, at the edge of the Delta quarter. It was now old and dilapidated and the Alexandrian branch of the family had been using it only for storing merchandise.

Joseph, studious and reflective, soon found a position as scribe in the synagogue of the quarter. And, contrary to what his father had feared, he also found a wife: Deborah, daughter of Lucius Tsophar, a jeweler.

As soon as the others had settled into their new lives, Gadias died, as if he had no more reason to go on living after carrying out his decision to leave Rome.

Joseph the lame and Deborah had two children, Judith and Abraham, and lived in the modest, peaceful way they preferred. Their lives would have continued to be as smooth as a beach in the morning if the Almighty had not stricken Alexandria with one of His worst calamities: an epidemic of the plague.

The whole city was plunged into agonizing distress. It was impossible to bury all the dead bodies that piled up in temples and public squares. Highly paid volunteers loaded some of them into boats and threw them into the sea, far away from shore, but there were not enough boats, and not even enough volunteers. The stench invaded houses in spite of curtains and perfume braziers.

In "Ezra's house," Miriam, one of Joseph's sisters, was the first to fall ill with the plague. She died a few days later and was followed by her son Appius Jacob. Then Judith discovered dark, ugly sores on her body. Joseph the lame sent for his son and gave him a satchel.

"This is all our savings," he said. "Take the next ship and go wherever you can. At least one of us must survive."

"But we're scribes, father: we must keep a record of what's happening."

"The first duty of anyone who wants to keep a record is to survive! Go, and be careful. Try to reach Caesarea and go from there to Tiberias, either riding a donkey or on foot. If you want to study at the Talmudic academy, I'll give you a letter of recommendation for Rabbi Yochanan, the most famous of the Amoraim. Listen to me, my son. If the Almighty doesn't give me the joy of seeing you again, remember that you'll find the Scroll of Abraham in the house of David, the *shammash* of the synagogue. Here, look at it. . . ." Joseph unrolled the papyrus. "Look, my son: here's Solomon, the rabbi of the synagogue of the Delta quarter. He was a sage; I've told you about him. He begat Miriam, Hannah, and Abraham.

"And here's Jacob, who made a voyage to Rome. He begat David.

"And Abraham, son of Solomon, begat Ezra and Judith.

"And Ezra begat Joseph, Rebecca, Sarah, and Enoch.

"During the reign of Emperor Caracalla, Enoch was the first of our family to receive Roman citizenship. He begat Judith and Theodoros.

"Gadias begat Miriam, your aunt—may God keep her soul—and me, Joseph, your father.

"Look at this line. I wrote it: 'Joseph the lame married Deborah and they had two children, Judith and Abraham.' May the Almighty give you long life and health, and an understanding heart to distinguish between right and wrong."

Father and son embraced weeping. Then, while Abraham began preparing to leave, Joseph went to his daughter and prayed for her. Her fever had risen to the point where it made her feel, she said, as if a fire were burning inside her.

Judith died the day after her brother left. And her father, his heart filled with tears, began looking for someone who could bury her: as a Levite, he was forbidden by the Law to do it himself. There were fewer and fewer gravediggers for more and more work, and Joseph the lame did not have the money to pay one of the reckless men who were trying to become rich at the risk of catching the plague.

Finally, after wandering through the streets for hours—a long step, then a short one—among the corpses abandoned to the black-and-white vultures, he encountered an Egyptian peasant carrying his dead daughter on his back. Joseph explained to him as best he could that he too wanted his daughter to be buried. Without a word, the peasant went to Joseph's house with him and picked up Judith's body to carry it off to the catacombs. Not knowing how to thank him for his compassion, Joseph looked attentively at his face. It was the homely face of a poor man grown old before his time, and Joseph was horrified to see that it bore the marks of the plague. The peasant had still said nothing; he smiled faintly and turned away. Joseph, overcome with emotion, stammered that he would pray for him and his daughter.

ABRAHAM FINALLY CAUGHT sight of Tiberias in the distance, through the haze. Ever since his arrival in Palestine, he had felt that his heart was beating to the rhythm of the drums of the prophetess Deborah: "To the Lord I will sing, I will make melody to the Lord, the God of Israel." The Plain of Jezreel, Mount Tabor, Megiddo . . . All those names now took on shapes and colors, and everything—even the dust of the road, the heat, the flies—seemed to him both marvelous and familiar.

Despite its colonnaded palace and the Greek pattern of its streets laid out in squares, Tiberias was the first really Jewish city that Abraham had ever seen. In the streets and on the shore of the Sea of Galilee, young Jews with prayer shawls on their shoulders, absorbed in discussing this or that passage in the Mishnah, were more numerous than the Romans and Greeks. The language spoken was either Hebrew or Aramaic.

Following the directions he had been given, Abraham walked to Yochanan ben Nappacha's *yeshiva,* a large building with a balcony. In the courtyard he was surrounded by a group of students.

"Who are you?" "Where are you from?" "Do you want to study here?"

"I'm Abraham ben Joseph, the Levite. I'm from Alexandria."

"Come here!" someone shouted. "A Jew from Alexandria!"

The circle widened and the students jostled each other around Abraham.

"Is it true there are no survivors?" "How did you escape from the plague?" "How long did it take you to come here?" "How well do you know the Mishnah?" "How long do you intend to stay in Tiberias?"

Abraham was dazed and bewildered, but deeply happy at the same time. He could have been any of those curious young men; he felt at home. He answered their questions as well as he could, and then he was taken to Rabbi Yochanan.

Tall as a Roman centurion, and handsome, with regular features, curly hair, and blue eyes, Rabbi Yochanan did not look like the rabbis Abraham had known in Alexandria.

Abraham was still more surprised when, after reading the letter of recommendation written by Joseph the lame, Rabbi Yochanan exclaimed, "So you're the son of Joseph ben Gadias of Alexandria! I'm very glad to welcome you here. I have great respect for your father. We've exchanged several letters and I've learned something from each one of his."

He took a papyrus from a shelf and unrolled it.

"This one, for example," he said. "Your father quotes a sentence from Exodus: 'You shall not oppress a stranger; you know the heart of a stranger, for you were strangers in the land of Egypt.' Question: Can this sentence be applied to those who are now, once again, strangers in Egypt? Yes, answers your father, because even if a man is oppressed himself, his oppression does not prevent him from wanting to assert his dominance over someone weaker than he is. Conclusion: This sentence from Exodus must be remembered in all times and places."

Abraham was dumbfounded. His father had never told him about his correspondence with Rabbi Yochanan. And the respect that one of the greatest *amoraim* showed for Joseph the lame filled his son with pride.

"You are welcome among us!" said Rabbi Yochanan.

The class was composed of about a hundred students who sat on twenty-seven rows of seats facing the rostrum, which was flanked by four assistants, the *meturganim*. On one side of the rostrum, in a seat slightly lower than Rabbi Yochanan's, was another rabbi: Simeon ben Lakish.

Abraham was placed in the thirteenth row, beside Judah, a thin young man with the sharp face of a greyhound.

He soon made a friend, Elhanan, who found a room for him in the house of a fisherman and his family, near the harbor. Every day at dawn, after reciting the morning prayer, he watched the fishing boats leave and then, while the sun rose behind the lake, he walked across the city, his heart swelling with happiness, to go to the *yeshiva*.

One morning Rabbi Yochanan welcomed his students, as usual, then offered them a theme for reflection: "Man needs God."

Rabbi Lakish immediately shook his head and said, "No, it's God who needs man."

"What I just said," replied Rabbi Yochanan, "is confirmed by a verse in Genesis: '. . . the God who has led me all my life long to this day . . .' We need God to lead us."

"In that same verse," said Rabbi Lakish, "is confirmation of my view: 'The God before whom my fathers Abraham and Isaac walked . . .' The King needs heralds to go before Him and clear the way."

After the two views had been repeated, the students were asked to give their opinions.

"I believe that Rabbi Yochanan is right," said Judah, the young man who sat beside Abraham, "because it is written in Deuteronomy, 'There is none like God, O Jeshurun, who rides through the heavens to your help.' "

"That's a misinterpretation," protested Rabbi Lakish. "It should be *with* your help,' not *to* your help.' "

"What's your opinion, Abraham ben Joseph?" asked Rabbi Yochanan.

In the two weeks that Abraham had spent at the *yeshiva*, this was the first time he had been asked a question. He stood up, intimidated. He knew what he wanted to say but it seemed to him that he would not succeed in expressing it. He coughed, shifted his weight first to one leg and then to the other, and finally took the plunge.

"I believe," he said without recognizing his own voice, "that you're both right, because it is written in the Psalms, referring to man, 'Thou hast given him dominion over the works of Thy hands; Thou hast put all things under his feet.' This shows that God needed man to help rule His creation, and also that man needed God because he would not be man without Him." He coughed again and added, "But perhaps I'm mistaken, rabbi."

Rabbi Yochanan smiled.

"Go on," he said. "Why would man not be man without God?"

"As long as man acknowledges God and respects His Law, he is different from and stronger than all the animals, and God can therefore need him. The Almighty said to Noah, 'The fear of you and the dread of you shall be upon every beast of the earth . . . into your hands are they delivered.' And so Cain said after his crime, 'Whoever finds me will slay me,' for it is only when man appears in the form of a beast that animals are able to dominate him."

Rabbi Yochanan smiled again and, satisfied, tugged at his beard.

The students applauded. It was a great day for Abraham ben Joseph.

He would have been perfectly happy during this period if he had had any news of his father. He had finally learned that the epidemic had ended in Alexandria, but he still did not know who had died and who had survived. He often dreamed of his father. He saw him walking—a short step, then a long one—in a city with empty streets. That city was Jerusalem, he was sure of it. How was he to interpret his dream?

After about six months of study and reflection at the *yeshiva,* he began thinking that he should go back to Alexandria. But, although he dared not admit it to himself, a reason other than his studies kept him in Tiberias: a girl he saw now and then in the morning, on his way to the *yeshiva.* She was sometimes alone, sometimes with a woman who might be her mother, evidently going to the waterfront to take a basket of food to a fisherman about to set out in his boat. The girl had red hair, and that was nearly all he knew about her, except that he could not look at her without being seized with a strange emotion.

One day he saw her on the waterfront, sitting on a pile of nets, alone. She was watching a boat, probably her father's, as it moved away from shore. He suddenly found himself beside her, standing first on one foot and then on the other, as he had done on the day when Rabbi Yochanan questioned him. His throat felt terribly dry. She looked at him with her green eyes, then burst out laughing. It was not a mocking laugh that would have made him want to die on the spot, but a pleasant, open, welcoming laugh, a laugh that included him in its gaiety.

"My name is Sarah," she told him.

"And mine is Abraham."

"Now we can begin," she said calmly.

She already knew Abraham and had been following his little game a long time: she was the sister of Elhanan, his best friend at the *yeshiva.*

They were married by Rabbi Yochanan himself, in the synagogue of the upper city. Since Abraham was eager to introduce his wife to his father—assuming that Joseph was still alive, as he hoped with all his heart that he was—they decided to leave for Alexandria after Shabuot.

ALEXANDRIA ITSELF had not changed, but not one family had been spared by the epidemic. The eyes of the survivors were still haunted by horror, to the point where it made one wonder how the trees, birds, and flowers had escaped the plague.

Joseph the lame was still alive, and so was Ptolomea, the old Greek servant. For his son's return, and in honor of Sarah, he held a reception at which Abraham was asked to tell about his journey and give a few examples of new commentaries on the Mishnah. Joseph said nothing, but he hung on each of his son's words and it was easy to see that he was proud of him.

After so many others, Abraham and Sarah began living in "Ezra's house," Sarah said that the cracks in the walls added to its charm: "This house is so full of history that it bursts out everywhere!" They both laughed, but Abraham promised himself that he would have some repairs done as soon as he could save up a little money.

Only a short time later, Joseph the lame reached the end of his days. He lay down, without regrets or complaints, and waited for death. Abraham piously watched over him; his father had known a great deal of loneliness in his life, but at least he would not be alone at that frightful moment.

Abraham watched his father's face and remembered the night when his mother, Deborah, had died. Joseph had taken him and his sister Judith by the hand and they had walked a long time, till they were near the lighthouse.

"Do you see that light disappearing and coming back, again and again?" Joseph had asked his children.

"Yes."

"It's like life. . . ."

Judith, a little girl at the time, had concluded, "Then Mama will come back!"

Joseph had been so surprised that a kind of laugh escaped from him.

As he looked at the cold, smooth stone of his father's face, Abraham recalled that laughter through tears, beyond anger and sorrow, unlike any other that he had ever heard. And he suddenly realized that Joseph the lame had died—discreetly and with dignity, as he had always lived.

After observing the seven days of mourning, Abraham searched the house for the Scroll of Abraham, asked his cousins about it, went to the *shammash*—in vain. The black wooden box seemed to have disappeared. Despite his grief, he regarded his father's death as being in the natural order of things, but he felt the disappearance of the scroll as a betrayal, an injustice. Since he could not imagine Joseph the lame destroying it or throwing it away, he was at a loss to explain what might have happened to it.

The mystery remained until his son was born, a year later. Holding a package against her bosom, Ptolomea, the servant, came to him and looked him in the eyes for the first time.

"Your father, God keep his soul," she said, "asked me to give you this as soon as your first child was born."

It was the Scroll of Abraham.

"Thank you, Ptolomea!"

Abraham might have kissed the old servant if she had not quickly turned and walked away.

"He was a good man," she said as she left.

That evening, after prayer, Abraham unrolled the papyrus and solemnly read it aloud, from beginning to end, before his wife and their sleeping son. Then, in the fine, clear handwriting that Joseph had taught him, he added, "Abraham married Sarah and they had a son, Ezra."

It was Sarah who had decided that the child should be named Ezra, after the house.

The Alexandria lighthouse was still blinking in the night: death, life, death, life . . .

EZRA HAD two brothers, Jonathan and Solomon, with whom he did not get along very well. One was a goldsmith, the other a cabinetmaker, and nothing seemed more important to them than the honor and prosperity of their guilds. Ezra was a scribe and taught Hebrew in a little school beside the synagogue. He married the mother of one of his pupils, a young widow named Miriam, who gave him five children: Judith, Ruth, Johanna, Theodoros, and Jacob.

Jacob, the youngest, was a difficult boy, unruly and pugnacious. He learned very quickly, and since it bored him to listen to the other pupils reciting a lesson that he already knew, he often slipped away from school and went off to loiter with a band of Greek boys in the waterfront quarter, among the coarse sailors and the piles of merchandise. One day, in an ugly brawl, he injured a young Christian, Clement, in the eye. As sometimes happens, the two adversaries became friends. They often met on the waterfront to watch the arrival of ships that had come from far away, laden with magic.

At that time the Christians were being persecuted because of the growing success of their religion, but Jacob and Clement never talked about things that might cause conflict between them. Nevertheless, Miriam worried about her youngest son, her favorite, and it seemed that Ezra scolded him only to satisfy the other children.

One day a great hunt for Christians swept across the city. Out of curiosity, Jacob joined the crowd of Greeks, Libyans, and drunken legionaries who were shouting, "Death to the Christians!" It occurred to him that he ought to shelter his friend Clement, but, dazed by the uproar and fascinated by that explosion of violence, he could not tear himself away from the mob. He was carried along to the theater, where, looking down from one of the upper rows of seats, he saw a white-haired old man being made to kneel while mockery and insults were hurled at him. Suddenly a sword flashed in the sunlight. Blood gushed from the old man's body and his head fell onto the yellow sand.

Jacob ran home. The family had gathered for the evening meal. His mother was alarmed by his pallor but he said nothing. That night he was unable to sleep; he kept seeing Clement in place of the white-haired Christian, and when the head rolled on the ground he recognized, at the corner of one eye, the scar left by the injury he had inflicted on his friend.

At dawn he went off to look for Clement, whom he had not seen the day before. There was no one in Clement's house. In answer to Jacob's questions, the neighbors said warily that they knew nothing. Had Clement and his parents been killed? Had they moved away? Jacob, of course, assumed the worst.

When he was about to leave, he looked into a courtyard and recognized a girl he had seen before, on the waterfront. She told him that she did not know what had happened to Clement, but he was touched that she had been willing to talk to him. Her name was Lydia and, with her slender body draped in a blue tunic, her eyes that seemed too big for her sharp face, and her long, straight nose, she looked like the drawings with which the Greek potters of Alexandria decorated their vases.

They saw each other again on the waterfront. She began to go there with him to spend the day waiting for ships. Her father was dead and her mother had great difficulty feeding her large brood of children. Lydia did not eat every day. Little by little, Jacob took her under his care; when necessary, he did not hesitate to steal a cake or a few dates from one of the merchants in the quarter.

Lydia came from a Christian family but her mother said that her husband's death proved that Christ was not as powerful as He was claimed to be. Lydia, however, liked the idea of a God who had come down to earth to redeem mankind, and she might have asked to be baptized if Jacob had not dissuaded her. Steeped in his family's warnings against the Christians and their errors, he was determined not to let her go astray. He had not saved Clement, but at least he could save Lydia. With the immense seriousness of his thirteen years, he told her that she should adopt the Jewish religion so that they could marry and live together forever.

It was a long, tiresome process. Jacob took Lydia to the synagogue. With great reluctance, the rabbi finally agreed to teach the Book to her, provided Jacob told his parents everything. Ezra was furious, Miriam wept, Jacob's brothers and sisters turned their backs on him: "Isn't there a Jewish girl who's good enough for you?" They said they would never accept a Christian in their home. They were so hostile that Jacob decided to disappear for a few days, to make them realize that they would lose him if they went on rejecting Lydia.

It took two years of teaching to bring Lydia to the day of the ceremony, two years of suspicion and solitude, but the rabbi could not have asked for a more conclusive test—especially since, in the meantime, the Christianity that Lydia had given up had become an official religion all over the Roman Empire.

At last, after all the precautions and warnings required by the Law, Lydia was taken to three rabbis wearing their white prayer shawls.

"What is your name?"

"Lydia, daughter of the merchant Apollonius, who died three years ago."

"What do you want?"

"To become Jewish."

"Don't you know that the people of Israel are now despised, in exile, and constantly afflicted with suffering?"

"Yes, I know."

"You can still change your mind."

"I've thought it over carefully. I'm ready to accept your faith and your commandments, as well as your afflictions—the afflictions of today's Jewish people."

The three bearded heads nodded and, one after another, the rabbis summarized the commandments of the Law, from the easiest to the most difficult, and pointed out their consequences.

Then, when they had finished, one of them asked her if she still wanted to become Jewish.

"Yes, rabbi," she replied.

"Then *mazel tov!*"

The next day she was purified by the ritual bath in rainwater, then she received her new name: Ruth.

Jacob, who had been waiting outside, took her by the hand and they walked together to his parents' house. He went in first and invited her to follow him. They were all there, his parents, his sisters, and his brother, waiting with expressionless faces.

"This is Ruth," said Jacob.

"Welcome, Ruth," Ezra was obliged to say.

They were married in the autumn of that year, when they were both fifteen. They lived in a room above a warehouse. Their first child, a boy, did not live, and Jacob's sisters could not help gloating. Their second child, also a boy, was splendidly healthy. They named him Aaron. It was he who really made Ruth one of the family. At Passover, Ezra invited his brothers, the cabinetmaker and the goldsmith, to come to his house for the *seder*. That evening, for the first time since he had seen a Christian beheaded in the theater, Jacob felt himself relieved of a terrible burden.

The evening was spent talking about the Christians. Because of Ruth, of course, but also because they were becoming more and more important.

"When people come to power," said Ezra, "they very seldom resist the temptation to impose their ideas on everyone else. The Christians are no different."

"But the Christians already control the whole city," said Solomon the cabinetmaker, who had put on his best clothes for the occasion, "and nothing bad has happened to us. Why should the situation change? They have power, they pray to their God, they collect taxes—what else do you think they want? To kill us? Christians don't kill Jews."

Ezra pursed his lips.

"But what if, in spite of everything, the Christians *do* begin killing Jews?"

There was a silence. Then, because he was the oldest brother, and because he was in his own house, Ezra read a passage from the

79

Passover Haggadah: "We were slaves of the pharaohs in Egypt and the Lord our God brought us out of Egypt with His mighty hand and His outstretched arm. If the Holy One, blessed be He, had not brought our ancestors out of Egypt, we, our children, and our grandchildren would still be there, in bondage to the pharaohs. That is why, even if we were all sages, all intelligent men, all experienced old men, all learned in the Torah, it would still be a duty for us to tell the story of the exodus from Egypt. The more we speak of it, the more we deserve praise."

Ezra let everyone meditate on the passage, then he added, "History is a teacher, and that's why I think we must go on hoping and fearing at the same time."

After the prayers, Ezra solemnly took out the Scroll of Abraham and, in front of everyone, wrote, "Today, the seventeenth day of the month of Nissan in the year 4075 (315) after the creation of the world by the Almighty, blessed be He, I, Ezra, son of Abraham the Levite, pray the Almighty to spare my people and my family the sufferings with which the future appears to me to be filled. May He make my apprehensions useless and my fears vain. Amen."

And then, with something in his eyes that looked like either affection or mischievous amusement, he added, "Jacob married Ruth and begat Samuel, who was stillborn, and Aaron."

"AND AARON begat a new Jacob.

"And Jacob begat Abraham-Alexander, Shulamith, and Rebecca.

"And Abraham-Alexander begat Saul, Judith, Ruth, and Ezra.

"And Saul begat Solomon."

Saul and Solomon, father and son, sat side by side at the table on which they had unrolled the ancient papyrus containing the names of their ancestors. Solomon felt intimidated when he saw his own name at the end of the list, after so many others; it was as if he already belonged to eternity.

"Now it's your turn," said Saul.

Solomon dissolved a little ink, wiped the pen on the wooden tabletop, and wrote, "And Solomon begat Elijah and Gamaliel."

Outside, the crowd was shouting, looking for Jews to convert or kill. In "Ezra's house," the two men made plans to survive in obscurity.

Their ancestor Ezra had been right, a hundred years earlier, to fear the worst. For several weeks now, priests had been going all over the city, preaching against the Jews. The Alexandrian crowd, always ready to riot, had quickly become aroused, especially since Bishop Cyril had refused to obey a summons from Prefect Orestes, whom he accused of having a Jewish mother and being kept by Philoxenus, "a Jew rich in gold, silver, servants, and animals." The prefect had placed soldiers in front of the synagogues, but that protection amounted to very little at a time when the bishop was urging the populace to crime, publicly expressing astonishment that "the Jews, being the murderers who crucified Christ, Son of the Living God, should be richer than the Christians."

Priests had begun visiting Jewish families and promising that the lives of those who converted would be saved. Then Joseph ben Obadiah, the young rabbi of the Canopus synagogue, was murdered. Disaster was on the march. . . .

Saul put his elbows on the table and rested his white-haired head between his hands, which were crossed by dark veins. He wished so much that he could have gone on peacefully growing old in the midst of his family. . . . A few months ago he had had extensive repair work done on "Ezra's house," and he now wondered if he would not have done better to keep that money to enable his family to flee.

Solomon reread what Ezra had written a hundred years earlier. He did not know what to say to comfort his father.

"What can we do against the power of the Church and the hatred of the crowd?"

Solomon had no answer. Should they stand fast? Leave? He wrote only these words under the names of his children: "May the Almighty, blessed be He, have pity on them!" And he added the date, for it seemed important to him: "4174 [414] after the creation of the world."

In front of the Caesareum, the temple built in honor of Caesar, young men burned papyrus scrolls that had been taken from synagogues. The soldiers of Prefect Orestes had been driven away; there was no longer any order in Alexandria. Bands of rioters roamed the streets, intoxicated with sunlight, sweat, and shouting. Near the Gymnasium, a woman carrying a baby crossed a street, and since she was running someone cried out, "A Jewess!" She was immediately caught and surrounded by the rabid mob and a few moments later she was left dead and bleeding on the ground beside her baby, whose skull had been crushed. There was blood, fire, and fear to stir up the madness that gripped the city. The little synagogue of the Delta quarter, not far from "Ezra's house," was set on fire, and the crowd applauded when the Jews who had taken refuge in it for one last prayer jumped through the windows, blazing like torches. On the other side of Alexandria, old men who had refused to convert were tied to the Column of Pompey and crosses were cut into their chests with knives. While their blood trickled across the paving stones, the crowd danced around them.

That day, a hundred Jews were killed before the legion took up positions in the city. What would happen the next day?

Night had fallen when there was a knock on the door of "Ezra's house." Solomon and his wife Miriam suddenly seemed to have been turned to stone. Then Solomon, without taking a step, moved his head forward a little. Miriam gripped him by the sleeve of his linen tunic.

"Don't go, Solomon! Don't open the door!"

They heard the knocking again and felt as if each blow were a stab in the heart. Then his uncle Ezra's hoarse voice called out, "It's me! Let me in!"

Ezra gave them news. Two of his friends had been stoned to death: Aristobulus and Eleazar the blacksmith, sons of Rabbi Enoch. It was said that Bishop Cyril had given the Jews six days to choose between conversion and exile; on the seventh day, those who had neither converted nor left would be killed.

But the most important news was that a Jewish sailor whose son wanted to marry Johanna, Ezra's daughter, was leaving the next day for Carthage, where he had cousins, and where the Jewish community was prosperous.

"He's willing to take us with him," said Ezra, "but we won't get out of the harbor unless we can raise twenty thousand sesterces."

The decision to leave was made without discussion. That night they collected the money they needed: they all took out their savings and Ezra sold his house to his neighbor. Although Saul refused to sell "Ezra's house"—"We'll need a home when we come back," he said—he bitterly regretted having spent money on repairs. Leaving was more painful for him than for any of the others. At the last moment they had to persuade him by insistently pointing out to him that saving a human life was a duty for every Jew. Solomon took with him the black wooden box that contained the family's memory.

THE SHIP reeked of fish and was adorned with a goose head on its stern. No one in the family had ever made a sea voyage. When he set foot on the rough planks of the deck, Saul laughed inwardly and told himself it might be less risky to stay in Alexandria.

The sun was already high in the sky when Amarantius, the Jewish sailor, gave the order to hoist the sail. The south wind pushed the ship out of the harbor between the Diabathea and the lighthouse, but it was the white city, bathed in a kind of pink mist, that seemed to be moving away. The family could not take their eyes off it.

Solomon put his hand on his father's shoulder. Saul sighed and, without looking at him, said in a voice weakened by age, "You see: it's easier than I would have thought. . . ."

But when green waves had filled the horizon, Saul leaned his white-haired head against his son's shoulder and sobbed like a child.

5

HIPPO

Elijah and Jemila

LONG BEFORE the ship landed, a fragrance of orange and jasmine wafted out to it and birds circled it as though to welcome the immigrants. Saul, the oldest member of the group, his brother Ezra, and Amarantius prayed that, with God's help, this new exile would not be too bitter for their families.

Carthage was a dazzling city. The Romans had planned it to be enormous, monumental, unforgettable, so that it would make a deep impression on all those they had conquered. Instead of ramparts, it was surrounded by a ring of gardens, villas, olive groves, and vineyards. As soon as the newcomers set foot on the dock, they were caught up in a bewildering swarm of people speaking different languages, not only Latin and Greek, but also Berber and a language that sounded like Hebrew: Punic. In the oppressive heat, with that whirlwind of races, customs, and beliefs, Carthage was Babel, and Saul quickly realized, from a certain sultriness in the air and the immodesty he saw in many eyes, that the sun, the sea, and history had combined to make this city a hotbed of that lust which the Jews regarded as a dangerous temptation and a terrible sin.

Amarantius did not even know if his cousins were still alive, but several people on the waterfront quickly took charge of the exiles and led them to the Jewish quarter, where Amarantius soon found his distant relatives: David, the *shammash* of a small synagogue, and Monica, a widow who traded in grain and olive oil with the help of her grown children.

For several days the Jewish community showered the newcomers with invitations to eat, pray, and spend the night, and lost no chance to question them. What was Alexandria like? Was it true that in Egypt the Christians persecuted the Jews? How had they escaped? What was a bushel of olives worth in Alexandria? David the *shammash* even blew the *shofar* in the synagogue so that the "sleepers" would know the misfortune that had struck their brothers in Alexandria, and the rabbi quoted the prophet Amos: "Is a trumpet blown in a city, and the people are not afraid?"

They spent the holiday of Rosh Hashanah in this way. The children delightedly explored the vast city, from Byrsa Hill to Maritime Square, walking along broad avenues lined with statues and columns, lingering in the forum or going to see the mosaic showing fabulous monsters: headless men, men with only one leg and a gigantic foot that sheltered them from the sun when they lay down and raised it above them . . .

But this state of idleness could not last. One day Amarantius's cousin Monica took her friends to see Mattos, a rich merchant who had several business enterprises in Carthage and wanted to open one in Hippo.*

"It's a good chance for you," Monica had said to Ezra. "Mattos will invest money, you'll work, and the two of you will share the profits. Try to make a good impression on him."

Ezra had accepted the idea even before he met Mattos and learned where Hippo was.

Mattos was a very stout man who hid his expressions in the folds of his fat. He had shrewd eyes and quick judgment. Without asking many questions, he declared himself willing to make a trial arrangement with Ezra.

"Hippo is a beautiful city," he said in his soft voice, as though this ought to be enough to make the whole family decide to pack up and go there.

Amarantius took them all aboard his ship and they went to Hippo, hugging the coast. It was indeed a beautiful city, sheltered at the back of a bay, facing east.

---

* Later Bona, now Annaba, Algeria.

Ezra went to see Sertius, Mattos's correspondent, who had been instructed to install him in the shop. It was in an arcade at one corner of the marketplace and consisted of a large square room opening onto the street, with a stone corner and a new *pondetarium,* a slab from which weights and measures were hung.

They found lodgings in a high, narrow house at the edge of the Jewish quarter, near the ramparts that overlooked the Seibus River. The ground floor was used by a Christian baker for storing firewood. Ezra and his family occupied the second floor—Johanna, separated from Amarantius's son Publius, who had remained in Carthage, wept a great deal—while Saul, Solomon, Solomon's wife Miriam, and their two sons, Elijah and Gamaliel, were crowded into the third floor.

How long were they going to stay in Hippo? Till the next persecution? Till the end of time?

As in Carthage, they were welcomed by the Jewish community with warmth and curiosity. Rabbi Joseph was strongly affected by the arrival of Saul and Solomon. Impressed by old Saul's knowledge, he introduced him in the synagogue as the sage of sages, a righteous man and a great scholar of the Mishnah who had come from Egypt, like Moses.

Rabbi Joseph was a man of slow speech and gestures. For years he had been unsuccessfully seeking permission from the city council to enlarge his synagogue, a square and rather dark building surrounded by cypress trees, at one end of the odorous Street of Bakers. It had become the great struggle of his life and he was glad to let Solomon take over the task of teaching the children of the quarter to read and write, so that he could devote himself entirely to persuading the city councilors.

And so a new life became organized. While Solomon taught, Ezra made his first purchases. But, obliged to deal with intermediaries, and exposed to the mistrust stirred up by his competitors, he was unable to buy on advantageous terms. He confided his difficulties to Sertius, who was as loquacious as Mattos was taciturn.

"You have to buy olive oil where it's pressed," said Sertius, "and grain where it's harvested. And where is it harvested? Where the peasants are. And where are the peasants?"

Asking and answering his own questions, he told Ezra that the best plan would be to rent two wagons and go to the market at

Cirta* or, still better, at Thamugadi,† which was far away from everything; at Thamugadi, prices defied all competition.

"You'll even find Jews there: Berbers who pray to the God of Israel!"

"How far is it?" asked Ezra, who could not see himself spending a long time on the road, at his age.

"That depends—on how fast you travel, on whether or not you're attacked by bandits, on how soon you want to come back. . . ." Sertius finally said, as if he were offering a price after a long session of bargaining, "A month to get there and back: is that all right?"

It was decided to send two wagons to the great springtime market at Thamugadi, in the southern mountains. Alexander, one of Ezra's sons, and Elijah, Solomon's older son, would make the journey with three men paid by Mattos.

Solomon soon had many pupils. The children liked the way he told them stories from the Book and added his own comments, some of which were a bit unorthodox. Rabbi Joseph was not always in agreement with those comments, but Solomon was attracting more pupils to the school and more worshipers to the synagogue, and Rabbi Joseph was able to use this as an argument in his efforts to obtain the permission he wanted from the city council.

"Our synagogue is shrinking, day by day!" he pleaded.

But it was as if the councilors were amused by his stubborn determination: they went on refusing to let him enlarge his synagogue, while the synagogue of the affluent quarter, between the sea and the hill, was treated with unfailing good will.

Gamaliel, who was rapidly growing up, began helping his father in the synagogue school. He read aloud and corrected the dictations. He was to remember all his life the happy times he spent there, teaching what he knew, in the course of days divided into periods by the times when bakers on the street took batches of bread from their ovens.

One day, a Sunday, Solomon and Gamaliel left the school later than usual. They hurried on their way home because they knew that Christians were bored on this day, not being allowed to do

---

* Now Constantine, Algeria.
† Now Timgad, near Batna, Algeria.

business or attend public entertainments, and that their boredom often incited them to provoke Jews or pagans.

This time Solomon and Gamaliel did not escape. A group of young men suddenly stepped in front of them.

"What's your hurry, Jews?" said one of them.

Solomon walked past him as if he and the others did not exist.

Another one, a tall young man with a square head, caught up with him.

"Just a minute, Jew. Do you think you're too good to talk to Christians?"

All at once he brutally pulled Solomon toward him by the front of his tunic and butted him in the face. Blood flowed immediately and the group ran away.

Gamaliel watched his father wash himself at the next fountain. He loved him very much, because he was his father, of course, but also because he was a gentle, cheerful man, always attentive to others, and it seemed to Gamaliel that he should have fought in his father's stead, or at least defended him, yet he had done nothing. This scene was also something he would never forget.

IN THE SPRING, Alexander, Elijah, and Mattos's three men left for Thamugadi, to the southwest. They were well supplied with food and urgent instructions from their mothers, which went from "Be careful not to catch a cold!" to "If bandits attack you, give them everything you have!" They had been warned about lions and wild dogs, and, perhaps even more dangerous, the bands of male and female brigands known as Circumcellions, heretical Christians who brought terror—pillage, fire, rape—to lands held by orthodox Christians. *"Deo laudes!"* [Praise to God!] was their war cry.

"For once, being Jews will be an advantage to us!" Elijah had said as a form of bravado.

The truth was, however, that the two cousins were a little uneasy as they watched the mules being hitched to the wagons before their early morning departure. Yet what an adventure it was to be young and go off to face unknown risks beyond the horizon!

After leaving Hippo they followed a road bordered by columns for a while. This was the military road that went straight to Tagaste* and Theveste† or, if one took the branch to the right, as

* Now Souk-Ahras, Algeria.
† Now Tebessa, Algeria.

they soon did, led to Lambessa. It was paved with broad stones near towns, but everywhere else it was covered only with pebbles. Optat, the youngest of Mattos's men, acted as the guide and led the wagon in which large earthenware jars for olive oil were firmly secured in place. Now and then they had to stop on the roadside to let a courier of the imperial post gallop past in a cloud of yellow dust.

They soon became used to the cadence of their days: occasional encounters, long stretches with nothing but the creaking of the axles to accompany their slow pursuit of the horizon. Sometimes they exchanged true or false stories, questioned each other—"Have you ever . . . had a woman?" "Who, me?" "Yes, you!"—or commented endlessly on an incident that had just happened, or on some odd feature of the landscape. After fertile plains and wooded valleys, they discovered plateaus where nothing grew except sparse grass, and where small herds of wandering donkeys fled as they approached. Unreal mountain ranges loomed in the distance. It seemed that the sky was vaster here than elsewhere, and the air purer.

When they were not lucky enough to be able to stop for the night at a caravansary—they could not know in advance what kind of mood the mules would be in, and therefore how far they would travel in a day—they stood guard one at a time, each of them taking his turn at being alone beneath the cold, white stars. It seemed to them that they must soon reach the other side of the earth. They sometimes met Roman patrols on the road and wondered what advantage the Romans could find in holding that wilderness under their administration. They knew that Alaric's army had captured and devastated Rome. In Hippo it was said that the empire was gradually disintegrating and that it was surviving better in Africa than anywhere else.

At last Thamugadi appeared through the haze, white and yellow against the purplish-blue background of the mountains on the horizon. Gaping in amazement, the two cousins discovered a true Roman city, a vast square divided into smaller squares, with broad column-lined avenues, a circus, a theater, a triumphal arch, and, on the north, a monumental gate, through which they entered.

The market, with its swarm of buyers, sellers, and onlookers, its shouts, animal cries, jugglers, dancers, and slave merchants, contrasted sharply with the pomposity of the city's architecture. As a result, Alexander and Elijah felt more at ease there.

They did not have time to make their purchases that day. After finding lodgings for themselves, they went off to reconnoiter. Camels and black goats, guarded by swarthy children, were penned at the edges of the marketplace. A little farther on were the tents of nomads who had come to sell their dates or olive oil.

"Are those the Jewish Berbers?" Alexander asked Optat.

"Not all Berbers are Jewish," replied Optat.

"Ask them."

Optat and the two cousins approached a group of young women waiting their turn at a well. When they saw the young men coming toward them, they began talking and laughing at the same time.

"My friend here," Optat said in Punic, "wants me to ask you if you're Jewish."

The laughter redoubled. One of the women was pushed forward by the others.

"We believe in one God, the God of Israel," she said.

"Then you *are* Jewish!"

Alexander smiled triumphantly, as if he had something to do with their being Jewish, and began putting on airs in front of the woman who had spoken. She modestly lowered her eyes. Her dark face was framed by braided blond hair and her loose dress was covered by a square of linen draped over her shoulders. The wind pressed the cloth against her slender body, which gave the impression of being lithe and vigorous. Standing motionless behind Optat and Alexander, Elijah seemed petrified with emotion.

"What's your name?" asked Alexander.

"Jemila."

"I'm Alexander and he's Optat."

Jemila raised her long eyelashes and looked at Elijah. He felt as if he were sinking into the ground.

"And what's *your* name?" she asked him.

She had golden eyes and he knew he could not live without her. He tried to say his name but, to his great embarrassment, he heard himself answer, "Jemila."

The others all burst out laughing. He turned and hurried away from them, almost running.

The next day, he, Alexander, and Optat went all over the market, talked with the merchants, and began making calculations: they could buy olive oil here for only half of what Ezra paid his wholesalers for it in Hippo!

Elijah did not see Jemila that day, and was therefore miserable.

The next day, *shabbat,* he saw her from the ramparts. She was with her family, among the tents of the camp. They stayed there all day without working, so they really were Jews. Strange Jews, those nomads who spent most of their time in the open air, with their camels and goats. Elijah would never have imagined such a thing. And as he was contemplating his beloved from the top of the ramparts, it seemed to him that she looked in his direction. . . . .

On Sunday, Alexander, Elijah, and Optat made their purchases. They preferred buying from the Jewish Berbers, whose leader was Tabet, Jemila's father. He gave them favorable terms.

That evening Elijah went off alone and wandered at the foot of the ramparts until he met Jemila, as if by chance. She was coming back from the well, with a water jug on her head.

"We have to leave tomorrow," he said.

"Then good-bye."

She went on walking, looking straight ahead.

"Why won't you stop?"

"Because my mother is waiting for this water. And because you're about to leave and we won't see each other again."

Elijah became frantic.

"I won't forget you," he said. "I'll come back!" He was now walking beside her. "Can I help you? Do you want me to carry your water?"

"No, that's women's work. We're almost there. Leave me now." She turned to him and said, as though challenging him, "I'll be here for the autumn market, and then I'll see if you've forgotten me!"

A sandstorm arose during the night and for three days Elijah and his companions were unable to leave for Hippo. When the sky finally cleared, the marketplace was deserted and, beneath the ramparts, the Berber camp had disappeared. Elijah vainly looked southward, toward the land of those mysterious Jews. The wind had wiped away their footprints. The awesome, desolate landscape was empty.

LIFE IN HIPPO gradually settled into an orderly sequence of activities, and life in Egypt began fading away like a childhood memory—even Miriam no longer spent her time making comparisons. Johanna, Ezra's daughter, and Publius, son of Amarantius the sailor, finally married. Amarantius was lost at sea soon afterward. Gamaliel was giving amorous looks to the daughter of Rabbi

Noah, who lived in the well-to-do quarter, and that important personage did not seem particularly happy about it.

One day Augustine, bishop of Hippo, sent someone to ask Rabbi Joseph if he would be willing to help him in a dispute concerning a new translation of the Bible. Rabbi Joseph's first impulse was to refuse, but then it occurred to him that the bishop might help him to obtain permission to enlarge his synagogue. He asked Saul to go with him.

The bishop was an eminent man among the Christians. Every day in the *secretarium* of the basilica or in the portico of the courtyard adjoining the church, he held sessions during which he acted as an arbitrator in the conflicts that frequently broke out among the contentious members of his flock.

Augustine must have been more than sixty-five at that time, and he had a fragile constitution, but he was constantly active: he preached, wrote, carried on an enormous correspondence, meditated, and engaged in exegesis with unflagging fervor. He had vigorously struggled against various heresies in Christianity and the authority he had acquired in this way had made him one of the leading lights of his time. He was not afraid to maintain relations with the Jews and he taught his priests to preach to them with love and humility. "We must not," he said, "haughtily raise ourselves above those broken branches of the tree of Christ."

Rabbi Joseph and Saul did not know how to interpret Augustine's request for help. They felt a little wary as they approached the *secretarium* of the Basilica Major.

When they came in, the bishop appeared to be exasperated by the pettiness of the cases submitted to him, and by the litigants' vehement recriminations.

"It seems to me," he was saying, "that you like lawsuits even when they're only a waste of time and a cause of trouble! It would be better to give money to your adversary than to go on wasting your time and destroying your peace of mind!"

"Do you want to encourage injustice?" asked the litigant to whom he had spoken.

The bishop swept away the objection with a quick movement of his arm.

"You know very well that the thief will be robbed in his turn by someone even more dishonest than he is!"

When he was told that Rabbi Joseph and Saul had arrived, he ordered that they be brought to him and greeted them warmly.

"Welcome to both of you," he said. "May Almighty God bless us all."

"Amen," replied Rabbi Joseph.

Glad to have a respite from his hearings, Augustine told them that a religious recluse named Jerome, in Bethlehem, had undertaken a new translation of the Bible in which he contradicted the Septuagint on several points. But Augustine did not subscribe to all of Jerome's innovations. The two men had been carrying on an animated correspondence with regard to the identity of the plant, called *kikayon* in Hebrew, that provided shade for the prophet Jonah.

"You know the passage, don't you?" he asked.

The two Jews knew it. They looked at each other and it was Saul who answered.

"I don't know what Rabbi Joseph thinks," he said, "but it's my opinion that the word *kikayon* designates a gourd."

Augustine smiled triumphantly.

"Jerome claims that it means 'ivy'!"

"I also think it means 'gourd,' " confirmed Rabbi Joseph. "But, if you like, I can write about it to the rabbis of Oea, in Tripolitana. They know much more than we do."

"Yes, please write to them," said Augustine. "Bring me your letter quickly, so that I can have it sent by the imperial post."

Before going back to his litigants, he asked Saul and Rabbi Joseph if there was anything he could do for them. Stammering with emotion, Rabbi Joseph told him that his synagogue had become too small and that the city councilors refused to let him enlarge it. The bishop promised that he would try to intervene and added with a smile, "If you enlarge your synagogue I'll have to build another church, because otherwise I'll lose my congregation to you!"

A few weeks later the councilors finally gave Rabbi Joseph the permission he had been seeking so long, and Augustine received the answer of the rabbis of Oea: they declared that a *kikayon* was a gourd. Because of this, Jerome referred to the bishop of Hippo and his Jewish translators as "cucurbitarians" (from *cucurbita,* the Latin word for "gourd").

Elijah and Jemila finally married, of course. There had to be two weddings: the first one in Hippo, with festivities that lasted seven days—Bishop Augustine sent a basket of fruit—and the second one in Thumar, in the Aurès Mountains, the following spring. Hundreds of Jewish Berbers came from neighboring camps. The ceremony was a mixture of Jewish and pagan rites that horrified old Saul.

Because he could not leave the shop, Ezra was unable to make the long journey to Thumar, but Saul, Solomon, Miriam, and Gamaliel wanted to accompany their grandson, son, and brother to the wilderness in which he had chosen to live. Tabet, Jemila's father, received them with elaborate honors and ceremonies. Then, when the wedding festivities were over, he announced that it was time to take the animals to new pastures. One morning the Berbers set off from the campsite, leaving behind only the old, the sick, and the visitors from Hippo.

The hordes of camels, goats, and donkeys, followed by families in disorder calling out to straggling children, headed into the rugged red-and-black mountains. Solomon and Miriam watched them till they had disappeared, then exchanged a look as though to assure each other that it was only a dream—how could they believe that their son now belonged to that world?

They did not accept it as reality until they were back in Hippo. But they had no regrets: Elijah and Jemila seemed happy together.

•　　•　　•

I WENT BACK to Jerusalem, where I was giving an exhibition of my paintings. Since I had a little time left over from hanging the paintings and keeping appointments with critics, I decided to visit the old rabbi who had told me, during our chance encounter one rainy day, that he owned a book printed by one of my ancestors.

I found him as I had left him, eternal, with his shtramel, his sidelocks, and his threadbare black caftan. He recognized me immediately.

"Welcome!" he said. "Have a seat. It was time you came." Realizing that I was thinking of his great age, he chuckled. "I'm in very good health. It's the neighborhood that's in bad shape!"

The Israelis had begun work on an extensive renovation project and I had had difficulty recognizing the street.

Without hesitation, from among several prayer books, he took a volume with a red cover darkened by humidity. It had been there within reach, as if Rab Chaim had expected me each day since our last conversation, a year earlier.

"Be careful," he said, "time has made it fragile." He seemed

reluctant to hand it to me. "It's a book of commentaries on the Talmud. Reading commentaries on the Talmud is never a waste of time, but you'll also find a letter. . . ."

"A letter?"

"A letter from your great-grandfather."

He put the book down on the table, opened it with the respect of a priest opening a tabernacle, and took out a sheet of paper folded in two, covered with elegant, slanted handwriting that was beginning to fade in some places.

"Look," he said excitedly. "Can you read it?"

He unfolded the letter on the table and read it to me solemnly, following the lines with his forefinger:

> To my dear brother, virtuous and full of wisdom, Rab Shlomo Levi, cantor of the Whitechapel synagogue, may long life be given to him.
>
> These few words are to tell you that I am, thank God, in good health and at peace. May Almighty God help us to hear only good things, good news, from each other, and may He give us health and solace. Amen.
>
> I learned a few days ago that we are related to the famous rabbi of Ger. His name is Isaac-Meir Alter. The H was supposedly added to our name by the French when our grandparents were allowed to be officially registered with the government. As you know, they lived in Strasbourg for a time during the reign of Napoleon. One of our ancestors, Samuel [illegible passage] in Poland. That is interesting news, is it not? I intend to go to Ger soon, to inform the rabbi of it, may long life be given to him. Do you remember the stories that our granduncle, Rab Abraham, told us about our family in Cordova? And the ones about Narbonne? And the ones [illegible passage] letters and memoirs that might give me information about that time? If the Almighty is willing, I will give you all the details of my research in my next letter.
>
> In the meantime, may God give you health. Give my regards to your beloved wife, her parents and your children.
>
> With friendship and best wishes from your brother.
>
> Meir-Ikhiel

THIS LETTER did not contain much that was new to me, but I had to incorporate its elements into my file cards in Paris. I asked

Rab Chaim for it but he would not part with it. At most, he consented to go with me to a small stationery shop near the King David Hotel, where a young Yemenite woman photocopied it. I promised to come back and tell him about my research, and thanked him warmly. Like many old people, he did not like a visitor to leave him; he gave me to understand that he might have other books printed by my great-grandfather.

That evening I went to see Professor Dov Sadan of the Hebrew University. Despite his name—dov means "bear" in Hebrew—he was small and lively, constantly in motion. With his crown of white hair, he made me think of David Ben-Gurion in a speeded-up film. His wife brought us coffee and cheesecake—a ritual in Israel. I showed them the copy of the letter from my great-grandfather. Dov Sadan got off his stool and waved his short arms.

"Your great-grandfather was mistaken," he said. "Alter isn't a real name, and the H doesn't date from the time of Napoleon. In German, Halter means 'keeper' and it used to mean 'shepherd' or 'herdsman,' but the Jews never kept flocks or herds in Germany, so it seems to me that Halter should be translated as 'keeper of the people and their laws.' "

"And why isn't Alter a real name?"

"That's a good question! Alter means 'old' in German. In the Middle Ages, a sick child was given the name of 'Old' to deceive the angel of death. When the angel came to take the child, the people around the cradle said to him, 'Why have you come for this person? He's Old and won't be of any use to you. Let him live out his few remaining days in peace.' "

"And did it work?"

"Apparently so. All tricks work at one time or another."

"But, Dov," I said, "some of my ancestors were real herdsmen."

He got back onto his stool, pushed his glasses up to his forehead, and looked at me as though trying to see if I was joking or not.

"Herdsmen? Real keepers of animals?"

"Yes," I said. "They even had camels. It was in the Aurès Mountains. My ancestor Elijah had just married Jemila. . . ."

6

HIPPO

Under the Rule of the Vandals

THE ROMAN Empire was dying. All sorts of disorders undermined the great body as its last strength deserted it, and it could not fail to be affected by the blows struck against the Church. Bonifacius, governor of Africa and commander of the Roman armed forces there, was a corrupt soldier who pillaged the region for his own benefit. The last expression of Roman order, insofar as it was bound up with Christianity, was Bishop Augustine of Hippo, who at the age of seventy-two had asked that he be allowed to devote himself at least partially to study.

But that was when the Vandals began to threaten. They had plundered Rome, marched across Gaul, and invaded Spain, and their hordes were now gathering at the Pillars of Hercules. This was like a signal to many less important looters. Wandering bands of reactivated Circumcellions, southern nomads, and Moors from the Atlas Mountains attacked one after another, as though determined to finish off the destruction of the Pax Romana. Bonifacius, overwhelmed, called on the Vandals for help. It was said that he had offered to share Africa with their king, Genseric.

The Vandal hordes surged into Africa and devastated Numidia. "Regions that were once prosperous and densely populated," wrote Bishop Augustine, "were turned into wastelands." Pillage,

97

slaughter, ruin. Populations fled like herds stampeded by fire and took refuge in fortified cities, which fell one by one.

In Hippo, Saul died at this time, as much from sadness as from old age. Solomon abruptly became the father, the figure of authority, and he felt it as a heavy burden. During the seven days of *shiva* he thought of his own son far away in the purple mountains, with his camels and date trees, and when *shiva* was over he told his family that the only way to escape from the Vandals was to leave Hippo and go to stay with Elijah.

Ezra, whose business was thriving because of the refugees, preferred to stay in Hippo. And so Solomon left with his wife Miriam, his second son Gamaliel, and his daughter-in-law Monica. After much hesitation he decided to take the Scroll of Abraham with him. It was now his responsibility and he felt that leaving it behind in a city that might be plundered and destroyed would be worse than exposing it to the dangers of travel.

Just then Bonifacius did another about-face: he proclaimed himself the defender of the Church and the empire and ensconced himself in Hippo. Solomon and his family barely had time to leave. As they began their journey, Solomon quoted from the Book of Lamentations: "Who has commanded and it came to pass, unless the Lord has ordained it? Is it not from the mouth of the Most High that good and evil come?"

THUMAR WAS a village perched on a cliff, overlooking a valley where life flowed: a stream and its oasis of date and tamarind trees. Solomon had hired a guide at Thamugadi and they had wasted no time on the way, yet when they reached the foot of the mountains in which Thumar was nestled they found the whole tribe of Jewish Berbers waiting for them, with Tabet in the forefront and Elijah, Jemila, and their newborn son Telilan close behind him. The women shouted greetings to them, the men beat small drums, and the children scurried around excitedly in the dust: events were rare.

When Elijah saw his parents, his brother, and his sister-in-law arrive in their city clothes, with their skin still showing little sign of being toughened by exposure to the elements, he realized how different he had become from them. He did his best to help them settle into their new living conditions. Tabet allotted them three cubes of brown earth, each with no other opening than its entrance, and they made themselves as comfortable as they could.

98

Every morning Tabet's mother, a wrinkled old woman, brought them cakes, dates, and a little sour milk.

Tabet treated his son-in-law's family with great respect, but saw to it that none of the tribe's customs and traditions were altered by contact with those city Jews. When winter came—a harsh, white, motionless winter—Solomon offered to teach Hebrew and the Torah to the children and anyone else who wanted to learn. Tabet felt that he could not refuse to allow it. He attended all the lessons himself, probably less to keep an eye on Solomon than to avoid the risk of someday knowing less than the people he commanded. His fear was not groundless: seeing that Solomon was such a learned man, the Berbers began questioning him, asking him for advice, and even abiding by his opinion in settling quarrels.

Elijah warned his father: "Tabet will think you're trying to take his power away from him. You ought to have a talk with him."

Solomon went to the chief of the Jewish Berbers and began by saying to him, "May the Almighty, blessed be He, protect you."

Tabet, sitting in front of a fire that had died down to embers, was rolling a string of amber beads between his fingers.

"Amen," he replied.

"I wanted to speak with you, Tabet."

"Then speak."

"My son and your daughter are married and already have a child, may God give him long life."

"Amen."

"You and your people have taken us in and given us food and shelter. We're grateful to you."

"You're all welcome here."

Tabet was keeping his distance.

"I wouldn't want you to think that we'd come to stay here permanently."

"Why are you telling me that?"

"To make it clear that I don't want to harm you in any way."

Tabet remained silent, watching the amber beads flowing in his hands.

"You're the leader in Thumar," said Solomon.

"You shouldn't be saying that to me, Solomon. You should say it to the people who are going to listen to you and become more learned than I am."

AS SOON AS WINTER was over, most of the Berbers left, driving their animals before them as they moved through the valley. No one stayed behind in the village but Solomon and his family, a few women, and the old men who took care of the date trees. Solomon felt as if he were the ruler of a deserted kingdom. Miriam learned to weave cloth for the black tents that kept out wind and rain. Gamaliel assiduously studied the Torah. His wife Monica was expecting a child.

The Vandals had come to the foot of the mountains, then left; they had better things to do in the cities. But it was said that they attacked only Christians and tried to gain support from the pagans, Donatists, and Jews. Now that the danger seemed to have passed, Solomon forgot his enthusiastic plans to provide schooling for all the Jewish Berber children and began thinking of going back to Hippo, though they would have to wait until after Monica's child had been born.

MONTHS LATER, when Monica had given birth to a daughter, the tribe returned in a whirlwind of dust and a tumult of mingled sounds: bleats, brays, the jingling of bells attached to animals' necks, the shrill shouts of women. As Solomon stood watching from the edge of the cliff, he suddenly understood the warmth with which nomads welcomed visitors in their remote wilderness: he himself felt like clapping his hands.

Tabet and Elijah greeted him with a serious expression and Jemila avoided his eyes.

Elijah took his father aside.

"I think it will be better if you and the others leave now."

Solomon stared at him in bewilderment.

"As soon as I tell you hello, you tell me to leave!" he said bitterly.

"Father, sheep have died without being sick, springs have dried up for the first time. . . . The wise men say that your presence has turned the gods against us."

"The gods? What gods? I know only one God, the Almighty, glory to Him and blessed be He!"

"The Jewish Berbers believe in the God of Israel and place Him above all others, but they say that Gurzil also exists, and Tanit. . . . Those other gods are angry with you because you want to teach the children Hebrew and the Torah."

Solomon was horrified.

"Elijah, my own son—don't tell me that you believe in Gurzil!"

"I believe in the God of Israel with all my heart and soul, but . . . But it's still true that sheep have died without being sick!"

Solomon went to Tabet, who seemed to have been expecting him.

"Tabet, I thank you for your hospitality, but we no longer have anything to fear from the Vandals and Monica's child has been born. . . ."

He had no doubt that Tabet had told Elijah to speak to him, feeling that this would be more tactful than a direct confrontation, but the chief remained inscrutable as he fingered his amber beads.

"You're leaving?" he asked. "That will probably be better for everyone. I like you and I've often been jealous of your knowledge, but the son of your son and my daughter is a Jewish Berber, like me, like my father Amri and my grandfather Mellag. For us, knowing how to follow trails, take care of date trees, and raise sheep is more important than knowing how to read and write. You're leaving and we'll be sad. That's how life is; we mustn't try to go against it."

Tabet gave them an escort to Thamugadi. Solomon looked back several times at the purple mountains where he was leaving part of himself behind: a son and a grandson. Would he ever see them again? Gamaliel was glad to be going back to the city. Miriam had wept when she left Elijah, but Fulvia, Monica's daughter, was enough to keep her attention occupied, with her belches and smiles. Solomon continued looking back until the mountains on the horizon had turned into a distant dark line.

At Thamugadi the Vandals stopped them. They were tall, had long blond or red hair, and they wore tight tunics and studded animal hides. Among themselves they spoke a harsh, rapid language that was unlike anything Solomon had ever heard before.

The interpreter who questioned Solomon and his family told them that Jews had nothing to fear from the Vandals and wished them a good journey. Solomon could scarcely believe what was happening: since when had barbarians stopped molesting Jews? He realized that there was a certain amount of self-interest in the invaders' attitude, but even so. . . .

HIPPO WAS unrecognizable: ramparts torn down, streets with their paving stripped away, gaping sewers, houses destroyed. The people had scarcely begun to rebuild the ruins. Ezra was dead; it was his son Alexander who told about the siege and capture of the city, and the death of old Bishop Augustine. Alexander had aged. He was now in charge of Mattos's shop.

The Vandals had changed nothing in the organization and civil law of the city. Life was gradually returning to normal. The work of enlarging Rabbi Joseph's synagogue had begun. Rabbi Noah, becoming increasingly tired, was preparing Gamaliel to be his successor in the synagogue of the well-to-do quarter. For the first time since they had been married, Solomon and Miriam found themselves alone. At holidays and sometimes on *shabbat,* they were visited by Monica and her children—she and Gamaliel now had three—or by their nephew Alexander, but they still lived alone and they saw people their age dying one by one. Time passed, lives passed; it was in the order of things.

SOLOMON OPENED his eyes. It was still night. He tried to move but a sharp pain pierced his heart. Was it a pain, or fear of a pain? If it was a pain, he would call Miriam; if it was fear . . . Poor Miriam, she was much sicker than he was. He tried to make out the contours of the room in the darkness, cautiously took a few shallow breaths, and became a little calmer. It was not this time that he would wake up dead, as his father used to say, jokingly. In his mind he again saw his father, Saul, the day they left Alexandria. It was . . . a whole lifetime ago. Daylight seemed to be approaching. "I thank You, O living and eternal King, for having, in Your love, given me back my soul. Great is Your fidelity." Those were the words of the morning prayer that men were required to say to thank the Almighty, blessed be He, for having brought them back to life after a night of sleep. But Solomon did not know if he was really awake. His eyes were open but he saw nothing. "Repent on the eve of your death," Rabbi Eleazar had said. But no one could know the day of his death, and that was why the sages added, "Therefore repent every day of your life." It seemed to Solomon that if he breathed too heavily, something inside him would be torn apart. Was this what it was like to be dying? He thought of his sons, Gamaliel and Elijah, as different from each other as it was possible to be, but two good sons, each in his own way. He had not seen Elijah since his stay with him in the mountains. That was during the time when the Vandals took Hippo, at least twenty-five years ago. Elijah probably had gray hair by now.

Every year, when he went to the great market in Thamugadi, Elijah asked travelers to bring his parents news of the tribe—his wife had given birth to another child, Telilan had married a young Jewish Berber woman named Tiski—but he had never said that he had gray hair. *My God, what's left of me when my son has gray hair? Come, Solomon, tell the truth: have you ever accepted, in your heart, Elijah's marriage to that daughter of the desert? Didn't your fascination prove that you regarded Tabet and his tribe as alien to you, with their barbaric gods and their curdled milk? I don't know, I swear I don't know, but one thing is certain: I did nothing to prevent that marriage or keep my son with me. . . .* Solomon struggled within himself. He knew that something terrible was happening to him but he had not yet accepted it. Even so, he wanted to feel that he had done right in his life. . . . He suddenly saw the face of Livia, Gamaliel's second daughter, who had one day gone off with a Syrian merchant. The family later learned that she had become one of the waterfront prostitutes in Carthage. *Gamaliel wanted to go and bring her back, but remember, Solomon, that it was you, the patriarch, who refused to let him go and said the prayer for the dead for her.* Solomon wept, for Livia, for himself, for misery and honor; he wept slow, burning tears. He had forgotten why he had been so unyielding. The words of Ezekiel came into his mind: "Have I any pleasure in the death of the wicked, says the Lord God, and not rather that he should turn from his way and live?" With all his heart, Solomon asked forgiveness of God, of Livia, of Gamaliel and Monica—but who had never made a mistake? He had not gone to Carthage that time, but he had gone there once before, when Jewish sailors had reported that Genseric, the Vandal king, was going to land there with war trophies, among which were the sacred objects that the Romans had long ago taken from the Temple in Jerusalem. The news had quickly spread. By the time Genseric landed and displayed his trophies as proof of his power, thousands of Jews had come from all over Numidia and Byzacium. They fell to their knees and prostrated themselves when the seven-branched candelabrum was shown. The barbarian king had smugly taken this as homage to himself. . . . Solomon could not help smiling. He recalled the Nubian slaves carrying the great candelabrum and the sacred vessels marked with Hebrew letters. What a turn of fate! He was overcome with gratitude to the Almighty and His unforeseeable designs. To bear witness . . . That candelabrum raised above the crowd in Carthage was a testimony.

. . . But now the images that appeared to him were becoming mixed: the purple mountains of Thumar, Amarantius's ship . . . Here, there . . . Solomon felt that the pain had taken up a position next to his heart and was waiting for its time to bite. . . . He would awaken his wife, his dear Miriam, and she would be able to calm him. But his arm was so heavy. . . . He was going to call out to her. . . . Why hadn't daylight come yet? He called out with all his strength, but did he even breathe a sigh?

MIRIAM DIED only a few days after Solomon; their lives had become too closely joined for either to continue alone. Gamaliel wrote to the rabbi of the little synagogue in Thamugadi, asking him to notify Elijah at the first opportunity, but travelers on their way to the wilderness where Elijah lived did not pass through Thamugadi every day. Soon after he had sent his letter, Gamaliel was visited by two nomads wearing striped garments of the kind he remembered seeing in the Aurès Mountains. He greeted them, thinking they must be members of his brother's tribe.

"Peace be with you," the older one said with his hand over his heart.

He was a lean, wiry man, straight as an arrow, with the slightly haughty and faraway look that was given to people of the desert by the contempt in which they held the demands of the body.

"Peace be with you," replied Gamaliel.

And suddenly he recognized Elijah. The two brothers threw their arms around each other, then Elijah introduced his son Telilan, who was also lean and straight, and blond, like Jemila.

"The last time you saw him," said Elijah, "his mother was still suckling him. Now he's our chief, and he has three children himself."

"God bless them."

"Amen," replied Telilan.

Gamaliel asked how the rabbi in Thamugadi had been able to notify them of Solomon's death so soon. But Elijah answered that the rabbi had not notified them of anything, that they had learned of it in another way.

"News travels faster than people," he said.

Gamaliel was unable to draw an explanation from him. The two of them went to the cemetery and said the prayer for the dead together. They felt closer to each other than ever before.

"One day," Gamaliel said abruptly, "I saw our father struck by a Christian. I was already a grown man but I didn't defend him."

"I'd been a grown man for a long time, and married," said Elijah, "when I let Tabet make him leave Thumar. But regrets are useless; they don't wipe away shame."

"Let's just pray that our sons won't forget us!"

Gamaliel was amazed at what his brother had become. His voice, his behavior, his gestures—everything about him had become extremely simple.

They went back to Gamaliel's house and looked at the Scroll of Abraham for a long time. Solomon had carefully kept it up to date and, no doubt hoping for many descendants, he had generously lengthened it. Gamaliel and Elijah sat side by side, leaning over what their father had called "the testament."

"Do your children know how to write?" asked Gamaliel.

"Yes, but not my grandchildren."

"How will you and your family know who you are?"

"There are different ways of remembering," said Elijah. "Footprints in the sand also write human history." He gripped his brother's arm. "And besides, *you're* here to write!"

Meanwhile Gamaliel's older son David, also a scribe, had introduced Telilan to the members of the family. They stared openly at that famous Berber cousin—all the more famous because he had just succeeded his grandfather, Tabet, as chief of the tribe. And that Berber chief, that odd kind of Jew, politely ate honey cakes that turned his stomach and dates that came from his homeland. He was so dignified and reserved that David could not help telling him, a few days later when they were about to part, that he would miss him.

"Come to see us," Telilan invited him.

"It's too far."

"No place is too far when you have time to go there."

"But I *don't* have time. I must write every day to earn my living."

"How much are you paid?"

"Twenty-five denarii for a hundred lines."

"Is that very much?"

"No, but it's enough for me."

Gamaliel and David watched Elijah and Telilan as they walked away with long, steady strides, holding themselves erect, as always, until they disappeared without having looked back.

HIPPO HAD NEVER recovered from the arrival of the Vandals. Besides its ramparts, it had lost its carefree attitude and that fragile equilibrium which had enabled different communities to prosper side by side. As a result of the constant, fluctuating warfare between the Vandals and Constantinople, there was no time to rebuild or replant.

These conditions were bad for business. Alexander, who had become a fat, disillusioned man, vainly waited for customers in his shop at one corner of the marketplace. David, however, was overloaded with work. He ceaselessly wrote copies of contracts, agreements, acknowledgments of debts—the more difficult the situation became, the harder businessmen tried to protect themselves against risks.

David had sent his son Abraham to a rabbi in Carthage, to assist him and learn from him. He sometimes regretted not having kept Abraham with him; there was easily enough work for both of them and he did not like the thought of growing old far away from his children and grandchildren. "Tell him to come back!" his wife Julia said to him now and then, forgetting that Abraham had a wife and four children in Carthage.

David endlessly mulled over regrets and plans as he copied documents. His hand, he said, was able to write on its own, and left his mind free.

Then his father, Gamaliel, died, and soon afterward so did his uncle, Elijah. Telilan sent him the news, without comment, in a letter written by the scribe of Thamugadi, adding only, as though to compensate for that death, that his wife had given birth to another daughter, named Yahia. David often thought of Telilan. "The sons have now become the fathers," he mused. He wondered if, like him, his Berber cousin had felt that emptiness in his chest since the death of his father. Several times he had begun walking toward Gamaliel's house, as he had done so often in the past, before remembering that his father would never be there again, and each time he had turned back with sudden pain in his soul and his body.

Shortly after Gamaliel's death, persecution of Christians began again in Hippo. The Vandals forbade them to go into their churches. The Christians were furious. For the festival of Floralia, they formed a large procession that made its way through the city until it reached the basilica. Vandal horsemen charged with their lances thrust forward. Some of the Christians were killed and, like a warning from heaven, a shower of hail came crackling down on the city.

The enraged Vandals hunted down Christians for several days, taking care to spare pagans and Jews.

Like all the Jews of Hippo, David the scribe and his wife Julia stayed at home with the door locked. One evening, when David was saying the *maariv* of Shabuot, there was a brutal knock on the door. He and Julia looked at each other. "Open!" said a voice. David and Julia had never been persecuted as Jews, but that knocking reawakened a memory much older than they were. David finally stood up, but just then the door was broken from its hinges. Torches, shadows, faces, voices. A dozen lances were pointed at his chest. The Vandals saw the prayer shawl on his shoulders.

"Jews?" asked one of them.

"Yes."

"Are you hiding any Christians here?"

"No."

David was afraid and wondered how he could feel guilty for no reason.

The soldiers left after taking a look into the next room. David and Julia heard them knocking at the house of their neighbors, who were also Jews.

David put the door back in place as best he could. For a long time, sitting beside each other, he and Julia listened to the night—there were shouts and rapid footsteps, sometimes far away, sometimes close by. Then Julia went to bed and David lit a lamp to write a few contracts. He could not sleep, and writing was his refuge.

After dissolving a tablet of ink, he trimmed a pen. How he loved those movements, and the smell of the ink, and the scratching of the pen on the papyrus! He loved to see the letters taking shape in orderly lines according to his will and his art, finally representing people, merchandise, parcels of land . . .

He wrote the date, year 488 of the Christian era, then became absorbed in his work. He was writing a contract in Latin. "Addressed to Marcus, son of Quintus, citizen of Hippo Regius, by Aurelius, son of Sectus. Of our own free will, we wish to buy from you . . ."

He heard a faint sound. Thinking the door had slipped out of

107

place after his makeshift repair, he stood up—and saw it slowly begin to open. A hand appeared, then a blue sleeve, and the face of a desperate woman. My God, he prayed inwardly, please help me. Seeing that he had not moved and was not threatening her, the woman became bolder. She came in and closed the door behind her.

"My brother has been killed," she said hurriedly. "I don't know where my husband is. I'm a Christian."

David had never before known fear of this kind. It seemed to him that his body was becoming liquid. He could not have run away if he had wanted to. Yet his first reaction was to signal the woman to speak softly: Julia was asleep in the next room.

The woman turned her frightened blue eyes to the papyrus lighted by the terra-cotta lamp.

"Am I disturbing you?" she asked.

She was interrupting his work, but that was not serious. What mattered was that her presence in his house endangered him, his wife, and even the whole community: if the Vandals took it into their heads that the Jews were protecting the Christians . . . But he heard himself say to her, "Sit down and catch your breath."

He pointed to a mat in one corner of the room and she sat down on it. He felt that he was living an unimaginable adventure. He thought of the Christians, the Vandals, his wife Julia, and his heart began pounding in his chest like an unknown drum.

"I must do some work," he said, instead of throwing her out.

He resumed his place in front of the papyrus. His hand wrote, but his mind prayed that the woman would leave.

"Don't worry, I won't interfere with your work," she said. "What are you doing?"

"I'm drawing up a contract for the sale of a piece of land."

"How much longer do you think the Vandals will stay in Hippo?"

"Only the Almighty knows, blessed be He."

The woman was becoming calmer. Her hands were now crossed over her knee. Did she have children? David recited to himself a passage from the Book of Job: "If my heart has been enticed to a woman, and I have lain in wait at my neighbor's door; then let my wife grind for another, and let others bow down upon her." With an effort, he began writing again: ". . . the ten-acre parcel of land situated . . ."

He thought he heard a sound from the street and for a moment he was on the alert. No, nothing. When he had finished his contract, he began another. Why didn't he have the courage to send that woman away while there was still time to avoid disaster? He questioned the Almighty with all his strength, but the Almighty did not answer him. And she was there, sitting motionless and looking at him gravely. All at once he realized that he desired her and his heart began pounding again. Perhaps it could be explained by the night and the shared danger, or the smell of her fear—how was he to know?

He finished his work toward dawn, after writing the concluding words: "I, David, son of Gamaliel, certify that I have written this for Marcellus, son of Cornelius, because he is illiterate." He put down his pen and stood up to relax his back.

The Christian woman also stood up. She came over to look at the completed contract, then unexpectedly took David's right hand and quickly kissed it. He stepped back in alarm.

"I must put more oil in the lamp," he said abruptly, pulling his hand away from her.

He took the terra-cotta lamp into the room where Julia was sleeping, and where the jar of oil was kept. Julia lay on her side with her cheek resting on the palm of her hand, her hair hidden by a gray scarf. He looked at her tenderly and noticed her wrinkles. He knew them all; he had watched them forming in the course of the long time that he and Julia had spent together—time erodes flesh as water erodes rock.

He picked up the jar and went back into the other room, trying to seem absorbed in what he was doing. Only when he had put down the jar and the lamp did he see that the woman was gone. He again heard shouts and rapid footsteps outside. He stood in the middle of the room with his arms hanging at his sides, feeling weary and empty. His hand burned where the woman had pressed her lips to it.

"DAVID, son of Gamaliel, begat Abraham and Rebecca.
"Abraham begat Hanan, Miriam, Aurelia, and Solomon.
"Solomon . . ."

7

HIPPO

Nomos the Red

"SOLOMON BEGAT Sarah, Ruth, and Jonathan.

"Sarah and Ruth were converted by force in the terrible year of 4295 [535] after the creation of the world by the Almighty, blessed be He. May their memory remain in the family and in the House of Israel.

"Jonathan begat Enoch and Elijah.

"Elijah begat David, Nomos, Judith, and Solomon."

It was the month of Tammuz in the year 4373 (613) and Elijah, the father, was reading to his assembled children the litany of the names of those from whom they were descended. Solomon, his grandfather, and Jonathan, his father, had passed on the Scroll of Abraham to him and urged him to add the names of his children to it, in accordance with family tradition, but they had not read it aloud to him. Elijah, however, had discovered that his ancestor Abraham, the scribe in Jerusalem, had expressly written, ". . . may the names that I have written on this scroll, and the names that others will write on it after me, be spoken aloud to rend the silence." The names therefore had to be read *aloud,* and Elijah, one of those rigidly scrupulous men who find fulfillment in the respectful observance of rituals, had gradually built up a whole ceremony around the reading of the Scroll of Abraham.

On the occasion of a death, a birth, or a *bar mitzvah*, he summoned the whole family to his house. They gathered in the big blue room, with the men on the right and the women on the left, as for prayer. With the ritual shawl on his head, Elijah made sure that everyone was present, then began reading from the scroll in the high-pitched voice of a *chazzan*.

This time there was neither a death to mourn nor a birth to celebrate, but the situation was serious. A wave of Jewish refugees from Spain had arrived in Hippo and Carthage, and the persecution from which they had fled was all the more disquieting because their story and that of the Jews in Numidia resembled each other as closely as two olive pits. It seemed quite possible that what had happened there would happen here.

As long as the Visigoths, having conquered Spain, had remained faithful to Arianism, the Jews had remained practically unharmed, but now that their leaders had accepted the authority of the pope they were stubbornly trying to convert the Jews. They had begun by taking children away from their families and sending them to Christian schools, then they had persecuted the parents—a certain Amarius, bishop of Toledo, had even baptized two rabbis, Joseph and Naphtali, by force.

In Hippo, the fate of the Jews depended on the outcome of the battles between the Vandals and the Byzantine armies. When Justinian, the emperor in Constantinople, had driven the Vandals from Africa—as he had driven the Ostrogoths from Italy and the Visigoths from part of Spain—he had issued a decree against the Jews and confiscated their synagogues. The decree had been abolished but not all of the synagogues had been restored to the Jews.

The arrival of the Spanish Jews (Sephardim), and the community council's request that each family take in one of those refugees, impressed Elijah as signs alarming enough to justify calling a family meeting around the Scroll of Abraham. His brother Enoch was there, with his wife and their son Aaron; his daughter Judith had come with her children; and finally there was his son Nomos the scribe, who modestly stood behind the others—as if there were any chance of his not being noticed. Not only was Nomos a very tall, broad-shouldered man with a likable face, but he had amazingly bright red hair. Unable to explain that phenomenon—it had never appeared in the family before—Elijah was not far from regarding it as a sign of bad luck for Nomos. After all, Nomos's wife Miriam had died the day after their wedding. And for the past fifteen years he had refused to remarry. According to the sages, "it is not good for a man to be alone," but all of Elijah's pious exhortations had left Nomos apparently indifferent. "Stop trying to get me married, father," he had once said. "Your other children have already made sure you'll have many descendants. The Almighty, blessed be He, deprived me of the wife I chose. He'll let me know His will, when the time comes."

When Elijah had finished reading Abraham's testament and the names of his descendants, shadows were beginning to lengthen. It was time for the *minhah,* the afternoon prayer: "I glorify You, O my God, my King, and I will bless Your name forever. . . ."

THE SPANISH JEWS had gathered in the courtyard of Rabbi Meir's synagogue, in the lower city. Sitting on bundles or standing with their arms at their sides, feeling out of place in their unfamiliar surroundings, overwhelmed with uncertainties, stiffening whenever anyone looked at them with curiosity, they remained somber and motionless: they had been told to wait.

Finally scribes recorded their names and volunteers assigned them to families. The last ones were assigned to the scribes. And so it was that Nomos took into his modest house a stern-faced woman, dressed all in black, and her young niece—very dark hair, intensely blue eyes, strikingly pale skin. From then on, Nomos spent his days copying the Torah at home, instead of working in the synagogue. He sat writing in the back room that faced the inner courtyard, where the Spanish women had reactivated a disused fountain. He was happy there; to him, the soft, mingled voices of the women and the fountain were like exquisite music.

Those who knew him observed the change in him with interest.

"Your pretty foreigner is strange," said his friend Paulus, a Christian scribe.

"Why do you think she's strange?"

"I don't know; maybe it's her fragility. . . . You need a woman, Nomos, not an angel!"

"She's so . . . so . . ."

"She's made you speechless! Remember what Bishop Augustine said: you must think very carefully before putting a chain on your feet."

A chain! Everyone saw that Nomos and Aster could no longer do without each other, even though they still scarcely dared to look at each other. She was sixteen and he was nearly forty, but they were bound together by one of those mysterious certainties of love, exciting and soothing at the same time.

When the community began to gossip, Elijah asked Nomos and Aster to marry. A year after the wedding, Nomos added the name of their first child, Abraham, to the family book.

IN THE MONTH of Tammuz, Elijah received a letter from his Berber cousin Tazir, written by the public writer of Thamugadi in clumsy Latin, with occasional Hebrew words such as *ben*, "son," and *shanah*, "year":

> To my cousin in Hippo Regius, Elijah ben Jonathan ben Solomon, from Tazir, son of Shakiya and Damya, grandson of Abraham and Diyia. We wish to tell you that we are in good health, with the aid of Yahweh and Gurzil, in our country. We hope that you and your family are also in good health and that you can send us the dates of the Jewish holy days for the coming *shanah*. Two moons from now, we will go down to the market in Thamugadi. The Almighty has granted me a new *ben* and a date harvest so large that even my father had never seen one like it. In His great fairness, the Almighty must have wanted to make up for the harvest of last *shanah*, which was so bad because of all our sins. Praise be to Him for His generosity. The man to whom you give your letter will find me at the market. Everyone knows Tazir ben Shakiya, chief of the Jewish Berbers. May the Lord of Hosts bless you. Your cousin, Tazir ben Shakiya ben Abraham.

Aster, whose whole family, except for her aunt, had been killed by the Visigoths, had gratefully adopted Nomos's uncles, aunts, cousins, nephews, and nieces, and she was delighted to discover that she also had Berber cousins.

"Do you know them?" she asked her husband. "How do they dress? Who's that Gurzil? What does Tazir mean when he says 'our country'?"

Nomos told her that a few years earlier the Berbers had proclaimed the independence of their territory in the Aurès Mountains and had been at war with the official government of Numidia ever since, whether it was Vandal or Byzantine; that he did not know how the Berbers of his cousin's tribe dressed; and the Gurzil was a pagan god.

113

"Then they're not real Jews!"

"They follow the precepts of the Torah, but they live far away from everything, so they must feel that they need extra protection. . . ."

Aster was silent for a moment; she seemed to be imagining herself in those faraway mountains. Nomos looked at her, touched by her youth. Suddenly her face became animated.

"Nomos, my husband," she said, "I'd love to go and visit your cousin Tazir!"

And the most surprising part of it was that Nomos, who had never left Hippo or even crossed the bridge over the Seibus, did not seriously consider opposing his young wife's whim. He raised a few objections dictated to him by his reason, but she swept them away with a gesture of her white hand. The child? Her aunt would take care of him while they were gone. The dangers of the journey? Nothing happened unless it was meant to happen. Fatigue? They would never be younger and stronger than they were now. As for his work, his friend Paulus would be glad to do any part of it that couldn't wait.

They left in the fall, while their family and neighbors looked on with either concern or disapproval. Nomos had borrowed his uncle Enoch's only cart, whose two wheels did not have the same diameter. "It limps!" said Aster. One wheel soon broke, then the other, and the improvised repairs did not hold up very long. They continued with only the two donkeys. Nomos walked most of the time.

Aster was curious about everything she saw and heard: herds of haughty camels, canals that crossed the plain like blue veins irrigating a body, whirlwinds of dust that reminded her of the way women danced in Cordova. . . . She suddenly became serious whenever she saw the remains of a burned house, or an abandoned estate overgrown with weeds.

They slept in inns, or what was left of them. "Look," an innkeeper said to them one evening, "this wing was burned by the Vandals, and that one by the legion. They each got their share!"

As they gradually became used to life on the road, each of them took on a healthier complexion and a heartier appetite. Their food seldom varied: dates and barley cakes, sometimes with a little milk. But what mattered was to keep moving forward.

They reached the land of red mountains and Aster felt as if she had returned to the environs of Cordova or Illiberis. Finally they were in Thamugadi. They scarcely took time to stop at the inn to

114

quench their thirst and leave their donkeys. Aster was so impatient, and so happy about everything!

They had arrived none too soon: the market was going to end in a day or two. The crowd of buyers, sellers, and onlookers was animated by a kind of stationary motion, like the sea, or like those big sand dunes that advance without seeming to move. Nomos and Aster let themselves be caught up in it. Water carriers, beggars, and sellers of talismans clutched at them from all sides.

The Sertius market was reached from the street by way of a little staircase. Around it was a stone wall surmounted by a row of windows with dozens of sleeping lizards on their sills, like a strange kind of lace. Inside, two semicircular courtyards were paved with light-colored stone. All around, in the porticoes, were shops whose merchandise overflowed into the passage. The central courtyard was an indescribable chaos in which all sorts of things were offered for sale: fruit, hides, olive oil, lamps, bags of barley, earthenware jars of wine, jewelry, toasted watermelon seeds, spices, fried cakes. . . . In one corner, criers were pushing back the crowd to make room for a fight between two black goats held on chains by their owners; farther on, a Nubian woman was whirling to the sound of drums and cymbals in the midst of spectators clapping their hands.

Aster suddenly took Nomos's arm and pointed to a man in striped clothes sitting not far away from them, in front of a basket filled with clusters of dates.

"I'm sure that's our cousin!" she said.

Nomos went up to him and asked him if he was Tazir. The man spat a date pit into the dust and shook his head.

Not at all disappointed, Aster turned to another "cousin." This one wore a white robe and was haggling over the price of some goat hides that he was trying to sell to a legionary. Nomos and Aster approached him.

"Ten sesterces for three hides," the legionary declared firmly.

"Ten for three? By Gurzil, you're trying to ruin me! Seven sesterces apiece, twenty-one for the three of them—that's my bottom price."

"I'll give you four apiece. That's all they're worth."

"Take them for seventeen and I'll go home."

"Fifteen!"

"Sixteen!"

Nomos waited till the legionary had paid for the hides and taken them away, then he asked the seller if he was Tazir, even though Nomos was sure he could not be his cousin.

"Tazir?" the seller said when he had finished counting his coins for the second time. "No, I'm not Tazir, but you'll find him farther down, in the date market." He turned to Aster, who still had her air of fragility and transparence despite her suntan. "Here, choose a hide for yourself and take it as a gift." He winked. "With the legionaries, business is good, and I want to thank the gods."

At the entrance to the date market a woman with tattoos on her face and an orange shawl over her hair was selling rings and bracelets that she wore on her fingers and wrists. She knew Tazir: they were cousins.

"He's our cousin too!" said Nomos.

She looked at them attentively.

"You're the Jewish cousins from Hippo? I didn't think you really existed!"

She took them to the camp of the Jewish Berbers, beyond the ramparts. Children quickly surrounded them. She went into the largest tent. A man came out of it a moment later. He was tall and bearded, with short brown hair, bright blue eyes, and a face the color of baked clay.

"Welcome!" he said in Punic, spreading his arms wide. "I was expecting you. Blessed be the Almighty for having guided you here!"

In the tent, several men were sitting on carpets. They stood up at the sight of the strangers, then bowed and left, one by one.

"Are you hungry, thirsty?" asked Tazir. "Please sit down. You're Nomos the Red, aren't you? How is your father, Elijah?"

"Yes, I'm Nomos. My father is well and sends you his greetings. But how do you know . . . ?"

"We don't know how to write," said Tazir, "but we know how to hear." A woman brought water and dates. He introduced her: "This is my sister Diya. My wife Zura stayed behind in Thumar. She'll be so sorry not to have been here! How are our brothers in Hippo?"

"The Christians tolerate them but don't accept them."

"Not many of those who preach justice practice it."

Sitting on the ground, Nomos felt at ease with his cousin Tazir.

"In Greek," he said, "the word for 'justice' is *eleemosyne,* which can also mean 'pity' or 'compassion,' while in Hebrew it's *tzedek,* which can also mean 'charity.' "

116

Tazir asked Nomos to repeat the words, then thought for a long time.

"I wouldn't want a kind of justice," he finally said, "that was only pity."

Aster had been closely following the conversation and examining everything around her. She looked back and forth between the Berber and her husband, trying to see a resemblance.

"In the mountains," Tazir went on, "I'm the chief. According to tradition, I give orders and decide matters of justice. I may sometimes be wrong, like anyone else, but . . ."

"Do you make your decisions alone?"

"The council of elders can give their opinion, but I'm their chief, and everyone fears the chief."

"There is justice," said Nomos, "only in fear of the Law, not in fear of its guardians."

"In our tribe, the Law is inseparable from God, and since we have several gods, each with his own law, it's the chief who decides. . . . Here, have a fritter."

Daylight was fading. Children stood in clusters outside the tent, looking in.

"Before we go back to the inn," said Nomos, "I'll tell you a story. A chief, a king, once built a palace. Everything about it was illusion: the doors, the windows, the rooms, and the wall around it. He ruled over his people from that palace of illusion. As you would expect, discontented and poverty-stricken people went to the palace to ask for justice. But they stopped in front of the gates, afraid to open them. One day a minister felt sorry for those people standing outside the palace without daring to come in. He told them that nothing really separated them from justice, because the gates, the wall, the locks, and the palace itself were only illusion."

Nomos fell silent.

"Well?" asked Tazir. "What happened then?"

"The story doesn't say."

Tazir smiled, then said with an embarrassed expression, "Your story makes a good point, but if I told it in Thumar I'd stop being the chief!"

NOMOS AND ASTER TALKED about that journey for years. As often happens with memories of travel, theirs were embellished as time went by. Each year their cousins in the Aurès Mountains sent a letter in which they gave news of themselves and asked for the dates of the holy days, and each year Nomos answered.

Years later—Nomos the Red now had gray hair but Aster's face still had the same luminous quality—they again had occasion to talk about Thamugadi and Thumar. One evening, Nomos was working on a copy of the psalms of David for the merchant Nehemiah, son of Janus, one of the *parnasim* of the community in Rusicade. He wrote with special care, not only because he liked the psalms of David but also because he was proud to have received an order from that foreign city. His wife and his two sons had long since gone to bed. Suddenly there was a knock on the door and a voice called out:

"Nomos! Nomos! It's Paulus, let me in!"

He went to the door. His friend Paulus seemed greatly distressed.

"Come in, Paulus. Sit down. What brings you here so late?"

"You could say 'so early.' It's nearly dawn."

"It's always too early for bad news. Take your time."

"You're right. As Bishop Augustine said, 'Benefits and calamities are intermingled. The former cannot be taken without the latter.' "

Paulus examined Nomos's work with his expert eye, then said abruptly, "Nomos, I don't know how to tell you this, but Emperor Heraclius has decreed that the Jews must convert."

Nomos made no reply.

"The leaders of the Jewish communities," Paulus went on, "will soon be summoned to Carthage. Messengers have already been sent to spread the news all over the empire."

"Then we still have a few days," said Nomos.

"What are you going to do?"

"Thank you, my friend, thank you. I don't know yet."

Paulus left. Nomos, very pale, went back to his place and resumed his work. At dawn he put down his pen and his scraper and slept briefly with his forehead on his arms. When he awoke, the sun was rising. He covered his head with his prayer shawl, turned toward Jerusalem, and recited in a clear voice, "My God, the soul You have placed in me is pure. You created it, You formed it, You breathed it into me, You preserve it within me. It is You who will take it from me, and restore it to me one day. As long as that soul is in me, I will give thanks to You, O Lord, my God and God of my fathers. . . ."

118

Then he called his wife and sons and told them about the decision of the emperor in Constantinople.

"May his name be cursed!" exclaimed Aster.

Abraham was twenty-one and planned to marry in the fall. His brother Maximus, two years younger, wanted to study in Carthage with Rabbi Yochanan.

"Let's leave the country!" said Abraham.

"And go where?" asked his brother.

"I don't know. Rome, Gaul. . . . There must be a country for us somewhere in the world!"

"Why not Babylonia?" Maximus proposed. "I've been told that there are famous schools of the Law in the land of the Parthians."

Aster intervened, as though struck by a revelation.

"Nomos, my husband," she said, "remember our journey to Thamugadi—why don't we go and stay with our Berber cousins?"

Nomos shook his head.

"I think," he said in a tone that was both determined and infinitely sad, "that we can't go on running away forever. Our ancestors ran away from Jerusalem, then from Alexandria. . . . It's time to learn to stay!"

"But how can we defend ourselves?" With her bright eyes widened by fear, Aster looked at her husband and her sons. "We don't know how to fight. We have no weapons."

"We have a proven weapon," Nomos replied firmly. "The word. It was with the word that the Almighty, blessed be He, created the world."

And Nomos went to war. He visited Jewish houses and spoke to people in the markets and public squares, saying that the Jews could not spend their lives running away, that everyone had the right to believe in his own God. He told Catholics to remember the time when they themselves had been persecuted by the Arian Vandals. He told Jews that a united and resolute population could not be converted by force.

He was followed by spies who listened to what he said and reported it to the authorities. "Be careful!" his Christian friend Paulus advised him, but Nomos replied that someone had to do what he was doing and say what he was saying. Rabbi Joshua, the *archisynagogos* of Hippo, had been ordered to prepare the community for conversion, and he was trying to gain time.

Nomos's older brother David, who had taken over the shop at one corner of the marketplace, clearly understood what Nomos wanted, but refused to support him: he could not afford to antagonize his customers. Some of them had already stopped greeting him and begun to avoid him.

One morning, as he was lifting the wooden bar that locked the shutters of his shop, David saw Joseph the butcher coming toward him.

"May the Almighty, blessed be He, protect you," said David. Joseph was furious.

"Not even the Almighty, blessed be He, can protect us if your brother goes on acting as if he were a prophet! Because of him, we can't even sell *kosher* meat anymore!" Joseph looked around him and lowered his voice: "We Jews are used to persecutions. We know we'll have to go through a time when things are bad for us, but in a few months it will all be over." His face took on a fierce expression beneath his bushy white eyebrows. "Unless Nomos stirs up the Christians against us!" He leaned toward David, as though to confide the secret of long life to him. "Believe me, what we have to do is avoid attracting attention to ourselves. We must become invisible."

Just then they heard shouts, rapid footsteps, and banging shutters. Joseph ran off toward the shop on the other side of the square. David was beginning to close his shutters again when he saw his wife Sarah and their son Simeon.

"David," she said, "we must hide! A riot has started! They're looking for Jews!"

David pushed Sarah and Simeon into the back of the shop, behind the jars of olive oil, made sure the doors and windows were tightly closed. He wondered where Nomos was. Through the crack between the shutters, he could see part of the square. People were pouring into it and gathering in groups to listen to the rabble-rousers who always came forward at such times. Suddenly there was the first cry, a terrible cry of fear, pain, and horror, and it was like a signal. The Christians rushed at the Jews who had not had time to hide or lock themselves in their shops. Displays were overturned, merchandise was trampled underfoot. David saw the mob break open the shutters of Joseph's shop and, with shouts of disgust, throw quarters of meat into the middle of the square. In his narrow field of vision he saw people passing in one direction or another, some armed with sticks, one even carrying an ax, but he could not see enough to give him an overall understanding of what was happening. He heard pounding on the door of the shop next to his, the vegetable shop owned by Flinius, son of Isaac. The blows reverberated through the wall and seemed to strike him in the chest.

"David," called Sarah, "what's happening?"

"Sh! Be quiet!"

More violent blows; this time they rattled David's shutters. He closed his eyes.

Suddenly shouts rang out.

"The legion! The legion!"

The square emptied as quickly as it had filled. When the soldiers burst into it, it was deserted except for a few dogs biting off chunks of Joseph's *kosher* meat and a few Jews in torn clothes struggling to their feet. David went outside. Rag dolls had been nailed to the doors of his shop and Flinius's.

IT WAS NEARLY NOON when soldiers came to arrest Nomos the Red. He was surprised, not that they had come for him, but that they had not come at dawn. "Men are arrested at daybreak," his father, God rest his soul, had once said to him, "so that their courage won't have time to become firm, and so that the consciences of the men who arrest them won't have time to awaken."

Aster clung to him with all her strength, not wanting him to leave without her. The soldiers struck her to make her let go. Later she slipped away from her sons and ran after Nomos as he walked between two horsemen with his hands tied. Abraham and Maximus caught up with her and brought her back, sobbing, crushed by the weight of her grief.

Nomos was taken to Carthage. An endless road, dust, heat, agonizing thirst. But what made him suffer most, more than his lacerated wrists or his bleeding feet, was that no one had come out to see him as he was crossing the city. None of his neighbors on the Street of God and the Street of the River, at the corner of which he lived, none of the people who had known him for more than fifty years! He had not expected them to try to save him, but at least they could have said something to him, told him that they would not forget him, that they would repeat his name, that they would pray for him not to be afraid at the hour of death, if it came to him, that they would . . . But there had been no one, Christian or Jew, and that made the road even harder for him to travel. He thought of the question in Ecclesiastes: "What does a man gain by all the toil at which he toils under the sun?"

121

For a long time he walked without being aware of it, having taken refuge in the depths of his pain. And when, in Carthage, he was thrown into an underground cell, he appreciated its darkness and dampness before sinking into unconsciousness. When he awoke, he felt terribly alone and without courage. Somewhere, someone was screaming. "For Thou dost not give me up to *sheol,*" he recited, "or let Thy godly one see the Pit. Thou dost show me the path of life; in Thy presence there is fullness of joy, in Thy right hand are pleasures for evermore."

Two indifferent soldiers came for him. They took him through long corridors with moisture oozing from their walls, up high steps of gray stone, and into a room with a vaulted ceiling where three judges sat, all dressed alike: each of them wore an embroidered outer tunic slit up the sides to reveal a bright red tunic underneath.

The judge in the middle accused Nomos of being an enemy of God, for there could be no other explanation for his having spoken against the authority of the Church. Nomos replied that he respected the Church and the Christian faith, but that he asked the Church to respect his own faith. The judges did not listen to him. He was told that he could save his life by accepting conversion.

"What value would a forced conversion have for you?" he asked. "Isn't faith a revelation? Do you believe that—"

He was ordered to be silent. Each of the judges spoke in turn. One of them told him that justice could be clement if he gave the names of his accomplices. Nomos raised his hand. The judge, suddenly interested, leaned toward him.

"Who gives you your orders? Tell us the name of your superior. Who is he?"

"The Almighty, blessed be He, God of Israel!"

Nomos learned that it was possible to feel like laughing in the face of death.

The chief judge, the one in the middle, read a few sentences from a document on the table in front of him. Nomos did not hear him. He knew he was going to die and he was thinking of his father, who had often said, "To receive a miracle, you must deserve it!" The thought of his father made him regret not having read the Scroll of Abraham in the midst of his family before he was taken away by the soldiers. But his sons were good sons, and they would carry on the tradition.

When that semblance of a trial was over, Nomos asked to speak.

122

"Christian judges," he said, "do not forget the demands of humanity!"

Again he was silenced. This time he was glad: what he had said was a quotation from Bishop Augustine! And Nomos learned that it was possible to be joyful in the face of death.

But when he was alone in his cell he wept convulsively for Aster, his sons, and himself. Then he regained his composure and, not knowing if it was morning or evening, chose to say the evening prayer: "Lord, it is You who come to our aid and our salvation. . . ." He fell asleep without realizing it, and when he awoke he learned that it was possible to be sleepy, hungry, and cold in the face of death.

Finally they came. He stood up on his wounded feet. He was trembling. "He will swallow up death forever," he recited, "and the Lord God will wipe away tears from all faces."

He walked along another gray stone corridor and came out into a small courtyard. It was dawn. He was made to kneel and bend forward, so that the back of his neck was horizontal. He wanted to pray. What prayer should he say? He saw the executioner move one foot back, to brace himself for his effort.

"The Lord is God!" Nomos had time to cry out.

THAT MORNING the governor of Carthage dictated two messages, one to the people of Hippo, the other to the emperor. They both said that the leader of the heretics, a man named Nomos, son of Elijah, known as Nomos the Red, had been beheaded, and that there was no longer any obstacle to the conversion of the Jews in accordance with the emperor's decree.

123

8

HIPPO

Abraham's Testimony

TODAY, ON the twenty-eighth day of the month of Tammuz in the year 4393 [633] after the creation of the world by the Almighty, blessed be He, I, Abraham, son of Nomos, son of Elijah, son of Jonathan, begin writing here the story of my life, in the hope that it will be instructive to my children and grandchildren.

Yesterday morning my brother Maximus came for me at the library and we went to the waterfront by way of the Street of the Bishop's Palace. Here and there we heard people shouting against the Jews, but no one molested us. On the wharf, some young Christians had put up an enormous cross. Everyone was looking at a burning ship not far from shore. Its sail, wrapped around the mast, was blazing like a torch. The mast broke in the middle and fell onto the deck. Three men jumped overboard and swam to the pier, but each time they tried to climb up on it the crowd pushed them back into the water. Some shouted, "Keep the Jews in the water!" Others wanted to take them out and crucify them.

That was when Maximus and I saw our father in the crowd. He seemed taller than usual as he made his way to the place where the three men were trying to climb out of the water. He turned his back to the sea and, alone before the crowd, raised his arms. Everyone fell silent.

"Didn't Christ preach mercy?" he asked loudly. "Have you Christians already forgotten that you were victims of persecution not so long ago?"

The wind carried his words to us. I felt like weeping.

When the first moment of surprise had passed, a Christian cried out, "What does this Jew want? What right does he have to talk about Christ?"

"I have the right of a man among men!" replied our father. "And now, take those men out of the water!"

After hesitating briefly, a sailor held out a pole and the three shipwrecked men climbed up on the pier. My brother Maximus wanted to go to our father but I held him back. I thought our father would rather we had not seen him. One day when I was a child, I unexpectedly came into the room where he was taking a bath in a tarred cloth tub. "Why do you have hair on your chest?" I asked him. "Uncle David doesn't have any." "Never mind, my son," he answered, "each of us has his own nudity."

Our father came home shortly after we did, and said nothing about the incident we had seen. He washed himself and prayed. My mother served him milk and cakes. It was then that the soldiers burst into the house and arrested him. Our mother tried to follow him and we had to hold her to prevent her from being wounded by the soldiers' spears. Our father, walking between two horses with his hands tied, looked back when he came to the end of the Street of God, our street, and then he disappeared.

TODAY IS the twenty-ninth day of the month of Tammuz. Paulus, a Christian, was the first to come and ask for news of our father, but even he waited two days. Then Rabbi Meir came. They are the only ones who have spoken to us since our father was arrested. "Don't judge," our father often said to us, "because you don't know the reasons." Even so, they are all cowards.

SEVENTEENTH DAY of the month of Av. We have just learned of our father's death. After long reflection, I have written in the Scroll of Abraham, "Nomos allowed himself to be beheaded for the glory of the Almighty, blessed be He, and the honor of the people of Israel, in the year 4393 after the creation of the world."

EIGHTEENTH DAY of the month of Av. Rabbi Joshua, the *archisynagogos* of Hippo, came to express his sadness and gratitude (those are his words). According to the news from Carthage, Heraclius's decree will not be applied in Africa. "Nomos has saved the community!" Rabbi Joshua said solemnly. "He will go down in our history as a martyr. He was a righteous man, never forget it!"

TWENTIETH DAY of the month of Av. I have become a scribe in the synagogue of the quarter of villas, and I have taken over all the work ordered from my father. I am now writing a copy of the Torah for the synagogue in Theveste.

SECOND DAY of the month of Elul. A caravanner from Thamugadi has brought us a letter from our Berber cousin Beruan. As usual, he asks us for the dates of next year's Jewish holy days. He too has heard of the multitudes on horseback who have left Tripolitana and are moving toward Byzacium. "The Berbers," he writes, "are preparing for war." Why should the Arabs do them any more harm than the Vandals did? For us Jews, the enemies are the emperor and the Church. The Arabs, God willing, can only free us from them. I would not be surprised if some of the young Jews I know opened the gates of Hippo to them.

TWENTY-SEVENTH DAY of the month of Elul. In two days a new year will begin, the first one that we will have to face without our father. We wanted to bury him in the cemetery of Hippo, in accordance with the laws of Israel, but we were unable to have his body returned to us. Although our mother no longer weeps, the light has left her face. She seems to be living very far away from here.

TWENTY-SEVENTH DAY of the month of Tishri in the year 4395 [635] after the creation of the world by the Almighty, blessed be He. Two years have passed since our father's death. Life goes on. Tomorrow I am going to marry Claudia. "A generation goes, and a generation comes, but the earth remains for ever," as it is written in Ecclesiastes.

SEVENTH DAY of the month of Heshvan in the year 4396 after the creation of the world by the Almighty, blessed be He. Claudia has given birth to a daughter whom we have named Miriam. I hope that our next child will be a son.

126

THIRD DAY of the month of Kislev. Our mother, Aster, is no longer with us. May the Almighty, blessed be He, have mercy on her soul. In spite of my age, I feel myself to be an orphan.

EIGHTH DAY of the month of Tevet in the year 4397 after the creation of the world by the Almighty, blessed be He. It is a day of mourning: Claudia gave birth to a son who died immediately. We were going to name him Ezra. Why, my God, why?

NINTH DAY of the month of Tevet in the year 4398 after the creation of the world by the Almighty, blessed be He. Nearly a year after Ezra's death, Claudia gave birth to another son. This one is alive, thank God, and we have named him Hanania.

THIRTEENTH DAY of the month of Elul in the year 4407 [647] after the creation of the world by the Almighty, blessed be He. The Arabs have inflicted a terrible defeat on the legions of Byzantium. In Hippo, there are people who maintain that the Eternal Lord of Hosts has avenged my father's death. The Arabs, they say, are only an instrument that the Almighty has used to stigmatize those who rule in injustice. Now that the passing of time has enabled these people to forget their cowardice, they have just discovered that in Greek *nomos* means "law," and they glorify my father, saying that the Almighty used him to remind them of the fidelity they owe to the Torah.

TWENTY-SIXTH DAY of the month of Elul. The Arabs have left Byzacium after receiving an indemnity of three hundred talents of gold. They are going back to Tripolitana.

TWENTY-SEVENTH DAY of the month of Elul. The Arabs had scarcely turned their backs before the Christians began accusing us of being their accomplices. Hanania has been beaten by children in the street.

ELEVENTH DAY of the month of Nissan in the year 4430 [670] after the creation of the world by the Almighty, blessed be He. Soon it will be Passover. I have not written anything here for twenty-three years! Work and everyday concerns have interfered with my plan. I was surprised when I reread what I had written.

All this is not as instructive as I would have wished. I have been a very poor witness. But perhaps my grandchildren will happen to read these lines anyway.

I do not know what tomorrow will bring. People no longer build with stone, as our fathers did. These hastily made clay buildings will fall apart with the first heavy rain. Will we again hear the earth tremble in the east beneath the hooves of those intrepid Arabs' small horses? Will they invade Africa in the name of a new faith? I know only that future generations will be composed of human beings, for such is the destiny of this world decreed by the Almighty, blessed be He.

I myself have little chance of seeing what will become of this tottering world. I am old. My daughter Miriam will soon be a grandmother. My son Hanania is now thirty-two. He is a scribe, like me, like my father and my grandfather. He is continuing the chain. But his older son, Nathan, rather than studying, wants to be a blacksmith to forge the weapons of Jewish soldiers. We have no soldiers, no army. "There are no soldiers because there are no weapons," he says. He is thirteen. It is his brother Joseph who will carry on our tradition. At eleven, he already knows several commentaries by heart.

Claudia is in poor health. I wonder which of us will be the first one called to the Almighty, blessed be He. I would want to go first if I did not dread leaving her alone.

•   •   •

WHILE THE CHRISTIANS—Byzantines, Vandals, or Visigoths—come to power and inevitably begin persecuting those who pray to a different God, the procession of fathers and sons files past, with the fathers bequeathing to the sons a memory and instructions for maintaining it.

Is my story thus always the same, through the centuries? It is true that I have chosen to simplify genealogical profusion by following the branch of the family that has the Scroll of Abraham in its keeping, and it is also true that, in a story of this kind, priority must be given to those who "have something happen to them." But while I feel the living presence of all those Elijahs and Gamaliels, that Nomos the Red, that Telilan the Berber and that Abraham who regretted having been such a poor witness, I am equally mindful of the anonymous members of the family, all those vegetable merchants,

128

carpenters, and so on, who led such quiet lives that they seem to have been made for silence and oblivion.

I think of Nathan, Hanania's older son and Nomos's great-grandson. At the age when children daydream, he wanted to be a blacksmith in order to arm the Jews. Nothing made him change his mind. He became a blacksmith while his younger brother Joseph carried on the family tradition by devoting himself to study. As it turned out, however, the Jews did not take up arms. Nathan swallowed his daydream and forged weapons for the new masters of North Africa, the Moslems.

For in 698 the Moslems had returned, this time to stay. Only the Berbers, led by a woman named Kahena, a Jewish Berber like my ancestors in Thumar, tried to resist them. A few legends and a regrettably small number of pages by the Arab historian ibn-Khaldun tell us that Queen Kahena, betrayed by a young Moslem to whom she had given hospitality, was wounded after long years of war, and that before dying she asked her people to convert to Islam, no doubt in order to save them from probable annihilation. I considered developing the extraordinary face of that Kahena, using my imagination where historical evidence was lacking, but I finally decided against it when I realized what a large and outstanding place she would occupy in my story. My characters are not heroes of history; they are sometimes obscure actors in it, and always witnesses to it.

Moving westward along the coast, the Arabs prepared to invade Spain. For two years they had clashed with the Christian Visigoths of King Witiza, who had preserved an African bridgehead at Ceuta. Witiza, having ordered the blinding of a duke of Cordova, was himself blinded and dethroned by the duke's son, Roderick. Roderick proclaimed himself king and, among other ruthless acts, abducted Florinda, daughter of Count Julian, governor of Andalusia and Ceuta, the man who was opposing the Arabs on the North African coast. Roderick accumulated enemies. Count Julian, the family of the former King Witiza, and Oppas, archbishop of Toledo, formed a coalition and asked the Arabs to rid them of their new master, promising that, in return Ceuta would not be defended.

To facilitate the consolidation of their power in Spain, the Arabs decided to take a few Jews with them and announced that synagogues would be restored to Jewish communities that the Visigoths had converted by force.

Among those Jews who went to Spain were two from my family:

Daniel and Abner, aged twenty-two and twenty. They were sons of Joseph the rabbi, but it was in the shop of Nathan the blacksmith, amid showers of sparks and the ringing of the anvil, that they met Ibrahim ibn-Shakiya, a Berber chief in his early thirties who had converted to Islam. He offered to let his distant cousins go to Spain with him. And so we are going to leave Hippo—where we arrived three centuries earlier with old Saul, his brother Ezra, and his son Solomon—with Tariq ibn-Ziyad, also a Berber, leader of the vast army setting off to conquer the Christian West.

P.S. What if the Scroll of Abraham should someday be destroyed by fire or stolen by pillagers? What if one of its custodians should fail to safeguard it? I am surprised that none of those scribes—wise, patient men, well aware of the risks to which they were exposed, and devoted to passing on what they had received—had yet thought to make a copy of it. "Two are better than one," says Ecclesiastes.

9

TOLEDO

Amir Tariq's Jew

RABBI JOSEPH, Nomos's great-grandson, had summoned the whole family, from his brother Nathan the blacksmith to Simeon the madman, who had never done anything but carry on an endless monologue while he tied and untied knots in a piece of string. That day, they were all celebrating the departure of Daniel and Abner, the rabbi's sons, for Spain.

Their mother Hannah, with a white shawl over her hair, served the thick, sweet wine ritually prepared by the Jewish winegrowers of Cirta. Unhappy that her sons were about to leave her, but happy that everyone was there, Hannah kept a sorrowful smile on her lips. Daniel and Abner wished they were already gone, but the farewells went on and on.

The men talked about everyday matters: the prices of things, their relations with the Arabs. Musa ibn-Nusayr, the governor of North Africa, had left a garrison in Hippo and established his headquarters in Carthage. The Hippo city council had remained intact; only a few councilors had felt obliged to convert to Islam. Nothing had changed except the currency—the new coins, called dinars, had no effigies on them—and taxes: there was now the land tax, *karaj,* and the poll tax, *dzizia.* But business was back to normal and some people did not hesitate to praise those conquerors who forced no one to become a Moslem.

Ibrahim ibn-Shakiya, who liked having discussions with his "cousin" Nathan the blacksmith, had asked him one day if he did not want to convert.

"Why should I?" Nathan had replied. "Would I be a better blacksmith? A better father? A better husband?"

"You'd be a better man."

"That's what the Christians used to tell us, but they had their share of sinners, robbers, and liars. My grandfather's father was beheaded for refusing to become a Christian, and my father Hanania—may their souls rest in peace—said that everyone should remain what he is and respect what others are."

"Islam respects other religions. 'Moslems, Jews, Sabians, and Christians,' it is said, 'those who believe in God and in the last days, and do charitable deeds, no fear is upon them, they will not be saddened.' "

Yet there were already rumors of a possible expulsion of Christians who refused to convert. In Rabbi Joseph's house, the men expected the worst. "The people in power always promise the Jews that they won't be molested," one of them said, "but experience shows that if they don't begin with the Jews, they end with them; in any case, they never forget them."

Daniel and Abner, eagerly looking forward to their journey, felt that this opinion was a great exaggeration. Cousin Ibrahim had become a Moslem, but they did not have to fear from their own relatives what the Romans had inflicted on the Jews for centuries. "A cousin is a cousin!" they said. They both faced their coming adventure unafraid, Daniel because he was pious and placed his life in God's hands, Abner because he was high-spirited and strong, and liked to fight. With their swarthy skin and curly hair, they looked alike; judging only from their appearance, no one could have imagined how different they were from each other.

FINALLY THEIR FATHER left the room and came back with a grave expression, holding the Scroll of Abraham as if it were a holy offering. Everyone stood up and there was a moment of silence.

"We thank the Almighty," said Joseph, "for having brought us together here today. May He give health and long life to us and to the whole people of Israel."

"Amen," the family replied in unison.

They raised their glasses to their lips. Rabbi Joseph was tense and solemn.

"Twice," he continued, "the Almighty has called on man for help. The first time, He spoke to Adam, who had sinned; the second time, to Moses, who had loved Him. This means that He needs us, whether we are innocent, like Moses, or guilty, like Adam, for the reprimand is transitory and the call is irreversible. In Spain the community is trying to be reborn from its ashes and someone must help it. Daniel and Abner have answered the call. They are going to follow, in the opposite direction, what was the path of exile for our ancestor Aster, and, God willing, they will be strengthened by contact with one of our origins."

Rabbi Joseph, who was known to be a rather proud man, seemed greatly affected by the departure of his two youngest sons. His voice faltered when he resumed: "May the Almighty, God of mercy, accompany them on their journey and protect them from aberrations of the heart and the evil ways of men, for the glory of the people of Israel, and . . . and . . ." If he had not been holding the Scroll of Abraham, perhaps he would have hidden his face in his hands; he finished his sentence almost in a whisper: ". . . and for me, their father. Amen."

"Amen," replied the family, deeply moved.

Rabbi Joseph regained his self-control and held up the Scroll of Abraham.

"As you all know," he said, "this is the story of those without whom we would not exist. I ask my sons not to forget what was written by our ancestor Abraham, son of Solomon, in Alexandria. He prayed for his sons as I pray for mine: may the Almighty give them an intelligent heart to distinguish between right and wrong."

"Amen," the family replied once again.

Rabbi Joseph gave each of his sons a prayer shawl. He seemed on the verge of tears. Suddenly he turned and hurried out of the room.

THE ARMY was about to set off. What an adventure, and what a sight! It had taken all night for the different units to come in from their quarters on the outskirts of the city and take up their marching positions: the green flags of Islam at the head, with the light troops of the vanguard, followed by the lancers on caparisoned horses who immediately preceded the amir (the leader of the army), his lieutenants, his relatives, and his advisers, amid the banners and drums. Then came the troop of Arabs, including both horsemen and foot soldiers; next, the converted Berbers—the bulk of the army—grouped by tribes, each preceded by its chief and its flag; finally, the mass of camels and wagons accompanied by auxiliaries: sutlers, wainwrights, carpenters, and cooks, protected by a rearguard unit. How happy and proud those warriors seemed when, after rising from prayer, they mounted their horses, drew themselves erect, and rode off in the light of dawn to conquer the world! They did not feel the slightest shadow of fear: Allah was with them!

Everyone in Hippo was out of bed when, for the pleasure of putting on an awesome display of force, the immense army crossed the whole city and went out through the western gate. The sun suddenly appeared and illuminated the silk of flags, the metal of weapons, the gleaming coats of horses, and the lustrous leather of magnificent trappings. The beating of the drums was like a steady, thunderous roar. Even the most reserved onlookers could not help feeling a strange kind of excitement. The people of Hippo went on watching a long time, till the last unit had disappeared.

Daniel and Abner were among the Jewish advisers in the retinue of Ibrahim ibn-Shakiya, one of Amir Tariq ibn-Ziyad's lieutenants. Everything surprised them, and even filled them with wonder. Surrounded by the fierce warriors of that mighty army, they felt invincible. Abner, the younger and less level-headed of the two brothers, had a strong urge to ask for a weapon. His ardor was tempered only by the pain and fatigue that tormented him for days on end. He and Daniel had begun practicing horseback riding as soon as they made their decision to leave with the army, but their practice had done little to prepare them for those long days in the saddle punctuated by the five prayers of Islam: el-Sabh, el-Qadr, el-Asar, el-Maghreb, and el-Leil.

Sitifis, Icosium, Caesarea, Cartennae . . . The sea on the right, the desert on the left, the earth and the sky stretching away to infinity; for the two young Jews, the journey had a strong taste of adventure and they no longer looked back. Like the others, they were consumed with impatience.

Finally they reached Ceuta, which was empty of enemy soldiers. The inhabitants came forward to meet them and showed them the two famous rocky promontories—Abyla on this side, Calpe on the other—known as the Pillars of Hercules, between which two seas were joined. Far off, in a kind of blue mist, was the coast of Spain.

It was evening. When the army came to a halt, a vast shout arose from it. Daniel and Abner added their voices to that formidable cry, which chilled their blood, and only then did they realize that it was a war cry. They did not sleep that night.

Now that they were about to invade another continent, the men thought back over their lives and wondered if they would ever return. The drums beat a long time, sustaining in the warriors' hearts a dark passion that hardened them and made them more eager to fight.

Daniel and Abner had to face the obvious fact: an army was not a caravan of merchants; its goal was war, pillage, booty, and ransom, and its glory was measured by the number of its victims. During the long march across Africa they had become better acquainted with their cousin Ibrahim. One day they had been horrified when he gave the order to cut off the right hand of one of his men who had been convicted of theft. "It's the law," he had told them. "An army that doesn't apply its own law has no chance of winning battles."

"But what if that man really wasn't guilty?"

"What matters is the cohesion of the army."

"A man is irreplaceable," Daniel had objected.

"So is victory, cousin, you'll see!"

The two brothers sometimes went several days without seeing Ibrahim, and sometimes he rode with them, lithe and slender on his gray horse, talking to them about the Aurès Mountains and the great oases where the Berbers pitched their black tents. Once he took them to Tariq ibn-Ziyad, in his splendid tent. The amir invited them to sit on the carpet that covered the ground. He questioned them about the organization of Jewish communities and asked if those communities could help in the administration of cities whose inhabitants were mostly Christians.

There were other Jewish advisers, some of whom Daniel and Abner knew. As they talked together, they discovered that they all had at least one ancestor who had come from Spain. Their journey was therefore a pilgrimage to cities and regions they knew only by name: Cordova, Toledo, Hispalis* . . . None of them could say if he would ever go back to Hippo.

_____
* Now Seville.

"ALLAHHU AKBAR!" [Allah is great!] cried the soldiers of Islam when they set foot on the Spanish coast. In honor of their leader, they gave the name of Jebal (Mount) Tariq* to the bare promontory that rose beside the strait. Then they went to Algeciras.

There, two men sent by Count Julian came to Amir Tariq in great secrecy. The count's message was that in the great battle between the Visigoths and the Moslems, he would help the Arab army. His plan was to place his forces to the right of King Roderick as usual, and then, if the Arabs attacked him first, he would draw back and Roderick's flank would be exposed.

"Why does he want to take vengeance on King Roderick?" asked Tariq.

"Because the king raped the count's daughter."

Tariq could not help smiling at the idea of losing a country because of a woman.

Jewish messengers came to assure the leaders of the Arab army that they would find the gates of Cordova, Toledo, and Málaga open to them. All the Jews who had been converted by force, they added, expected the Arabs to keep their promise to reopen the synagogues.

"First let us win the battle," replied Tariq.

THE BATTLE was fought on the Jerez plain, between the Gaudalete River and a village surrounded by olive trees.

The Visigoths had left their wagons among the olive trees and taken a stand with their backs to the hills. They formed a dense, compact, dark wall, colored only by the red of their shields. It was like a grim, immutable element of the landscape, a barrier so forbidding that only a madman would try to break through it.

While his scouts and vanguard troops were crossing the river, Tariq ibn-Ziyad had his tent pitched on the near side of it, on an arid hill where only a few cypress trees grew. He kept his keen eyes on the army of the Visigoths. Perhaps he was trying to spot King Roderick; that was where he would have to strike: at the head. Or perhaps he was trying to guess, with the instinct of a desert hunter, whether or not Count Julian's promise was a trap.

The advisers were on that same hill. Daniel and Abner watched the Arab army slowly crossing the river. Here the archers, there

---

* Now Gibraltar.

the light cavalry, over there the lancers. They paid special attention to Ibrahim and his Berbers, wearing blue turbans. That morning they had seen them transfigured by the approach of battle and had realized that there would be two combats: that of the army as a whole, which would end in victory or defeat, and that of each warrior, which would decide whether he lived or died. As they watched Ibrahim moving away from them, they could not help praying for him. He was now a Moslem, since his conversion, but he was born a Jew, and there must still be something Jewish left in him. The Eternal God of Israel had perhaps not completely banished him from the Book of Life. . . .

Suddenly they saw that the thick wall of enemies was in motion. The Visigoths had waited for the time when the Arab army, having crossed the river, would be looking for its positions. They hoped to take it by surprise before it could form a battle front. And their formidable charge shook the earth. The wall advanced uniformly, implacably, raising an immense cloud of yellowish dust.

Daniel and Abner closed their eyes, sure that the slender Berbers on their light horses would simply be crushed beneath the heavy gallop of their countless enemies. They were seized with deep fear. When they dared to look again, they realized that the Arabs had eluded the charge, having neither the weight nor the inclination for one of those brutal clashes that were like a head-to-head collision between two angry buffalo. They were quick, skilled, and cruel, striking where they were not expected, whirling, pretending to flee, coming back. Cavalry units abruptly swerved aside, uncovering three ranks of archers who loosed a lethal rain of arrows. Riderless horses rode off in all directions, whinnying. The clang of metal against metal, shouts, moans, frantic cries for help . . . Tariq's legions did not let the Visigoths regroup. That chaos of mingled men and horses was just what they wanted.

Suddenly Ibrahim and his Berbers, acting in perfect unison and uttering a single cry, charged Count Julian's army. And, as promised, Count Julian's army fell back and uncovered King Roderick's flank. The king of the Visigoths was there, in his famous ivory chariot, among his personal guards on big white horses. When Tariq saw him, he signaled to his men, leapt into the saddle, and rode down the hill.

Daniel and Abner saw him cross the river. Knowing somehow that he was coming, his warriors moved aside as he approached, and he advanced along a kind of corridor that opened before him.

137

The battle was now general. The Arabs were encircling the Visigoths. It became impossible to understand anything about that furious melee, except that the losing side would not recover from it for a long time.

Roderick's army struggled tenaciously, like a massive animal that a tiger was trying to bring down, and it was not until evening that it collapsed, emptied of its blood. Those still on their feet ran away; the wounded were finished off with shouts of joy. Then came the taking of booty.

Daniel and Abner, as exhausted as if they too had been fighting, went down to the river. Corpses were floating in the current and trickles of blood were dissolving in the clear, cool water. The ground was covered with hundreds and hundreds of dead and wounded men. The victorious soldiers prostrated themselves on the ground for the evening prayer.

IBRAHIM IBN-SHAKIYA had been mortally wounded. He would not return to his mountains. He sent for his Jewish cousins. He had been taken, along with other wounded chiefs, to the amir's tent. Daniel and Abner approached him. His robe was bloodstained and his face seemed even thinner. He was barely able to speak.

"May Allah protect you!" he said. "May the God of Israel protect you!"

He closed his eyes for a long time, but he was still breathing weakly. Daniel was ashamed of the excitement he had felt when he saw Ibrahim charge into the thick of the enemy ranks with his sword raised.

"Cousins," Ibrahim said feebly, "protect our amir, Tariq. Advise him. Be wary of the men around him. They are . . . jackals. . . ." He paused, but he still had one more thing to say: "Be proud of me. . . . I struck the first blow at King Roderick."

Ibrahim the Berber died during the night and was buried at dawn. That morning, Daniel and Abner were summoned to the amir's tent, where messengers were hurrying in and out.

"Salam ala ikum," Tariq greeted them.

"Ala ikum es-salam," they replied.

"We've won a great victory," said the amir, "but this is a day of mourning. We've gained a world and lost a friend, may Allah have mercy on him. . . . Do you understand what I'm saying?"

138

Thanks to their knowledge of Hebrew and Aramaic, the two brothers had learned everyday Arabic rather easily.

"Tomorrow," Tariq went on, "we leave for the north. The enemy army has scattered, many noblemen are throwing in their lot with us, and Jewish communities everywhere are waiting for us as liberators. It's now time for you to begin serving your function: establishing relations between them and us, and helping them to take control of the administration of their cities. Until Musa ibn-Nusayr joins us, we won't have enough men to make war and govern at the same time. Where do you prefer to go? Toledo? Cordova?"

"Our family came from Cordova," replied Daniel. "But what about you? Where are you going?"

"To Toledo. Roderick has disappeared. Only his horse and his silver buskins have been found. But Toledo was his capital and I'm going to take Toledo."

"Then we'll go there with you, amir!"

Tariq, who had many visitors waiting to see him, became impatient.

"Why?" he asked curtly.

"It was the wish of your faithful lieutenant, and our cousin, Ibrahim ibn-Shakiya."

Tariq had no more time to waste. He pointed to each of the brothers in turn.

"You," he said to Abner, "will come with me." And to Daniel: "You'll go to Cordova with Mugueiz el-Rumi. *Ma es-salama.*"

CORDOVA SURRENDERED without a fight. It was a large city, hospitable yet secretive, with palaces and public squares, an enormous Roman bridge over the Guadalquivir, a labyrinth of narrow streets lined by whitewashed houses, gardens filled with the fragrance of flowers and fruit, and fountains flowing in the shade of closed courtyards.

Daniel immediately felt at home there; he even found the house where Aster, wife of his ancestor Nomos, had lived. His first official act was to notify the converted Jews that they could return to their religion and begin attending the synagogues again. Jews and Christians were given the status of *dhimmis:* protégés of Islam. Daniel was welcomed as if he himself, armed with the force of God, had overthrown the Visigoths. His troubles began when the Jews were allowed to recover certain pieces of property that had been out of their possession for several generations and therefore gave rise to enormous disputes. Daniel always did his best to be patient and fair before presenting his proposed solutions to the governor. He thus made many friends and many enemies, which is no doubt the fate of influential advisers.

The Jews lived between the cathedral—now transformed into a mosque—and the river. This quarter was known as the Medina El-Yahudi, the City of the Jews. Daniel lived in an outbuilding of the magnificent palace formerly occupied by Visigothic sovereigns. He had written a long letter to Hippo and sent it by army messengers, but he had no way of knowing if it had arrived, or even if it ever would arrive. He sometimes thought of his family: his father, so stiff in his dignity; his mother, so affectionate, as though to restore the balance; Simeon the madman and his piece of string. It was like another life. . . .

HALF EMPTY, standing on its granite pedestal, Toledo was mirrored in the slow, red water of the Tagus. When Amir Tariq arrived there after short but violent battles, part of the population had fled and those who remained in the city opened its gates to him. The conquerors seized the treasures of the Visigothic kings, including the fabled "King Solomon's table," which was said to have been brought from Jerusalem to Rome by Titus, and from Rome to Toledo by the Goths. It was made of solid gold and silver decorated with pearls and coral, and with emeralds that formed the twelve signs of the zodiac.

Like Cordova, Toledo found a new equilibrium. Mosques were built, synagogues were reopened, and Jews returned to the religion of their fathers. Like his brother Daniel, Abner served as a link between the reviving Jewish community and the Moslem rulers. Every evening he went to the restored synagogue that had become the meeting place for the community. He was always treated with consideration and plied with questions. His judgment was sound with regard to matters that came within his duties; but he enjoyed being honored, and at the age of twenty he fell into all the traps of power. He had already had to change his residence to escape from his overly numerous feminine conquests. He lived from day to day, frenziedly but without gaiety. He had little liking for Toledo, with its gray stone walls under oppressive skies and its stepped streets along which dirty water flowed down to the Tagus. But he knew he would not grow old there.

It soon became known that Musa ibn-Nusayr, the caliph's envoy, was on his way to Spain. He was a haughty, capricious nobleman, jealous of Tariq's military glory, and relations between the two men had never been either good or simple.

"Do you know who's coming to Toledo?" Tariq asked Abner one day.

"Yes, amir, everyone's talking about it."

"What are they saying?"

"That you ought to be on your guard."

"Why?"

"Because jealous men should always be mistrusted."

Tariq was as much at ease among the marble statues of the palace as in his tent.

"What if I were to give him Roderick's treasures so that he could take them to the caliph himself?"

"You'd deprive him of the pleasure of taking them away from you."

Tariq laughed heartily and asked, "What's your advice?"

"If I were you, amir, I'd give him the treasures, but, to keep him from claiming that he'd taken the city himself, I'd hold something back—one leg of King Solomon's table, for example."

Tariq smiled.

"Ibrahim, may Allah keep him in His holy care, wasn't mistaken about you! Thank you for that advice!"

Abner told the amir about one of his own concerns. Taxes were being collected by a Jew named Yoseh ibn-Ezra. He had collected taxes for King Roderick, after converting to Christianity, and had kept the same position after becoming a Jew again when the Arabs arrived. He was merciless: even though the law exempted them from it, he had cripples pay the monthly tax of forty-eight dinars imposed on all other citizens of Toledo. Abner wanted him to be replaced.

"Why?" asked Tariq. "He does his work."

"But he's a Jew, amir."

"Well, what of it? Aren't you also a Jew?"

"Amir, when a Jew does dirty work, he soon arouses a kind of hostility that can turn against the whole community at any moment."

"I don't think tax collectors are ever very popular, Abner, whether they're Jewish or not."

141

Abner withdrew but he knew he was right: Yoseh ibn-Ezra's conduct was a threat to Tariq. He decided to visit him.

Yoseh ibn-Ezra lived in a big, austere house that would have been completely lacking in warmth if it had not been for the thick wool carpets on its floors. He was a lean, stiffly erect man of about forty, with gray hair and black eyebrows, which gave a singular hardness to his gaze. After his wife's death, he had sent his daughter to stay with his sister in Murcia.

He received Abner in a room furnished only with a marble table on which stood a basket of fruit whose colors seemed to concentrate all the light from the two large bay windows.

"I'm pleased to see you, counselor. How do you like our city?"

"It's beautiful," replied Abner, ill at ease.

"Do you know that Toledo's name comes from the Hebrew word *toldot*, 'genealogy'?"

"No, I didn't know that."

"It's said that on the fourth day of creation, when the Almighty, blessed be He, made the sun, He placed it over Toledo, and that's why we have the best-lighted city in the world."

Abner suddenly realized that this man would not listen to him. Nothing could make him change his way of exercising power.

"You wanted to speak with me about something important?" asked Yoseh ibn-Ezra.

"No. . . . Yes. . . . Actually, I only wanted to say . . . 'Where there is no guidance, a people falls.' "

"You're quoting from Proverbs, young counselor. Do you know what comes next? 'But in an abundance of counselors there is safety.' Good-bye. I hope you enjoy your stay in Toledo."

Abner went home, humiliated, furious, and more firmly convinced than ever that Yoseh ibn-Ezra would be the cause of an uprising among the people.

MEANWHILE, in Cordova, Daniel was also becoming an increasingly popular adviser. Unlike his brother Abner, however, he maintained an unassuming attitude and drew enough satisfaction from his work to be happy without wanting anything more.

It was during this period that he married. One day he took a stroll in the market, as was his habit. He looked at the peddlers, the street singers, the conjurers, the performers of shadow plays. From the mood of the market, he could gauge how things were going in the city. He listened to people, spoke with them, questioned them about business, supplies, taxes. They knew who he was but they answered his questions because they appreciated his good-will.

On this day he watched an old Jew and a dark young woman as they sat near the fortress, weaving baskets and hats. He was fascinated by the agile dance of their fingers among the blades of esparto grass. Soon after he had struck up a conversation with him, he discovered that the old basketmaker, Naphtali, was also related to Rabbi Kalonymos, father of Daniel's ancestor Aster. It seemed to him that his journey to Spain was suddenly justified: it was as if he had brought together the two edges of a rift in time. And, almost as a matter of course, he married Naphtali's daughter Dulcia—was it not written that every Jew must some day marry and create a home? They moved into the house where Kalonymos had once lived, which Daniel's post as an adviser in the palace enabled him to rent. He then wrote another letter to Hippo, inviting his parents to Cordova, if they wanted to come there.

ABNER FOUND little satisfaction in the pleasures of his new life but he could not give them up. What was he to do? Study? He had no inclination for it. Marry? More than one father had offered him his daughter but he was in no hurry to make a choice. The administration of the city was now well organized and Tariq no longer needed him very often. He sometimes found himself wanting to leave Toledo. To go where? He did not know, but at his age, and in his frame of mind, going away was enough in itself.

Then he met Yoseh ibn-Ezra's daughter at a reception in the palace. She was dark and slender, like her father, and behind her veil she appeared to be rather pretty. As soon as he learned who she was, he began trying to win her favor.

"I didn't know," he said to her, "that our tax collector had such a beautiful daughter!"

"Beautiful? What can you see of me through my veil?"

Her voice was amused and provocative at the same time.

"I can't see you with my eyes, but I see you with my heart."

"Thank you. You speak well, counselor."

She bowed ironically, then turned away and disappeared. He looked for her in vain all evening. When he had returned home and gone to bed, alone for once, he could not sleep. Wanting to know more about her, he waited impatiently for morning.

When it came, he learned that her name was Rachel and that the reason he had not seen her before was that since her mother's death she had been living with her aunt in Murcia. "Rachel!" he repeated to himself. "Rachel!" It had become the most beautiful name in the world. He would not rest until Rachel belonged to him. Would he have to marry her? He would do it gladly. It was, in fact, exactly what he wanted to do. He would hurry to Yoseh ibn-Ezra's house and ask for his daughter's hand. . . .

But he did not go there. That Yoseh ibn-Ezra frightened him. Abner was no longer thinking clearly enough to realize that Rachel could first of all provide him with a chance to take revenge for the humiliation inflicted on him by her father.

He saw her again several times; he attracted her attention, amused her, interested her, dazzled her.

Then Yoseh ibn-Ezra unexpectedly paid Abner a visit. His dark eyes rapidly examined the room, as if he were estimating the prices of the furs and tapestries.

"You have a fine house," he said.

"Have a seat," Abner invited.

"No, this won't take long. Counselor, I know you've talked against me to Amir Tariq. You've said that by collecting taxes I'm harming the Jews, that they'll all suffer from the hatred I arouse. But what are you, counselor, except a *dhimmi* who's tolerated for the moment by the men in power? You're young, intelligent, and ambitious, but your future depends on the future of a Berber chief —may God protect him! The Jews' great mistake is to believe in peace when the enemy is only catching his breath. There will be no peace for us, counselor. So let me be what I am and do what I do."

Abner felt himself blushing at this reprimand. The taste of the first humiliation returned to him and he did not know what to answer.

"I'm not interested in anything you have to say," Yoseh ibn-Ezra continued. "I've come here to tell you one thing: my daughter Rachel is the only person in the world I care about. Leave her alone!" He turned to go. "Don't show me to the door. I know the way."

Abner did not go out that day. He was discovering in himself a feeling he had never known before: hatred. He could not help thinking of those brutes who were paid a few dinars to rid someone of an enemy. Was he going to have Yoseh ibn-Ezra murdered? He was ashamed and wept bitterly. What else could he do, then? Run away?

He would probably have done it if Tariq had not sent him, in great secrecy, one of the legs of King Solomon's table. Musa ibn-Nusayr, the governor of North Africa, was about to arrive, and Tariq, following Abner's advice, was taking his precautions.

He did well to take them. No sooner had Musa come to Toledo than he began criticizing nearly everything Tariq had done. He was surprised that there were so many *dhimmis* in the local administration, regretted that mosques had been built here and not there, complained that the city stank . . .

In the course of a great celebration in Musa's honor, the day after his arrival, Tariq gave him most of the treasures of the Visigothic kings, including King Solomon's table—minus one leg. Musa took the treasures as if he were confiscating them, dismissed Tariq from his position, then had him beaten with rods and thrown into prison.

A shock wave ran through the whole city. Everyone immediately turned away from Tariq's courtiers and advisers. Abner was still greeted, but only from a distance. No one spoke to him and he received no more invitations; fathers no longer offered him their daughters in marriage. When he walked through the streets of the city or along the bank of the Tagus, he was no longer assailed by petitioners, as he had been in the past. He felt that freedom as solitude. He would have liked to go to see his brother in Cordova, but he held proof that it was not Musa who had taken the treasures of the Goths, and his loyalty to Tariq required him to wait until he knew Tariq's fate.

One day a servant came to tell him that her mistress wanted to see him.

"And who is your mistress?"

"The woman you're forbidden to meet."

With painstaking precautions, the servant took him to a house where Rachel was waiting for him, lying on cushions in front of a fireplace. She had not, it seemed, doubted for one moment that he would come.

"You wanted to see me?" he asked, his heart pounding.

He had never seen her so beautiful. Strange flames danced in her eyes; perhaps they were only reflections of the fire, but they might also be pride, or defiance, or even love—who could say?

She did not answer. Embarrassed, he asked again, "Why did you want to see me?"

145

"My father forbade me to do it. That's reason enough, don't you think?"

THEY SAW each other again, often, and not only because of Yoseh ibn-Ezra's prohibition. Perhaps they were in love, or perhaps there was love only between their bodies. In any case, they did not tire of each other.

At the end of winter, messengers arrived from Damascus with instructions from Caliph Walid. Dissatisfied with Musa's conduct, the caliph ordered him to free Tariq ibn-Ziyad and continue the conquest with him.

Tariq was released from prison, but Musa refused to go with him. While Tariq moved down the Ebro, took Tortosa and then advanced to Murcia, Musa went north to Galicia. Caliph Walid was quickly informed of this. Furious, he summoned the two men to Damascus. Before leaving Spain, Tariq briefly returned to Toledo, where Abner gave him the leg from King Solomon's table and wished him good luck.

"I hope we'll see each other again, here," said Tariq. "May Allah protect you!"

For the moment, only Rachel kept Abner in Toledo. They were meeting more and more often, and sometimes forgot to observe the rules of caution that they had set for themselves. One night as he was hurrying home through the dark streets, he suddenly found himself surrounded by three men. He knew them: three of the brutes employed by Yoseh ibn-Ezra to force payment from those who could not afford it.

This time they did not demand money. Without a word, they began systematically battering Abner's head, belly, and back, grunting from their exertions. He fell to his knees, then rolled into the stream of filth that flowed down the middle of the sloping street.

The coolness of morning awoke him. He was barely able to breath. Excruciating pains pierced his body like blades. With a great effort of will, he laboriously raised himself on all fours, like a broken-down old horse, and crawled to the shelter of a bush. He saw that he was on the bank of the Tagus and realized that he had been thrown from the ramparts. The red water of the river seemed motionless. Not far away, big black oxen were rolling in the ashy dust.

He lay under the bush, recovering his strength, until the next

146

morning. He then stood up, dragged himself to the old Roman bridge, and staggered across it. That was how he left Toledo, without looking back. His only regret was that he had to leave behind the prayer shawl his father had given him in Hippo.

ka coksinnm. He then would run, dragging behind, to the house.
Bright, blah magos many up in... I lay was one. (your) Telma is...
her of my splerdes, He of myself. ... Hizi. the home. and of myself.
...pockey magelpes Lerry, ... oxise yourself.

10

CORDOVA

Passover in Peace

ON THE way from Toledo to Cordova, Abner paid for all his past
and future sins. He was no longer an adulated counselor, or even a
former counselor. He was a poor man, wounded in body and mind,
who chewed bitter herbs as he plodded toward the horizon. If he
survived, he thought, he would be changed forever.

He survived. Cordova seemed to him the most hospitable city on
earth. Dulcia, Daniel's wife, took care of him as if he were her
firstborn son. He claimed to have been robbed and beaten by bandits. A dozen times a day, while he was resting, Dulcia brought
him herb tea. Floating in a pleasant fog, he heard his brother's
voice, which alternately lulled him to sleep and awakened him.

"Do you know that Pesach is in two weeks? Do you remember
our last *seder* together, in Hippo? Who could have said, then, that
we'd be together in Spain? We never know what the Almighty,
blessed be He, holds in store for us. . . . When you're back on
your feet, I'll show you around Cordova. It's a magnificent city! Its
central part alone has seven gates, and there are twenty-one quarters in the suburbs! The Guadalquivir is three times as wide as the
Seibus. The climate here is the same as in Hippo. The Jews in
Cordova are happy. In less than a year, five synagogues and two
Talmud Torahs have been built here in the Jewish quarter. We're

Wali Hosein's most trusted advisers. 'Present yourselves as protectors, not as conquerors,' we suggested to him, knowing that the Moslems don't have enough soldiers to hold all the conquered cities. And Wali Hosein understood: the archbishop is regularly received in the palace. Do you know that the Arabs are well educated? I've found some remarkable men among them, men who know Philo of Alexandria as well as I do, and know much more than I do about medicine and science. I've sent a message to the exilarch* of Babylonia, asking him to send us the Mishnah and the Halacha. Did you hear in Toledo that the Christian kings are regrouping their armies in Septimania, to drive the Arabs back to North Africa? How much longer will Jews be advisers to rulers? But maybe you'd like to sleep awhile, Abner. I can see I'm tiring you with my stories. I'll let you rest, and I'll ask Dulcia to bring you some herb tea."

THREE DAYS BEFORE Passover, Daniel and Abner had the happy surprise of seeing their family arrive from Hippo: their father Rabbi Joseph, their mother Hannah, their older brother Jeroboam with his wife Ruth and their children Azariah and Rachel. Bringing their belongings—mainly papyrus and parchment scrolls —in a trunk, they had traveled with one of the caravans that had been going from Carthage to Spain once or twice a year since the conquest. Nathan the blacksmith was taking care of their house in Hippo until they decided whether or not they would return. Joseph and Hannah were glad that Daniel had become an adviser to the wali and that he already had a son. And Joseph had been so worried about not arriving in time for Passover that merely being there would have been enough to make him happy for the moment.

It was he, of course, who presided over the *seder*. Everyone was there, including Dulcia's father Naphtali and his two brothers Jaco and Phatri, the latter with his wife Artemisia. The flames of the candles cast joyous, dancing reflections on all faces. Abner was deeply moved to see his father, whose hair and beard were now white, make the traditional gestures and speak the ritual words.

"This is the bread of affliction that our fathers ate in Egypt," he said as he uncovered the *matzot*. "Let all who are hungry come and

---

* Also known as the prince of the exile. Presumably a descendant of the House of David, he was the leader of Babylonian Jewry and administered the Jewish communities of the empire.

eat. Let all who are needy come and celebrate Pesach with us. This year, here; next year, in the land of Israel! This year, slaves; next year, free men!"

"Amen."

It was Azariah, Jeroboam's son, who asked the first ritual question.

"Why is this night different from all other nights?"

Abner smiled. For years, as the youngest son, he had been the one who asked the Passover questions, and he knew the answer by heart: "Because it commemorates what God did for us when we came out of Egypt. . . ." In renewing contact with his childhood, Abner felt that he was also renewing contact, beyond his adventures in Toledo, with the best part of himself.

Rabbi Joseph took a sip from his glass and recited: "Blessed be You, Lord, our God of the universe, who delivered us and our fathers from Egypt and brought us to this night when we eat unleavened bread and bitter herbs. May You let us live until the next solemnities, O Lord our God and God of our fathers. May we celebrate them in peace and have the joy of seeing Your city rebuilt and Your worship restored."

"Amen."

A SHORT TIME LATER, at a reception in the house of the cadi, to which Daniel had taken him, Abner became acquainted with a manufacturer of luxurious cloths who invited him to visit his workshops. His name was Rosemundo. He was a plump, round-faced, outspoken man, and although he was a Christian he dressed and lived in the Arab fashion.

In Rosemundo's workshops, Abner admired brocades and silks and took such an interest in their making, finishing, and sale that the merchant proposed a partnership with him. Abner asked Daniel to borrow two hundred dinars for him and persuaded Rosemundo to dress not only people and walls, but also horses. Knowing the Arab rulers' taste for ostentatious display, he believed they would constitute an important market. He and Rosemundo gave Wali Hosein their first brocade saddle and a silk horsecloth stitched with gold thread. The wali was pleased with this gift and it quickly set a fashion: all the rich horsemen in Cordova wanted the same kind of adornment for their mounts. Within a few months, Rosemundo and Abner were receiving orders from Hispalis and Saragossa.

150

FINALLY THERE WAS NEWS of Tariq and Musa ibn-Nusayr, who had gone to appear before the caliph in Damascus. As expected, Musa had presented the caliph with the treasures of the Goths and claimed that he had taken them from the enemy himself. Tariq had then easily established the truth by producing the missing leg of King Solomon's table. Musa had had to pay a large fine and submit to the indignity of being placed on public display for a whole day.

Abner, who had never returned to Toledo, considered going back there just for the pleasure of seeing the bowing and scraping of those who had turned their backs on him when Tariq was thrown into prison. But he quickly gave up that idea; perhaps he was still afraid of Yoseh ibn-Ezra—or of his daughter.

He had things to do in Cordova. To his family's surprise, after repaying his loan he bought a small mill in which he ground the leaves and seeds of coloring plants, trying to invent and stabilize new tints. He spent all his time on these efforts. Again he succeeded, and before long the light blue silk from the little cloth works in Cordova was in great demand all over el-Andalus.

"You're working too much, my son," his father said to him one day. "You think of nothing but your dyes. I hope you haven't forgotten the Torah."

"Don't worry, father, I haven't forgotten the Torah."

"I know, I know. But why not stop awhile to marry and begin a family, like your brother Daniel? His wife is already expecting their second child. You have more than enough money. . . ."

"You know money doesn't interest me."

Abner had just given a small fortune to a man named Jacob of Tortosa, who was engaged in buying the freedom of Jewish slaves. What interested him in his work was inventing, gambling, and winning. In Hippo he had helped his brother-in-law Ezra with his shop, and his first purchases—a few jars of olive oil, a few measures of barley—had filled him with excitement: he was captivated by the game of guessing the seller's thoughts, foiling his strategy, being shrewder and more quick-witted than someone who nevertheless had to be regarded as equally shrewd and quick-witted. Abner felt it was basically true to say that by buying or selling jars of olive oil, one could discover what one really was. He remembered old Joad, who owned several shops in the Hippo market and was said to be unbeatable in business dealings. Joad lived modestly with his wife and their daughter, who had been born mute, in a small house on the outskirts of the city, and gave most of the money he earned to the community for works of charity. He was once asked why he worked when he could have done quite well without it; he replied that real pleasure came from doing what was not required.

"Remember Ecclesiastes, my son," said Rabbi Joseph: " 'Then I considered all that my hands had done and the toil I had spent doing it, and behold, all was vanity and a striving after wind, and there was nothing to be gained under the sun.' "

"It was a sour old man who wrote that."

"Take care that *you* don't become old before you've begun your family," Joseph said with a sigh.

Abner vaguely felt a desire to have children when Dulcia gave birth to his brother's second son. He was struck by the fervor with which Rabbi Joseph looked at his sleeping grandson. The rabbi finally shook his head as if he were awakening from a dream and murmured, "May the Almighty spare him the ordeals of the desert!"

"Amen," said Abner.

A week later, the whole family was waiting for the new little Solomon in the synagogue of the Jewish quarter in Cordova. When he was carried in by his godmother, Sarah, wife of Rabbi Yochanan, everyone greeted him with a loud *"Baruch haba!"* [Welcome!] Not only was the family there, but also friends, the pupils of the Talmud Torah where Daniel taught, and the *parnasim* of the community. They were all proud of the new synagogue and took pleasure in reading the psalms engraved at the base of the walls or the inscription in Arabic on the corbel supporting the pointed arch: "To the Everlasting, reigning and all-powerful."

Rabbi Joseph officiated. He stretched out his arms toward the baby.

"Here," he said, "is a prince for the City of the Jews. He has come to seal the covenant with the Almighty, blessed be He."

He took little Solomon and placed him on the white silk cushion on the lap of his godfather, Daniel's friend Judah el-Karui, a scribe. The *mohel* uncovered the little body and said, "Blessed be He who ordained circumcision." With two fingers of his left hand, he gently pulled the baby's delicate foreskin, then deftly cut it off.

Daniel gave thanks "to Him who commanded us to make the child enter into the covenant of Abraham, our father," and the others all said in unison, "As he has entered into the covenant, may he grow up for the Torah, the *chuppah,* and acts of charity."

The baby was crying. Rabbi Joseph leaned his white beard toward him and said softly, "You are now marked in your flesh with the indelible seal of the covenant with the Creator of the world. This sign must not only mark your body, but also constantly remind you that you were created imperfect so that you could perfect yourself."

The child stopped crying, as if he were meditating, thought Abner, on what his grandfather had just said.

That evening, when all the guests had gone home, Rabbi Joseph, his wife, and their three sons remained together on the patio, around the fountain. The children were all in bed. The fragrance of plants was reviving in the coolness of the oncoming night. The five of them were silent for a time, then Rabbi Joseph said, "Man is like a breath, his days are like a passing shadow."

But instead of continuing the psalm, he quietly sang an old Jewish song that spoke of the passing of time. He sang in the silence around him, and sometimes his voice broke, to convey the melancholy that was left unspoken at ordinary times, when it was daylight and the children were listening.

Abner now realized that he did not know his father. He was amazed that this man of duty and prayer could so truly express what he himself felt. And when Rabbi Joseph proposed that they all go and open the Scroll of Abraham, Abner followed him with curiosity.

Dulcia brought a lamp.

"Bring the light closer, my daughter," Joseph told her. Then, evidently having sensed Abner's mood, he said to him, "Come here and help me."

Together they unrolled the papyrus. The lamplight revealed columns of names—Abraham, Gamaliel, Sarah and Ruth, David, Nomos, Judith—as though it were momentarily drawing them out of the shadows of eternity.

Rabbi Joseph did not read from the scroll. He only made sure that Abner saw his own name written after those of his brothers and sisters, then he rolled up the papyrus and recited, "His kingdom is an everlasting kingdom, and his dominion is from generation to generation."

Abner strongly felt how comforting it was to be part of that chain. He also felt a desire to continue it himself, and for the first time he did not try to reject that desire.

His fate might have been decided that evening—he was going to marry and have children who would grow in age and wisdom while he peacefully moved toward the end of his days—if he had not learned soon afterward that Yoseh ibn-Ezra had died in Toledo.

With his ruthless behavior and offensive manner, the tax collector had made so many enemies and aroused so much hatred and rancor that the inevitable had finally happened. Some of his victims had stirred up a riot against him. His house was invaded and ransacked. He barely had time to hide in his cellar, where he smeared his face with dirt in an effort to escape from those who were looking for "the Jew." When they found him, they insulted him and beat him to death, then nailed his body to one of the city gates. The wali immediately called in the Berbers from a nearby garrison. This restored calm, but the episode brought fear into every Jewish home in Spain.

As soon as he heard the news, Abner knew he would go back to Toledo. Ever since his abrupt departure he had often thought of Rachel, even though he was sometimes unable to recall her face; three years earlier, he would have bet his life that he would never forget it.

And so he left, saying that he was going off to look for new markets and new ideas. During his absence, his brother Jeroboam would handle his business affairs with Rosemundo.

Toledo had not changed: still haughty and austere, overlooking the desolate landscape from its rocky foundation. Abner entered the city in the middle of a caravan of merchants and went with them to take lodgings at an inn where he would not be recognized. He was convinced that he could not cross the street without being greeted and praised as the brilliant Jewish adviser who had enabled Amir Tariq to triumph over his enemy Musa ibn-Nusayr. He quickly realized, however, that no one even turned to look at him and that Toledo had completely forgotten him. He was both relieved and mortified.

He went to his former servant Alfonso to ask for news. Alfonso, at least, greeted him by falling to his knees; but perhaps he thought he was seeing a ghost. He told Abner that Tariq had sent a messenger from Damascus to thank him and assure him of his friendship; that Rachel, Yoseh ibn-Ezra's daughter, was married and had a child. Then the old servant opened a chest and took out the prayer shawl that Abner had abandoned when he fled from Toledo.

Abner was about to leave when the old man lowered his eyes and said that Rachel had named her son Abner.

Abner thanked Alfonso and gave him the piece of magnificent cloth that he had intended for Rachel.

"You can give it to your daughter," he said, "or your granddaughter. If you think it's beautiful, pray for me."

He left Toledo the next day, with the caravan of merchants in which he had arrived. It belonged to a man named Yakub el-Bejer, who earned his living by organizing travel for merchants from one city to another. It moved slowly, with the five daily stops required for prayer. It was going first to Saragossa, then on to Narbonne, from where Jewish merchants were said to go to India and China as readily as Cordovans went to Toledo.

To my father, Rabbi Joseph of Hippo, to my mother, to my brothers. May the Almighty, blessed be He, give you long life.

I must first tell you that I am in good health, and I hope the same is true of you. I have lost a little weight and my skin is suntanned. I left Toledo with a caravan of merchants and I have made a friend: Ambros, a former Jew who became a Christian and even a monk. He admitted to me that he had been tired of fearing God without being assured of His love, and that he found it unjust to risk persecution without receiving anything in return, whereas the Christian religion is based on love and forgiveness and is also triumphant. I protested, as you can well imagine, but the journey was long. We soon decided to leave the caravan because it went too slowly to suit us, and I bought two mules.

Near Jaén, Ambros showed me a cemetery full of children's graves, with a seven-branched candelabrum on each tombstone, and told me the story behind it. The local lord dreamed that Jews were killing his son. He had neither a son nor a daughter, but when he woke up he had all Jewish children under the age of thirteen taken from their homes and beheaded. The Arab authorities punished him by destroying the houses on his estate, devastating his fields, and sending him to Africa as a slave. Then they had the seven-branched candelabrum carved on the tombstones of the Jewish children, because everyone must be honored according to his religion.

155

Later we were attacked by bandits who took our mules and all our other belongings. But, thanks to the Almighty, they left us alive and we finally reached the monastery of my friend Ambros, near Saragossa. I had to explain to the monks there that the Jews observe the Law not to be rewarded for it, but simply to be human.

So I am writing to you from a Christian monastery! I will give this letter to the monks and they will have it delivered to you the next time some of them go to Cordova. I will go on to Barcelona and follow the coast into Septimania. I hope that Jeroboam and Rosemundo are getting along well, that Moses and Solomon are growing, and that the Almighty, blessed be He, will allow us to see each other again in a prosperous and peaceful world.

Your son and brother, Abner.

11

NARBONNE

Abner the African

NARBONNE WAS the capital of Septimania, which the Arabs, at the end of their surge, had taken from the Goths. Their presence there was light: a wali and a garrison. To Abner, what mattered most was that Narbonne was near the sea. As he strolled along the waterfront, recalling the smells and sounds of his childhood in Hippo, he realized that in Toledo and Cordova he had missed the flapping of sails and the promises of the open sea.

Narbonne was the point of departure for most of the merchants who sailed to Farama, formed camel caravans there to reach Kolzum, on the Red Sea, from where they sailed to El-Jar and Jidda, and went from there to Sind, India, and China. When they returned from the East, they brought with them musk, aloes, camphor, and unknown spices, and sold their wares to anyone willing to buy them, from the emperor in Constantinople to the chiefs of the Franks. Abner immediately thought of forming a partnership with one of those merchants. But first he would have to settle down and become accepted: although his brocades and his cloths in inimitable colors were known in Narbonne, he was still "the cloth maker from Cordova," an outsider.

In a conversation with Abner one day, Rabbi Bonjusas, an influential man in the Narbonne Jewish community, casually remarked that his daughter Dossa was now old enough to marry; he then went on to describe his difficulties in financing the enlargement of the Old Schools, a group of buildings that included synagogues and houses of study. Abner quickly thought over the situation. Marrying Rabbi Bonjusas's daughter would integrate him into the community and gratify his father, Rabbi Joseph, who wanted him to begin a family.

His hesitation ended when he saw Dossa: she was ravishing. And so he married her; or, more precisely, he married Bonjusas's family, which included a swarm of uncles, aunts, and cousins, another daughter, and a son, Capdepin, a slave merchant.

With the next caravan that left for Cordova, he sent a message informing his father of his marriage and asking his brother Jeroboam to send him the money he would need to set up a mill and a workshop in Narbonne, on the model of those that were already functioning so well in Spain.

He was soon earning so much money that Rabbi Bonjusas began planning to add a ritual bath and a house for old people to his synagogue and school. Abner had also formed a partnership with two Radhanites* who made journeys to the East that lasted two or three years. Their names were Joab and Bonisac, and anyone seeing them together understood that they were inseparable: one was short, fat, and gloomy, and the other tall, thin, and cheerful; one liked to sell, the other to buy; one spoke foreign languages that were a mystery to the other. On their next journey, they would take cloths made in Narbonne by Abner.

BUT ABNER'S financial success did not bring him social acceptance. The Jews of Narbonne had been settled there so long, each in his exact place, that the community continued to be wary of that Jew from Africa who had come with the Moslems and showed too much generosity not to have an ulterior motive. They greeted him, they appreciated his skill in making money, but they kept him at a distance—whereas his brother-in-law Capdepin, the slave merchant, was welcomed everywhere as if he were a son or a brother. Rabbi Bonjusas, delighted at finally being able to make his old dreams come true, was not aware of Abner's uncomfortable situation. He judged the tree by its fruit: Dossa had given birth to a son,

* Jewish merchants who carried on trade between the East and the West in the eighth and ninth centuries. (The origin of the word is unclear.)

Vidal, and the work of enlarging the Old Schools was under way. As for Dossa herself, the beautiful and ironic Dossa, she was on closer terms with her brother than with that curly-haired husband whom she sometimes called "our African," as though to set him apart. She never asked him about his work, plans, and successes, and whenever he talked to her about them of his own accord he clearly saw that she was not listening to him. Nor had she ever gone to that famous workshop where, in everyone's opinion, the most beautiful and luxurious cloths in Narbonne were woven.

What had to happen finally did happen. One day a young Christian woman came to the mill to ask for work; her husband had just died, leaving her alone with a mother and two children. What Abner first noticed about her were two exciting breasts, "like clusters of the vine," moving beneath her shabby tunic. Because of those breasts, he put on a great display of charm, told her amusing stories, and did everything he could to please her. Her name was Angevina. Instead of hiring her, he installed her, with her mother and her two sons, in a little house on Paterte Street where he could go without much risk of being noticed.

His visits to Angevina soon fell into a pattern. He often stopped by in the morning, before going to do business on the waterfront or at the mill. She served him hot milk with honey, they made love, and then they talked about all sorts of things; he was always full of plans, she was always full of questions. She affectionately called him "my Jew" and gave him an image of love and admiration, knowing that he needed her for what he did not find in his wife: attention and tenderness.

Remembering his meetings with Rachel in Toledo and how they had been discovered, Abner redoubled his precautions. But in Narbonne, as in all sunny cities where people lingered on their doorsteps, rumors sprang up quickly. Before long, everyone knew about the misfortune of Rabbi Bonjusas's daughter. Alerted by a blind man on the waterfront to whom he often gave alms, Abner decided not to visit Angevina for several days. During that time he went to Lunel, where he had heard about a fulling mill that was for sale. His wife, Dossa, was on the verge of giving birth and he intended to be back before *shabbat*. But he was detained by business and did not return home until two days after *shabbat*.

He arrived in Narbonne at siesta time, and since the streets were empty he hurried to Angevina's house on Paterte Street. She was not there.

"Where is she?" he asked her mother.

Her mother immediately became alarmed.

"I thought she was with you!"

A chill gripped Abner's heart. He questioned the frightened old woman and learned that two men had come for Angevina, saying that he had sent them to take her to him in Lunel.

"She was so happy!" added her mother. "So happy!"

"Who were those men? Had you ever seen them before? What did they look like?"

Angevina's mother sank into the terrible resignation of poor people accustomed to injustice and misfortune.

"I told her it was too good to last," she said. "With Jews, you have to be on your guard. They bring bad luck. . . ."

Abner hurried away from her and went home.

"You've come back very late," remarked Dossa.

She was lying down with her hands on her belly while a servant bathed her temples with diluted vinegar.

"I finally bought the mill," he replied, "and I had to stay in Lunel for *shabbat.*"

Dossa's face suddenly tensed.

"The pains have begun," she said, breathing deeply. She gave him a strange look and, fearing that he might notice it, began talking to him as she had never done before. "It must be a boy: only boys hurt their mothers this way. . . . You seem very pale, Abner. Are you ill? Are you sorry you bought that mill? I've already told you that you work too hard, that you try to do too many things. Aren't you satisfied with what you already have? Are you leaving, Abner? Where are you going? You haven't even told me about your trip to Lunel. Abner! I'm about to give you another son and you're leaving!"

Abner did not know if his wife was making fun of him or if, only a short time away from childbirth, she needed his presence. He left the house without a word, skirted the Belveze quarter, walked along Aludiere Street to the waterfront, and began looking for Gozolas, his blind beggar. Two of the big-bellied ships known as *marakibs* had just arrived from Africa. Slaves were laying sacks of grain on the ground and other slaves were loading them onto the backs of mules. The caravan would go to Toulouse, where the cotton it carried would be put aboard ships that would reach the Atlantic by way of the Garonne, sail along the coast, and finally go to England and Ireland. Abner was jostled from all directions.

Ordinarily he liked to let himself be swept along by the waves and eddies of the crowd on the waterfront, but this time he struggled and tried to free himself; he was still looking for Gozolas.

It was Gozolas who found him.

"Hello, Abner ben Joseph," he said.

The old blind man had mastered the trick of recognizing people by their voices, their footsteps, and even, he claimed, the rustling of their clothes. He said that people were so vain, and so pleased at being recognized by a blind man, that his ability substantially increased the alms he received.

"I'm glad I've found you, Gozolas," replied Abner. "I need you."

"I already know what you want to know, Abner ben Joseph."

"Then tell me."

Abner reached into his robe for a coin but he was stopped by Gozolas's voice.

"You can give me charity another time. What I have to tell you will hurt you. You'd be sorry you paid me for it."

"Don't worry about hurting me, just tell me what you know."

The blind man shook his old head.

"People are impatient to know their misfortune, then when they've heard about it, they wish they hadn't."

Gozolas told Abner how Angevina had been taken aboard a slave ship by force, and how the ship had immediately set sail.

Abner said nothing.

"Don't ask me the name of the slave merchant," Gozolas continued. "I have no enemies here. . . . Think carefully about what you're going to do, Abner ben Joseph. Think carefully."

With his dead eyes seeming to watch some invisible star in the sky, he walked away, tapping his stick on the pavement.

Abner had understood what Gozolas refused to tell him. He was a solid mass of contempt and sorrow.

He went straight to his brother-in-law Capdepin, who had a beautiful house in the Belveze quarter, overlooking the waterfront and the river.

Capdepin received him as if he were the wali himself.

"Baruch haba!"

Tall, with regular features, he resembled his sister, and, like her, he had a haughty manner that kept people at a distance. This time, however, he was affable. He took out two silver goblets.

"Have a seat, Abner. Would you like something to drink?"

161

Abner examined him as if he had never seen him before. Beneath that silent scrutiny, Capdepin lost his composure.

"And how's my sister?" he asked. "Has the baby been born yet?"

"Capdepin," said Abner, "I hate you! I hate you for what you've done! I hate you for what you are! I hate you!"

His words were like blows. He hurled them at Capdepin to hurt him, wound him, punish him. Capdepin had stepped back, but now, pretending great detachment, he poured sweetened fruit juice into his goblet.

"Abner," he said, "I won't let you insult me in my own house. I did what I did because it was decided by the family: Dossa, our parents, and I myself. Everyone in Narbonne was making fun of us! You'd been humiliating us with that woman for months, so don't come here now and say we did wrong! As for my occupation, I admit that it's not as noble as yours. But the Torah doesn't forbid it. The Torah even specifies the rights of slaves: they must be considered members of the family they work for, and be allowed to rest on *shabbat*. They can inherit their master's property if he dies without direct heirs. The murder of a slave is punished in the same way as the murder of a free man. This is what Exodus says on the subject: 'When a man strikes his slave, male or female, with a rod and the slave dies under his hand, he shall be punished.'"

Capdepin had justified himself; a buyer and seller of human beings who did his work honestly could have a clear conscience.

"The Torah doesn't forbid slavery," he repeated, and he added, before emptying his goblet, "but it does condemn adultery. So you see, my dear brother-in-law, that if one of us has a right to reprimand the other . . ."

Abner was beside himself with rage.

"Stop!" he ordered. "Don't talk to me about the Torah! I'll let you be judged by the Almighty, the God of justice and vengeance. But I know that the laws of this city forbid selling a free person as a slave. And if the seller is a Jew . . ."

He turned and hurried down the stairs. When he reached the street, he saw Gozolas walking away from him. "Think carefully," the blind man had urged him. Perhaps he had come to learn if Abner had followed his advice.

Abner took a few steps but his legs were trembling so much, from agitation or anger, that he had to sit down on the doorstep of a house. He was still sitting there when his servant Shemaya came running up to him.

"I've been looking everywhere for you, master! It's a boy! *Mazel tov!*"

THE BABY was named Sabrono. A few days later the whole family, including Capdepin, gathered in the synagogue for the *brit milah.* No one seemed ever to have heard of Angevina, and since Abner himself did nothing—denouncing a Jew might have endangered the whole community—silence closed over her and her fate like deep water.

Abner returned one last time to the house on Paterte Street, to give a well-filled purse to Angevina's mother, for the children. Then, after walking around the house for a few minutes, like a dog looking for its lost master, he went to the waterfront. There he gave alms to the blind Gozolas, strolled aimlessly, watched a sailor caulking a boat, listened to another sailor singing:

> *Three months at sea,*
> *Never touching land.*
> *Aboard a galley,*
> *Time is slow.*

He walked to the bridge over the Aude, then went home and wrote to his brother Daniel. Without Angevina he was lonely in Narbonne and he needed to renew contact with his family. But before he could send his letter—he had to wait for the caravan that left from Narbonne for Saragossa, Toledo, Cordova, and Hispalis every two months or so—a merchant with whom he was on friendly terms brought him a letter from Daniel. It informed him that Rabbi Joseph had died and that his wife Hannah had died a few days later, crushed by the death of the man from whom she had not been separated for a single day since their wedding in Hippo fifty years earlier. Daniel added that as the result of action taken by certain Moslem officials protesting against what they saw as the excessive number of *dhimmis* in the administration of Cordova, he had been forced to give up his position as adviser to the wali. The workshop was thriving, however, and Jeroboam intended to enlarge it if Abner gave his consent.

Abner reread the letter several times, as though trying to discern some hidden meaning between its lines or behind its words. But no, there was nothing other than what he had read: his parents were dead and life was continuing. He wept. Then he asked his servant Shemaya to tell his customers and clerks that he was in mourning, and hurried to the synagogue.

It was late morning and the sun was high. In the synagogue, two or three Jews were praying. Not even a *minyan*, he thought. He said the *kaddish*. "Glory and sanctification to the name of the Lord, who will renew the world and resuscitate the dead. May His reign be proclaimed in our days and in the lifetime of all the House of Israel, today and forever. . . ." He spent the rest of the day softly singing the hymns that Rabbi Joseph had taught him and that he had last heard in Cordova, the evening of his nephew's *brit milah*. At nightfall, when the synagogue was filled for evening prayer, he mingled his voice with the others, then went home. Dossa showed compassion for him but he felt even lonelier with her than when he was alone. He wrote another letter to his brother and invited him to come and live in Narbonne.

DANIEL DID NOT ARRIVE until two years later, in the year 4485 (725) after the creation of the world by the Almighty, blessed be He, with his wife Dulcia and their two grown children Moses and Solomon.

Abner was amazed to see that his brother's hair was beginning to turn gray: at thirty-seven, Daniel was only two years ahead of him! Life is passing, he thought, and I must hurry to do what I haven't yet done. But since Angevina's disappearance, a part of him, the most cheerful and enterprising part, seemed to have died forever. He let his business affairs go their own way; he no longer struggled, created, or dreamed. So what difference did it make if he was thirty-five or seventy?

BECAUSE OF HIS KNOWLEDGE and his modesty, Daniel was quickly accepted by the Jewish community in Narbonne. Old Rabbi Bonjusas warmly recommended him and even introduced him to the wali and the bishop, with whom he was on excellent terms. Daniel liked Narbonne and soon had the idea of beginning a Talmud Torah there.

"No community," he said to his brother one evening, "can do without the divine presence, but that presence isn't manifested by sadness, laziness, laughter, idle talk, or vanity: it's manifested by the wholehearted joy of doing good deeds and studying the Torah."

Rabbi Bonjusas supported the idea of that Talmud Torah and Abner agreed to pay for construction of the building that would house it. After summoning Daniel so that they could hear some scholarly commentaries from him in person, the members of the community council gave their approval.

Abner was glad that Daniel and his family had settled in Narbonne. He found them a large house for forty-eight dirhems a year, on Coyran Street, near the Aude, between the Belveze quarter and the fish pond. Nearly the whole street belonged to Dalmas of Vinassan, a Goth with whom Abner had business dealings.

For their first *shabbat* in their new home, Daniel and Dulcia invited Abner and Dossa to dinner. After the meal, the two brothers remained alone together at the table. They looked at each other in silence, and years of separation were suddenly abolished—they were children again and in a little while they would run to the bridge over the Seibus. . . .

Finally Daniel asked, "What are you thinking?"

"The same as you."

"Why don't we tell Jeroboam to come?"

In the time it took for the caravan to go to Cordova and back, Jeroboam arrived in Narbonne. He was alone. Daniel and Abner presented the city to him in a wondrous light: they wanted him to stay and live there. Jeroboam was hesitant. In Cordova, his partner Rosemundo was becoming tired and wanted to stop working, and his sons were willing to sell their shares of the business. Jeroboam was inclined to buy them; he liked the thought of being sole head of the business.

Because floods had made all the rivers rise, Jeroboam had to delay his departure and his answer. He spent Passover in Narbonne. Dossa, amused by the presence of the three brothers—they were called either "the Spaniards" or "the Africans"—offered to celebrate the *seder* in her house.

Uncles, cousins, sisters-in-law, children of all ages. . . . There were sixty-two of them that night in the big room on the first floor, sitting around the gold-embroidered white tablecloths, listening to little Vidal ask his grandfather Rabbi Bonjusas the four questions, listening to the Passover story, and finally drinking to life: *Lechaim!*

After the meal, when the children were in bed, the men sang hymns. The melodies were not the same in Narbonne as in Cordova, and this sometimes caused a little confusion.

"We Jews," remarked Daniel, "are a strange people, scattered all over the world: we all sing the same words, but not always the same songs."

Rabbi Bonjusas was as proud of Daniel as if he were his own son or his pupil, and never missed a chance to have him speak in front of his guests.

"Daniel," he said, "will you remind us of that famous *midrash* about the evil inclination?"

Daniel willingly did as the rabbi asked; he was always glad of a chance to make others better acquainted with the word of God or the commentaries of the sages of Israel.

"Rabbi Yochanan," he said, "teaches that one day the Almighty will seize the evil inclination and destroy it before the righteous and the impious. To the righteous, it will appear as a high mountain; to the impious, as a thin thread. Both will shed tears, the righteous wondering how they were able to conquer that lofty peak, the impious wondering why they were unable to master that little piece of thread."

When he had finished, everyone meditated. Nothing was heard but the sputtering of the oil lamps. Rabbi Bonjusas was greatly pleased with himself. He liked to celebrate knowledge, reflection, and memory for the edification of all.

"In our African friends' family," he said, "a chronicle of generations, handed down from father to son, has been kept since the destruction of the Temple, and Daniel is now the one who's carrying on the tradition. Isn't that right, Daniel?"

"Yes, rabbi, but . . ."

"You and your family read it together on important occasions, don't you?"

"Yes, rabbi."

"This is an important occasion, isn't it?"

Daniel had to go to his house for the Scroll of Abraham. He felt uneasy at the thought of reading it in front of those strangers. But, after all, they were his brother's wife's family.

"It's our custom," he said when he had returned with the scroll, "to stand when it's read."

Rabbi Bonjusas pressed his hands against the white tablecloth as he rose to his feet. The others also stood up, pushing back the benches, while Daniel unrolled the papyrus. With his brothers Abner and Jeroboam beside him, he began reading aloud.

"Abraham, son of Solomon the Levite, lived in Jerusalem and

the name of his wife was Judith. Elijah, his first son, became a scribe like his father. Gamaliel was the second son.

"Elijah begat . . ."

Abner watched all those strangers gravely listening to the succession of names and dates, and he realized that the Scroll of Abraham was more than a family history. It was the whole Jewish memory. Ezra, Judith, Gamaliel, Nomos—it was not the names themselves that mattered, but the continuity they exemplified. Because of what underlay that continuity, sixty-two Jews in Narbonne felt that the history of centuries of Jewish life in Alexandria, Hippo, and Cordova was the history of their own past.

JEROBOAM FINALLY DECIDED to go back to Cordova. "That way," he said, "someone from the family will be there to honor our parents' graves." The fact was that he could not resist the temptation to be in sole command of the workshop and the mill. To each his own destiny.

Daniel was highly successful as the head of the Talmud Torah. One of his most diligent pupils was his son Moses, and for this he constantly thanked the Almighty, blessed be He.

Abner no longer traveled or made plans. Skeptical and embittered, he contemplated the world's ambitions and, rereading Ecclesiastes, finally understood the writer he had once called a sour old man: "All was vanity and a striving after wind."

He still refused to speak to Capdepin the slave merchant. Although he now had a daughter, named Hannah after his mother, he still regarded his wife Dossa as a kind of stranger, and was surprised that their lives could have been bound together in that way.

THE ONLY EVENTS that continued to arouse his interest were confrontations that pitted one people against another. News of them always made him relive the battle of the Jerez plain and remember his Berber cousin Ibrahim charging into the enemy ranks.

Firmly anchored in Spain, the Arabs were held in check at the borders of Septimania, particularly by Eudes, duke of Aquitaine, who was sometimes an ally and sometimes an enemy. A new amir, Abd-er-Rahman, tried to resume the Arab conquest at the head of a powerful army. He clashed with Eudes on the bank of the Dordogne and forced him to retreat. The duke requested help from one of his adversaries, the chief of the Franks: Charles, son of Pepin of Herstal.

Survivors of Abd-er-Rahman's army came to Narbonne with news of the Arabs' defeat near Poitiers. Abd-er-Rahman had been killed and nothing was left of his superb army. In Narbonne, the wali had the city's defenses strengthened: victors were seldom satisfied with a single victory, and an assault by the Franks probably had to be expected.

Charles Martel and his soldiers reached Narbonne and laid siege to it, confident that their reputation as invincible fighters would soon make the city surrender.

"THE FRANKS are stupid," Abner said gruffly. "Narbonne isn't a city they ought to besiege. Its supplies come in from the sea and it can still carry on its trade by means of ships. What are they hoping? That the wali will be frightened into surrender? That a traitor will open the gates? All they've accomplished is to prevent the Jews from going to the cemetery on the Jewish Mountain!"

The siege was so ineffective that Vidal, Abner's older son, who had decided to visit his uncle Jeroboam in Cordova to learn more about cloth making, did not change his plans, except that instead of leaving by land with the caravan, he took a ship to Barcelona.

Abner told his son good-bye as if he would never see him again, and quoted Ecclesiastes to him: "Whatever your hand finds to do, do it with your might; for there is no work or thought or knowledge or wisdom in *sheol,* to which you are going."

AND HE NEVER DID see Vidal again. Abner fell ill and took to his bed. His fever left him a few days later, but he remained in bed. He seemed to have lost interest in life. Though he still asked Sabrono, his younger son, to keep him informed on the state of the siege, he spoke of nothing else. Completely turned in on himself, he felt the throbbing of two unhealed wounds: Rachel and Angevina. There was nothing to say, nothing to do; there was only regret.

A week before Rosh Hashanah, Sabrono excitedly came to tell his father that Charles Martel's Franks had abandoned the siege.

"Then the road to the Jewish Mountain is open now," said Abner, and made no other comment.

The next day he was found dead in his bed.

12

NARBONNE

The Jewish King

THE FRANKS came back. It was in the year 4512 (752) after the creation of the world by the Almighty, blessed be He, and their leader was no longer Charles Martel but his son Pepin, who, with the support of the pope, had just had himself elected king at Soissons.

When the Franks arrived at Narbonne, the Jews were just finishing their celebration of Purim, commemorating an episode of the exile in Persia: When Mordecai refused to bow down to Haman, King Ahasuerus's favorite, Haman persuaded the king to order that Mordecai and all other Jews in the kingdom be killed. But then Queen Esther, Mordecai's adopted daughter, intervened. After prayer and fasting she was able to make the king change his mind. He rescinded his order to kill the Jews and had Haman hanged.

Since then, Jews had celebrated Purim, or the Feast of Lots, every year in the month of Adar. Children wearing masks and disguised as Ahasuerus, Esther, and Mordecai danced in the streets and chanted Haman's name to the rhythm of sticks or stones struck against each other.

That year, at the end of the celebration, the formidable army of savage Frankish warriors paraded in front of Narbonne, as if that awesome display would be enough to bring down the walls of the city and overwhelm its defenders. The Jews could not fail to see a sign in this coincidence: if they placed themselves under the protection of the Almighty, the Lord of Hosts, then affliction would be turned into gladness, and cries of anguish into tears of joy.

The community council convened and decreed that a day of fasting ought to be sufficient. Most of the *parnasim* were persuaded that Pepin, like his father twelve years earlier, would stop the siege as soon as he realized it was futile. Furthermore the wali, with whom they were on good terms, had told them not to worry.

Yet the Franks seemed to have settled in to stay forever. Exasperating winter rains, sweltering summer heat, the boredom of long, empty days—nothing shook their determination. Although Narbonne could bring in supplies by sea, it was cut off from inland cities. The drawbacks of the situation were considered tolerable at first, but a season passed, then another, then still another . . . The Narbonnese felt as if they were living on an island.

King Pepin had said he was firmly resolved to take Narbonne and would never give up. But when it finally became apparent that waiting would not be enough, the Gothic Count Milo sent Miletius, one of his counselors, to Narbonne to confer with the Jews and try to find some way of putting an end to the siege. Practically speaking, his mission was to learn whether or not the Jewish and Christian civilians would be willing to help the Franks take the city.

It was now the year 758 by the Christian calendar. Rabbi Bonjusas and Daniel the sage were dead, Dossa was an old woman, and Daniel's and Abner's children already had children of their own. "A generation goes, and a generation comes. . . ." At forty-five, Daniel's son Moses was the oldest of the generation that had not known Africa: he and his brother Solomon were born in Cordova, while the children of Abner and Dossa were born in Narbonne.

Moses was a scholarly scribe who respected learning. The family had entrusted the Scroll of Abraham to him, with the responsibility of keeping it up to date and finally passing it on. He was a member of the community council, and it was in this capacity that he one day summoned his brother Solomon and his cousins Vidal and Sabrono to a meeting in his house.

"This evening," he said, "the council must decide on the answer we'll give to the Goths. Are we with the Goths against the Arabs?

170

With the Arabs against the Franks? Our position in the city enables us to play a part that may be decisive. We must make the right choice."

The four men were grave.

"Let's try," Moses continued, "to decide among ourselves what I should propose to the council this evening."

Sabrono, a round little man with a sparse beard and shrewd eyes who managed the mill at Casal, raised his hand.

"There are two points to consider," he said.

The three others burst out laughing: Sabrono had the habit of splitting every problem into two parts. He was not offended, and even joined in the laughter; then he returned to his reasoning.

"The first one is clear: till now, the Arabs have never given us any cause for complaint. The second one is equally clear: to the Arabs, we're only *dhimmis,* people under their protection."

"What's your conclusion?" asked Moses.

"My conclusion is that we should calmly examine the situation in the light of those two obvious points."

More laughter.

"That solves our problem!" Vidal was finally able to say. "Thank you, Sabrono! What would we do without you?"

Solomon the carpenter wiped his eyes with his big, square hands.

"What Sabrono has done is very good: he's made us laugh. Now we can have a serious discussion without becoming too tense."

"Who would like to begin?" asked Moses.

It was a cold day. The north wind had taken possession of the city. It could be heard hissing at the corners of houses, howling in the narrow streets, and roaring like a blacksmith's forge in the covered passages. That terrible wind was said always to last three, six, or nine days, and Moses thought that everything would be settled, for better or worse, by the time it ended.

He looked at his brother and his cousins. Through the years, the four of them had built up a large fund of shared experiences, common memories, and tacit understandings, and even though their characters had become more distinct with the passing of time, Moses believed that the others' opinions would be fairly close to his own. After careful reflection he had concluded that the Jews of Narbonne could not betray the Moslems, who had never persecuted or even threatened them, and ally themselves with the Goths, who in the past had converted Jews by force. To him, it was a clear-cut matter of justice.

Vidal raised his hand. He was a tall, thin man with prominent cheekbones and gray eyes like those of his mother, Dossa.

"When I have to decide something for myself," he said, "I compare the advantages with the disadvantages. In this case, we have to decide whether or not it's in our interest to continue being dependent on the Moslems. On the one hand, it's true that they don't mistreat us. But on the other hand, they give us almost no commercial outlets in Spain, and each time they've fought against the Franks, they've lost. If we go over to the Franks, we'll open up for ourselves not only Aquitaine and Provence, but also the countries to the north, with large cities as well as regions that are still relatively unknown, and we'll be under the protection of the strongest armies. From the standpoint of our own interest, I think our choice is clear."

"So what you're proposing," said Moses, scarcely able to believe what he had just heard, "is that we surrender to the Franks."

"Yes," replied Vidal, "and the sooner the better—provided we won't simply say, 'We surrender.' We'll say that we're willing to make it easier for the Franks to take Narbonne, in exchange for certain advantages."

"I agree: the sooner the better," said Sabrono. "The Arabs are divided into two opposing camps, the Ommiads and the Abbassides. Someday we'd have to choose between them. And whichever one we chose, we'd be choosing only half of the Arabs' strength."

He stressed his words with quick movements of his pudgy hands. Solomon the carpenter, however, spoke with his hands laid flat on the table.

"I don't look as far ahead as Sabrono does," he said, "but I know one thing: if we're not with the Goths when they open the city to the Franks, we'll be against them, and against the Franks to boot."

"But if we remain loyal to the Arabs and help them defend the ramparts," Moses objected, "the Franks won't be able to take Narbonne!"

He was appalled. He could never have imagined that members of his own family would let self-interest and fear make them disregard such things as loyalty, a shared past, the experience of living side by side for many years. He felt that there was a kinship between the sons of Israel and the sons of Ishmael, a childhood in the desert, a common heritage of landscapes, sunlight, and customs, whereas those big, blond barbarians, those pork eaters brought up

172

in the forests, were completely foreign to them. But how was he to express all that?

"You know very well," he said, "that the Christians have always persecuted us and that the Goths have tried to convert us!"

"That's in the past," replied Vidal. "We're living in the present."

Moses, who did not see very well, squinted to scrutinize the faces of his brother and his cousins. It seemed to him that they had changed, that they were no longer the men he had known. How could a Jew, he wondered, not take the past into account? He strongly felt that in the decision they were about to make they should consider their responsibility to their ancestors as well as to their grandchildren.

"Do you think Narbonne belongs to you," he asked, "and that you can do with it as you please?"

What he said had little relation to what he wanted to say. Something in this situation escaped him completely.

"Would you rather wait for others to decide for us?"

Vidal's tone was brusque, almost hostile. Moses realized that he must not try to persuade him: nothing would be left of that man if the shell of rudimentary truths that composed him were changed.

"I don't know . . ." said Moses. "I thought . . ."

The discussion took up the whole afternoon and involved all the good and bad reasons that people put forward when they are concerned with both their well-being and their safety.

Darkness was falling when Moses stated the outcome of their debate:

"I'll propose to the council that we ally ourselves with the Goths to open Narbonne to the Franks, provided King Pepin promises to respect our autonomy, our laws, and our religion, and guarantees our right to hereditary possession of property: land, buildings, and so on. Do you all agree to that?"

"Yes, I agree," said Sabrono, "but be sure to specify mills as one of the kinds of property we can own."

"I agree too," said Vidal.

"So do I," said Solomon the carpenter. "May the Almighty, blessed be He, help you and the other council members to make the right decision."

"Amen," replied Moses.

When they left, the wind nearly snatched the door from Moses's hand as he held it open for the others. They folded back their hoods, leaned into the wind to reach the shelter of the wall across the street, and then separated. Moses went to the synagogue, where the council was holding its meeting.

It was quickly established that the Jews had an important part to play, as Moses had said: if they sided with the Arabs, it would probably mean that Pepin could have no hope of taking the city in the near future. After an emotional debate, the council came to a decision that coincided with the recommendation that Moses, sick at heart, had presented in the name of his brother and his cousins: the Jews would help the Goths to open the gates and hold the garrison in check while the Franks took the city, provided that Pepin met the demands of the *parnasim*. Three council members would go to Pepin's camp the next morning to negotiate the conditions under which the Jews would help him.

To try to attenuate his deep feeling of betrayal, Moses asked that the wali be informed of the whole maneuver.

"Since you all feel that he has no chance of victory," he said, "let's warn him, so that he won't send his men to be killed for nothing—or so that he can withdraw to Spain, if he wants to."

He insisted so forcefully that the council finally gave in. After all, his plan had its advantages: the *parnasim* would have not only the satisfaction of being on the winning side, but also the pleasure of keeping a clear conscience. And when it was time to decide who would go to the wali's palace the next day, the council naturally chose Moses, without concealing the risks of his mission.

It was a clear night. That devilish wind had driven all impurities from the sky and the stars were shining as they must have done at the beginning of the world. Moses came home and found his wife waiting up for him. When he had told her about the day's discussions, she said he had been right to advocate acting in accordance with the teachings of the Law. He asked her to go and wake up their son Bonmacip.

Bonmacip, Moses's only son, was also a scribe. At eighteen, he was a slender young man with delicate features framed by stiff black hair. The expression of his eyes was a surprising combination of innocence and gravity.

"My son," said Moses, "I'm going to the wali's palace tomorrow morning. Perhaps the Almighty, blessed be He, will decide to shame the other members of the council by not allowing me to return. If so, you'll take my place in this house as the guardian of our memory."

He took out the cordovan leather case in which the Scroll of

174

Abraham was now kept. They put on their prayer shawls and reverently looked at the columns of names, sometimes accompanied by comments, to which Bonmacip might soon have to add a few lines—dying under those conditions was a way of remaining alive.

In the morning, Moses embraced his wife and son and set off for the palace. The wind had not weakened. The wali, who had sensed that something was afoot, received him immediately. He was an irascible but basically spineless man, embittered by the feeling that for the past six years he had been abandoned by the Arabs in Spain.

Moses told him that the siege had already lasted too long, that no help could be expected, and that it would be best to negotiate with the Franks—which the Goths and the Jews had decided to do, on their own if necessary.

The wali flew into a rage. He swore that he would rather have Narbonne destroyed, and all its inhabitants slaughtered, than submit to the infamy of surrender.

"I'm going to take hostages," he shouted, "and I'll cut off their heads myself if your people and the Goths betray me! And you're the first hostage!"

He had Moses thrown into a dungeon cell in the basement of the palace.

He did not know that the Jews had already sent three men to negotiate in Pepin's camp. When they came back the following night they reported that the king had given them a friendly reception and asked them what they were offering and what they wanted in exchange. It was Jacob the Radhanite who had answered. The Jews of Narbonne, he had said, would help the Goths to open the city and its port to the Franks; they would pay the Franks the yearly tribute of seven thousand marks of silver that they had till now been paying to the Arabs; and they would place their knowledge, which was priceless, at the king's disposal. In exchange, Pepin had consented to satisfy the Jews' demands concerning their rights and their laws. He had ordered his scribes to put all the terms of the agreement into writing, then he had set his Latin seal to the document and the Jews had signed it in Hebrew.

And so it came about that on a February night in the year 759 of the Christian era, the Goths and the Jews seized the Arab guards and opened the western gate, known as the royal gate. The Frankish soldiers advanced to the Aude along the Straight Street, by way

175

of the old market. By morning, they had taken possession of the whole city, almost peacefully.

The Jews went to free those among them who had been held as hostages by the wali and took them to the synagogue in a procession. Moses was taken there with the others, but several families openly turned their backs on him and accused him of having endangered the lives of fathers or brothers by warning the wali of what was going to be done. Moses made no reply. His heart was filled with sadness. He squinted and looked for his son's face in the crowd, but Bonmacip was not there.

Moses left the synagogue and began walking home. He noticed that the wind had stopped during the night; it had lasted six days, during which the city had changed masters and human nature had been revealed.

Bonmacip was lying on his bed with his face swollen and his body painfully bruised: he had been attacked in the street and beaten with sticks. He would not name the men who had attacked him but Moses knew all too well why they had done it.

"They all thought I'd betrayed the Jews," he said.

"I don't think that," replied Bonmacip. *"They're* the traitors: they've betrayed the Law."

"Weren't you afraid?"

With his wounded lips, Bonmacip quoted from a psalm and the words brought tears to Moses's eyes: "Out of my distress I called on the Lord; the Lord answered me and set me free. With the Lord on my side I do not fear."

It was finally learned that the wali had refrained from ordering the garrison to fight because Moses's warning had discouraged him in advance. He admitted this himself when King Pepin questioned him. The Jews of Narbonne immediately changed their attitude toward Moses and his family. Many of them praised his wisdom and courage; some told him that they regretted not having supported him from the start, or having said things they did not mean. Moses answered only that they should all be thankful to the Almighty, blessed be He, for subjecting them to trials that enabled them to realize the uncertainty of human judgment. He also thought, though he did not say it, that the wild wind that sometimes blew from the mountains made the people of Narbonne do strange things.

THE GOTH MILO became the first count of Narbonne and struck coins bearing his name, like a sovereign. Old Bishop Aribert received, in the name of the Church, most of the Arab property in the city. King Pepin kept his promise to the Jews: they were left in possession of their land, houses, mills, saltworks, and even their vineyards, despite the opposition of the Church. They also obtained recognition of their council, to be headed by a nasi whom the king would acknowledge as their sole leader.

After six years of isolation, Narbonne renewed its links with the rest of Septimania and with Aquitaine, which the king soon annexed to the kingdom he was to divide several years later between his two sons, Charles and Carloman.

Life in the city had scarcely changed, except that muezzins no longer called the Moslem faithful to prayer and the sound of bells was heard from newly built Christian churches. The authorities gave the Jews complete autonomy. Rabbi Bondavin took advantage of it to add a library to the imposing buildings of the Old Schools, to which Abner, peace be with him, had allotted so much money. The rabbi closely followed the construction work and the pupils of the school were amused to see him pick up a shovel and enthusiastically mix mortar whenever he had a few spare moments.

Everything had been going well for the Jewish community when, after Pepin's death, Pope Stephen reprimanded Bishop Aribert for the friendliness of relations between Jews and Christians and denounced the way in which Jews were allowed to inherit property, saying that it would be advantageous for the king to require payment for his consent to it.

It was urgent for the Jews to have the new kings, Charles and Carloman, confirm the privileges granted to them by Pepin. They then realized that no one had yet been designated as the nasi mentioned in the document signed by the king. The council had not been able to agree on the method of designating him, the nature of his functions, or the extent of his power, and the community was still represented by delegations whose members often lost sight of the general interest in their efforts to make their own particular interests prevail.

The council met in the Old Schools. There was apprehension in the air: if the pope had his way, the Jews of Narbonne would be dispossessed of their property. But they could not demand that the pact signed by Pepin be respected unless they first conformed to its terms themselves; they therefore had to choose their nasi.

"I propose," Moses began, after the prayer with which the meeting had opened, "that we really try to forget our usual arguments and come to an agreement."

In the ten years since the Franks had entered Narbonne, he had held a preponderant position in the council. His hair had turned white and he was nearly blind; he could no longer write and he was able to read, slowly and laboriously, only by holding the text very close to his eyes. He usually asked his son Bonmacip to read him this or that passage in the Scriptures; it was an added comfort for him to hear his son's voice speaking the words of God.

"The survival of our community is at stake," he continued.

But this time, as always before, the council again failed to agree on the choice of a nasi. Every proposal gave rise to a counterproposal. Then a newcomer to Narbonne, Rabbi Meir, son of Isaac, who had arrived from Arles a short time earlier to teach in the school, discreetly asked to speak.

He was a thin, stooped old man with a white beard that jutted out in front of him like a dangerous weapon. He coughed twice, as befitted a scholar, and said in a scarcely audible voice that made everyone else fall silent to listen, "In my opinion, the new king of the Franks will renew your pact if at least one of the three following conditions is fulfilled." The silence was complete. It obviously gave Rabbi Meir great pleasure. "The first one is that he consider himself bound by the commitments his father made. I think it's unrealistic to count on that. The second one is that he consider it more important to have peace with the Jews of Narbonne than to be able to draw money from them. But it's futile to try to reason on the basis of what a young king may regard as being in his own best interest. The third one . . ." He paused, to build suspense, and again coughed twice. "The third one is respect."

"Respect?" Rabbi Bondavin asked as if he had just heard that word for the first time.

"Our sages teach us that we cannot use gold to control someone richer than we are, and the Arabs say that kings treat only with kings. We must therefore find a king."

There was a chorus of exclamations.

"A king?" "What king?" "King of what?"

Rabbi Meir obviously knew where he was going. His voice became even fainter, and the others listened to him all the more intently.

"You've heard of the rivalries in Babylonia between the exilarchs and the *geonim*. . . ."

The *geonim* were great and revered teachers who headed the famous academies at Sura and Pumbedita. Several years earlier, a *gaon* named Malka had tried to replace the reigning exilarch, Zakkai bar Ahunai, with another descendant of David, Natronai bar Habibai, a distinguished scholar. But the exilarch foiled the maneuver; the *gaon* was dismissed from his functions and died shortly afterward. As for Natronai bar Habibai, he had to leave Babylonia.

"And do you know, people of Narbonne, where Natronai bar Habibai is today? He's in Cordova, and he's bored there. Let's invite him to come here, offer to make him the head of a Talmudic academy, and"—Rabbi Meir looked at each of his listeners and concluded almost gaily—"and proclaim him our king! Then we can send to the descendant of King Pepin a descendant of King David! Who could better deserve respect than he?"

Hubbub, exclamations, questions. With his beard thrust forward, Rabbi Meir was like a juggler basking in applause.

"But what if he won't come?" asked Rabbi Bondavin, who was already imagining plans for the new academy that would have to be built.

The answer was peremptory: "He'll come if it's the will of the Almighty."

"Amen," said the members of the council.

NATRONAI BAR HABIBAI—also known as Nakhir, which the Narbonnese soon turned into Makhir, "Knower" in Hebrew—arrived by sea with his family, five of his disciples, and boxes full of papyrus and parchment scrolls. Children ran through the streets, calling the population, and there was a real crowd on the waterfront when Natronai appeared.

He stood on the deck of the ship, majestic and straight as a cedar, wearing a brocade turban, like a caliph, and a flowing, gold-embroidered tunic of white velvet, closed at the top by an impressive clasp. In response to the shouts of welcome he raised his arms, which two of his disciples immediately supported, and he remained that way for a long time, like Moses in the desert with his arms held up by Hur and Aaron.

Thus there was in Narbonne a Jewish king of David's lineage.

No sooner had he settled into the residence prepared for him in part of the Old Schools than he was asked to pay a visit to King Charles. He made ready for a long journey because King Charles—Charlemagne—seldom stayed very long in one place: he held court at Aix, Compiègne, or Attigny, waged war in Lombardy, Spain, Germany . . . The Jewish king was finishing his preparations when Count Milo was notified by Charlemagne that the pact concluded between King Pepin and the Jews of Narbonne was still in effect. As for Pope Stephen's threats, nothing more was heard about them.

"You see what respect can do!" Rabbi Meir said modestly but triumphantly. "The Frankish king didn't want to make the descendant of David take the trouble to go and see him!"

Natronai bar Habibai, king of the Jews of Narbonne, was an erudite and witty old man, and so benevolent that he accepted many more students than the school could hold. Bonmacip, Moses's son, was given the task of making a final selection from among the applicants. Since Makhir's reputation had quicky become known all over the West, young men came from Lyon, Mâcon, Vienne, Arles, and even Frankfurt, to study at the academy in Narbonne. Bonmacip questioned them on the Torah, tried to judge which of them would be most likely to benefit from Makhir's teaching, and rejected the others. To those he sent away, he sometimes gave food or even a little money (of which he had scarcely any to spare), and always a copy of a *midrash* from the Talmud, so that they would not feel humiliated at returning home empty-handed.

He spent the rest of his time copying the chapters of the Mishnah that Natronai had brought from Babylonia, having completed them, it was said, from memory. Bonmacip was now married, and had named his first son Abraham.

On the whole, it was a happy time for the Jews of Narbonne: they were developing their schools and strengthening their commercial relations. But Charlemagne, intent on merging the temporal and the spiritual in his kingdom, was unifying the Church and exalting Christianity, and the Jews realized that in those circumstances it was better not to attract much attention.

Before dying at an advanced age and totally blind, Moses had said to his son Bonmacip, "The Torah also belongs to the Christians, but not the Talmud. The Talmud is our stronghold, our refuge, with a surrounding wall to protect our history. That's why

180

the Church, now that it's in power, can't tolerate the enclosure in which we take refuge. Remember that, my son, and teach it to your own son."

Abraham, Bonmacip's son, also became a scribe. He and Bonmacip worked side by side, each at his own writing desk, stopping now and then to exchange a few words while they relieved the stiffness in their fingers or legs. They looked so much alike that they were sometimes taken for two brothers.

"This morning," Abraham said to his father one day, "someone thought I was you."

"You know what the Talmud says: that before Abraham, old age was unknown. People who saw Abraham said, 'There's Isaac,' and people who saw Isaac said, 'There's Abraham.' To avoid that confusion, Abraham prayed that he could become old. That's the meaning of the verse in Genesis: 'Now Abraham was old.' "

They worked for a time in silence, then Abraham said, "Father, would you have wanted me to become something other than what I am?"

"Why do you ask that?"

"Because everyone says we're alike, but maybe it's not true."

Bonmacip put down the sharpened reed that served as his pen, threw back his shoulders to relax his back, and replied with a quotation from Proverbs: "My son, if your heart is wise, my heart too will be glad." He looked at Abraham thoughtfully. "I've sometimes dreamed of another kind of life, like the life of your cousin Davin, son of Levi, a traveler to distant places, a man who knows all roads and markets, meets all sorts of people, faces danger and survives. Other cities, other horizons. . . . Baghdad, Cracow, Samarkand, Kiev . . ."

Abraham was wide-eyed with surprise. This was the first time his father had ever made such an admission to him. But he, Abraham, was perfectly satisfied with being a scribe and was not at all envious of his cousin Davin's uncertain life.

"Don't worry, my son," said Bonmacip the scribe. "I was thinking of myself, not of you."

And he resumed his work, leaning over his parchment.

13

NARBONNE

Charlemagne's Diplomatic Mission

THE ADVENTUROUS Davin, whose travels inspired the prudent Bonmacip's daydreams, became sensitive to cold and fond of comfort as he grew old. Now it was his turn to watch young men setting off for faraway destinations, and he did all his traveling in stories.

His grandchildren and the grandchildren of his brothers and cousins never missed a chance to have him tell about this or that episode in his life as a great wanderer. The children would gather around him—in winter, before the fire; in summer, on the front steps of the house or in the shade of the arbor—and one of them would say, "Grandfather, Jacob—or Ezra, or Moses—doesn't believe that you. . . ."

This time it was an autumn evening, after the end of *shabbat*. Davin had finished reciting the blessings: for the wine, a symbol of joy; for the spices that his wife Esther kept in a wooden box; for the fire, to recall the creation of light at the beginning of the world, and thus look forward to the beginning of a new week. Esther put down on the table a decanter of sweet wine and a tray of fruit. For a few minutes the grown-ups talked about the state of the world and wondered what would come of it all. Then, taking advantage of a prolonged silence, the children left their places and went over to Davin.

"Grandfather Davin," said little Ezra, who was actually Abraham's grandson, "Jacob doesn't believe that the caliph had you bring an iliphant to Emperor Charlemagne!"

"It's *elephant,* not *iliphant,*" Davin corrected him, unaware that he was being deliberately goaded. "But the story is too long to tell now."

To the children, it was a familiar ritual. They had long known that a good storyteller always made a show of being reluctant to begin.

"Grandfather Davin," asked the frail, dark-haired Abigail, "is it true that an elephant couldn't fit into a house?"

Davin smiled and put his hand on her head.

"It depends on which house you're talking about, and which elephant."

"I'm talking about your elephant, Grandfather Davin, the one the caliph gave you."

"The caliph didn't actually *give* me an elephant, Abigail. But the story begins a long time before that, when Isaac the Radhanite and I were traveling . . ."

Now that he had finally launched into his story, Davin told how he and Isaac, young merchants in search of important customers, went to Charlemagne's court in the hope of selling the merchandise they had brought back from the East. Not only did they sell everything—precious silks, spices, ivory, chests made of fragrant wood—but, when he learned that they were at his court, Charlemagne summoned them and asked them if they would be willing to go to Baghdad with the diplomatic mission he was planning to send to Caliph Harun al-Rashid.

"But why you and Isaac, Grandfather Davin?"

"Maybe because we knew the languages and the roads, or simply because we were there that day and it was the will of the Almighty, blessed be He."

"Then you saw Charlemagne, and talked to him?"

Davin spread his arms.

"It would have been hard not to see him! Everything about him is big: his height, his stomach, his voice, his nose, his appetite, his ambition . . ."

He seemed to be reliving the prodigious encounter, and now no one could have stopped him. He told how they had left from Aix with two important emissaries, several servants, and a whole caravan of wagons, to take Charlemagne's gifts to the caliph.

"What a journey it was, my dear children! We were spared nothing: sickness, wolves, bandits . . ."

One of the two Christian emissaries died of a fever and the other was killed in an ambush by bandits. Davin and Isaac went through all sorts of ordeals and reached Baghdad only by the grace of the Almighty—and after two and a half years of traveling. Harun al-Rashid gave them a splendid reception, showing them through his palaces and letting them admire his treasures, so that they could tell Charlemagne about all the things they had seen that testified to the caliph's power.

"Is Baghdad bigger than Narbonne, Grandfather Davin?"

"Ah, Baghdad . . ."

No one could surpass Davin in describing Baghdad: the brick rampart with a hundred and sixty-three towers, the recently finished palaces and mosques, the stone-paved streets, the gardens, the libraries, the caliph's court, the court of his wife Zobeidah. . . . His eyes, his hands, and his words evoked masterpieces of the goldsmith's art, precious enamels, unknown colors, ineffable wonders.

Because flooding rivers had made the roads impassable, he said, Harun al-Rashid kept them a whole winter. He then gave them twelve ivory-inlaid chests filled with superb gifts for King Charlemagne, including the first clock ever seen in the West, the keys to the church of the Holy Sepulcher in Jerusalem, and a large quantity of jewelry with special settings.

"And what about the elephant, Grandfather Davin?"

Davin struck his forehead with the heel of his hand.

"Yes, of course! I was forgetting Abdul Aziz!"

"It's lucky you didn't forget him along the way!" Abigail remarked in her tart little voice.

"Abdul Aziz didn't let anyone forget him, Abigail, believe me! There was a special caravan of water and food for him, and on days when he decided not to walk we just had to wait for him to change his mind."

That elephant had become the main character in Davin's story. Depending on his audience and his mood, Davin endowed him with either admirable virtues or exasperating faults, and made him the hero or the villain of various adventures. An elephant, a real elephant!

After crossing cities and deserts at the pace set by Abdul Aziz's majestic stride, the mission reached Byzacium and stopped at Kairouan, from where its escort went back to Baghdad. Dreading the length of a return by way of Spain, Davin and Isaac had the wali of Kairouan send a messenger to Charlemagne to ask for a ship and an escort, which would enable them to return by way of Italy and the Alps.

And so the expedition landed at Patovenere. There it was met by Erchimbar, one of Charlemagne's secretaries, who had been made responsible for the last part of the journey. But not even a secretary of Charlemagne himself could induce Abdul Aziz to walk in the snow; they had to wait through the winter in Vercelli, at the foot of the Alps, before finally going on to Aix, which the king, having meanwhile become Emperor Charlemagne, had made the capital of the West. The whole journey had lasted nearly six years!

"And what did the emperor say?"

"He said that the Jews deserved to be honored for building a bridge between the Christian world and the Moslem world."

"And what did you answer?"

"I answered that the Almighty, blessed be He, had ordained that we were to act as an arbiter among nations."

"And what became of Abdul Aziz, Grandfather Davin?"

"I don't know, children. He too is part of the divine creation, and I don't want to say anything that wouldn't be the exact truth."

THE TRUTH, as everyone knew, was that Davin of Narbonne, son of Levi, son of Vidal, had not gone to Baghdad with Charlemagne's diplomatic mission. His friend Isaac the Radhanite had taken part in the expedition and told him about it when he returned. Davin had always regretted not having gone with him, and now that he was old he told the story of the journey to Baghdad over and over again.

Perhaps by now he really believed that he had gone there with Isaac. A dream of a cake is a dream, not a cake, but a dream of a journey is itself a kind of journey.

14

The Song of Songs

DANIEL, THE scribe and scholar who had gone from Hippo to Cordova with the Arab army, then from Cordova to Narbonne, had begotten Moses, and Moses had begotten Bonmacip, and Bonmacip had begotten Abraham—they were scribes from father to son.

Abraham, son of Bonmacip, had begotten Ezra, Abomar, and Resplendina. In the middle of his life, perhaps to carry out his father's unrealized dream of travel, he decided to follow, in reverse, the course that had taken his ancestor Daniel from Hippo to Narbonne. When he reached Cordova he found descendants of Jeroboam who still owned the cloth workshop and the mill for making dye from plants, and were prominent members of the council and the community. In Hippo, great-great-grandsons of Rabbi Joseph's sister owned the shop at one corner of the marketplace. But he had his most memorable experience in Kairouan, a city built by the Arabs to be their capital in North Africa. It was there that he met a distant cousin, a descendant of Nathan the blacksmith of Hippo, who was the head of a Talmudic academy. When Abraham arrived, his cousin was embroiled in a controversy with the sect of the Karaites—in Hebrew, *kara* means "to read"—who rejected all oral tradition, even if it had been put into writing, as in the Tal-

186

mud, and followed only the written Law, the Torah. Abraham was fascinated by the debate and spent several months in Kairouan. While he was there he contracted a malignant fever that repeatedly disappeared, then returned when he thought he was cured, leaving him a little weaker each time. He thought of death and decided to go back to his family in Narbonne.

He went to bed at the end of his strength, as soon as he arrived. He was glad to see his wife, his sons Ezra and Abomar, his daughter Resplendina, his daughter-in-law Asturga, his grandsons Simon and Elijah, and his friend Stephen, a cleric who often came to discuss the Scriptures with him. He asked his older son to write in the Scroll of Abraham that he had made a pilgrimage to Hippo. Feeling that he had fulfilled his obligations to everyone and everything, he asked for thyme tea sweetened with honey, perhaps because it reminded him of his childhood. When his wife came in with the steaming cup, he smiled and died.

That same day, at the end of January in the year 814 by the Christian calendar, the news of Charlemagne's death reached Narbonne. The bells of all the churches in the West, each calling to another, sounded an endless knell for the old emperor. People stopped what they were doing and hurried to the usual gathering places in markets or in front of churches, feeling as if they had lost someone close to them, yet struck by this reminder that death did not spare even the greatest and most powerful of men.

The whole seven-day period of Ezra's formal mourning for his father was marked by that steady, melancholy, inescapable tolling. He could not decide whether to take the coincidence as a good or a bad omen, and finally came to regard it as what it was: a coincidence.

As soon as he was no longer occupied with the common prayers for the peace of Charlemagne's soul, Stephen, the cleric, came to visit Ezra and Abomar. They spoke of life and death, God's will, man's precarious condition on earth, and their gratitude to the emperor for having enabled Christians and Jews to live together in peace and respect.

But, they wondered apprehensively, what would happen now that Charlemagne was dead? A few years earlier, he had divided his dominions among his three sons, Charles, Pepin, and Louis, but the first two had died, leaving Louis as the sole heir. He was known as Louis the Pious and his policies, totally dedicated to the

Church, were soon to justify the fears expressed by Ezra and Stephen.

SINCE THE DESCENDANTS of Sabrono, son of Abner, had died without heirs, part of their property went to Abraham's children: Ezra, Abomar, and Resplendina. As his share, Ezra received the New Mill, located downstream from the Old Mill, with fishing rights and the "handful right," which entitled him to take a handful of flour from each bag. Being a scribe, he had no use for the mill, and so he rented it until his son Simon was old enough to run it.

Simon had a real passion for the mill. At the age of twelve, he was already wielding the heavy hammer used for dressing the millstones; at fourteen, he was able to work the winch by means of which the sluice gates were opened to an extent that depended on agreements with the owners of other mills, upstream and downstream. At seventeen, he took sole responsibility for the mill, keeping only two men to work with him. He married, but his wife died in giving birth to a son, Vivas, whom he brought up with the help of a woman servant.

He began his days as early, and ended them as late, as the regulations allowed. He lived happily to the sound of the clanking water wheel and the grinding millstones. His customers liked him because he liked his mill and never took more than his due. The slightest rise of the water level kept him awake at night, imagining he heard the stone foundations cracking. Every Sunday, when work was forbidden, he inspected the framework and mechanism of the mill, looked for signs of wear in the wooden gears and, when he had nothing else to do, watched the swift green water of the millrace.

His two millstones were meant for grinding wheat, and there was not always enough work to keep both of them in use. He therefore decided to use one of them, dressed with a relatively smooth finish, for wheat, and the other, with a rougher finish, for barley and even beans, which his customers often had to be satisfied with toward the end of winter. When he asked them about this idea, they showed great interest. He began altering his installation. The only one who did not approve was his mistress Bonadona, a young widow, who would have liked to see him more often and for longer periods of time. But her brother Benedict, a courier at the bishop's palace, sometimes came to help Simon and encouraged him to innovate. It had become a kind of game between them to see whether Bonadona or the mill would win the competition for Simon's heart and time.

One day Simon had to dive under the mill to clear away some branches that were clogging the grate of the millrace. He saw that they were freshly cut branches and wondered who might have let them fall into the stream. When he went to dry himself in the room he lived in, above the millstones, he noticed a certain disorder and thought that Bonadona must be there. He looked all over the mill for her without finding her, and his workers confirmed that she had not come.

The next day, a secretary from the bishop's palace came to ask him to pay the ecclesiastical tithe. He refused.

"Jews pay their tithes in synagogues," he said, "just as Christians pay theirs in churches. And I also pay a viscontal tithe, even though it's not obligatory!"

Two days later Vincent, one of his workmen, came to shout in his ear, to be heard above the loud rumble of the millstones, that someone wanted to see him outside. Simon went out to the open shed where loads of grain were brought. Two guards from the bishop's palace were waiting for him there. They told him to come with them, bringing his deed to the mill. He went up to his room to get the deed and opened the oak box in which he kept it; it was not there, even though he was sure he had not taken it out. After asking Vincent to tell Bonadona that he was going to the bishop's palace, he rejoined the two guards. They chose to take him with them, even without the deed, rather than return completely empty-handed.

They walked around the church of Saint John of Jerusalem and went into the palace, which Simon knew only from having passed in front of it each time he took the road to Toulouse. They followed a long corridor where groups of people, evidently waiting for something, turned to look at them as they went by. Simon was a startling sight between the two guards: his clothes were covered with a fine layer of flour, from his hat to his sandals, and even his black, bushy beard had been turned white.

He was taken into a small room where he sat down on a wooden bench and waited to be called. He wondered why he had been brought to the palace by guards, as if he were a criminal. Was it because of the tithe he had refused to pay? He should have told his father about it, or the community council. Had Vincent found Bonadona?

Finally he was taken to another room, where a man with a bald, uneven skull, seated behind a table, looked up and signaled to a scribe who stood at his writing desk, pen in hand.

"Are you the Jew Simon, son of Ezra," he asked harshly, "operator of the mill known as the New Mill?"

"Yes, I'm Simon, son of Ezra."

The cleric looked him up and down.

"You don't have your deed to the mill?"

"I couldn't find it and I didn't want to keep the guards waiting."

"You'll bring it to me later. In the meantime, I want you to swear on the Pentateuch that what you say is true." The cleric pointed to a scroll on the table. "Put your hand on it. Do you swear by God, the Father Almighty, Adonai, that you will tell the truth? Answer, 'I swear.' "

"I swear."

"Do you swear by God, the Father Almighty, who said, 'I am the Lord'? Answer, 'I swear.' "

"I swear."

"Do you swear by the ten commandments of God and the seven names of God? Answer, 'I swear.' "

"I swear."

"Do you swear by God the Father, Elohim? Answer, 'I swear.' "

"I swear."

"Do you swear by the whole Law that God gave to Moses? Answer, 'I swear.' "

"I swear."

"Know, Simon, son of Ezra, that if you lie under oath you will be doomed to daily fever, loss of sight, and anguish of soul. Now, let's examine your case. The bishop's tax collector has informed me that you refuse to pay the ecclesiastical tithe owed by all inhabitants of this country. What do you say to that?"

Just then the guard standing at the door announced, "Bishop Nibridius!"

The bishop was a frail old man whose benevolent smile concealed great strength of character.

"Gaucelm," he said in his gentle voice, "what's happening here?"

The cleric stood up. His face and skull had turned red from surprise.

190

"This Jew refuses to pay the tithe and claims he's lost his deed. And he's insolent, like all Jews."

Bishop Nibridius turned his thin face toward Simon, silently inviting him to answer. But Simon was so astonished at hearing himself referred to as a Jew, rather than as a miller, that he blurted out a passage from the Bible that his father had often repeated to him: "The Lord is my light and my salvation; whom shall I fear?"

Gaucelm called the bishop to witness: "This Jew is a true son of the sullied, shriveled, and repudiated synagogue!"

Bishop Nibridius was still smiling.

"I recognize the words of my friend Agobard, archbishop of Lyon. I see that you've also received his letter. Well, Gaucelm, if you want to practice that catechism, I won't prevent you from going to Lyon. As for me, I've promised, in the name of Jesus our Savior and our God of mercy, to show kindness to the Jews of our city, and I won't break that promise."

The bishop stepped toward the door. He was as light as an angel.

"You're free," he said to Simon as he was leaving. "May God keep you."

Simon walked out of the room without looking at Gaucelm. Bonadona and Benedict were waiting for him in the corridor. After being told by Vincent that Simon had been taken to the palace, Bonadona had gone there to notify Benedict, who had in turn notified Bishop Nibridius.

News of the incident quickly spread through the city, awakening forgotten anxieties in the hearts of the Jews. That evening the community council gathered around the nasi, Natronai, great-grandson of the famous Makhir who had been called the king of the Jews. The councilors sat in chairs with carved backs and armrests. The nasi was enthroned under a blue-and-white canopy. The *shammash* seated Simon on a stool, facing the nasi.

Simon the miller was intimidated by all those white-bearded dignitaries. Although he was somewhat reassured by the presence of his uncle, Elijah the scribe, who was to record what was said at the meeting, he scarcely dared to look at him. At the nasi's request, he told how he had been asked to pay the ecclesiastical tithe and how he had discovered the disappearance of the deed to his mill. What he had not realized at the time was now clear to him: the incident was the result of nothing less than a plot against the Jews, and Gaucelm was the agent of that plot in Narbonne. He, Simon, had been its first victim, probably because his mill was outside the

191

Jewish quarter and anyone who wanted to go into it could do so without difficulty. It had been a simple matter to throw branches into the millrace and then steal the deed while he was removing them.

Bishop Nibridius had referred to the instigator of the plot, and the nasi confirmed his identity to the council: he was Agobard, archbishop of Lyon, who had written and begun circulating a letter against the Jews. Bishop Nibridius had shown the nasi a copy of the letter that afternoon. In it, after a series of insults, Agobard demonstrated to his own satisfaction that there was a fundamental antagonism between the Church and the Jews, and concluded by asking Christians to break off all relations with those infidels. Gaucelm had been a little overzealous, but there would no doubt be others like him.

Beneath his heavy blue brocade turban, Natronai, the nasi, seemed deeply sad.

"I wonder," he said, "how many more times it will be given to us to sing the song of Moses: 'Thy right hand, O Lord, glorious in power, thy right hand, O Lord, shatters the enemy.'"

The rabbi of Posquières quoted from Proverbs, "When the wicked rise, men hide themselves," and added, "I hope we won't have to hide again."

The nasi passed his long white fingers over his heavy eyelids.

"The Almighty," he said, "makes us die only once, but He hasn't limited the number of our exiles."

"But if the Christians exile us, rabbi," said Samuel of Sales, a slender, handsome old man, "it will harm them as much as us. We have our place in their community."

"That's true, Samuel, son of Jacob, but if people thought of others while thinking of themselves, and if they were preoccupied with themselves while being preoccupied with others, they would never harm anyone."

Elijah the scribe was so interested in the discussion that he wiped his pen on his beard and asked, "But what will King Louis say?"

The nasi shrugged.

"We have nothing to fear from kings, so long as they have the desire and the power to make others respect our rights." He raised his hands in a prophetic gesture. "But woe to us if their power or their will should weaken! Ambitious little princes would use us and then bury us under the ruins of our communities; the Church would throw us to the hostile crowd; the kingdom would become impoverished and divided."

Elijah was no longer writing. It seemed to him that the nasi was announcing the upheavals that would precede the end of time.

The nasi stood up and, in his powerful voice, called on the God of Israel for help: "May the Almighty protect us against those who persecute us, and against those who speak evil of us. Blessed be the Almighty."

"Amen," the councilors responded fervently.

Simon the miller was trembling with emotion.

IN THE YEARS that followed, the three sons of emperor Louis the Pious dispossessed their father and dismembered Charlemagne's empire, behaving like dogs fighting over a fallen quarry. Local lords took advantage of the disorder to settle old quarrels. The count of Toulouse used an Arab army from Spain to force Septimania to accept the rule of Pepin, the former king of Aquitaine. Warfare, destruction . . . In Narbonne, the suburb of Saint Paul and the Villeneuve quarter, beyond the Gate of Saint Stephen, were burned. Fields and orchards were devastated, yet refugees from the surrounding villages had to be taken in and fed.

At Verdun, the three warring brothers agreed to a division of territory. Septimania, along with the whole western part of the empire, went to Charles the Bald. Its people had to decide whether to grant their loyalty to Charles or to Pepin of Aquitaine.

Elijah asked the men of the family to meet in his house to discuss this question. Among those who came were Simon the miller and his son Vivas, who was now old enough to be a partner in running the mill; but while Simon liked working in the mill itself, with its gears and millstones, Vivas preferred to look for new customers, make deliveries, keep the accounts, and manage the fishery. Also there were Balid, son of Astruc, Vidal the goldsmith and his son Azac, and Elijah's two sons, Solomon and Comprat. Solomon was a scribe, like his father, and already an erudite young man. Comprat had gone to Cordova to learn how to cut and bind sheets of parchment to make them into books, which were easier to handle than large scrolls. Elijah was greatly pleased with his sons, but he worried about his daughter Dulcia: at fifteen, she was inquisitive, impudent, and even rebellious; she did not keep her place as a woman and wanted to know everything that was taught to boys.

Once when he had come home unexpectedly, he had found her in his study, reading his scrolls. Since anger was not in his character, he had merely shown her a text that he had seen and copied one day in the workshop of a group of scribes in Carcassonne: "May those who reproduce the commandments of the sacred Law combine their efforts here; may they abstain from all frivolous v·rds, lest their hands also stray into frivolities; may they strive for accuracy in their work, and may their pens follow the correct path."

"Why," Elijah asked his daughter, "did you come in here without at least asking my permission?"

"Would you have given it to me?"

Elijah was a wise and patient man, but he felt completely disarmed before Dulcia. The best that a man could expect from a woman, he thought, was that she give him children and add luster to his home.

"While Adam learned," he quoted, "Eve spun."

Dulcia lowered her eyes, as was proper. But she was not one to maintain a respectful silence for very long.

"Didn't the prophetess Miriam take part in the deliberations of her brothers Moses and Aaron?" she asked.

"Who told you that?"

"I read it."

"Where?"

"Here."

"Dulcia, I thank the Almighty, blessed be His name, for having given me an intelligent daughter, but your place is not in this room."

She undoubtedly was intelligent: she asked her father to forgive her, straightened her gray hat on her almost red hair, and left.

But Elijah now had other matters on his mind. When all the men had arrived for the meeting, he asked the Almighty to help them make the right decision, and then the discussion began. Unknown to all of them—the possibility had not occurred even to Elijah—young Dulcia had her ear to the wall and was listening to everything they said. She easily identified them by their voices; it was strange, people reduced to their voices. . . . "Who does Pepin think he is?" asked Balid, son of Astruc, in his nasal voice. Then she heard her father, Elijah: "We Jews must respect the law, as long as the law respects us." Delighted and excited at being able to follow the discussion perfectly, Dulcia brought a stool to the

194

wall and made herself more comfortable. "You're forgetting the Bodo affair!" Dulcia sighed with happiness: this was the voice of her cousin Vivas, the man her heart had chosen, her beloved, the object of all her thoughts and dreams. It seemed to her that she had always loved him, even when she had been a bony little girl with freckles all over her face. One day when she was about ten, she had told him that she wanted to live with him, that he would be a miller and she would be his wife. He had laughed indulgently —he might have been fifteen at the time—and she had become angry.

"Don't make fun of me, Vivas. The sages say that when you make fun of people, it's like killing them."

"Excuse me, I didn't want to kill you."

She had taken his hand, kissed it violently, and then run away, with her face bright red.

Since then, she had grown up and she clearly saw that men were troubled by her body. At family gatherings she constantly looked at Vivas, whom she had chosen once and for all, and it seemed to her that he was not completely indifferent to her. She was now old enough to marry; if he did not soon realize that by himself, she would have to tell him. She knew what love was like; she had read about it in the Bible. She knew the Song of Songs by heart.

> *Behold, you are beautiful, my love;*
> *behold, you are beautiful;*
> *your eyes are doves.*
> *Behold, you are beautiful, my beloved,*
> *truly lovely.*
> *Our couch is green. . . .*

From the other side of the wall, she heard voices deploring the ruin and destruction caused by war.

"We can still get silk from Spain by sea," said Balid, son of Astruc, "but we can't sell it."

"We'll soon have to ask help from the community."

"May the Almighty, blessed be He, preserve us from being reduced to begging!"

"Mutual aid within the community has nothing to do with begging!"

Dulcia recognized her father's tone as much as his voice. It was her uncle Simon who answered.

"I know, Elijah, but it's still unpleasant to be dependent on others."

"Not on others, Simon," Elijah insisted, "but on ourselves."

Sitting with her ear pressed to the wall, Dulcia felt her attention gradually beginning to wander. She was thinking of Vivas. When would she see him? One day he would come for her and take her away. He would come into her bedroom and say to her, as in the Song of Songs:

> Arise, my love, my fair one,
> and come away;
> for lo, the winter is past,
> the rain is over and gone.
> The flowers appear on the earth,
> the time of singing has come. . . .

For some reason she had the idea that if the Jews of Narbonne decided to remain loyal to King Charles, they ought to tell him so. She imagined Vivas going to the court and impressing the king by his handsomeness and noble bearing. And Vivas was speaking now.

> I slept, but my heart was awake.
> Hark! my beloved is knocking.
> "Open to me, my sister, my love,
> my dove, my perfect one;
> for my head is wet with dew,
> my locks with the drops of the night."
> My beloved put his hand to the latch,
> and my heart was thrilled within me.

Dulcia was sleeping as one sleeps at fifteen. She did not hear the men in the next room stand up, take leave of each other, open the door—and stop at the sight of that young woman asleep with her head on her shoulder and the shadow of a tender smile on her lips.

She again heard the voice of her beloved, but this time he was not speaking of love.

"No, uncle, don't wake her. Isn't it our fault? We should have invited her to take part in the discussion. I'm sure she would have said things worth listening to."

What was he talking about? She heard her father's voice answer curtly, "Girls have no place in that kind of discussion!"

And suddenly, breathless from the shock of having understood, she woke up. They were all there, standing around her in a semicircle: father, uncles, cousins, white beards and dark beards, in the yellow light of an oil lamp. Vivas was there too, looking rather amused. She ran away. This was the second time she had run away from him, and as she hid her head under her pillow she swore to herself that it would be the last.

NEXT MORNING, the first thing Elijah did when he came back from the synagogue was to call his daughter.

"May I come in, father?" she asked.

"Come in and sit down here." He seemed more grave than angry. "I've been thinking, Dulcia, and I want to apologize. You have as much right as your brothers and cousins to know what's happening."

"But father . . ."

"Was there anything said last night that you didn't understand, or couldn't hear?"

"Yes. Vivas mentioned someone named Bodo. Who is he?"

"Bodo? He was a deacon at the court of King Louis and he had great influence, which wasn't always good for the Jews. Then one day he decided to convert to Judaism. A pilgrimage to Rome gave him his chance: he let his beard and hair grow, had himself circumcised, took the name of Eleazar, married a young Italian Jewish woman, and went to live in Saragossa."

"What happened then?"

"I don't know what happened to Bodo. But Archbishop Amolon, who had replaced the famous Agobard, may his name be cursed, learned about Bodo's conversion and proposed measures against the Jews at the council of Meaux. At the same time, he wrote to King Charles to ask for his support."

"And what did the king do?"

"So far he's done nothing, because the Almighty, in His kindness, never sends an affliction without a means of remedying it, and King Charles's war with the other two kings has made him forget about Bodo."

Dulcia was silent for a moment, then she asked, "But why did that Bodo want to become a Jew, father?"

Elijah smiled thoughtfully, as if this were an odd question.

"I'm going to tell you a story," he said, "as I used to do when you were little. The sages say that Nebuzaradan, chief executioner of Nebuchadnezzar, king of Babylonia, discovered the blood of the prophet Zachariah in the temple and saw that it was still bubbling. 'What is this blood?' he asked the other executioners. 'The blood of the sacrifice,' they answered. Seized with doubt, he had sacrificial blood brought to him and saw that it had a different color. 'Tell me the truth,' he said to the executioners, 'or I'll have iron harrows dragged across your bodies!' And one of the executioners answered, 'There was a prophet who accused us of being sinful men. We killed him. That was many years ago, and his blood has still not stopped bubbling.' 'I'll make it stop!' said Nebuzaradan. He sent for the members of the Great Sanhedrin and had their throats cut over Zachariah's blood. It did not stop bubbling. He had adolescent boys and girls killed, and still the blood bubbled. 'Zachariah, Zachariah,' he cried out, 'I've already killed the best of them! Do you want me to kill them all?' As soon as he said these words, the blood stopped bubbling. And he thought, If one human soul, unjustly put to death, thus demands vengeance, how will it be for me, the murderer of thousands and thousands of human souls?"

"And then?" asked Dulcia.

"Then he ran away, sent his will to his family, and converted to Judaism."

Elijah and his daughter had never before felt so close to each other, but he shook off his tender emotion.

"Even though I've apologized to you," he said, "you must apologize to your uncles and cousins. It's not right to spy on people that way."

"But you didn't let me explain, father. I wasn't spying. I . . . I only wanted to hear Vivas's voice. . . ."

"Vivas's voice?" echoed Elijah, staring at her in bewilderment.

With Dulcia, he thought, he should always expect the unexpected.

ELIJAH HAD TAKEN a long time to realize that his daughter was old enough to marry and that she had chosen her future husband on her own.

The wedding took place as soon as peace had returned to the region. It was the fifth day of the month of Elul in the year 4608 (848) after the creation of the world by the Almighty, blessed be

He. Solomon, Dulcia's older brother, prepared the *ketubah* himself, and it was Comprat, her other brother, who decorated it.

That summer without war was superb; the entire family was able to rejoice wholeheartedly.

15

NARBONNE

The Four Millers

A YEAR after the wedding of Vivas and Dulcia, in October 849 by the Christian calendar, King Charles, known as Charles the Bald, came to Narbonne to assure the loyalty of Septimania and confirm the privileges granted by his predecessors. Simon and Vivas took advantage of his visit to have a new deed drawn up, attesting to their ownership of the New Mill.

THE MILLSTONES turned and time passed. Vivas and Dulcia had a son and two daughters. The son, Abraham, eventually took over the mill, married and had four sons of his own, who became inseparable: Samuel, the oldest; Moses, who had red hair; Isaac, who was always laughing; and the tender-hearted Levi. Samuel married, but the close friendship that united the four brothers remained unchanged.

One evening in the autumn of the year 900 their cousin David, grandson of Dulcia's brother Solomon, came running to the mill. It was the first time he had run since he became a scribe and stopped playing with the four brothers. He held his hat on his head with one hand as he ran, and the first to see him was Isaac, who burst out laughing.

"Quiet!" Isaac's red-haired brother Moses said to him. "He's probably bringing bad news."

When David had caught his breath, the brothers learned that the news he had brought was not only bad but also incredible: Bishop Erifons had gone to the king to request property for his Saint Quentin parish, and King Charles, known as Charles the Simple, had quite simply given the bishop all mills downstream from the Old Bridge!

"Not *our* mill!" cried Levi.

"Yes, cousin. *All* mills."

"But it belongs to us! We have a deed signed by the king!"

"What the king does, the king can undo."

"Where did you hear about it?" Samuel asked David.

"In the council. We were in the middle of a meeting when a messenger from the bishop came to tell us what had happened and ask the nasi to urge you to be sensible about it. The bishop is giving you till Saint Martin's Day to leave the mill."

The news was such that the brothers, expert practical jokers, might have believed that their cousin was in turn playing a joke on them, if that cousin had not been the sober and solemn David. When they realized that they had to consider themselves as having been dispossessed of the mill, they washed themselves, put on their best *shabbat* robes, combed their beards, and went to see the nasi.

Nasi Kalonymos was a scholarly old man, more inclined toward writing commentaries and studying than toward fighting, even if the fighting was only a legal battle. He kept repeating that no one could seize legally acquired property whose ownership had been guaranteed by the king.

"But, nasi, if the king himself . . ."

"No one! If words still have meaning, *no one* can seize legally acquired property."

The nasi felt as if the ground had collapsed beneath his feet. Nevertheless, he told the four millers that he had laid the matter before the royal tribunal and the ecclesiastical tribunal. He cautioned them against any kind of violence and promised to notify them as soon as the tribunals had reached a decision.

As they left the Old Schools, the brothers realized that their plight was beyond their control. They walked along Aludiere Street, as they had done in their childhood when they went to the waterfront in search of a chance to fight. It was raining.

"It's lucky we washed ourselves," remarked Isaac. "If we

hadn't, the rain would be turning the flour in our beards into dough!"

Levi was shocked: "Our mill is being taken away from us and you make silly jokes! How can you laugh at a time like this?"

"There's a time for laughing and a time for weeping, little brother."

"But what are we going to do?"

"Do you remember the verse in Psalms?" asked Moses.

"Which verse?"

"This one: 'If they plan evil against you, if they devise mischief, they will not succeed.' "

"May the Almighty, blessed be He, grant that it will be true for us!" said Samuel.

"Amen," replied his three brothers.

They decided to go to La Fourche, residence of the lord who had jurisdiction over their mill and to whom they had regularly paid the viscontal tithe.

Viscount Francon had died from overeating at a hunting banquet, leaving his wife with two sons, a half-built castle, and a great number of debts. The viscountess had sent her sons to stay with her cousin, the count of Toulouse, to learn what young men ought to know: how to serve the sovereign, fight, hunt, and pray. Living alone, she was now doing her best to pay the debts left by her husband, who had been one of those men always trying to get their hands on money in order to double it and then spend three times the original sum.

She gave the four millers a friendly welcome. She did not know them, but she had known their father: when Francon had taken her on a tour of his domain soon after their wedding, Abraham had shown them the mill. Viscountess Arsinde was no longer very young but, with her blue eyes, luxuriant dark hair, regular features, and simple but elegant clothes, she had a beauty that did not depend on youth.

No, she said, she had not heard of the king's gift to Bishop Erifons, but it seemed strange to her. The brothers asked if she could help them, at least by testifying that they had always paid the viscontal tithe and never given her any cause for complaint. She promised to have the viscontal tribunal render a judgment on the matter. They could come back in two days and she would give them a copy of the judgment.

Two days later, Samuel had another meeting with the nasi,

Moses and Isaac were working at the mill, and it was therefore young Levi who went to the castle of La Fourche. The viscountess greeted him graciously.

"Things are going well for you," she said. "Come."

She led him into the great hall of the castle, which was the room where she spent most of her time. Chests, furs, benches placed perpendicular to the vast fireplace, a loom and, near one of the two windows, a writing desk at which a scribe was working.

"As you can see," she said, "Gautier is making a copy of the judgment."

Levi stepped forward to read it, but it was in Latin. He could not help showing his disappointment.

"Are you wishing you knew how to read?" asked the viscountess, amused.

Levi bristled, as if she had insulted him.

"I *do* know how to read, but not Latin. The language of my fathers is Hebrew."

"Where did you learn it?"

"In school. We all learn it."

"What do you read?"

"The Book, and chapters of the Mishnah."

"How is Hebrew written?"

What a question! He was amazed that a woman like the viscountess did not know how Hebrew was written.

"Well," he said, "in relation to Hebrew, Latin is written backward, from left to right. . . . I'll bring you something written in Hebrew, so you can see how beautiful it is."

In the meantime, she read the judgment of the viscontal tribunal to him: inasmuch as a royal deed guaranteed ownership of the mill to the Jew Simon, to his son Vivas, and to the latter's descendants, the mill belonged to them; inasmuch as no one had ever lodged a complaint against them, and they had no debts, and they had always paid the viscontal tithe regularly, nothing could justify the expropriation of their property. The text was signed by the twelve judges and bore the viscontal seal, placed on it by the scribe.

Levi would have liked to stay longer but he was eager to report the judgment of the tribunal to his brothers.

"I thank you, your ladyship," he said. "You have a sense of justice."

"There's not much more I can do," she replied, "but let me know what happens."

Levi promised that he would.

The millers had their cousin David make a second copy of the judgment and took the first one to Nasi Kalonymos, who immediately requested an audience with the archbishop.

Levi often thought of the viscountess. One morning he awoke with a plan already formed in his mind. At the first opportunity, he slipped into David's house and took the Scroll of Abraham in its cordovan leather case. With his heart pounding, he went back to the mill and hid the scroll there. This was the first time he had ever concealed anything from his brothers. He felt no great remorse, but he was afraid to think of what would happen if it was discovered that he had taken the scroll.

The next day he suggested that he should go to La Fourche and give the viscountess two bags of flour to thank her for her help. Isaac laughed. Moses and Samuel looked at each other and Levi felt as if they had read his mind. But what mattered was to have a pretext for going to La Fourche.

When he arrived there, leading the pack mule, Arsinde was at the top of the stone steps. She said she was glad to see him, thanked him for the flour, and asked him how matters stood with the mill.

"The archbishop is going to discuss it with the bishop," he replied, then stopped short: he had not come there to talk about the bishop. "Your ladyship, I wanted to show you this."

He took the Scroll of Abraham from the cloth bag slung over his shoulder.

"Come in, miller," she said.

There was no one else in the great hall, which smelled of smoke and soup. Levi went to the writing desk and put the scroll on it. Arsinde came over to look at it.

"Ever since the destruction of the Temple of Jerusalem by Titus," he said, "we've been recording all births in the family, and all important events that affect us." He realized that the Scroll of Abraham was something quite different from a cold record of facts, but he did not know how to express it. "It's . . . it's my history for the last nine centuries," he finally added.

It seemed to him that Arsinde was now looking at him differently. It was as if that written memory bestowed a kind of nobility on him. She leaned over the scroll.

"How do you read Hebrew?" she asked.

Pointing out each word to her with his finger, he enunciated slowly: ". . . so . . . that . . . none . . . will . . . be . . . forgotten . . . on . . . the . . . day . . . of . . . forgiveness . . . I . . . inscribe . . . the . . . names . . . of . . . my . . . sons . . ." He showed her the letters one by one, *aleph, beth, gimel,* and she amused herself by trying to find them in other lines.

They leaned forward, side by side. Their fingers brushed against each other, their laughter was mingled, their shoulders soon touched. They were so troubled by what was happening to them, the lady and the miller, that they no longer paid any attention to what they were reading. Desire was equally heavy in both of them. Even when his left hand had taken her right hand, they did not dare to look at each other. Finally they turned their faces and their eyes met. And when the viscountess pressed her lips to his, Levi the miller felt as if he were about to faint. He thought briefly of putting the Scroll of Abraham back into its case; he regarded it as a sacred text for which he must never fail to show proper respect. But it was too late. He was already caught up in a whirlpool like those that ran through the mill when the Aude was flooding.

WHO DENOUNCED THEM? A maid or a stableman from the castle? In any case, the rumor quickly spread through the wash-houses, markets, street stalls, and lines of people waiting at fountains and mills: the viscountess and a miller young enough to be her son . . .

"He's one of the Jews from the New Mill."

"Are you sure it's only one? Remember Francon's orgies. . . ."

"Wasn't it from Jews, Sabrono and Barala, that she borrowed a thousand sous and put up the freeholds of Magric and Cuxac as security?"

"I won't be surprised if it turns out that the Jews cast a spell on her, poor woman."

How else could it be explained that a woman of her rank had fallen so low?

The story soon reached the mill. And although the incorrigible Isaac jokingly referred to his young brother as "Viscount Levi," the others took the matter very seriously, especially since it had come at a bad time. The three tribunals of Narbonne—royal, ecclesiastic, and viscontal—had ruled that the dispossession of Samuel and his brothers was illegal, the archbishop had intervened at the nasi's request, and Bishop Erifons had finally listened to reason: in exchange for an annual donation of flour and fish for the poor of his parish, he had given up his claim to the New Mill. Levi could therefore not have chosen a worse time to attract attention to himself and his brothers by becoming involved in such a scandal.

Levi was horrified and bewildered. How was it possible for evil to arise from good? He and the viscountess were united by something so strong, simple, and miraculous that he did not understand how it could have been transformed into a disgrace and an abomination. The time they spent together left them happy and enriched, each from the other, from the other's desire and pleasure, the sound of the other's voice, the touch of the other's skin. And when she asked, "Will you always love me?" and he replied by asking her the same question, it meant "We'll always love each other."

Once again cousin David ran to the mill. This time he had come to announce, tragically, that the archbishop had told the nasi he was afraid the scandal would eventually cause violence between the Christian and Jewish communities. Wouldn't it be a good idea for Levi to go away? The whole community shouldn't be made to pay for one man's sin.

"Sin?" Levi said indignantly. "How have I sinned? Arsinde is a widow and I'm not married!"

"We're not reprimanding you for anything, cousin, nor even your exploits; after all, they're the kind of thing that has to be expected from a man your age. Our sages say that someone who has never sinned can't understand the profundity of the Commandments. It's because sin is possible that the Law is necessary. But this doesn't concern only you, cousin: it concerns all of us. Nasi Kalonymos and the members of the council agree with the archbishop's opinion that you ought to leave Narbonne for a time. Especially since the viscountess's two sons might learn what's happening and come back from Toulouse to . . . correct the situation."

It seemed to Levi that the millstones were grinding his heart. He scarcely heard David talking about a letter of introduction from Nasi Kalonymos to his cousin Rabbi Kalonymos bar Meshulam in Mainz, on the Rhine. He wanted to die. . . .

"Aren't you going to say anything, little brother?"

"What is there for me to say, Samuel?"

Levi left his brothers and went to sit, with his legs dangling, on the flat stone above the downstream millrace in which the water became calm after having been churned by the paddles of the great wheel. The clear water was striped by the black backs of trout.

Levi felt like shouting to the world that he was miserable and that no one could understand him. What was he to do? He had heard of Kairouan, a city in Africa where part of his family lived; he suddenly thought of going there with Arsinde. He was already making plans when his brothers called him.

Samuel, the oldest, with his wife Rachel beside him, put his robust hand on Levi's shoulder.

"You'll have to go away, little brother. It will be better for you, for her, and for all of us."

Being betrayed by his brothers was the last thing Levi would have expected.

"So you're . . . abandoning me?"

Samuel, Moses, and Isaac seemed to be thinking of something else.

"Would you like me to go with you?" Isaac asked casually. "All right, then, I will."

Levi looked at him without understanding.

"That's an idea," said the red-haired Moses. "I may as well go too."

"In that case," said Samuel, "there's no reason for me to stay here."

Levi shrugged his shoulders. He was furious.

"You ought to be ashamed of yourselves for making fun of me when . . ."

"If you don't mind," said Rachel, "I'd like to come along too. A wife should always go with her husband."

First Isaac burst out laughing, then Samuel, Moses, and Rachel. And now Levi understood. No, they were not abandoning him to his fate: loyal to the brotherly solidarity that united them and was stronger than anything else, they had chosen to give up the mill rather than let him leave Narbonne by himself. The four brothers clasped each other's hands. Then Levi was abruptly overcome with emotion; he hid his face in Samuel's beard and, for the first time since their father's death, he wept.

SAMUEL, Moses, Isaac, and Levi, sons of Abraham, sold the freehold they had inherited from their father—the mill and its outbuildings, the millstones, the fishery, the aqueduct and the land —to William the Levite and Belcom, abbot of Saint Paul, for the sum of a hundred and fifty sous, paid in cash.

They then loaded their few belongings into a wagon drawn by

two mules, promised David the scribe that he would hear from them, and set off northward, away from the sea.

Levi had not gone to tell Arsinde good-bye. Only now did he realize that he would never see her again.

16

NARBONNE

Fears of the Year One Thousand

TWO YEARS passed before David the scribe had any direct news of the four brothers. In the meantime, he had learned from a traveler that they had joined a convoy of merchants and that the convoy had been attacked by one of those troops of bandits that lurked in the forest. The traveler had seen them defend themselves; Levi, the youngest, he said, had fought like a madman, constantly risking his life as though he wanted to die on the spot. As for the traveler himself, he had run away after saving himself by handing over his money and his merchandise. He therefore did not know how the battle had ended, and David heard nothing more about it. He prayed for his cousins every day.

Finally, shortly before the second Chanukah after the brothers' departure, David received a letter dictated by Samuel, the oldest of the four, to a scribe in the city of Troyes, in Champagne, where he was now living: "As you know, my dear cousin, I have never liked to write. . . ." Samuel informed David that his three brothers had been killed by bandits and that Levi had sacrificed himself to save Rachel. Samuel had survived only by a miracle. He and Rachel had finally reached Troyes, ragged and destitute, like two vagabonds. The Jewish community had treated them with warmth and generosity, giving them food and shelter until Samuel found work in a mill whose owner, an elderly man, had no heirs. Perhaps he would someday be able to buy the mill. Meanwhile, Rachel had given him a son, named Levi after his youngest brother. Samuel ended his letter by asking David to pray for the souls of Moses, Isaac, and Levi, and adding that since the letter would be sent to a scribe, David's colleague in Troyes had refused to take any payment for writing it. "But I would have preferred to pay him and have better news to give you."

This was the first time that death had suddenly burst into David's life and he was deeply affected by it. Because he wanted to have a large number of people praying for his cousins, he invited all his Narbonnese relatives to celebrate Chanukah at his house. It happened that several uncles and cousins who did not live in Narbonne were now staying there briefly, on their way to other places: Moses and Judas, who spent a great deal of time traveling between the workshop in Cordova and the fairs in Germany, where their silks were more and more highly valued; Ezra, Judas's oldest son, who had returned a few weeks earlier from the academy at Sura, in Babylonia, where he had gone with his Spanish cousin Ezra of Cordova to follow the struggle of the learned Saadia Gaon against the Karaites; Azac, David's older son, who had just come back from a visit to his cousins in Kairouan. David's sister Mairona was also there, with her husband Bonisaac, a salt maker who, tired of constantly being in conflict with the archdiocese that had jurisdiction over his saltworks, had just sold it and was now going to Metz to form a partnership with one of his brothers there, a moneylender. And finally there was Meir, son of Moses the silk merchant, who had agreed to delay his departure for Palestine; he intended to spend the rest of his life there, and he proclaimed that the Jews should never have let themselves be exiled from their homeland.

They all gathered in David's house for Chanukah. For the children, he recalled the victory of the Maccabees over Antiochus Epiphanes and the purification of the Temple, desecrated by the pagans and sanctified by the miracle of light. Then he lit the first of the eight oil lamps and gave the benediction: "You have made a great and holy renown for Yourself in Your world and for Your people, Israel. You have wrought salvation and deliverance, as on this day. . . ." And he added, "May Your name be sanctioned for all that You decide in Your mercy and justice. Forget neither those who have gathered here today nor those whom You have called to Your eternity."

The little flame of the first lamp was reflected in his eyes, which showed sorrow mingled with pity. He wanted to cite the names of his three cousins but he was silenced by a lump in his throat. He felt intimidated by all those people looking at him. With a gesture, he invited them to come to the table on which engraved silver ewers had been placed, and he poured water scented with rosemary on their hands. He dried his fingers with a white cloth, then broke the bread, gave everyone a piece of it sprinkled with salt, and praised "Him who draws bread from the earth." The others all replied, "Amen," and prepared to eat the meal.

While bowls of boiled barley seasoned with garlic, cumin, and pepper were being served, David tried in vain to shake off an immense sadness. Even when the travelers began exchanging stories about people they had met and landscapes they had seen, he could not help thinking about the four brothers.

Judas the merchant told how, in Cordova, he had become acquainted with Rabbi Chasdai ibn-Shaprut, an eminent scholar, physician to Caliph Abd-er-Rahman and head of the customs service. Words failed Ezra when he tried to describe the exilarch's palace in Baghdad, with its Jewish guards. Meir, Moses's son, who was going to Palestine, announced the decline of Babylonia. "Soon," he said, "the Jews will no longer have a center. There will only be a choice between Palestine and dispersion." At the other end of the table, Bonisaac, the former salt maker, repudiated his twenty years of work at his trade. Through his brother, he had discovered money. "Till then," he explained with the faith of a new convert, "I sold merchandise and was interested only in merchandise. From now on, I'll be in contact with human beings. Money will bring me closer to them and let me learn about them, whether they're borrowers or lenders. . . . What did you say? A slave? No, it's just the opposite. Without money, the master disposes of the man, his property. With money, the man is released from his obligations in exchange for a sum whose size is determined by mutual agreement. Believe me, money is a means of liberation."

David's wife Sarah served him a piece of meat on a thick slice of bread. He forced himself to eat, so that she would not worry about him.

Ezra was now telling how a ship on its way to Constantinople had been stopped and plundered by the fleet of the caliph of Cordova. Gold and other valuables were seized and the passengers were sold as slaves. Among them were four prominent Jewish scholars who had been collecting money from Jewish communities on the Mediterranean for the Talmudic academies in Babylonia. The news spread so rapidly that in each port where the Saracens dropped anchor a delegation of Jews was waiting to buy a scholar's freedom. Rabbi Moses was freed in this way by the Spanish Jews, Rabbi Hochiel by the Jews of Kairouan, and Rabbi Shomriahu ben Elhanan by the Jews of Alexandria. Only the fourth rabbi had disappeared.

"Saadia Gaon," Ezra said sententiously, "maintains that the Holy One, blessed be He, never leaves a generation of His people without a scholar whom He inspires and enlightens, so that the scholar can teach the people and enable them to prosper."

Three saved and one lost: it was the opposite of what had happened with the four millers, and David could not help seeing that coincidence as a kind of sign. But he knew that the justice of the Almighty, blessed be His name, was impenetrable, and that he had to accept its decrees. At that point in the celebration, when Sarah was pouring sweet wine and Bonisaac was asking for more meat, David decided not to ask anyone to pray for Moses with the red hair, Isaac who was always laughing, and "Viscount Levi." Later, however, when the guests had all left and Sarah and a servant were taking off the soiled tablecloth, he called his sons Azac and Eliazar.

The three of them put on their prayer shawls and David took the Scroll of Abraham from its case. At his writing desk, he dissolved a tablet of ink, sharpened his pen, and, after his own name, added these words: "whose cousins Samuel, Moses, Isaac, and Levi, sons of Abraham, were millers in Narbonne."

"AND DAVID BEGAT Azac and Eliazar.

"And Eliazar married Shulamite and begat Ester, Bonina, and Benjamin.

"And Benjamin married Leah and begat Astruc, Yoseh, Sarah, and Zipporah.

"And Astruc married Rachel and begat Vidal."

FOR THE FIRST TIME after celebrating Rosh Hashanah with his family, as a good Jew should, Vidal the scribe dated a contract with the number of the new year: 4760 after the creation of the world by the Almighty, blessed be He. He realized that this would be the thousandth year of the Christian calendar and wondered what it would bring for the Jews.

212

According to a text in what the Christians called the New Testament, after a thousand years Satan would be loosed upon the world, there would be terrible calamities and a battle between good and evil, and then would come the end of time. But the year 1000 went by with no more famine, misery, and war than usual. As the result of invasions and the dismemberment of the empire since Charlemagne, the Christian West had become a jungle in which the strongest and least scrupulous prevailed. The idea that a millennium had ended took several years to sink deeply into the minds of the people, but then they were seized with fear, even terror, of the end of the world and the Last Judgment.

Signs were seen everywhere: a comet with the shape of a sword streaked across the sky; there were rains of shooting stars; the sun was obscured by the moon "from the sixth to the eighth hour, and it was truly terrible"; Pope Benedict died, and so did Basil, emperor of the Greeks; Hakim, the Fatimid caliph, destroyed the church of the Holy Sepulcher in Jerusalem.

Wild-eyed preachers who quoted from the Book of Revelation and called for expiation began appearing in public squares, at crossroads, and in front of churches. Their inflammatory words sowed madness in the crowds that listened to them. And since there had to be guilt somewhere, they began suggesting that the Jewish people might be that Satan who had been loosed upon the world, or that if it was not the Jews, they were still to blame for what was happening—after all, they had crucified the Son of God.

For the moment, the Jews were protected by the law. But while they could not legally be killed, the fact that they were Jews was not forgotten. To make them expiate the death of Christ, in some cities a Jew had to be publicly slapped in front of a church every year on Good Friday. Once, in Toulouse, Chaplain Hugo wore an iron glove for the occasion and delivered the slap so effectively that he knocked out his victim's brains and eyes.

Whenever Vidal the scribe heard about one of these scenes, he told his son Bonjusef that the Almighty, blessed be He, used them as a means of reminding Jews who had become absorbed in worldly pleasures, to the point of forgetting to study the Torah, that they were still in exile.

In Orléans, when the Christians learned that Caliph Hakim had destroyed the church of the Holy Sepulcher, they wondered how such an abomination could have taken place. They soon had an answer. A vagabond named Robert, a serf who had escaped from a monastery, claimed that the Jews of Orléans had paid him to go to the Holy Land with a letter for Caliph Hakim. And what did the letter say? That if the caliph did not quickly destroy the church of the Holy Sepulcher, Christians from all over the West would make a pilgrimage to it and ravage the country. Robert was burned at the stake and a large number of Jews left Orléans. Not far away, in Limoges, Bishop Audoin published an edict requiring the Jews either to become Christians or to leave. When many of them refused to choose, the bishop's guards assembled the whole community—men, women, children—in front of the cathedral to convert them by force. But, witnesses reported, the Jews chose to commit collective suicide rather than deny the God of their fathers: the head of each family killed his wife and children, and then himself. Before dying, they sang in such poignant, ethereal voices that the Christians who heard them trembled. "Guardian of Israel," they cried out, "preserve the rest of Your people! Do not let them perish, they who proclaim, *'Shema Yisrael!'* " And they died saying, "The Lord is our God, the Lord is one!" as Rabbi Akiba had affirmed in the time of Emperor Hadrian.

When Vidal heard this story, he did not know what to think. It was a beautiful day in early summer. The air smelled sweetly of new-mown hay and children were making wreaths of daisies and poppies. Through the open window, he heard the voices of pupils in the Talmud Torah. Narbonne was so far away from Orléans and Limoges!

Even so, he decided to go and ask Nasi Saul ben David Kalonymos to explain the meaning of what had happened in Limoges. The city was just emerging from the torpor of the afternoon siesta. Not wanting to arrive too early, Vidal took his time. He slowly walked up the Street of Shipbuilders, along the Jewish quarter under the jurisdiction of the viscount, and, as was his habit, touched the cloth in the stall of his cousin Solomon, son of Hanania the draper, as he passed. He listened to the sound of gold being beaten into thin sheets in the jeweler's shop next door, then turned into Aludiere Street, where he had bought his parchment for more than twenty years.

He went to Saint Zacharias Island, opposite the viscontal palace, to greet his friend Joseph, son of Bonjudas, a distinguished Talmudic scholar and the supervisor of the Jewish almshouse: he had promised him his daughter Esther for his son Enoch. Finally he came to the synagogue, where he expected to find the nasi at this hour. He read, as if it were a prayer, the sentence engraved on the façade: "If the sky and the skies of the skies cannot contain You, how much less this house that I have built."

The nasi still had sleep in his eyes. He too had heard about the suicides in Limoges. There had also been atrocities in Rouen, he said, but he would wait until he had confirmation of them before stating a firm conclusion. He was afraid that difficult times were coming. As though speaking to himself, he recited, "O Lord, make haste to help me! Let them be put to shame and confusion who seek my life! Let them be turned back and brought to dishonor who desire my hurt!"

Then he asked Vidal to copy two *takhanot* by Rabbi Gershom of Mainz, who had just sent them to him. Vidal went home. Meir-Ikhiel, son of his son Bonjusef, had just awakened in his crib and was babbling happily.

Vidal set to work. One of the two *takhanot* dealt with the rights of women, the other with the prohibition of polygamy. Narbonne really was far away from Limoges.

AFTER VIDAL, Bonjusef, and so many others, Meir-Ikhiel became a scribe and the guardian of the family tradition. He would have preferred to travel but he was the older son, already ten when his brother was born, and by then everything had been decided—it was his brother Azac who traveled.

Meir-Ikhiel married Lia, whose father had a wickerwork shop on the waterfront. He did not choose her because of the wickerwork shop, but because she had gazelle eyes and because he had once heard her sing. This was in the time when he often went to the waterfront to watch the departure of ships that he would never board.

Many ships had left since then, and while Lia almost never sang anymore, she had given him three children. Their names were inscribed in the Scroll of Abraham: Sarah, Abraham, and Jacob. Thanks to the Almighty, blessed be He, they grew and acquired wisdom with age.

There had been a succession of kings on the French throne: Hugh Capet, Robert the Pious, Henry, Philip. They were less powerful than their great vassals but they tried to expand their kingdom by means of war, guile, or money, depending on their respective characters. The duke of Normandy, William, had conquered England. Knights dreamed of combat and, at any call to action, formed armies and went off to fight here or there—in Spain, for example, where the pope had sent them to confront the troops of the caliph of Cordova.

One night in the year 4830 (1070) after the creation of the world by the Almighty, blessed be He, Meir-Ikhiel awoke with a start. He seemed to hear noises from the street. He got up quietly, to avoid alarming Lia, went to the dormer window, and lifted its curtain. Lights were appearing and disappearing on the other side of the Aude: torches, banners, a crowd.

Meir-Ikhiel suddenly felt cold. He pulled his nightcap farther down on his head, put on a short robe over his thick nightshift, lit a small oil lamp, and tiptoed into the next room. Sarah was asleep but her brothers Abraham and Jacob had not come home. He blew out the flame, went back to the window, and waited for his eyes to become accustomed to the dark. The city was enveloped in a light mist. Faint sounds of shouting men and whinnying horses were moving closer to the bridge.

"Is that you, Meir-Ikhiel?"

"Yes, Lia."

"You frightened me. Why are you standing at the window?"

"A crowd is coming into the city."

"At night? Who opened the gate?"

"I don't know."

"But what about the guards, Meir-Ikhiel? Where are they?"

Lia wrapped a shawl around her shoulders and joined him at the window, already prepared for the worst.

"Boats full of men are coming down the Aude," said Meir-Ikhiel.

"I hear hoofbeats. Horses are coming this way. . . . May the Almighty Creator protect us from harm!" Lia suddenly put her hand over her heart. "Abraham and Jacob—have they come home yet?"

"Don't worry, Lia, they're big boys now. Rabbi Joshua must have kept them later than usual."

Lia groped her way into the room where Sarah was sleeping.

The sounds were louder now: the tramping of feet and hooves, the clatter of metal, men calling out to each other, obviously not trying to pass unnoticed.

Meir-Ikhiel heard someone running. He told Lia to get dressed, wake up Sarah, and have her get dressed too. Then there was a rapid knocking on the door.

"Father! Father! Let us in!"

Meir-Ikhiel unbarred the door. Abraham and Jacob rushed in, jostling each other. Lia had been so afraid that she could not help scolding them: "This is no time to be coming home! Your father was worried to death!"

Abraham and Jacob reported that they had been in the synagogue, learning songs, when a messenger from Viscount Beranger arrived and asked the nasi to go to the palace without delay. The nasi left immediately and came back later to say that a troop of Christian soldiers and pilgrims on their way to Spain had come into the city, contrary to established agreements, and would probably soon begin making their usual exactions; the viscount had recommended that the Jews barricade themselves in their homes. The nasi then ordered everyone who was in the synagogue to run through the streets of the Jewish quarter and give the alarm.

"There are riders in scale armor and pilgrims going to Santiago de Compostela," said Abraham.

"They came in by way of the market town and blocked the bridge behind them," said Jacob.

"Then they divided into two groups. Some of them went through the Gate of the Pope and the others . . ."

"Then chased us—"

Just then they heard voices in the street, near the house. A torch appeared in front of the window, then vanished. The voices were speaking a harsh language that Meir-Ikhiel did not understand. He went to make sure the door was solidly barred, so frightened that he felt physical pain.

"We must pray," he said softly.

They heard a woman ask, "What do you want?"

It was Avelina, who lived next door with her husband John, a manuscript illuminator. They were Christians and had always been on good terms with Meir-Ikhiel and Lia.

The door was shaken by violent pounding.

"Why do you want to go into that house?" asked Avelina.

Jud! Jud!

"There's no *Jud* here," said Avelina. "Here, take these coins." She must have realized that they did not understand. "You, buy candle. Candle: understand? Light candle at Santiago de Compostela."

They evidently took the money, because the pounding stopped and the voices faded into the distance.

"May the Almighty in His mercy never forget Avelina and her husband!" said Meir-Ikhiel, barely able to speak. He had just been confronted with violence for the first time in his life.

His sons wanted to go outside, "to see." He told them to stay in the house and sternly reminded them that they would do better to join him in thanking the Almighty.

All night long they heard shouts, running footsteps, and other disquieting sounds. Who was being pursued by whom?

Finally, in the morning, a town crier passed by, announcing, "In the name of Beranger, viscount of Narbonne, you can come out now, good people. The city is safe." The streets were quickly filled. Lia went to Avelina, threw her arms around her, and wept.

Details of what had happened gradually became known. The pope had asked that Christian knights go to Spain to fight against the Arabs. A large group of German pilgrims going to Santiago de Compostela had encountered a troop of Burgundian knights and begun traveling with them. Before reaching Narbonne, they had sent emissaries to ask if the city could sell them food. The viscount had consented, provided they did not come through the gates. But a band of them had entered the outskirts of the city, looking for "enemies of Christ." Pilgrims had tried to convert Jews, and soldiers had pillaged several houses on the Straight Street, near the Almshouse of the Cross. Outrageous acts had been committed. "I saw women dragged to baptismal fonts by the hair," testified the *shammash,* Jacob ben Hanan. "I saw fathers, with their heads covered as a sign of mourning, take their sons to baptism to avoid having them killed by the Christians. With my own eyes I saw those horrible things, and many others, done to the Jews." This might have happened all over the city if Viscount Beranger and his guards had not succeeded in dividing the invaders and forcing them to leave Narbonne. The pope was later to commend the viscount for what he had done, and reprimand Archbishop Guifred for not having opposed the outrages.

Seven Jews had died, victims of either murder or suicide resulting from their refusal to be baptized. The Jewish community gave care to the wounded, took in the orphans, and raised money to repair the damage done to houses and other property. Then all the men went to the synagogue and spent two days there, fasting and praying before the Holy Ark, which was veiled in black as though for the ninth day of the month of Av, when Jews everywhere mourned the destruction of the Temple.

Then life resumed its course, but the Jews of Narbonne had an incurable wound in their hearts. They had been spared persecution for so long that they had finally come to believe they were safe from what Jews were undergoing in other parts of the world. Some of them left.

Despite all this, a few months later there were two weddings in Meir-Ikhiel's family: first that of his daughter Sarah, who married Jacob ben Hanan, the *shammash;* then that of Ezra, son of his brother Azac, who married the daughter of Astruc of Florensac, manager of a large fishery. But these weddings were celebrated discreetly, in honor of the seven martyrs.

Jacob, a highly skilled scribe, copied on parchment the whole Narbonnese part of the Scroll of Abraham, and his brother Abraham, who was a bookbinder, cut the parchment into sheets of equal size, assembled them in sections, sewed them together, and bound them in leather-covered wood. They concealed the volume from their father: they wanted to give it to him as a present for the thousandth anniversary of that ninth of Av, a year after the destruction of the Temple, when Abraham the scribe had written the first lines of the scroll.

When he received their gift, Meir-Ikhiel was more deeply moved than he wanted to show. He thanked them for the book itself and for having thought of making it. Later, after they had left him, he looked at the Scroll of Abraham for a long time. Tears came into his eyes and he did not know whether he was weeping for the destruction of the Temple, his sons' devotion, or the ten centuries of exile that were made bearable only by those ten centuries of memory.

He spent the night thinking about the destiny of human beings on earth and the precariousness of their condition, but also about their invincible ability to survive. That night brought him a kind of solace and serenity, a confidence in the all-powerful God who held the human race in the palm of His hand.

One consequence of Meir-Ikhiel's new attitude appeared a few months later, when he received a letter from Jeremiah, a descendant of Samuel, the miller who had gone from Narbonne to Troyes, in Champagne. Jeremiah, who said he had "a shop with a window on the street," had spoken to Rabbi Solomon ben Isaac, known as Rashi, about a family document that had been described to him by his father and grandfather, though they had never seen it. The rabbi had shown great interest. Jeremiah wanted to know if the document, assuming it still existed, could be sent to Troyes, perhaps in the keeping of a merchant traveling there.

That evening Meir-Ikhiel read the letter to his wife and sons and, even though he had already made his decision, asked them for their opinion.

"I don't think we should part with the Scroll of Abraham," said Jacob the scribe.

"If you feel we should send it to Rabbi Solomon," said Abraham, "I can take it myself. I've never traveled."

Meir-Ikhiel turned to Lia.

"Do as you think best," she said. "But I wouldn't like Abraham to travel alone."

For the first time since the night of the pilgrims, Meir-Ikhiel smiled.

"I'm going to put you all in agreement. We won't abandon the Scroll of Abraham." He paused for dramatic effect. "Since we're all going to Troyes!"

NASI TODROS DID NOT try to dissuade them. On the contrary, he said they were lucky to have that opportunity to meet Rashi, whose knowledge was so great that he was already known as Rabbenu, "Our Teacher." He advised them to leave during the month of Tammuz in order to reach Troyes before Rosh Hashanah. More specifically, he advised them to leave on the seventeenth day of Tammuz: in Hebrew, each letter has a numerical value, and the number seventeen represents the word *tov,* "good." It would make them feel safer, said the nasi, to begin their journey on a good day.

17

The Ambush
According to Joshua

MONTPELLIER, NÎMES, Avignon, Lyon, Dijon . . . What a journey! What an adventure, for people who had never left Narbonne, to keep moving toward the horizon from dawn to dusk, in sunshine and rain! After the first week, when their bodies had become used to the discomforts of life on the road, Meir-Ikhiel and his family began to develop a taste for traveling, for looking, feeling, evaluating distances, guessing what the weather was going to be, seeing how the landscape changed from one valley or ridge to another, noticing the colors of stones, the shapes of houses, people's clothes, faces, languages, food . . . In short, they began to see the world.

Meir-Ikhiel realized that, like his father Bonjusef and his sons Jacob and Abraham, he had developed his knowledge only through the Scriptures. It suddenly appeared to him that this was a kind of inadequacy, because revelation had occurred in nature before man recorded it in signs on clay tablets, papyrus, and parchment. Was it by chance that the Almighty, blessed be He, had chosen a tribe of nomads, rather than sedentary city dwellers, to transmit His Law to the human race? And when He had given them that promised land on the other side of the desert, what had He wanted them to do there: take up a settled, stationary life, or remain faithful to themselves? Rabbi Judas had said, "Those houses built for eternity —in Tiberias, named for Tiberius, in Alexandria, named for Alexander—will be their sepulcher."

The Jews, thought Meir-Ikhiel, were people of movement who went from place to place while others slept, like herdsmen taking their cattle through villages at night. "Your servants have been keepers of cattle from our youth even until now, both we and our fathers," it was written in Genesis. The only difference now was that people like him, Meir-Ikhiel, kept herds of letters and words.

The morning mists (they found autumn between Lyon and Dijon), the tumult of birds, the smell of cut grass or windblown smoke, the taste of an apple eaten on the road—these were new little delights for them. During their overnight stops, or at fountains where they drank like vagabonds, they had unforeseeable encounters. A money changer told them the rates of exchange among florins, deniers parisis, deniers viennois, and livres provinoises. A horse breeder explained to them that everything in his occupation had changed when the throat collar for horses was replaced by the shoulder collar with a rigid framework: whether they were hitched to wagons or plows, horses could now pull harder and longer with less fatigue. A cloth merchant used samples to show them how to distinguish among the cloths of Bruges, Troyes, and Lyon. In Dijon, a traveler from Poland told them that several thousand Jews had settled there and were living quite well, despite the harshness of the climate, because they were protected by Prince Wladislaus, whose wife was Jewish.

They paid for all this by being frightened now and then: when they heard wolves howling in the distance, when a suspicious-looking troop appeared on the road, when a toll collector demanded three times the normal price for crossing a stream, or when the sky was ablaze with lightning. They tried always to travel in company with others and each morning they had their route explained to them in detail, to avoid the risk of going astray at a crossroads.

When they arrived at a town or city in the evening, they nearly always found a Jewish family who took them in for the night. They thus brought news from one community to another. When their hosts learned that they were going to Troyes, they gave them long lists of questions for Rashi.

Two or three times, night overtook them while they were still on the road and they had to sleep in the wagon, afraid to light a fire because they felt so defenseless that they did not want to draw attention to themselves. On the whole, they took their hardships with good humor. They laughed at their lack of experience, their sunburns, and the voracious appetites they acquired in the open air. One morning, after a night when they had thought they were going to die of cold, Meir-Ikhiel said nothing and kept his lips firmly pressed together until the sun rose. Only then did he open his mouth to say jokingly that he had kept it closed while he waited for the air to turn a little warmer, because he was afraid the cold would crack his teeth and make them all fall out. Lia and her sons were often amazed to see their husband and father so relaxed and lighthearted.

They climbed up to Langres and then went down to the plain. The weather was still cold. At Chaumont, where they spent the night in the house of Rabbi Jeziel, they parted with the travelers who had accompanied them for several days and were going to Metz, to the northeast. Meir-Ikhiel and his family were told that they could expect to reach Troyes in three days.

They soon entered a forest where only a little sunlight was able to filter through the tops of the enormous trees. The road wound its way among ponds and all sounds were muffled by the dead leaves that already covered the ground. A kind of vague apprehension gradually came over them. Even the mules became nervous and kept pricking up their ears. There was something malevolent about that forest.

Just as they were wondering if they should stop and wait for other travelers to come along, a hush fell over the forest. No birds sang, no leaves rustled. Silence, anxiety.

And suddenly everything exploded. With bloodcurdling shouts, bandits charged toward them from nowhere and everywhere. They were quickly encircled. One of the bandits seized the mules by their bridles while another leapt onto the wagon with a vicious-looking scythe in his hand. There were both men and women, all shabbily dressed and armed with various kinds of weapons: daggers, clubs, hooks. One man, wearing a torn green velvet tunic, was surrounded by three dwarfs who seemed to be his personal bodyguards.

"O Lord," Meir-Ikhiel recited, "consume them in wrath, consume them till they are no more, that men may know that God rules over Jacob. . . ."

"What's he saying, Tonsure?" asked the man in the green tunic, obviously the leader.

"It's Hebrew," replied Tonsure, who was no doubt a former monk. "They're Jews."

He spat to show his contempt.

"Get out of your wagon, all of you!" ordered the leader.

Since they did not obey quickly enough, they were pushed and sent sprawling on the ground. Meir-Ikhiel helped Lia to her feet. His knee hurt where it had been jabbed with the point of a knife. The four of them stood huddled together. They would never reach Troyes, thought Meir-Ikhiel, and they would never see Narbonne again. There was nothing to be done. . . .

The three dwarfs climbed into the wagon, took hold of the first chest they saw, and pried open its lock with a crowbar. They immediately began decking themselves out in the clothes it contained, clowning with prayer shawls and men's underwear while their companions laughed uproariously. Then they played awhile with tunics and breeches and finally tossed them to the others. When they found Lia's underwear, they were beside themselves with joy. Meir-Ikhiel was ashamed. Blood was trickling down his leg.

"The other chest!" ordered the leader.

The second lock was pried open. This chest contained books, writing and binding materials, sacred texts, and the Scroll of Abraham. One of the dwarfs unrolled the parchment, took on a self-important expression, and pretended to read.

"Noble lords . . ." he began in a shrill voice.

"Quiet!" said the leader. "And put that back!" He turned to Meir-Ikhiel. "Which means more to you: your life or your belongings?"

Meir-Ikhiel closed his eyes without answering.

"Search them," ordered the man in the green tunic.

The four of them were seized and held tightly while rough hands felt them all over and took their money, their cloaks, and even their shoes. The three dwarfs danced grotesquely around Lia, singing:

> *Jewess, my Jewess,*
> *Will you love me?*
> *Tra-la-la!*
> *Will you love me?*
> *Tra-la-la!*
> *Jewess, my Jewess. . . .*

"Where are you going?" the leader asked Meir-Ikhiel.

"To Troyes."

"If your God is with you, you'll get there sooner or later. But be on the lookout for robbers!"

He burst into peals of laughter, then put two fingers into his mouth and whistled loudly. The bandits regrouped. The dwarfs got into the wagon and took the reins.

A few moments later Meir-Ikhiel, his wife, and his two sons were alone in that hostile forest that was too vast for them, too high, too deep, too far away from everything. Why had they left Narbonne, where all their certainties were?

Meir-Ikhiel wept. Not because of the pain in his knee, or the loss of their wagon and money. He wept slow, silent tears for the Scroll of Abraham. He had not been able to defend and keep it. What kind of herdsman was he, to have lost his herd? He thought of those ten centuries of memory and history, ten centuries since Jerusalem, Alexandria, Hippo, Cordova, Narbonne . . . A thousand years of fidelity, tradition, and respect that represented a victory over oblivion and the shortness of human life, a thousand years that had been brutally disrupted by impious hands in a forest in Champagne.

He also wept for all victims of violence and injustice, and for their tormentors as well, because those who needed to rob, rape, and humiliate were greatly to be pitied.

"Father," said Jacob, "we must catch up with them."

"Hurry, let's leave now," said Abraham.

Meir-Ikhiel looked at his sons. What a comfort, O Lord, what a joy!

"We must thank the Almighty," he said, drying his tears, "for having spared our lives."

"Amen."

BEFORE EVENING they were overtaken by a convoy composed of money changers from Vaud and merchants from Lyon, Milan, Naples, and Genoa, accompanied by a dozen armed men whom they had hired to protect them. Seeing that Meir-Ikhiel and his family were exhausted and that their feet were bleeding, Ansaldo, a Jew from Genoa, offered to let them ride in his three carts. Everyone listened to their story and tried to console them. When they had been given wine and warm clothes, they got into the heavily loaded carts.

"Don't worry," said Ansaldo, "they're strong enough to hold you: they've crossed the Alps twice!"

He was tall, thin, and loquacious. He wore a waterproof wool cloak and his black felt hat was pulled down to his bushy eyebrows.

The convoy set off. Ansaldo, who had taken Meir-Ikhiel into the cart with him, talked steadily, passing without transition from the disappearance of the Jewish kingdom of the Khazars, on the road to China, to the birth of his first granddaughter, Ruth, daughter of his son Jacob, back in Genoa.

"Long life to Ruth!" wished Meir-Ikhiel, fully appreciating the proverb according to which good news that comes from far away is like water to a thirsty man.

They stopped at Vendeuvre for the last night before reaching Troyes. While the merchants went to the inn, Meir-Ikhiel and his family were taken in by Judas ben Abraham, one of Rashi's students who, like his teacher, spent a great deal of time cultivating grapevines. Judas, a slender little man with a very long reddish beard, was overwhelmed by the loss of the Scroll of Abraham.

"Something has to be done!" he said, scarcely able to contain his agitation. "Let's think about it, Meir-Ikhiel. What can those bandits—curses on them!—do with texts in Hebrew? If they're ignorant louts, they may burn them because they think they're worthless. If they're . . ."

"One of them," said Abraham, "was called Tonsure. He must have been a monk at one time."

"Good! Hurrah for Tonsure!" Judas exclaimed jubilantly. "If he's a former monk, he'll realize the importance of what they've stolen, and they'll try to get a good price for it." He spread his arms with his palms upward. "Then they come to us as brooks come to the river! I'll alert all the Jewish communities from here to Ramerupt, and Dampierre, and Vitry, and Meaux. . . ."

"Judas ben Abraham," said Meir-Ikhiel, "you've given me hope."

"Meir-Ikhiel, son of Bonjusef of Narbonne, you ought to know that we should never lose hope. Trust in the Almighty, blessed be He. He punishes the foolish and protects the wise."

The next morning, Judas gave Meir-Ikhiel a purse with several coins jingling in it.

"But, rabbi . . ."

"Don't protest, Meir-Ikhiel! I have no doubt that you'll repay me soon. We'll surely see each other again in Rashi's house. It was he, my master, who taught me that if we see someone suffering and don't help him, we're as guilty as if we'd harmed him with our own hand. To understand Rashi, you people from Narbonne must know that when someone says to him, 'May the Lord be merciful to you,' he answers, 'May the Lord make you merciful.' "

TROYES, A CITY divided into four quarters nestled in a bend of the Seine, differed from Narbonne in every way. The sunlight was not the same, and neither were the houses nor the people, who were generally taller and calmer, had lighter complexions, and spoke more slowly.

When the convoy arrived there, Troyes was preparing for the autumn fair and the beginning of the grape harvest. And since the count of Champagne was expected to come soon, the houses were decorated with brightly colored banners and hangings. The streets had the animation that always filled them just before a festival: vendors who had not yet finished arranging their wares in the booths reserved for them were working feverishly, while those who were ready strolled around the market, looking at their competitors' displays, joking, and buying drinks for their friends.

Ansaldo took Meir-Ikhiel and his family to the cloth market, near the consular house, where he found one of his Jewish friends who in turn took them to Jeremiah's shop in the Jewish quarter—known as the Jews' Thicket because it was built on land originally covered with thickets—between the Girouarde Gate and the count's castle. Jeremiah, a dark, stocky, curly-haired man, greeted them with exclamations of incredulity that were succeeded by lamentations when he learned that the Scroll of Abraham, about which he had written to Meir-Ikhiel, had been stolen.

"It's my fault!" he said. "It's my fault!"

He abruptly stopped moaning, told his wife to take care of Lia and his clerk to take charge of the shop and, as if he were going off to war, left with Meir-Ikhiel and his sons to see the fairmaster. As they pushed through the crowds in the narrow streets, he explained that the merchants of Troyes, to encourage more people to come to the fair, sometimes donated money to pay for merchandise stolen on the way to it.

But Meir-Ikhiel was not a merchant, and the fairmaster, a big, placid man with unwavering blue eyes, declared that the matter was outside his jurisdiction. Even so, he asked for a description of the bandits. The three dwarfs would have been enough to identify them if he had ever heard of them before, but they were unknown to him.

"How much are your writings worth?" he slowly asked Meir-Ikhiel.

As if the Scroll of Abraham had a commercial value! For Meir-Ikhiel, things were happening a little too quickly and unexpectedly, as in a bad dream. His wounded knee was hurting him.

"The Scroll of Abraham is priceless," he said. "It's the history of my family."

"Then it *does* have a value—to you."

"Yes, but also to everyone."

The fairmaster unclasped his thick hands and laid them flat on the green velvet of the table, as though to say that the discussion was over and he had other things to do.

"If you find your bandits," he said, "I'll be glad to deal with them. But I know Jeremiah. Remember this, both of you: I don't want any trouble or scandal during the whole time of the festival and the fair!"

He lowered his eyelids for the first time, and it was as if he had closed a door.

As soon as they had left him, Jeremiah rubbed his hands together.

"He told us in so many words that we can deal with the bandits ourselves. He's a real friend! Come, we're going to draw up our plan of attack!"

The first step in the plan of attack was a search for allies. Meir-Ikhiel, whose knee was becoming more and more painful, stayed in the shop with Lia and Jacob while Abraham went off with Jeremiah. First they looked for Moses, a cousin who taught at the *yeshiva* and was a *parnas* on the community council; when they finally found him, he promised to do everything he could to find the scroll that Rashi had said he wanted to see. Next they hurried to a cousin who was a goldsmith, and in his shop they met another cousin, a Vitry winegrower who had come to Troyes for the festival. They looked in vain for other relatives and friends: preparations for the festival had thrown the city into turmoil. They came back exhausted.

"One thing," said Jeremiah, "is already sure: tomorrow, Moses will ask all the students at the *yeshiva* to find out anything they can about the scroll, and he'll discuss it with the council this evening."

Moses came at dawn the next morning, with the furtive air of a conspirator. The council, he said, keeping his voice lowered, had suggested that they ask for help from a Jewish thief named Joshua and nicknamed Kountrass, whose specialty was dealing in stolen Latin and Hebrew manuscripts, genuine and forged documents, and parchments sold as new after the writing on them had been scratched off. He was suspected of seeking out students in Mainz and Worms who needed money and paying them to work at collecting, falsifying, and selling his merchandise. He was a strange man: he knew the Book of Joshua by heart and would quote from it at the drop of a hat. The council, after wanting for a long time to be rid of that troublesome Kountrass, had finally found a chance to make use of his talents, but . . .

Moses looked around and lowered his voice still more: "But no one must ever find out that the idea came from the council." A look of fear came into his eyes. "If it became known that the community council had used the services of a thief, that would be the end of our honor and our influence in the city."

Moses's departure was closely followed by the arrival of a well-dressed young man with delicate features and an angelic expression.

"My name is Joshua," he said in a gentle voice, "but I'm called Kountrass. I may be able to help you recover the chest that was stolen from you."

"May the Almighty, blessed be He, grant that you'll succeed!" said Meir-Ikhiel.

Inwardly, he was shocked at the idea that anyone would scratch the writing off parchments to make them seem new. He had such respect for writing that although he sometimes took out a letter or a word to make a correction, he would never destroy a whole text.

"How will you go about it?" asked Jeremiah. "Do you need us?"

Joshua, known as Kountrass, lifted his hand and quoted, "Be strong and of good courage; be not frightened, neither be dismayed; for the Lord your God is with you wherever you go." And he added, smiling, "Joshua 1:9. . . . Can someone who has a little money come with me?"

Meir-Ikhiel's knee was now so painful that he could no longer walk. It was Abraham who volunteered to go with Kountrass. He took the purse that the rabbi in Vendeuvre had given them.

"This is your first visit to Troyes?" Kountrass asked him graciously. "Then don't judge the city by what you're about to see."

"The Talmud says that the Almighty spread a disease, evil, but immediately invented the remedy for it, the Law."

"I'm afraid that today we'll have more to do with evil than with the Law!"

After going through the Girouarde Gate, also called the Jews' Gate, they joined the gathering crowd and walked to a small public square beside the wooden Saint Arbois church. Jugglers were beginning to perform and barkers were exercising their voices. Kountrass went toward the stone fountain in the middle of the square and stopped in front of a lanky, red-nosed man who was selling remedies.

"I gathered these herbs myself," the vendor was saying, "between the towers of Abilant, three leagues from Jerusalem, in the garden where the Jew Corbilaz forged the thirty pieces of silver for which God was sold. My herbs cure tertian fever, quartan fever, scabies, blisters, and smallpox. Buy them if you want to be cured, ignore them if you want to die!"

Kountrass raised his hand to catch the vendor's attention.

"Do you still have some of that medicine for diarrhea?"

"Is it for you?"

"No; I'm cured now, thanks to you. It's for my mother."

"Is she very sick?"

"Yes, very."

"Then the medicine will cost you a sou."

"Five deniers."

"For five deniers you'll only get half as much."

"I'll take it. Pay him, Abraham."

Kountrass had spoken more loudly than necessary and, as a result, several passersby had stopped. He moved closer to the vendor. Abraham heard them whispering.

"What are you looking for, Kountrass?"

"A chest containing parchment manuscripts in Hebrew was stolen from my friend. Someone will try to sell them."

"See Piaudou, the man with the trained monkeys."

Kountrass took the little jar of medicine. The vendor straightened up and began hawking his wares again.

"Who's next? Who wants to buy my potions, herbs, and ointments? Take them if you want them, leave them if you don't!"

Kountrass and Abraham found Piaudou behind the church of Our Lady of Nuns. He lay under a cart, either drunk already or not yet sober from the night before. Two little monkeys dressed in red were busily searching for lice on him and eating those they found. They seemed to be guarding him, because they chattered and bared their teeth whenever anyone came close to him.

"Piaudou!" Kountrass called out.

Piaudou was snoring, with a long lock of sticky gray hair across his forehead. Kountrass reached out to shake him but stopped when the monkeys began hopping up and down, screeching and spitting. Then he saw women standing in line to take water from a nearby fountain. He borrowed a bucket, filled it, and tossed its contents onto Piaudou and his monkeys. One of the monkeys furiously charged at Abraham and gave him a vicious bite on the hand. Piaudou laboriously sat up, trying to understand what was happening.

Kountrass squatted beside him.

"Piaudou, it's me, Kountrass. Listen to me."

The drunkard grunted and tried to lie down again. Kountrass lifted his hand and quoted, "Arise, why have you thus fallen on your face?" Pleased with himself, he gave the source, "That's Joshua 7:10," and leaned toward Piaudou. "If you don't listen to me, I'll empty another bucket on you."

"No! No more water! Throw as much wine on me as you want, Kountrass, but no more water!"

Piaudou slowly passed his hand over his face and shook his head. Seeing that he was awake, the two monkeys huddled against him.

"I'm looking for manuscripts in Hebrew," said Kountrass. "I've been told that someone here in Troyes is offering them for sale."

"In Hebrew?"

"Give him a few deniers," Joshua said to Abraham.

Abraham dropped five deniers into the outstretched dirty hand. Piaudou's memory suddenly returned.

"Ah, yes, Hebrew! Now I remember. Bonebreaker has some Hebrew manuscripts for sale."

"Bonebreaker? The champion?"

"Yes. He'll be in the Butchers' Tavern all day."

Joshua and Abraham left Piaudou blinking his eyes as he sat in the dust with his monkeys beside him. At the fountain, Abraham washed his bitten hand. Robbed by bandits, bitten by a monkey— the world outside of Narbonne was full of adventure!

Joshua explained to Abraham that the man called Bonebreaker was a professional champion, a brute who was hired to represent others in trials by combat. Joshua had never heard that he was a manuscript thief, or even a thief at all; the bandits who had attacked Abraham and his family in the forest were probably strangers in Troyes, and they must have hired Bonebreaker to make sure that no one would try to cheat them when they sold their booty.

Before turning into the Street of Butchers, they agreed that Joshua would go into the tavern by himself; Abraham would follow a little later and see if he recognized any of the bandits. Still wearing his angelic expression, Kountrass walked off along the street where animals were being slaughtered in great numbers for the evening's feasts. Dogs fought each other to drink the steaming blood that flowed in the gutter. The sickening smell, the butchers' coarse jokes, the death cries of calves, pigs, and sheep, the grating of knives on whetstones—faced with all this, Abraham struggled against the nausea rising inside him. How was Joshua able to seem so far above that loathsome reality?

He saw Joshua approach the tavern, which was on one corner of the street, and go into it without looking back. As they had agreed, Abraham gave him time to find Bonebreaker, then discreetly followed him in. When he stepped into the dimly lit room filled with an uproar of harsh voices and the stench of herring and bad wine, he felt as if he had collided with a wall. Taking a long breath, he slipped behind a wooden pillar, waited till his eyes had adjusted to the semidarkness, and then looked around at the tables. In the short light of the oil lamps he saw hands throwing dice and mouths gluttonously taking in huge quantities of food and wine. At one table he spotted Kountrass sitting opposite a reddish-blond giant, and beside the giant was a man he immediately recognized as Tonsure, the ex-monk who had been with the bandits. With his heart pounding, he hurried out of the tavern and went to wait at the far end of the Street of Butchers.

A few minutes later Kountrass casually walked up to him and said, "Come, we're going to your cousin Jeremiah's house. There's no time to lose."

BY NIGHTFALL, Troyes had abandoned itself to wild revelry. The count of Champagne had gone through the main streets while his almoner followed him, throwing handfuls of small coins to the crowd, and he had ordered that what was left of last year's wine be given out free, since the new grape harvest promised to be abundant. The poor people of the city seized that rare opportunity and drank to the count's health—again and again. The merchants, ready for the opening of the fair the next day, relaxed and enjoyed themselves. Except for thieves and prostitutes, no one was working now. The only lights came from taverns, churches, and a few torches carried along the streets by staggering carousers at the risk of setting fire to the city.

Kountrass, Abraham, and Jacob went into the Butchers' Tavern together. Preferring to wait till wine had claimed as many victims as possible, Kountrass had tried to calm the two brothers' impatience by explaining that confusion would be their ally. Once again he had lifted his hand and quoted from Joshua: "And the sun stood still, and the moon stayed, until the nation took vengeance on their enemies."

Kountrass showed his face openly but Abraham and Jacob concealed theirs beneath large hoods. The three of them sat down at the table where Bonebreaker and Tonsure were waiting. The tavernkeeper immediately brought wooden goblets and a pitcher of wine. Kountrass seemed blithely unaware of the bellowing drunkards around him and the overpowering mixture of smells that hung in the air.

"God be with you, Bonebreaker," he said affably.

"With you too, Jew Kountrass."

"I've brought my customers. Do you have the chest?"

"Are you here to steal it or pay for it?"

"I'm only an intermediary. I just have to make sure the chest isn't empty."

"It's not. And what about their purse?"

From the folds of his tunic, Abraham took out a big leather bag attached to his waist. He let Bonebreaker see it for a moment, then hid it again. He and Jacob had still not shown their faces.

"Open the chest," suggested Kountrass, "and they'll open their purse."

Bonebreaker turned halfway around.

"Bring the chest!"

The three dwarfs came out from under the next table, pushing and pulling a chest that Abraham and Jacob instantly recognized. But while they were leaning over it, Bonebreaker suddenly reached out and pulled back their hoods. Tonsure pointed at them and the dwarfs began shouting excitedly. Abraham and Jacob dashed toward the door, overturning their bench, while men stood up here and there to stop them.

Jacob was grabbed by a hand that pulled off one of his sleeves, but the two brothers reached the door, flung it open, and ran down the Street of Butchers. How many men were pursuing them? Ten, maybe fifteen not counting the three dwarfs—probably all the bandits, led by the man in the green tunic. Bonebreaker came through the doorway, filling both its height and its width with his enormous body. After running a certain distance he stopped and tried to understand what had happened.

Bumping aside everyone in their way, Abraham and Jacob raced toward the Seine—and their pursuers fell into a carefully prepared ambush. Waiting for them were the students employed by Kountrass and a group of robust winegrowers recruited by the cousin from Vitry. Some of the pursuers escaped; for the rest, the chase ended in the Seine, which was very cold at that time of year.

Kountrass had found the idea for the ambush in Joshua 8:1–23, where it is written that the Almighty, blessed be He, commanded Joshua, son of Nun, to use a stratagem that enabled Israel to take the city of Ai and its king. "So Joshua arose, and all the fighting men, to go up to Ai; and Joshua chose thirty thousand mighty men of valor, and sent them forth by night. And he commanded them, 'Behold, you shall lie in ambush against the city, behind it. . . .'" Kountrass had simply reduced the number of mighty men of valor and replaced the city of Ai with the grain market of Troyes. Otherwise, he had followed the biblical plan, with the additional detail of having Jacob and Abraham hide their faces: he knew that Bonebreaker would want to know whom he was dealing with and that the brothers would therefore have a pretext for running away, which would make Bonebreaker and the bandits go after them, leaving the chest unguarded.

When Abraham and Jacob returned to Jeremiah's shop, their father Meir-Ikhiel was holding the Scroll of Abraham.

Jeremiah, as agreed, had waited outside the tavern. When he saw his cousins rush out with a pack of pursuers behind them, he had gone in. Kountrass, more angelic than ever, had pointed to the chest and said, "In Joshua 22:8 it is written, 'Divide the spoil of your enemies with your brethren.' You can take the document that interests your cousin and I'll take the rest. Then each of us will go his own way, and each will have his own heritage." Jeremiah had recognized the leather case containing the Scroll of Abraham and the book bound by Abraham in Narbonne. He had taken it, leaving the chest to the mysterious Kountrass. As Jeremiah was leaving the tavern, Bonebreaker had come in, immense and furious, clutching a short club in his monstrous fist. Jeremiah had not stayed to chat with him.

Kountrass did not come back that night or the next morning. Had he fled with the chest?

During the day, Jeremiah was summoned by the fairmaster. The man with the pale, unblinking eyes was sitting in the same place with his hands crossed on the green velvet of the table, as if he had not moved since Jeremiah's last visit to him. Speaking slowly as always, he asked Jeremiah if he had heard of a brawl the night before, between a group of Jews and some bandits from the forest. Three dwarfs had drowned in the Seine, he said, and a notorious Jewish thief and forger had been found dead on the Street of Butchers, with his skull crushed. His name was Kountrass and he was known as Joshua, or maybe it was the other way around.

Jeremiah turned pale and replied that a respectable licensed merchant had better things to do, on the night before a fair, than waste his time in disreputable parts of the city. As a matter of fact, he added, he still had work to do and would therefore have to end his visit.

"Long life to you," he said in conclusion. "I hope no one else will disturb the public peace."

"So do I. Long life to you too."

As Jeremiah was turning to leave, he was stopped by the fairmaster's calm voice.

"You haven't said anything more about the parchments stolen from your cousins. Have they recovered them?"

"Yes, they have, thanks to the Almighty. I forgot to tell you."

"Blessed be the Almighty."

Jeremiah took a few steps toward the door, slowed down, stopped, and turned around.

"Perhaps we should arrange to have a decent burial for that Jew with the broken skull. Even a thief is entitled to a grave."

"I think that's an excellent idea," said the fairmaster. "Excellent."

He uncrossed his hands and his pale eyes blinked once. Everything had been said; the conversation was over.

SOLOMON BEN ISAAC, known as Rashi, known as Shlomo Rabbenu ("Solomon Our Teacher"), swayed backward and forward as he read the Scroll of Abraham. He was a tall, broad-

235

shouldered man with gray eyes, even features, and a heavy black beard.

He had received his visitors in a room with whitewashed walls of clay mixed with straw. Scrolls and bound books were piled on shelves. He sat behind a table composed of a pine board supported by two trestles. The only window opened onto a carefully weeded vineyard with leaves turned red by autumn.

People who came to listen to him, sometimes from far away, sat down if there was still room for them on the chests and the two benches; if not, they stood leaning against the walls and looking over Rashi's shoulder at the text he was reading. Everyone went in and out of the room without ceremony. Even the presence of such eminent figures as Zerah ben Abraham or Solomon ben Samson of Vitry—or, as on this day, Rabbi Isaac Halevi, head of the *yeshiva* in Worms—did not deter Rashi's three little girls from doing as they pleased, as if they were alone with their father. He always excused them, smiling.

A woman came in to ask a question about *kashrut.* The baker next door brought in an apple tart still hot from the oven. Rashi cut it into pieces and handed them out. Meir-Ikhiel, sitting between his two sons, had imagined much greater solemnity. That general simplicity, those scholars dressed like peasants, that Hebrew interspersed with Frankish words—he was so surprised by all this that he felt vaguely disappointed. He recalled the jewels and blue brocade turban of the nasi in Narbonne, and thought nostalgically of the sonorous, richly colored language spoken in that sunny region.

Rashi had resumed reading the Scroll of Abraham. "What a memorial!" he murmured now and then.

When he had finished, he read the last inscription aloud: "And Meir-Ikhiel married Lia, and their children were Sarah, Jacob, and Abraham." He was thoughtful for a few moments. Everyone looked at Meir-Ikhiel and his sons, as if they were the heroes of an amazing adventure, while they felt that they held a kind of privilege and had been invested with a sacred responsibility.

Rashi finally spoke: "In the *Midrash Tanchumah,* Rabbi Yitzchak says, 'The Torah should have begun with "Why?" ' "

Everyone had fallen silent at the sound of his gentle, melodious voice.

"Do you know," he continued, "what is at the beginning of the manuscript our friends from Narbonne call the Scroll of Abraham?

236

It begins with an exodus! I've always agreed with Rabbi Yitzchak in thinking that our history, the Torah, should have begun with the Exodus. Everything develops around the Exodus, and our first *mitzvah,* our covenant with the Almighty, blessed be His name, was born of the Exodus."

With a hand roughened by his work in the vineyard, he caressed the papyrus that had been carefully chosen long ago, by Abraham the scribe. He turned his eyes to Meir-Ikhiel and his sons.

"What do you think about that?"

Meir-Ikhiel was intimidated. It was Jacob who answered by asking another question.

"Why does the Chumash begin with the Creation?"

"Your son, Meir-Ikhiel ben Bonjusef, has asked an excellent question. Why does the Torah begin by revealing what was created on the first day, the second day, the third day, or the sixth day? It does so in order to make other peoples, the *goyim,* understand that although the story speaks of one people, Israel, it actually applies to the whole world, the world created by the Holy One, blessed be He, according to His will."

Just then the door was flung open and a voice thundered, "Arise, Jews! I bring you the news, the good news! The Messiah has come!"

"Don't worry, it's only Mordecai," those who knew the poor madman said to those who did not yet know him and had been startled by his noisy arrival.

"Peace be with you," said Rashi.

Mordecai walked with a crutch because one of his feet was missing. Bandits had tortured him to make him tell where he kept his hoard of money. He had not told them, and for a good reason: they had confused him with a rich merchant. Unable to tell what he did not know, he had gone mad, and his burned, smashed foot had had to be amputated. Since then, he had been looking for the Messiah.

"The Messiah has come!" he repeated. "Arise, Jews! I've met the Messiah!"

He took a seat by letting himself slide down the wall beside the door.

"Have you really met him?" Rashi asked gently.

"No, I haven't yet found him, Solomon Our Teacher, but I *will* find him."

Rashi observed him for a moment and shook his head.

"He'll find . . ." he murmured. Then, without finishing his sentence, he turned back to Jacob. "Do you have any more questions, Jacob ben Meir-Ikhiel?"

•   •   •

MEIR-IKHIEL ben Bonjusef's arrival in Troyes brings me back to the discussion I had in the Jerusalem home of Professor Dov Sadan when I was trying to find the origin of my name, either Alter or Halter.

"Halter: there's a name, a real name!" Dov Sadan said enthusiastically. "But the use of last names really isn't very old among the Jews. Genealogies are traced through first names. What's yours?"

"Marek."

"Yes, I know. But in Hebrew?"

"Meir-Ikhiel, the same as my great-grandfather's."

Dov Sadan leapt off his stool.

"That's an important element. Let's look for Halters and Meir-Ikhiels. Maybe chance will put us on the right track."

"Would you like some more coffee?" asked his wife.

"Yes, thank you," I said.

I do not remember how, but the conversation turned to Kafka. The professor detested him and considered him dangerous.

"He's partly responsible for our passive attitude toward the rise of Nazism," he said, "because he made us become used to the idea that man can be transformed into an animal. Furthermore, Kafka himself was aware that his writings were dangerous. Don't forget that on his deathbed he asked Max Brod to burn all his manuscripts."

"And Max Brod didn't do it."

"No, and it's a pity he didn't!"

"Professor," I said, "let me remind you that in Metamorphosis *the animal isn't the kind of cruel beast you've referred to. He's a strange creature who, because he's different, becomes a victim: a victim of the world, of society, of his own family. If you mean that our ability to resist is weakened when we become used to seeing people transformed into cruel beasts, then we'll have to say that all of Europe had a passive attitude toward the rise of Nazism. Like you, I believe in the power of words, but I wonder if we should attribute so much power to a writer whose works, admirable though they are, were almost unknown before the war."*

Dov Sadan was not listening. He nervously paced the floor, stopped to drink his coffee without sitting down, rummaged in his

238

pockets, took an ashtray from one place and put it down in another. This did not prevent him from pursuing his train of thought.

"One day," he said, "when Martin Buber was passing through Prague, he went to see Max Brod. Brod talked about Kafka, as usual, and offered to read Buber a passage from one of his manuscripts. But as soon as he found the page he was looking for, the room went dark: the electricity had gone out. And not just the room, but the whole apartment, and even the whole city of Prague. It was as if God hadn't wanted that manuscript to be read!"

"That's a good story," I said.

"Good and true!"

"Isn't it enough for it to be good?"

"It's too good to have been invented. But excuse me, we're forgetting your ancestors. . . . Do you know if any Halters have been writers? After all, publishers, printers, and writers belong to the same family, and they need each other. Somewhere I have a bibliography of all Hebrew authors up to the beginning of this century." He laughed heartily, as though at a good joke. "I've willed all my books and papers to the Hebrew University, but they won't get them till after my death! I'll be back in a minute."

He left the room. His wife made conversation with me. She talked about her husband's disorderliness, said she had been told by someone who heard it on television that there was a good chance it would snow in Jerusalem that winter, asked me again if I would like more coffee, and went off to make it just as Dov came back with a pile of books. He put them down on the table, looking as if he had won a prize in the lottery.

"Here they are!" He took a big volume and began leafing through it. "Halter, Halter," he repeated, "Halter . . . Ah!"

Just then we were plunged into darkness.

"Dov!" his wife called out from the kitchen.

"Light a candle, Hannale."

A yellow glow appeared in the doorway, lighting the lower part of Hannah Sadan's face.

"Excuse me," she said, "I plugged in the kumkum *for the coffee, and . . ."*

A kumkum kashmali *is one of the electric kettles found on all Israeli tables.*

"The fuses have blown," Dov decided. He fumbled in a drawer, then handed me a pack of fuses. "Since you're tall . . ."

When the lights had come on again, I could not help saying, "What an odd coincidence!"

Dov went back to his alphabetical list and I rejoined him. I felt a kind of anxiety when a Halter caught my eye. It was as if that Halter, whose existence I had not even suspected, had brought me a message from the depths of time. I read that his first name was Mosheh, that he had lived in Piotrkow, Poland, and that he had written several books.

"Now," said Dov, "I'll have to get the titles of his works, and descriptions of them, from somewhere else."

I had time to drink a glass of orange juice while he went to get the book he had in mind. Hannah was afraid even to mention coffee again.

When Dov returned, he had already found the right page: Mosheh Halter had written commentaries on the Talmud and a funeral oration in memory of Rabbi Meir-Ikhiel Lifszic of Ostrowiec.

Dov was elated. That Meir-Ikhiel was venerated as a saint by his devotees. Believing that people could not live without sinning, he had fasted twenty years to induce God to grant that he would commit only a venial sin each day, rather than eventually making himself guilty of a mortal sin. During all those years, his only nourishment was the sugared coffee he drank every morning.

Rabbi Meir-Ikhiel of Ostrowiec was related to another rabbi, who was said to have taken a further step toward God. His first name was also Meir-Ikhiel, and his last name was Halevi. He had fasted only twelve years before giving up the ghost, but, convinced that fasting without temptation was not worthy of accompanying a prayer to the Almighty, he paid a young man to eat at his table every day. He served the young man himself and said to him, "Eat, eat so that I can fast and take upon myself all the sins of my people, may they live in peace."

Dov Sadan rubbed his hands together.

"A Halter and two heavyweight Meir-Ikhiels in one day—isn't that fantastic?" he said. "Now we have to find the works of that Mosheh Halter."

"Dov," Hannah intervened firmly, "it's late. You know what the doctor said. . . ."

I left Jerusalem without seeing Dov Sadan again. The next time I returned, I learned that he had gone to teach in the United States. I still have not seen him again, but I think of him each time I encounter a Meir-Ikhiel in my story, and whenever a failure of electricity

240

plunges me into darkness. Strangely enough, meir *in Hebrew means "light."*

THE FIRST *Meir-Ikhiel in my story—the Narbonnese scribe, son of Bonjusef—finally decided to stay in Troyes. First because his wounded knee made him unable to walk for a long time, and then because he gradually came to admire the vast wisdom of Rashi— that peasant rabbi who rejected ostentation of any kind—and hoped to become his regular scribe.*

His cousin Jeremiah found him a house to rent. It was on the Street of Jews, near the castle, and belonged to the Saint Loup monastery. The Jewish community helped him to settle into his new home, and one of Jeremiah's uncles, a banker in Metz who was another descendant of Samuel the miller, lent him money until he and his sons could find work.

But nothing in Troyes happened as expected. Rashi finally chose to give Jacob the position his father wanted. At the request of the community, but not without a certain bitterness, Meir-Ikhiel established a Talmud Torah for young children, in his house. Abraham had to give up bookbinding because the guilds, which were just being formed at that time, were placed under the protection of a patron saint and this excluded Jews from the various crafts. The banker in Metz offered to let Abraham come and work with him but he preferred to help Jeremiah in his wine and fruit business, so that he could remain near Rashi.

Abraham was in love with the beautiful Chavah, daughter of Zerah ben Abraham, but everyone believed that Zerah and his daughter both preferred Jacob, who had become an eminent figure in Rashi's entourage. Again the unexpected happened. Ansaldo, the Genoa cloth merchant, came to the autumn fair as usual, but this time he brought his daughter, the ravishing Miriam. He said he wanted to show her the world; later, however, no one doubted that he had had an ulterior motive: when he left Troyes, Jacob went with him, as Miriam's husband. Thus, to the splendor of his fortune, Ansaldo added the prestige of one of the closest disciples of Rabbi Solomon ben Isaac of Troyes.

After Jacob's departure Rashi realized that although Abraham was humbler than his brother, he was no less erudite, and he made him a reader at the yeshiva, *a position he shared with his friend Joseph bar Simeon. Abraham helped Rashi during the grape harvest* and, with the same faith, took part in pressing the grapes, decanting the wine, sweetening it, and putting it into barrels.

Then old Zerah came to speak to him about marriage—was it not written that a man without a wife is deprived of happiness, joy, and blessings? And so, after taking over Jacob's position in Rashi's entourage, Abraham married Chavah, whom he had expected his brother to marry.

Happy days in Troyes. But this took place in 1072. In less than twenty-five years Pope Urban would come to Clermont to preach what later came to be known as the First Crusade, which gave rise to the first great massacre of Jews by Western Christians. Does history never stop?

P.S. THE SCROLL of Abraham is still in Meir-Ikhiel's possession. According to established custom, he will keep it until his death. It will then be kept by Abraham, since Jacob has lost his right to it by going off with the ravishing Miriam.

I still do not understand why no one has made several copies of the Scroll of Abraham, even after its theft and the difficulty of recovering it. Surely my ancestors in Troyes knew the Champagne proverb: "The roof tiles that protect you from rain were made in fair weather."

18

TROYES

I Saw Peter the Hermit

ABRAHAM HAD aged. He was thin from fasting, round-shouldered from leaning over his writing desk, and gray-faced from working far into the night. During one of Rashi's absences he wrote to his brother Jacob, whom he had not seen since Jacob's departure for Genoa twenty-five years earlier.

"MY DEAR BROTHER, may God protect you. Since your father-in-law Ansaldo became too old to go to the fairs in Troyes, we have had no news of you, but I hope with all my heart that this letter will find you and your family in good health. Yesterday was the anniversary of our father's death and we lit a *ner tamid* in his memory. The twins, Meir and Ezra, are now more than twenty years old, and they have promised that they will both marry at the same time. But who can still speak of joy? As you must already realize, the purpose of this letter is not to tell you about everyday matters. I wrote my previous one with tears in my eyes, to inform you of our father's death. This time I no longer have enough tears. As the prophet Jeremiah said, 'The joy of our hearts has ceased; our dancing has been turned to mourning.'

"You probably know that at the beginning of winter the pope of Rome came to call on Christians to go to Jerusalem to free what

243

they call their holy places. You must also know how well his call was answered. As soon as we realized that large masses of people were going to be in motion, we feared for our lives. We sent three of our sages to meet the pope in Limoges, where he was celebrating the Christian holy day known as Christmas. He received them as sages ought to be received, and reassured them: his appeal was addressed only to lords and knights, whose armies were disciplined, and so there was no reason for us to be alarmed. His legate, the bishop of Puy, even asked us to contribute to the provisioning of those armies when they went through cities where our communities are prosperous. Nevertheless we alerted our brothers in the Rhine valley, knowing that Christians would be traveling there; we urged them to fast, do penance, and pray in order to ward off danger. Do you know, my dear brother, what they answered? That the Christians were their friends, that the bishops protected them, that they were not afraid. Woe to those of us who never believe the warnings that the Almighty, blessed be He, gives to us in His mercy!

"But while the lords were preparing to leave, an obscure monk called Peter the Hermit began going to cities, towns, and villages, shouting that it was time to set off, that God had sent him a letter and that Jerusalem could wait no longer. I saw him myself, and heard him, when he passed through Troyes at the head of a terrible horde. He is a dark, thin little man who keeps his feet and arms uncovered even in winter and eats nothing but bread. When he speaks, the Christians act as if they had gone mad. They pull hairs from his head to keep as relics, abandon their homes and property, sew a red cloth cross on their shoulders—some of them even have a cross tattooed on their foreheads—and follow him without knowing if they will ever come back. He asked us for a letter stating that he had not done any damage to our city or harmed the Jews in any way, and calling on the communities of Ashkenazim to give them provisions when they passed through. We wrote that letter for him. Woe to us!

"How can anyone forget that crowds on the march always attack the Jews? It began in Rouen, in Normandy, where Jews were slaughtered—may God keep them in His holy care. Then Godfrey of Bouillon, duke of Lotharingia, asked why Christians should go to fight infidels in the East and leave other infidels behind them. The Jewish communities of Mainz and Worms each sent him five

244

hundred marks of silver, and the emperor ordered all his vassals to protect the Jews. Woe to us if we believe those promises!

"Peter the Hermit and his multitude left in spring, whereas the pope had set the departure for the middle of summer. Bandits and mad monks, claiming to have been sent by God or the pope, followed Peter's example. Behind each of them was a mob ready to kill. In Metz, one of those mobs ordered the Jews to forsake the faith of their fathers. Those who refused to be baptized were killed. The victims included Rabbi Samuel, the community's treasurer, and twenty-one other men. Our cousin Abel, son of Naphtali the banker—you may remember that Naphtali offered to let me work with him soon after we came to Troyes—was sullied by the impure water of the Christians. But Rashi has declared that such forced conversions are invalid, and so has the emperor. Woe to us who are forced to deny our fathers!

"You are about to learn what happened afterward, my dear brother. Here in Troyes we have received written accounts from Worms, Mainz, and Darmstadt. We moaned and wept as we read them, and I moan and weep as I copy them to send to those who have been spared disaster, so that they will know and not forget. Pray and fast, my dear brother. Woe to us who live in exile and have not finished expiating the sins of Israel!

"Here, then, are passages from the chronicles of Solomon bar Simeon, Eliezer bar Nathan, and a scribe in Darmstadt who has not left us his name. Withdraw into seclusion, my dear brother, and weep for Israel!"

What we are going to tell here in memory of those who let themselves be massacred in the name of the Holy One took place in the year 4856 [1096] and therefore in the one thousand and twenty-eighth year of our exile, in the eleventh year of the two hundred and fifty-sixth lunar cycle, in the course of which we expected the Messiah, as announced by Jeremiah. But the joy of expectation was transformed into grief and moaning.

THE POPE of infamous Rome having called for Christians to go to Jerusalem, there suddenly arose a ferocious horde of Frenchmen and Germans who volunteered to leave for Jerusalem and the sepulcher of the hanged bastard. They attached an abject sign, a cross, to their clothing. Satan joined them, and they were more numerous than the grains of sand on the shore or the grasshoppers on the surface of the earth. Their voices were the voice of a storm. They accused the Jews of having crucified Christ, and they reached hateful agreement among themselves. "Why," they said, "should we tolerate these unbelievers before going off to fight against others? Let us first take vengeance on them and exterminate them if they refuse to convert."

The madmen came, horde after horde. They issued a call to action: anyone who killed a Jew would have remission of all his sins. A count named Dithmar swore that he would not leave the country without having killed at least one Jew. Several princes of the country sided with him.

Then the Jews did what our fathers had done. They repented, prayed, and performed acts of charity; hiding in the most secret rooms of their houses, they purified themselves by three days of fasting, until their skin clung to their bones and they were as dry as wood. But the Father hid in the clouds, did not listen to them, and banished them from His sight. The punishment had been announced long before.

Worms, tenth day of Iyar [Monday, May 5].

The enemies dug up a corpse that had been buried thirty days and carried it through the city, showing it to the crowd. "Look," they shouted, "see what the Jews did to our neighbor! They boiled this Christian in water, then poured the water into our well to poison us!"

The enemies and the crowd went mad. "The time has come," they said, "to avenge the death of Christ, whom their fathers crucified. This time, no one will escape!"

The Jewish community of Worms then became divided. Some stayed in their homes, convinced that in case of danger the burghers of the city would come to their aid; the others, less trusting, took refuge in the palace of Bishop Adalbert.

On the twenty-third day of Iyar [Sunday, May 18], the wolves from the steppes exterminated those who had stayed in their houses, even old people and children. They took the scrolls of the Torah and trampled them underfoot. After killing, they plundered.

The first victims had left their property to people of the city who had promised them protection but betrayed them. Some

246

Jews preferred to convert so that they could bury their brothers and free the children whom the lunatics had abducted to bring them up in their religion.

The cross-wearers had completely undressed their first victims. The Jews who had taken refuge in the palace gave clothes to the survivors so that they could cover the dead, and consoled those who had converted.

On the day of the new moon of Sivan [Sunday, May 25] the lunatics attacked the palace. The Jews who had taken refuge in it exposed their necks to the attackers' swords, or committed suicide, or killed each other. One killed his brother, another his parents, his wife, or his children; one killed his fiancée, another his bride; a woman killed the man she loved. They all accepted their misfortune and died crying out, "The Lord is our God, the Lord is one!"

A young man named Meshulam bar Isaac addressed the others in front of his wife Zipporah.

"Listen to me, all of you. God granted me this son, my wife Zipporah gave birth to him and his name is Isaac. I am going to sacrifice him as Abraham sacrificed his son Isaac."

Zipporah intervened.

"My lord, my lord, don't kill my son! Kill me first, so I won't see my child die!"

But Meshulam remained inflexible.

"Let Him who gave him to me take him back!" he said.

He picked up a knife and said a blessing over it. His son replied, "Amen," and he killed him. His wife screamed. He took her by the hand and they left the room. Outside, the lunatics seized them and killed them.

There was also a young man named Isaac, son of Daniel. When he refused to convert, they put a rope around his neck and dragged him through the mud of the streets to the church.

"You can still be saved. Will you change your faith?"

Half strangled, unable to speak, he made a gesture telling them to cut his throat. They cut off his head.

There was also Simcha the rabbi, son of Isaac the scholar. They tried to make him let himself be sullied by their putrid water.

"Look: there are all the members of your family, dead and naked. Accept baptism and you'll be saved."

"I'll do as you want," replied Simcha, "but first take me to the bishop."

They led him to the palace, where a sermon was preached to him in front of the bishop's nephew and several notables. Then he took out a knife and, like a lion attacking its prey, stabbed the bishop's nephew and two other men before the knife broke in his hand. Seeing him unarmed, the notables rushed at him and put him to death.

Others let themselves be killed without putting up any resistance, saying that it was the Lord's will. This was the case with Minna, a woman who was respected all over the city and who frequented powerful people. She had taken refuge in a cellar. Those who found her tried to convince her.

"Since you're a sensible woman, you must realize that your God can't save you. Consider the people who have been killed, lying naked and unburied. Let yourself be baptized."

"Far be it from me," she answered, "to deny the One God. For the love of Him and His holy Torah, I ask you to kill me without delay."

And they killed her.

In two days, nearly eight hundred Jews were put to death and buried naked. Only a very small number accepted baptism.

The other Jewish communities in Germany quickly learned of the massacres in Worms. Their hands were weakened and their hearts turned to water.

That same day, the bandits of Count Emich—may his bones be ground by iron millstones!—came into the good city of Mainz. A few Christians tried to protect the Jews, but they were killed by the bandits.

Count Emich had invented the story that an emissary of the hanged man had come to him and marked him with a sign in his flesh to show that he had been chosen. He was the enemy of all Jews, sparing neither babies nor invalids and cutting open the bellies of pregnant women.

While his troops were entering the city, the Jews learned that Bishop Ruthard was preparing to leave on a journey. Those who had entrusted money to him begged him to stay. He assembled the community in his palace, and he and the

248

burgrave gave them a solemn promise: "We will either save you or die with you."

The community decided to send money—seven pounds of gold—to Emich, and letters urging other communities along his way to give him a good reception. But this proved to be futile: we were less respected than Sodom and Gomorrah.

Mainz, third day of Sivan [Tuesday, May 27], a day of darkness.

The Jews were gathered in the bishop's palace when the wrath of the Almighty was kindled against His people. Toward noon the infamous Emich—may his bones be ground to dust!—arrived with his army before the gate of the city, which was immediately opened to him.

"Look," said the lunatics, "the gate opened by itself, a sign that the Crucified One wants us to avenge his blood on the Jews."

With banners flying they marched on the bishop's palace and, because of our sins, were able to penetrate it. Menachem, son of Rabbi David the Levite, comforted the Jews who prepared to fight.

"Honor the great God and His awesome Name with all your heart!"

Rabbi Kalonymos bar Meshulam led those who fought. The bishop's men fled and abandoned them to the enemy. The bishop himself fled. But Rabbi Kalonymos and fifty-three of his followers were able to escape.

When our enemies burst into the courtyard, they found Rabbi Isaac bar Mosheh. He showed them the back of his neck and they cut off his head.

Woe to that day when our souls were filled with anguish.

"Hurry," cried the Jews inside the palace, "let us sacrifice ourselves to the Almighty! Let those who have a sacrificial sword make sure it is not nicked.* They will sacrifice the rest of us, and then themselves."

The Jews who were in the courtyard had put on their prayer shawls and phylacteries. The thought of taking refuge in the palace to live one more hour did not interest them.

---

* According to the Law, the slightest blemish on the edge of the blade invalidated sacrifices in the time of the Temple in Jerusalem.

They sat down on the ground, ready to submit to the will of their Creator. The cross-wearers assaulted them.

Witnessing this martyrdom of the righteous, those watching from the windows of the palace decided to kill each other. They quarreled over the question of who would be the first to die. Women threw coins into the courtyard to delay their enemies and thus gain time to kill their sons and daughters.

The last Jews to resist threw stones at the cross-wearers and mocked them.

"Do you know what you believe in? You believe in a decomposing man, a stinking corpse!"

Rachel, daughter of Isaac bar Asher, wife of Jehudah, a just and pious woman, said to her friends, "I have four children and I don't want the Christians to take them alive. Don't spare them."

One of her friends came forward, took the sacrificial knife, and prepared to begin by killing Isaac, Rachel's younger son, a handsome boy. Rachel screamed and beat her face and bosom.

"Where is Your pity, Lord?" She implored her friend, "By your life, don't kill Isaac in front of his brother Aaron!"

But the woman sacrificed Isaac and his blood flowed onto Rachel's sleeves. Aaron shrieked in terror.

"Mama, mama, don't kill me!"

He ran away and crawled under a cabinet. Rachel's two daughters, Bella and Matrona, took the knife themselves, sharpened it, gave it to their mother, and bowed their heads. Rachel cut their throats, then went to look for her last child.

"Aaron, where are you hiding? I can't spare you or take pity on you."

She found him, pulled him out from under the cabinet by one foot, and sacrificed him. Then she lay down on the floor beside her children, whose bodies were still quivering. When the cross-wearers came into the room, they thought she was hiding a treasure under her long sleeves.

"Show us the money you're hiding!"

She showed them her children and they killed her. Then the father saw his dead children. He threw himself facedown on the floor, with the point of his knife against his belly.

The enemies also assaulted the burgrave's courtyard, where

other Jews had taken refuge. There, too, they slaughtered everyone.

Mosheh bar Shelbo, who had two sons, said to them, "My sons, heaven and hell are both open to you at this moment. Where do you want to go?"

"To heaven."

The three of them showed their necks to the attackers and were killed.

The lunatics tore to pieces a scroll of the Torah. A group of pure and saintly women who witnessed the sacrilege cried out to alert the men. David, son of Rabbi Menachem, said to the men, "Brothers, tear your clothes in honor of the Torah!"

They immediately did so. Just then a cross-wearer came into the room. They all stood up, men and women, and stoned him to death. The attackers then climbed onto the roof and began breaking through it.

Jacob bar Sulam was there. He came from a humble family and was the son of a non-Jewish mother. He spoke to everyone.

"Till now, you haven't held me in very high regard. But watch what I'm going to do."

He took a knife, pressed it against his throat, and killed himself before everyone, in the name of the Almighty.

Another man, old Samuel bar Mordecai, cried out, "Look, brothers, at what I now do for the sanctification of the Almighty."

He cut open his belly with his knife, and his intestines fell to the floor. He collapsed and died for the oneness of God.

Elsewhere, the lunatics and the people of the city stopped before the courtyard of a farmhouse belonging to a priest, in which Mar David bar Nathanael, a financier, had taken refuge with his wife, his children, and his servants.

"You can save your family and your fortune," the priest said to him. "You have only to convert."

"Go to those cross-wearers and tell them to come here."

Believing that he had convinced him to convert, the priest told the people what he had said. They rejoiced and came closer to hear Mar David bar Nathanael.

"It's you who are the infidels!" he shouted to them from the window. "You believe in a God of nothingness, while I believe in the all-powerful God who lives in the sky. I have always

251

trusted Him and I will go on trusting Him until my soul leaves my body. I know with certainty that if they kill me, my soul will rest in heaven in the light of life, while you, to your eternal shame, will sink into the abyss of corruption and putrescence, with your God who is nothing but the son of a prostitute!"

The cross-wearers stormed the house and killed him, along with his wife, his daughter, his son-in-law, his maidservant, and his menservants, in the name of the hanged man. Their bodies were thrown out the windows.

In another house, they tried to force Samuel bar Naeman and his family to let themselves be sullied by their stinking water. When they refused, they slaughtered them and trampled on them.

After the massacres, the uncircumcised undressed the Jews and threw them out the windows, even those whose souls were still attached to their bodies. When those who were dying asked for something to drink, they offered to take care of them and save them if they accepted a different God. But the dying shook their heads or refused with a gesture of their hands.

Eleven hundred were thus sacrificed in one day. Among them were great scholars, exegesists of the Torah, men who feared God, men of faith.

The people of the city buried them, naked and piled on top of each other, but at least they did bury them. They dug nine pits and laid them in together, men and women, fathers and sons, mistresses and servants.

Why was the sky not darkened? Why did the stars not lose their splendor? Why did the sun and the moon not hide themselves when so many saints perished? They accepted death out of love and fidelity. May their merits bear witness for us before the sublime Being, may they save us from banishment and rebuild the walls of Jerusalem, may they reunite the sons of Judah and Israel scattered over the earth!

"YOU HAVE READ, my dear brother Jacob, and now you know. Copy what you have read, so that others will know and no one will forget. For, like Rabbi Akiba and our ancestor Nomos the Red, the martyrs of Worms and Mainz refused all compromise and gave their lives to sanctify the Name. I believe, my brother, that this

252

ancient form of resistance will leave its mark on future generations. God grant that they will be spared such ordeals!

"When I read those terrible accounts, I asked myself how I would have behaved in similar circumstances, and I have not found the answer. Would I have been able to sacrifice my wife and sons? But can we foresee how much strength the Master of the world will give us at the time of His choice?

"Dawn is near, my fingers are stiff, and my eyes are weeping. I hear sounds from the bedroom: my sons are getting up, for life goes on. Today, we will return to work in the vineyard of Solomon Our Teacher. It comforts us in a way that is difficult to explain. Yesterday, when we were weeding the ground around the vines, Rashi reminded us of Jeremiah's words in Lamentations: 'But Thou, O Lord, dost reign for ever; thy throne endures to all generations. Why dost Thou forget us for ever, why dost Thou so long forsake us? Restore us to Thyself, O Lord, that we may be restored! Renew our days as of old!'

"I pray that you and I, my dear brother, will again know days like those of old. Embrace your family for your brother Abraham the scribe, in Troyes."

19

TROYES

The Judgment of Abraham

IT WAS still true that nothing in Troyes happened as expected. Abraham had feared that the whole region would be put to fire and the sword, as in the Rhineland, but the armies went off to the faraway East and then there were no more ragged cutthroats wearing crosses and shouting, "It's God's will!" Their departure was followed by several years of calm and prosperity.

In the morning, when the campanator—this was the name used in Troyes for the *shammash,* who had the duty of announcing the hour of prayer—knocked four times on the door of each Jewish house, it no longer marked the beginning of a day of anguish and terror. The agonizing affliction that had gripped the Jews of France gradually gave way to everyday concerns, discussions, and work.

As they had promised, Ezra and Meir, the twin sons of Abraham and Chavah, were married on the same day. Ezra's wife Rebecca was dark; Meir's wife Judith, Rebecca's cousin, was blond. Judith gave birth to a daughter, Rebecca to a son. This prompted a renewal of the old debate on whether it was better for the firstborn child to be a boy or a girl. Many couples regarded it as a blessing when their first child was a boy, even though he was more vulnerable than a girl to the evil eye; others wanted to have a girl first, so that she could later help to take care of her brothers and sisters.

One day when Meir and Ezra were debating the question in front of Rashi, he said in his gentle voice that if the first child was a girl, then later, when the mother had sons, she would be less envied—and therefore less likely to be exposed to the evil eye.

In any case, since his grandson Jacob had just been born, Rashi brought a jug of wine from the cellar and they all—fathers of sons and fathers of daughters—joyously drank to life: *"Lechaim!"*

Manesses, the archbishop of Reims, had received letters from his friend Anselm of Ribemont, who had taken the cross. The archbishop had these letters read in the churches, and so the news in them circulated: the Christian army had passed Constantinople, taken Nicaea, triumphed over the Turks, besieged Antioch. . . . Then came the news that Anselm of Ribemont had died. Later, the pealing of all the bells in Christendom announced that the army had reached its goal: Jerusalem. The Christians rejoiced in the streets, burned candles in the churches, sang hymns of thanksgiving. That day, for the first time, Abraham heard Rashi speak with irritation.

"If the Christians respond to the Moslems' holy war with another holy war, that's their affair. But why Jerusalem? Doesn't the land of Israel belong first and foremost to the people of Israel?"

Mordecai the madman held up his crutch and, with his eyes rolled back, began turning more and more rapidly on his one foot, shouting "Jerusalem! Jerusalem!" again and again. Finally he collapsed, exhausted and panting. "Now he'll . . . have to . . . come," he said between sobs of joy. "He must . . . come . . . now. . . ."

To Abraham, it was more or less a matter of indifference that the Christians had taken Jerusalem, since they had taken it from the Moslems and the Jews had been exiled from it. But the massacre perpetrated by the knights of Godfrey of Bouillon had left no survivors: there was no longer one single Jew in Jerusalem! As if by a kind of compensation, it was soon learned that Pope Urban had died. And what a death! It had come just after the taking of Jerusalem, but just before messengers arrived to bring him the news. Abraham saw this as a sign sent to the Jews by the Almighty.

Soon afterward the victorious warriors began returning, laden with relics and trophies, welcomed and honored everywhere. Also soon afterward Chavah, Abraham's wife, the diligent and modest companion of his life, disappeared from the house. Abraham and his sons looked for her a whole day and night. They finally found

255

her, haggard, her gown stained with earth, wandering in the Jewish cemetery beyond the Comporte Gate. She was speaking to the dead. When she had been brought back home, she smiled: she thought she was in heaven. She refused to eat anything and died a week later.

"The Lord gave, and the Lord has taken away," Rashi said to Abraham, quoting Job.

As if his grief were not enough, Abraham soon learned what gossiping women were whispering to each other in washhouses and at fountains: Chavah had been a *strea,* with the power to make the dead leave their graves. While they were at it, some women claimed to know from an absolutely reliable source that just before dying Chavah had tried to pull hair from the heads of her daughters-in-law and suck their blood. If her daughters-in-law had let her do as she wanted, Chavah would still be alive.

What was Abraham to do? Pray, work, and close his heart to bitterness and hatred. The Almighty did not inflict ordeals on His servants without a reason.

For a time, Ezra and Meir stood by their father and consoled him as much as they could, but their youth and the plans they had formed quickly made them forget, and then Abraham found himself alone. His cousin Jeremiah often invited him to visit and even asked him to come and live with him, but Abraham, having come to Troyes as a stranger, did not want to feel himself a stranger in Jeremiah's house.

He spent all his afternoons with Rashi. Since Rashi was now nearly sixty-five and easily tired from writing his columns of commentaries on facing pages of the Gemara, he often dictated to Abraham.

One afternoon Abraham found him lying down, which had never happened before. His daughters and sons-in-law were beside the bed, along with two doctors in purple robes, with desolate faces beneath their hoods.

"May He who can do anything give long life to Solomon Our Teacher!" said Abraham.

Rashi heard him and weakly moved his hand.

"May the Almighty, blessed be He, give health to Abraham ben Meir-Ikhiel," he murmured.

His old hand, roughened by the many years he had spent laboring to grow grapevines in the soil of Champagne, gestured as though to say that nothing more could be expected of it. Then he opened his gray eyes and looked out the window.

"Is the wind from the north, Abraham? Make a note of it. . . . It is written, as you remember, that 'four winds blow every day and the north wind accompanies them all; otherwise the world could not exist, even for an hour.' You can add that the north wind is neither too hot nor too cold, that it tempers the others and makes them bearable."

He said little more before dying a few hours later, on the twentieth day of the month of Tammuz in the year 4865 (1105) after the creation of the world by the Almighty, blessed be He. Abraham was not surprised that Rashi had spoken of the north wind: in Hebrew one word, *ruach,* means both "wind" and "spirit." And he was perhaps the only one not surprised at the news of another death: that of Mordecai the madman, whom Rashi had never ridiculed. In despair because the Jews would not listen to him, Mordecai had gone off into the countryside to announce the coming of the Messiah, and had so exasperated the Christians that a group of farmers had beaten him with sticks. Mortally wounded, he had dragged himself to a road where he was found by Moses, son of Benjamin, a farmer. Moses had put him on his big plowhorse, but Mordecai had died before reaching Troyes. Despite his aberrations, the community decided to give him a burial worthy of a good Jew, and accompanied him to his last resting place.

Abraham was overwhelmed by that succession of tragedies. There had been so many deaths around him since he came to Troyes! First Kountrass, then the three dwarfs drowned in the Seine, his father, his mother, Chavah, Rashi, Mordecai the madman. . . . Since he did not want his sadness to be a burden on his children, he settled into a solitude from which nothing could divert him. His sister had remained in Narbonne, his brother had gone to Genoa. Did they feel cut off from everything, as he did? While Rashi was alive, Abraham had not felt the anguish of growing old alone, alien to everyone. It was as if Rashi had been both his teacher and his country.

One morning he awoke with a longing to be back in Narbonne. He recalled the smell of the waterfront, the streets of his childhood, the play of bright sunlight on stones. He closed his eyes and saw the cypress trees around the Jewish Mountain, where his father Meir-Ikhiel had taken him to pray over the graves of his ancestors.

On the following *shabbat* he told his children that he was going to Narbonne.

"I don't know if I'll come back," he said. "When we came to Troyes, we didn't intend to stay here. The Almighty decided once, and He will decide again."

His only concern was the Scroll of Abraham. Not wanting to endanger it again, he had decided to hand it on to one of his sons. But which one? They were both the same age, both scribes, both pious, both married. They resembled each other physically, being twins—at first even their wives had sometimes confused them with each other, before learning to tell them apart—but Meir was more brilliant, more ambitious, and perhaps greedier. Abraham considered Ezra more loyal, more strongly attached to the simple things of life, and on the whole he recognized himself better in him, whereas Meir reminded him of his brother Jacob, who in childhood had been successful in everything he did.

"My sons," he said, "I'm going to give the Scroll of Abraham to one of you. Ezra, could you take it and continue it?"

"I'd be honored, father, if you feel I'm capable of it. But maybe Meir could do it better."

"And you, Meir?"

"I think I'm worthy of keeping it, father. My writing is more regular than Ezra's."

Abraham took on an uncertain expression. He had thought a long time about the fairest way to settle the matter.

"Each of you has an equal right to the scroll. To avoid wronging either of you, I'll divide it in two. Then each of you will have half of our history. What do you think of that?"

"If Ezra has no objection," Meir said quickly, "I'd rather have the first part, the one that begins in Jerusalem."

"Do you agree to that, Ezra?" asked Abraham.

"Father, I think it would be a great pity to divide the Scroll of Abraham. I'd rather let Meir have all of it."

Meir suddenly turned pale, realizing that he had fallen into the trap of "the judgment of Solomon": when two women both claimed to be the mother of the same child, Solomon proposed cutting it in half; only the real mother refused, preferring to have her child live, even with the other woman. Blinded by his greed, Meir had not seen the subterfuge. He contritely quoted from the First Book of Kings: "Then the king answered and said, 'Give the living child to the first woman. . . .'"

258

"You've said it yourself, my son. I'm not King Solomon, but what was good enough for him is good enough for me. Ezra will be the guardian of the Scroll of Abraham."

They put on their prayer shawls and Abraham read the names of their ancestors one last time. Then he took a pen, made sure it had a good point, and added after his own name: "who in Troyes, in Champagne, knew Rabbi Solomon ben Isaac and Mordecai the madman."

HE LEFT at the first opportunity: the arrival in Troyes of two rabbis, Judas ben Abraham and Moses ben Isaac, who had come from Amsterdam and were on their way to Cordova. They were traveling in a wagon drawn by two horses and would not listen to those who warned them about winter. When they left Troyes with Abraham, it was a sunny, pleasant day, excellent weather for setting off on a journey. Their guide, Simon, had given them an itinerary: Auxerre, Bourges, Châteauroux, Limoges, Périgueux, and Bordeaux, where they had things to do. For Abraham he had drawn a sketchy map on the ground and told him that he would have to leave his companions at either Limoges or Périgueux and go on from there to Narbonne.

How happy the three of them were, bundled up in their furs beneath the coarse cloth cover of the wagon, beard to beard, saying the daily prayers and discussing the Torah! When they put their heads outside they always saw the same landscape of dark forests, and they quickly closed the cloth, as though not to hear the thud of woodsmen's axes or the distant howl of a wolf looking for his pack. Abraham, Moses, and Judas told each other story after story, repeated comments they had read in the margins of sacred texts, savored the remarks, conjectures, and answers of great rabbis. They were impatient whenever they had to stop to take care of the horses or pay a toll. They usually stayed overnight with Jewish community leaders in the towns and cities through which they passed, and on those occasions Simon always asked detailed questions about the road ahead and the next stages of their journey.

At Limoges, Abraham decided to continue on to Périgueux with his new friends. But there he had to leave them: he had nothing to do in Bordeaux and it was out of his way. As he watched the wobbling wagon move away from him, he felt almost as lonely as he had felt at the death of Rashi, God keep him in His holy care.

"May you be blessed at your arrival and your departure!" he shouted, but his words were carried away by the wind.

He had been told to go to Terrasson, where he could cross the Vézère. Though he suddenly realized how helpless he was in that unknown region, without even a donkey or a dog, he set off at a brisk pace, gratefully using the staff that Simon had given him and listening with childish pleasure to the sound of his heels striking the frozen ground. Everything he had brought with him was in a bag slung over his shoulder: underwear, a virgin parchment, his writing materials, and a piece of bread given to him by the rabbi in Périgueux, an ardent and knowledgeable admirer of Rashi's commentaries, with whom he had stayed overnight.

Toward the middle of the day, when he saw a flock of wild geese fly past, high in the sky, he remembered what was said to children: "When it snows, the angels are plucking the feathers of geese in heaven." Soon afterward it began to snow. He was now going through a thin forest. Seeing no shelter, he quickened his pace.

The light flakes became denser and fell more rapidly. Abraham's hat, shoulders, and beard were covered with snow. He could scarcely make out the road in front of him. The silence was absolute, terrifying. No animal cries, no birdcalls, nothing.

When he felt the cold penetrating him, he decided to eat half of his bread. He tried to remember a commentary on bread but he had forgotten all of it except the part concerning bread eaten in the morning, which was said to have thirteen qualities: "It protects against heat, cold, evil spirits, and demons. It makes the simpleminded clever. It helps those who learn and those who teach the Torah. It makes others listen to their words. The studies of the man who has eaten it are not forgotten, his flesh gives off no bad odor, he is attached to his wife and does not covet other women. . . ." Two qualities were still missing.

Absorbed in searching his memory, Abraham had not heard the muffled hoofbeats of two horses approaching from behind him. He started violently when a voice called out, "Who goes there?"

"Twelve: it destroys tapeworms," he muttered in his snowy beard. "And thirteen: it makes love arrive."

He now saw two big black horses ridden by terribly tall and massive men.

"Where are you going?" asked one of the men, pushing the collar of his cloak away from his face.

He had the roughhewn features of a man of war, and Abraham

saw a heavy sword hanging from the pommel of his saddle. The other man had baggage behind his saddle. They were evidently a knight and his squire.

"This road," replied Abraham, "should take me to Terrasson. From there I intend to go to Narbonne, if the Almighty goes with me."

"Then one of us has lost his way in this cursed snow," said the knight. "I'm going to Agen."

Just then they heard a wolf howl in the distance, and then another.

"They're on our trail," said the squire.

"Are you coming with us?" asked the knight. "If you go on alone, you'll die."

Now that they had stopped moving, the snow was covering them more thickly. Abraham felt the cold rising in his body.

"Are you a Christian knight?" he asked.

"Yes. I've come from Jerusalem. My name is Raymond Pilet and I serve Raymond de Turenne."

"My name is Abraham, son of Meir-Ikhiel. I'm a scribe and I serve the Almighty, the God of Israel." Seeing that the two men had not reached for their swords, he added, "I'm a Jew."

"Maybe so, but if you stay in this forest alone, you won't be a Jew much longer. You're old and half frozen. Come, climb up!"

He reached out a powerful hand. Abraham suddenly felt himself lifted off the ground. A moment later he was seated unsteadily behind the saddle. The knight clicked his tongue, the horse started off, and Abraham nearly fell backward. The squire rode ahead.

It occurred to Abraham that perhaps the man whose broad back was sheltering him had killed Jews. Should he ask about it? He remained silent. The snow, blotting out everything around him, seemed to take away all reality from what he was experiencing. His world was reduced to a smell of leather and wet wool, and the pleasant feeling of rest after a long walk.

When they came out of the forest they were attacked by an icy wind that blew snow under their collars and sleeves. They heard more wolf howls, then there was silence; the pack was probably following them from a distance. Abraham felt safe and, swaying with the regular gait of the big horse, he even began to be drowsy. He clenched his teeth to keep from falling asleep. He thought of the wolves and looked back. The snow had already covered the horses' tracks. Those swirling flakes made him feel dizzy. He closed his eyes and saw himself in Narbonne, as a child, running in the sunlight along a street that led to the waterfront. . . . Then with Rashi, in the vineyard behind the house. . . .

"There's smoke in the wind," the squire said much later, when it was nearly dark.

The horses had smelled it and veered toward it. A few minutes later they nearly collided with a tight cluster of houses that suddenly appeared in front of them.

"I don't know where our horses have brought us," said Raymond Pilet, "but we've found shelter."

Hearing no answer, he looked back over his shoulder. The old Jew was no longer there.

Behind the knight and his squire, the falling snow was like a white wall. They crossed themselves.

20

TROYES

Esther's Sin

LEVI, EZRA'S son and Abraham's first grandson, had three good friends: Rashi's grandson Jacob, Eliakim the tall, and Absalom the fat. And on the day when his marriage was decided, he hurried to bring them the news before telling it to anyone else.

"Who is she?" asked Absalom, always curious.

"Esther, daughter of Shemariah ben Jacob, of Ramerupt."

"She's beautiful," Eliakim said appreciatively. "When will the wedding be?"

"At the next moon."

"Mazel tov! Let's go and celebrate!"

"Are you coming with us, Jacob?"

"I have to study."

"But that's all you ever do!"

"The Talmud is a vast domain."

"You know it as well as the streets of Troyes!"

Jacob laughed at the comparison.

"Anyway, *mazel tov!"* he said, raising his thin face toward his friend Levi. "I hope you didn't do what Isaac ben Oshaya did!"

"What did he do?"

"You don't know?"

"No."

"Well, Isaac ben Oshaya wanted to marry the daughter of a rich Englishman named Morel. He went to him and said simply, 'I'd like your daughter to be my wife.' "

"What was wrong with that?"

"Only that he didn't say whether he meant the older daughter or the younger one. Because of that, their engagement was declared invalid by the rabbis."

Levi laughed.

"Esther has no sister!"

"Then may He who holds our fate in His hands give you great happiness!"

"And may He give you the same, Jacob. I'll see you tomorrow."

Levi was a tall, slender young man with dark, lively eyes and a curly beard. He liked laughter and all sorts of amusements. The carnival season had just begun and he was looking forward to enjoying himself with Eliakim and Absalom.

They first went to Saint Arbois Square, where a troupe of actors were putting up their stage and musicians were tuning their instruments.

"Did you hire them to perform for your fiancée, Levi?" Absalom asked jokingly.

Levi did not have time to answer. They were caught up in a group of dancers who took them to Maldanyon Street, at the edge of the Bourg l'Evêque quarter, where the dance ended amid shouts and laughter. Levi and his friends went to the bishop's palace and saw a procession with crosses, torches, and banners coming from the Quail Gate and going toward the hospital. They joined the people walking behind the procession; that long line of torches moving through the city was not something that could be seen every day.

The heart of the procession was a gigantic personage in a striped satin robe. With one hand he held a double-edged ax and with the other he led an elephant covered with silk. In a structure on the elephant's back stood a lady wearing a cloak and the white hat of a young nun. At each crossroads and public square, the procession stopped and the lady sang:

> Come to my aid, and falter not.
> Weep for my woes: I am the Church.

264

"I wonder why she's asking for help," said Eliakim.

"You can see for yourself," replied Levi. "The giant represents the Saracens who want to subjugate the Church."

"The Saracens and the Jews!" said a voice close behind them.

Levi, Eliakim, and Absalom suddenly became motionless.

"And the Jews!" the voice insisted. "Don't forget the Jews!"

Levi turned around and saw a figure wearing a bird mask. He clenched his fist and hammered at the mask until it split and fell off, revealing an ordinary man with ordinary hatred in his eyes. Levi swung his fist again, with all his strength, with all his fear. His friends tried to hold him back but other men intervened and started a brawl that quickly spread. Levi felt himself grabbed by the feet and pulled down to the pavement. He struggled frantically when he saw a glittering blade.

Suddenly a loud, clear voice rang out: "Sword against sword! Turn and face me!"

Actually, the man who had been about to attack Levi held a dagger, and the elegantly dressed young man who had come to his rescue held a weapon of a kind not known in Champagne: a cross between a sword and a stiletto. The two men took their guard but some of the spectators separated them and others quickly began dancing a farandole that swept everyone toward the receding procession.

"May all the plagues of Egypt fall on their heads!" stormed Eliakim. "They tore my surcoat!"

"My nose is bleeding," moaned Absalom.

"Wipe it and thank God you're still alive!" said Levi. "We've had a narrow escape!"

"Who was that man who saved you?"

"Here I am!"

They could not see very much, now that the torches were gone, but they recognized the young man's voice and shape.

"Who are you?"

"Jacob of Ascoli."

"You're a Jew?"

"Yes, and a banker. This is the first time I've ever been in Troyes."

"Come," said Levi, "we'll celebrate our meeting."

"And your marriage!" added Absalom, wiping the blood from his nose.

"You're getting married?" asked Jacob of Ascoli.

265

"At the next moon."

"I'll still be in Troyes then. If you invite me . . ."

"You've invited!"

"Then let's go and have a drink!"

They went to the Butchers' Tavern, where Levi never failed to tell the story of Kountrass, his grandfather Abraham, the three dwarfs, and the stolen scroll.

"What scroll?"

"I'll tell you about it."

In front of the tavern, beneath the hoop that served as its sign, a woman was calling out to the passersby: "Are you hungry? Come in and eat! Are you thirsty? Come in and drink!"

The four of them went in and shared a table with three men playing dice.

"My God, twelve!" cried one of them.

"Two fours and a two: that makes ten, not twelve!"

"Who asked you? A curse on anyone who's afraid of losing after a ten!"

Four goblets and a pitcher of purple wine were put down on the table.

Jacob of Ascoli represented Italian sellers of alum, a product used as a mordant in the making of textiles. The three *yeshiva* students had never heard of it before. But Jacob of Ascoli was not fascinated by alum. He was mainly interested in weapons, he said, and collected fine specimens of them. In the last few days he had bought a horn crossbow of the kind made in Montbéliard, and another one made of yew, from Valenciennes.

He had very pale skin and was clean-shaven like most Christian noblemen. Although he made a first impression of being charming and likable, there was a certain smugness in the way he quoted the Greek and Latin poets he knew by heart. Levi had not yet told the story of his grandfather Abraham in the Butchers' Tavern but he no longer wanted to tell it, or to have Jacob of Ascoli come to his wedding. But he could not take back his invitation.

WHEN THE CAMPANATOR knocked on the door—once, twice, once—to announce that it was time for prayer, Levi was already awake. Simeon ben Samson, rabbi of the synagogue of the Jews' Thicket, personally came to take him to the house of the Almighty amid the crowd of relatives and friends holding candles.

After calling him to the Torah, he left him in the courtyard to wait for the bride.

It was a sunny day. Levi was deeply moved. Suddenly the zithers and flutes began playing: the bride was coming. She was beautiful in her white cape. Levi told himself that he was a lucky man.

Esther was surrounded by her family. Ezra, Levi's father, and Jacob, his friend, each took her by an arm and, preceded by Rabbi Simeon, led her toward the groom. Jacob of Ascoli had come to the wedding, as he had said he would. He walked behind the bride, between Eliakim and Absalom, wearing his sword and his brightly colored clothes, dazzling as an Oriental consul.

Levi took Esther's hand. The crowd of relatives and friends threw handfuls of grain and shouted, "Be fruitful and multiply!" They all went into the synagogue. The bride and groom sat under a canopy. In accordance with tradition, Levi had not eaten since the day before. He felt weak and tried in vain to remember the order of gestures and words.

They came out into the courtyard. Levi let himself be led. He was taken home and dressed in new clothes, a woman's hood was placed on his head as a sign of mortification and repentance, so that he would feel as new as his clothes, and then he was taken back to the synagogue.

After the morning prayer, the *shaharith,* Levi stood on a platform and ashes were poured onto his head. Only then, surrounded by the sages of the city, did he go to his bride, who was still waiting in the courtyard among the musicians, with her face veiled.

From here on it seemed to Levi that he saw and heard everything through a fog. He and Esther went into the synagogue, where the whole community was now waiting. Esther was on his right, as it is written in the psalm. Four men lifted the groom's hood and put it on the bride's head. Rabbi Simeon blessed the wine, then held out the cup to Esther and Levi. As custom required, Levi threw it against the north wall.

"Tov! Mazel tov!"

He was light, airy, perfectly happy. He thought of a sentence in a rabbinic *midrash* on Ecclesiastes: "No man leaves this world after fulfilling half of his desire." But Levi desired nothing more than what he was experiencing at this moment.

They moved through the streets, dancing to the sound of timbrels. People gave way to them, leaving them the upper part of the pavement so that they would not have to dance in the filth of the gutter.

Levi drank with his friends and with his friends' friends; he drank with Jacob of Ascoli, and again with Jacob of Ascoli. He danced a great deal. Once for a round dance, Esther placed herself between him and Jacob of Ascoli. At the end of the dance he kissed his wife, and Jacob of Ascoli kissed her too. Levi scarcely knew Esther—they had only exchanged a few kisses—but they had the rest of their lives for coming to know each other better.

He found her even more beautiful than in his memory, but also more distant, and she seemed a little apprehensive.

The night ended without him: he had finally sunk into drunken sleep. When he awoke, with his skull vibrating and nausea in his throat, he stood up and walked unsteadily out of the room.

His mother Rebecca was preparing the meal.

"Where's Esther?" he asked.

"She went out."

"She went out? So early?"

"She's young. She wanted to go and see her parents."

"How did she go to Ramerupt?"

"Our neighbor, Hanoch, was supposed to go to La Chapelle today. He must have taken her with him."

"Where's father?"

"At the *yeshiva.*"

Levi went into the courtyard, filled a bucket with water, rinsed his arms and face, shook his head to drive away the vapors of the night, then went back to his room to say the morning prayer.

That evening, Esther still had not returned and Levi was beginning to worry.

"Wait till Hanoch comes back," his mother told her. "I'm sure she didn't walk all the way!"

A servant brought a parchment sealed with red wax. It was a letter from Jacob of Ascoli in which he announced his departure for Geneva with a convoy of merchants from Vaud, said that he thanked the Almighty for having let him meet Levi, and asked Levi to forgive him for the harm he had done him. Preoccupied as he was, Levi did not understand what Jacob of Ascoli meant by that, or how to interpret the quotation that followed: "David said to Nathan, 'I have sinned against the Lord.' And Nathan said to David, 'The Lord also has put away your sin; you shall not die.' "

Levi watched for Hanoch's return. When at last he heard the

268

rumble of wheels, he rushed outside. The old man was alone. No, he had not seen Esther, either that morning or that evening.

Levi walked all over the city, as if his wife might be strolling in the streets. He did not come back until curfew and he refused to share the festive meal, which was actually like a gathering of mourners. He took refuge in his room.

For a long time he lay on his bed with his eyes open in the darkness, listening intently. He knew that Esther could not come back from Ramerupt before the next day, but each sound startled him and seemed foreign or hostile even after he had recognized it. He recalled that hope was not among the commandments received by Moses on Mount Sinai, for it gave no protection and healed nothing; it only delayed the awareness of affliction.

When his father went to bed, Levi got up to pray. Outside, the sloping street was dark and deserted. The ancients said that this was the time of night when the dead gathered in the synagogue to say the *chatzot* and mourn the destruction of the Temple. He remembered the death of his grandmother Chavah and shuddered.

He could neither pray nor sleep. Suddenly, among the images assailing him, he saw Esther dancing between him and Jacob of Ascoli, kissing one and then the other. Violent suspicion bit his heart and it seemed to him that in the darkness he could make out two sweaty bodies coupling. He started convulsively. Everything became clear, obvious, including the letter from Jacob of Ascoli. But how were such things possible?

The night seemed endless but finally the campanator knocked on the door. Levi hurried to Hanoch's house, borrowed a horse from him, and galloped off toward Ramerupt. He rode through the town of La Chapelle without slowing down. Maybe he was mistaken, maybe Esther was simply visiting her parents. His horse was foaming by the time he dismounted at the house of Shemariah, son of Jacob. His doubts were quickly dispelled: no, Esther was not there. Poor Shemariah silently opened and closed his mouth like a fish out of water.

Levi headed back toward Troyes but his exhausted horse was scarcely able to move and he decided to stay overnight in La Chapelle. In the public square before the church, men were piling up fagots. Someone was going to be burned at the stake, probably the next morning. Levi found himself fiercely hoping that the victim would be his sinful wife Esther. And he hoped that Jacob of Ascoli would be tortured with red-hot pincers, that his bones would be ground between millstones, that his name would be cursed to the thirteenth generation.

At the inn, he was lodged in a room with four beds. He ate a bowl of soup and fell asleep soon afterward. He dreamed that Esther was dying, smothered by a bloody sheet wrapped around her body. He woke up gasping for breath. Did Esther really have to die for her sin? Wasn't it enough that she had lost her peace of soul forever and was doomed after her death to wander barefoot till the end of time? According to Rashi, the real sinner in the garden of Eden was not Eve but the serpent, because he knew what he was doing. Levi resolved that if Jacob of Ascoli ever fell into his hands, he would cut him to pieces so that he could never go to heaven, then burn his flesh and scatter his ashes all over the country. His rage finally exhausted him and he went back to sleep.

THE BELLS of the nearby church awakened him. He remembered, and his heart filled with ashes. He went downstairs, washed, and said his prayer. Then he returned to his room and stood at the window. A crowd was gathering in the square to watch the execution. A man in a red tunic, evidently the executioner, was giving orders to assistants dressed in white. A stake had been set up, with logs, fagots, and bundles of straw carefully piled around it. Someone was about to die. Levi again began thinking that it might be Esther. Suddenly a murmur ran through the crowd: "Here she comes!" The room where Levi stood was now full of people trying to see out the window.

Preceded and followed by guards, the woman was naked. With her long, dark, disheveled hair and the unreal whiteness of her skin in the midst of all those colors, she seemed to be some sort of strange, unearthly creature. The guards let her through a gap left in the firewood. She climbed a low stepladder and docilely stood with her back to the stake. That resignation made a stronger impression than struggles or cries of revolt would have done.

The executioner's assistants made her put on a robe impregnated with sulfur and attached her to the stake with ropes around her neck and ankles and a chain around the middle of her body. Now that she was no longer naked, her face was seen more distinctly. She had broad cheekbones, her mouth was half open, and her eyes stared straight ahead, above the men filling in the gap through which she had come to the stake. The wind played with her hair.

A tonsured monk stood at the edge of the pyre, unrolled a

parchment, and read the condemnation. "In the case at hand . . . the said defendant . . . having prostituted herself and having once had carnal intercourse with the devil . . ." The crowd cried out in horror; people made the sign of the cross, or spat on the ground, or crossed their fingers to ward off an evil spell. "In view of the evidence and testimony . . . burned by fire . . ." There was an outburst of insults and applause, then silence fell over the crowd because death was approaching.

From the woman's gray lips came a long, blood-chilling wail. Levi resisted an impulse to put his hands over his ears and regretted with all his heart that he had thought of Esther when he saw the pyre.

The executioner threw the first torch into the straw. A high yellow flame immediately sprang up. His assistants set fire to the four corners of the pyre. Surrounded by fire and smoke, the woman stood still with her head thrown back as far as the rope would allow and continued her wail until her breath was exhausted, then she took another breath and the wail began again, unvarying and obsessive.

The flames were like lithe, high-spirited red-and-yellow animals boldly closing in on their prey. One of them bit the woman and her robe was set ablaze. Her wail became a shriek. More than one onlooker turned away.

Fighting back nausea, Levi elbowed his way through the people tightly packed together at the window, went downstairs, ran to the stable, and saddled his horse. The woman was no longer shrieking. The air smelled of sulfur and burned flesh. The silence was total. Levi rode off at a gallop.

ESTHER HAD STILL not come back. Levi had to resign himself to his fate. His friends tried to console him.

"Maybe she was abducted," suggested Absalom the fat.

"You can ask for a *get* [bill of divorce] and remarry," said Eliakim the tall. "There's no shortage of girls in Troyes!"

"What if she comes back?" asked Jacob. "What will you do?"

Levi made no reply; he did not know whether he would turn his back on her or fall at her feet.

"You could punish her," said Absalom.

Jacob stood up, slowly unfolding his frail body, and moved closer to Levi.

"Do you know why, after the first couple's sin in the garden of

271

Eden, the Almighty, blessed be His name, asked the man, 'Where are you?' It was a useless question, since He always knows where all His creatures are, but He asked it as a way of opening a conversation, so that the man would speak without fear."

"Yet the Almighty still banished him from the earthly paradise," remarked Levi.

"That's true, but only after giving him a chance to repent."

For a week they kept discussing every possibility, again and again. They worked in a cramped little room where most of the space was taken up by the furniture: two writing desks, a table, two benches, and a set of shelves. Levi and Eliakim stood at the writing desks, copying commentaries by Rashi. Absalom and Jacob studied scrolls. Despite his youth, Jacob's reputation promised to equal that of his grandfather, Rashi, and there was already talk of making him the head of the academy in Troyes.

He sometimes came to sleep in Levi's house. Perhaps because he had made very little effort to find one, he still had no house of his own where he could keep his books and other belongings, most of which his creditors had forced him to leave in Ramerupt.

One evening about a week after Esther's disappearance, Levi brought Jacob home with him, walking in a warm summer rain. As soon as they opened the door they knew that Esther had come back. The whole family was there, standing around her. She was gray in her gray dress, rain-soaked, motionless, indifferent to everyone.

When she saw Levi she bowed her head and said in a soft but clear voice, "I've sinned, I've sinned! May the Almighty forgive me, and may my husband be merciful to me."

With her eyes fixed on the floor, she walked stiffly toward Levi, then fell at his feet.

"She came a few minutes ago, in the rain," Ezra said to Levi, "and she refused to move till you were here."

Levi looked down at his wife as she lay on the floor like a pile of abandoned clothes, waiting without knowing whether or not he was going to send her away. The image of the woman burned at the stake in La Chapelle flashed into his mind. He bent down and stroked Esther's hair. Overwhelmed, she began sobbing with a mixture of distress and happiness.

Jacob, who had been thoughtfully following the scene, quoted from one of Rashi's writings: "In the beginning, the Almighty, blessed be He, conceived the idea of creating the world according

272

to the attribute of rigor, but He saw that the world could not subsist. He then gave precedence to the attribute of mercy, mingled with the attribute of rigor."

Levi looked at his friend and their eyes met. He straightened up, but Esther clung to his hand.

"I've forgiven her," he said. "She's paid for the pain she inflicted on me. For her affront to the Almighty, blessed be He, she will do penance."

"What penance?" Jacob asked gently.

"Speech, which enables us to know and communicate, and enabled the Almighty to create the world, must be reserved for the righteous in the coming days. . . ." Tears came into Levi's eyes but he felt the weight of all the attention centered on him and continued: "Esther will be deprived of speech until the fast of the next Yom Kippur. She will be deprived of hearing. She will neither speak nor listen to speech. She will be among us and apart from us, like a deaf-mute. She will be apart from our communication, but among us in the prayer that will absolve her sins in the eyes of the Holy One, blessed be He."

"Amen," replied his family.

Esther pressed her lips to his hand. Her father, Shemariah ben Jacob, who had not spoken her name since her disappearance, stretched out his arms toward her and sank to the floor, unconscious.

YOM KIPPUR PASSED, with its ceremonies of expiation, but Esther still remained deaf and mute, as if her voice were imprisoned in her body with a sin that was impossible to expel. She had a miscarriage, then gave birth to a stillborn child. She did not weep, because her penance was not yet over.

Levi spent his time helping Jacob at the academy, where there was no lack of students. They came from Lyon, Blois, and Narbonne, and even from Germany and Bohemia. At home, he told his wife that her punishment had ended, that it was time to live normally, that he wanted a child. Although she continued to be walled up inside herself, she at least gave him the son he wanted. In the autumn of the year 4884 (1124) after the creation of the world by the Almighty, blessed be He, a plump, bawling, and babbling baby was born. Levi named him Elijah and inscribed his name after his own in the Scroll of Abraham. Then he hurried off to the synagogue to thank Him who gives life.

273

21

TROYES

The Jew with the Sword

ELIJAH, SON of Levi and Esther, grew up in his mother's silence. She spoke to him with her eyes and hands, with the food she prepared for him, with the herb tea she brought him when he was feverish, but she never even said his name. He finally became old enough to realize that her silence was a form of expiation. He did not try to guess the reason for it, and no one dared to explain it to him—he would never hear anything about Jacob of Ascoli.

As a result of all this, he developed a hardness of character, a sensitive pride, and a quickness to take offense that made him different from the other men in the family over many generations. At eighteen, he thus became one of the first Jews to wear a sword; there was no prohibition against it, and he had reason to doubt the power of words alone.

"How will you defend yourselves," he asked in assemblies of Jews, "if the Christians again try to convert you, or decide to kill you?"

He was twenty-one when the full meaning of his question became apparent. That year, the very pious King Louis of France took the cross to go with King Conrad to the Holy Land. This time the Christians' purpose was not to take Jerusalem, but to defend it against Moslem attack.

As in the past, there was now an eminent authority—Peter, abbot of Cluny—who asked, "Why go to the end of the earth to fight the Saracens, at an immense cost in men and money, when we allow other infidels, guilty of a much greater offense against Christ, to live among us?" That was enough to make isolated bands immediately begin attacking Jews.

Jacob, Rashi's grandson, now known as Rabbenu Tam ("Our Righteous Teacher"), was in his house in Ramerupt one day when a group of pilgrims invaded it, pillaged and broke everything, and ripped a scroll of the Torah to pieces in front of him. Then they took him into a field, insulted him, and began beating him. "Since you're the greatest of the Jews," they said, "we're going to avenge Christ on you. We'll give you the five wounds that the Jews inflicted on Our Lord."

Rabbenu Tam was close to death that day, but, he later said, the Almighty took pity on him and made it possible for him to call out to a powerful nobleman who was passing by. Rabbenu promised to give him a horse worth five pieces of gold if he saved him. The nobleman said to the pilgrims, "Leave him to me for today and I'll speak to him. Perhaps I can make him change his faith. If not, I'll turn him over to you tomorrow." And so Rabbenu Tam was saved. But he did not like to talk about that episode.

"What are my wounds," he said, "in comparison with all those deaths, all those ravaged communities?"

THE JEWS OF FRANCE were not too greatly afflicted when that new Christian army set off for the Holy Land; again it was the German communities that suffered from the passage of the "soldiers of Christ." The depredations were such that Bernard, abbot of Clairvaux, who had preached the expedition, had to hurry to Mainz to ask Radulf, a monk who was leading an army of German pilgrims, to stop persecuting the Jews.

"We must learn to defend ourselves!" Elijah repeatedly told the students and rabbis at the *yeshiva*.

"No," Rabbenu Tam replied to the son of his friend Levi. "No, Elijah, we'll always be so outnumbered that we'll have no chance of defending ourselves successfully. Our future depends more surely on our unity and our respect for the Commandments. Some of us have been going to complain to the *goyim*, or having differences settled by their judges, which makes them feel that they have power over us. That must stop. We are answerable for our acts only to the Almighty, the God of Israel, and no one else. That is our strength."

"How are we to establish those rules and make our brothers accept them?" asked Elijah.

"Since the situation is urgent," said Rabbenu Tam, "we must impose them."

"How?"

"By using *cherem* [excommunication]."

THUS WAS BORN the idea of the first French Jewish synod. It was held in Troyes four years later during the period of the summer fairs, when the roads between Champagne and Flanders resounded with the gallop of riders carrying correspondence and bills of exchange, when the markets and inns were overflowing with merchandise and travelers, when bargaining was done in the varied accents of merchants from Montpellier, Barcelona, Valencia, Lérida, Geneva, Ypres, Genoa, Picardy, and Auvergne. Into the midst of that throng came a hundred and fifty eminent rabbis representing Jewish communities all over the country.

The assembly made Levi weep for joy. Twenty years earlier a Church council had been held in Troyes, at the urging of Bernard of Clairvaux. This time it was the Jews' turn to pool their talents and give their efforts a common direction. They were going to define rules that would be binding on all Jews in France. Elijah was impressed by the strength this gathering of a hundred and fifty rabbis represented, even though that strength was not an army and a hundred and fifty brutes could easily have cut off their hundred and fifty heads.

In a week of work, the synod gave shape to the principles enunciated by Rabbenu Tam: "We have therefore convened this council, we the elders and sages of Troyes and its environs, the sages of Dijon and its environs, the leaders of Auxerre and Sens and its suburbs, the elders of Orléans and its environs, our brothers the inhabitants of Chalon-sur-Saône, the sages of the Rhineland, our teachers in Paris and their neighbors, the scholars of Melun and Etampes, the inhabitants of Normandy and the seashore, of Anjou and Poitou, the greatest men of our generation, the inhabitants of Lorraine . . . We have voted, decreed, ordained that . . ."

Written accounts of the decisions made in Troyes were taken to the various communities by the rabbis themselves, *yeshiva* students, merchants, occasional couriers, and regular travelers. And for a long time afterward the official text, which had the force of law, was read in the tribunals of Jewish communities.

The counts of Champagne were not alarmed by the fact that the Jews of Troyes had thus taken the leadership of a movement openly affirming their difference. They were glad, in fact, since the Jews existed, that the Troyes academy was one of the most famous in France and that Rabbenu Tam, after Rashi, was from Troyes. Champagne was open not only to the winter winds, but also to different currents of thought. Clairvaux was not far from Troyes, and at the distance of a day's journey by horseback Abelard had founded the Paraclete monastery, where he critically examined the dogmas of the Church in the light of reason.

Elijah saw that this success reduced the validity of his calls to arms but he went on wearing the sword that was now familiar to everyone in Troyes. During the day he worked as a scribe with his father Levi and in the evening he practiced to improve his skills in the use of weapons with a group of robust young men who were training for tournaments. Not rich enough to buy a warhorse, he offered his services to riders who owned several of them and were always looking for volunteers to help them train for combat. He was called either "the scribe" or "the Jew," and to those thick-necked jousters who loved nothing so much as battling each other for money, honor, or simply the pleasure of striking harder than their adversaries, it seemed that being a scribe and being a Jew were equally strange.

Elijah often came home battered and bruised. His mother, and later his wife, when he was married, had to rub him with arnica ointment or snake balm. He always said that no worthwhile achievement came easily, and that he felt stronger than the time before.

"The enemies of the Jews had better watch their step!" Levi once remarked when his son came home with a dislocated shoulder.

He was joking, but with great affection and admiration, because he understood what Elijah wanted.

"Those noblemen," Elijah had said to him, "respect only strong muscles, skill in riding a big horse, indifference to pain, and contempt of death. But I can assure you that the men I fight are also learning to respect the Jews, and to me that's worth a little blood and fatigue."

His wife Bathsheba gave birth to a son whom he named Solomon, in memory of Rashi, because his interests were not limited to

277

weapons and fighting. When he was past thirty and had become less hot-blooded, when he no longer went to the square enclosure beside the Seine where young men trained for war and tournaments, he combined his knowledge of knights, his fidelity to Jewish tradition, and his skill as a scribe by writing stories of chivalry in which the heroes were taken from the Bible. One of them began in this way:

KING DAVID SUMMONED his valiant knight Joab to appear before him.

"Joab, my friend," he said to him, "the Ammonites are gathering in the city of Rabbah and preparing to do battle against us. Place yourself at the head of the army and hurl back our foes."

"Sire," replied the dauntless Joab, "there is no need for you to speak at length. If it please God, I shall win that battle!"

WHEN ELIJAH WAS FORTY, his father Levi died. Since his son Solomon was not yet old enough to help him in his work as a scribe, he carried on alone. His free time was now so limited that he stopped writing his stories of chivalry, just as he had stopped jousting ten years earlier. But he continued to wear a sword at his side, and although it was not as heavy as a war sword, it still aroused respect.

One day Rabbenu Tam asked Elijah to go with him to the castle to which the count of Champagne, known as Henry the Generous, invited the sages of the Jewish community once or twice a year. Henry and his wife Mary were patrons of the *trouvères*. They commissioned works by such authors as Chrétien de Troyes and paid them handsomely. Rabbenu Tam, now nearly seventy, was a lean, lively old man. His mind was as quick and sharp as ever, and the count enjoyed asking him questions containing artfully devised traps, which Rabbenu evaded without appearing to see them.

This was the first time Elijah had been inside the walls of the castle in whose shadow he had always lived. He wanted to stop in front of everything he passed: the kennels, the forge, the stables, the falcon roost. But Rabbenu, walking with his rapid little steps, led him up a staircase cut into the rock, to the high courtyard dominated by the massive fortified tower.

The stone-paved esplanade was as busy as a beehive. Elijah was dazzled by the way all those noblemen and their ladies were dressed: rare cloths embroidered with gold or spangled with silver,

jewelry, precious stones . . . Henry the Generous greeted his
Jews warmly and told them to make themselves at home. His wife,
he said, was occupied with a Court of Love and would be absent
until the verdict had been decided. Meanwhile, he beckoned to the
nearest guests with both hands, and when a circle had formed
around them he asked Rabbenu a question that he had no doubt
prepared long in advance.

"Saul," he said, "had sinned less than David, yet it was David
whom God preferred. Do you know the reason for that, my dear
rabbi?"

His eyes narrowed with mischievous pleasure, but there was
equal pleasure in the old rabbi's eyes when he answered, "One day
King David was taken prisoner, then released on his promise to
pay a large ransom. But instead of paying the promised sum of
money, his servants used it to buy a province, which they gave to
him. Valuing his honor much more highly than the most beautiful
province in the world, David sternly reprimanded his servants.
Saul, however, in other circumstances, was tempted by the abundant booty taken at Amalek and kept it for himself, disobeying
God's order to destroy everything. Those are the reasons for the
choice made by the Almighty, blessed be He."

"Honor and faith above all!" the count summarized.

He called the onlookers to witness, delighted that Rabbenu Tam
had once again known the right answer.

"It seems that the rabbi has read Chrétien's romances!" a young
man in a green silk tunic remarked mockingly.

"I don't know if he's read my romances," replied Chrétien, who
was rather frail and wore a quilted blue brocade doublet with white
fur on the shoulders, "but I'll be greatly surprised if he's read
yours, Gautier!"

The count put his hand on Rabbenu Tam's arm, leaned toward
him, and asked, "How do you explain that those men, who write
such refined, courtly works for our pleasure, quarrel with each
other like stablemen? And yet they're inseparable!"

"In friendship," answered Rabbenu Tam, "we must leave a little
room for quarreling, and in quarreling we must leave room for
reconciliation."

Elijah admired the old rabbi's ease and total lack of affectation.
Rabbenu Tam's back was bent, his complexion was sallow, his
beard was sparse and white, his clothes were dark and threadbare,
and yet he was a radiant presence in the midst of the elegance,

279

youth, and wealth that surrounded him. Elijah recalled the debates on the respective powers of knowledge and the sword that he had had with his father, God rest his soul, twenty years earlier. How life passed!

When Elijah and Rabbenu Tam had arrived, they had seen the *trouvères* dividing among themselves the subjects of poems and the guests to be honored during supper. In the meantime, a young woman recited "The Women Weavers' Lament":

> *We shall always weave silk cloth*
> *And never be better dressed.*
> *We shall always be poor and unclothed*
> *And always hungry and thirsty.*
> *We shall never earn enough*
> *To buy more and better food.*

A poem about poverty might have seemed out of place in that luxurious setting, but Henry the Generous took it as a matter of course and his attitude no longer surprised anyone. There was applause at the end of the recitation:

> *They threaten to beat us*
> *If we rest,*
> *And so we dare not rest.*

The young woman bowed, picked up a lute, played a chord on it, and pointed to the author of the poem, Chrétien de Troyes. He took on a modest expression. Gautier d'Arras did not miss this chance for a sarcastic thrust.

"Our great poet," he said, "feels that a poem can be cut from any cloth!"

The two friendly enemies resumed their running quarrel. Rabbenu Tam led Elijah to the count's residence, next to the castle. The main door opened into an immense hall decorated with tapestries, hunting trophies, and murals. A platform had been erected in the middle of the room, and on this platform several dozen noble ladies had gathered for what Rabbenu Tam described as "the most curious thing anyone could imagine": a Court of Love. The ladies periodically met to debate a question and then pass judgment on it. Today's question, Chancellor Haice de Plancy told Rabbenu Tam and Elijah, was: "Is not marriage the enemy of real love?" But the debate was over and Mary of Champagne was about to announce the decision of the court.

Just then Gautier d'Arras rejoined Rabbenu Tam and Elijah and asked them if they knew the Jews of Blois, where he spent most of his time because he was a protégé of Count Thibaut. Rabbenu Tam replied that he carried on a correspondence with Rabbi Yechiel ben David. Gautier asked him if he knew that the count had a Jewish mistress, Polcelina, and that the Jews of the city had great advantages because of her. Rabbenu Tam gave Elijah a skeptical look. Gautier went on talking, without waiting for an answer, and asked why the Jews, who wrote so much, never wrote chivalric romances.

Rabbenu Tam gestured toward Elijah.

"The only Jew who ever wrote any, to the best of my knowledge," he said, "is standing before you."

Gautier d'Arras was speechless with surprise. Elijah acknowledged that years ago he had written some chivalric romances, but in Hebrew. They would have to be translated.

There was a call for silence: Countess Mary was standing on the platform, ready to speak. She wore a robe of heavy blue silk and a diadem glittered in her hair, which was arranged in long braids interwoven with threads of gold. In a firm, clear voice, she stated the judgment of the Court of Love.

"We hereby declare that love cannot exercise its rights between husband and wife. Lovers grant everything to each other freely, without the constraint of obligation, whereas each member of a married couple is bound by duty to yield to the other's will. We pronounce this judgment after hearing the arguments of a number of ladies. It is to be regarded as an established and incontrovertible truth."

Rabbenu Tam was greatly amused but no one noticed it except Elijah, who knew him well. The old rabbi soon told him that it was time to leave, since, for religious reasons, they could not share the enormous meal of roasted meats and game in sauce, whose powerful aroma had begun drawing the guests toward the table. Before Rabbenu Tam headed for the stairs, hurrying away from that promise of a lavish feast as though fleeing from sin, Gautier d'Arras had time to ask Elijah if he would like to come to Blois with one of his chivalric romances. Elijah replied that he would be delighted to come.

"I'll have you invited by the count," said Gautier.

THE INVITATION arrived a year later. Gautier d'Arras reminded Elijah of their meeting in Troyes and told him that the count of Blois, Thibaut, had expressed a keen desire to know "the Jew with the sword."

Elijah was overjoyed. He had just finished translating one of his romances, originally written in Hebrew, into French octameter verse. At eighteen, his son Solomon was capable of doing his everyday work for him while he was away, and of taking responsibility for the three women in the house: his mother Bathsheba, his sister Ruth, and his grandmother Esther, who was still voluntarily mute. Elijah went to one of the jousters in the field beside the Seine and bought from him, at a favorable price, an old white saddle horse that had been retired from military service. He then set off for Blois.

As he rode along, alone with his horse, his sword, and his chivalric romance, he had a strange sense of detachment from his ordinary life and wondered if his true destiny might not have been to become one of those *trouvère* knights who went from battle to battle, from castle to castle, from heart to heart, and saw nothing but deadly boredom in living without danger or luxurious clothes. But he wisely resisted the temptation to indulge in futile regrets. Between Orléans and Blois he spent hours looking at the light morning and evening mists and the slow, slate-gray water of the Loire. How far away Troyes now seemed to him! He did not regret being a scribe, even though he realized that he could have become many other Elijahs than the one he was. He told himself that what mattered was to fight, by the pen if not by the sword, against injustice and oblivion.

Night was falling when he came within sight of Blois. He decided it was too late to go to the castle where Gautier d'Arras was presumably expecting him, or even to the house of Rabbi Yechiel ben David, for whom he had messages from Rabbenu Tam. He began riding toward the house of the brothers Gabriel and Hedin ben Moses, winegrowers who had formerly lived in Troyes and now cultivated a whole hillside two miles outside of Blois. He had been told that they were somewhat coarse, and he had also been warned against their habit of insisting that visitors drink vast quantities of their wines.

The door was barred and the house was silent, but white smoke rising from the chimney in the gathering darkness showed that someone was there. Elijah knocked on the door, then on the window shutter. In vain. He called out his name.

"I'm Elijah, son of Levi. I'm from Troyes, like you. If you hear me, please let me in."

He sensed that he was being watched through some sort of opening, then he heard the heavy wooden bar being pushed back and saw the door slowly swing on its hinges. The two brothers appeared, each holding a prayer shawl in his hand. From what Elijah could see of them, they were stocky, suntanned peasants, almost as broad as they were tall. They motioned him to come inside. He tied his horse to the ring beside the door and stepped into the dark house.

"If you want to sleep here," said one of the brothers, "you'll have to put your horse in the barn."

"But if you don't want to risk your life," said the other, "you'd better go straight back to Troyes!"

In the darkness, Elijah was led by the arm to a bench. He sat down. He was handed a goblet of cool wine and drank it with pleasure. Only then did Gabriel and Hedin speak again.

"It's because of Polcelina. . . ."

"That whore!"

"She came from Tours to be the count's mistress, and . . ."

"And now the countess is taking her revenge—on all the Jews in Blois!"

Elijah remembered how Rabbenu Tam had grimaced when Gautier d'Arras mentioned the count's Jewish mistress. The old sage's apprehension had proved to be justified. Elijah learned what had happened from the alternating voices of the two brothers, whose faces were invisible to him now that night had completely fallen.

Two days earlier, a servant in the castle had declared under oath that he had seen the carpenter Isaac ben Eleazar lead his donkey to the Loire and throw the body of a Christian boy into the water. A search was made for the body, without success. The carpenter admitted that he had taken his donkey to drink from the Loire, but denied the rest. The witness was subjected to trial by ordeal: he was thrown into a vat of holy water deep enough to make him drown if he had lied; he stayed afloat, and his good faith was therefore established. Rabbi Yechiel went to the castle to defend the carpenter but was put into a dungeon cell. There were attacks against Jews, and demands that all the Jews in Blois be baptized. Those who refused were imprisoned. Gabriel and Hedin had so far been spared only because they lived outside the city, and perhaps no one had yet thought of them.

"What will you do if they come to baptize you?" asked Elijah.

"We've never put water in our wine . . ." one brother began.

"And we won't let it be put on our heads!" the other finished.

"All because of a woman. . . ."

"That whore!"

Elijah calmed them. He told them he knew influential people in the castle; he would go there next morning and have all the imprisoned Jews released.

HE LEFT AT DAWN. The castle was even more impressive than the one in Troyes. From the postern gate, where he asked for Gautier d'Arras, he saw the river and the three suburbs: Foix, Bourg-Moyen, and Saint-Jean-en-Grève.

Gautier's eyes were still puffy from sleep. When he recognized Elijah, he hesitated, then approached him with obvious reluctance.

"You've come at a very bad time!" he said. "You'd better leave, before they—"

"I want to see the count," Elijah interrupted. "Tell him I'm here."

Gautier retreated a few steps.

"A Jew, a merchant from Orléans, came here yesterday to offer a ransom. The count nearly had him thrown into prison with the others. Take my advice and leave immediately. When things have calmed down, I'll write to you again."

He turned his back on Elijah and hurried away. Elijah found it hard to believe that this man had written chivalric romances.

The transparent morning air brought sounds and smells to him. Everything seemed peaceful, ordinary. What were they thinking, he wondered, those Jews who had been imprisoned because they were Jews? Did they still have hope? If so, from whom did they expect help to come?

Elijah mounted his horse and rode away. He wanted to think about what should be done. Finding a solution would be all the harder because the count was evidently ready to buy his wife's forgiveness by letting her take vengeance on the Jews.

Elijah rode toward the Loire, then decided to go back to the brothers Gabriel and Hedin ben Moses. They ate a meal of bread and goat's-milk cheese together, and for once the winegrowers refrained from drinking wine, which for them was the harshest form

284

of fasting. After their meal they prayed to the Almighty, asking Him to strike down the enemies of Israel.

Then an agitated man arrived and introduced himself as Baruch ben David, a merchant from Orléans. It was he who had gone to the count the day before and offered to pay a ransom for the release of the prisoners. He had already sent two messengers at his own expense: one to notify the king of France, Louis, of what was happening, and the other to ask Nathan ben Meshulam, in Paris, to collect money in case the count should finally listen to reason.

But what he had come to say, out of breath, was that the prisoners had been taken out of the castle and locked in a barn near the Loire, just outside the suburb of Saint-Jean-en-Grève. The count's soldiers were guarding them. Baruch ben David now came to the worst part of his story: the prisoners had been condemned to death by burning and there was reason to believe that, to save the expense of a pyre, the count intended to let them be killed by a mob.

Elijah, the merchant from Orléans, and the two winegrowers looked at each other. What should they do? They were only four men, too few to take action themselves, and they did not have time to bring help.

Elijah stood up, tightened his sword belt, slipped his sword into its sheath, and steadied himself on his feet.

"Don't do anything foolish," said Baruch ben David. "You'd only add your death to all the others."

"I'm just going to see," said Elijah.

He patted the neck of his old white horse with almost cheerful affection. The man, the horse, and the sword soon reached the slowly swirling waters of the Loire.

Elijah was guided by the shouts of the crowd that had gathered outside the barn in which the prisoners were enclosed. The count's guards were holding off people who wanted to go into the barn, but how much longer could they resist? Was it even intended that they would resist very long?

Elijah rode into the crowd, forcing people to step aside from his horse. He reached the guards and approached their leader.

"What's happening?" he asked. "Who are the prisoners you're guarding?"

"Jews."

"What have they done?"

"They kill Christian children and throw their bodies into the Loire."

"Are you sure of that? Have you seen it with your own eyes?"

"I haven't seen it, but it's been proved at a trial."

Just then a tall, blond, rather young man aggressively asked Elijah, "Who are you? We don't know you here."

"The count invited me to visit him," replied Elijah.

"I saw you this morning at the postern gate," said one of the guards. "Gautier d'Arras didn't let you come into the castle."

While the guards were occupied with Elijah, men behind them were bringing fagots and bundles of straw. Still sitting on his horse, Elijah saw what they were doing.

"They're going to set fire to the barn!" he said, to warn the guards.

"Burn the Jews!" cried the blond man. "They're all Judases!"

The crowd encouraged him: "That's right, Jeannot! Tell them what they are!"

"Murderers of Jesus!" bellowed Jeannot, and Elijah saw his neck swell.

"Murderers of Jesus!" echoed the crowd.

"More bestial than beasts!"

"More bestial than beasts!"

"Kill them!"

"Kill them!"

A torch was thrown into the straw, instantly setting it ablaze. The crowd applauded joyously, as though at a bonfire. Women called for everyone to dance. Everything that could be found was used to feed the flames: pieces of wood, rags, branches. Children threw stones at the burning barn. A few men undressed and tossed their clothes into the fire. The crowd roared savagely.

Elijah suddenly urged his horse forward and, after knocking down several of the guards, stopped at the door of the barn. There he turned around.

"My name," he said loudly, "is Elijah ben Levi and I'm a scribe in Troyes, in Champagne." His voice became choked with emotion. "I too am a Jew, and if these Jews must die, I will die with them."

He dismounted from his horse. While the people near enough to see him stared in amazement, he pushed open the barn door.

Flames were greedily biting into the planks and acrid smoke was billowing upward.

"Death to the Jews!" cried Jeannot.

"Death to the Jews!" the crowd repeated faithfully.

Then Elijah came out of the smoke, sword in hand, like an

avenging angel emerging from storm clouds. Seemingly indifferent to the fire, he went to Jeannot, pressed the point of his sword against his throat, and forced him to go into the blazing barn with him.

"Save Jeannot!" someone shouted.

"Save Jeannot!"

But no one moved. Then the crowd stepped back at the sweet, ethereal, unforgettable sound of a hymn rising above the roar of the flames. *The Jews were singing.*

Suddenly, in an explosion of sparks, the roof and the beams collapsed.

"May God forgive us our sins!" said someone.

The Christians all crossed themselves.

IN ACCORDANCE with the proposal put forward by Rabbi Jacob ben Meir, Rabbenu Tam, it was established that the twentieth of Sivan, 4931 (May 27, 1171), the day of the martyrdom of the Jews of Blois, would henceforth be commemorated by a fast. The Jewish community of Tours instituted measures that were also adopted in Champagne and Lorraine for three months: at weddings, there would be no guests from outside the family, unless more men were needed to form the *minyan;* men and women would refrain from wearing silk garments; men would fast on Monday and Thursday. An anonymous *trouvère* wrote a "Lament of Blois" that was taken from city to city by *yeshiva* students:

> And he came alone with his sword,
> Like David before the terrible Goliath,
> Like the hand of the angry Almighty,
> And he died as a martyr to quell his wrath
> In the flames of a pyre.
> O God, let us contemplate Your splendor!

A few days later the body of Polcelina was found in the Loire, but no one could say whether she had drowned herself or been thrown into the water.

22

TROYES

And Saul Became Paul

ELIJAH HAD begotten Solomon, who begat Samuel, who begat Saul—born in Troyes in the autumn of the year 4952 [1192] after the creation of the world by the Almighty, blessed be He—Yochanan, Bathsheba, Esther, and Miriam.

Saul, the oldest of Elijah's great-grandchildren, soon came to feel that he was big enough, and rich enough in knowledge and will, to stand on his own feet without leaning on the memory of that glorious ancestor who was constantly cited as an example. Time and time again, members of his family had read to him what his grandfather Solomon had written in the Scroll of Abraham at the age of eighteen: "He died by fire in Blois, sanctifying the Name to the glory of the people of Israel, who are, among the nations, like the heart in the body, the part that is both the healthiest and the sickest. May the Almighty grant that they will survive."

It was said that Elijah's mother, having become mute before his birth, had regained the power of speech at the news of his death: "The Almighty has made me pay by taking away what I held most dear, blessed be He," she had said before letting herself die of grief and starvation.

To Saul, all this was only one of those dark stories from the past. As far as he was concerned, the peace in which the Jews now lived

—those of his age had never known any other condition—did not justify the ceaseless exaltation of Elijah's memory. And it was more or less natural that when his father Samuel had planned a life for him that would be worthy of his ancestor, he chose a different one. Despite his aptitude for commentary and the hopes he had aroused in the most famous Tosaphists of the time—such as Isaac ben Joseph of Corbeil, and Judas ben Joseph of Paris, with whom he had studied—he abruptly decided to abandon the world of scholarship. He went to see his cousin Asher ben Moses, a banker in Metz, and proposed opening a branch of his establishment in Troyes. Asher ben Moses accepted the proposal on a trial basis. Without regret, Saul let his younger brother Yochanan take over the responsibility of carrying on the family tradition.

He installed a table at the Place au Change, between two other men: Ponce de Chaponnay, from Lyon, and Tolomei, from Sienna. The latter worked mainly with abbeys, which left him such religious objects as valuable crosses or gold ciboria as security for the money he lent them. As for Ponce de Chaponnay, most of his clients were either local noblemen or men who regularly attended the Champagne fairs. Usury was condemned by the Church: no one could lend money for interest, since that was a way of putting time to work, and time belonged only to God. But Tolomei and Ponce de Chaponnay were not hindered by that condemnation.

The widow of Duke Eudes, Alix de Vergy, who seldom succeeded in making her large income cover her great expenditures, borrowed five hundred livres provinoises from Ponce de Chaponnay and promised to repay it at the time of the next fair. Not only was she unable to keep her promise, but she asked for an additional loan of a thousand marks of silver. It was an enormous sum and Ponce de Chaponnay flatly refused to lend it to her. From his table, Saul saw the duchess's face take on a look of dismay and humiliation. He stood up and, without hesitation, offered her his services. How much did she want to borrow? A thousand marks? For what security? Till when?

She looked condescendingly at the modest moneylender. He introduced himself.

"I'm Saul," he said, "son of Samuel the scribe. And cousin of the Metz banker Asher ben Moses. I represent him in Troyes."

Probably as much out of spite against Ponce de Chaponnay as because she needed the money, the duchess gave the impression that she was delighted to borrow from Jews.

Saul was so eager to arrange the loan that he immediately rented a horse and rode to Metz at full speed. He was able to present the case convincingly to his cousin. As a result, having left Troyes as a humble moneylender, he returned as a banker who was going to manage several freeholds and tithe two villages near Vitry, for these represented the security and interest to which the duchess had agreed.

Instead of happily congratulating Saul on having made such a brilliant start, his family treated him even a little more coldly than when he had abandoned his studies. Resentment? Jealousy? Because his cousins, uncles, friends, and neighbors behaved toward him as if he had contracted a dangerous disease, he preferred to go and spend the Rosh Hashanah holidays with Asher ben Moses in Metz. Soon after he came back, he moved out of the family house and rented lodgings for himself with some of the money from his first earnings.

On the date when the duchess had promised to repay her debt, Saul received a visit from her wardrobe maid, a young woman with a fair complexion and blond braids. She had come to ask that he allow the duchess to postpone payment. Common sense told him that he should either refuse or demand additional security, but the young woman stirred such powerful feelings in him that he said yes and had no thought of regretting it.

They exchanged only a few words that day but from then on he thought about her constantly. He saw her again, by chance, on Holy Innocents' Day. It was snowing. He was following a procession of people wearing disguises, on their way to perform a farce in the square in front of the Saint-Etienne Church. Darkness had fallen and the snowflakes glittered in the torchlight with wondrous beauty. It was one of those evenings when the festive spirit was irresistible.

He did not recognize her immediately. Her blond hair was hidden by a wimple and she wore a long, warmly lined green surcoat with ornamental trimming.

"What are *you* doing here?" she asked, laughing.

"I like celebrations."

"But this one is for a Christian holiday!"

"What's the difference? I'm enjoying myself like everyone else."

"You're a strange kind of Jew!"

A stage made of boards laid across trestles had been set up in the square. While they waited for the actors to appear on it, the spectators sang and clapped their hands, with a little white cloud in front of every mouth. A song ordered everyone to take the arm of the person next to him, and the chains formed in this way rose and fell like waves, out of time with the music.

"My name is Mathilde," she said. "Come, Saul."

She took him by the arm and they joined the movement of one of the chains. He was trembling with excitement, dazzled by the thought that since she had spoken his name, she must love him.

The movement took on such amplitude that the human waves began to break up. Participants who were unsteady on their feet slipped in the mud amid shouts of joy. Saul caught Mathilde just in time and pressed her against him. Their faces met.

"You mustn't," she said.

He kissed her anyway. The celebration was swirling around them. She drew him aside.

"I must go now." She smiled and added, "There's snow in your beard."

She hurried away from him, then looked back for an instant and waved discreetly.

He did not see her for a whole month. One evening when he was reading the Sefer Chasidim by candlelight, there was a knock on his door. It was Mathilde, holding a package wrapped in blue cloth.

"Good evening, Saul," she said. "The duchess wanted a safe hiding place for these books and I thought of you."

"Books?"

"Yes, two books forbidden by the Church."

Saul would have given all the books in the world for the courage to take Mathilde in his arms; instead, he unwrapped the package and saw Aristotle's *Physics* and *Metaphysics*.

"These books were translated from the Arabic by Jews," he could not help saying.

"Then they're not forbidden among the Jews?"

"Not yet. But some people are already beginning to attack Maimonides, a sage from Cordova who tried to reconcile faith and reason, Judaism and Aristotle. . . ."

"What were you reading when I disturbed you?"

"You didn't disturb me! I was reading a book on the secret of God."

"Who can know the secret of God?" Mathilde asked with surprise.

"Those who fear Him, according to this book."

"I want you to explain it to me, Saul, but another time. I can't stay any longer now."

He took her hands between his. She blushed slightly and told him that she had talked about him with her brother, who was the abbot of Notre-Dame-aux-Nonnains.

"He'd like to meet you," she said. "Would you be willing to visit him?"

She left without giving him time to answer.

LIKE A FLY buzzing around in a jar, a rumor soon began circulating in the Jewish community that Saul the banker, a descendant of the martyred Elijah, was regularly going to the abbey of Notre-Dame-aux-Nonnains and having long discussions with Guyard, the abbot. One day when Saul visited his father at the same time as Jacob, the rabbi who was known as the teacher of the Jews of Troyes, his father asked him if it was true. Saul replied that it was, but that he saw nothing wrong with it and was in no danger.

"In the fear of the Lord one has strong confidence," he quoted.

"My son," asked Samuel, "do you fear Him enough, blessed be He?"

"It is written in Isaiah, 'The sinners in Zion are afraid,' which means that he who avoids sin has nothing to fear, because the Shechinah stands before him and protects him. And I haven't sinned, father."

Samuel looked at his son sadly. His little Saul had become a robust, broad-shouldered man with a thick beard and forthright green eyes.

"So much knowledge wasted!" murmured Samuel.

"It's not wasted, father, since I share it with others."

"How many seeds shared with the earth produce no fruit!"

From then on, only Saul's younger brother Yochanan continued to see him, bringing him news of the family: for example, that cousin Bonmacip and his daughter Sarah had been killed in Narbonne during a campaign by northern Christians against southern Christians, or that his father was ill but did not want him to visit.

Less than a year after his meeting with Rabbi Jacob—that is, in the year 4974 [1214] after the creation of the world by the Almighty, blessed be He—it was learned in Troyes that Saul was going to marry the duchess's wardrobe maid and that he wanted to become a Christian. Yochanan hurried to him and tried to dissuade him. Samuel wept, and the whole family went into mourning for a week. It was a deep wound.

At the duchess's request, Saul was baptized Paul by Bishop John himself, a tall, pale nobleman with drooping eyelids and a strained way of speaking.

"Paul, what do you expect of God's Church?"

"Faith."

"Paul, do you renounce Satan?"

"I renounce him."

"And his works?"

"I renounce them."

"And his vanities?"

"I renounce them."

How simple it all was! Well prepared for the ceremony by Mathilde's brother, the abbot of Notre-Dame-aux-Nonnains, Saul deeply felt the meaning of each word, gesture, and symbol in the ritual. And he devoutly received the water and salt of his new birth.

"Paul, I baptize you in the name of the Father, the Son, and the Holy Spirit."

When he looked up, Saul's eyes met the sorrowful gaze of the gigantic painted wooden statue of Christ above the altar. He told himself that from now on he too was going to have a cross to bear.

At first it was rather easy. He married Mathilde and their love for each other was as strong as ever. In the middle of summer they learned of the great victory won by the king of France at Bouvines: Philip, supported by contingents from the militias of the communes, had defeated the coalition formed by Emperor Otto, the king of England, the count of Flanders, and the count of Boulogne. This provided subjects for endless discussions, on the part played by the communes, on the new relations to be established with Flanders, on the character of that farsighted and ambitious king. During the whole time that was spent trying to decide whether or not the victory at Bouvines was "good for the Jews," Saul and Mathilde lived in peace.

Guyard arranged for his brother-in-law to be employed as a scribe in the bishop's palace, and so every day Saul walked along the edge of the Jewish quarter and saw former friends and neighbors who looked away from him as he passed. At first he amused himself by calling out to them, then he was annoyed, saddened, and offended by their silent hostility. He felt like taking hold of them and forcing them to look at him, making them recognize that although he had changed his religion he was still the same man: whether he was called Saul or Paul, he was the son of Samuel, son of Solomon, son of Elijah the martyr.

Mathilde gave birth to a boy, Matthieu, who had his father's dark hair and green eyes. Yochanan was the only member of the family who came to see him, and he did it in secret. Saul finally came to hate those stubborn Jews, enclosed in their own little world, who made the air of his native city unbreathable for him. Yochanan was now the only Jew who ever talked with him, during his rare visits. His life was centered around his work, his wife, his son, and his new friends; there was no longer any place in it for the Jews.

A YEAR LATER he went to Rome with his brother-in-law, the abbot, for the Fourth Lateran Council.

That gathering of seventy-one archbishops, four hundred and ten bishops, and eight hundred abbots testified to the power of the Church. With the ardor of a convert, Saul was thrilled simply by the sight of all the crimson, white, and gold in the chancel of the great church, and he took a passionate interest in all the debates, even the least important and the hardest to follow. Then the Jews came under discussion, and each word entered into his body.

"In regions where Christians are not distinguished from Jews or Saracens by their clothing," said a bishop, "relations have taken place between Christian men and Jewish or Saracen women, and vice versa. To make it impossible for such abominations to be excused by a claim of error, it would be desirable to have Jews of both sexes set apart from other people by their clothing."

The proposal was adopted: Jews would be required to wear a circular badge of yellow cloth sewn to their clothes, over the chest.

Saul needed air. He slipped out of the Church of Saint John Lateran and walked aimlessly through the streets of Rome. He knew from the Scroll of Abraham that some of his ancestors had once lived here. In the Jewish quarter, near the Colosseum, he tried to picture them to himself. He imagined them with the faces of the Jews who had already learned the news and were now coming out into the dirty streets, vehemently talking and gesticulating, with somber expressions.

It was on that day, at that moment, that he decided to have nothing more in common with those Jews tightly packed into a little island moored in the Tiber. From now on, his life was going to be free of narrow boundaries, like a ship on the high seas. During that brief time spent wandering in Rome, Paul shook off Saul. And it was Paul who went back to the church, where Guyard was waiting for him.

THE YELLOW BADGE soon became obligatory for Jews in Languedoc, Normandy, and Provence, but it still had not been imposed in Champagne twenty years later, when Paul and his wife Mathilde died in one of the winter epidemics that were depopulating the cities.

Their son Matthieu, now married and the father of three sons, took Paul's place as a scribe in the bishop's palace. He had an open, curious mind, never willing to accept conventional ideas without examination. One of the first disputes he had with his friends concerned the Jews. A few families of Jewish refugees had just come to Troyes after being expelled from Brittany by Duke John the Red. Matthieu felt that the way the Christians treated the Jews was unjust, and said so. He quoted Saint Augustine: "The Jew has the book from which the Christian draws his faith."

"The Jews have abandoned that book for the Talmud, and we're now the only heirs to it," replied one of his friends.

"Not long ago, here in Troyes," said Matthieu, "Rabbi Solomon was writing new commentaries on the Bible."

The others then remembered that Paul, Matthieu's father, had been born Saul, and this reminded them of the proverb "The apple never falls very far away from the tree."

Matthieu's wife Marie gently scolded him.

"You have three children," she said, "and a good position in the bishop's palace—why make enemies for yourself by meddling in those foreigners' affairs?"

"But the Jews aren't foreigners!"

"They're not like us, Matthieu, and you know it."

"Are you forgetting that my father was a Jew?"

"He was born a Jew, but later he was baptized, and that changes everything!"

It distressed Matthieu that Marie, ordinarily so fair-minded and generous, did not understand him. He sometimes went to Bishop Eustace for comfort, when he could approach him during his work. One day, despite all his benevolence, the bishop advised him not to go too far in defending the Jews, since they were a treacherous, usurious people even though a few of them were exceptions to the rule.

Matthieu replied with a quotation from the Gospels: "For with the judgment you pronounce you will be judged, and the measure you give will be the measure you get."

"Take care, my son! As you know, Dominic's monks are trying to ferret out heretics everywhere. Your conduct and your words might be judged harshly."

"Then must I smother my sense of justice and my love of my fellow man? Jesus said, 'Love your enemies, do good to those who hate you, bless those who curse you, pray for those who abuse you. . . . If you love those who love you, what credit is that to you?' "

Wanting to give Matthieu a different outlook and help him to avoid sinking into solitude, as he seemed in danger of doing, the bishop asked him to go to Paris and deliver a document to Benedict, the abbot of Saint-Victor. He advised him to stay there a few days, if his wife had no objection: Paris had become the meeting place for students from all over the West, and a mind like his would surely find nourishment there.

WHAT A CITY, and what a life! Matthieu had been given lodgings in the abbey of Saint-Victor, near the student quarter on the left bank of the Seine. Students crowded into courses on the seven liberal arts or improvised debates in the meadows along the river, outside the walls, upstream from the tanneries and dye works. It was June and the weather was superb. The short nights scarcely gave the city time to calm down before resuming its feverish agitation at dawn. The great cathedral dedicated to Our Lady (Notre Dame) was practically finished. People came to it as much to admire as to pray. Its proportions, the soaring height made possible by the new technique of flying buttresses, the profusion of statues and gargoyles—everything combined to exalt the glory of God and enhance the rapture of the faithful, and when sunlight set one of the great stained-glass windows ablaze with color, how natural it was to fall to one's knees!

But after a few days Matthieu had to think of going back to Troyes. He was about to leave when he heard that all copies of the Talmud within the royal domain were being seized by order of King Louis IX. Matthieu was so appalled that he could hardly believe his ears. What could be so dangerous about that book? And if it contained untruths, would it not be better to refute them? It was said that the copies were going to be burned the next day at the Place de Grève.

He got up early and saw the city awakening. The first boats of the powerful guild of merchants who brought goods into Paris by water were beginning to be unloaded; peasants were arriving, leading donkeys laden with early-ripened fruits and vegetables; butchers were killing animals in front of their stalls; beggars had already begun their quest for alms—the first alms of the day, they swore, brought good luck to the giver as well as the receiver. Matthieu was lingering at the foot of the Saint-Séverin Church on the Rue Erembourg-de-Brie, watching the bookbinders and illuminators open their shops, when there was a large movement of people toward the Rue Saint-Jacques.

Preceded by sergeants of the municipal guard, recognizable by their breastplates and yellow tunics, carts were bringing the books to be burned. "Writings of Satan!" murmured the man next to Matthieu, crossing himself. Matthieu counted the carts, as if their number mattered. Fifteen, sixteen, seventeen . . . He was in the crowd that followed them to the Place de Grève, across the Petit-Pont, past the Grand Châtelet, and through the Outre-Grand-Pont quarter.

The pyre had already been prepared. Curious onlookers, with beggars and thieves mingling among them, were rapidly filling the square. Hearing a group of men talking with a Champagne accent, Matthieu followed close behind them. They wore no distinctive signs, but their sorrowful tone, their long beards, and their hunted look made him think that they were Jews.

Trumpets sounded and the crowd parted to make way for dignitaries of the Church and representatives of the king. From where he was standing, Matthieu could not hear the reading of the judgment but he saw the first flames. The spectators were not affected as they would have been if a human being were about to be burned; there were only a few scattered cries.

When the flames were high enough, the books from the first cart were thrown into them. The parchment burned, giving off thick black smoke. Matthieu looked at the faces of the men he believed to be Jews from Champagne. One of them had his teeth clenched, another was quietly reciting a prayer. The one nearest to Matthieu was silently weeping.

"Why are you weeping?" asked Matthieu.

The man sniffled, wiped his eyes, and looked at him sadly.

"I'm a scribe," he said. "Each of those books represents the work of a man's life."

"I'm also a scribe," said Matthieu. "At the bishop's palace in Troyes, in Champagne."

"Troyes!" the man exclaimed. "I'm from there too! Blessed be the Almighty for bringing us together here, since such is His will."

As soon as one cart was empty, another was brought forward and the executioners threw armfuls of books into the fire. The burning pages writhed as if they were suffering, and heavy swirls of smoke darkened the sky.

"May His name be glorified and sanctified in the world He created according to His will. May He . . ."

The man was praying in an undertone, aware that he had nothing to fear from Matthieu.

"You're a Jew, aren't you?" Matthieu asked him when he had finished.

"Yes. My name is Abraham, son of Yochanan. A few days ago we were notified that the king of France was having all copies of the Talmud seized. We were safe in Troyes, but several of us came here to see with our own eyes if the Almighty would permit . . . But He must want to give a new warning to His people."

His regular features, very dark beard, and green eyes seemed familiar to Matthieu.

"Why?" asked Abraham. "Why are people sometimes so cruel? Why don't they obey the Law? Why do they show so little love for each other? Why?"

"Come," said Matthieu. "Call your friends and we'll go back to Troyes."

"You're right. May the Holy One, blessed be He, forgive us."

They were already on the road to Troyes when Matthieu asked Abraham, "What was your grandfather's name?"

"Samuel."

"That was also my grandfather's name."

Abraham was silent for a long time, then he dared to ask, "Are you the son of that Saul who converted?"

"I am, cousin," replied Matthieu, overwhelmed with emotion.

IN TROYES, the Jews wore mourning and some of them had sewn the round yellow badge onto their clothes even though they were not obliged to do so. The Christians were divided on the question of whether or not the king's decision had been justified. If it was

298

true that the Talmud contained abominations against Jesus, the king was probably right to have it burned. But if it was not true, if the Talmud was nothing less than the word of God, then there was reason to fear His anger.

Matthieu questioned Bishop Eustace at the first opportunity.

"Is it certain that the Talmud contains attacks against Christ and the Christians?"

"Yes, Matthieu."

"How was it proved?"

"Two years ago the king ordered four rabbis to debate the question with Eudes de Châteauroux and a converted Jew named Nicolas Donin. Blanche of Castile herself presided over the debate."

"What was said in it?"

"From what I've been told, Nicolas Donin easily confounded the rabbis."

"But did he really prove that there are blasphemies against Our Lord in the Talmud?"

The bishop made a gesture of impatience.

"The matter was decided by people better qualified than either of us, Matthieu. I can understand your desire to help the oppressed, but the Jews are different from other victims of oppression. Listen to the words of Christ: 'Let them alone; they are blind guides. And if a blind man leads a blind man, both will fall into a pit.'"

Matthieu did not mention the Talmud again. He worked hard, spent hours praying in the Saint-Etienne Church, and at night, when everyone else in his house was asleep, he read for a long time by the light of an oil lamp.

One morning his arrival at the bishop's palace caused a commotion. He went to work as if everything were the same as usual, but a report soon reached Bishop Eustace and he came to see for himself: Matthieu was wearing a yellow badge on his surcoat.

"WE, THE BROTHERS of the blessed Dominican Order, have been instructed to judge the case of Matthieu, a scribe in the bishop's palace, guilty of rebellion against our Holy Mother the Church."

The monks, in white cowled robes, sat in a semicircle around him. Their stern faces had the patient and inexorable look that distinguished those charged with administering God's justice. The voice resounded beneath the vaulted stone ceiling.

"We consider, however, that the Church must not cast out any repentant sinner and we call upon you to renounce your errors, to reject the pestilence of heresy, and to denounce before this tribunal those who led you into sin, in order to save yourself from human punishment and the eternal flames."

What was he to answer? These men who spoke in the name of Christ were betraying Christ: they had no love in them.

He simply said, "I am not a heretic."

"Did you or did you not wear the insignia of the Jews?"

"I did."

"Who incited you to do it? A Jew?"

"Yes," said Matthieu.

"What is his name?"

"Jesus of Nazareth."

The inquisitor's thin lips quivered.

"Brothers, how do you judge that reply?" he asked.

"Blasphemy!" said a voice on the right.

"Blasphemy!" said a voice on the left.

"Blasphemy! Blasphemy!"

The monks facing Matthieu, as stiff and motionless as if they were made of stone, suddenly seemed larger and closer together. He remembered what Bishop Eustace had said to him: "If they take you before their tribunal, there will be nothing I can do for you, except to pray." Fear clutched his heart but he still could not say the opposite of what he knew, with all his faith, to be the truth.

MATTHIEU COULD NOT MOVE. Tied hand and foot, he was hanging upside down from the chain of a well. Each time the inquisitor gave the order, he was lowered into the water, then pulled up just before he was asphyxiated. His torturers were waiting for him to speak, to denounce, and then they would free him. It was as if they needed a certain number of victims. How could God allow such things to be done? That unanswered question was the worst part of the ordeal; it plunged Matthieu into the same despair that Christ had known when he cried out on the cross, *"Eli, Eli, lama sabachthani?"* (My God, my God, why hast thou forsaken me?)

The clatter of the chain on the drum, the water streaming from his clothes, the sound of his breathing and moaning amplified by the well, in which maidenhair ferns grew between the stones—all this soon lost its reality. "Lord," he prayed, "please help me." If he denounced someone, anyone, he would be saved. He thought of Abraham, his Jewish cousin, and his silent tears at the Place de Grève in Paris. If he denounced no one, he would be burned as a heretic. What a mockery. . . .

HE WAS SUBMERGED once too often, or too long, in the water of the well. When he was pulled up, he had ceased to live. He was buried in secret, with no one present but his three sons, his wife Marie, and an old priest from La Chapelle.

Abraham had been notified by Marie. He watched the burial without letting himself be seen and said the *kaddish*. That same evening, he and his wife and their children decided to leave Troyes.

23

STRASBOURG

The Money of the Commune

ABRAHAM, HIS wife Nana, and their sons Samuel and Nathan arrived in Strasbourg at the end of that same year, 5002 [1242] after the creation of the world by the Almighty, blessed be He. The Strasbourg Jewish community took them in until they found lodgings and work.

Abraham was an upright, faithful, and honest man. Except for his journey to Paris, his life had been uneventful and he had known adventure only vicariously, through reading the family scroll that enabled him to follow the tribulations of his ancestors. When he arrived in Strasbourg he felt that he must be reliving what other Abrahams had known when they arrived in Alexandria, Hippo, Cordova, Narbonne, or Troyes: an unknown city with ramparts to be explored, a river with bridges to be crossed, new customs and manners to be discovered, a new language to be learned; the only certainty and comfort came from the warmth and daily routine of the Jewish quarter, the shared prayers, the synagogue anchoring the whole community. Then life went on, month after month, year after year; your children grew up and you finally blended in with the people of Alexandria, or Cordova, or Strasbourg—and no one could tell from your grandchildren's accent that you had come from somewhere else.

Strasbourg suited Abraham: there he met sensible people with a strong sense of community. He was hired as a scribe in the synagogue and rented a small house nearby, on the Street of Carpenters. His wife Nana, however, soon began to languish. She could not get used to the Alamannic language spoken in Strasbourg and she missed the relatives she had left behind in Troyes. To his great sadness, Abraham saw that she was wasting away. Did he realize that she would soon die, and he with her? In any case, without mentioning it to anyone, not even his sons, he decided to bring the Scroll of Abraham up to date.

This placed him in a dilemma. His extreme modesty made him reluctant to write about himself in such a precious document; he regarded his life as being without interest. But his sense of duty won out over his humility. Although he had done nothing that was noteworthy in itself—and in this he was like those dozens and dozens of ancestors whose names were the only information about them given in the scroll—he felt that he should at least bear witness to matters that concerned everyone's conscience. He thought a long time about the best formulation, then wrote in a firm hand, after his name, "who begat Nathan and Samuel; was a scribe in Troyes, in Champagne, like his father; saw in Paris the fire in which the king of France, Louis the Ninth, burned all copies of the Talmud that he had been able to seize; and, not wanting to stay in a city where a righteous man had sacrificed his life according to his faith, left Troyes and went with his family to Strasbourg, to live there and serve the Almighty, blessed be His name."

He was not surprised when Nana's life ended like the flame of a lamp that had burned low and then quietly gone out. And those close to him were not surprised when he too died, exactly a year later, without having given anyone cause to worry.

His two sons had already decided on the work they wanted to do. Nathan, the younger, became a scribe. Samuel went to Metz to learn banking and came back a few years later to set himself up as a banker in Strasbourg. They were totally different from each other but they both remained devoted to the memory of their parents, knowing that they had left Troyes less out of fear than in order to obey their conscience, and they thanked them for it each year when they lit a *ner tamid* in memory of them.

TWENTY YEARS after their arrival in Strasbourg, Nathan and Samuel again had reason to be glad that their parents had brought them there. Lenit of Offenburg, a merchant, reported to them that in Troyes a Jew—Meir ben Samson, a goldsmith in the Jewish quarter, whom they had known as children—had been accused of profaning the Eucharist. He had been saved in the nick of time by a ransom of a hundred and fifty marks that the community had hastily collected.

In Strasbourg also, things were not always easy for the Jews, but, thank heaven, there was never any serious trouble. And what Jew, anywhere in the world, was not exposed to some sort of harassment?

Samuel the banker wondered how it would be best for him to react if his son Menachem were accused of profaning the Eucharist. He had been working on his accounts since dawn, making calculations by moving copper counters on his reckoning board and writing figures in columns on parchment. Having brought his records up to date, he was wiping his pen and thinking of his son when he heard hurried footsteps on the stairs.

It was Vogel, his clerk.

"We have a visitor, sir," said Vogel, catching his breath. "It's Reinbold Liebenzeller, the patrician."

"What does he want?"

"The same thing as everyone else, I suppose: money."

For a few moments Samuel thoughtfully tugged at his beard and chewed on a few of the graying whiskers that grew around his lips, then he straightened his purple surcoat over his gray tunic.

"Show him in," he said.

Reinbold Liebenzeller was a tall, wide man with a vast paunch. His brown hair straggled out from under his hood, which had a velvet crest the same shade of red as the gloves he tossed onto a table. Despite the mild weather, he wore a fur-trimmed cloak. He greeted Samuel with a broad smile, then sprawled on the bench without having been invited to sit down, making it creak beneath his weight.

"We need you, Samuel of Troyes, the most honest of bankers!" he announced in a solemn tone.

"We?"

"We, the patricians of the council: Heinrich Eichen, Burkard Spender, Berthold Ruses, Hugo Kuchenmeister . . ."

Samuel took on a look of surprise.

"What can I, a poor Jew, do for the most powerful burghers of Strasbourg?"

"You can lend us money."

"Money? But you're the richest men in the city!"

"What we have isn't enough."

"Then my money is all you lack!" Samuel said with a sigh. "Money, money, always money! Where could I get it? Haven't we already paid our taxes to the emperor, the bishop, and the city council, not to mention the forced loans that will never be repaid?"

"Come, come, banker! Haven't I always paid back the loans you've given me?"

Samuel leaned against the high, carved oak back of his chair.

"It's true, Herr Liebenzeller, that with you I haven't lost anything. But I haven't gained anything, either."

"You'll have the interest I promised you!"

"I don't doubt the word of a Strasbourg patrician. I only pray that I won't die in poverty before I've been able to profit from that word."

Reinbold Liebenzeller let out a booming laugh.

"You've got a sense of humor, Jew! But this time it's the council that's asking you for money, and the council is powerful enough to give you certain advantages."

"Powerful, powerful . . ." Samuel repeated. "I have no doubt of it, personally, but the new bishop doesn't seem to believe very much in the council's power."

Liebenzeller smiled grimly.

"You're well informed, Jew!"

Samuel spread his arms as though to stress an obvious fact.

"Our lives depend on it."

"And that's why you must help us," said the patrician, becoming more animated. "If the bishop and his followers take over the city, that will be the end of your privileges."

"Our privileges? What privileges?" Samuel asked with surprise. "We're not allowed to work at any craft! The Christians restrict us to dealing in money, so they can borrow from us and hate us more! What privileges are you talking about, Herr Liebenzeller? The truth is that we have only obligations."

Embarrassed, the patrician let his eyes wander over the dark, heavy furniture and the large silver objects. Samuel coughed.

"But why do you need money so urgently?"

A smile spread across Liebenzeller's broad face.

"Then you'll help us?"

"If I can, if I can. . . ."

"You can. Here's the situation. Bishop Gautier is assembling an army near Holtzheim. Several noblemen are supporting him: Rudolf of Rapperschwyl, for example, and Berthold of Saint Gall, the bishop's uncle. We don't want to avoid a battle, but we need weapons and soldiers, and therefore money."

"How much?"

"Two thousand marks, guaranteed by the council."

"Guaranteed if you win. But what if you lose?"

"We'll win." Liebenzeller took a deep breath. "I'll fight in the battle myself!"

"Two thousand marks. . . . That's a big sum."

"You belong to an association of bankers, don't you? Why not ask them to help?"

"That will take time."

"How long?"

"Two weeks, maybe more."

The patrician passed his hand, laden with rings, over the back of his thick neck.

"That's a long time!"

Samuel opened the strongbox behind him, took out a bag, and put it down on the table, beside the reckoning board.

"Here's five hundred. You can take it now and I'll get the rest for you as soon as possible."

Liebenzeller leapt to his feet.

"You're our savior!"

"I hope so," replied Samuel, "because if the bishop wins the battle. . . ." He took a sheet of parchment, made sure his pen was in good condition, dipped it into the inkwell, and handed it to the patrician. "I'd like you to sign a receipt."

"Of course, of course! In the name of the council, naturally."

"No, in the name of Reinbold Liebenzeller. After all, you're the one who's here. And I prefer to deal with a man I know, rather than an institution in which I'd never find anyone to talk to."

When Liebenzeller was gone, Samuel locked the receipt in his strongbox and asked Vogel to tell Menachem that he was leaving for Metz that same day. Then he put on his pointed hat, the distinctive sign of German Jews, and went to ask his younger brother Nathan for his opinion.

Nathan the scribe lived near the building known as the "Jewish bath," which also contained the synagogue. Thin, ascetic, his face illuminated by big green eyes, he devoted all his strength and time to study. He was surprised by his brother's arrival.

"May the Almighty, blessed be He, protect you. What brings you here, Samuel?"

"News. And I need advice."

"I'll do what I can. Come in and sit down."

Samuel told him about Reinbold Liebenzeller's visit.

"You don't need advice!" said Nathan.

"Why not?"

"Because advice is useful before a decision, not after it, and you've already made your decision. All we can do now is pray that the burghers will defeat the bishop. If they win, I think that a man like Liebenzeller may become an important support for the community."

"We've already placed that same hope in so many noblemen!"

"Remember this text: 'Man strikes many coins with a single stamp, and they are all alike, but the Holy One, blessed be He, strikes all men with the stamp of Adam, and not one is like another.' "

"Yet they all kill, rob, and persecute us," Samuel replied bitterly.

"Imagine what it would be like if all men weren't descended from the same man and didn't have the feeling of committing fratricide, like Cain, when they killed a fellow man! So let's thank the Almighty for having created us in His image. Let's also thank Him for having preserved us from evil here in Strasbourg, till now. Aren't we much better off than our brothers in Paris, Troyes, and Mainz?" Nathan stood up, pulled his *tzitzit*, the woolen fringes attached to his garment, and said cheerfully, "Do you know that Rachel, my son Elijah's wife, is about to give birth? It will be my first grandson."

"And what if it's a girl?"

Samuel did not yet have a grandson. His older son Menachem had just lost a child for the third time, and his younger son Isaac only had two daughters. For reasons that escaped him, he found it abnormal that his younger brother should hope to be the first to have that blessing of the Almighty: a grandson.

But that was what happened. Rachel gave birth to Chaim, and Samuel had to wait two years before Bella, Menachem's wife, finally gave birth to a boy, a fine, robust boy who suckled like two babies and bawled like four. He was named Mosselin.

The war between the bishop and the burghers of Strasbourg,

who had equipped their army partly with the money lent by Samuel, had not yet ended, and although winter had delayed battle between the two sides, it had not cooled their ardor.

On the day in March 1262 when Samuel's grandson was born, his younger son Isaac rode off to join a small group of volunteers who were going to try to destroy the steeple of Mundelsheim, which served as an observation post for the bishop's soldiers and enabled them to keep watch on the road from Strasbourg to Haguenau. Samuel had tried to dissuade his son from enrolling in the army, but the Jews had to supply soldiers to the commune and Isaac did not want to be accused of shirking.

The group was composed of about a hundred men, followed by sappers. They were spotted by the lookouts in the steeple, who gave the alarm. Bells were rung in all the villages of the plain, mobilizing knights and foot soldiers. A few men, Isaac among them, were ordered to go back and inform the council that the bishop's army was assembling.

In the past two years the same maneuvers had been repeated a dozen times, with Bishop Gautier watching from the high ground of Musau while the burghers' troops deployed their banners on the Hausbergen hills. But this time, misled by his adversaries' detour to avoid the trench between Ober and Mittelhausbergen, the bishop thought they were falling back. Hoping to take them from the rear, he rode off at the head of his horsemen without waiting for the bulk of his foot soldiers.

But the burghers turned and stood fast. A battle began. The two sides were more or less evenly matched until the city's last troops, commanded by Nikolaus Zorn the elder, arrived as reinforcements. The bishop's foot soldiers then drew their bows. A thick black cloud hissed across the sky. "Arrows!" someone shouted near Isaac. The knights held their shields over their heads. Isaac felt a sharp, burning pain at the junction of his neck and his shoulder. He touched the place with his hand: blood. His sight dimmed and he had to make an effort to keep from sliding off his horse.

Berthold the carpenter took him back to the city. His wife Mina sent for Samuel and the doctor, Süskind. With the other men of the community, they had been praying in the synagogue since morning. While she waited for them, Mina cut away Isaac's clothes around the arrow.

Süskind, who was always humming—even when someone was talking to him, even when he was operating—pulled out the arrow without seeming to have any idea that it might hurt. He then cut an X across the wound, poured plum brandy over it, and, seeing that Isaac was about to faint, held the bottle to his pale lips.

"Will he live?" asked Samuel.

"If the Almighty decides that he'll live, then he'll live!"

Night had fallen when Ellenhardt, treasurer of the Brotherhood of Our Lady, who had been sent by Reinbold Liebenzeller, came to ask about Isaac's condition and tell how the bishop had finally been defeated after having two horses killed under him. He had been able to flee under the protection of a few knights. About sixty enemy knights and noblemen had been killed and stripped of their clothes on the battlefield.

The commune of Strasbourg had won. It was in a free city that Isaac recovered from his wound and little Mosselin spent his childhood.

MOSSELIN WAS nine years old when he failed to come home one evening. This had never happened before. His mother quickly became alarmed and sent for her husband Menachem. He hurried to the palace of the Müllenheims, where Mosselin often went to play with little Rudolf, who was also nine.

The Müllenheims were one of the most powerful families in Strasbourg, and one of the most influential in the council. Their palace stood at the corner of Sand Street and the Street of Scriveners, a hundred paces from the Jewish quarter. One day Rudolf had slipped away from the servants taking care of him and fallen into the Ill River. Mosselin, who had been playing nearby, had saved him by holding out to him the stick that served as his sword. Hugo Müllenheim, Rudolf's father, had been overwhelmed with gratitude and sworn that as long as Mosselin lived he would always be welcome in the palace. From then on, Mosselin had often gone there to play, and Rudolf's servants had always sent him home at supper time.

And so, that evening, Menachem went straight to the palace. Yes, he was told, Mosselin had come there, but he had left at the usual time. After going back home and learning that Mosselin had still not come, Menachem returned to the palace. Hugo Müllenheim placed ten men at his disposal to search the banks of the Ill and the thickets beside them. Menachem then ran—he had to hurry because night was falling—to the synagogue, where he found a few young men willing to help him and a few men too old to run;

the latter began praying. Samuel, who was also there, promised to fast until his only grandson returned.

Darkness came. No trace of Mosselin had been found. Nothing in the morning, still nothing by the following night. Had he fallen into the Ill? Had the current carried away his little body without its being seen by the tanners, weavers, and dye makers?

Bella stayed at home, with the women of her family and the neighborhood doing what they could to sustain and comfort her. Menachem went back to all the places where he had gone the day before, thinking that maybe . . . Samuel fasted and prayed. For two days Nathan the scribe, Mosselin's granduncle, went to the streets and markets where women gossiped and men stopped after work. He repeated Mosselin's description everywhere: at Saint Peter the Elder, behind the Franciscan monastery, on the Street of Locksmiths, at Under Metzingern. With his tall, gaunt body, his long arms, and his green eyes, he was one of those strange and somewhat fascinating personages who make others feel that they have always known them.

No one could give Nathan any information but he was not discouraged: God did not abandon seekers; even Adam did not know if the time of his travail would be reckoned according to human time or the time of God, in which one day is a thousand human years.

On the third day a boy came to him, asked him to follow him, and led him in the direction of the slaughterhouse. They walked under the vast awning of the butchers' open-air stalls, passed the Herring Fountain, and went down to the ancient Roman ditch, now a veritable cesspool that received all the sewage of the quarter. There, the boy turned and ran away.

Nathan remained alone with clouds of flies. It was a disquieting place but he was not worried. Soon he saw a butcher's helper coming toward him, wiping his bloody hands on his already reddened apron. He had a round head and a pale face.

"Is this the first time you've ever come to Albergrien?" he asked in a hoarse voice, after looking around to make sure no one was watching them. Then, evidently feeling that he had spent enough time on polite conversation, he said, "I know where the child is. How much will you pay?"

"There is no more just reward than the satisfaction of having done a good deed," replied Nathan. "Having said that, I'll ask you how much you want." He reached under his belt and took out three coins. "Here's a heller, and another heller, and a river. That's all I have on me."

"It will do."

Nathan did not press him. Flies were clustering on the abominable apron and the stench of the cesspool was overpowering, but Nathan, in his long gray tunic, seemed calm and patient.

"Once a week," said the man, "I take meat to the Hangman's Tower. This morning I went there as usual and I came to the postern gate at the same time as Gerhardt, the priest of Saint Martin. While we were waiting for the guards to raise the portcullis, we talked a little. He said he'd come to baptize a Jewish child. There, I've told you what I know."

"Bless you, butcher, bless you!"

Nathan walked away with long strides, his loose tunic fluttering like a pair of wings. Without informing Samuel and Menachem of what he had learned, he went to see Ellenhardt, treasurer of the Brotherhood of Our Lady, who had come to ask about Isaac during the battle against the bishop. Nathan had been on good terms with him since then.

Ellenhardt knew about Mosselin's disappearance but he could not believe there had been any kind of foul play. He and Nathan went to look for Gerhardt, the priest.

In front of the chapel of Saint Martin, where Nathan waited for Ellenhardt, the money changers were clearing their tables. When the bells rang for vespers, the square quickly emptied. Finally Ellenhardt came back, with the look of someone who had important news to tell.

"I believe that child is your Mosselin," he said. "And I believe I know why he's in the Hangman's Tower." He took Nathan by the elbow. "Your Mosselin is a friend of the Müllenheims' heir, isn't he?"

"Yes. He often goes to the palace to play with him."

Ellenhardt nodded.

"Just as I thought. If a child who's in your care disappears, you'll be responsible, won't you? And if that child is initiated into another religion, who will be accused? You will. Now, who has a reason for wanting to harm the Müllenheims? If you can find that out, you can guess who abducted your Mosselin. Good luck, my dear Nathan. May the Almighty help you!"

Nathan hurried to Samuel's house, where the whole family had gathered. Samuel himself was sitting motionless in his usual place,

311

leaning against the high back of his chair. On the table in front of him was the Scroll of Abraham. It was Nathan who, being a scribe, periodically brought it up to date, but Samuel kept it in his strongbox. Menachem and Bella, standing beside each other, were livid.

"Thanks to the Almighty, blessed be He, Mosselin is alive!" Nathan announced when he came in.

He described everything that had happened and ended with Ellenhardt's question. Who had a reason for wanting to harm the Müllenheims? He knew the answer perfectly well, as did Ellenhardt and everyone else in the city: the Zorn family. Nikolaus Zorn, the patriarch, known as Zorn the elder, was a stubborn, irascible man. He had posted spies to watch the Müllenheims' palace and try to discover something that could be used against them. He had thus learned about Mosselin's frequent visits to Rudolf Müllenheim, and before the city council he had accused his adversaries of being dependent on Jewish money. With his morbid jealousy, he was quite capable of having conceived the devious idea of using Mosselin to bring the Müllenheims into disrepute.

"That old Zorn follows the path of the devil!" said Nathan, summing up the others' thoughts.

"What can we do?" asked Menachem, torn between the joy of knowing his son was alive and the anguish of being unable to rescue him.

"I don't know," replied Nathan. "May the Holy One, blessed be He, protect us."

He turned to Samuel, who sat with his lips pressed tightly together.

"Every course of action that I can imagine," the banker finally said in a toneless voice, "would be ineffective and dangerous: meeting with Zorn, placing the matter before the council, asking the Müllenheims for help. They have Mosselin as a hostage, we mustn't forget that. If they demanded a ransom. . . . But money doesn't disarm hatred."

"But we can't just stay here and do nothing!" exclaimed Menachem.

His wife Bella wrung her hands. After several moments of silence, Nathan spoke abruptly, with unshakable determination in his green eyes.

"Mosselin will come back to us, safe and sound," he said.

"What makes you so sure of that?" asked Menachem.

"My faith."

312

* * *

WHEN HUGO MÜLLENHEIM LEARNED that Nikolaus Zorn was holding Mosselin in confinement, he made it his personal concern and, as Samuel had feared, sent his men to surround the Hangman's Tower. One of them killed one of Zorn's guards with a crossbow. Zorn immediately sent word to Hugo Müllenheim that any attempt to storm the tower would result in the child's death.

Samuel left his house—it was his fourth day of fasting and he felt a little light-headed—and went to see Reinbold Liebenzeller. The enormous patrician had gained even more weight and width. He stood with his back to the gigantic fireplace, in which a thick log was burning. His massive legs were like two tree trunks and he gave the impression that nothing on earth could uproot him.

"What do you want me to do, for God's sake?" he thundered. "The council is divided exactly in two. And Zorn is my friend, and so is Müllenheim! And you too, Jew, you're my friend! Have I ever failed you in the whole time we've known each other?"

"No, maybe because I've never asked you to do anything for me."

"You still have your sense of humor, Jew!"

"Herr Liebenzeller, I'd like you to call a meeting of the council."

"Why? To make war break out in the meeting hall?"

"Call a meeting, Herr Liebenzeller, and announce that I'll cancel the debt the council has owed me for the last ten years if my grandson is brought back before tonight."

The patrician stood for a moment with his mouth open and his arms hanging at his sides.

"You'll give up two thousand marks?"

"Yes."

"And the ten years' interest on it?"

"Yes."

"By God, Jew, you're not the kind of man I thought you were! For two thousand marks, the councilors would make the devil himself listen to reason!"

The council meeting lasted all afternoon. During that time, Müllenheim continued bringing men and weapons to the moats that protected the Hangman's Tower. Isaac ran back and forth between the tower and the council.

Müllenheim's men had already succeeded in putting together a pontoon bridge when two municipal horsemen arrived. One of them blew a trumpet and the other ordered the men, in the name

313

of the council of the commune of Strasbourg, to lay down their arms.

REINBOLD LIEBENZELLER laboriously climbed the wooden stairs. Samuel stood up to greet him but kept his pointed hat on his head. His cheeks were sunken and he felt very weak.

Despite his puffing and wheezing, Liebenzeller was beaming with self-satisfaction.

"By God, I kept my word!" he said, tossing his red gloves onto the table. "And it wasn't easy, believe me!" He sat down heavily on the bench, which bent but luckily did not break. "You should have heard me talking about your grandson, my dear Samuel!"

"You forgot to invite me, Herr Liebenzeller."

The patrician guffawed.

"I've always said you had a great sense of humor, Jew!" He loudly slapped his thighs and pulled on a cord to open his green velvet cloak. "Do you know the main complaint that old Zorn made about the Müllenheims?"

"No."

"As you know, their palace is near the town hall: he said they've been taking advantage of that fact to scheme against him. And do you know what we decided?"

"No."

"To build a new town hall, halfway between the two palaces. And do you know what Zorn demanded?"

"No."

"He said there would have to be two separate staircases: one on the north side for him, and one on the south side for the Müllenheims!"

Evening shadows were invading the room. For a few moments, hunger stopped tormenting Samuel. He felt an airy lightness and deep inner peace, but there was still room in his mind for the bitter conviction that people were not yet anywhere near being able to live together.

"And what about the money?" he asked.

"The money? Ah, yes, the money! The council accepted your proposal."

"For the interest too?"

"Of course. Isn't that what we agreed on?"

"Yes," replied Samuel.

"In exchange, your grandson has been returned to his parents."

"That's true."

"And his baptism will be annulled, since that's what you want. So everything has turned out well."

"That's true."

Reinbold Liebenzeller noisily cleared his throat, spat into the fireplace, and stood up, seeming to fill the room.

"Don't forget the receipt I signed for you," he said.

Samuel turned around, opened his strongbox, and took out a rolled sheet of parchment tied with a red string.

"Here it is, Herr Liebenzeller."

The patrician put on his gloves.

"What are you going to do now?" he asked.

"Say the evening prayer."

24

STRASBOURG

Ziporia's Victory

THE CENTURY was drawing to a close, as though for the end of the world. A book, the Zohar, had come to Strasbourg. It was said to have been written in Galilee by Simeon bar Yochai, a famous second-century rabbi, but many believed it to be the work of Moses of León, whom a distant cousin of Samuel and Nathan had recently met in Cordova. The Zohar, or Book of Splendors, dealt with mysteries in the Bible and the hidden meanings of the Law and divine revelation. It immediately gave rise to impassioned discussions within all Jewish communities. In Strasbourg these discussions were made even more ardent by the arrival of Moses of Turckheim, a merchant who claimed to have been told by a Jewish pilgrim coming from Jerusalem and Acre, where he had visited Rabbi Yechiel's great school, that many signs announcing the Messiah and liberation had recently been observed there.

Signs were also abundant in the West. In Troyes, for example, a Jew, Isaac the castellan, was accused of having killed a young Christian—a "ritual murder," said the Dominicans, who proceeded to burn thirteen Jews. In Strasbourg, Löwe the *shammash* had a simpleminded daughter named Güttelin, who at the age of twenty had seldom been heard to speak. One *shabbat,* at the end of services in the synagogue, she cried out, "Woe unto you! Find your salvation before it is too late!" The next day there was a crowd of visitors in front of Löwe's house. He took his daughter, dressed as though for a wedding, to the meeting hall next to the synagogue, opposite the building of the carpenters' guild. She was questioned as if she were an oracle, several people who had open sores asked her to touch them, and Löwe had to have her protected by a group of husky young men.

Then one evening Hirtz the hunchback, a beggar who for a long time had seemed to have taken root in front of the synagogue, left his usual place, went inside, and said excitedly that he too heard the *shofar* announcing the Messiah. People gathered around him. Trembling, he stared at a bare wall and said he saw a chariot of fire coming toward him, the same one that had carried away Elijah. He trembled more and more violently, then fell as if he had been struck by lightning. It took a bucket of water to bring him back to his senses.

Then it was learned that Rabbi Meir of Rothenburg, spiritual leader of the German Jews and a disciple of Rabbi Yechiel of Jerusalem, was going to Palestine. Dozens of families decided to go with him. They set off as the Christians had done two hundred years earlier, behind Peter the Hermit. But they did not reach Jerusalem: not wanting to lose his Jews and the profit he drew from them, Rudolf of Hapsburg sent his soldiers to catch up with them and bring them back home. When Rabbi Meir said he was going to leave again, Rudolf ordered that he be confined in the Ensisheim fortress until the end of the world that he was announcing—unless a ransom of fifteen hundred marks was paid for his release. The Jewish communities of Alsace joined together to raise the money. Since Samuel the banker was now too old to travel, Menachem and Mosselin assembled the large sum, whereupon Rabbi Meir declared that he refused to be ransomed, because he wanted to discourage what was nothing but a form of banditry.

Meanwhile Löwe the *shammash* had decided to have his daughter Güttelin marry Hirtz the hunchback, so that their prophetic strength would be doubled. Güttelin, who now sang hymns in languages she had never learned, was delighted, and the wedding took place a week later. Money donated by the community enabled the newlyweds to move into a little house at one end of the Street of Jews. But the money was misspent and the community's hopes were disappointed, because Güttelin and Hirtz, completely absorbed in their marital bliss, stopped having visions.

317

Old Samuel, shrunken by age, so that his high-backed oak chair now seemed even larger when he sat in it, was deeply affected by these happenings. As he had done at the time of Mosselin's disappearance, he undertook a fast of purification and expiation.

"If the Messiah will soon be here," he said, "I may as well take part in his coming."

His brother Nathan's long body had become as gnarled and twisted as the trunk of an old olive tree; only his green eyes remained unchanged. He did not believe in the imminent coming of the Messiah.

"The Messiah," he said gruffly, "won't come furtively, like a thief in the night! He'll announce himself to the world, and the world will recognize Him with blinding clarity!"

Samuel did not withstand the strain of his fast very long. Just before he died, he gave his son Menachem the key to his strongbox and asked him to come closer.

"My son," he said to him, "do you know the first question asked of someone who appears before the tribunal of the Almighty? It's 'Have you been honest in your transactions?' Never forget, my son, that Jerusalem was destroyed because honest people had disappeared from within its walls."

His brother Nathan scarcely had time to record his death in the Scroll of Abraham, writing with an unsteady hand, before he himself gave up the ghost. Their respective ages were seventy-seven and seventy-six.

Ten years later, the Messiah still had not appeared, but the Almighty showed His people that He had not forgotten them. A fire ravaged Strasbourg, destroying the Street of Drapers, the Street of Halberds, the fish market, and part of the great arcade. The immense cathedral narrowly escaped destruction. It had been under construction for more than a hundred years, and Erwin of Steinbach, aided by his son and his daughter, had undertaken to give it an openwork stone spire that would be unequaled anywhere in the West. The Christians of Strasbourg had been so afraid for the cathedral—some of the scaffoldings had caught fire!—that they immediately thought of attributing the fire to the malevolence of the Jews. Luckily Rudolf Müllenheim, whom Mosselin had once saved from drowning and who was now an important member of the city council, was able to have an investigation conducted, and the man responsible for the fire was discovered: he was a stableman who had left a lighted candle in the stable of the Kalkenkeller inn. And so, for the fast of Tishah B'Av in the year 5058 [1298] after the creation of the world, the Jews mourned their exile, but they also thanked the Holy One, blessed be He, the God of mercy, for keeping them under His protection.

MOSSELIN HAD MARRIED Ziporia, who had given him three daughters in succession and then, when he had lost hope, a son, whom he named Samuel-Elijah in memory of his grandfather.

At the death of his father Menachem, Mosselin received the key to Samuel's strongbox. He took over the table and the high-backed chair on the second floor, where Samuel had spent so much of his time. It was a favorable period for bankers. The council had decided to build a wall and a moat around the new quarters. Patricians borrowed a great deal so that they could imitate princes, and craftsmen borrowed a great deal so that they could imitate patricians; as for the poor, they were always a pfennig short of being able to wait till they received their next wages. Trade in money was flourishing. Mosselin hired two clerks.

Suddenly a wave of refugees burst into the city. The Jews had been expelled from France by King Philip the Fair, who confiscated their property and demanded that the money owed to them be paid to him instead. Some of them went to the Rhineland, others to Spain. The Narbonne branch of the family split up; some joined their Spanish relatives in Cordova, some went to North Africa, where they had relatives in Hippo and Kairouan, and two students accompanied Rabbi Estori Parhi, a geographer, to the banks of the Jordan. The Troyes branch came to stay with Mosselin and his cousin Chaim the scribe. Their houses were filled with dejected men, weeping women, and noisy children excited by the change.

The *parnasim* decided that the community would take care of the refugees and give them work. Community taxes and contributions were increased. Mosselin did not complain; he could afford it, thank the Almighty.

One day he received a visit from Ammeister Wilhelm, the guild leader. Wilhelm, a carpenter, was a crude man who had been chosen for his position more because of his violent character than because of his perspicacity. He climbed the staircase as if it were a scaling ladder, and Heimon, the clerk, was reluctant to leave him alone with Mosselin. But Mosselin smiled, invited Ammeister Wilhelm to have a seat, and asked him why he had come. For a moment, Wilhelm seemed disconcerted at having no pretext for launching an attack. His gnarled fingers clutched the arms of his chair.

"Banker," he said, "we need you."

"For what?"

"For your money."

"That's usually why people come to see me. But who is 'we'?"

"The craftsmen."

"Why do the craftsmen need money? Aren't the guilds rich enough?"

Wilhelm tightened his grip on the arms of his chair. Mosselin noticed that everything about him was angular: shoulders, knees, chin.

"The guilds are rich," Wilhelm said in a restrained voice, "but not rich enough to oppose the patricians."

"Oppose them? Are you going to make war on them?"

"No. But we want to share their power."

"You won't do it without war."

Wilhelm leapt to his feet and leaned across the table, behind which Mosselin sat impassively with his hands folded.

"That's none of your business, Jew!"

"You still won't do it without war."

Wilhelm picked up a wooden ruler and broke it in half, as if it were Mosselin.

"We want money. Will you lend it to us or not?"

"Yes, but . . ."

"You can ask me for security, Jew, but you can't ask me what I intend to do with the money!"

"And what security will you give me?"

"The dues of the guilds."

"Who will sign the receipt?"

"I will."

"How much do you need?"

"Fifteen hundred marks."

"That's a large sum. I don't have it in my possession."

"You belong to an association. . . ."

"It takes time."

Banking was a demanding occupation, Mosselin thought calmly. He had enough experience to know that although his transactions followed a kind of ritual, each case was different from the others. And while he had not yet tried to foresee the difficulties that

320

awaited him this time, he already knew that he would not come out of the operation unscathed.

"We have no time!" Wilhelm said belligerently.

Mosselin took a sheet of parchment, dipped his pen in ink, and wrote a few figures. He could not refuse to lend money to the guilds, but he did not want to help them fight the patricians: among the patricians were his friend Rudolf and old Liebenzeller, to whom the Jews owed a great deal.

On another sheet, he wrote the text of a receipt.

"Have this signed by your amtman, then come back this evening and sign it yourself. I'll give you half of the amount you want this evening, and the rest later."

"Thank you, banker," said Wilhelm, making it sound like a threat. "You won't lose anything by helping us!"

When Wilhelm had left, Mosselin closed his eyes, suddenly weary. It was true that the patricians behaved unjustly and arrogantly toward the population and that the guilds were closed to Jews, but how was he to choose between those who had power and those who might soon have it?

Whom could he ask for advice? Ziporia, his wife, was at the market. His clerks? They would not understand his dilemma. The members of the community council? There were too many of them; they were always chattering and could not keep a secret. He put on his pointed hat, went downstairs, and hurried to the house of his cousin Chaim, Nathan's grandson. Although he did not know banking, Chaim knew the Scriptures, and he had given Mosselin good advice in the past.

"Baruch haba!" said Chaim the scribe, opening the door.

He led Mosselin to the small attic room, full of books and scrolls, where he worked. This was his refuge, his citadel. Mosselin had come there once before and Chaim had shown him the Scroll of Abraham, which he kept in a strongbox with other precious writings. What certainties, what peace! For a moment he envied Chaim. Then he told him about the craftsmen's request for a loan and asked him what he should do. Chaim—as tall and thin as his grandfather, with a high forehead and hands that were always in motion, like butterflies—did not think very long before giving his answer.

"You must do both," he said.

"Both? What do you mean?"

"Give the money to Ammeister Wilhelm and tell Rudolf Müllenheim about it."

"Do you think that's very . . . ethical?"

The butterflies fluttered.

"I think our situation is very sad. We owe our friendship to those who have given us theirs, but we must also be prepared for change: if we refused to help the craftsmen and they took power, our community would be swept away by the flood. . . ."

"The flood?"

"The sages say that when God said to Noah, 'Make yourself an ark of gopher wood,' Noah planted cypress trees. 'What are you going to do with those cypress trees?' Noah was asked, and he answered, 'The Holy One, blessed be He, is going to cause a flood to cover the earth and He told me to save myself and my family by building an ark.' Everyone laughed at him but he went on watering his cypress trees. When he judged that they were big enough, he cut them down and sawed them into planks. 'What are you doing?' he was asked. He repeated the warning but no one believed him. And so God decided to cause the flood."

"But we'll be accused of playing a double game."

"No, we won't—not if you're the one who lends money to the craftsmen and I'm the one who tells the patricians about it."

"That's a strange way of building our ark!"

AT THE END of May in the year 1308 by the Christian calendar, on the day after Ascension Day, a troop of armed craftsmen attacked the tavern in which the patricians had gathered. But the patricians were expecting them. The battle lasted all night. Sixteen craftsmen were killed. Calm returned to the city.

Mosselin and Chaim had not seen each other again. But on the following Yom Kippur they both wept bitterly, each in his own house, when they said the ritual words "Lord, our God, forgive the sin that we have committed before You, either under constraint or freely, and the sin that we have committed before You out of the hardness of our hearts."

FOUR YEARS LATER an unknown disease swept over Strasbourg. Chaim was among the first to contract it. His sons Vifelin and Marx called in Babel the healer but he said there was nothing he could do. Neighbors brought herbs guaranteed to be from Palestine. Bayle, Chaim's wife, boiled them and gave him the decoction

322

to drink. He swallowed the hot, bitter liquid and vomited blood. In desperation, Bayle sent for Güttelin and Hirtz; although they had long since stopped having visions, they were said to be still able to work miracles. But there was no miracle. Vifelin called on Mosselin for help. Mosselin went to Chaim's house with Philip Baumhauer, a doctor who had studied in Paris, but the disease was unlike any that Baumhauer had ever encountered before and he merely advised purifying the air around the patient by burning balsamic essences.

Later, no one could explain how an incense burner had overturned and set fire to the rug. When Mosselin arrived, the house was already burning. Vifelin and Marx had just carried their father's body out of it. Bayle was weeping in the arms of the woman who lived next door. Men were passing buckets of water to each other.

Mosselin suddenly thought of the strongbox containing the Scroll of Abraham, in the attic room. He looked around for Vifelin and Marx but did not see them. Flames were licking at the half-timbered façade. He rushed into the house and felt a hot breath on his face. With his heart pounding, he ran up the stairs. The little room that had been Chaim's haven and ivory tower had not changed, with its smell of ink and parchment and its light from the sky. He picked up the strongbox and tried to go back down the stairs, but the flames had already begun climbing them. He opened the overhead window and lifted the strongbox with an effort. It was too wide to go through the window. The heat in the room was now overpowering. The house was cracking, the fire was roaring. He noticed a velvet curtain, pulled it down, threw the manuscripts from the strongbox into it, tied it into a bundle, and pushed it through the window. The door was beginning to burn when he climbed out onto the roof.

MOSSELIN LIVED seven more years. Seven years that he spent in his bed with his body like dead wood and his mind alert, wondering whether or not he and Chaim had been punished by the Almighty.

His three daughters were married. His son Samuel-Elijah, called Samueli, would soon be twenty and was studying at the *yeshiva*. In the evening he helped his mother Ziporia to put the bank's accounts in order. The frail, discreet Ziporia was firmly in control of the household. She took care of her helpless husband, received clients, and made decisions both quickly and well; she sometimes asked Mosselin for advice but he realized that she did it only out of charity.

Like dead wood. Only his eyes moved, and no one but Ziporia could understand what he was trying to make them express. Every day she came to tell him the news of the world. When the king of France, Louis, successor of Philip the Fair—cursed be his name!—allowed the Jews to return to France and gave them back their houses, synagogues, and cemeteries, all of which was done at his people's request, Ziporia recited to Mosselin a poem written by a man named Geoffroi:

> *Poor people are all complaining,*
> *For in business dealings*
> *The Jews were much more tenderhearted*
> *Than the Christians are now!*

Like dead wood. A fly alighted on Mosselin's forehead. He felt it walking, stopping, walking, and could do nothing to escape from what was becoming a kind of torture. Why these sufferings? he wondered. What am I—I who can do nothing against a fly? He had often heard people say in his presence that the worst life was better than the best death, but did those kind souls know what he endured as he lay there like a stick?

A kind of cramp seized his stomach. It became more violent and he could not hold back his excrement. He would now have to wait for the maidservant to come in and wash him like a newborn baby. The humiliation was new each time. He closed his eyes. Perhaps because it was such a beautiful day outside, he wanted to die.

As soon as Ziporia came into the room, she knew that Mosselin was no longer alive. She screamed, then fainted.

"LADY," said Ammeister Ruhlmann Schwarber, "I've come to borrow money."

Straight and thin, her face white beneath her white wimple, Ziporia looked at the man in front of her, on the other side of the table. Everything about him was average, anonymous, unobtrusive, almost blurred, except for his intensely blue eyes. For the moment, he did not know where to look. Ziporia was used to that. Men did not like having to talk about money with a woman.

"Lending money is my occupation," she said.

"My predecessor," said Ruhlmann Schwarber, "once borrowed some in this same house."

"That was twenty-three years ago, Herr Schwarber. And the money wasn't very useful to you."

"We paid it back to the last pfennig, didn't we?"

"How much do you need?"

"Two thousand. Two thousand marks."

"That's a sizable amount. Your predecessor only asked for fifteen hundred."

This man, with his blue eyes like windows opening onto the sky, seemed trustworthy to Ziporia. Perhaps he sensed it.

"Lady, you're the only one who can help us quickly."

She did not hesitate. She would have liked to consult her son Samueli, but she said, "You'll have your money, Herr Schwarber. Tomorrow evening. Bring me the signatures of the amtman and the meister. I assume that the security is the dues of the guilds."

Ruhlmann Schwarber was delighted. This woman knew what she wanted. He blinked his eyes like an owl.

A few moments after he left, Samueli came in.

"I just saw Schwarber leaving the house," he said. "What did he want?"

"Money, of course."

"Do they want to fight the patricians again?"

"I suppose so."

"Shall we tell the patricians?"

"Why should we? Liebenzeller and Rudolf Müllenheim are dead, may their souls rest in peace. Their successors don't know us. Have they ever helped us? Have they ever done us any good? We owe them nothing."

"And the guilds?"

"I can see, my son, that the time has come when the men of the guilds are going to take power. For once, let's bet on the winning side."

Samueli had total confidence in his mother's judgment.

"Shall we tell the *parnasim?*"

"No. They couldn't keep it to themselves. We'll tell only Rabbi Gumbrecht, and ask him not to repeat it to anyone." She made a short gesture with her bony hand, as though brushing aside a matter of no importance. "How is your son Jacob?"

"He's preparing for his *bar mitzvah.* The rabbi is very proud of him."

Only then did Ziporia smile, and she suddenly seemed disarmed, completely vulnerable—a grandmother.

BEFORE RUHLMANN SCHWARBER'S CRAFTSMEN launched their attack, Louis of Bavaria announced that he was taking the Jews of Strasbourg under his personal protection and guaranteeing their rights and property, in exchange for an annual tax of sixty marks. Most of the influential members of the Jewish community rejoiced. "Now we have nothing to fear from either side," they said. "Nothing except . . ."

Less than a year later the emperor simply sold the contract to his vassals, the counts of Oettingen, for seven hundred marks—to be collected from the Jews themselves!

The law of the strongest, the most cynical, and the most unjust continued to prevail when, on May 20, 1332, by the Christian calendar, the patricians of the city council and their families gathered for a banquet in the garden of a house belonging to a patrician family, the Ochensteins, on the Burned Street. In the course of the banquet a quarrel broke out between two men, one a member of the Zorn faction, the other of the Müllenheim faction. Angry words led to blows, then to drawn swords. Other men joined the fight and it overflowed from the garden into the streets of the neighborhood. As night was falling, reinforcements rushed to the scene. Then the fighting spread all over the city. At dawn supporters of both sides, responding to urgent messages, poured in from the nearby towns and villages, and the result was carnage.

When the patricians paused to catch their breath, they discovered that the guild leaders had taken over the city hall and demanded that the mayor give them the seal, banner, and keys of the city. And it was the new council, headed by Ruhlmann Schwarber as acting mayor, that imposed peace on the patricians and disarmed them.

A few weeks later, in the middle of summer, the new council set about drawing up a new constitution, but first expelled from Strasbourg the patricians who had disrupted public order. For the inhabitants of the city it was the beginning of a new era in which each of them would supposedly be able to make his voice heard. And when the time came for the guilds to repay their loan, Ziporia refused to take any interest on it. This was, no doubt, her way of taking part in the change.

The new constitution was finally written. A date was set for its promulgation and for Ruhlmann Schwarber to be succeeded by the newly elected mayor, who was none other than his younger brother Berthold. On the day before that date, the council was notified that Jews who had fled from villages in the direction of Ruffach were asking for asylum in the city. Johann Zimberlin and his "leather arms," so called because they all wore a leather wristband in imitation of their leader, had been pursuing Jews, beheading those they could catch, burning houses, and ravaging vineyards.

The "leather arms" were abominable bandits, but those intent on killing, robbing, or expelling Jews never lack allies or justifications. Hatred of Jews is a smoldering fire that can be fanned into flames by any Zimberlin who comes along. In Strasbourg and elsewhere, Leather Arm encountered sympathizers, and it was clear to everyone that the new mayor would be judged by the way he settled the matter.

It was winter. Darkness had long since fallen when it appeared that a majority of the council members would vote against taking in the Jewish refugees. Ruhlmann Schwarber used the darkness and the snow that was beginning to fall as a pretext for suspending the discussion. The refugees would spend the night outside, under the ramparts, but that was a lesser evil. He ordered that hot drinks be given to them and went home with his two brothers.

The three of them closely resembled each other, with their round, nebulous faces and extraordinarily blue eyes, except that the second one was a head taller than the oldest, and the third was a head taller than the second. They shook the snow off their capes and sat down with their feet on the andirons to think over the situation.

The next morning was gray and cold. The snow had stopped but the streets were freezing. The delegations of the various guilds, dressed in black and preceded by their leaders dressed in white, took their places in the square in front of the cathedral, to the sound of fanfares. All around them was a cordon of armed troops. A large platform covered by a red-and-white canopy—the colors of Strasbourg—had been set up before the entrance of the cathedral. On it sat the members of the magistracy and representatives of the nobility. The cathedral bell rang and a bailiff dressed in red and white stepped forward to the edge of the platform.

"Honorable burghers," he said loudly, "approach and, in the name of God, listen. . . ."

Ruhlmann Schwarber was shivering under his cape. He glanced

327

at the unfinished cathedral spire, whose top was hidden by low clouds. When it was his turn to speak, he firmly read the text of the new constitution, then swore in the new mayor, his brother Berthold. The spectators fervently repeated his words, and it was to them that he addressed the end of his speech:

"May God give you prosperity, happiness, and long life!"

That same day, two criers read the first proclamation of the new council and mayor: "We, Mayor Berthold Schwarber and the council, hereby make known that we will take under our protection the German Jews requesting asylum in Strasbourg, as part of those who pay a thousand pounds for five years, if they consent to remit to us . . ."

For that was the solution devised by the three brothers: to present the arrival of those new Jews as an opportunity to make them pay part of the city's expenses.

Ziporia realized that the Schwarbers had found a way to pay her the interest she had refused to take.

JOHANN ZIMBERLIN AND HIS "leather arms" continued their ravages. They had come to the gates of Strasbourg, denounced the craftsmen for protecting the Jews, and sworn vengeance. Prompted by Berthold Schwarber, a number of cities—notably Strasbourg, Haguenau, Kolmar, Schlettstadt, Obernai, Mülhausen, and Neuerburg—agreed to wage war against the "leather arms," relentlessly pursue Zimberlin and his secondary leaders, and punish anyone who gave them asylum.

Louis of Bavaria, who had sold his "right" over the Jews, took them under his protection again and demanded in exchange that each of them, except for children under the age of thirteen, pay an additional tax of one florin per year.

It was at this time that Vifelin, son of Chaim the scribe and second cousin of Mosselin and Ziporia, was abducted. He was nearly sixty and had retired when his grandson Abraham took over his work with his son Matis. A man of vigorous temperament, he had taken little satisfaction in spending his time at a writing desk, leaning over parchments. He now took every chance to go out, visit friends, and improvise activities to fill his days between morning and evening prayer.

One day when Abraham was going to Haguenau to deliver some texts to Rabbi Meir, Vifelin decided to go with him. Near Truchtersheim they were waylaid by the "leather arms." Abraham spurred his horse and succeeded in escaping to go and bring help from Strasbourg.

Berthold Schwarber personally led the armed men who rode off toward Truchtersheim. By attacking two of the Strasbourg Jews under his protection, Zimberlin had openly defied him.

Long before the steeple of Truchtersheim came into view, Schwarber and his men saw smoke rising into the pale sky above the dark forest. They spurred their horses.

The stake had been set up in the church square. The man tied to it was alternately hidden and revealed as gusts of wind blew the high flames in different directions. Berthold Schwarber and his men made the crowd move aside and rode toward the fire until the heat became so intense that their horses refused to go any farther. The smell of burning flesh was already in the air when a powerful voice came from the flames.

"Curses on you! May the Almighty make all the plagues of Egypt fall on you with my ashes!"

Everyone in the crowd shuddered and quickly stepped back. Raindrops began falling, but it was too late.

THE FAMILY BEGAN *shiva,* the seven-day period of formal mourning. The neighbors, the *parnasim,* and even Jews from the environs sat on the floor, recalled memories of Vifelin, and sang psalms.

On the seventh day, with his tunic torn as a sign of mourning, and with ashes on his head, even though that ancient custom was now seldom observed, Matis opened his strongbox, took out the Scroll of Abraham—the papyruses and the book—and, swaying back and forth, read it while his listeners remained standing: ". . . may the names that I have written on this scroll, and the names that others will write on it after me, be spoken aloud. . . ."

When he had finished, he asked his sons Abraham and Moses to help him wrap the documents and put them back in place. He then had them carry the strongbox into the garden, where a hole had been dug under a tree.

"This story," Matis said gravely, "is our story. I have a presentiment that difficult times are coming. Only the Creator of the world, the all-powerful God of Israel, knows what lies in store for us. After consulting my brother Elijah and my uncle Samueli, I have decided to bury the strongbox here, so that our past will not be at the mercy of our enemies of today or tomorrow. You will know where to find it if, God forbid, misfortune should strike. The responsibility for continuing the story will then be yours."

He put on his prayer shawl and phylacteries and murmured, "O God, You have rejected and dispersed us, You have turned Your anger against us; restore us to Your favor!"

25

STRASBOURG

The Black Death

THE PLAGUE came from the East, aboard Genoese ships that put ashore dying crews and putrid cargoes infested with rats. Wherever it landed, life stopped: Haifa, Constantinople, Messina, Genoa, Marseille . . . Only the plague did not stop. Nothing stopped it.

The "leather arms" had been overcome. It had taken only the will and the means to combat them. They had been cruel bandits, but only cruel bandits, one scourge among so many others. The plague was different. It did not fear armed men, searches, ambushes, or even prayers and exorcisms. All efforts to ward it off—putting up barricades, filling moats, raising drawbridges, lowering portcullises, closing shutters, blocking windows—were futile. One day it was suddenly there, and horror followed.

IN STRASBOURG, it was on a sunny morning in August 1348, by the Christian calendar, that the marks of the plague were recognized on people who had died during the night. The city council had it announced in the streets, so that everyone could take whatever precautions were considered necessary, and asked that all suspicious deaths be reported at the city hall.

The people of Strasbourg were either stunned or panic-stricken.

331

Some of them piled a few belongings into a cart and fled—perhaps to a place where the plague was waiting for them. Others, who had nowhere to go, resigned themselves to staying at home and waiting for God's verdict. Matis could not make up his mind. His neighbor, Samuel of Marmoutier, a baker, left to join his wife's family in Rosheim. Should he come to a decision alone? Consult the members of his family at the risk of losing time? His son Moses, who was about to marry Esther, daughter of Rabbi Samuel of Weissenburg, would surely refuse to leave the city. Matis hesitated. Finally he put his prayer shawl over his head and shoulders, like a shield, and went to see his uncle Samueli the banker.

He was not the first to arrive. Aunts, cousins, and serious-eyed children were gathered around Samueli in the big room that contained his reckoning tables. Should they stay or leave? Joshua the *shammash* had died, and so had Levi the carpenter and his wife, and . . . They spoke in hushed voices: the plague was prowling in the city and they did not want to attract its attention. But where could they go? Little Elijah, Abraham's son, suddenly suggested Benfeld, simply because he wanted to see his cousin Jacob, son of Dyrel the butcher, who had come to visit for the last holiday. Benfeld was a long day's walking distance away, on the road to Schlettstadt. In everyone's name, Samueli thanked the Master of the world; it was known that He sometimes expressed Himself through the mouths of the innocent.

BENFELD HAD TWO CENTERS: the market and the church. With Dyrel's recommendation, Samueli was able to rent half of a high, narrow house: a kitchen, a bedroom with a fireplace, and a cellar. Thirty-one people had to squeeze into it, but it was better than nothing. The owner of the house, an ill-tempered man named Elward Mersvin, who was a member of the village council, did not ask if they were Jews or where they came from. Uncle Babel and his brood of children moved into Dyrel's house. Abraham, his mother Leah, and his wife Sarah shared the cellar with his brother Moses, who had left Strasbourg only because he could not bring himself to defy his father's authority.

A miniature Jewish community was implanted in Benfeld, near the market, with a little synagogue, a butcher, and a baker. The others, who seemed to be living on air, did whatever they could: one peddled trinkets, another borrowed here and lent there, another repaired carts at the owners' homes, even though Jews were

332

forbidden to practice manual trades. The Jews of Benfeld were well integrated into the life of the village, and perhaps the only thing that made the Christians laugh at them was the language they spoke: Yiddish, with its mixture of German and Hebrew words.

The inhabitants of Benfeld, both Christians and Jews, spent long hours praying. To the prayers and psalms, some young villagers added frenzied dances, filling themselves with "joyousness," as they put it, so that the plague could not enter into them. And the fact is that it did not come to Benfeld. It came to Matzenheim, five miles away, and killed dozens of people, but it stopped there.

Moses was filled with bitterness and sorrow at having left Esther, his beloved fiancée, in Strasbourg. What had become of her? It was as if he had been cut in half. How could his father not have understood? A rooster crowing, a dog barking, the church bell ringing for a new day—everything that gave evidence of life made him unhappy. One morning he could stand it no longer. He left the musty darkness of the cellar before dawn, slipped into the kitchen and took a piece of bread, tiptoed out of the house, walked across the deserted marketplace, and went to the postern gate.

"Who goes there?" asked the guard.

"I'm going to Strasbourg."

"Anyone who leaves doesn't come back, my friend!"

"I won't come back."

"Do you know what you're saying? Do you know what you're doing?"

"I won't come back."

"God keep you, then!"

The guard stepped aside and pulled the lever that lifted the portcullis. Moses went out. He heard the thud of the portcullis falling behind him.

STRASBOURG WAS GRIPPED by the silence of death. No ringing of anvils in blacksmiths' shops, no clamor from the marketplace, no shouts of men selling wine or trying to bring customers into inns, no braying of donkeys—only the tolling of the knell, the voices of crows, the rumble of carts loaded with corpses.

Moses came into a city with empty, abandoned streets and flapping shutters, and he realized that the plague was there. In the alleys, the air was foul with the stench of urine and vomit. Time seemed motionless in the thick summer heat.

At the corner of the Street of Jews and the Street of Virgins, where Esther lived, Moses encountered two men whose faces were hidden by hoods. They were knocking on doors and asking, "Are there any corpses here?" They looked at him through the narrow openings of their hoods, without speaking to him, and watched him till he had gone into Esther's house.

Semidarkness and closed shutters, a smell of incense and sickness.

"Esther?" he called out in a hollow voice.

He opened the shutters.

Esther was lying on the kitchen floor, near the table. Her long black hair had been cut. On her neck, just below her ear, he immediately saw a kind of blackish abscess. Her breathing was labored.

Moses fell to his knees, not knowing what to do and not daring to touch the woman he loved. He waved his hand to drive a fly away from his face, then he thought of Simon, son of Moses, a doctor who had studied at Montpellier and had been a friend of his grandfather Vifelin.

He ran out of the house and down the street. In front of the cathedral he stopped and listened. He heard shouting, singing, and moaning. In the square he saw several dozen people, naked to the waist, moving steadily in a circle and flagellating their already bleeding backs to call forth God's pity. Coming closer, he saw that small metal blades were attached to their whips. Around them, forming a wider circle, women were singing:

> Lord, help us by the blood
> You shed on the cross
> For our redemption. . . .

Moses turned into Perche Street, opposite the ramparts. Simon the doctor opened his door. He looked like a specter in his purple robe with a fur-lined hood. He was unsteady on his feet.

"Ah, it's you, Moses," he said in an infinitely weary voice. "Why have you come here, my boy?"

"Esther," replied Moses. "She's sick."

"We're all sick. We're all going to die."

Simon stumbled on the threshold and his pointed hat nearly fell off. He looked at the crimson disk of the sun just above the rooftops, blinked his eyes, and quoted from Jeremiah: "O that my head were waters, and my eyes a fountain of tears, that I might weep day and night for the slain of the daughter of my people!" He suddenly seemed to see Moses for the first time. "Ah, yes, you want me to treat Esther."

"Please."

"It's too late, my boy. May the Almighty, blessed be He, forgive me, but I'm already dead. I've done everything, tried everything, I wanted so much to save everyone. . . . But it wasn't the will of Him who sees everything. Look." He pulled his collar away from his neck and Moses recognized the same horrible blackish swelling that he had seen on Esther. "Go, my boy, and pray for me. If Esther is meant to recover, she'll recover. If she's meant to die, she'll die. We can do nothing against the divine will."

Moses fled. In front of the cathedral, the penitents were now lying on the ground, reddening the dust with their blood. Clouds of flies swirled above their bleeding wounds. The women were singing in unearthly voices:

> *Jesus was given gall to drink.*
> *Let us all fall to the ground*
> *With our arms outstretched*
> *To form a cross!*

At one end of the Street of Jews a cart drawn by two oxen stopped and hooded men began throwing bodies into it. The cathedral bell was tolling very slowly.

Esther had regained consciousness, gone to her bed, and lain down on it.

"It's you, Moses," she said as if she had been expecting him all that time.

"Yes, Esther. Is there anything I can bring you? Water? Would you like me to tell you a story?"

"We were going to be married, Moses. My father wouldn't let me go to you."

She held out her hand to him. He took it in his. Her eyes were bright with fever. She slowly drew his hand toward her and placed it over her breast. He was filled with sudden warmth.

"Lie down beside me," she said softly.

He hesitated.

"Lie down beside me," she repeated.

He took her in his arms and kissed her burning lips.

MOSES HEARD A knocking on the door and felt it inside his body. He tried to stand up, in vain.

"In the name of the mayor and the city council," cried a voice, "are there any corpses here?"

Moses wanted to answer. He opened his mouth but no sound came from it.

"Are there any corpses here?" the voice asked again.

Moses took a deep breath.

"Yes," he finally answered. "Yes."

IT WAS ESTIMATED that thirty-two thousand people died in Strasbourg between the middle of summer and the middle of winter. Thirty-two thousand people who died abominably and whose bodies were thrown into pits, without prayers or ceremonies. Thirty-two thousand deaths for which the survivors felt a need to hold someone responsible. A letter was brought to the mayor, who was then Konrad Kuntz. He read it with his two deputies, Goff Sturm and Peter Schwarber, youngest of the three Schwarber brothers and the only one who had survived.

The letter was signed by the consul of the city of Bern; he had sent the same letter to Basel and Cologne. He had proof, he wrote, that the Elders of Zion had met in Toledo long before the plague to elaborate a plot against Christendom. This plot had been carried out in Savoy, more specifically in the town of Chambéry, at the foot of the Alps, by the Jew Jacob Pascate, the Jew Fairatt, a rabbi, and the young Jew Aboget. They had invented a poison made of toads' feet, snakes' heads, women's hair, and wolves' semen. It was a kind of black, stinking liquid, horrible to smell and see. They had given it to a number of lepers and told them to drop it into wells and fountains. In Bern several Jews had confessed under torture.

The letter was read to the council by Mayor Konrad Kuntz.

"It's absurd!" exclaimed Peter Schwarber.

"Maybe, but where there's smoke there's fire," Hanselin Campser said slowly. "Let's at least hold an inquiry."

He was one of those men whose cleverness consists in seeming to state only obvious, commonplace truths, thus making themselves spokesmen for the majority.

Peter Schwarber opened his blue eyes wide and stared at him in amazement.

336

"But you know as well as I do that the plague was just as deadly to Jews as it was to Christians!"

"It's true that Jews died too. But who can say it wasn't a ruse?"

"A ruse?"

"I'm not saying it was a ruse, Herr Schwarber. To know whether it was or not, we'd need an inquiry. What I *am* saying is that if the consul of Bern is right—and I see no reason to doubt his accusations before we've held an inquiry—then having Jews die in the plague, along with Christians, would have been the best way to avert suspicion."

"By God and all the saints, that's madness!"

After a long debate, the council decided to seal off the public fountain and ask the survivors to take their water from the river. In Peter Schwarber's mind, this was a means of disarming everyone like Hanselin Campser. But Campser was easily able to insinuate that the reason for closing the fountain was that its water might have been poisoned. The next day, an angry crowd gathered in front of the town hall and the Jews had to be asked not to leave their quarter.

THE CHRISTIANS SPENT Christmas and Epiphany without festivities. Bishops and priests read from the pulpit a papal bull by Clement VI refuting the accusations made against the Jews. This prompted the often-repeated remark that the Jews must be very powerful, to have the pope in their service.

In Benfeld, Samueli and Matis received a letter from Peter Schwarber in which he told them about his apprehensions and, "in memory of Ziporia," urged them to leave the region. He suggested that they go to stay with his cousin Arnold, at Barr, on the bank of the Rhine, near Marckolsheim. Samueli and Matis did not hesitate. They packed their belongings and left that same day.

Not long afterward a large conference was held in Benfeld, attended by Swiss and Alsatian authorities, to decide whether or not the Jews had poisoned wells. Against Peter Schwarber's opposition, the conference recommended "the extermination of all Israelites in the cities, towns, and seigniories of the upper valley of the Rhine."

PETER SCHWARBER, to whom Mayor Konrad Kuntz had left the task of defending the Jews, was jeered when he returned to the city hall. "Schwarber the Jew!" he heard.

The council was convened. Hanselin Campser asked to speak and the mayor consented. With an affected air of simplicity, raising his eyebrows and showing the palms of his hands as though to prove that he was not concealing any bad intentions, Campser turned to Schwarber.

"The survivors in this city are angry with you, Schwarber! And with the rest of us too, because of you!"

Schwarber tried to keep calm.

"Didn't we guarantee the Jews that they would be safe in Strasbourg as long as they obeyed the laws of the city?"

"Yes, we did," Campser admitted readily. "But between that promise and today, we've had thousands of deaths and no family has been spared."

"A promise is a promise."

Just then shouts arose outside. A guard came in to announce that a delegation of craftsmen was asking to be heard. Feeling that the situation was going beyond his control, the mayor looked around at the councilors, silently asking them for advice, but they lowered their eyes.

"I'll see them downstairs with my deputies," he said.

Johann Botschold, leader of the butchers' guild and head of the delegation, had a mouth twisted by hatred.

"The council is protecting the Jews!" he said aggressively.

"The council," replied the mayor, "accepted the Jews' money, guaranteed their safety, and gave them letters of protection. You mustn't forget that, Herr Botschold."

"And what about the decision of the Benfeld conference?"

"Each city is free to accept it or reject it. That's precisely the question we were debating."

"You've all sold out to the Jews!" cried a tall, gaunt man standing behind the others.

"Be calm, my friends, be calm!"

"Jews! The Jews have bribed you! You're working for those sons of Satan!"

"Guards!" called the mayor.

The craftsmen left the city hall with the guards' halberds against their backs.

The mayor and his two deputies went back to the meeting hall of the council. The councilors were standing, looking embarrassed.

"What's happening here?" asked the mayor.

338

It was Albert Hutten, a jeweler known for his moderation, who answered. His chin was quivering.

"We've decided to go home," he said.

"Go home? But you're members of the city council. You've been elected. Your duty is to govern. Sit down and let's talk."

Albert Hutten looked in the direction of Hanselin Campser, who came to his rescue.

"You're right, it's our duty to govern the city," Campser said to the mayor, "and God knows we're trying. Govern it, yes, but not divide it."

"We don't want to divide it either, as you know very well. We're protecting citizens in danger."

"Forgive me, Mayor Kuntz, but nothing on earth could make me take part in a war of Christians fighting Christians because of Jews!"

Campser walked out and the other councilors followed him. Konrad Kuntz, Goff Sturm, and Peter Schwarber found themselves alone.

Albert Hutten, the jeweler, came back and stayed just long enough to plead, "Try to understand us! Don't hold it against us. . . ."

The mayor gave orders to reinforce the guards at the entrances of the city hall, then the three men tried to decide what to do. Should they assemble the Jews there in the city hall, which was easy to defend? How many of them were left now? Two thousand? Three thousand?

Standing at the window, Schwarber saw Bishop Berthold von Bucheck coming. He was a short man with long white hair under his skullcap, and lively eyes. He wasted no time on greetings.

"I have bad news for you," he said. "The patricians and the guilds are stirring up the crowd in front of the cathedral. They want to put the Jews on trial. They asked me to give them my blessing and I refused."

"Who's haranguing them?" asked the mayor.

"I saw mainly Nikolaus von Bulach and Gosso Engelbrecht. They were speaking in the name of the nobility."

"They're the ones who have borrowed most from Jewish bankers," remarked Schwarber.

"Johann Botschold, the butcher, also spoke," continued the bishop. "When I saw the councilors arrive without you, I understood. . . . I've come here in the hope that my presence may dissuade them from attacking the city hall."

The mayor shook his head.

"If they attack . . ." he began.

He did not finish his sentence. He no doubt meant to say that nothing worse could happen.

THAT EVENING the crowd surrounded the city hall. The guards defended it loyally. The bishop also fought and was wounded in the arm. Peter Schwarber was stabbed in the thigh.

The council was declared dissolved. The new council that replaced it, presided over by Nikolaus von Bulach, Gosso Engelbrecht, and Johann Botschold, put Peter Schwarber on trial, confiscated his fortune, and expelled him from the city.

On the morning of February 14, 1349, while the Jews were celebrating *shabbat,* a mob invaded their quarter.

Five hundred Jews were baptized by force that day. The others were taken to where their cemetery was, between the city wall and the Quay of the False Rampart. An immense pyre was built and set aflame, and the Jews were all thrown into it. There were perhaps two thousand of them—may the Almighty keep them in the abode of the blessed!

It was Saint Valentine's Day. The plague had long since gone, but someone had to pay for all those deaths, that fear, those horrors, and the smell of urine and vomit that still haunted the nights of those who had known that scourge of God, the Black Death.

•   •   •

AT THE END OF a meeting on human rights, in Paris, a woman approached me.

"My maiden name was Halter," she said by way of introducing herself.

Neither of us had much time that evening, but she told me that she was Alsatian and Catholic, that she knew other Halters in Alsace, and that her grandmother probably knew more than she did about the origin of her—our—name.

I gave her my phone number and she promised to call me. As soon as she had disappeared into the crowd moving along the boulevard, I was sorry I had not kept her longer. This was the first time that chance had offered me a flesh-and-blood lead, perhaps the key to my whole story, and instead of holding on to that young woman and getting her address, the name of the village where she was born, and the name of her grandmother, I had let her disappear.

Two weeks went by before my Catholic "cousin" announced herself to me on the phone in a playful tone. She had seen her grandmother, who at the age of eighty-two still had a perfectly clear mind and maintained that the ancestral home of the Halters was Haguenau. She remembered that one part of the family had left Alsace and gone to the United States at the beginning of the century, while the other part had settled in Strasbourg and the surrounding region.

"Did you ask your grandmother if she knew any Jewish Halters?"

"She doesn't know any, but she advises you to talk about it with Raymond Halter, in Haguenau."

"Raymond Halter? Who is he? What does he do?"

She laughed gaily, sure of her dramatic effect.

"He's a priest," she said.

I went to Strasbourg the next day. My "cousin" had given me several phone numbers and assured me that the phone books of the Bas-Rhin and Haut-Rhin departments were full of Halters.

Within a few days I traveled hundreds of kilometers and met dozens of Halters: businessmen, craftsmen, civil servants, peasants, and even a gendarme and a railroad gatekeeper. Raymond Halter, the priest, was away on a pilgrimage to Lourdes. At first, those I talked with listened to my explanation with thinly disguised mistrust, then they became more sociable, though they were still divided between genuine family patriotism and uneasiness at being involved in a Jewish undertaking. One of them was Elisée Halter, originally from Bischheim, whom I met in an inn near Haguenau. He told me that several times he had heard his grandfather, who had died five years earlier, say that "the Jews were also part of the family," but he did not know what he had meant by that.

My initial excitement was beginning to die down. I was now used to leaping from one Halter to another and catching only air. And sometimes, as I had lunch in country inns among traveling salesmen, I felt like a traveler following a road without knowing where it was taking him. When I was about to go back to Paris, I met one more Halter, a retired professor in Strasbourg. He believed he belonged to a Jewish family that had converted centuries ago, and advised me to look up all the conversions mentioned in the records of Jewish communities in Alsace. One of his cousins—"But he's not a

341

Halter," he said apologetically—worked in the Haut-Rhin Record Office. He was kind enough to notify him that I would visit him.

M.S. was a man near retirement age, with slow movements and a vague look in his eyes. We met in the Kammerzell, on the Place de la Cathédrale. He watched the legs of a passing woman, turned the stem of his glass between his fingers, and fondly contemplated the cathedral.

"Seven hundred years ago," I said, "I saw the spire built."

M.S. looked at me attentively without showing the slightest emotion.

"When do you believe you come to Strasbourg?"

"In 1242."

"And where did you come from?"

"Troyes."

"In 1242," he remarked amiably, "the spire hadn't yet been begun. Master Erwin didn't start work on it till 1277."

"That's true," I said. "His son Johann and his daughter Sabine continued it after him."

We were both satisfied with ourselves. M.S. finished his white wine. His face turned pink, like the stone of the cathedral.

"After my cousin called me," he said, "I did a little research. I found a Halter at the beginning of the seventeenth century. His first name was Johann and he was an executioner."

I called the waiter. M.S. ordered another glass of white wine. I imagined him slowly rolling a cigarette.

"Do you smoke?" I asked.

"No, thanks."

"Do you think Johann Halter might have been Jewish?"

"No, he couldn't have been. As an executioner, he held an important position and Jews were barred from it." He abruptly changed the subject. "I saw you on television one night. . . . Have you visited the Rue des Juifs [Street of Jews]? It's near here, just behind us. There's still one house on it that dates from the twelfth century." He slowly turned his eyes to me. "You'll recognize it!" Then, suddenly, "Do you know where your name comes from?"

"I know that in German it means 'holder' or 'keeper,' " I answered. "In Jerusalem a professor told me that in the Middle Ages a halter was the keeper of a herd or a flock: a herdsman or shepherd."

M.S. gave a kind of joyless laugh.

"A keeper, yes, but not of a herd. In Alsace, a halter kept a register."

That was how I learned der Halter *had been the man who kept the register of a village; it was an honorary position that could be hereditary. M.S. thought that the* halter *must have kept Jewish records, since Christian records of births, baptisms, and burials had long since begun to be kept in churches.*

"I think you're right: this is where you were born," he said to me.

He stood up heavily. I gave him my address, in case he should discover new information, and thanked him warmly. He slowly walked toward the cathedral.

I went to the Rue des Juifs, thinking of Chaim the scribe, Vifelin, Matis, young Moses, who had come to die with Esther. If it had not been for the plague, Moses would have become der Halter, *after his father Matis. Was he I? Was I he? At the corner of the Rue des Charpentiers, I found myself looking for the circle of bleeding flagellants.*

343

26

STRASBOURG

The Jews Will Pay

ALMOST BEFORE the ashes of the pyre had cooled, the city council decided that Jews would be forbidden to live in Strasbourg for two hundred years. They would be tolerated there two days a week, if they had an official pass.

Samueli and Matis chose to return to Benfeld. It had been spared by the plague and was once again the peaceful village they had known before. This time they were able to rent all of Councilor Elward Mersvin's house. The Jewish children of Benfeld came there every morning and Matis taught them the Torah. On days when they were allowed to enter Strasbourg, Abraham and his granduncle Samueli left Benfeld before dawn, in a cart, and arrived in the city before noon. They stopped at the inspection station on the Saint Nicholas bridge, went through the fish market and past the slaughterhouses—sometimes making a detour to see their former house, in which the council had placed an old couple—and came to Saint Martin Square. There, behind a moat, stood the Müsse, the building containing the offices of the communal services. They greeted the money changers who were already at their tables: Lombards, Flemings, and Jews; only the latter had had to pay, like Abraham and Samueli, two deniers for an entrance pass, plus two schillings for each horse. They set up their trestle table and began calling out to prospective customers across the moat. Samueli offered loans against security and Abraham worked as a scrivener, writing contracts and bills of exchange.

THERE WAS NOW scarcely ever any mention of the plague or the Great Pyre, except to divide time into before and after. Strasbourg, half emptied of its inhabitants by the Black Death, like a body drained of its strength, needed to forget in order to resume living, conceiving children, and making plans.

Abraham's wife Sarah was about to give birth to her third child. She and her family were waiting for the first pains. After so many deaths, each birth was important, and everything possible had to be done to increase the odds in favor of life.

The pains began on a Tuesday. Abraham spent the day reciting psalms with his cousins, uncles, and aunts. Leah, his mother, drew a chalk circle around Sarah's bed and wrote, "Adam and Eve. Out of here, Lilith!" on each of the four walls, as well as the names of three guardian angels: Sini, Sincini, and Smangalof. While the women heated water and prepared clean cloths, Matis, the future grandfather, explained the custom to the children.

"When God had created Adam," he said, "He saw that it was not good for man to be alone, and so He created a wife for him, out of mud. The wife's name was Lilith. Almost as soon as she was created, she began quarreling with Adam. But when she realized that she couldn't get the better of him, she spoke the ineffable name of God, rose into the air, and flew away."

The children stood facing Matis with open mouths and round eyes, listening with rapt attention—even those who already knew the story.

"God told three angels, Sini, Sincini, and Smangalof, to go after Lilith," Matis continued. "They caught up with her in the middle of a river and ordered her to come back. 'Leave me alone,' she begged them, 'because I was created to destroy newborn babies, eight days after their birth if they're boys, twenty days if they're girls.' But the angels again ordered her to come back, this time more sternly. Then she said, 'I swear to you by the name of the all-powerful living God that each time I see you, or your names or images on an amulet, I will do no harm to the child in that place.' That's why your grandmother Leah wrote the names of the three angels on the bedroom walls. When the child is born, Lilith will come, see the names, and remember the oath she swore."

Sarah gave birth to a boy. Abraham named him Vifelin, in memory of the grandfather who had been burned by the "leather arms." Matis wept for joy.

And so life gradually returned to its normal course and people fixed themselves in the stream of time with new roots. Samueli soon died, but only because he had reached the end of his allotted span of life. Abraham disliked traveling to Strasbourg alone and finally stopped going there. In Benfeld he found enough work as a scrivener to keep him busy, especially since he also kept the register of the Jewish community: births, arrivals, departures, deaths. He was called Abraham *der Halter*, Abraham the register keeper. Matis had nearly stopped writing because his sight was no longer very good.

One day at noon, when little Vifelin was ten years old, the earth shook. It was so brief, violent, and inconceivable that some of those who experienced it were left with a feeling of unreality and wondered if it had all been a dream: those houses suddenly collapsing in clouds of dust, those trees uprooted, that terrible dizziness in the body, those cries of panic-stricken animals. But no, the rubble remained rubble, the fallen trees remained lying on the ground. . . .

Abraham, on his way back from the synagogue, had the feeling that the street was twisting beneath his feet; then he heard screams. When he realized what had happened, he ran home. The house was still standing. He went inside. His wife was waiting for him, wringing her hands.

"Thank God you've come back!" she said.

"Has anyone been . . ."

"Your father, Abraham."

"My father?"

"He was with the children, near the oven, when the earth shook. He fell backward. It may have been his heart."

"Is he . . ."

"No, Abraham. He's waiting for you."

Between his snow-white hair and beard, Matis's broad face was peaceful. He smiled weakly when his son came in, then asked for water and said that he wanted the whole family to come to him. When Sarah put down a basin of warm water beside him, he dipped his fingers into it and carefully dried them with the big white towel that she held out to him. He beckoned to Abraham, who stepped toward him and knelt at his bedside. Matis put his hand on his son's head.

346

"May the Almighty," he said, breathing in quick little gasps, "turn His face to you . . . and give you peace. May the spirit of God . . . rest on you . . . the spirit of wisdom, intelligence . . . and knowledge of the fear of God."

Abraham stood up, deathly pale. Matis closed his eyes, as though to summon up his last strength. His voice was firm when he said, "Come closer, all of you. . . . Until now, with the . . . help of the Almighty . . . I have been the guardian of our family history. You trusted me . . . when I decided . . . to bury the Scroll of Abraham . . . in our garden in Strasbourg. Now it's my turn . . . to trust you. Don't abandon it!"

It was a man with his earthly affairs in order who died quietly a few moments later. His family knew he was dead when they saw that he was no longer breathing. Abraham closed his father's eyes.

Then he went to the writing desk, drew a simple map of the garden of their house in Strasbourg, and marked the location of the linden tree under which Matis, God rest his soul, had buried the family scroll, as if he had known what was going to happen. In case he should not be able to return there before his death, Abraham made his three children, Elijah, Vifelin, and Miriam, learn the map by heart, draw it again from memory, recite the number of steps from the entrance of the garden to the trunk of the tree, then from there to the place where the scroll was buried, and repeat all this until they could do it without hesitation. Standing before his father's body, he made them promise to hand on the map to their own children if they were unable to use it themselves. Only then, when he was sure that all precautions had been taken, did he begin mourning the death of his father Matis.

ELIJAH WAS TWENTY-THREE and Vifelin eighteen when Alsace, still recovering from the Black Death, was ravaged by a new scourge. This time it was roving bands of the mercenaries who had fought for France and England. Peace had abruptly left them without work or money. The bands were composed of Englishmen, Bretons, Frenchmen, Welshmen, Flemings, and Germans, under the command of leaders chosen for their courage, savagery, or greed. Not only did they pillage but, as if to make their victims pay for regarding them with horror, they burned what they could not take, cut down fruit trees, and killed children. Many unfortified villages were completely abandoned at the news of their approach.

Between Saverne and Bouxwiller, whole families fled as though running away from a fire. In Benfeld, where the guard had been doubled on the ramparts, Abraham *der Halter* scrupulously recorded the names of all the Jews who passed through. These refugees asked for a meal or a place to sleep for the night, and in exchange they gave the latest news. It was in this way that Abraham learned that King Charles V of France had authorized Rabbi Matatiahou ben Joseph, from Provence, to establish a *yeshiva* in Paris, but that persecution had resumed in Castile after the deaths of Don Pedro, son of King Alfonso, and his Jewish minister Samuel ben Meir Halevi.

Now and then Abraham took refugees into his house. Many of them were on their way to Poland, where, they said, King Casimir was well disposed toward the Jews, as was shown by the fact that the four children he had by his Jewish mistress were evenly divided: two Catholic sons and two Jewish daughters! Others had chosen Italy, where they were confident that certain towns of the Piedmont region, such as Asti and Montecalvo, would give them a warm welcome. One or the other of these two currents sometimes swept along an entire family, and sometimes a young man in search of change or adventure. Thus Jacob the jeweler, Samueli's son, went to Poland with his family, while his brothers Deyot and Simon, tombstone engravers, left Benfeld for Italy.

Those who stayed in Benfeld still felt a little like exiles from Strasbourg. After many discussions within the community, Abraham was instructed to write a letter, whose text was approved by everyone, to the city council: "To the honorable masters and council of Strasbourg, we offer our greetings and our humble services. We beg you to cease your rancor against us and allow us to come and live among you, as our ancestors lived among yours." The letter was delivered by Abraham's sons Elijah and Vifelin.

The council addressed Heinrich of Salmatingen, steward of the dukes of Oettingen, who had jurisdiction over Benfeld: would his masters allow their Jews to go to Strasbourg? Heinrich of Salmatingen replied that the dukes of Oettingen would permit the Jews to leave if Strasbourg agreed to pay the dukes an annuity of ten marks for the first ten years and then give them the capital.

Strasbourg and the Jewish community of Benfeld accepted this bargain. The council decided to take in six families, who would be given the same protection as other citizens. The six families were specified by the names of the men who headed them: Abraham *der Halter;* his older son Elijah, a money changer; Vifelin, a scrivener;

Mannekint; his brother-in-law Jacob of Speyer; and another Vifelin, brother of Mannen of Worms.

Abraham, Elijah, Vifelin, and their families once again loaded their belongings into a cart and set off for Strasbourg. Elward Mersvin, the old councilor who had been their landlord in Benfeld, laughed mockingly to himself as he watched them leave, and said in an undertone, "I'll keep the house for you—you'll be back!"

In Strasbourg, the city council allowed Abraham and his sons to return to their old house, with an increase in rent and an additional tax on their furniture. Elijah, who had left the city at an early age, and Vifelin, born in Benfeld, learned the streets and public squares of Strasbourg. The cathedral was now finished. A man named Hultz, from Cologne, had completed the spire of elaborately carved stone two centuries after another master had planned it.

No one talked to them about the Great Pyre or their expulsion. A few days after their return, since things had been going smoothly, they decided that they could dig up the Scroll of Abraham without risk. They did it one *shabbat* evening. Abraham put his prayer shawl over his shoulders and his sons took turns working with a pick and shovel. The linden tree was blossoming, and their emotion was so great when they heard the pick strike wood that for the rest of their lives they associated the Scroll of Abraham with the smell of linden blossoms.

They read the scroll that same evening, from one end to the other. "Abraham, son of Solomon the Levite, lived in Jerusalem and the name of his wife was Judith. Elijah, his first son, became a scribe like his father. . . ." When he had finished, Abraham added the names of his children Miriam, Elijah, and Vifelin, his brother Moses, "who died because he could not bear to live without his fiancée Esther, daughter of Rabbi Samuel of Weissenburg," and finally his father Matis, "thanks to whom the family scroll escaped the Great Pyre of the year 5109 [1349] after the creation of the world by the Almighty, blessed be He."

Abraham and his sons were aware not only of fulfilling Matis's last wish, but also of carrying on a work whose foundations had been laid long before those of the Strasbourg Cathedral, a work that, with the aid of the Almighty, would rise much higher into the sky than any stone spire.

VIFELIN, WHO HAD MARRIED just before coming to Strasbourg, already had two daughters when the mercenaries again appeared in the region. This time they came by way of Saverne and Belfort, and were commanded by Sir Enguerrand de Coucy. Demanding his share of the inheritance left by his grandfather Leopold I of Austria, he sent his troops to pillage some forty villages in Sundgau. They then proceeded to slaughter the inhabitants of Wattwiller and burn the Thann monastery. Advancing on Strasbourg, they took the suburb of Koenigshoffen, but were stopped by the ramparts of the city.

"You see: they don't kill only Jews!" Vifelin remarked to his father Abraham.

"That's good news for lunatics!" replied Abraham.

"It doesn't make me glad to know that Christians are being killed, father, but you must admit that when the sons of Esau fight each other, they give the Jews a respite."

"Come, come, my son, haven't you noticed that when Christians go to war against each other the Jews always pay for it, in one way or another?"

That was exactly what happened again this time. Even though the city had recently acquired firearms, the council decided to pay Enguerrand de Coucy's mercenaries to go elsewhere. The sum of three thousand florins was agreed on and the council ordered Abraham, as a representative of the Jewish community, to collect the money.

The six families were thrown into panic. Mannekint and Jacob openly expressed regret at having left Benfeld. How were they going to raise three thousand florins?

It was Elijah the money changer who found the solution. He proposed taking a two-year loan from the burghers, against security.

"But what security can we give?" asked Abraham, who had never understood anything about financial affairs.

"Our own money."

"We don't have any!"

"That's why we'll ask the council to let us postpone our payments for two years: the five hundred Strasbourg pounds for our rent, the thirty marks per person that we must pay to the bishop, and the ten we must pay to the dukes of Oettingen."

Abraham thought this over for a few moments, then asked, "But after two years, when you've paid back the loan, with interest, where will you get the money for the payments we'll have postponed?"

"We'll have earned more money in the meantime. The loan will give us the three thousand florins to ransom the city. Postponing our payments of rent and taxes will leave us with a large sum at our disposal for two years, and we'll make profitable use of it."

"I'm not sure I understand everything you said, my son, but if your plan succeeds you'll deserve to be something more than a poor money changer!"

"May the Almighty, blessed be He, grant that you're right, father!"

The council accepted Elijah's proposal, asking that all members of the Strasbourg Jewish community sign the agreement stipulating that the sums in question were to be paid in two years, on Saint Martin's Day of the year 1377 by the Christian calendar, and that the interest was to be paid on Saint John's Day of the same year.

AFTER TAKING their three thousand florins, Enguerrand de Coucy's mercenaries left Strasbourg and went into Switzerland, where they were beaten by the Bernese.

Satisfied with its Jews, the Strasbourg city council gave them permission to bring in a rabbi: Samuel Schlettstadt, so called because his father had been a rabbi in Schlettstadt. The community gradually increased, and the council issued a new decree concerning the Jews: "The mayor and the council will take them under their protection and severely punish anyone who mistreats them in any way. The Jews themselves will be tried in the same manner as other burghers in cases of misdemeanors or crimes."

Abraham stopped working as a scrivener and established a school in his house. His son Vifelin was now *der Halter*. Vifelin's wife had given birth to a child, then another, then a third. The Jews of Strasbourg had not forgotten, but life in the city was so good that it was easy for them to believe that the time of tribulations had ended.

When Leopold Sturm, a councilor whom Abraham had known as a child, came to tell him in secret that the council was about to banish the Jews again, it was like another earthquake. "Why?" moaned Abraham. "Why?" Was it simply intolerance? A way of eliminating a living remorse and forgetting the Great Pyre? A means of making the Jews pay again for the privilege of returning? No reason that Abraham could think of seemed to justify that new expulsion. But once again he and the others had to pack a few belongings in haste. They had just celebrated the *bar mitzvah* of Vifelin's youngest child Aaron.

By the time the expulsion was announced in the streets by town criers, the family had already made sure that the house in Benfeld was still vacant. Councilor Elward Mersvin was dead now, but his son, who already seemed as old as his father, had faithfully kept it for them, calling it "the Jews' house." They had discreetly taken some furniture to it, along with the Scroll of Abraham. They had been right to make preparations in advance: they had to leave Strasbourg as quickly as they could, running with their hands raised to protect themselves from insults, jeers, and spittle.

Abraham was overwhelmed. He stopped writing and left the house in Benfeld only to go to the synagogue. He read and reread the family history, perhaps trying to find in it the meaning of his destiny, or of the destiny of the Jewish people.

One day young Aaron brought him a blank page and handed it to him without a word. Abraham ran his finger over it, smelled it, felt its weight, thickness, and grain. It was light, thin, and fragile, and he could not identify it as anything he knew; it was neither parchment nor papyrus.

"It came from Troyes," said Aaron, as if he were giving him a hint.

"From Troyes?"

"Yes. It's made from rags of linen and hemp."

"Rags? Don't make fun of me, Aaron. I'm your grandfather. I have to pray now and I can't waste any more time with your foolishness."

Afraid that Abraham might fall back into his melancholy, Aaron told him the name of that new material.

"It's called paper, grandfather."

27

BENFELD

A Man Named
Hans Gensfleisch

WHEN AARON became engaged to Guthil the lame, daughter of Lowelin the innkeeper, paper was still only a curiosity.

Guthil's infirmity, which the children of the village mocked by imitating her walk, filled Aaron's heart with inexhaustible tenderness. He was deeply happy when the *chazzan*—there was no rabbi in Benfeld—put into the engagement contract the amount of the dowry and the list of presents that the two parties promised to each other, and when he broke a pitcher to show, according to tradition, that "just as this pitcher cannot be put back together, so this agreement cannot be broken." Aaron then took the *chezzan*'s place before the assembly of families to give his word that he would faithfully abide by all the terms of the contract.

Ordinarily, an engagement did not last longer than a year, but in this case the wedding had to be postponed because Abraham died suddenly and quietly, while rereading the Scroll of Abraham for the hundredth time, or perhaps the thousandth. He still had found no answer to the question he had repeated so often: "Why?"

THE WEDDING was finally celebrated the following spring. The whole village took part in it, along with Jews from the environs, who came with their sons and daughters of marriageable age. Since the plague and the Great Pyre, weddings had been celebrated more fervently than funerals, so important did it seem that life should prevail over death.

The first child was slow in coming. He did not make his presence known until two years later, and never saw the light of day. The second, a girl, died shortly after birth. The third, a boy, died the day after his *brit milah*. The fourth and fifth died in an epidemic when they were one and two years old, respectively.

When Guthil became pregnant for the sixth time, the whole village prayed for her. Her father fasted two days a week and Aaron did penance. They went to Haguenau to bring Loser the *shormer,* who was said to be able to exorcise the worst demons. He was a short, round-faced Jew with a gentle voice. For two days he recited magic formulas to a certain rhythm. Then he put a coral necklace on Guthil to protect her from the evil eye. Finally he proclaimed at the top of his lungs, "I *shorm* so that evil will withdraw from your flesh, and so that the God of Israel will grant His protection to the child you bear."

He left at dawn on the third day, refusing to take any payment.

The child was born in pain at the beginning of summer, two days before Shabuot in the year 5178 [1418] after the creation of the world by the Almighty, blessed be He. He lived past the first day, the first week, the first month. His name was Gabriel. He was beautiful and smiling and his parents contemplated him as if he were a miracle.

When Gabriel was three years old his father taught him the *aleph-beth,* and after his *bar mitzvah* his father took him to Mainz to see the famous Rabbi Jacob ben Moses Halevi Mölln, commonly known as Maharil. The rabbi judged the boy to be very knowledgeable for his age and accepted him as a pupil. After two years, Gabriel wrote to Benfeld that he was going to stay another two years. At the end of that time he wrote another letter to his parents: he wanted to spend more time with Maharil, whom he was helping to copy his book, the Sefer Minhagim. Meanwhile, a shepherdess from Lorraine went to war in the name of God against the English and had a king crowned, but was burned at the stake in Rouen. The Jews of Benfeld saw this as one more proof that "whoever burns a Jew will finally burn a *goy.*"

At last Gabriel came back to Benfeld. His mother Guthil scarcely recognized her child in that tall, slender, dark-haired man with limpid eyes and a willful chin shaded by a light beard. Under his green cape he wore a green tunic taken in at the wrists and closed in front by a row of small buttons that were a gift from Maharil. Guthil the lame was intimidated by her son. He could be as lively, playful, and lighthearted as any young man his age, but sometimes he became serious, almost grave, and a furrow appeared between his eyes. He then said things that Guthil did not understand very well. She thanked God that he had become so learned without ceasing to be himself.

His reputation followed him. People came to hear him chant prayers to a melody composed by Maharil. He received orders, sometimes from far away, for copies of the Megillat Esther or chapters from the Book of Psalms, which he transcribed in an elegant hand and illuminated in colored inks that he had learned to make from plants. The hours in a day were not enough for him because, in the time not spent on his work, he tried to satisfy his curiosity about everything and his eagerness for new discoveries and experiences.

One day he heard about a paper mill that had been set up near the priory of Saint Arbogast, a little outside of Strasbourg. He went there as soon as he could. The mill was isolated, and the man he saw standing in a cart, unloading bundles of rags, seemed suspicious of him.

"What do you want?"

"I've come from Benfeld," replied Gabriel. "I'm a scribe. I've seen sheets of paper, but I'd like to know how you make it."

"You haven't come to buy?"

"It depends on the price."

The man's face brightened.

"Then come in. My name is Andres Heilman."

"And I'm Gabriel, son of Aaron, the *Halter* of Benfeld."

They went into the mill. Gabriel was surprised by an unpleasant smell and a kind of dull, thudding sound.

"You have to get used to it," said Andres Heilman. "Look: this is where we cut the rags into narrow strips. Then we soak them and pile them up in what we call the steeping vat, in the cellar. When they've begun to ferment, we put them in that tank of water, where they're pounded and shredded by those spiked mallets."

Gabriel looked at the drive shaft that moved the mallets, and the gears that connected it to the mill wheel. Andres Heilman continued his explanation.

"The pounding goes on till the rags are turned into a milky

355

paste. That's the beginning of paper. Then all that needs to be done is . . . Look."

Workers were pouring some of the paste into a mold closed by a strainer. Water dripped from it. When it had become thick enough, it was spread onto pieces of cloth that were piled up and placed in a press.

"As you can see," said Heilman, "the press forces out the rest of the water. And now we have paper. The sheets are strong enough to dry in those small bundles over there on the drying rack that we call the treble. . . . Believe me, paper is the writing material of the future! Do you doubt it? You're not convinced?"

Gabriel was holding a flawless sheet of paper between his fingers. It had a smooth, uniform texture and was almost perfectly white.

"Yes," he said, "I'm convinced. But I wonder if it's permissible for us, the Jews, to use paper for copying our sacred texts."

Just then a massive man of about forty, with broad shoulders and a broad face, came into the room. His light blue eyes were set far apart and he blinked them when he talked. He seemed rather disagreeable, like those obsessed with a single idea. He glanced at Gabriel's pointed hat, then turned to Heilman.

"I have to talk to you, Andres."

Heilman nodded toward Gabriel and said, "We were wondering if it was permissible for the Jews to write their sacred texts on paper."

"That would be a good market, wouldn't it, Andres?" the man said with a brief laugh. "Who are you?" he asked Gabriel.

"My name is Gabriel. I'm a scribe in Benfeld and I recently came back from Mainz."

"Mainz? That's where I'm from. What were you doing there?"

"Studying with Rabbi Jacob ben Moses Halevi Mölln. I learned to work with ink and colors, and I also learned a little engraving."

"Engraving?"

The man seemed to doubt that Gabriel had really studied engraving. It was perhaps a touch of vanity that made Gabriel try to impress him.

"I've always wondered," he said, "if it was possible to make wood engravings of the whole text of a book and then reproduce it many times. Till now, my only difficulty was finding the right material for the reproductions. Parchment isn't suitable. But paper is exactly what's needed."

The man seemed both interested and disdainful.

"Paper doesn't solve all problems, take my word for it. Cutting letters in relief on a slab of wood takes a great deal of work and the results are disappointing. Several people have already tried it." He put his hand under his red hat and scratched his head. "If you're interested in such things, come back. I'm often here. Andres and I are partners. My name is Hans Gensfleisch. Will you remember it?"

HANS GENSFLEISCH DID NOT have a good reputation. He lived with his servant Lorenz in an isolated house; he worked with Andreas Dritzehen, a burgher of Strasbourg, on some sort of research unknown to everyone else; he claimed to be a goldsmith, and he belonged to the artists' guild.

At the family table that evening, when Gabriel told about his visit, everyone urged him to be careful.

"They say he's trying to make gold," said Lowelin, his father-in-law.

"And precious stones," added Aaron.

"I've heard talk of sorcery," said Symunt, Guthil's brother, showing his buckteeth.

Gabriel was disappointed. He looked at the family scene: those men bristling with suspicion, his mother limping between the table and the fireplace, the blackened ceiling, the walls oozing moisture. Although he knew the value of tradition and prudence, he was keenly aware of the limits imposed by convention, fear of the unknown, and lack of daring. He loved his family, with their determination to perpetuate what they were and what they knew, but he felt a kind of obligation to broaden his horizon and strive for better things, even at the risk of mistakes and misadventures.

That was why, despite his father's warnings, he went to see Hans Gensfleisch one day. A house at the edge of the forest, a surly servant who refused to let him come in, chained dogs, pigeons on the roof. Gensfleisch came to the door and recognized Gabriel.

"Ah, it's you. How did you find out where I live?"

"Everyone knows."

"Everyone?"

"Everyone, at least, who says you live in this isolated house because you make gold and practice sorcery."

Gensfleisch repeated his familiar gesture of putting his hand under his red hat.

"Those people will make trouble for me someday," he muttered. "And you, what do you think of those stories?"

"I'm sure that a man who's interested in paper and engraving," replied Gabriel, "doesn't have time to waste on trying to make gold."

Gensfleisch blinked his eyes rapidly.

"And I'm sure you'll die less innocent than you were when you were born! Come in."

The fireplace seemed to take up most of the room. Beside it, a woman sat in semidarkness, shelling beans. One staircase led upward, another downward. They took the descending one and came into a vaulted cellar where Gabriel's nostrils were seized by an acrid smell. Two men were working beside a caldron on a tripod, with glowing embers under it and ugly yellow vapor rising from it. They turned their reddened faces toward Gabriel. One of them seemed furious.

"Why have you brought a Jew here?" he asked Gensfleisch.

"He can help us. Let's go upstairs and have a stein of beer."

While the two men were lifting the caldron off its tripod and putting away their tools, Gensfleisch went over to a workbench on which Gabriel recognized the chisels, gouges, and points of a wood engraver. Gensfleisch handed him a block carved in relief.

"This is what you were talking about," he said. "You spread ink on the letters, put a sheet of paper over them and press it, and the letters are reproduced."

He carried out the process he had just described and Gabriel, delighted to see in reality what he had previously seen only in imagination, was able to read the words *Scriptura manent*.

" 'Writings remain,' " he translated. And he added impulsively, "This is the greatest day of my life!"

"Come. You can explain that to us."

They went up to the first floor and sat down at the table. The woman brought them steins of thick beer. She had taken off her hat and, in the light of the big oil lamp, Gabriel saw her blond, wavy hair and the low-cut neckline of her blue robe, which revealed a generous portion of her white breasts. He realized that she had seen him staring at her. She did not seem troubled by it—not as much as he was, in any case.

"This is Andreas Dritzehen," said Hans Gensfleisch. "He's the one who doesn't like Jews. And this is Hans Dünne. We're partners."

"It's not that I don't like Jews, Gutenberg," Dritzehen said impatiently. "But we're already suspected of sorcery, so you can imagine what it will be like if a Jew is seen here!"

"Then we'll all burn together!" replied Gensfleisch.

The woman let out a peal of laughter and quickly put her hand in front of her mouth. Dritzehen gave her a withering look.

Gensfleisch put his broad, acid-stained hand on Gabriel's arm. "Now, my friend, tell us what brought you here."

Gabriel could not help looking at the woman again, and he became aware that he wanted to speak to her, not to the three men.

"In my family," he said, "we've been scribes from generation to generation. My father, Aaron, is the *Halter* of Benfeld. My ancestor Abraham was a scribe in Jerusalem. . . . I studied in Mainz. I now copy scrolls of the Torah, and the days are too short for my work. Ever since hundreds of copies of the Talmud were burned, scribes have spent whole lifetimes making new copies from the few old ones that were saved. My father has been working on one book for the last four years. . . . That's why I spoke to Herr Gensfleisch—"

"Everyone calls me Gutenberg."

"—to Herr Gutenberg about the possibility of reproducing many copies of a text from one engraving. That way, the text could be read by a much larger number of people."

The three others looked at each other knowingly.

"Your dream, young man, is also ours," said Gutenberg. "But wood engraving isn't the solution. I have an idea, and my friends here are helping me to put it into practice. They're not only workers, they're also my financial backers. If you'd like to join us. . . ."

"I'm afraid I'm in no position to give you any financial backing," Gabriel replied quickly.

"Then you'll be a worker."

WHENEVER HE COULD, Gabriel saddled his horse and, in spite of the warnings his father still repeated, rode to Gutenberg's house. Sometimes he found everyone there—the three partners, the servant Lorenz, and his wife—and sometimes only Lorenz's wife. It had become clear to him that she was not overly fond of her ill-natured husband and that she and Gutenberg were on intimate terms; he had seen them exchange looks and gestures that left no doubt about the nature of their relations. This did not stop him from staring at her. He knew she could not fail to see that she excited him. It seemed to amuse her and he had the impression that she sometimes did it deliberately, when she leaned toward him or slowly climbed the cellar stairs while he remained below. He felt that he was like a man who stood at the edge of a cliff and, instead of stepping back, prayed God not to let him fall.

As soon as he took out his tools, however, he thought of nothing but his work.

Gutenberg had conceived the idea of pouring molten metal into molds with the shapes of letters. When the metal cooled, he had letters in relief; he could then put them together to form words, ink them, and press a sheet of paper onto them. The principle seemed sound, but the problem was to find a metal, or an alloy of different metals, capable of forming letters that would not be broken or crushed by the force of the press. That was the problem he and his partners were trying to solve in the cellar. They mixed lead, antimony, and tin in various proportions. The antimony increased the hardness of the metals with which it was alloyed, but also made them more brittle.

Gabriel's work was making the molds into which the molten alloys were poured. He concentrated on it with patience and passion. Gutenberg was a harsh man, sometimes unfair, quick to express contempt, and stingy with compliments, but Gabriel could see that he was pleased with him.

In the year 1438, two weeks before Christmas—the day after Chanukah—they tried an alloy whose proportions had been carefully noted by Hans Dünne. Melting, molding, cooling, removal from the molds—how often they had repeated those operations! Gutenberg asked Gabriel to bring the molds for the letters of the usual words, *Scriptura manent,* and poured the liquid metal into them. He and the others then drank beer while they waited for the metal to cool. Always the same wait, the same hope. When the letters had been taken out of the molds, Gabriel secured them in the press and placed a sheet of paper over them. Gutenberg worked the press, examined the sheet, inspected the metal, signaled for another sheet. . . .

Scriptura manent. Scriptura manent. Scriptura manent. This time the alloy was not too brittle, or too friable, or too soft, or too . . . *Scriptura manent. Scriptura manent.* Ten times, twenty times, three hundred times the press did its work, and three hundred times Gutenberg saw that the reproduction was satisfactory.

When he finally motioned that they could stop, they were all silent for a moment. Then he threw his red hat into the air with a triumphant shout, Hans Dünne began dancing first on one foot and them on the other, and Dritzehen sat down, overwhelmed with emotion. Gabriel felt tears welling up in his eyes. He quickly wiped them away when Lorenz's wife came down to hug each of the four men in turn. It seemed to Gabriel that she kept her firm breasts against him a little longer than was proper.

Gutenberg raised an enormous beer stein toward the vaulted ceiling of the cellar.

"Praise the Lord," he thundered, "we've succeeded!"

GABRIEL TOOK one of the three hundred proofs and hurried to show it to his father. Aaron slowly shook his head. He did not doubt Gutenberg's success, but that very success saddened him.

"Writing," he finally said, "is a human act, an act of the hand and the eye. It takes sustained attention, patience, taste . . ."

"But father, the reproduction is the same, and it's done by human beings like you and me. The only difference is that it's writing done without a pen, and much faster."

"No, Gabriel, no. This thing you've shown me is not for people like you and me."

"Why not?"

Gabriel had wanted so much for his father to realize the advantages of writing something only once and then making three hundred copies of it!

"Our work, Gabriel, transcribing scrolls of the Torah, is *malechet hakodesh* [sacred work], as you know better than I, since you studied with Maharil, may God preserve him from all harm. We take part in making the parchment, we make our own ink, and each time we write the venerated Name we first stop for a moment and think about the holiness of the word we're about to write with a freshly dipped pen. You can't have all that, my son, with your metal letters and wooden press!"

"But father, paper is made by men! And there's no reason you can't stop and meditate when you compose the name of the Almighty, blessed be He, with metal letters."

"How will you scratch your paper if you find a mistake?"

"People who practice the trade will solve the problems that arise in it."

"I'm not talking about a trade, I'm talking about the mission of the scribe, our mission. It demands all our loyalty and our whole lives. It's a simple mission: transcribing the word of the Lord and making known His Law. Nothing else. Do you understand? Nothing else!"

"A printer can do the same thing."

"Don't interrupt me, my son. A printer can do the same thing and much more. He can preserve the Law, but he can also preserve the words of madmen. And in many copies! The printer's art will serve everyone: the faithful and the unfaithful, the righteous and the wicked. And as you know from having read it, 'The wicked are like the tossing sea, for it cannot rest.' God grant that we won't have to regret this new invention. . . . Listen, there's Isekin: it's time to go to prayer."

ANDREAS DRITZEHEN'S HEART could not withstand his emotion. He died two weeks later, on Christmas night. His two brothers, Klaus and Georg, wanted to take his place in the partnership, but Gutenberg refused. They then demanded five hundred florins, which they judged to be the value of their brother's share. Again Gutenberg refused. The agreement that he and Andreas Dritzehen had signed, he said, had no stipulation concerning heirs. The brothers filed a lawsuit against him.

Gabriel was disappointed. Disappointed that an invention making it possible to reproduce hundreds of copies of the word of the Holy One, blessed be He, should lead to legal wrangling. Disappointed that a man who had had the ingenuity and patience to follow his idea through to the end should behave with such pettiness. He went to the courtroom where the case was being heard and listened to the witnesses and the lawyers, surprised that the legal proceedings were limited to determine how much Gutenberg owed to Andreas Dritzehen, without taking any account of what the human race owed to Hans Gensfleisch, known as Gutenberg. Finally the old judge, Cune Nope, councilor of the city of Strasbourg, ordered Gutenberg to pay Georg and Klaus Dritzehen the sum of fifteen florins, after which there was to be no more legal action concerning the partnership between Gutenberg and Andreas Dritzehen, or the enterprise they had founded together.

TOWARD THE END OF the Gutenberg lawsuit, Guthil the lame was going down the cellar stairs when she missed a step and fell onto the large earthenware jar of olive oil that she had intended to bring up. She lay for a long time without being able to move or even call for help. Finally Aaron, worried by her absence, went to look for her. He found her that evening, in alarming condition. He and Gabriel carried her up the stairs. She died a few days later.

Soon afterward, Gutenberg went back to Mainz without even saying good-bye to those who had supported or helped him. Gabriel briefly considered going with him but decided to stay a little longer with his father, whose strength seemed to be failing. Aaron had been aged by the shock and grief of his wife's death, and his conversation with Gabriel about the new way of reproducing texts had taken away his taste for writing. It was as if the invention of printing had made everything futile for him: his work as a scribe, his whole life, the history of his family. He even refused to record Guthil's death in the Scroll of Abraham. Weakened and embittered, he scarcely ever left the house and spent his days in prayer. No one was surprised when he died the following winter.

During the week he spent in *shiva,* Gabriel had time to think about what he was going to do with his life. His plans were centered around one idea: to get money and buy a press, ink, lead, tin, antimony, and paper. But he had no desire to stay in Benfeld; except for his parents' graves, there was nothing to keep him there. He thought of returning to Mainz but could not make up his mind to do it.

The first chance offered by fate was the one he chose. It came in the form of a letter addressed to "Aaron, son of Vifelin, *Halter* of Benfeld" and brought from Italy by Jacob Ashkenazi, a Talmudic scholar from Cremona. It was written by a cousin named Elijah, grandson of the Deyot who, with his brother, had left Alsace and gone to Italy seventy years earlier. He lived in Soncino, where he was a tombstone engraver. Soncino, he wrote, was a good place for Jews to live, since they enjoyed the protection of the duke of Milan. He asked for news of his relatives in Benfeld and said, without phrasing it as an explicit invitation, that the Jewish community in Soncino needed a good scribe because "marriage contracts are not as well written or illuminated here as they are in Mantua."

Gabriel took this letter as a sign from heaven and decided to go to Soncino—wherever that might be. His family raised no objection to his decision. Although, according to custom, he was the only one entitled to have the Scroll of Abraham in his keeping, he was asked not to expose it to the risks of whatever adventures he might encounter.

"We'll send it to you," promised his granduncle Judel, "as soon as, with the help of the Almighty, blessed be He, you've settled somewhere."

Gabriel left Benfeld at the end of May in the year 1440 by the Christian calendar. He took the road that followed the Rhine, in the direction of Basel. He felt as light as the white clouds moving southward with him, like an escort.

•　　　•　　　•

I HAD JUST FINISHED writing chapter 27, in which my hero becomes acquainted with Gutenberg, and I had chosen to name that ancestor Abraham, symbolically, like the initiator of our story, Abraham the scribe. Then I received a letter from M.S., the Strasbourg archivist I had met in the Kammerzell. I clearly remembered the man with slow movements and vague eyes who had fondly contemplated the pink stone cathedral and I was surprised to see that his handwriting was fine, precise, and elegant. He told me that he had found a bill of sale registered by a Jewish scrivener in Benfeld named Gabriel, but that the date at the bottom of it was illegible.

This new personage had turned up in Benfeld just as my story was leaving Alsace. I immediately decided to go back over chapter 27 and give the name of Gabriel, rather than Abraham, to the son of Aaron and Guthil the lame. So it is now Gabriel who meets Gutenberg and leaves for Italy. I could not let that real-life Gabriel go to waste.

A rather wild idea came into my mind: maybe that Gabriel revealed to me by chance actually did meet Gutenberg. I wrote to my Strasbourg archivist and asked him if he knew of any surviving records of the many lawsuits brought against Gutenberg by his partners and creditors.

Was that story real or imaginary? A kind of unknown anxiety came over me. I had already been working on this book for three years and I still saw no end to it. I know of no other activity that devours time as irretrievably as writing does. I get up early, go over a few documents, write a few pages, and it is already night. I sleep awhile, take my pen and put down a few words on paper, a few characters appear, and it is day again.

The old scribes lived and died to the rhythm of time. The dream of today's writer is to stand on the banks of time and watch it pass; his ultimate ambition is to immobilize it and make it his own. What anguish, all that time slipping away from me!

364

The source of my story is Jerusalem, and I go there, in one way or another, each time my story bogs down. This time I went back over my notes on a strange meeting with Rabbi Adin Szteinzaltz, director of the Institute of Talmudic Publications. On the telephone, he had told me that he lived on a little street near the Mishkenoth Shaananim, the house for guests of the city, where I was staying at the time.

It was only a little past six o'clock but darkness had already fallen. I walked around a block and questioned several passersby; none of them seemed ever to have heard of that street. Then a postal worker gave me directions, but they turned out to be wrong. When I finally found the building, which dated from the turn of the century, it was only by chance. I was late but the rabbi took it as a matter of course. No one who came to see him was ever on time, he explained.

I was surprised to see how young he was because I had imagined an elderly man, probably by association of ideas: rabbi-wisdom-age. His sparse beard was reddish-brown, like his hair, sidelocks, face, and eyes. He seemed extremely gentle and patient. I began telling him about the project I had undertaken; at that time it was still at an early stage. He listened attentively. Now and then he stopped me with a gesture and said, "Interesting, very interesting. It seems to me that Kant wrote somewhere. . . . I'll look it up," or, "Wait a second. What you just said reminds me of a story by Joyce." He would always look it up, and he was always right.

One thing about our conversation was disconcerting to me: rather than trying to give me answers, Rabbi Szteinzaltz tried to understand my questions. He imposed nothing on me; he only helped me to follow each of my thoughts to its end. "Ah, ah," he would say, tugging at his thin beard, "what you say is very interesting. Let's try to see where your reasoning will take us." He would then go on from there, with gracious courtesy and implacable logic, until I realized that my idea would not hold water. "Ah, ah, that's interesting," he would say when I put forward another one.

At midnight, we were still there.

"Let's sum up," Rabbi Szteinzaltz suggested. "You know that you're descended from a family in which men were printers from generation to generation, but you don't know how long ago it began. You know only that the earliest Halter print shop you've heard of was in either Lublin or Warsaw. Now all you have to do is to retrace the itineraries of the several dynasties of Jewish printers known to *have existed from the fifteenth century onward, and see which one of them eventually came to Lublin or Warsaw."*

How simple it all seemed!

"Furthermore," the rabbi went on, "it's reasonable to assume that the first people to realize the value of printing were closely involved with writing. We know that there were also dynasties of scribes in which the techniques of writing and the mystique of knowledge were passed on from father to son. And so, my friend, you must connect a dynasty of scribes with a dynasty of printers, at a time probably not long after Gutenberg's invention."

"If what you say is true . . ."

The rabbi slowly shook his head.

"I'm not the one who said it: you are. I've only listened to you and suggested solutions—your solutions."

"Now we have a guiding thread."

"Don't let go of it or you'll get lost in your maze!" Rabbi Szteinzaltz said with a kind, gentle laugh.

That conversation took place before I had written the first page of this book.

I had now reached the exact place where the two stories—the one before Gutenberg and the one after—could be joined.

What if that Gabriel were the missing link? Yes, but what if he were not? Would each of my two stories follow its own course without ever encountering the other?

While I was waiting for an answer from M.S., the Strasbourg archivist, I went back to my hero—now named Gabriel—at the time of his departure from Benfeld. I would not be risking anything by following him to Soncino.

Pursuing my reasoning in the manner of Rabbi Szteinzaltz, I had concluded that Gabriel, knowing the secret of reproducing texts, would be sure to dream of setting up a print shop. Did he have the means for it? Certainly not. Was it permissible for him? We have no record of any Jewish print shops in Alsace at that time—or even in France or Germany. In Italy, however, Jewish print shops are known to have existed in 1475 at Reggio di Calabria and Pieve di Sacco, then at Ferrara and Bologna, and, in 1483, at Soncino. Only the one at Soncino, as far as we know, was established by Jews from the Rhineland.

It was therefore in accordance with Rabbi Szteinzaltz's logic that Gabriel should go to that ocher village between Cremona and Milan.

P.S. I CANNOT HELP regretting that Aaron's only son set off for Soncino without a qualm, leaving behind the Scroll of Abraham just when he had inherited the responsibility of keeping it. It seems to me that he took a very casual attitude toward thirteen centuries of history and fidelity.

Why is there still only a single copy of the scroll? It is as if there had to be no more than one, for some reason that escapes me.

28

BENFELD-SONCINO

Gabriele di Strasburgo

GABRIEL WAS then twenty-two and he had devoted more than
ten years to reflection and study. As he rode his horse from one
horizon to another, he felt carefree again, after such a long time.
. . . He had not forgotten what he owed to his parents and to his
teachers, Maharil and Gutenberg, and he was aware that he who
knows has more duties than he who does not know, but the gravity
of a young scholar was now giving way to the curiosity, enthusiasm, and happiness of living in the present, and the light excitement of a traveler without baggage.

He had to go around Colmar because Jews had been banished
from there after being wrongly accused of having supported the
heretic Jan Hus. He reached Basel in time for *shabbat* and went to
the house of Bele of Freiburg, a money changer for whom his
cousin Mennelin had given him a letter of introduction. After *shabbat,* Bele took him on a tour of the city, or rather the two half-
cities separated by the Rhine and connected by a wide wooden
bridge. He saw his first clock, heard it strike eight, and waited,
filled with wonder, for it to strike nine.

The next evening, when he and Bele came out of the synagogue
to which they had gone for prayer, they met two slender men
wearing red *cappuccios*—turban-shaped hats reinforced with cork

—and loose, short blue-velvet surcoats with flowing sleeves; they looked like two insects in superb shells that were too big for them. Bele greeted them with deference. They were Zinatano and his son Jekutiel, bankers from Reggio nell'Emilia who had come to Basel on business and intended to leave within two days at the most. Jekutiel showed great interest when he learned that "Gabriele" had studied with Maharil: he knew by heart whole passages of the Sefer Minhagim that Gabriel had copied in Mainz.

After a brief discussion, the father and son made a proposal in their Italian-accented Hebrew: if it was agreeable to the young scribe from Benfeld who was about to go beyond the Alps for the first time, they would take him with them and, rather than traveling by way of Balzano as they usually did, they would skirt Lake Garda in the direction of Brescia and go through Cremona, a "delightful city" that had a "very attractive synagogue" and was only a day's journey from Soncino.

And so Gabriel left with them. The two bankers, accompanied by attentive servants, were charming, considerate, and amiable companions. Gabriel was never bored with them.

At Trento, on the Adige River, the small Jewish community was more Italian than German, and for the first time Gabriel felt that he was really in a foreign country, especially since the Jews here did not wear pointed hats but, instead, had round yellow badges sewn to their clothes, except for a few privileged people, including the two bankers, who were protected by Duke Lionel d'Este. Thanks to his knowledge of Latin, Gabriel understood a few words of the rapid, melodious language to which he listened, fascinated, in the narrow streets near the cathedral. The bankers asked for directions to a Jewish inn. There they were finally able to have a normal—that is, *kosher*—meal.

Everything seemed to favor Zinatano and his son: money, people, and the weather. When the road rose between mountains still capped with snow, the sun came out to warm the travelers, and when they went down into valleys, a breeze sprang up to cool them. It seemed that with them it could not be otherwise. Near Gardone, at the edge of the lake, they passed peasants singing as they pushed blue handcarts full of cackling chickens.

Suddenly one of the servants, who had been riding ahead, came back at a gallop.

"War!" he shouted. "War!"

They went to the top of a rise. Through a dip in the landscape they saw galleys fighting on a lake and, on the nearest shore, a tumultuous battle between two troops of soldiers dressed in bright colors.

"Probably *condottieri,*" Zinatano said in his thin voice. Then he explained to Gabriel. *"Condottieri* are leaders of mercenary soldiers hired by princes. From the banners, it seems to me that Piccinino, who serves Milan, is fighting against Sforza, who serves Venice. He'll have his hands full."

Looking down from their vantage point, they saw a team of horses laboriously pulling what Zinatano said was a cannon. Gabriel had heard of cannons but had never seen one before. They watched it being installed in its position and loaded. It was like a ballet, with men coming and going, making false starts and then returning, while one of them directed the operation with broad, theatrical gestures.

Gabriel could not take that war seriously. The blue water of the lake, the deep calm of the mountains, the meadows with black-and-white cows grazing in them, the resplendent colors of the uniforms—all this formed a springtime scene from which tragedy seemed to be excluded; Gabriel even had the feeling that the bodies lying in the thick grass would stand up when the game was over.

Suddenly the cannon thundered, ejecting an enormous cloud of smoke and a ball that fell in the midst of its own soldiers. It still had the desired effect: the enemy soldiers immediately scattered in small groups and headed into the mountains.

"We'd better get away from here," said Zinatano. "We'll go back to where the road branches off toward Iseo, and from there we'll go down to Milan." He had already turned his horse around. As though to excuse what Gabriel might regard as cowardice, he added, "The *condottieri* are magnanimous only if they're victorious. Be careful of those who have been defeated and want revenge for it!"

Soon after they started back in the direction from which they had come, they rounded a bend in the road and found it blocked by the blue handcarts full of chickens that they had passed earlier. Tragic silence hung over the mutilated bodies of the peasants. Scraps of torn clothing lay on the ground beside them and white feathers stirred uneasily in the wind.

THEY REACHED MILAN on a Monday. The city had spread beyond its ramparts, thrusting out crowded, bustling districts into the countryside. To enter it, they crossed a drawbridge guarded by soldiers wearing striped uniforms and plumed hats. What noisy, teeming streets! Zinatano's servants led the way and it was amazing to see the crowd open, like the Red Sea opening before Moses, at the approach of the gaudily dressed little banker. Via dei Profumieri, Via dei Pennachiari, Via dei Orefici . . . It was on that Street of Goldsmiths that they stopped, at the shop of Niccolò Malavolti, from whom Zinatano wanted to order a piece of jewelry for his daughter.

"Signor banker! What an honor!"

"How is your work going, Niccolò?"

"I have enough to keep me busy, thank God. The more wars destroy, the more people build and buy. It's as if they were running a race."

"Have you heard any news lately?"

"Our duke has offered his daughter in marriage to Francesco Sforza, the *condottiere.*"

"But he's his enemy!"

"Precisely. Have you ever seen the powerful of this world offer anything to a friend? A friend is someone who serves them: it's their enemies who must be bought off!"

Zinatano pointed his finger, adorned with a crimson ring, to the design he wanted on his daughter's jewelry, then he led Jekutiel and Gabriel to the Piazza Mercanti to see if he could find any important men there. The piazza, connected by six streets to the main districts of the city, was a square paved with bricks and surrounded by luxurious palaces with arcades and porticoes. Zinatano asked Gabriel to excuse him and his son while they went into the Broletto Nuovo for a few moments. While they were gone, Gabriel explored the piazza, drifting with the crowd, stocking his memory with words, smells, colors, faces, looks. . . . What a difference between this crowd and those in the north!

Zinatano and Jekutiel soon came back, accompanied by a stern-faced man with white, curly hair that emerged from his back *cappuccio* and hung down over the high collar of his red surcoat. Tall and broad, he formed such a contrast with the two frail bankers that he seemed to belong to a different species. Zinatano made the introductions.

"This is Samuel of Speyer, a banker in Soncino, and this is Gabriel of Benfeld, a scribe, a scholar in the Law, and a disciple of the

371

famous Maharil of Mainz. He's on his way to Soncino to stay with one of his cousins."

Samuel the banker knew Gabriel's cousin Elijah.

"He's a good craftsman," he said appreciatively in his booming voice, "a learned man and a good Jew!"

They all left together and reached Marignano before nightfall. Since Milan had no Jewish community, they could not have found a place to spend the night there. Jews on their way to or from Milan stopped at Marignano to eat and sleep in the famous inn kept by Joseph of Casalmaggiore, on the bank of the Lambro River.

Marignano was a fortified town perched on a mountaintop overlooking the river. In the inn they met Simon, Samuel's partner. Not only was he from Soncino, but his cousin was the partner of Gabriel's cousin! Simon was an expansive, good-natured fat man who instantly became friendly.

"Why are you wearing that ridiculous hat?" he asked Gabriel. "I must have a blue *cappuccio* in my baggage. It should fit you very well."

He snapped his fingers; a servant left and came back a little later with the *cappuccio* in question. Gabriel put it on. It suddenly seemed to him that he had become someone else.

They had dinner at the innkeeper's family table in the large trellised arbor. The evening was mild, the conversation pleasant. Surrounded by his children, some of whom were already married, Joseph of Casalmaggiore broke the bread, as was done in Benfeld, dipped it into the salt, and praised "Him who brings out bread from the earth." Despite his happiness at having become acquainted with so many new things, Gabriel felt a pang in his heart.

SONCINO, AT LAST. Gabriel had warmly thanked Zinatano and his son Jekutiel when he left them, and they had repeatedly invited him to come and visit them. He arrived in Soncino with Samuel and Simon the bankers, who took him to the house of his cousin Elijah.

Soncino, with its red brick wall and towers, stood in a green basin decorated with a wavy blue line: the Oglio River. Behind the wall were brick streets, brick houses with ogival doors, palaces adorned with colored mosaics and terra-cotta bas-reliefs, and the remains of an ancient citadel. In Soncino, everyone always seemed to be outdoors.

Elijah lived in a one-storied house with narrow doors and windows on a little street that had no official name but was called the Street of Jews because the small Jewish community was grouped there. Elijah's father, Moses, had turned one room of his house into a synagogue. He could not assemble more than one *minyan* for prayer, even on great occasions, because the community's thirtysome members belonged to only two families and included many women and children. When other families had expressed a desire to settle in Soncino, the town council had refused them permission. The nearest Jewish community outside of Soncino was in Orzinuovi, on the other side of Oglio, but it might as well have been on the other side of the earth because there was ceaseless quarreling between Soncino and Brescia over rights to the bridge that crossed the river.

Gabriel settled into Elijah's house, where he had been eagerly and joyfully welcomed, as if he were the greatest scholar the world had ever known. Elijah was short and plump, but as quick and agile as a lizard. His workshop was in the courtyard. There he engraved tombstones with great skill and amazing speed made necessary by the habit he had acquired, despite the remonstrances of his partner Giacobo, of not beginning work on a tombstone until it was supposed to be delivered.

Gabriel worked for a time with Elijah and Giacobo. As he cut into the stone before him with his graver, he thought of the hours he had spent in Gutenberg's cellar, making molds for letters in the same way. Engraving letters seemed to be his fate! During this period he decided what to put on the first page he would compose and print—for he had no doubt that he would someday print books. It was a passage in Job: "Oh that my words were written! Oh that they were inscribed in a book! Oh that with an iron pen and lead they were graven in the rock for ever!"

Embarrassed at seeing a scholar like Gabriel kneeling in the dust with a graver in one hand and a mallet in the other, Elijah suggested to him that until his abilities became more widely known, he could teach the Torah, and even the Talmud, to the children and adults of the community who wanted to learn from him. One day a lay brother named Ambrosino da Tormoli, a great specialist in stained glass who had a workshop in Soncino, came to ask Gabriel to give him Hebrew lessons so that he could read the Old Testament in its original language. Word of the lessons spread, and Hebrew became fashionable in Soncino.

373

Gabriel was still trying to find a way to finance a print shop. Elijah had quickly understood the importance of that project but he could not help to finance it, since he was never able to put aside a single ducat. He had, in fact, done something that greatly delayed the time when the project could be carried out: he had arranged a marriage betwen Gabriel and Estelina, daughter of his partner Giacobo. Gabriel, now known as Gabriele di Strasburgo, named his first son Abramo.

Because Elijah's house had now become a little cramped, Gabriel and Estelina moved to the corner of Orefici Street and San Antonio Street, where a goldsmith rented them one floor of his house. It seemed to Gabriel that nothing had ever happened in his life as important as the birth of his son Abramo. Since then, he had no longer been the same.

"The fathers shall not be put to death for the children, nor shall the children be put to death for the fathers; every man shall be put to death for his own sin." Gabriel had often copied that passage in Deuteronomy. He understood that a child did not have to die for his father's sins, but he firmly believed that a father was guilty of his child's sins. Otherwise, why would it be a *mitzvah* for a father to lead his son along the path laid down by the Almighty, blessed be He, proclaimed on Mount Sinai and recorded in the Torah? Yes, he thought, a father had to answer for his son and for his son's sons. That was how nations were preserved, for they could wither and die like individuals.

He now missed the Scroll of Abraham. Things would not be in order until his son's name was written after his own, and after those of Vifelin, Abraham, Matis. . . .

GABRIELE DI STRASBURGO'S great project did not begin to take shape until Israel-Nathan, son of Samuel the banker, returned from Padua. He was a thin, grave man with burning eyes beneath bushy gray eyebrows. A physician and a Talmudic scholar, he shared certain passions and convictions with Gabriel, notably with regard to the Cabala. They both regretted that at a time when the world was opening to the future and rediscovering the past, many Jews were taking refuge behind Jewish mysticism and becoming prisoners of it. They saw only one way to keep alive the values that had enabled the Jews to come through the centuries: reproduce books and make them known and available to everyone.

Israel-Nathan persuaded his father to advance the money

needed to install a press and buy metals. The white-haired banker deserved all the credit for parting with his ducats because he did not believe in printing. Gabriel decided to set up his shop in Elijah's cellar, where he would not have to worry about bothering the neighbors. Elijah and Giacobo offered to help; their skills made them highly qualified for designing and cutting letters. Isaiah the carpenter made the press according to Gabriel's instructions. It turned out that Gabriel had to reinvent everything that Gutenberg had developed after years and years of trial and error. He had the advantage over Gutenberg of knowing that printing was not just a dream, but he knew little about working with molten metal. His only certainty was that he had to mix lead, tin, and antimony. How he regretted not having followed the experiments that Hans Dünne recorded so meticulously!

His first efforts produced letters so fragile that the press broke them. The press itself was too rigid; its functioning had to be improved by means of leather straps that gave it a certain flexibility. After several months he had still not succeeded in making letters that could be used—except by Elijah's children, who played at being printers before the occupation existed.

Suddenly, in the year 1446 by the Christian calendar, an army of five thousand horsemen and a thousand foot soldiers, led by the *condottiere* Francesco Piccinino, came to Soncino. The town surrendered before a single cannon shot was fired. Piccinino represented the duke of Milan at that time.

The real war took place inside Soncino without weapons or soldiers, between the partisans of Milan and those of Venice, the Covis and the Barbos. The two sides spied on each other, dramatically denounced each other, and circulated insidious rumors. The "Milanese" soon spread the story that those comings and goings in the Jewish engraver's house, those noxious fumes that escaped through the cellar window, and those sounds unlike anything known were obviously evidence of a plot by the "Venetians." Israel-Nathan and Gabriel had to resign themselves to "closing up shop," as Elijah put it, and waiting for better days.

A few months later the *condottiere* Michele Attendolo took Soncino for the "Venetians" and Gabriel believed it was safe for him to go back to work. But then the "Venetians" accused him of fomenting some sort of mysterious scheme in favor of the "Milanese" and again he had to "close up shop."

Tents in the colors of Venice were pitched between the river and the ramparts. A stream of merchants, craftsmen, and travelers again began moving along the road from Bergamo to Cremona, which went through Soncino before dividing into two branches, one going toward Bologna and Ancona, the other toward Florence. Since Samuel and Simon were the only bankers in the town, their business prospered and their influence grew. They obtained permission for a Jewish butcher and a Jewish baker to live in Soncino, so that *kosher* meat would not have to be brought from Lodi and the women would be spared the work of making bread, *matzot* for Passover, and sweets for Rosh Hashanah. The butcher came from Pavia and the baker, at Gabriel's suggestion, from Benfeld: Gabriel had chosen his cousin Borack.

Borack reached Soncino in the summer of the year 5207 [1447] after the creation of the world by the Almighty, blessed be He. It was the first time he had ever left Benfeld and he was taken aback by the glaring sunlight, the tumult in the streets, and the excitability of the Italian people. He was further dismayed by the fact that there was no oven for him to use; he had to wait till one was built. Only after he had baked his first batch of bread, with the whole community eagerly following his every move, did Borack the baker become himself again.

Borack's arrival was especially important to Gabriel because he had brought with him the box containing the Scroll of Abraham, the "testimony" of another Abraham in Hippo, and the Narbonnese segment that had been copied on parchment and bound.

That evening, between the silent press and the cold melting pot, Gabriel read the scroll from beginning to end, without skipping over any of the names or dates. By the time he had finished, his sight was beginning to blur. He had weak eyes, but the tears trickling down his cheeks were not caused only by fatigue. He was filled with deep emotion when he thought of what the scroll represented: respect for tradition, the duty to bear witness, determination to pass on the heritage, the hope that had sustained the enterprise from one century to the next and still showed through in every line. He felt all this as a stirring victory over the tragedies of the human condition: savagery, death, oblivion. And it strengthened his resolve to print and distribute books.

Samuel the banker, who wanted his son Israel-Nathan to go back to practicing medicine, had refused to finance any more experiments. Gabriel had decided to visit Zinatano and Jekutiel, the bankers of Reggio nell'Emilia. They were men of knowledge and taste and he regretted not having told them about the new invention. But he had to postpone his visit to them because his wife Estelina was about to give birth and he wanted to be with her when their second child was born.

One day when Gabriel was helping his cousin Elijah to engrave a tombstone, little Giuseppe, Elijah's oldest son, came running up to them. He was a bold, resourceful boy of ten and, like many children in Soncino, he earned a little money by doing light work for travelers without servants. His round, freckled face was now flushed with excitement. Without waiting to catch his breath, he told the two men that after his lesson with Gabriel he had joined his friends and gone with them as usual to the place behind the San Giacomo Church where barbers shaved their customers in the open air. While the customers were waiting, the children brushed their breeches or polished the scabbards of their swords. Giuseppe had been at the feet of a man sitting on a stool when he overheard a conversation between a man who looked like a bandit and a young nobleman in a green doublet. They were talking about a payment of forty ducats for something to be done that night. Convinced that a crime was being planned, Giuseppe followed the young nobleman and saw him go into the palace of the Barbos, the "Venetians." Giuseppe then went back to the barbers behind the San Giacomo Church and saw that the man who looked like a bandit was still being shaved. When he left, Giuseppe followed him and saw him go into a tavern on Mercanti Street.

"Well, what of it?" asked Elijah.

"Don't you understand, father? There's going to be a murder in Soncino!"

"The fact that a young nobleman promised someone forty ducats doesn't prove anything, though I'll admit that it's a large sum. Who is there in Soncino that anyone would want to kill?"

"Sforza, the *condottiere!*" Giuseppe answered without hesitation.

Francesco Sforza had been in Soncino for several days. To everyone's surprise, he had refused to stay with Count Barbo, a leader of the "Venetians," and had gone instead to the palace of Count Covi, who was known for his Milanese sympathies. Francesco Sforza was an almost mythical figure: the ideal of knights, the hero of children, the dream of young women. He was as brilliantly successful in palaces as on the battlefield.

Gabriel and Elijah did not know what to make of Giuseppe's

377

story. The only way they could investigate it was to find out if young Lorenzo Barbo was wearing a green doublet that day. Since Elijah refused to leave his work, Gabriel went with Giuseppe to the Barbos' palace. They stood watching it through part of that afternoon. Finally Giuseppe tugged at Gabriel's sleeve. A young man in a green doublet, with a somber, vindictive expression, rode out of the palace, accompanied by several liveried servants who opened a path for him through the crowd.

"Who is that magnificent young lord?" Gabriel asked of the guards.

The guard eyed him disdainfully.

"Count Barbo's son, *il signore* Lorenzo."

When Gabriel came back and reported this to him, Elijah was panic-stricken.

"Then it's true! My God, what are we going to do? Should we keep quiet? Warn Sforza?"

"It's like a situation in Strasbourg," remarked Gabriel.

"What situation?"

"The family scroll tells about it. Strasbourg was also divided between two rival families, the Müllenheims and the Zorns, and we, the Jews, were always mixed up in their quarrels whether we liked it or not."

"Have we ever let anyone be killed when we could have prevented it?"

"No."

"Then," concluded Elijah, "we must go to Count Covi's palace and warn Sforza."

Shadows were already lengthening and there was no time to lose. Since Elijah would have no chance of being allowed into the palace —a tombstone engraver!—Gabriel put on his *lucco,* a long overgarment of ordinary black cloth that hung down to his heels, and went to see Manfredo Fieschi, an old nobleman to whose grandson he gave Hebrew lessons.

Manfredo Fieschi went to the palace with Gabriel and vouched for him. The commander of the guards, Falamesca da Castaleone, took them into a richly decorated room with historiated tapestries on the walls. Count Iacopo Covi, a thin, round-shouldered man with a pointed white beard, came forward to meet them. He warmly greeted his old friend Manfredo Fieschi, who introduced "Gabriele di Strasburgo, the famous writer."

"You're the man who's trying to invent a press for reproducing writing, aren't you?" said the count. He laughed at Gabriel's amazement and took him by the elbow to lead him toward the garden. "I had to have you spied on because there were rumors that you were the ringleader of a plot against Milan. . . . Why have you come to me today?"

"To tell you about another plot, this time a real one."

Gabriel reported what Giuseppe had overheard. The count listened very attentively.

"Wait here a moment," he said.

He came back accompanied by a man of imposing appearance, with a gold cup in his hand and an Oriental dagger in his belt, wearing a trim-fitting red satin doublet and black velvet breeches that molded his powerful thighs.

"This is Francesco Sforza," said the count. "Tell him what you just told me."

As he spoke, Gabriel looked at Sforza's muscular neck, willful chin, and aquiline nose. That man gave an impression of extraordinary strength and authority. When Gabriel had finished, the *condottiere* made no comment, but questioned him about the Cabala and asked him why the Jews did not use bills of exchange. Then he said, "The count tells me that you've invented a way of writing without a pen."

"I didn't invent it. I worked with the man who invented it, a goldsmith from Mainz. I'm now trying to rediscover his secret."

"If you succeed, come to see me. Perhaps in Milan, who knows? Perhaps in Venice." Sforza patted Count Covi on the shoulder, and the count responded with a rather forced laugh. "In any case, thank you, writer! I won't forget you. Can you show one of my men the tavern my . . . 'assassin' went into?"

THE NEXT DAY, the death of Filippo Maria Visconti, duke of Milan, became known in Soncino. Milan was now ready to be taken, and Francesco Sforza ordered his army to prepare for departure.

Before leaving Soncino, he stopped by Elijah's house to give Giuseppe a bag of money and thank Gabriel, who was in the cellar, melting a new mixture of lead, tin, and antimony. The *condottiere* was fascinated by Gabriel's work and asked him to explain in detail the technique of printing and the problems that still had to be solved. Gabriel composed the name *Sforza,* coated the metal letters with ink, placed a sheet of paper over them, and printed them by rubbing the paper with a brush. Sforza was as happy as a child when Gabriel gave him the sheet with his name printed on it.

Before mounting his horse and going off to conquer Milan, Francesco Sforza put his strong hand on Gabriel's shoulder.

"Thank you again, my friend. I'll always be obliged to you. The man has confessed, and so has his accomplice."

"What have you done with him?"

"Chi e morto non pensa alla vendetta" [He who is dead does not think of revenge].

"And young Lorenzo?"

"I talked to him," replied Sforza. Seeing Gabriel's surprise, he explained. "Words, strength, and authority are usually enough to persuade an individual. What I'm about to do now is much more difficult: conquering the multitude. Wish me good luck!"

NEARLY THREE YEARS PASSED before Francesco Sforza was able to make his victorious entry into Milan, acclaimed by the populace: *"Duca! Duca Sforza!"* This was in February of the year 1450 by the Christian calendar. Gabriel was then thirty-one and had three children: Abramo, Solomon, and Rachel.

Gabriel's progress in his work depended on the size of the sums he was able to procure. But four years later, when a peace agreement had finally been signed in Lodi between the "Milanese" and the "Venetians" and Francesco Sforza had taken possession of Soncino with the title of duke of Milan, the press was ready to function and seven complete sets of letters had been assembled: four in Hebrew and three in Latin.

Now the only problem was to find enough money to print the first book. Simon and Samuel the bankers had been practically ruined by the establishment of a pawnshop in Soncino, a form of usury tolerated by the Church. And Gabriel could not hope that sales would cover the expenses of the first book he intended to print, because it was the Scroll of Abraham.

It was only after Samuel's death that his son Israel-Nathan used the remains of the family fortune to buy enough lead and paper for a year of work. Israel-Nathan's two sons, Mosè and Giosuè-Salomone, did not appreciate the trade of usurer any more than their father did, and they set to work in Elijah's cellar without regret. They had both studied at the Talmudic academy in Cremona. Mosè had returned from Cremona with a wife and a son, Gershom, and had caught Gabriel's passion for printing as if it were a disease.

When the first page of the Scroll of Abraham finally came from their press, it was Israel-Nathan who took it in his hand. The ink on it was not yet completely dry. He looked at it both lovingly and critically, then showed it to the others. It bore the brief introduction that Gabriel had written:

"Today, the second day of the month of Adar in the year 5226 [March 8, 1466] after the creation of the world by the Almighty, blessed be He, I, Gabriele di Strasburgo, son of Aaron der Halter of Benfeld, have reproduced, with devices of iron and tin, seven copies of the testament of my ancestor Abraham, son of Solomon of Jerusalem. I pray to the Everlasting that this document will be as sacred to my sons and my sons' sons as it has been to me, my father, and my fathers' fathers."

The others had already read this a dozen times before it was set in type, but as they listened to Israel-Nathan reading it aloud they were all seized with an emotion that may have been a mixture of joy at having finally succeeded and excitement at seeing, for the first time, printed words in that language which to them was much more than a language.

Israel-Nathan was transfigured. His austere face was radiant.

"We're going to produce books!" he exclaimed. "We'll sell them at such a low price that even the poorest Jews will be able to buy them!" He raised his forefinger toward heaven, as though calling the Creator to witness, and in a solemn tone he gave an altered version of a passage in Isaiah: "For out of Zion shall go forth the Law, and out of Soncino the word of the Almighty!"

They surrounded Gabriel, clapping their hands. He had tears in his eyes and suddenly he felt the weight of all his past fatigue and disappointments. Elijah brought wine. *"Mazel tov! Mazel tov!"* they said to each other. They began dancing behind Israel-Nathan as he held the printed page above his head, like a scroll of the Law. They danced and laughed and wept, those Jewish printers, and sang their own versions of the Simchat Torah songs they had learned in childhood:

> *Abraham rejoiced*
> *In the gift of the Torah.*
> *Let us go and bring a sheaf*
> *In the name of the Torah.*

Their voices resounded under the vaulted ceiling of the cellar, intoxicating them more surely than wine.

> *Israel-Nathan, Giosuè-Salomone,*
> *Elijah, Giacobo, Gabriel, and Mosè*
> *Rejoice in the gift of the Law.*
> *Let us go and bring a sheaf*
> *For the celebration of the Torah!*

•   •   •

THIS MORNING I received a bulky package in the mail. On the wrapping paper I recognized the slanting, elegant handwriting of M.S., the Strasbourg archivist who had provided me with the name of Gabriel. It was a thick bundle of bad photocopies held by a rubber band. With it was a note written on a large sheet of paper folded in half:

> *Enclosed are records of the main lawsuits instituted by and against Gutenberg in Strasbourg between 1434 and 1439. I did not have time to read them in detail, but it seems to me that your Gabriel's name was cited in the case in which Gutenberg was opposed by the wood merchant Hans Schulheis and his wife Ennel (ff 13 and 14).*
>
> *I remain at your disposal for any help that I may be able to give you in your undertaking, within my modest competence.*

> *And, after the signature:*

> *P.S. The cost of the photocopies, plus postage, is 187 francs. Please pay that amount, preferably by postal check, to the Chief Treasurer and Paymaster of the Haut-Rhin.*

So Gabriel really did meet Gutenberg. My head is spinning. Where is reality? And where is fiction?

29

SONCINO

The Printers' House

"NEVER TOUCH another man's wife. Never strike one of your servants; or, if you do, send him far away. Finally, never ride a hard-mouthed horse or one that tends to lose its shoes." Francesco Sforza had learned those maxims from his father, also a respected *condottiere,* who felt that they dealt with the three main dangers to which men like them were exposed. But Francesco Sforza, the "undefeated man," did encounter two defeats: the first when his wife killed his mistress; the second when, at the age of sixty-five, he let death take him. He was mourned by many, in Milan and elsewhere.

Gabriel was disappointed, because he had intended to ask the duke for help at one time or another, but above all he was sad. Like everyone else present when Sforza, still a *condottiere,* had come into the cellar of Elijah's house, Gabriel had been deeply affected by his meetings with him. Giuseppe, who had saved money given to him by Sforza, burned an enormous candle in his memory, and the good-hearted Elijah wept as he had done when his father died.

Galeazzo Maria Sforza, Francesco's son, who had inherited his strength, shrewdness, and imposing appearance, succeeded him at the age of twenty-two. As soon as he arrived in Milan, the new duke surrounded himself with a splendid court devoted to the satisfaction of his passions.

SEVERAL BOOKS printed by Gutenberg in Mainz had crossed the Alps, notably a Bible dated 1454. Israel-Nathan bought a copy of it. The printing was of good quality but Gabriel felt that the results they achieved in their cellar could easily stand comparison with it. Print shops were being set up in many different places, but each new printer had to travel the slow road of discovery. Israel-Nathan and Gabriel were in the vanguard. They had decided to publish only in Hebrew.

In 1475 they printed *Sheva Enaim* by Rabbi Gedaliah ben David ben Yahya. The project took nearly a year of work and left them without a ducat. They took special care to avoid mistakes; it was Gabriel's son Abramo who did the proofreading. The appetite for knowledge was so prodigious at this time that all nine hundred thirty copies of the big volume were sold in less than two weeks, as if it had been a chivalric romance.

Israel-Nathan, who was in charge of accounting and distribution, calculated that sales had brought in two hundred forty-three ducats, which was only forty-three ducats more than the cost of the paper alone. That was not enough to pay the other expenses, such as lead and candles, and support a large family. There were six men working in what had come to be known as the *casa degli stampatori,* the printers' house: Israel-Nathan and his sons Mosè and Giosuè-Salomone, Gabriel and his older son Abramo, and Elijah. Elijah and Gabriel occasionally went back to engraving tombstones to feed their wives and children.

But publication of *Sheva Enaim* did help to make them better known. One day they received a letter from Guglielmo di Portaleone, Galeazzo Maria Sforza's Jewish physician. The duke of Milan, he wrote, intended to establish a print shop and wanted to see the Soncino printers "for advice."

"At last!" cried Giosuè-Salomone, who was ardently dedicated to printing and did not understand why all the rich men in Italy were not offering to finance their work.

"This may be our chance," said his father. "At least someone now knows we exist."

"Anything can happen!" was Gabriel's only comment.

He was already imagining a larger and less damp shop than Elijah's cellar, a new press, different cases for storing type. . . .

"Before we go to Milan," suggested Mosè, "maybe we should visit the print shops in Ferrara and Bologna."

Giosuè-Salomone frowned.

"We have nothing to learn from anyone, Mosè!"

"Mosè is right," Israel-Nathan said decisively. "Pride is a sin punished by the Almighty, blessed be He."

And so Giosuè-Salomone and Mosè went to Ferrara and Bologna. They brought back drawings of tools, tables, and details of presses, but the main conclusion they drew from their journey was that they were ahead of their competitors, primarily because of the work that Gabriel had done with Gutenberg. This suggested the idea of sending Mosè's son Gershom, now sixteen and gifted for the trade, to go and study a few years in Mainz. Gutenberg was dead now, but his print shops—the one he had owned at the time of his death and the one that had been taken away from him by his partners—were still outstanding examples.

"It will help us to keep our head-start," said Israel-Nathan. "Every technique makes progress, every art changes. We'll be the best so long as we're not satisfied with ourselves. It's easy for us to be the best in Soncino, but what do we care about that? Each book we publish must be finer and less expensive than any book published anywhere else at the same time."

They had begun work on *Massechtah Berachot* but they did not have enough money to buy the paper they needed; the invitation to visit the duke of Milan seemed to them a promise sent by the Almighty.

It was decided that Gabriel and Israel-Nathan would go to Milan together. They left in the middle of December, just after the last candle of Chanukah. This was the first time Gabriel had been away from Soncino since he arrived there some thirty-five years earlier. His memories from that time—Zinatano the superbly dressed little banker, the battle on the lake—were vague and seemed to belong to another life. He had not seen time slipping past. Like everyone completely intent on moving toward a single goal, he had left a great deal of himself along the way. His hair and beard were now almost white, his children had grown up and married before he had had time to know them, his wife had become an old woman without his noticing it. He was not inclined toward regret or melancholy; he considered that in devoting his life to printing he had only acted in accordance with the will of the Almighty. The Jews would have their inexpensive books, and could glorify the Everlasting.

Because of their age, and because they were not used to long hours of horseback riding, Gabriel and Israel-Nathan did not travel very fast. Weary and aching, they decided to stop at the inn of Joseph of Casalmaggiore, where Gabriel remembered having eaten, long ago, with Zinatano, Jekutiel, Samuel, and Simon. But Joseph was dead and it was his nephew Mano who now kept the inn. In the afternoon, Gabriel insisted on resting awhile in the arbor, where pale sunlight enabled him to forget that it was winter. Exposure to the chilly air was evidently too much for a man who had seldom come out of his cellar, because the next morning he had a high fever and could not get up.

Israel-Nathan went back to Soncino to bring his son Giosuè-Salomone, who had studied medicine before becoming a printer.

The weather had turned bitterly cold. Gabriel's bed had been pulled close to the fireplace. He was delirious; in his fever, he kept repeating that printing had to be done in bigger letters, because big letters could be read by people with good eyes, while small ones could not be read by people with bad eyes. "Bigger! Make the letters bigger!" he mumbled. "Use a larger type and reduce the space between letters if necessary. Bigger!" Now and then he would talk about money and the price of paper.

Giosuè-Salomone limited his treatment to taking ice from the nearby pond and putting pieces of it on Gabriel's forehead and wrists and over his heart. Gabriel was delirious for six days. During that time he never spoke of anything but printing and books, except for one evening when he called for "Lorenz's wife" and asked her to bring him beer. "Lean toward me!" he said "Lower!" Israel-Nathan, who was sitting at his bedside, turned his head away and put his hands over his ears.

On the morning of the seventh day—the Christians had rung church bells for Christmas all night—Gabriel woke up cured. His forehead was cool, his eyes were clear. He simply felt very weak.

"I know," he said, "what we must add to our print shop: movable signs to show the vowel sounds, above and below the letters. What do you think of that?"

It was now his son Abramo who sat at his bedside. He stared at Gabriel in bewilderment, as if he did not understand what he had said. Only then did Gabriel look around him.

"But. . . . Where are we?"

He had to be told how he had fallen ill and become delirious. He also had to be told that there was now no reason to go to Milan: Duke Galeazzo Maria Sforza had been killed by three noblemen who could no longer tolerate his caprices and contempt.

"May the Almighty deliver us from evil!" said Gabriel.

He stayed at the inn till he had completely recovered, then he and Abramo headed for Soncino. When they arrived, they found Israel-Nathan and his sons plunged in gloom. The three of them were sitting in the cellar, looking at each other without speaking, when Gabriel came in, delighted to be back with the smell of ink and lead.

"What's the matter, my friends?" he asked. "Does it make you so sad to see me again?"

Israel-Nathan pointed to a book on the table in front of Giosuè-Salomone. Gabriel picked it up. A heavy, well-bound volume, printed in Hebrew; skillfully done, but without imagination. It was a collection of religious precepts by Rabbi Jacob ben Asher. Gabriel knew immediately that this book had not been printed on *his* press. He looked at the colophon. The letters were small and he had to hold the book farther away from his eyes to read: ". . . I am the crown of all the sciences, a secret hidden from all. I write clearly, without a pen, and I am composed in sections, without a scribe. Ink covers me all at once. I write straight, with no need of lines. . . ." The book had been printed in Pieve di Sacco by a physician, Meshulam ben Mosè Giaccobo Cusi, and was dated 5235 [1475].

"But we printed before that!" said Gabriel.

The others looked at him. They had known he would be indignant when he read that colophon.

"No, Gabriel," said Israel-Nathan. "Our first book, *Sheva Enaim,* has the same date."

"But we printed the Scroll of Abraham nearly ten years ago!"

"Seven copies, Gabriel, seven! We're the only ones who have ever seen it."

Gabriel's face was ashen. He suddenly stood up.

"I'm leaving today to see Zinatano the banker. Let's pray that he's still alive. If the Almighty, blessed be He, is willing, I'll come back with money and we'll show them things they've never even imagined!"

387

GABRIEL'S PLAN was to publish the complete text of the Jewish Bible with signs above and below the consonants to indicate the vowels, as was done with the texts of prayers, and as he had thought of doing during his delirium. Hebrew is usually written only with consonants and the reader must mentally insert the vowels. Gabriel's edition of the Bible would have the advantage of being easier to read, which would make it accessible to more people, and it would also have the advantage of avoiding misinterpretations. A given combination of consonants can have different meanings, depending on the vowels attributed to it. The combination *daleth-waw-daleth,* for example, can be read as *dod, dud,* or *David,* and can mean, besides the name David, "uncle" or "barrel." But who was to choose among different possible readings when the text was the work of the Almighty? Israel-Nathan persuaded the highly respected Rabbi Chaim to undertake the task of placing vowel signs all through the Bible.

Rabbi Chaim collaborated with Gabriel's son Abramo, who did the proofreading. Gabriel had cast the letters and vowel signs; Giosuè-Salomone and Mosè experimented with the reproduction of engravings; Israel-Nathan traveled over the whole region in search of more and more money. Zinatano had been generous, but his son Jekutiel claimed that his father's mind was no longer clear and emphatically told the Soncino printers not to come back.

Rabbi Chaim's work went very slowly. It sometimes went far beyond typography, since some words that could be interpreted in different ways had always been a matter of dispute among supporters of various schools of thought. Gabriel and the others had to accept the need to publish another book while they waited for that Bible in which they placed so much hope.

The book was *Massechtah Berachot,* the treatise on benedictions, and it was published in 1484 by the Christian calendar. The printing was perfect: the inking was neither too dark nor too light, and parchment friskets prevented any smudging around the columns of text, which stood out with just the right degree of sharpness—"like the stripes on a prayer shawl," said Elijah. It had been decided not to use vowel signs in this book, so as to keep the effect of surprise for the Bible. The innovation lay in the engravings, or, more precisely, the quality of the engravings, which was the result of Giosuè-Salomone's diligent, painstaking work. In the colophon, he had coyly identified himself in an acrostic: the first letters of lines one, three, five, seven, etc. formed his name.

The book was very well received. Important people, whether they were scholars or not—in that time, all prominent figures prided themselves on knowing Latin, Hebrew, and Greek—sent their servants to the "printers' house" in Soncino to buy one or two copies of the highly praised treatise.

GABRIEL DID NOT LIVE to see the Soncino Bible: he died just after the publication of *Massechtah Berachot.* One afternoon he felt more tired than usual, but he still wanted to finish printing the first proofs of the first page of the Bible. Gershom, now back from Mainz, had designed an engraving around the first word of Genesis, *Bereshit* ["In the beginning"], in ornate letters intended both to glorify the Almighty who created all things and to inspire the respect with which the text should be read. Gabriel locked up the metal form, inked it, covered it with a sheet of paper, and once again pushed the movable part of the little press made for that purpose. He did not finish his act. Sudden pain gripped his chest and he fell lifeless at the foot of the press.

AFTER A LONG PERIOD of mourning for Gabriel's death, Giosuè-Salomone replaced him, and he in turn was replaced in his former work by his nephew Gershom, who had more skill and imagination than all the others in the *casa degli stampatori* combined. Rabbi Chaim patiently continued his laborious work and Abramo remained the best proofreader in Italy.

Abramo did not measure up to his father, perhaps because Gabriel had always treated him like a kind of servant. He was now past forty and had three children—Meshulam, Daniel, and Yochanan—but he had no other ambition in life than escaping now and then from the tyranny of his wife Deborah.

A year older than Abramo, beautiful and majestic, Deborah was one of those women who knew everything, controlled everything, and constantly gave the members of their families, particularly the men, the feeling that if they had not devoted themselves to them, they could have reached unimaginable heights of fame and glory. Deborah knew the Talmud and the commentaries on it, and, like all well-read people of the time, she could quote Vergil, Horace, and Petrarch. She dreamed of transforming the "printers' house" into a center of literary discussion and activity, but she had always been stopped by the indifference, and even the refusal, of the print-ers themselves, who were much too busy with such matters as alloys, inking, and production costs to think of glory.

She had held her father-in-law Gabriel in a certain esteem, not so much because of his achievements as because he had worked with Gutenberg himself. As for the others, she placed them on the same level as her husband: they were incapable of attracting visi-tors more important than some bookseller from Milan or some rabbi who was curious to see those men who printed books in Hebrew. Abramo had long since stopped pretending to appreciate her Greek and Latin quotations, which left him cold.

Every day, as soon as he could, he went down into the cellar to correct proofs, or went to work with Rabbi Chaim, who was still preparing the text of the Bible. He was then able to exercise his unmatched talent for spotting the slightest mistake. He had "a sharp eye," as his father had said. Deborah considered it a minor talent but he knew there was no good book without a good proof-reader, and the respect of Giosuè-Salomone and Gershom was enough for him.

One day Moses of Speyer, a Venice silk merchant and an ardent booklover, stopped to visit the print shop on his way through Soncino. When Israel-Nathan expressed regret at not being able to invest more money in the shop, Moses offered to introduce one of the printers to a well-known banker in Venice, Hayim Meshulam del Banco, who often helped artists. But Israel-Nathan had become too old for such a journey, the others were too busy at that time, and there was no more talk of Venice.

Jews driven from Spain by new persecutions were beginning to arrive in Italy. Among all her other activities, Deborah naturally devoted herself to receiving the refugees in Soncino. She took in a doctor from Toledo, Don Jacob Senior, and his daughter Sarah. The doctor, his wife, and their daughter had converted to Chris-tianity, but the persecutions did not spare even the Marranos, as the new Christians were called—they themselves preferred the term Anusim, "forced ones," because they were forced to live a lie. The doctor's wife had been denounced for observing the law of *kashrut* by never serving milk and meat in the same meal, which obviously meant that she had converted only in words and not from the heart. When questioned, she had answered that she did not like the taste of milk and meat together, and she had held to that answer until she died under torture.

While Don Jacob Senior was telling this story to Deborah—everyone always turned to Deborah to tell stories—Abramo looked at Sarah, a pale, dark-haired young woman with a sorrowful expression, and had an impulse to take her hand. He scarcely heard what was being said. As she and her father were leaving, she smiled sadly at Abramo.

The next day Deborah told Abramo that she had arranged for Don Jacob Senior and Sarah to go horseback riding, and asked him to take them to the hostler at the San Giuseppe Gate. Abramo took Sarah's elbow to help her mount her white mare, but one of them made a wrong movement and his hand imprisoned a breast as soft, warm, and palpitating as a dove. Don Jacob Senior was looking elsewhere. Sarah blushed; Abramo opened his hand and released the dove.

"You shouldn't have done that," she murmured.

But the smile that accompanied her words excited him still more.

ABRAMO DID NOT SEE Don Jacob and Sarah again before they left for Venice, where they were going to stay with a close friend, Jacob Mancino.

So that his wife Deborah would not see a connection, Abramo had the patience to wait several days before announcing—falsely—that Rabbi Chaim's work, which he alone had been following, was nearly finished.

"Now we absolutely must have more money," said Giosuè-Salomone.

"What was the name of that merchant from Speyer who knew a banker in Milan?" asked Abramo.

"Moses. Moses of Speyer. And it was Venice, not Milan."

"One of us should go there," suggested Gershom.

Giosuè-Salomone and Israel-Nathan agreed on this; they had little hope that that unknown banker would help them, but nothing ventured, nothing gained.

"Which of us will go?" asked Giosuè-Salomone.

Following his plan, Abramo answered, "I think Gershom and I should go together. He'll give the banker a copy of *Massechtah Berachot* and I'll give him one of the seven copies of the Scroll of Abraham. The perfection of the first and the fidelity of the second ought to be enough to persuade him that helping us will be a work of piety."

There was nothing to be said against this, and even Deborah could not prevent Abramo from going to Venice with Gershom, although her expression clearly showed that she thought her poor husband would cut a pitiful figure among the Venetian bankers.

MOSES OF SPEYER, the silk merchant, shared a business house in Venice with two other German Jewish merchants. He lodged Abramo and Gershom in his modest palazzo at one end of the Campo San Canciano.

They had arrived during the carnival season and that strange city with liquid streets was full of people wearing disguises. White masks, black capes, swirling dances, loud singing—Abramo and Gershom dreamed of joining in that wild celebration whose purpose was perhaps to make it possible to forget the tenacious smell of sludge and death. Moses of Speyer showed Venice to the two dazzled provincials from Soncino.

Claiming that he was tired from his journey, Abramo let Moses and Gershom continue their sightseeing without him. He then made inquiries and learned that Jacob Mancino lived in a dark yellow house on the Campo San Polo, behind the Casa Bernardo, at the edge of the Gran Canale. At the thought that Sarah was there, his heart leapt in his breast. But how was he to let her know that he was in Venice, that he had come there to see her, and that he was waiting for her? He remembered that Moses had spoken of "love messengers" who could be found strolling with courtesans in the arcade of the Procuratie.

"Prudentissima signorina, scialom," he wrote. "I am now in Venice and I would very much like to see you. . . ." When he had finished, he went to the Procuratie, blushing with embarrassment, to have a "love messenger" deliver his note and bring back an answer.

He then went to the Rialto Bridge, where the messenger had agreed to meet him when he returned. The crowd was dense and Oriental fragrances were mingled with the odor of salt and iodine. Canal boats and barges were loading and unloading all sorts of merchandise. Gondolas with gracefully curved bows and sterns, covered with brightly colored cloth, were discharging passengers— white masks, black capes—who merged into the crowd. Abramo saw German Jewish merchants dressed like Moses of Speyer: long velvet cloaks and big, wide-brimmed black hats over crimson skull-caps. Suddenly he recognized his messenger.

"Did you give her my note?" he asked.

"Sì, signore."

"Did she say anything?"

"No, signore."

"Did she read it?"

"Yes, in front of me."

"How did she act?"

"She seemed perturbed, *signore.*"

"What did she do with the note?"

"She hid it inside her dress."

"That's all?"

"That's all."

"Could you deliver another note?"

"Of course, *signore,* if you pay me."

They went to Moses's house. The messenger waited downstairs while Abramo feverishly wrote words that came from his heart: *"Perfetta colomba, signorina mia carissima, scialom.* My heart is breaking. Why have you not written a few lines to reassure me? Why. . . ?"

This note, like the one before it, went unanswered. He thought of going to Jacob Mancino's house to see her, but then Moses and Gershom came back. They had made an appointment with the banker for the next day.

As soon as he awoke the following morning, Abramo wrote a third note: *"Diletto del cor mio, scialom.* You cannot imagine the power of my desire to see you again. Why this silence? When I think that we are leaving Venice after *shabbat.* . . . Have pity on me, *colomba mia!"* He would not deliver the note himself: he had no wish to encounter Sarah's father. But this time he had to succeed, because he was already running out of money.

The carnival awakened toward noon—white masks, black capes. There was dancing in the public squares and in the *calli,* those narrow little streets that wound their way among houses and stopped at canals or dead ends. Abramo had found his "love messenger" again, but Sarah still had not answered.

In the afternoon Moses of Speyer took his two printers to the palace of Hayim Meshulam del Banco. They went there in a gondola and Abramo violently regretted that Sarah was not beside him. They entered the palace through a carved wooden portico painted dark green, the same color as the water of the lagoon. White marble steps. On the second floor the banker, an affable man in a green brocade robe, was waiting for them. He thanked them warmly for the two books they had sent him, and especially for the Scroll of Abraham, which he would read from beginning to end, he promised, because he was deeply moved by its story.

He led them into a vast room with bay windows overlooking the lagoon, marble pillars, precious tapestries, paintings, iridescent stained-glass windows. . . . Abramo, entranced, thought of his wife Deborah—what would she not have given to be in his place!

The banker introduced them to a small group of men and women who suspended their conversation.

"These are the printers from Soncino whose books you see here."

An elegant young man with curly hair and whiskers stepped toward them.

"This is Count Pico della Mirandola," announced the banker. "He's said to know everything that a human mind can know today."

Pico della Mirandola made a graceful gesture with his hand, as though to brush aside the compliment, and congratulated Gershom and Abramo.

"Your work is remarkable. I've been told that one of you studied in Mainz."

"Yes, I did," replied Gershom. "But Abramo's father worked with Gutenberg."

"Really?"

"In Strasbourg," said Abramo, now feeling perfectly at ease.

Another man came forward. He had a grave manner, long hair, and heavy features. He gave Abramo a friendly look.

"Your family book," he said, "is extraordinary. Anyone who doesn't know its story *vivit et est vitae nescius ipse suae:* lives, but is not aware of what he lives."

"Ovid!" a third man said triumphantly, then launched into a long speech in Greek.

The conversation continued in several languages. Abramo had difficulty following it and remembering the names of all the important people who were introduced to him: Elia del Medigo, the only Jew who taught at the University of Padua; Antonio Zerliga, prothonotary of the Cathedral of Saint Mark; Aldo Manuzio, who told him about the paintings on the walls: a view of Venice by Vittore Carpaccio, a portrait of a *condottiere* by Gentile Bellini, conservator of the Grand Palace. . . .

Abramo was jubilant. He could not help thinking of his wife again and it was because of her that he tried to remember all those names, knowing that when she heard them she would be tortured unmercifully by excruciating pangs of jealousy.

Count Pico della Mirandola began discussing the Cabala with him, and had just said that he saw the essential basis of Christianity in it when Elia del Medigo came to take leave of them.

"May the Master of the world bless the work you've undertaken!" he said to Abramo, embracing him. "It's sacred work."

"And why," asked Pico della Mirandola, "should the art of printing be more sacred than any of the others?"

"Because it strives to transmit wisdom. What do you think of that?"

The question was addressed to Abramo.

"I can only speak for myself," he said. "But for centuries my ancestors copied the same texts at the same rate, one by one. That was as true of my own grandfather, may God keep his soul, as it was of Abraham the scribe in Jerusalem, more than a thousand years ago."

People who represented the cream of Venetian intellectual life had formed a circle around Abramo, the printer from Soncino. He did not know if his words would hold their attention, but he knew exactly what he wanted to say.

"Today," he continued, "thanks to Gutenberg of Mainz and my father, may God keep his soul, who worked with him, in a few months we can reproduce hundreds of copies of what it took a whole lifetime to copy once. If life on earth is a race between good and evil, between light and darkness, it's important to spread the divine word as rapidly as possible."

Gershom stared round-eyed at Abramo. And Abramo peremptorily ended his oration:

"Then the world will be saved!"

Pico della Mirandola was speechless. Elia del Medigo again clasped Abramo to his broad chest.

"You've explained, much better than I could have done, why printing is a sacred art. God bless you!"

THEY WENT BACK TO Moses's house, happy as children: Gershom because the banker had given them a substantial sum for the print shop in Soncino, Abramo because he felt in luck and was sure he would see Sarah.

An answer from her was waiting for him. "You are mad," she wrote, "but I will meet you this evening near the Fondaco dei Turqui, opposite the San Marcuala Church, at the hour of vespers."

It was as if impatience were burning the soles of his feet. He left far ahead of time, crossed the canal on the Rialto Bridge, and mingled with the disguised revelers—white masks, black capes— who were still tirelessly running, leaping, and dancing.

He saw her get out of a gondola. She wore a black silk cape and her face was covered by a veil, also of black silk, but he recognized her instantly.

"Prudentissima signorina!" he exclaimed. *"Beezrat ha-Shem* [with God's help], you've come!"

"Don't shout," she said in an undertone. "My father has found your notes."

Abramo did not hear her.

"Signorina! Vita che ami da morte. . . ."

"I've come to ask you to stop writing to me."

"Amor mio! Amor mio!"

Unable to restrain himself any longer, he took her in his arms and pressed her against him. She abandoned herself for a moment, then halfheartedly pushed him away.

"You shouldn't have done that," she said, as she had said in Soncino.

Just then a terribly large man stepped between Abramo and Sarah. He wore a black cape and a sad white mask.

"You're forcing your attentions on this young lady!"

"No, I'm not! Leave us alone! We're together!"

The man drew his dagger. There were screams. Sarah backed away till she came to the gondola that had brought her, then she turned and got into it.

"Sarah!"

The man in the sad white mask put the point of his dagger against Abramo's chest. Abramo saw the gondola moving away from the dock. He suddenly pushed the dagger aside, shoved the man backward, and began running along the Fondamenta. He caught up with the gondola, saw his beloved, and jumped.

When he realized that he was not going to land on the deck of the gondola, he took a few disorderly steps in the air, as if he were trying to go back, and then plunged into the green water of the canal, splashing the disguised dancers—white masks, black capes —who applauded his spectacular exit.

"WHY DID YOU JUMP into the water?" Gershom asked him for the tenth time.

"Gershom, I swear I didn't jump into the water! I jumped: that's one thing; and I fell into the water: that's another."

"It seems you're the first one to do that since the opening of the carnival."

"Well, someone had to begin!"

THEY LEFT VENICE the next day. When they arrived in Soncino they learned that immediately after their departure Venice had declared war on the duke of Ferrara, who was supported by Milan, Naples, and Florence. This did not change life in the printers' house. They made good use of the Venetian banker's money by publishing seven books in succession, including a theological work by Joseph Albo and the *Pirke Abot*.

Abramo had settled back into his ordinary life. The names he had scrupulously reported to his wife were still like so many thorns in her flesh. She had listened to them, tight-lipped, and then reacted with a scathing Latin quotation: *"Margaritas ante porcos!"* [Pearls before swine!]

Rabbi Chaim finally finished preparing the text of the Bible and the printers began setting it in type.

Abramo's three sons had returned. The first two, Meshulam and Daniel, had been in Padua, where, at Deborah's insistence, they had studied with the famous Rabbi Mintz. Almost as soon as he came back, Meshulam had married the timid Rachel, Giosuè-Salomone's daughter. Yochanan, the youngest of the three, had spent two years with the painter David of Lodi and had learned engraving in Donatello's studio. It was he who drew and engraved most of the ornamental capitals and frontispieces that Gershom had not had time to make for the Bible on which they were all working.

One day they were visited by Abraham ben Chaim, a Jewish printer from Bologna, who examined what they had done and asked to join them. He was taciturn but he worked with something that went beyond talent, skill, and perseverance: he put love into what he did.

"Anyone who reproduces the word of the Almighty with such

fervor and capability has the Shechinah in him!" said Israel-Nathan, nodding his white-haired head.

The composition, printing, and binding—five hundred eighty sheets, each bearing two thirty-line columns—were finished on the day after Rosh Hashanah in the year 5248 [1488] after the creation of the world by the Almighty, blessed be He.

It was late afternoon; the light of the setting sun came into the cellar through the small window.

Giosuè-Salomone spread a white cloth over one corner of the table and placed on it the first bound copy of what would come to be known as the Soncino Bible. All the men who had worked to produce it stood there motionless, with their arms hanging at their sides, and their work clothes seemed to be festive garments.

Old Israel-Nathan stepped toward the Book to pick it up, but it was too heavy for him. He stroked it with his fingertips and blessed those around him. Then he bent over the Book and kissed it with his pale lips. He straightened up, thanked the Holy One, blessed be He, for His mercy, and turned the thick leather cover. He saw the superbly engraved page on which Gabriel had been working when he died, the page that announced, *"Bereshit. . . ."* [In the beginning. . . .]

And Israel-Nathan burst out sobbing.

• • •

I HAD WRITTEN part of the next chapter when the sky fell on my head, in the form of mail from Italy: bibliographic documents concerning works printed in Soncino between 1484 and 1492. I was already familiar with most of them, having read either the documents themselves or descriptions of them. It was in Professor Di Rossi's scholarly study, for example, that I had learned of the acrostic giving Giosuè-Salomone's name. But I had not read the colophon of Massechtah Berachot and did not know that it was actually composed of three parts.

Now that I had it before my eyes, in Hebrew with a facing Latin translation, I saw that the first part, in prose, praised and thanked God; that the second part, in verse, secretly named Giosuè-Salomone; and that the third part, in prose, describing the work put into that edition of Massechtah Berachot, was simply signed "Gabriel, son of Aaron, known as Gabriel of Strasbourg."

A kind of tingling ran through my body. I stood up with my mind empty and went to make coffee for myself. Then, without going back to my desk, I went out to walk awhile in the street. I stopped at the Petit Béarn for a sandwich. I was alone at the counter. For a few moments, through the open door, I watched gendarmes going in and out of the barracks across the street. I was really, almost physically, aware of being at the exact point of intersection of two stories: the horizontal story of the present and the vertical story of the past.

Suddenly I wanted to have another look at that photocopy I had received from Italy. I was seized with a kind of delayed-action excitement: reality had unquestionably confirmed what the logic of my thought processes, or my intuition, or my memory—but then what is memory made of?—had incorporated into my narrative.

I reread "Gabriel, son of Aaron, known as Gabriel of Strasbourg." No doubt of it: Gabriel was really there. He had waited five hundred years for me on the last page of that Treatise on Benedictions, one of the earliest known printed Hebrew books. I could not help calling my close friends, as well as Robert Laffont, because I was certain that the project I had undertaken, backed by their confidence, had now been suddenly and undeniably justified.*

I then went back to work with renewed energy. I decided to alter my plan and close the first part of my book at this point, as though closing a circle, going from Jerusalem to Soncino by way of Alexandria, Hippo, Toledo, Cordova, Narbonne, Troyes, Strasbourg. . . . The half-written chapter would become the first chapter of the second part, with Abramo the proofreader, holder of the Scroll and Book of Abraham, as its guiding thread.

I was mechanically rereading the Hebrew and Latin texts of the second part of the colophon when I suddenly realized—though I normally have little ability to discern such things—that there was a pattern in the beginnings of the last six lines of the Latin translation:

> *Opportune veniens . . .*
> *Memoratam . . .*
> *Mentis addita conjunctis . . .*
> *Robore suo tradetur . . .*
> *Brakhot tractatum . . .*
> *Ad erudiendum . . .*

---

* Publisher of the French edition of this book—Trans.

399

If the first letter is taken from each line, starting at the bottom, the result is *ABRMMO*. And if the first two words of the third line are reversed (addita mentis *instead of* mentis addita), *ABRMMO* becomes *ABRAMO*.

So my ancestors were all there, hidden in words, concealed between lines, as in those fairy tales in which the right word at the right time turns a toad into a prince, or like those dry, gray buds that respond to water by opening and reviving—they are called, I believe, roses of Jericho.

This time my excitement was so great that I called Rabbi Szteinzaltz in Jerusalem and told him about my adventures.

"That's very interesting," he said. "As you can see, the course you took was justified. Now you must let yourself be carried along by that Gabriel's descendants."

I imagined his gentle expression, his sparse red beard, his lively eyes.

"And then?" I asked.

"Then, if all goes well, Marek Halter, you'll finally succeed in rejoining yourself!"

Part Two

30

SONCINO

Letters to a Father

THE SONCINO bible was well received by the humanists. They praised its engravings, the quality of its printing, and the great care that had been taken in proofreading it, though their opinions were divided on the innovation of indicating vowel sounds by means of special signs. Pico della Mirandola bought a copy of the book and wrote to Abramo and Gershom to express his enthusiasm. When Deborah saw his letter, she could scarcely believe her eyes.

The Soncino printers now turned their attention to drawing up a schedule for the next few years. Gershom wanted to publish Petrarch and Abstemio. His father Mosè and his uncle Giosuè-Salomone were opposed to it.

"Anyone can publish books in Latin nowadays," said Mosè. "It's our duty to go on publishing inexpensive books in Hebrew."

"But a print shop must also keep up with the times," objected Gershom. "Can we live among the people of other nations without sharing their joys, sorrows, wisdom, and passions?"

"We *do* share them!" said Giosuè-Salomone. "But we're now the only ones who can share our own!"

"That sharing can't go in only one direction, uncle."

Disputes of this kind were repeated more and more often. It soon became clear that the Soncino printers would have to dissolve their partnership. They made the decision together, taking account not only of their differences but also of everything they had in common, which they were determined to preserve. Abramo brought a big jug of wine that day and they drank to life— *"Lechaim!"*—knowing that a new adventure was about to begin for each of them.

That evening Abramo washed himself and put on his *shabbat* clothes. Without answering Deborah when she asked him if he had lost his reason, he took out four of the six remaining copies of the Scroll of Abraham printed by his father Gabriel.

"My children," he said, "before life separates us, I want to give you this book."

His voice faltered, but not at the idea of separation. His emotion came from that continuity, that permanence, that victory over time and oblivion, which it was now his responsibility to embody before his descendants.

"I'm giving it to you," he went on, "so that it will serve you as a guide. Here's your copy of it, Meshulam; and yours, Daniel; and yours, Yochanan; and yours, Esther. Respect it, and life will respect you."

"Amen," replied his children.

Abramo could have continued speaking but it seemed to him that he had already said what really mattered. Now it was up to each of them—Meshulam the printer, Daniel the Cabalist, Yochanan the architect, and Esther—to carry on, each according to his or her conscience and destiny, beneath the gaze of the Almighty, blessed be He.

THE SONCINO PRINTERS published a few more books together, then Mosè died, and it was like a signal. Giosuè-Salomone went to Naples, where he took over the print shop of Joseph Gunzerhauser, one of their competitors, and began working on an edition of the Pentateuch. Gershom, a great traveler, went to France, then was invited by Count Martinengo to set up a shop in Brescia. Abramo wanted to join him there but Deborah refused to leave Soncino and it was their son Meshulam who went to Brescia. Yochanan went to Florence, where his friend the sculptor and architect Luca Fancelli, whom he had met in Mantua, wanted his help in making a monument commissioned by the Medicis.

There remained only the very old Israel-Nathan, Abramo, and his second son Daniel, who was much more interested in the Cabala than in printing. With the help of a printer staying in Soncino only temporarily, Israel-Nathan and Abramo published Maimonides's *Yad ha-Chazakah,* then Israel-Nathan died. Abramo abandoned the next project—the poems of Judah Halevi—and began earning his living by teaching Hebrew grammar to the sons of some of the city's noble families.

Deborah now spent nearly all her time in bed. No one knew if she was ill—she complained of pains in her back, feet, and heart—or if it was her way of saying that she regretted not having had the kind of life for which she was made. Abramo sometimes let her call him several times before going to see what she wanted: an extra pillow, which she would soon push aside; a book, which she would stop reading because it was too heavy; a compress, which she would find too hot or too cold . . .

When his son Daniel or his daughter Esther came for a visit, Abramo was relieved of his obligation to take care of Deborah. During those respites he went out to stroll around the ramparts, walking with slow little steps as if he were already an old man. He always stopped in front of the livery stable at the San Giuseppe Gate; memories of what had happened there made his hand feel warm, and he looked at it as if he expected to see some trace of the marvelous breast it had held. Then he went home happy. Deborah could call him as much as she liked.

Sometimes, at night (Deborah was a sound sleeper), he took a candle and went down to the deserted print shop where everything —even the smell of ink, it seemed to him—was slowly mildewing. He would reread old proofs or put a tray of type in order. He scarcely disturbed the spiders, yet he had the feeling that the print shop was coming back to life around him. Ah, what rich, beautiful hours he and the other Soncino printers had lived there!

A LARGE GROUP OF Jewish refugees soon arrived from Spain, having been expelled by a royal decree after the fall of Granada. There were many Cabalists among them, including the man who had put forward the greatest number of arguments to prove that the Messianic era was about to begin: Isaac ben Judah Abrabanel, former treasurer of King Alfonso V of Portugal. He reached Naples by sea and went from there to Venice. Daniel, who was one of his fervent admirers, decided to give up everything and join him. And so Abramo was left without any of his three sons at home.

Now and then a traveler brought him a letter filled with news from elsewhere. Yochanan, for example, told a remarkable story: the king of Spain had sent ships to explore the other side of the ocean, and the leader of the expedition, a Genoese named Christopher Columbus, had "discovered several islands, notably a very large one toward the east, with beautiful rivers, formidable mountains, and extremely fertile land, inhabited by men and women who were quite handsome, though entirely naked, except for a few who covered their genitals with a piece of cotton."

Christopher Columbus, reported Yochanan, had written a letter to his friend the financier Gabriel Sanchez, a Marrano, telling him about his extraordinary voyage and noting that "the land was rich in gold and the people were generous with their possessions," that "there were abundant palms and more than half a dozen spices, impressively tall trees and many islands, five of them with names, and one almost as large as Italy," and that "the rivers carried gold, there was a great deal of copper but no iron, and many other wonders were to be seen."

Gabriel Sanchez, Yochanan continued, had sent this letter to his brother Juan, who lived in Florence. Juan Sanchez had given it to his cousin Leonardo de Coscon, who then translated it and sent it to the sculptor Luca Fancelli. That was when Yochanan had read it. He had immediately thought of sending it to Gershom or Giosuè-Salomone so that they could print and distribute it, but Luca Fancelli had given the letter, and the idea of printing it, to his patron, the marquis of Mantua, who quickly had it published and sold in large quantities by a Florentine printer. Angered by this unscrupulous behavior, Yochanan had left Luca Fancelli. He was now staying in Rome, from where he was writing to his parents. He ended by wishing them good health for a long time, with the help of the Almighty, blessed be He.

Each time a letter came to break the monotony of his days, Abramo first read it for himself, then went to read it to Deborah, and finally put it away in the box that held the Scroll of Abraham and the two remaining copies of the Book of Abraham. He intended, if he received enough letters, to publish them before his death. He would have the printing done by someone else, but he would choose the format, the paper, and the type, and do the proofreading himself—he still had "a sharp eye."

Letter from Meshulam, in Brescia, to his father Abramo, in Soncino.

406

To my father Abramo, son of Gabriel. May the Almighty, blessed be He, grant that this letter will find you and my mother in good health.

After leaving you, we went to Milan, where, at the city gate, we happened to witness the meeting between Duke Ludovico, brother of Galeazzo Maria, and Beatrice d'Este. What a spectacle! The leaders of the nobility were dressed in their most magnificent clothes and the duke wore a gold brocade doublet. The walls and the streets, where they were not painted, were hung with rich brocades and festoons of flowers. On either side of the street along which the duke passed, there were figures on horseback wearing the finest armor made in the city —if you had seen them, you would have sworn they were alive.

The representatives of Bologna were squeezed into a triumphal chariot drawn by stags and unicorns, the Este animals. As he rode along, Ludovico Sforza was surrounded by twelve knights in black-and-gold Moorish costumes, each holding a shield adorned with a Moor's head. Galeazzo's soldiers were disguised as savages, but when they presented themselves before the dukes and duchesses they took off their costumes and appeared in splendid armor. A gigantic Moor then came forward and praised Beatrice in verse. The costumes were designed by Leonardo da Vinci.

It has now been a long time since I saw that spectacle, but I have forgotten none of its details, none of its colors.

From Milan we went to Brescia, where Gershom had begun setting up a print shop with the help of the count of Martinengo, a truly charming man. I am sending you—by the merchant Nathan of Mantua, who has agreed to pass through Soncino to bring you this letter—a copy of the Bible we have just printed. You will be an expert judge of its quality. I hope you will not find too many mistakes in it!

We would now like to publish some original works, and so we have decided to go to the city of Chambéry in Savoy, where, we have been told, there are collections of rabbinical writings radiant with wisdom, yet unknown to nearly everyone.

May the Holy One, blessed be He, protect you, my mother, and Esther.

Your son Meshulam
Written in Brescia on the day before Pesach, that is, the third day of April in
the year 1497 by the Christian calendar

Letter from Yochanan, in Rome, to his father Abramo, in Soncino.

To my father and my mother, may their lives be long and honored.

I have not written to you in a long time, father, because moving from Florence to Rome was no simple matter for me. You know how little I worry about the future ("It is pitiful to torment oneself uselessly," as Cicero says), but I knew no one in Rome when I came here. Even so, I felt at home as soon as I saw this city where ancient ruins stand among fields and vineyards, where flocks of goats with tinkling bells move slowly through the maze of narrow streets, where stalls invade the pavement and balconies jut out above it, and where incredibly beautiful monuments and palaces overlook the Tiber.

Not knowing where to go, I asked for directions to the synagogue. On the way to it I saw a curious German-style house with a high tower bearing the inscription *Argentina,* which means "Strasbourg." The poor have nothing to lose, I told myself, so I had the servant at the door announce me as Yochanan, son of Abramo di Strasburgo, an artist.

The master of the house received me almost immediately. He was a tall, solemn man wearing a black velvet robe trimmed with ermine. I told him that my family had come from Strasbourg and Benfeld and that my grandfather Gabriel had worked with Gutenberg, then I told him about the books we had printed in Soncino.

After asking me what I knew how to do and what I wanted to do, he invited me to come back and see him the following week. I still did not know who he was. Only when I questioned the servant as I was leaving did I learn that he was Johann Burchard, master of ceremonies of Pope Alexander VI!

And the amazing part of it is that he took me under his

patronage and recommended me to a famous architect, Bramante d'Urbino, who is now employing me to oversee work on the chancellery that he designed. In taking a Jew like me under his wing, Master Burchard was following current fashion: the pope himself takes Hebrew lessons from Obadiah of Sforno, and Cardinal Egidio da Viterbo is being initiated into the Cabala by Elijah Levita, who is also, I believe, of Alsatian origin. Levita is a remarkable man. He knows Cicero and Petrarch as well as the Talmud, and music as well as Latin. He has just translated into Yiddish (of which I have only a sketchy knowledge, even though it was the language spoken by our ancestors in Benfeld) the famous poem about Bevis of Hampton. He has entitled his version the *Bovo Buch,* and expects to have it published.

I often meet important people and regret that my mother, may the Almighty protect her, is not with me. I am living with a family of Jewish goldsmiths of Spanish origin, very kind and pious people who are determined to arrange a marriage for me. Perhaps they will succeed.

There are many other things I could tell you, but "the true art of writing is knowing when to stop," so I will now tell you good-bye and pray that the Lord will give you health and happiness.

Your son Yochanan
Written in Rome on this fifteenth day of
Kislev in the year 5260 [1500] after the
creation of the world by the Almighty,
blessed be He

Letter from Meshulam, in Fano, to his father Abramo, in Soncino.

To my father Abramo, son of Gabriel. May the Almighty, blessed be He, grant that this letter will find you in good health. I have just learned from Jacob ben David the proofreader, who passed through Soncino a few months ago, that my mother is no longer alive. I have wept a great deal. Peace to her soul! The house must seem terribly empty to you. Rachel and I would be glad to have you come and live with us, but I doubt that you are willing to leave Soncino; and there is also the fact that we live a little like vagabonds.

We have returned to Italy, *beezrat ha-Shem,* with a number of manuscripts and another child, a daughter named Leah. She was born during our journey, in the house of a Christian lawyer, Aimon Burnier-Fontanelle, may the Almighty bless him. He took us in when we had just lost one of the wheels of our wagon and Rachel was beginning to have labor pains. So one generation passes on and is replaced by another. With the help of the Holy One, blessed be He, you are now the grandfather of Abbahu, Leah, and Isaac. Gershom has three sons: Mosè, Giosuè, and Eleazaro, may the Almighty give them long life.

We met with all sorts of adventures in our travels. After going through cities from which the Jews had been expelled, we were driven back to Geneva and we then lived for nearly three years in Chambéry. Several decades ago the duke of Savoy, Amadeus VIII, who later became the leader of the Christians under the name of Felix V, ordered the apostate Louis of Nice to examine the contents of our sacred manuscripts. Fearing his severity, Jews in the communities of Montmélian, Yenne, Aiguebelle, and Saint-Genix hid many manuscripts, and, with the help of the Almighty, I was able to find them.

We are now in Fano, near the sea, between Ancona and Rimini, and have begun printing the manuscripts we gathered in the course of our travels. *Vita Epaminundae,* a work by Abstemio, was the first to be finished. The next one will be Petrarch's *Rime,* which Gershom has always wanted to publish, and the one after that will be Kimchi's grammar, which we brought from Chambéry.

Francesco da Bologna, the best engraver in Italy, is working with us. He designed a new, slightly slanted type for us and Gershom called it "cursive." We were greatly pleased with it and had no inkling of the quarrel that was going to follow. Aldo Manuzio—you must remember him: you and Gershom met him in Venice and gave him a taste for printing—set up a print shop, discovered our new type, shamelessly took it as his own, and named it Aldine, after himself. Knowing Gershom's touchiness and hot temper as you do, you can imagine how furious he was. He wrote to Aldo Manuzio and also to Prince Borgia (I have copied part of that letter for you).

410

The prince promised to look into the matter and the Florentine ambassador spoke about it to the doge of Venice. But, far from apologizing to us, Aldo Manuzio complained about us to the Venetian senate! What *chutzpah!*

Gershom wants to leave Fano when we have finished Kimchi's grammar. I have never seen him so full of rancor. He is thinking of going to Salonika. Only the Almighty knows where I will write my next letter to you!

I have learned that Daniel is living in Venice and Yochanan in Rome. Perhaps I will see them. May the Almighty protect you, my sister Esther, and her husband Lazzaro, and give you all health and long life.

Your son Meshulam
Written in Fano on the twenty-seventh
day of December in the year 1503

Excerpts from the letter written by Gershom of Soncino to Prince Cesare Borgia.

Two years ago, Most Excellent and Invincible Prince, having been pleased by the general atmosphere, the site, and the fertility of your pious city of Fano, as well as by the talents and enjoyable company of its inhabitants, I resolved to live here and exercise my art, which is the printing of books. . . .

I have brought here not only some of the most outstanding typesetters and proofreaders in Italy, but also a superlative engraver of Latin, Greek, and Hebrew letters named Francesco da Bologna, whose talent is so great that he surely has no equal. He invented for me a new style of letters that I called cursive, but it was appropriated by Aldo Manuzio and others. I wish to inform you that Francesco da Bologna is the sole inventor of all forms of letters ever used by Aldo Manuzio, who is incapable of creating such grace and beauty.

Because we are all Your Excellency's humble and devoted servants, and because, in our absolute submission, it is fitting for us to call upon the protection of our Most Illustrious and Clement Prince, we hereby ask for justice. . . .

Written in Fano in the month of July,
1503

To my father Abramo, son of Gabriel, may long life be given to him.

In the past few years I have written several letters to you and entrusted them to Menachem, son of Abner, messenger of Nathan the banker, but I have just learned that he never delivered them: he died yesterday and they were found in his house. His wife came to tell me about them. If he were still alive, I would try to have him punished as he deserved. What an ungrateful son you must have thought me to be!

I am, *baruch ha-Shem,* in good health, and teaching at the *yeshiva* in Venice. I am greatly distressed, however, by what is happening around me. First of all the war, with its thousands of victims. It is lucky that Soncino was spared by the battle at Marignano between the French and the armies of Massimiliano Sforza.

Is that war a sign? In any case one thing, of which you have surely not yet heard in Soncino, is unquestionably a sign: the senate has passed a law requiring that the whole Jewish population of Venice be confined in one quarter, the Ghetto Nuovo, in the San Girolamo parish. It is a dark, dismal island, surrounded by canals, north of the city. Only physicians will be allowed to leave it after nightfall.

May the Almighty grant that this will be our last period of darkness and that we will finally come into the light! "What is the light for which the people of Israel hope?" asks the Talmud. And it answers, "It is the light of the Messiah, for it is written, 'And God saw that the light was good.' This teaches us that the Holy One, blessed be He, envisaged the Messiah and his acts even before He created the world."

I often think of what Rabbi Yochanan said: "In the age when the Son of David comes, there will be many difficulties, and wicked decrees will again be promulgated; and each bad event will happen quickly, before the previous one has ended." My teacher Abrabanel was right: the time is approaching.

Do you know, father, how my brother Yochanan is faring? May God have mercy on that pagan who reproduces images in temples of the Gentiles!

Blessings on you, my sister Esther, and her husband Lazzaro.

Your son Daniel
Written in Venice on the twenty-fourth
day of Nissan in the year 5276 [1516]
after the creation of the world by the
Almighty, blessed be He

Letter from Daniel, in Venice, to his father Abramo, in Soncino.

To my father Abramo, son of Gabriel, may the Master of the world protect him.

We seem fated to have strange events come between us. Ten or twelve years ago, when I thought you had been regularly receiving letters from me, I discovered that that bank messenger, whose name I have forgotten, had kept all my letters without delivering them. This time, a traveler passing through Venice told me—be ready for a shock!—that you were dead. That was quite a long time ago. I sat *shiva* for you in deep sorrow, and every year afterward I piously lit a *ner tamid* in your memory. Imagine my joy this morning when I learned, through the son of the goldsmith who rented the house to us, that the Soncino printer who had died was not you, but Giosuè-Salomone!

It is sad for Giosuè-Salomone, of course, but I am all the happier for you because I have good news to tell you. He has come. My teacher Abrabanel was not mistaken.

"In thy light do we see light," says the psalm. I have seen him. He stepped onto the Pier of the Slavonians from a sailing ship that had just arrived from Egypt. He is dark-skinned because he comes from the East, and his black eyes reflect the sunlight like mirrors. He is always dressed in white, as befits the Messenger, and he speaks the harsh Hebrew of our ancestors. His servants call him Sar David Reubeni and say that he comes from a faraway kingdom.

When I was able to approach him, I felt such strength emanating from him that I knew he was the Messenger. He is preceded and followed by servants carrying banners on which the initials of the words *Who then has Your power, Lord?* are embroidered in gold thread.

You know how eagerly I had awaited him, father. From the

413

moment he set foot in Venice, I never left him. I followed him into the great hall near the synagogue, where the most important Jews of the city came to question him. Their mistrust and disrespect wounded me to the depths of my soul. I remembered a sentence in the treatise entitled Sanhedrin: "The Messiah will not come as long as there is still one vain man in Israel," and I found myself (may Adonai, the God of Israel, forgive me) wishing that they would die. But the Messenger remained calm, dignified, and steady as a rock. The sound of his voice made the notables quiver and they were astonished at what he said: his name was David, son of Solomon, of the tribe of Reuben, and he had come from the desert of Khaibar, sent by the seventy elders of a kingdom whose king was his brother Joseph. He had a secret message for the pope because, he said, the time was near.

Some refused to hear any more. Rabbi Simeon ben Asher Meshulam, however, offered him an escort of soldiers to accompany him when he went through Romagna, where a war was being fought. He refused the offer: he had come, he said, for all Jews, and could not accept help against the will of part of the community.

He discerned my zeal and told me to go and wait for him in Pesaro. I left that same day, with my wife and children. In Pesaro I notified the community. They all went to greet him when he arrived on a completely white ship. What fervor! They crowded around the man who had come to announce the Messiah, trying to touch his robe and kiss the ground on which he stepped. He refused all invitations and accepted only a few horses and mules. He chose a white horse for himself and gave me a mule.

We traveled to Rome without fatigue. Whole families joined us. Exiles from Spain, living in Marches with the pope's permission, came to the Messenger in great numbers and plied him with questions. He told them that he had no secret, but the more brusquely he spoke to them, the more they feared him and believed in him. I recalled this passage in the Zohar: "Rabbi Simeon bar Yochai sat down and wept, then he said, 'Woe to me if I reveal these secrets, and woe to me if I do not reveal them!' The companions who were present remained silent, then Rabbi Abba stood up and said, 'If our Master wishes to reveal these things, is it not written that the secret of the Lord belongs to those who fear Him?' "

Father, I am now resuming this letter after having interrupted it long ago. I had it with me through many tribulations. I always intended to add a few lines to it, but hours and days were snatched away from me.

First let me tell you that, thanks to the Holy One, blessed be He, my family and I are in good health. May the Lord always thus assist me in His mercy and judge me worthy of seeing the coming of the Messiah, so that this verse in Isaiah may be confirmed in us: "Rejoice with Jerusalem, and be glad for her, all you who love her; rejoice with her in joy, all you who mourn over her." Amen, amen!

When we reached Rome, thousands of men and women were waiting for us in the rain. The Messenger was immediately received by the *fattori,* that is, the three leaders of the Jewish community: Obadiah of Sforno, who taught Hebrew and the Cabala to Pope Alexander; Giuseppe Zarfati, a physician; and Daniel of Pisa, a rabbi and banker. They were all struck by his answers, which he gave in either Latin or Italian without a foreign accent. Two days later he was received by Pope Clement, of the Medici family.

I later learned that the Messenger proposed to Pope Clement an alliance with his brother Joseph, king of Khaibar, against the Turks. He asked for artillery, which is unknown in Khaibar, and the right to raise an army among the Jews living in Christian countries. In exchange, he promised to give the pope possession of Constantinople and all of Greece. From his conquests, he would keep only Jerusalem and the Holy Land.

You know, father, how I abhor the sword. I would accept the use of force only in the case described in Numbers: "when you go to war in your land against the adversary who oppresses you." I was therefore troubled, but my apprehensions were dispelled by the support that the Messenger received from the most illustrious rabbis, and by the gifts sent from Naples by Benvenida, daughter-in-law of my lamented teacher Isaac Abrabanel, may his memory endure forever.

Favorably impressed by David Reubeni and his plan, the pope gave him credentials for King João of Portugal. I was among those he took with him. I will spare you all the accidents and adventures of the journey, but I will tell you that when Almaria appeared to us in the distance, glittering in the sunlight, a sentence from the Second Book of Kings came into my mind: "If we say, 'Let us enter the city,' the famine is in the city, and we shall die there." And since we should always make hope prevail over doubt, I immediately said to myself, "We're going straight into the Assyrians' camp, and if they don't kill us, we'll live." So you see, father, that as long as the Messiah has not delivered us, our lives will always depend on the goodwill of other nations.

The king's ministers promised the Messenger their support and assured him that they would look after the Portuguese Jews and send them to the coast of Palestine in their own ships. For the moment, everything was going well. But the ways of Him who decides our fate are impenetrable. A noble, very handsome young man named Diogo Pires, who held the position of royal secretary, fell in love with David Reubeni. He had visions, began studying Hebrew and the Cabala, circumcised himself, and took the name of Solomon Molcho.

The Messenger realized the danger immediately. He asked the young man to go to Turkey as soon as possible to make preparations for our arrival. But it was already too late: our enemies accused us of trying to convert Christians and demanded that a great tribunal of the Inquisition be established in Portugal. So instead of taking command of a Jewish legion, we had to flee as if we were criminals, leaving our baggage behind. In my own baggage was the copy of the Book of Abraham that you gave me in Soncino. I hope that you and my ancestors will forgive me.

Meanwhile Solomon Molcho was going from country to country, announcing that the Messiah would come when Rome fell. It happened that Emperor Charles V took Rome during this time. You can imagine how David Reubeni was then received when he appeared, still dressed in white, among the smoking ruins. People were seized with a kind of madness. I can still see Solomon Molcho, also dressed in white, welcoming the Messiah in front of the Castelnuovo synagogue. That was when I realized that Solomon Molcho had come to regard himself as the Messenger, while David Reubeni had succumbed to all that worshipful acclaim to the point where he believed he was the Messiah himself. Feeling disoriented, I took refuge in my brother Yochanan's house. He persuaded me not to go with David Reubeni and Solomon Molcho to Avignon.

I have just reread this letter and it has made me even more strongly aware of the contrast between the elation I felt at the beginning and the disappointment I feel today. But I console myself by repeating what is written in Habakkuk: "For still the vision awaits its time. . . . If it seem slow, wait for it."

I pray that this letter will find all of you in good health: you, father, my sister Esther, her husband Lazzaro, and, if it has been God's will, their children. Amen.

Your son Daniel
Rome, on this twenty-fourth day of Elul in the year 5288 [1528] after the creation of the world by the Almighty, blessed be He

Letter from Yochanan, in Rome, to his father Abramo, in Soncino.

To my father Abramo, son of Gabriel, may peace be with him.

Daniel gave you news of me in his last letter, and now I will give you news of him. He is doing quite well, in spite of his disappointment. At least he can thank that David Reubeni for having kept him away from Rome while Charles V was besieging us. By the time he came back from Portugal it was all over; the famine and the dead had been forgotten.

Daniel still thinks about David Reubeni constantly. He reminds me of the passage where Aristotle describes a hunter who pursued a hare up and down mountains and in ravines, through heat and cold, and wanted it as long as it kept eluding him, then despised it when he finally caught it. The other day, without telling him where we were going, I took him to the statue of Moses by Michelangelo, who seems able to turn stone into flesh. I think Daniel was as deeply moved as anyone else by that representation of the man who saw the face of the Creator, but afterward he began a long fast of purification.

My next news will surely not leave you indifferent. I will begin at the beginning. A German scholar named Johann Reuchlin learned Hebrew and studied the Cabala in Rome. When he returned to his country, he denounced the Dominicans, who had set out to wage war against the Jews and the

417

Talmud. He was able to have the books spared, and demanded that two professors of Hebrew be appointed in each university! Our enemies then published a scurrilous pamphlet against him, entitled *Handspiegel [Hand Mirror]* and he wrote a brilliant reply: *Augenspiegel [Eye Mirror]*.

The controversy divided the Church and the universities. Emperor Maximilian declared in favor of Reuchlin, and King Louis XII of France against him. However, all the humanists —those people so vehemently scorned by Daniel, our Cabalist —came to the defense of the Jews: all of them, from Erasmus to Martin Luther, a monk who has written an essay entitled "That Jesus Christ Was a Born Jew." Pope Leo X, despite the repeated requests of his Jewish friend and physician Bonetto de Lattes, refused to settle the dispute, but he asked Daniel Bomberg, a Christian printer from Antwerp who had established himself in Venice, to publish a complete edition of the Talmud.

That young Martin Luther has attracted a great deal of attention. He has translated the Bible into German so that everyone in his country can read it. And do you know which Hebrew text he used? He mentions it in the colophon: the Soncino Bible! And not just any copy of it, either. It was the one that Count Pico della Mirandola bought from you; it came into Johann Reuchlin's possession and he gave it to Luther. This shows that any path may be taken to disseminate the word of the Almighty, so that, as Isaiah says, "it may be for the time to come as a witness for ever."

And now for the best news, which I have saved for last. My hosts finally succeeded in arranging a marriage for me. My wife's name is Monica and we have two sons, Elhanan and David, may the Holy One, blessed be He, protect them.

My health is good and I am now doing a series of engravings for a new edition of the poems of Vergil.

May God protect you, father, as well as my sister, her husband, and their children.

Your son Yochanan
Written in Rome on the fourth of June
in the year 1528

Letter from Meshulam, in Rimini, to his father Abramo, in Soncino.

To my father Abramo, may God be merciful to him.

First I must tell you, my dear father, that my wife Rachel has died. Blessed be the memory of a righteous woman.

Forgive me, father, if it is not too late, for not having done my duty as a son, for not having written to you more often, for not having been concerned about your loneliness. How you must have cursed me!

I have no excuse, but since you know the art of printing, since you know how much time and passionate devotion it demands, at least you will understand how one book follows close behind another, giving no respite or leisure. I scarcely saw my own children growing up, and now my older son Abbahu has just given you your third great-grandson, may long life be granted to him, amen.

Gershom and I are now living in Rimini, which is near the sea, between Ancona and Ravenna. Wanting to have a print shop here that will contribute to its glory, the city council has given us certain privileges: exemption from the tithe and the salt tax, free use of a stall on the San Pietro bridge during the feast of San Giuliano, twelve ducats a year to pay the rent for our house. We have published nearly forty books here, including Rashi's commentary on the Pentateuch and a treatise by Elijah Levita, who taught Hebrew to Cardinal Egidio da Viterbo, that great friend of the Jews, blessed be his memory.

Altogether, Gershom and I have published about a hundred books, twenty of them in Hebrew. As you might expect, Gershom's character has not mellowed with age. He has quarreled with practically all the printers in Italy. Only Daniel Bomberg, a printer who came to Italy from Antwerp, has escaped his anger, by the grace of God. Bomberg has told us how much he respects our work, and the work of all the Soncino printers, so the compliment is also addressed to you.

In Padua we met a very likable man, Rabbi Mordecai Joffe, who comes from the city of Lublin, in Poland. He talked with us a long time about that country. He told us that the Jews live in peace there and that it would be a good place in which to open several large print shops. But Gershom will not even consider going to Poland. He says that living in snow is only for barbarians and that he is too old to go and mingle with barbarians. He sometimes thinks of joining his sons in Salonika, where it seems that Eleazaro, the oldest, has founded an excellent print shop.

But most of the time Gershom simply threatens to abandon his trade. He says that printers are no more respected than street peddlers and that their enemies keep trying to make them stumble at every step. I often admonish him and remind him of what Rabbi Tarphon says in *Chapters of the Fathers:* "You are not required to finish the task, but you have no right to shirk it."

Father, I calculate that you must now be about eighty. I pray that you will be able to read this letter and forgive me. May the Almighty give you many more years of life, and protect my sister Esther, her husband Lazzaro, and their children.

> Your son Meshulam
> Written in Rimini on the day before
> Rosh Hashanah of the year 5286 [1526]
> after the creation of the world by the
> Almighty, blessed be He

When he read this letter, Abramo di Soncino, son of Gabriele di Strasburgo, had been living for years with his daughter Esther. Generations of children had become used to seeing him sitting on the stone bench near the door, like an immutable element of the landscape. He was one of those thin old men who seemed fragile, almost brittle, but are endowed with mysterious strength.

From their reports at distant intervals, Abramo had followed the way his sons went through life, each according to his destiny: Meshulam in Gershom's shadow, Daniel misled by the Cabala, Yochanan floating like a cork among the Gentiles. Their letters always set him to daydreaming, and his daydreams always took him back to the brief Venetian escapade that still glowed in his hazy memory.

One morning, in his eighty-seventh year, he was found dead. Esther and her husband Lazzaro asked their youngest son, Giacobbo the goldsmith, who already had children of his own, to go to Rimini, from where Meshulam's last letter had been sent, and give him the legacy to which he was entitled as Abramo's oldest son: the box containing the Scroll of Abraham, a few manuscripts, and the last two copies of the Book of Abraham.

In Rimini, Giacobbo found Meshulam and Gershom packing. They had decided to go to Salonika.

31

SALONIKA

Two Ordinary Jews

WHAT JOYOUS, tumultuous chaos! Nowhere else in their travels had Gershom, Meshulam, and Abbahu, Meshulam's older son, heard such an uproar or seen such frenzied shoving and jostling. As soon as they stepped off the ship they were caught up in a whirlwind of bawling children, bales of cotton, cages of terrified chickens, porters, peddlers, beggars, and thieves. Strangers embraced them and affectionately slapped them on the back while others picked their pockets. They stared at the sea of faces beneath the multicolored foam of turbans, caps, and felt hats. A huge black ox at the front of a caravan plowed through the human waves like a disdainful figurehead. Golden dust rose from the turmoil, into the purplish-blue sky of Salonika.

Meshulam and Gershom were separated, then found each other again, but without Abbahu, beside a drinking trough for animals near the waterfront gate, where they had been brought by a powerful current of horses, cows, donkeys, and sheep. They felt drunk with noise and strong smells.

"Father! Meshulam! Peace be with you!"

The greeting came from Eleazaro, Gershom's son. He embraced each of the two men. Behind him were strangers who eagerly approached them and stepped on their feet while offering to take them into their respective synagogues. Then Abbahu appeared, laden with baggage. Eleazaro took it from him and gave it to the zealous recruiters to carry.

"Now they'll leave us alone," he said to his father, with a wink. "In Salonika, no one can talk without using his hands!"

Gershom frowned and looked at the mob around him without indulgence.

"This is no city!" he said scornfully. "I didn't know my son lived in an overgrown village!"

When Abbahu had found his wife and children, they all set off for Eleazaro's house in a group that collected curious onlookers along the way.

They went through a little door that was the only opening in the high, stern wall of the house. Then the newcomers discovered a large patio where fountains splashed musically among fig, jujube, and sorb trees. The walls were covered with roses and honeysuckle. On the ground floor, glazed doors opened into the garden, and above them, on the second floor, were loggias and enclosed balconies.

Joseph, Sarah, and Abraham, Abbahu's children, seemed astonished and rather intimidated by those imposing men, wearing doublets decorated with braid and breeches held by broad belts, who called themselves their uncles. Cakes and sweetened fruit juices were served. Gershom scarcely deigned to taste them. He had already made his decision: he would never be a printer in an overgrown village!

"But more than twenty thousand Jews live in Salonika, father. Twenty thousand!"

"Yes, but what Jews!"

"It's true that most of them are poor. But didn't the Soncino printers choose to publish inexpensive books so that the wisdom of Israel would be accessible to even the poorest Jews?"

Gershom's only answer was to shake his head and make a hissing sound between his teeth.

The next day he was taken on a walk through the city, from a synagogue to a print shop, from the bazaar to the Via Egnatia, the main street parallel to the sea. It was all in vain: he still thought only of taking the next ship out of Salonika.

He left for Constantinople two days later, after *shabbat*. As he had done for more than thirty years, Meshulam went with him, and so did Giosuè, his youngest son. Abbahu stayed behind with his wife Ruth and their children, Joseph, Sarah, and Abraham. Eleazaro had asked him to work with him in the print shop he had established with a partner who was now gone. Abbahu and his family moved into the part of Eleazaro's house abandoned by Meshulam.

Abbahu was at this time a man of thirty-five with a dull complexion, gentle brown eyes, and a long, thick beard. He worked at his trade with a humble, demanding passion, but while he and his father Meshulam had learned a great deal from Gershom, the old printer's irascible authority had not allowed either of them to be himself. Abbahu hoped he would get along well with Eleazaro, who had an easygoing nature but showed a certain lack of imagination in his work. "Be careful," his wife, Ruth, had said to him, "Eleazaro isn't a man who can fight against adversity. If you have difficulties, you'll find yourself alone." Abbahu had great confidence in Ruth's judgment, but he told himself that no one ever got through life without having to struggle now and then. And he was looking forward to working without the burden of Gershom's overpowering presence.

He spent several days becoming acquainted with the city that was now his own. Turks, Greeks, and Jews lived in both parts of it: the lower one, which was commercial and densely populated, and the upper one, whose houses were spaciously spread over the hill, with many gardens. The large Jewish population had been built up by separate waves of immigration. First had come the Bavarians, who established an Ashkenazi community, then the Spaniards and Portuguese, many of whom were Marranos, which often raised problems with regard to Halacha. The rabbinic tribunal of Salonika had decided to consider the Marranos as Jews in all matters of marriage and divorce.

Mainly merchants and artisans, the Jews had an intense community life. Some thirty congregations were grouped in a federation. A special committee decided how much each community would contribute toward the total amount of taxes that had to be paid to the Turks. And the Turks seldom missed a chance to impose a tax. Abbahu learned that besides the yearly general tax there was a tax for maintaining the army, an inheritance tax, a tax for the upkeep of the imperial pastures, a tax on meat, a tax for the maintenance of hunting falcons, a tax for the chief rabbi, a tax for exemption from military service, a tax for the imperial couriers, a tax for supplying furs to the sultan. . . . "In exchange for all that," said

Eleazaro, "we're free to practice our religion and make our communities prosper."

On the eve of Tishah B'Av, the anniversary of the destruction of the Temple, Abbahu joined the long procession that left from the upper part of the city and moved toward the waterfront. At the head of it were four rabbis carrying a stretcher on which a child lay. Thousands of Jews followed. There was deep sadness in their eyes and each of them carried, at the end of a pole, a perforated hollow gourd with a candle burning inside it.

"They are going, the seven brothers!" the rabbis chanted in Spanish.

And the crowd answered, "Alas, what sorrow!"

"They are going to the gallows."

"Alas, what sorrow!"

The Greeks and Turks standing along the route of the procession also took up the slow, mournful chant. All those mingled voices, and the swaying of all those lights in the darkness, brought the tragic reality of exile into the hearts of the Jews.

"Alas, what sorrow!"

Abbahu and his children came home overwhelmed with emotion.

The next day, friends and neighbors gathered in Eleazaro's garden. They stayed there till evening, sitting on their heels, chanting the lamentations of Jeremiah, the sufferings of Job, the psalms of mourning. "If I forget you, O Jerusalem, let my right hand wither!"

ELEAZARO'S PRINT SHOP—small and rather disorderly, but still a pleasant place in which to work—was below the Via Egnatia, between the Talmud Torah and Francomahalla, the former Frankish quarter where merchants originally from Venice, Genoa, and Marseille now lived. There was another print shop in Salonika, belonging to Judah Gdalia, a Portuguese who had arrived a few years earlier.

While Eleazaro and Abbahu were printing a *machzor*, a festival prayer book, Judah Gdalia chose to publish the sermons of Solomon Molcho, the self-styled Messenger of the Messiah, whom Daniel the Cabalist had known in Italy and Portugal. At first the *machzor* was quite successful; Samuel Achemeoni the peddler had no difficulty in selling it. Then the news of Solomon Molcho's death reached Salonika. He and David Reubeni had gone to Germany to ask Emperor Charles V to help them reconquer Palestine. The emperor had apparently shown great interest in the plan until the harebrained Molcho suggested to him that he become a Jew. Furious, the emperor had Molcho and Reubeni arrested and taken in chains to a church in Mantua where an ecclesiastic tribunal sentenced Molcho to be burned at the stake for apostasy and heresy. The Church feared his words so much that he was taken to the stake with a gag in his mouth; he died without having been able to voice the name of the Holy One, blessed be He.

He had once visited Salonika and many Jews there still held him in high regard. When his death became known, sales of the collection of his sermons published by Judah Gdalia increased sharply and from then on Samuel Achemeoni the peddler was unable to sell a single copy of the *machzor*.

Eleazaro and Abbahu became so short of money that they had to borrow in order to publish Kimchi's grammar, which the schools needed. Its steady sales enabled them to survive while they waited for better times.

Abbahu liked Salonika. He had become used to the loud speech and exuberant gestures that were the rule there (people could not say hello to each other without deeming to exchange serious insults), to the purple sky, to the wind that blew from the Vardar River, and to the drink called *kahve* in Turkish, a black, bitter liquid to which cloves were added.

He had become a close friend of Rabbi Benjamin Halevi Eskenazi. He visited him often and asked him to perform the ceremony when his daughter Sarah married David, son of Rabbi Joseph ben Lev, a thin, excitable little man who wore clothes too big for him and had a stock of terrifying quotations that he uttered with his forefinger threateningly raised. Luckily for Sarah, his son was a peaceful young man who worked for the federation of Jewish communities.

Abbahu's older son Joseph had not wanted to become a printer. To him, what was essential in the family tradition did not lie in reproducing comments on the Law, but in transmitting the Law itself. He had become a scribe and, as so many of his ancestors had done, he continued copying scrolls of the Torah, painstakingly covering sheets of parchment with letters that experts compared to rows of pearls and sapphires. It was his younger brother Abraham who had joined Abbahu in the print shop.

Gershom died in Constantinople and his death was closely followed by Meshulam's—inseparable to the end, the two old men made that last journey together. Some time later a Venetian merchant passing through Salonika delivered the box containing the Book and the Scroll of Abraham, as well as a copy of Kimchi's *Michlol** printed by Gershom, Meshulam, and Giosuè. Gershom had added a note at the end of the volume: "From my youth until my old age I traveled, at the cost of great fatigue, to find precious Hebrew manuscripts, which I brought into the light of day by printing them; most of those priceless works had fallen into obscurity and been forgotten. A large number of Talmudic works were printed through my efforts, more than twenty-three treatises, along with the commentaries of Rashi that are customarily studied in our small academies. The printers of Venice shamelessly copied them and would have reduced me to ruin if the Almighty, blessed be He, had not sustained me. He who knows all things will recall the sacrifices I have made, the dangers I have faced, and my efforts to help my brothers from Spain and Portugal who were forced to abandon the religion of Zion. In the evening of my life I therefore place my confidence in God and in His blessed name."

Gershom and Meshulam were buried in the cemetery of Egri Capu, outside the walls in the direction of Balat, which was also the resting place of Moses Capsali, last of the great rabbis of the Byzantine period. May God protect the memory of the righteous.

Eleazaro and Abbahu swore to go and visit their fathers' graves as soon as possible, but while one was able to keep his promise, the other unfortunately never saw Constantinople. They were about to be plunged into a tragic episode that would leave few people in Salonika unaffected by it.

For Abbahu it began one evening when Eleazaro left the shop, saying he was going to deliver some books that had been ordered by the Italian synagogue. A short time later, Abbahu saw that Eleazaro had forgotten to take the books with him. He hurried after him but did not see him on the way, and at the synagogue he was told that Eleazaro had not been there. As he was walking back toward the shop, puzzled, he saw Eleazaro talking with Nissim the

---

* A treatise on Hebrew philology by David Kimchi (1160–1235), also known as Radak, an abbreviation of his name (Rabbi David Kimchi). A grammarian, exegesist, and teacher born in Narbonne, France, he codified the rules of Hebrew grammar and was the first to introduce such refinements as the distinction between long and short Hebrew vowels.

Aragonese, a notorious criminal. Without thinking, he hid in a doorway, from where he saw Eleazaro give Nissim a purse. Should he intervene? Did he have a right to meddle in Eleazaro's affairs? And wasn't it a sin to spy on a friend this way?

Deeply troubled, he returned to the print shop. The sky was overcast and the humid air felt as if it were clinging to his skin. Muezzins were calling the Moslem faithful to evening prayer. Isaac Pinto, who lived next door to the shop, had come out onto his front steps for a breath of fresh air. Abbahu stopped to greet him and they talked about the heat.

"Your lead will soon be melting by itself, printer!" said Isaac Pinto, fanning himself.

He was a jovial man, a "retired shipowner," as he described himself, who had just sold his only ship and was living modestly on the small sum he had saved from his profits.

Abbahu sat down beside him on the warm stone step.

"I just saw Nissim the Aragonese," he said. "I thought he was in prison."

Isaac Pinto spat into the dust.

"He deserves to be there for the rest of his life. But he's protected."

"By the Turks?"

"Not only by the Turks!" Pinto was no longer smiling. He looked left and right and lowered his voice. "He's one of that cursed Baruch's men."

Baruch was a merchant who sold supplies to the Turkish army and therefore had many friends among army commanders and government officials. But his commercial activities concealed a different kind of enterprise: he had built up a powerful organization that extorted money from merchants and artisans "for protection against bandits." He was shrewd enough to choose only Jewish victims, knowing they would not dare to denounce him to the Turkish authorities. And the Turks closed their eyes—let the Jews settle their differences among themselves!

Abbahu had heard of Baruch, but money had never been demanded of him and it had not occurred to him to wonder why; he was only surprised that there could be Jews who robbed other Jews.

Isaac Pinto leaned closer to him.

"Don't ever talk about Baruch, printer," he said. "He'd be sure

428

to find out about it and take revenge, by either raising your payments or burning your shop."

Abbahu stood up. He had just realized that it would be abnormal if the print shop were exempt from payments for Baruch's "protection." And if such payments were being exacted, then it was Eleazaro who . . .

He left Isaac Pinto without saying good-bye. He did not see Eleazaro again that evening, and spent the night tossing restlessly on his bed.

The next morning he left to go and see his friend Rabbi Benjamin Halevi Eskenazi. It still had not rained. The sultry heat slowed everyone's movements. Animals lay on their sides in the shadows of houses and passersby had to kick them to make them get out of the way. Vultures soared above the city in broad circles.

Rabbi Eskenazi was speaking to his students about the conduct of human beings and the conduct of the Holy One, blessed be He, Master of the world. He quoted a passage by Rabbi Josse Hagligi in the Talmud: "When a man has been offended by another man, he sinks into his anger to the point of taking the offender's life. The Holy One, blessed be He, does not behave in that way. He cursed the serpent, but if the serpent climbs onto a roof he has food within reach, and if he goes down to the ground he still has food within reach. God cursed Canaan and condemned him to slavery, but Canaan eats what his master eats and drinks what his master drinks. . . . God cursed woman, but all men desire her. . . . God cursed the earth, but all living creatures are fed by it."

A pale young man stood up.

"When one man has rightfully cursed another," he asked, "who will carry out the judgment?"

"He who decides everything: the Master of the world," Rabbi Eskenazi replied in his calm voice.

Then he saw Abbahu beside the door and smiled at him.

Yes, he said a little later, when they were alone, he knew about Baruch, but no one had ever lodged a complaint against him. It would be possible to bring up the matter at the next meeting of the community council, but there, too, complaints and proof would be needed. He quoted Isaiah: "Woe to those who decree iniquitous decrees."

Abbahu went back to the print shop. He watched Eleazaro locking up a form and sliding it off the marble-topped table. Should he speak to him? But it was written, "Sin is couching by the door; its

429

desire is for you, but you must master it." Eleazaro would have to confront that problem alone. But they were partners in the print shop, and the problem concerned them both.

"Eleazaro," he said, "has Baruch ever offered you his protection?"

Poor Eleazaro was so perturbed that he dropped a tray of composed type.

"Baruch?"

"Yes, Baruch the extortionist."

"The extortionist?"

Abbahu took pity on him.

"Eleazaro, I saw you give a purse to Nissim the Aragonese. And later, when I talked about it with Isaac Pinto, I realized that you've been paying Baruch."

Eleazaro wiped his hands on his wide trousers. His chin quivered when he answered, "Yes, I've been paying him! I pay him so I can go on working! I pay him so you can work too! I pay him so his men won't burn this shop where we print books to the glory of the Almighty, blessed be He! I didn't tell you about it because I wanted to spare you all the torment I've been through, but now, like me, you'll have to wait for a messenger—a child, an old woman, anyone—to tell us how much we have to pay, and where to bring the money."

He was weeping. Abbahu turned to the apprentices, on the other side of the shop, and motioned them to leave.

"And besides everything else, it's too hot," Eleazaro said wretchedly.

TWO DAYS LATER, Isaac Pinto's house burned down.

As soon as he learned of it, Abbahu went to Rabbi Eskenazi.

"Rabbi," he said, "I have no proof. No one has any proof, I know that. But since we can't have Baruch arrested, can't we at least excommunicate him? That's the only weapon we *rayas* have."

Rabbi Eskenazi was standing in front of his collection of books, one of the finest in Salonika.

"In the name of the Almighty, blessed be He, calm yourself, Abbahu! Remember what is written in Proverbs: 'He who is slow to anger has great understanding, but he who has a hasty temper exalts folly.'"

For the first time, his voice was stern. But Abbahu did not soften his attitude.

"What's to be done, rabbi, with a criminal who can't be brought to trial?"

"He will be judged by the supreme Judge, the King of the world," answered Rabbi Eskenazi. His eyes glowed with deep conviction and Abbahu admired his faith. "Come back tomorrow, Abbahu, and we'll discuss all this calmly. 'The hope of the righteous ends in gladness.'"

That evening it was learned that the Turkish administration had made Baruch a *kehaya,* which meant that he would have responsibility for collecting taxes from the Jews of Salonika and be in charge of their relations with the authorities. Abbahu was so choked with indignation that he could not eat. His wife Ruth tried to reason with him.

"There's no use fighting against things that can't be changed, Abbahu. Baruch, may God curse him, has all the Turks with him. Do what everyone else does: pretend to accept his authority but reject it in your heart."

The next day, when Abbahu went to Rabbi Eskenazi's house, another rabbi was already there: David Benveniste, a thin, austere man with white hair hanging down below his white hat.

Rabbi Benveniste agreed with Abbahu in thinking that something had to be done, and with Rabbi Eskenazi in thinking that caution was essential. He proposed writing a long letter to Moses Hamon, who had been his teacher and was now the personal physician of Suleiman the Magnificent and a friend of Rustam Pasha, the grand vizier. The purpose of this first step would be simply to ask for advice. Rabbi Benveniste suggested having the letter delivered by his cousin Jeremiah, who regularly went to Constantinople on business.

The letter was written and sent. Jeremiah brought back an answer from Moses Hamon a month later. The physician sternly condemned Baruch's extortion and urged the rabbis to begin by trying persuasion. "Send for him," he wrote, "and urge him to mend his ways. Then, if necessary, threaten to have him severely punished by the sultan." He added that he had ordered two men to keep watch on Baruch's activities so that a formal accusation against him, if one should be needed, could be solidly supported. "Do not fear the venom of the wicked," he wrote in conclusion. "Aim your arrows and strike down the evildoer. I will always fight with all my strength for the triumph of justice."

The two rabbis followed Moses Hamon's advice and sent for

Baruch the *kehaya*. He placidly told them that he did not understand the accusations they were making against him. He did his work as well as he could, he said, and tried to prevent problems from arising between the Jewish communities and the Turkish administration. Threats? Extortion? Arson? Did they really think he was guilty of all that? Who could have told them such lies about him?

"Is it reasonable to believe," he asked, "that one Jew could dominate twenty thousand others against their will? As for the fires you've mentioned, they're practically inevitable, considering that the air is often dry here, that many houses are made of wood, and that people are sometimes careless. Even this magnificent library of yours, rabbi, might be destroyed by fire: it would take only a spark, a candle knocked over by a child. . . ."

Later, when Rabbi Eskenazi had reported this conversation to him, Abbahu asked, "But what kind of a man is he?"

Rabbi Eskenazi looked at his books, which included a copy of the Soncino Bible.

"He's an ordinary Jew, my friend, just as you are. He sends his children to the Talmud Torah and never eats a young goat boiled in its mother's milk. You and he are both ordinary Jews, but in you the Almighty, blessed be He, has placed the spirit of good, and in him the spirit of evil."

Rabbi Eskenazi and Rabbi Benveniste again wrote to Moses Hamon, reporting Baruch's veiled threat. Since the two men ordered by Moses Hamon to keep watch on Baruch had gathered conclusive evidence against him, Rustam Pasha, the grand vizier, told the cadi of Salonika to send him to Constantinople. Rabbis Eskenazi and Benveniste, who had investigated the case, were summoned to testify.

The community began breathing more easily. In Baruch's absence, his henchmen disappeared. Money was raised to rebuild Isaac Pinto's house. To relieve his conscience, Eleazaro went to him and asked him to forgive him: yes, it was he who had told Nissim about Abbahu's conversation with Isaac Pinto.

"But why did you tell him?" asked Abbahu.

"I thought it would keep him from coming back to the print shop," replied Eleazaro. "And in fact he hasn't come back, as you've seen."

In the past few weeks the poor man had become pitifully thin and his hair had begun turning gray.

The outcome of Baruch's trial in Constantinople was soon made public: he had been sentenced to death, then pardoned. The details became known when Rabbis Eskenazi and Benveniste returned. The trial had been honestly conducted, but after being sentenced to death Baruch had humbly begged for mercy, and Rabbi Solomon ibn-Hasson, an eminent Talmudic scholar from Salonika, had spoken in his favor.

"And what about you?" Abbahu asked Rabbi Eskenazi.

"I, too, asked that Baruch be pardoned."

"But you must know very well that . . ."

"We must know how to punish, my friend, but we must also learn how to forgive."

"Must we wait for justice 'until cities lie waste without inhabitant, and houses without men, and the land is utterly desolate'?" asked Abbahu, quoting from Isaiah.

Rabbi Eskenazi's eyes again showed the light of certainty that had so strongly impressed Abbahu.

"We must place our trust in the Almighty, blessed be He."

ONE MORNING Eleazaro came into the print shop with his face deathly pale.

"They've given me a warning."

"Who?"

"You know who. They sent a beggar with the message. If I don't pay by tomorrow, they'll burn down the shop."

Abbahu felt as if molten lead had suddenly been poured into his heart. He looked around the room at the trays of type, the forms, the press, the stocks of paper and ink, the proofs of the book now being printed. . . .

"How much do they want?"

"They're not asking for much, Abbahu. They're reasonable."

Abbahu was ashamed of having asked the question. He left Eleazaro and went to Rabbi Eskenazi's house, but his friend was not there. Looking at the faces of the people he passed in the street, he wondered if this one paid, if that one paid. . . . His steps took him to the house of his daughter's father-in-law, Rabbi Joseph ben Lev, an eccentric, irascible old scholar who had very few social relations.

Rabbi Joseph seemed lost in the colored *feredge* he wore over his black satin dolman. He listened to Abbahu, then drew his short body erect and raised his forefinger.

433

"Rise up, O judge of the earth," he quoted melodramatically; "render to the proud their deserts! O Lord, how long shall the wicked, how long shall the wicked exult?"

He stopped to listen to the call of a muezzin, as if it concerned him.

"Come with me," he said.

He went to lay the Baruch case before the rabbinic tribunal. The tribunal, he was told, would meet the next day. Abbahu agreed to testify.

He went back to the print shop. Eleazaro seemed relaxed now, though he avoided Abbahu's eyes. Abbahu realized that he had gone to pay Baruch but he said nothing.

The next day, Abbahu and Rabbi Joseph went to the rabbinic tribunal together. In front of the door, they were stopped by Rabbi Solomon ibn-Hasson, who was said to be in Baruch's pay.

"It will be better for the community," he said to Joseph ben Lev, "if you withdraw your complaint. If you don't, the Gentiles will slander us again, and laugh at us."

Old Joseph ben Lev turned red with anger, pushed Solomon ibn-Hasson aside, and went through the doorway, with Abbahu behind him.

He asked the assembled rabbis to examine the Baruch case calmly and impartially, without concern for reprisals, then render a fair judgment in accordance with the Law.

The tribunal deliberated for several days. The case was discussed within all families. Some young men, including Abbahu's son Abraham, wanted to oppose violence with violence and have Baruch put to death. Abbahu was indignant.

"Remember the commandment: 'You shall not kill,' " he said to Abraham.

"But there's also another commandment, father: 'You shall not steal.' "

Abraham and his friends stood guard in front of the print shop and Rabbi Joseph's house. They had no illusions, and their elders had not answered their blunt question: "How are we going to fight against Baruch?"

The rabbis of the tribunal finally reached a decision: they sternly censured Baruch but refused to excommunicate him because, they said, everyone had to be given a chance to repent and return to the ways of God.

Two days later the body of David ben Joseph, Rabbi Joseph ben

Lev's son and Abbahu's son-in-law, was found at dawn on the road to Livadia. He had left home the previous evening to go to the synagogue. His skull was shattered.

The cadi's police claimed to believe that the crime had been committed by a Greek bandit, but this deceived no one. In the Jewish quarters, people were so shocked and horrified that they spoke in hushed voices, without ever mentioning Baruch by name.

Abbahu stayed at home, in seclusion. He tried to pray but was unable to put his thoughts into words. Had he been wrong not to accept Baruch's evil power? And if he had been right, why had poor David had to pay with his life? "See," it was written in Deuteronomy, "I have set before you this day life and good, death and evil."

He took out the Scroll of Abraham and began reading it with his prayer shawl on his head and tears in his eyes. As he went through the long succession of names, a certainty took shape in his mind. Some of his ancestors had died—one was beheaded in Carthage, another was burned in Blois—to defend something higher and greater than the placid course of everyday life. And who could say if, without those martyrs, the family would have survived? Or if, without people like them, the human race would not already have returned to the savagery of Cain?

He was overwhelmed with sadness because he felt that he did not have the makings of a hero, but he now knew that he had been right. He also knew that he could not turn back.

His wife Ruth had gone to bring their daughter Sarah, who was about to give birth. Her husband's death had left her prostrate, unable to speak and scarcely able to move. In spite of everything, Abbahu felt terribly guilty. He decided to begin a penitential fast, then went to Rabbi Joseph's house to sit *shiva* with him.

Sarah gave birth, in pain, to a son whom she named Daniel. Life resumed in Salonika, as if everything were now settled, clear and peaceful. Abbahu was surprised that most people had that ability to forget—unless it was simply cowardice. And Rabbi Joseph, whom he often visited and accompanied to the synagogue or the cemetery, sometimes stopped, looked at the crowd, and quoted from Psalms: "Fools, when will you be wise?"

One day, just as they were passing the shop of Abraham Catalano the apothecary, Baruch came out of it with some of his men.

"What a lucky meeting!" he said mockingly when he saw Rabbi Joseph.

Once again Abbahu was amazed to see that Baruch really was an ordinary man: there was nothing about him to show that he was any different from others.

Furious as a fighting cock, Rabbi Joseph tried to approach Baruch and curse him to his face, but he was tripped by a man behind him. He fell and lost consciousness when his head struck the pavement. There was an outburst of coarse laughter.

Abbahu knelt beside him. Then he looked at Baruch and spoke words that came from some unknown part of himself: "If human justice doesn't punish you, Baruch, may God's justice do its work!"

"Amen!" said a voice from the crowd that had gathered.

A PLAGUE BROKE OUT a month later, in the midst of the Passover celebration. It struck all parts of the city at once, rich and poor. On the first day there were three hundred and fourteen victims among the Jews, and Cabalists were quick to point out that 314 was the numerical value of Shaddai, one of the names of God. Several families left Salonika and headed for one or another of the surrounding villages, but the plague caught them before they arrived. The dead were buried in common graves, without ceremony or prayer. There was a shortage of quicklime.

As if this were not enough, at the beginning of summer Abraham Catalano the apothecary stumbled with a lamp in his hand, setting fire to his shop—the shop in front of which Rabbi Joseph had fallen—and the flames spread with terrifying speed. All the survivors of the plague came into the streets and passed buckets of water from hand to hand. Their efforts were futile. Within six hours, nearly five thousand houses and eighteen synagogues had burned.

There was now no doubt in anyone's mind that the terrible justice of God had passed over Salonika: despite all his power, Baruch lay in one of the common graves.

Rabbi Benjamin Halevi Eskenazi, whose library had been destroyed by the fire, wrote an elegy that was included in the ritual mournfully recited by the Ashkenazim on the anniversary of the destruction of the Temple: "Those who fell were lofty as cypresses. And we, the sad, drifting survivors, are condemned to ruin, without a guide, a leader, or a priest. Our homes and our riches have perished and we wander without shelter or fortune, without clothing or food. . . ."

Abbahu did not have an occasion to recite Rabbi Eskenazi's elegy. He buried Eleazaro and his family, who had died in the wreckage of their burning house, and boarded a ship for Constantinople with his wife, his children, and Rabbi Joseph ben Lev.

32

CONSTANTINOPLE

Doña Gracia
Mendes

ABBAHU THE printer never found his place in Constantinople. He continued to be haunted by the plague that had punished the city of Salonika and the fire that had purified it. Had he been the voice that provoked the curse of the Almighty? Should he have remained silent and let Baruch and his men go on tyrannizing decent people? He had no answers to the questions that gnawed at his conscience. Sometimes he comforted himself with the idea that some people were chosen to say and do certain things, and that it was then their duty to carry out the mission assigned to them. If he had been vainglorious or fanatical, he would have been proud of what he had done, but he was a modest man who found himself in a situation that overwhelmed him.

One of the first things he did after arriving in Constantinople was to go with his son Abraham to the grave of his father Meshulam in the Egri Capu cemetery, beyond the Kalligaria Gate. It was an ancient cemetery with gravestones that had been eroded by time. Many of the Hebrew inscriptions were now indecipherable, like time itself and the history of the Jews.

Standing with his son beside him, Abbahu put his prayer shawl over his shoulders, took the fragile family parchment from the box in which he had carried it, and began reading it in a muted voice.

Praise be to You, O Lord our God, God of our fathers. You have turned away from us because of our sins. You have abandoned us. The world You made for us still exists, and we, for whom You made it, are disappearing. But we are still Your people. Our memory is the abode of Your Law. By the letter and the word, by prayer and fasting, we will maintain love and respect for Your commandments. So that no one of my lineage will repudiate Your name in the suffering of exile, and so that none will be forgotten on the day of forgiveness, I inscribe the names of my sons on this scroll. I hope and desire that it will be preserved after my death and continued by my descendants from generation to generation, until the day of Your reconciliation. . . .

When he had stopped reading, he felt a tear trickling down his cheek. He did not wipe it away and let it cling to his beard.

Abraham looked at his father in silence. He saw him put the scroll back into the box and take out a copy of the family book printed by Gabriel in Soncino. Abbahu carefully opened it and, name after name, evoked the memory of their ancestors in the old cemetery: and Gabriel begat Abramo, and Abramo begat Meshulam, and Meshulam begat Abbahu, and Abbahu begat Abraham. . . .

A light wind from the sea ruffled the fringes of the two men's prayer shawls and bent the dry grass. Abraham, who had grown up in Salonika after being born in Rimini, found himself thinking that he was at home in that Constantinople cemetery, among those stones and names emerging from history. The Turks had taken the city from the Greeks, who had taken it from the Franks, who had taken it from the Greeks, and all through that time gravestones were being added to gravestones and names to names.

As if he had been following Abraham's thoughts, Abbahu quoted from Psalms: "So teach us to number our days that we may get a heart of wisdom."

"Amen," replied Abraham.

ABBAHU DID NOT ACCEPT the invitation of Gershom's oldest son, Eleazaro, to work with him in the print shop. He wanted to study and pray, and above all he wanted to devote his remaining days to transcribing the word of the Creator as his distant ancestors had done: with pen and ink, on parchment. Not that he had suddenly become opposed to printing; but printers had the task of propagating human knowledge and opinion, and he considered it his duty to preserve the wisdom that God had given to the whole human race. "The eternal Torah," he said, "can't be treated in the same way as those ideas that appear and pass away like the seasons, and change as they spread from one place to another."

And so Abbahu became a scribe. It was his son Abraham who began working in Eleazaro's print shop, and moved into lodgings above it. Abbahu, his wife, their widowed daughter, and their grandson Daniel lived with Rabbi Joseph ben Lev in one of the buildings that had been placed at his disposal for the new *yeshiva* he was going to found.

At first Abbahu intended to teach at the *yeshiva,* but he soon came to feel that this would be too great a burden for him. While Rabbi Joseph gave the impression that he had been granted a second youth, Abbahu became increasingly uncommunicative. Each day he isolated himself a little more from the world, whose constant clamor seemed to him as meaningless as the splashing of waves against a shore. He gradually withdrew into solitary silence and fervent prayer. His fear that God might have abandoned him was dispelled when his widowed daughter Sarah married Eleazaro, himself a widower. Life had healed the wounds of the past.

Unlike his father, Abraham felt perfectly at ease in Constantinople. His room above the print shop was spacious, with two windows overlooking the Golden Horn and the shipyard beyond, from which the wind sometimes brought a smell of tar. In the morning, at the first call of the muezzins, he got up, said his prayer, ate breakfast, and went off to work with a happy heart. Eleazaro had been giving him more and more responsibility in the shop because he wanted to devote himself to study, like his younger brother Giosuè, who had become a rabbi. This suited Abraham quite well.

He worked hard in the shop, but outside it he was easygoing and unconcerned. When there was no family gathering or amorous rendezvous to take up his free time, he liked to stroll through that imposing city, observing people and things, stopping by to see Isaac Akresh the rare-book dealer, exploring the great bazaar, or going as far as Besiktas, from where ships left for the Asian shore of the Bosporus. In Constantinople, with its mixed population of Turks, Greeks, and Jews, the style of living was almost the same as the one he had known in Salonika, and he liked it.

SEVERAL YEARS AFTER the family had come to Constantinople, Doña Gracia Mendes, a great lady of the city, invited Abbahu and Rabbi Joseph to her house. But since Abbahu still preferred to live in seclusion, he asked his son, who was now twenty-five, to go in his place. Abraham was glad to oblige him.

Doña Gracia was a Marrano who had recently arrived in Constantinople. Spanish by birth, she had married a Portuguese who headed a banking establishment with headquarters in Antwerp and a large enterprise that dealt in precious stones. After her husband's death she left Lisbon and went to Antwerp, where she set up an organization to oppose the activities of the Inquisition and help Marranos escape from Portugal. When her brother-in-law Diogo died, the family fortune was partially confiscated, but she was able to leave Antwerp surreptitiously and go to Venice. There, her sister Reyna denounced her for secretly practicing the Jewish religion. She then went to Ferrara, continued helping Portuguese Marranos to escape, and openly returned to Judaism.

She came to Constantinople at the invitation of the sultan himself, with a retinue of forty horsemen and forty wagons filled with servants and Spanish ladies. Her master of ceremonies was a Spanish duke. By special permission of the sultan, the members of her entourage were not required to wear distinctively Jewish clothes. For one ducat a day, she rented a magnificent estate in Pera, the elegant quarter where most of the Franks* lived. She maintained a veritable court of noblemen, diplomats, scholars—and paupers. It was said that every day she received eighty indigent people and treated them like royalty while distinguished visitors waited in the anteroom. Rabbi Joseph, who had visited her several times, gave her his highest praise: "She's a *tzaddik* [righteous woman]."

The streets of Galata, on the other shore of the Golden Horn, were wider than those of Stambul; it was even possible to ride through them on horseback. The buildings were less tightly packed together and there were no *baltadgis,* those "axemen" who, when a fire broke out, demolished the houses around it, beginning ten, twenty, or thirty houses away from the one that was burning, depending on the speed of the fire and the wind.

Doña Gracia's estate was on a hilltop with a view of the Seraglio and the Sea of Marmara in one direction and the Bosporus in

* Westerners in general were referred to as Franks.

another. Through the heavy iron gate, slow-moving figures could be seen working in the garden.

Doña Gracia stood in the doorway of a semicircular room to greet Rabbi Joseph and Abraham. Despite the youthfulness of her face, she gave an impression of majestic dignity. With a gracious gesture she invited the two men to come in.

"May the all-powerful God of Israel bless you for having come so soon." Her voice was melodious and she spoke Hebrew with a lilting accent. She examined Abraham attentively. "You're the son of Abbahu the printer? You work with Eleazaro of Soncino, don't you? And your father has sent you in his place?"

Abraham looked at her, spellbound, without answering her questions.

"I greatly admire the courage your father and Rabbi Joseph showed in Salonika," she went on. "I know how difficult it is to oppose evil." The wrinkles in her face were so fine that they could be seen only from close up. She turned to Rabbi Joseph. "Have you read this, rabbi?" she asked, taking a sheet of paper from a table and handing it to him. "It's *Cum Nimis Absurdum,* the bull that the new pope has just issued."

Rabbi Joseph began reading it aloud: "It is too absurd and unseemly that the Jews, condemned by God to eternal slavery because of their sin, should, on the pretext that they are treated with love by the Christians and permitted to live among them, be so ungrateful as to insult them instead of thanking them, and so insolent as to claim the status of masters where they ought to be subjects. We have been informed that in Rome and elsewhere they carry audacity to the point of living among Christians in the vicinity of churches without wearing their distinctive sign, that they rent houses on elegant streets and around public squares in the cities, towns, and villages where they live, acquire and possess real estate, have Christian maidservants and nurses as well as other paid servants, and commit other misdeeds, to their shame and in contempt of the Christian name. . . ."

Rabbi Joseph seemed to be enraged by each word he read. He stopped abruptly, raised his forefinger, and said vehemently, "May all Your enemies perish, O Lord!" Then he was seized with deep dejection. "What can we do, *señora,* what can we do? Nothing, except to place our trust in Him who can do anything. . . . It is written, 'With the Lord on my side I do not fear.' "

A servant brought three cups of *kahve* on a silver tray and they

442

sat down around a low table. Doña Gracia's bodice, whose high collar was spangled with precious stones, revealed a triangle of white skin that fascinated Abraham.

"As a result of that papal bull," she said, "harsh measures have been taken against the Jews in all cities under pontifical domination: they're forced to wear yellow hats and live in ghettos that have only one entrance and exit, they're forbidden to have Christian servants, they're required to use only Latin or Italian in keeping their accounts. . . . In Ancona, the pope's representative has been given full power to prosecute Portuguese Marranos who have returned to the God of Israel, as I have done. About a hundred of them have been arrested. I know them all: I made it possible for them to leave Portugal and I sent them to Ancona, where the previous popes, Paul III and Julius III, had guaranteed their safety and freedom of worship. And now . . ."

She went on to say that only the day before she had been received by the sultan and that he had promised to demand the release of all prisoners who were Turkish subjects or were affiliated with Turkish commercial enterprises. But Abraham was not really listening. Looking into the garden, he saw a young woman wearing a short-sleeved purple tunic over a long robe with a broad cloth belt. Her hair was held by a bluish-green headdress with two lace ribbons hanging from it. Walking slowly beside a child, she seemed absorbed in thought, as if she did not know she was being observed. Abraham looked at her and told himself that he loved her. He did not feel the excitement that usually drove him to conquer women. This time he felt the deep calm of certainty: he knew he would never forget her.

"Rabbi," Doña Gracia was saying, "I expect you to organize prayers and inform all the Jews of Constantinople. If the sultan's efforts fail, we must try to act on our own." She turned to Abraham and took him by surprise. "Don't you agree, Abraham ben Abbahu?"

Abraham, whose thoughts were still in the garden, said the first thing that came into his mind.

"Ancona is a seaport. Let's stop sending our ships and merchandise there."

Doña Gracia fixed her dark eyes on him and frowned.

"Explain yourself, young man."

"Well, it seems to me that since the Jews in Ancona have been imprisoned, we won't do them any harm if we stop trading with the city." His idea suddenly seemed brilliant to him. "In Salonika, my father Abbahu and Rabbi Joseph showed that the Almighty helps those who help themselves, and not those who do nothing but wait, weeping and moaning."

Doña Gracia smiled briefly.

"You're absolutely right, but we'll at least wait to see the outcome of the sultan's efforts."

When they had left Doña Gracia's house, Abraham turned away from Rabbi Joseph and walked toward the young woman he had seen from the window. She had a puzzled expression as she watched him approaching her, and it seemed to him that he would never cover the distance between them.

"Shalom," he finally said to her.

"May the Creator, King of the world, protect you," she replied.

"Who are you?"

"I came from Portugal a few weeks ago and Doña Gracia was kind enough to take me in."

"But what's your name?"

"Beatrice."

Abraham felt as if she had just given him the best news he had ever heard in his life. He took leave of her and rejoined Rabbi Joseph, who was muttering obscure curses in his beard.

That afternoon he asked one of the printers at the shop, who was also from Portugal, to go to Doña Gracia's house and make discreet inquiries. When the printer returned at the end of the day, Abraham learned that this Beatrice was an aguna. Having converted to Christianity to escape persecution, she had married another convert, a man much older than herself. When Doña Gracia's organization gave her a chance to leave Portugal she took it without hesitation, even though her husband refused to go with her, preferring to stay in his own country and remain a Christian. She left with a group of other Marranos and went first to Ferrara, then to Constantinople, where she publicly returned to the religion of her ancestors. Was the child hers? No, she was only taking care of it.

In the print shop that evening, Abraham described Beatrice's situation to Eleazaro and asked him if she was free to remarry.

"Certainly not, Abraham! A woman can't have two husbands!"

"But what if her first husband is no longer a Jew?"

Eleazaro quoted the Talmud: "A wife can be repudiated whether

444

she consents to it or not, but a husband can be repudiated only with his consent."

"The Almighty gave us the Law, and we have to make the best of it!"

"The Law is the same for everyone, Abraham. One person has no right to . . ."

ABRAHAM CONSULTED nearly all the rabbis in the city, without finding a single one who was willing to marry him to Beatrice.

"Bring witnesses," said Rabbi Meshulam Halevi, "who will testify that the husband either gives his consent or is dead."

"But I don't even know where he lives, rabbi!"

"The Law is the Law."

Eliezer ben Nahmias, the community council leader who drew up bills of divorce, told Abraham that Beatrice's marriage could not be declared null and void, even though it had taken place within a religion imposed by violence.

"So says the Law."

The Law, the Law. . . . Abraham finally discovered a Greek merchant in Galata, named Nicos Polyandrou, who was about to go to Portugal on business and agreed to find Beatrice's husband and have him sign the divorce document that Meshulam Halevi had prepared.

"Where does he live?" asked Polyandrou. "What's his name?"

Abraham, who had not seen Beatrice again, could not answer these questions. He went back to Doña Gracia's house in Pera, but this time he stopped at the gate and asked a gardener to bring Beatrice to him. She came a few minutes later, still accompanied by the small child, as she had been the first time he saw her. She smiled when she recognized him.

"Beatrice, I need to know the name of your first husband."

"My *first* husband? I've had only one."

She had golden eyes—how had he not noticed it before?

"I'll be the second one," he said. And, suddenly intimidated, he added, "If you're willing."

RABBI JOSEPH STILL SAW Abraham regularly but preferred not to become involved in his efforts to marry Beatrice. It was through him that Abraham learned of developments in the Ancona affair. As he had promised, the sultan demanded the release of Jewish prisoners affiliated with Turkish commercial enterprises.

445

The non-Jewish merchants of Ancona then sent an emissary to the pope to express their concern over the possibility of losing their trade with Turkey. Nothing had yet been won or lost when thirty of the hundred prisoners succeeded in escaping and going to the neighboring—and rival—city of Pesaro.

The pope appointed a new representative, Cesare della Nave, a fanatic who conducted the trial of the remaining prisoners according to the methods of the Inquisition. Under torture, some of the Marranos confessed to having converted in order to save their lives. Twenty-four of them were sentenced to be strangled and burned.

It was spring when the news reached Constantinople, throwing the Jewish community into consternation. Doña Gracia's nephew, Joseph Nasi, hurried to the grand vizier, who summoned the leader of the Ancona merchants to tell him that all those disturbances were harmful to his master's affairs and that he demanded the immediate release of Turkish subjects and Doña Gracia's agents. If he did not obtain satisfaction, he said, he would take reprisals. As a first step, he ordered all Ancona merchants in Turkish territory to keep their ships ready to put to sea.

The French and Florentines in Constantinople were afraid that the affair would have adverse effects on international commerce. The French ambassador sent his secretary, Pierre Cochard, to the pope with a letter from the sultan himself.

Whenever he had a little free time, Abraham went to the waterfront in the hope of seeing his Greek merchant return from Portugal. He waited impatiently and remembered what Nicos Polyandrou had said to him before leaving: "I'm sure I won't be gone more than six months. Or maybe a year. I won't come back any later than that, unless my business in Portugal keeps me longer." What a precise schedule!

At the print shop, where Eleazaro now appeared only on rare occasions, Abraham was setting type for an edition of *Amadis of Gaul*, a story of love and adventure, in the translation by Rabbi Jacob, son of Moses al-Gave. Yearning for Beatrice, he sometimes made additions to the text in which he declared his passionate love for the woman he regarded as his fiancée, and he felt that this writing was superior to the author's.

Nicos Polyandrou unexpectedly arrived at the print shop on one of the few days when Abraham had not gone to the waterfront. He woefully announced that he had not been able to have Beatrice's husband give his consent to a divorce, but, he added, his face brightening, he had found two witnesses willing to sign a declaration of his death. He again took on a mournful expression, then burst out laughing when Abraham leapt into the air and began running around the shop like a child, shouting jubilantly, "He's dead! He's dead!"

He took the declaration, gave Polyandrou the money he had promised him, ran down the three steps that led to the street, and went on running till he reached the house of the chief rabbi, Menachem Bahar Samuel, a tall, stout, solemn man with an impressive square beard. Abraham interrupted his meditation and showed him the declaration, which was written in Portuguese. The chief rabbi read it and turned it over, as if he expected to see something written on the other side of the paper. Then he gave Abraham a look of commiseration.

"Where's the declaration certifying that the dead man had no brother?"

Abraham was staggered by this question. He knew that the Law required a widow to give priority to her dead husband's brother if she wanted to remarry, but in Beatrice's situation that requirement bordered on absurdity. He protested, pleaded, flew into a rage—in vain. The chief rabbi met all his objections with the same answer: "The Law is the Law."

And that was the only answer he got from all the other rabbis in the city, whether they were Portuguese, Italian, Hungarian, or German. They seemed to believe that if they consented to marry Abraham and Beatrice the Almighty would cover the earth with darkness, ashes, and blood, and the whole world, lacking the support of the Law, would collapse.

Meanwhile news had reached Constantinople that about half of the prisoners in Ancona had been executed.

Pierre Cochard had arrived in Rome too late, with letters from the sultan and the French ambassador in Constantinople. The letters were not completely ineffective, however: the pope replied to the sultan that all Turkish subjects who were still prisoners in Ancona would be released, and that the confiscation of Doña Gracia's property would be abolished. But he refused to release the condemned Marranos, including Doña Gracia's agent in Ancona, Jacob Mosso. Ignoring all pleas, he let the executioner do his work: on June 6, 1556, eight Marranos sentenced to death for apostasy were burned at the stake, and a week later the last three, one of whom was Jacob Mosso, died in the same way.

Doña Gracia Mendes summoned all the rabbis and other important Jews of Constantinople to her house in Pera. The Señora, as she was called, was dressed in strict mourning. She stood on a low platform, facing the assembled men.

"My friends and teachers," she said, "listen to the voice of the Jews of Ancona: 'Who will rise up for us against the wicked?' Twenty-four of our people have perished; may the Almighty give them eternal rest. Where will the man of Rome strike next? How long are we going to wait without putting up any resistance? Must the Jews live in helpless fear of a pope?"

There was total silence. Chief Rabbi Menachem Bahar Samuel wiped his damp hands with a square piece of cloth and then put it back under his shirt, next to his skin, in the Turkish fashion. The poet Solomon ben Mazeltov hid his face in his hands. Rabbi Joseph ben Lev was breathing rapidly but those who saw him could not tell whether he was holding back tears or anger.

"We have sent letters and petitions to the leader of the Christians," Doña Gracia continued, "and the sultan himself, God bless him, supported us. Neither entreaties nor threats have had any effect. The murder of Jews in Ancona has been the only answer from that man—may he be forever cursed!"

She did not speak loudly but her inner strength and conviction were such that no one missed a single word of what she said. Abraham, who had come with Rabbi Joseph and modestly taken a place at the back of the room, was still fascinated by her. She was able to charm and command at the same time. He saw her standing before him, slender and erect, like an indomitable flame.

"One of those who escaped from Ancona and took refuge in Pesaro," she said, "arrived in Constantinople yesterday. I ask you to listen to his testimony. His name is Judah Faraj."

A round little man, moving so slowly that one could not help wondering how he had been able to escape, joined the Señora on the platform and described what had been inflicted on the Jews in Ancona since the election of the new pope. He spoke simply, carefully choosing his words, and this made his story seem all the more horrible. Such cruelty, such iniquity! When Judah Faraj had finished, few of his listeners had dry eyes.

"My friends and teachers," said Doña Gracia, "you have heard what I have heard. Shall we do nothing but weep? No, we must act. We have no army to attack Ancona, but we can ruin it. A seaport without ships will wither and die. In trying to enrich themselves through us, the nations have given us a weapon against them. Let us use it. I propose that from now on no Jewish ship will enter the harbor of Ancona, that no Jewish merchant will stop at Ancona, that no business will be conducted between a Jew and a merchant at Ancona. We will quarantine the city of Ancona, as if it were stricken by the plague."

A moment of dazed silence was followed by loud commotion. Exclamations of surprise and approval. Apprehension and excitement were mingled. Chief Rabbi Menachem Bahar Samuel took out his handkerchief.

Doña Gracia held out her hands and silence gradually returned. In answer to questions, she suggested that the quarantine remain in effect for eight months, until Passover, and that another meeting then be held to decide what would be done next. She also suggested that all trade normally carried on with Ancona be transferred to Pesaro, whose duke, said Judah Faraj, was friendly to Jews in general and Marranos in particular. Any Jews who traded with Ancona would be fined, and for a second offense they might be punished with excommunication.

Thus was decided the boycott of Ancona by the Jews of Constantinople, Salonika, Adrianople, and Brusa, in Asia Minor. All rabbis in the Turkish empire received a letter from Doña Gracia asking them to see to it that no merchant broke the rule. Abraham printed a notice of the boycott that was distributed in all Jewish communities.

This gave him several opportunities to go to Pera—and see Beatrice. She had not been excessively grieved when she read the declaration of her husband's death: she was acquainted with one of the two men who had signed it, and knew that he would do anything for money. In any case, her husband had no brother. But she could not prove it.

Doña Gracia had learned of the romance between Abraham and Beatrice. She broached the subject to him one day when he brought her a proof to read.

"How do you intend to get the testimony you must have before you can marry Beatrice?" she asked.

Abraham told her that he was discouraged and did not understand the rabbis' blindness.

"Even Rabbi Joseph," he said. "He's a friend of my father and he's like an uncle to me, yet he keeps repeating that he can't transgress the Law!"

"If a rabbi transgresses the Law, who will respect it?" asked Doña Gracia. She made a slight gesture with her hand. "That's what they answer. But sometimes it's possible to compromise with the Law. We Marranos, driven from one community to another, from one exile to another, learned to do it because it was often a matter of life and death for us. As a result, the rules concerning the rights and duties of Marranos aren't the same in all places. In Salonika, for example, marriages between Marranos are considered to be invalid."

Her dark eyes sparkled gaily when she saw that Abraham had understood.

IN ANCONA, the effects of the boycott began to be felt in the middle of summer. Travelers coming from Italy reported that there were many bankruptcies and that clothing intended to be sent to Turkey was piling up on docks and in workshops, while products from Turkey, such as hides and ore, were selling at incredibly high prices. The situation was so serious that the Ancona city council sent a letter to the pope begging for his help.

The Marranos of Pesaro wrote to Doña Gracia, asking her to express their gratitude to the Jews of the Ottoman Empire, who had, they said, "broken the arms" of the wicked people who lived in "the city of blood."

During this respite, Rabbi Joseph granted Abraham's request that he make a quick voyage to Salonika. The three of them boarded a ship together: Abraham and Beatrice to be married, Rabbi Joseph to perform the ceremony. The old man had readily consented; after all, Salonika was his native city, and he was curious to see what had become of it.

He had a feeling of affectionate recognition when he again found himself surrounded by the bustle and uproar of the Salonika waterfront. The parts of the city destroyed ten years earlier had been rebuilt.

In a new synagogue, among his distant relatives, he performed the wedding ceremony that united Abraham and Beatrice. But a few days were enough for him. His life was now in Constantinople, he missed his pupils, and he wanted to be back where he could have direct news of the boycott.

AFTER ROSH HASHANAH, the admirable unity of the Jews began to crumble. The Jews of Ancona who were not Marranos, and were therefore allowed to carry on their commercial activities, found themselves on the verge of ruin. Their rabbi, Mosè Bassaola, wrote to all the rabbis in Turkey, asking them to have the boycott stopped. The merchants of Brusa maintained that the financial interests at stake had been underestimated and that the port of Pesaro was not equipped to receive their large ships. Violations of the boycott became known, notably those committed by a Salonika merchant named Solomon Bonsenior.

The Jews of Pesaro became apprehensive and wrote to Doña Gracia. They were tolerated by the duke, they told her, only because of their promise to develop the city; he had committed great resources to enlarging the port and authorized certain arrangements to facilitate credit. If the boycott of Ancona ceased to be effective, they added, they would have to fear for their own safety.

Doña Gracia, who still favored the boycott and its continuation, could count on the Spanish and Portuguese communities, but the Italian, German, and Greek communities were inclined to side with the non-Marrano Jews of Ancona and advocate the resumption of commerce. She asked Judah Faraj to draw up a manifesto and talked with the most important rabbis in Constantinople, telling them again and again that Jewish solidarity would lose all credibility if it became incomplete and failed to produce concrete results. She gave Rabbi Joseph the task of having Judah Faraj's manifesto signed by the most important Jewish merchants and public figures.

Rabbi Joseph went to work with fiery zeal. To him, each new signature was a victory over the forces of evil. He even made Abraham Jerushalmi, rabbi of the Greek community, sign the manifesto on his deathbed. Chief Rabbi Menachem Bahar Samuel insisted on remaining neutral. Doña Gracia's greatest adversary proved to be the rabbi of the main synagogue, Giosuè, son of Gershom the printer, known as Giosuè of Soncino. Not only did he refuse to sign, but he had his brother Eleazaro print a pamphlet in which he gave the reasons for his refusal. The boycott, he explained, was not in conformity with Jewish law, because it was wrong for one man to protect himself at the expense of another, and the Marranos of Pesaro should not be supported to the detriment of the Jews of Ancona; if the Marranos of Pesaro felt that they were in danger, they could come and settle in the Ottoman Empire, a land of tolerance, instead of continuing to live under Christian rule.

At Passover, supporters and opponents of the boycott gathered in Doña Gracia's house. She had invited all those who considered themselves her friends or owed her something. Since she was too deeply committed to act as an impartial mediator, she asked Chief Rabbi Menachem Bahar Samuel to preside over the discussion. This enabled him to go on maintaining his neutrality.

The debate continued all day without bringing forth a single new idea; the arguments had all been heard before, and positions were firmly established.

"Every day I pray that the Almighty, the God of Israel, the God of vengeance, will punish the guilty," said Rabbi Giosuè of Soncino. "My heart, like that of Doña Gracia, bleeds at the thought of the sufferings inflicted on our brothers, and I do not forget the flames that have seared their tortured bodies. But it sometimes happens that when we blow on a fire to extinguish it, we make it burn more fiercely instead. Attacking the leader of Christianity means running the risk of stirring up violence against the Jews in all Christian countries."

Rabbi Joseph leapt to his feet.

"Shame!" he cried out. "Shame! What does Giosuè of Soncino want to safeguard? Our meager privileges? Those who think that way are slaves, like our ancestors in Egypt!" He began stuttering with exasperation. "They're n-n-not yet f-f-free, and they're already weeping f-f-for their lost chains!"

Judah Faraj passionately defended the principles of solidarity with the martyrs of Ancona. Rabbi Giosuè interrupted him.

"Don't you realize that you're saying for the duke of Pesaro what he doesn't dare to say for himself? The ruin of Ancona will make him rich."

Judah Faraj, speaking slowly as always, quoted from the Talmud: "Master of the world, I will accept these sufferings with all the satisfaction of my soul and all the joy of my heart, provided that no one in Israel shall perish."

"I too would accept all suffering," said Rabbi Giosuè, "if I were sure that our action would not cause anyone in Israel to perish. But I'm afraid that if we continued our war, it would cost Israel more lives than have already been lost in Ancona."

There was a chorus of exclamations from his listeners.

Doña Gracia raised her voice: "I'm disappointed. As Rabbi Joseph ben Lev has said, you're in chains, and instead of seizing a chance to free yourselves, you sit and ask, 'Who will give us meat to eat?' Remember Baruch, the bandit who extorted money from the poor people of Salonika. Two men rose up against him, and that was enough to cause his downfall.''

Abraham felt his heart swelling in his chest. The Señora was absolutely right and he was ashamed of the timorous attitude of those rabbis more concerned with the prosperity of their communities than with justice.

"I'm disappointed," Doña Gracia continued, "but I'll carry on the struggle. Alone, if necessary, with the help of the Almighty."

THE BOYCOTT WAS NOT renewed and the port of Ancona began returning to its normal level of activity. Soon it lacked only the ships and agents of Doña Gracia Mendes.

RABBI JOSEPH SUDDENLY became bent by age and accepted the fact that he was an old man. Abraham resumed his usual work at the print shop. He and Beatrice lived above the shop and they would have been the happiest couple in the world if spiteful people —probably enemies of Doña Gracia—had not begun saying that the marriage ceremony performed in Salonika by Rabbi Joseph was fraudulent. In the bazaar and at fountains, Beatrice heard innuendoes and disguised insults. One day she came home with her face pale and drawn.

"Abraham," she said, "I won't stay in this city any longer! We have to leave! I won't stay here!"

"Calm yourself, Beatrice, and tell me—"

"They say I commit adultery every day!"

"You mustn't pay any attention to that kind of malicious gossip. It never lasts very long here. In a few days it will all be forgotten."

Beatrice held back her sobs.

"You're mistaken, Abraham. You don't know what hatred is like. You've never pretended to be something you weren't, as we Marranos had to do. You've never been pointed at, wherever you went. I know that hatred doesn't fade away. It takes root in the heart, and grows. . . ."

Abraham understood. Would they also have to flee from Jews? He took his wife in his arms.

"If you want us to leave Constantinople, my darling, we will."

"When?"

"Where do you want to go?"

"Far away."

They decided to leave in a week. Abraham settled the accounts of the print shop with Eleazaro, wrote a long letter to Doña Gracia, who was away from Constantinople at the time, spent a *shabbat* with his family, and went to say good-bye to Abbahu in the retreat he no longer left for any reason. Abraham looked at his father and was deeply moved. This thin old man, with almost transparent skin, had been able to resist the temptation of cowardice.

They prayed together and embraced, then Abbahu slowly walked to the box containing the Scroll and the Book of Abraham, took them out, and put them on the table. Abraham unrolled the parchment with awe; he had never done it before. He was surprised to recognize his father's handwriting at the bottom of the scroll. He leaned over it and read:

ON THIS NINTH DAY of the month of Av, one thousand four hundred and eighty-six years after the fall of Jerusalem, one thousand four hundred and eighty-five years after the first Abraham of my lineage wrote his name and those of his sons Elijah and Gamaliel on this parchment, after one thousand four hundred and eighty-six years of exile, love, and prayer, the stones of the Temple are still disjoined. How long, O Lord, how long?

Is it because we have sinned so much that we have not yet received any sign of Your reconciliation? Have You, unknown to us, chosen an invisible Temple whose contours are gradually revealed more fully to the mind's eye through the words of Your Book, rather than a visible Temple made of stone and wood? And have we scribes taken the place of priests as the guardians of Your house? But how long, O Lord, how long?

Prayers are added to prayers, commentaries and hymns of praise abound, books accumulate, libraries are filled with wisdom, and Your new house becomes larger and more beautiful than the old one. But how heavy that house is, O Lord, when it must be carried from exile to exile, and how hard it is to defend against Your enemies and the discouragement of Your people!

We will continue, according to Your will, to write the words of Your Law and deepen their imprint among the nations, but give us a little hope, O Lord, show us Your generosity, so that my sons' sons and the generations after them will never be afflicted with despair. Holy, holy, holy, You are the Almighty. Amen.

When Abraham had finished reading, Abbahu said quietly, "I want you to take the scroll and the last two copies of the Book of Abraham."

"But father. . . ."

"I feel as if I'd already left this world," said Abbahu. "And besides, if it's the will of the Almighty, blessed be He, you'll need the scroll when the time comes for you to write the names of my grandchildren."

•   •   •

AFTER LEAVING—fleeing from—Constantinople, Abraham and Beatrice went to Italy, where Abraham had been born. He found work in Venice, in Giovanni da Gara's print shop on the Fondamenta Pescaria, at the corner of the Ghetto Vecchio. Giovanni da Gara was not Jewish, but he hoped to fill the vacancy left by the disappearance of the great print shops specializing in Hebrew books.

Abraham and Beatrice stayed in Venice for several years and had two sons, Isaac and Jeremiah. Then, for reasons unknown to me, they went to Poland. Perhaps their reputation as an illegitimate couple had caught up with them. The Jews lived in a closed world filled with waves of feverish agitation and gossip, and Abraham's commitment to Doña Gracia Mendes may have brought him some strong and lasting enmities.

Two years after the end of the boycott, Doña Gracia had the bitter satisfaction of being proven right: the duke of Pesaro banished the Marranos from his territory. Some of them found refuge in other parts of Italy or in Turkey, and some wandered for the rest of their lives, but they were all forbidden ever to enter the port of Ancona.

Petitions, signatures, boycotts, appeals of all kinds—how close that story seems to me, and how well I know the good reasons of those who refuse to sign!

In connection with Doña Gracia Mendes, I am reminded that a few years ago I talked with Pierre Mendès-France about our respective ancestors. His were Portuguese Marranos who had settled in Bordeaux and I suggested to him that my scribes from Strasbourg might have met his merchants from Bordeaux. He loved talking about that period of his family history; his face became animated and his pale fingers danced in front of him.

"My dear Marek Halter," he said with a glint of irony in his eyes, "don't forget that in those days the Sephardim were the aristocracy of the Jewish people—it's hard for me to imagine my ancestors having social relations with modest Alsatian scribes."

When, following Abbahu and Abraham, I arrived in Constantinople, where Doña Gracia had just settled, I wrote to Pierre Mendès-France that if our ancestors had not met between Bordeaux and Strasbourg, they might have met between the Bosporus and the Golden Horn. He answered four days later, in a letter dated April 6, 1981:

> My dear friend,
> I am touched by your letter of April 2. Yes, it is quite possible that our families met at some time in the distant past. But I am sorry to say that I am not a descendant of Doña Gracia Mendes, who once played an important part in history. The similarity between our names is only a coincidence, and I regret that a little. . . .

PROBABLY AMUSED BY MY persistence, he expressed the hope that I would "have the last word." But I believe that our families actually met only once. It was in Paris in the twentieth century—more specifically, in May 1967, just before the Israeli-Arab war of that year. He and I, among many others, spoke of peace.

33

LUBLIN

A Love Story

LUBLIN WAS a fortified market town surrounded by fields and marshes. Abraham and Beatrice realized all too well how far they had come from palaces overlooking the Bosporus, from purple seas, and even from the yellow, timeworn façades of the Ghetto Vecchio. The springtime afternoon was rainy and almost dark. They looked at each other sadly and felt like weeping.

It was Rabbi Mordecai Joffe who, during a brief stay in Venice, had suggested to Abraham that he go to Poland. Life was good there, he said, and King Sigismund had exempted the Jews from wearing a distinctive sign. Mordecai Joffe lived in Lublin, where, since the death of the famous Solomon Luria—may the Almighty keep his righteous soul—he had been fulfilling the functions of rabbi and head of the *yeshiva*.

He told Abraham that dozens of rabbis and their pupils came to fairs in Lublin from villages all over Poland, sometimes even from Lithuania, and left without having been able to find any books except those that had to be brought from Cracow or faraway Prague. Abraham hesitated. Then Mordecai Joffe said that his son Kalonymos wanted to set up a print shop but needed a partner who knew the trade. Abraham decided to go to Lublin.

And now, after having gone through a gray suburb made of

slanting little wooden houses on muddy slopes, he and Beatrice were waiting in front of a town gateway clogged with low carts, broad-rumped horses, and men dressed in faded linsey-woolsey who seemed indifferent to the rain. So this was Poland. . . .

* * *

POLAND. That name brings back the smell and taste of my childhood. When I was born there, before the war, one Pole in ten was Jewish (3,250,000 Jews in a total population of 32,183,000). Some villages and regions were practically a hundred percent Jewish, and Jews had been living there for nearly a thousand years.

Warsaw, my native city, had nearly a million inhabitants, of whom 368,000 were Jews, with their thirteen primary schools, dozens of yeshivot, six theatrical companies, two film production companies, six daily newspapers, and dozens of weekly and monthly magazines, as well as fifteen publishing houses and about the same number of political parties. And all this in Yiddish, my native language, which my ancestors learned at Benfeld in the fourteenth century.

But there were also two Jewish dailies in Polish, ten literary and political journals, and a multitude of writers, thinkers, and scientists, university graduates despite the restricted quotas of Jewish students, whose creative work enriched the cultural heritage of Poland, their homeland.

In Warsaw, the Jewish streets were like all other Jewish streets in the cities, towns, and villages of Central Europe. The houses smelled of fresh bread and pickled herring. In parks and public squares, men commented on the day's events with broad gestures. Women with their hair hidden by colored shawls washed their laundry in courtyards where children played. Cafés, clubs, and libraries were filled with enthusiastic young people eager for knowledge. Adolescents who had just left their yeshivot chased each other, laughing, with their sidelocks dancing to the rhythm of their steps. On crowded, commercial Nalewki Street the hubbub was punctuated by the shouts of newspaper sellers and the cackling of chickens. I remember an old hunchbacked Jew who had always been waiting for someone to buy the pair of unmatched shoes he offered for sale, and the tens of thousands of bearded Jews who filled the street one May Day, singing the "Internationale" in Yiddish. Two thousand of them went off to fight against fascism in Spain, as others had fought on the barricades of Saint Petersburg, or in Paris during the French Revolution, or in the American Revolution.

Those Jews no longer exist. They have been obliterated, and their traces have been erased from the history of Poland by the Polish People's Republic. Thus, to the few visitors who now go to the Auschwitz camp, the guides talk about the three million Poles killed by the Nazis, but not about the Jews, as if there were an attempt to deprive those Jews even of their death and their place in our memory.

My friends are surprised that since coming to Paris in 1950 I have had no desire to go back to Poland. They do not understand that without that warm, lively restless world in which I am rooted by my memories, Poland is for me a colorless landscape, a body with withered limbs, a nameless being. It is painful for me to return there, even in imagination, with Abraham and Beatrice and all the printers who afterward lived, worked, and hoped there for centuries.

When I think of the towns and villages burned by anti-Semitic bands in the seventeenth, eighteenth, and nineteenth centuries, I always see Warsaw in flames. "I will light a candle for each Jew in Warsaw," said Hitler. And whenever I must describe a pogrom or some other murder of innocent victims, I am haunted by the image of the white-bearded old man my mother tried to save from a wave of arrests at the beginning of the German occupation: men in gray-green uniforms burst into the house, pulled him out of the closet where he was hiding, and dragged him by the feet down the marble steps, on which his brain left yellowish streaks.

That is why I find it so hard to begin writing about the Polish period of my family history. But without it this story would not be what it should be. And I would not be what I am.

•   •   •

IN THEIR WAGON, with their children Isaac and Jeremiah sleeping huddled against each other, Abraham and Beatrice were finally able to pass through the congested gateway. From there, bouncing along on disjoined paving stones, they skirted a deserted marketplace by way of Bramowa Street and turned into Grodzka Street, which led them to another congested gateway, the Jews' Gate. The crowd was different here: black caftans and caps, baggy trousers over short boots.

In front of Abraham and Beatrice was Rabbi Mordecai Joffe's wagon. The crowd opened before it.

"Make way for the rabbi! Make way for the rabbi!"

On the other side of the Jews' Gate was a bridge over a wide ditch that the people of Lublin, explained the driver, who was from Radom, regarded as a river and called the Bistryca.

The Jewish section of the town was surrounded by a high wooden fence. Its streets were even narrower and muddier than those of the Christian section. Only the main thoroughfare was paved. The horses slipped and floundered in unspeakable filth. The wooden houses were pressed tightly together, as though to avoid sliding into the slimy street. Above them rose a bare hill topped by a massive building and a square tower that seemed to be holding up the sky.

Abraham and Beatrice followed a stream, the Czechowka, on whose banks women were washing clothes in the rain. Signboards with Hebrew letters swayed in the gusty wind, the buckets hanging at the rear of the wagon loudly banged against each other, lightning streaked across the sky, invisible dogs barked in courtyards. Here and there, water dripped through the cloth cover of the wagon. Finally they stopped.

"Welcome!" said a tall, thin man with a fan-shaped beard and yellow catlike eyes. "I'm Kalonymos, Rabbi Mordecai's son. Come in and make yourselves at home."

ABRAHAM WAS AWAKENED by a ray of sunlight coming into the bedroom. He got up without making any noise. Isaac and Jeremiah lay close beside their mother. Abraham went out onto a balcony sheltered by a projection of the thatched roof. A smell of tree bark rose from the steaming earth. The wind was drying the mud, making signboards dance, and hissing through cracks in the house. High in the sky, a flock of wild geese flew past. In the street, children in black caftans were laughing and jostling each other around a water carrier whose two buckets bent the pole resting on his shoulders. From the kitchen on the first floor came a cheerful song in Yiddish and the fragrance of hot pancakes. Everything was new to Abraham, yet he did not really feel that he was in strange surroundings.

The house belonged to Kalonymos. It was near the *yeshiva* and had large outbuildings. One of them, a decrepit structure heated by a blue enameled stove, stood next to the chicken coop and contained the scantily equipped print shop. The printer, Eliezer ben

Yitzhak, was a short man, round as a barrel, who never stopped talking.

"So you're Abraham, the printer from Venice! Welcome! Do you know why the Jews have a prayer for the beginning of a journey but don't have one for its end? No? It's because the Jews are always leaving but haven't yet arrived anywhere! Wait, there's more. You must know this passage in Genesis: 'Jacob went on his way and the Angels of God met him; and when Jacob saw them he said, "This is God's army!" So he called the name of that place Mahanaim [Two Camps].' Well, do you know that that passage is part of the prayer for beginning a journey? And do you know that Mahanaim is here in Lublin? We have two cities, one Jewish and the other Christian: two camps. And do you know. . . ."

At this point Kalonymos came to Abraham's rescue. He was accompanied by his two sons, Tzvi-Hirsch and Chaim.

"What do you think of the shop?" he asked. "We've come to begin work, under your guidance."

"God bless you!" replied Abraham.

THE TEN YEARS THAT followed the arrival of Abraham and Beatrice in Lublin were peaceful and therefore happy, thanks to the Almighty, blessed be He. Abraham and Kalonymos gradually improved the print shop until it could stand comparison with the one in Venice. They printed in Hebrew and also in Yiddish, a rich language that Abraham had to learn; his children spoke it fluently, but Beatrice the Portuguese never really mastered it.

They had adopted the habits, clothes, songs, and food of the Lublin Jews. They no longer told stories on the front steps of the house, but around the stove; they knew the deep silence of snowy nights, and the powerful urge to live that rose in everyone when the spring thaw awakened the earth. Isaac—now called Yitzhak—and Jeremiah, having arrived as children, were indistinguishable from young men born in Lublin.

Ten years! They had a little anniversary celebration and Abraham made everyone laugh when he told how he and Beatrice had first come to Lublin, wet and disappointed, and nearly turned back without even getting out of their wagon. They spoke of Rabbi Mordecai, Kalonymos's father, who had died of a winter fever; they spoke of Abbahu, Abraham's father, who had died in Constantinople three years earlier; they spoke of Eleazaro, who had gone off to Safad, in faraway Palestine. . . . Candles were lit and, at Kalonymos's request, Abraham read passages from the book of his ancestor the Jerusalem scribe. Hippo, Cordova, Narbonne . . . Magic words of memory. Roots. Certainties.

As it had done ten years earlier, the snow turned into mud that was soon dried by the sun and the wind. The roads became animated. From all directions, wagons converged on Lublin for the great fair. Cattle came from Muscovy; from the Netherlands came caravans of horses laden with bales of cloth; from Hungary, creaking carts carrying barrels of almost black wine. Livestock dealers gathered around the herds to bargain. Herring peddlers circulated in the crowd.

Yitzhak, who was now seventeen, liked the atmosphere of the fair, the exclamations in Polish, Yiddish, Turkish, and Hebrew, the harsh smells of wool grease and freshly tanned furs, the fragrance of cinnamon and cloves that came from the Kapanica, the building where royal agents verified the authenticity of goods brought by Jewish merchants from Turkey and Greece.

He was looking for a traveler from Constantinople who might have news of his aunt Sarah and uncle Joseph. At one corner of Olejna Street, a resourceful man had put up a target and was renting his bow and arrows to anyone who wanted to practice a little or challenge his friends. Yitzhak was drawn to the scene by exclamations. He mingled with the onlookers. Two *szlachcics* [Polish noblemen], one old and the other young, were about to compete against each other, with a bet at stake. For *szlachcics* too, the fair was an opportunity to meet friends, make purchases, or have lawsuits settled by the royal tribunal that held sessions in Lublin. They came from Gdansk, Poznan, Lvov, Cracow, and Warsaw, with grave faces, loud voices, and imposing mustaches, wearing fur-lined silk cloaks. Each of them carried a martel-de-fer as a sign of rank and wore a saber whose hilt was set with precious stones. It was said that a *szlachcic* took off his saber only when he went to bed, and that not all of them took it off even then. Yitzhak saw them from close up only at fairs and had never spoken to one of them.

The old *szlachcic* took aim for a long time but his hand was unsteady; his arrow hit the edge of the target. Then the young one shot quickly, almost casually, and his arrow sank into the outer part of the bull's-eye. The onlookers applauded.

"You win," said the old one, "but you'll have to give me another chance when we're both drunk!"

The young *szlachcic* laughed with pleasure. He was tall and luxuriously dressed. His skull was shaved, except for a tuft of blond hair in the middle, which swayed in the wind. Holding up his bow, he made a circular gesture to the crowd.

"Does anyone want to try to do better?"

Suddenly ill at ease, the men looked away from him and shifted their weight from one foot to the other.

"No one? You're all afraid to try? You have nothing to lose. . . . You, over there!"

The man who had been singled out was standing in front of Yitzhak. He abruptly turned and hurried away, blushing with embarrassment. The *szlachcic* then saw Yitzhak.

"Come here," he said.

"Are you talking to me?" asked Yitzhak.

"Yes. What's your name?"

"Yitzhak, son of Abraham."

"You're a Jew?"

"Yes."

"Have you ever used a bow?"

"No."

The young nobleman examined Yitzhak from head to toe.

"You seem strong," he said. "If you're as talented as you are handsome, you'll do very well. Watch me."

Yitzhak followed the lesson attentively, then took the bow in his hands; it was not as heavy as he had thought. Unafraid, but determined not to make himself ridiculous, he rolled up the sleeves of his caftan, put the arrow in place, and drew the bow, trying to reproduce the young Pole's stance and movements exactly. When the arrow left the bow, he closed his eyes. A moment later he heard exclamations and felt a hand grip his shoulder. He looked at the target: the arrow, planted in the middle of the bull's-eye, was still quivering.

"Thank the Lord!" he murmured.

The young *szlachcic* laughed wholeheartedly.

"Bravo, Jew! You've beaten me! The pupil has outdone the teacher after the first lesson! Bravo!"

He put on his fur hat and led Yitzhak outside the circle of spectators.

"You're not like other Jews," he said. "What do you do?"

"I'm a printer. But what makes you think I'm not like other Jews?"

"A printer? You're from Lublin?"

"I live here but I was born in Venice, in Italy."

"Do you speak Italian?"

"A little, yes."

"And Latin?"

"Yes."

The young Pole stared at Yitzhak in surprise.

"You know more than . . . How old are you?"

"Seventeen."

"I'm eighteen. My name is Jan Ostrowski. Do you know Ostrow?"

"No."

"It's near Leczna. We have Jews on our estate. You'll have to come and visit me there some day."

YITZHAK AND JAN OSTROWSKI did not see each other again until the following winter. On a very cold day, when Yitzhak was walking in the middle of an icy street, he heard jingling bells behind him, turned, and saw a sleigh drawn by two magnificent horses speeding toward him. He leapt aside, slipped, and fell. The runners of the sleigh grated on the ice.

"May the devil take you!" he shouted angrily as he stood up.

A man in gray fur jumped out of the sleigh.

"Why, it's my expert archer!"

Yitzhak recognized Jan Ostrowski. The young nobleman came up to him.

"Forgive me. But it's rash of you to walk in the middle of the street. . . . Come, let me introduce you to my sister."

They went to the sleigh together. Between a gray fur blanket and a white hat, Yitzhak saw two dark, sparkling eyes looking at him with curiosity.

"Elena, this is Yitzhak, the Jewish printer I told you about—the one who beat me in an archery contest!"

Yitzhak then heard Elena's voice and it was like heavenly music to him.

"Yes, it's true that Jan told me about you. He said you were born in Venice. I'm glad of this chance to become acquainted with you."

"Get in," said Jan. "We'll take you to where you're going."

Yitzhak hesitated, then climbed into the sleigh. He found himself sitting between the brother and sister, with his legs under the thick fur blanket.

"Go!" Jan ordered the driver.

The sleigh set off and was soon moving at great speed. The bells jingled and the runners made a faint squealing sound. Puffs of vapor rose from the horses' nostrils. Yitzhak felt the warmth of Elena's body against his. He sat motionless, as if he were afraid of awakening from a dream.

"I love to go fast," Elena said to him. "Do you?"

THE NEWS CAUSED A great stir in the Jewish quarter: the son of Abraham the printer had been taken to his home on Broad Street, near the synagogue, by the son of Pan Ostrowski, in his sleigh. The community was still shocked by the death of Mordkhe the innkeeper, who had been accused of killing a Christian child with the help of his son Aaron, his son-in-law Aizik, and his servant Joachim. The royal tribunal had sentenced him to be drawn and quartered, despite the testimony of shepherds who had found the child's body slashed by the teeth of wolves.

Since then, the community had kept to itself as much as possible. The Jews of Lublin spent more time in their synagogues than before, leaving them only when necessary, trying not to attract any attention. In those circumstances, Yitzhak's sleigh ride might be regarded as either a foolish blunder or a provocation, or even as a kind of betrayal.

Abraham did not mention it at the family table, but the next evening, when they were on their way to the synagogue for *shabbat* services, he said to Yitzhak, "It's not good, my son, to associate with Poles when Mordkhe, may God have mercy on his soul, has just been drawn and quartered only because he was a Jew."

"But father, not all Poles are—"

Abraham cut him short: "I know, I know!"

It was snowing. Jews were coming out of all doors. They headed for the synagogue and greeted each other: *"Shabbat shalom! Shabbat shalom!"* The snow sang beneath their feet.

TWO WEEKS LATER, Jan Ostrowski's sleigh stopped in front of the print shop. The young *szlachcic* went in. Abraham, Kalonymos, Tzvi-Hirsch, and Chaim interrupted their work and turned toward him. He stopped, suddenly embarrassed.

"Good morning," he said.

Yitzhak came forward and introduced him to Abraham and the others. They greeted him politely.

"I've come to invite you to a sleigh ride with music," he told Yitzhak. "It's next week. I'll stop by for you."

In the street, a crowd was gathering around the sleigh. Faces were pressed against the windows of the shop.

"With your permission," Jan said to Abraham. "I'll come back someday to see how books are printed. But today I don't have time."

Yitzhak accompanied him to the doorway, where he was chilled by the bitter cold outside. Jan leaned toward him.

"Inviting you wasn't my idea," he said. "It was Elena's."

He laughed and jumped into the sleigh, which started off and quickly gathered speed. His happy laughter mingled with the sound of the bells.

THE RUNNERS OF THE sleigh hissed as they glided through the snow. In other sleighs, ahead and behind, musicians—Jews—were playing pieces of music that had been assigned to them. As before, Yitzhak was seated between Jan and Elena. The wind, the infinite space around them, the music, and the clouds of glittering, powdery snow raised by the horses' hooves made the young people feel like laughing and shouting.

"How are the girls in Venice?" Elena asked Yitzhak with a rather provocative laugh.

"I left Venice when I was only seven," he replied. "I hadn't yet begun looking at girls."

"And now?"

He did not know what to answer. Under the fur blanket, he felt Elena's warm thigh next to his own.

"Why are you Jews so serious? Don't you ever enjoy yourselves? Listen to the musicians: their music is as sad as a funeral. . . ."

"You mustn't jump to conclusions, little sister," said Jan. "Their music is sad because it's slow, and it's slow because their fingers are cold, that's all!"

"Luckily I have enough gaiety for three of us!" said Elena.

They stopped in front of an isolated church whose two spires were covered with frost that sparkled in the pale sunlight. The door was wide open and the glow of dozens of candles could be seen inside. The women got out of the sleighs, formed groups, and knelt in the snow before going into the church. Most of the men only crossed themselves and waited outside. The musicians

466

stopped playing. Jan lifted the blanket from his lap and stepped into the snow.

"I'm going to see if Father has come," he said. "You two can take a little ride and come back for me."

When the sleigh had taken Elena and Yitzhak away from the church, she asked abruptly, "Do you like me?"

"You know I do," he answered.

"Really?"

"Really."

"Very much?"

"Yes, very much. And you?"

"I feel drawn to you," she said, "and I don't know why. Is that love?" Her eyes shone like flames. "Do the Jews know any love stories?"

Yitzhak recited: "Behold, you are beautiful, my love! Your eyes are doves, your two breasts are like two fawns, twins of a gazelle, that feed among the lilies. . . ."

Elena's cheeks turned bright red and she moved away from him a little.

"Where did you learn that?"

"From the Bible."

"It's in the Bible?"

"Yes. It's King Solomon talking to a shepherdess, the Shulamite."

"What happened to them?"

"They loved each other, then they parted."

"Why?"

"Because everything separated them."

"That's sad. I knew the Jews were sad."

She moved close to him again. He smelled perfume.

"It's not that the Jews are sad," he said, "it's that love stories are sad."

He took her in his arms. She turned her face toward him, with her eyes closed. Their lips joined and time was abolished. Under the fur, she pressed her tense body against him.

Then they heard bells: the sleigh had brought them back to the church. The space in front of the church was now crowded with people singing hymns and holding crude statues and wooden crosses.

Yitzhak let go of Elena's hands. He was reluctant to get out of

467

the sleigh; this ceremony did not concern him. He saw Jan coming toward them with a tall, broad man wearing an ermine cloak.

"Father," said Jan, "this is our Jewish printer."

"You're the young man who's such a good shot with a bow? You must come and try your skill against me someday. Jan will bring you."

Krzysztof Ostrowski had a deep voice that rumbled formidably in his chest. He turned to his daughter.

"Elena, go to your mother in the church."

He winked at Yitzhak as though asking him, man to man, to take note of his authority over his women, then he walked away with the heavy, rolling gait of a bear. "God save Poland!" sang a group of young *szlachcics* kneeling in the snow.

THREE WEEKS LATER, when Jan again came for Yitzhak, Abraham and Beatrice had mixed feelings of anxiety and pride as they watched their son leave. They were impressed by the fact that a nobleman had invited him to his home, but they both recalled the Turkish proverb: "Associating with the great brings great troubles."

It was less cold now, and patches of snow were sliding off the roof of the Ostrowski family's enormous house, exposing the shingles here and there. Jan led Yitzhak into a vast room. Yitzhak was unpleasantly surprised: the room was full of people. Clean-shaven faces, luxurious clothes, a hubbub of voices. Weapons of many different origins—clubs, spears, daggers—were displayed on the walls. Beside the gigantic fireplace, in which massive logs were burning, Yitzhak saw Elena surrounded by a group of young men. In her brightly colored bodice, tapered at the waist, and with her two blond braids resting sedately on her shoulders, she seemed so different from the ardent Elena in the sleigh. . . .

Yitzhak suddenly heard Krzysztof Ostrowski's powerful voice.

"Ah, here's our young Jew!"

Half the people in the room fell silent. Yitzhak wondered what he was doing there.

"Yitzhak is a printer," said Jan. "He was born in Venice and he speaks several languages."

"Does he know how to hunt bears?" asked a ruddy-faced man with a small head and a bulging paunch.

There were several outbursts of laughter.

"I don't know if he hunts bears," answered Jan, "but at the Lublin fair he beat me in an archery contest."

Krzysztof Ostrowski laid his heavy hand on Yitzhak's shoulder. "Come, have a drink and a piece of sausage with us!"

"Excuse me, sir," Yitzhak had to reply, "but my religion forbids me to—"

"He's talking about the Talmud," explained a tall, thin man whose blond mustache was wet with mead.

"So the Jews are allowed to do business with Christians," said the fat bear hunter, "and cheat them if possible, but not to share a sausage with them!"

Jan pulled Yitzhak by the sleeve.

"Let's go, I want to show you the rest of the house."

"Let the young Jew answer!" protested the bear hunter. "We're not doing him any harm!"

He blinked his eyes when Yitzhak looked at him intently.

"The Talmud says nothing about Christians," Yitzhak said in a calm voice.

"Who does it mention, then?"

"It speaks of idolaters."

"For you Jews, Christians are idolaters! But I don't understand why the Jews, who are usually so clever, made the foolish mistake of denying the only Son of God. Why didn't they realize that the future belonged to the Christians?"

"Everyone is entitled to have his own religion," said Yitzhak.

He wanted to avoid a discussion, especially since he could see that these people had all been drinking heavily. He thought of Mordkhe, the Jew who had been drawn and quartered, and suddenly wondered if he had fallen into a trap.

Krzysztof Ostrowski suggested that they give Yitzhak time to get his bearings before drawing him into a serious conversation, but the bear hunter persisted.

"I'd like this son of Abraham to explain why, in his opinion, the Christians persecute the Jews."

"That's for the Christians to explain," said Yitzhak. "For my part, I do my best to observe the Law I received from my forefathers."

"Does that Law command the Jews to despise the Christians?"

"This is a ridiculous discussion!" exclaimed an old man with a wide beard.

The thin man who had first mentioned the Talmud took another sip of mead and said with a knowing look, "When you listen to the stories that Jews tell each other. . . ."

Everyone had now gathered around them. Elena was standing beside Jan. They both seemed upset. She smiled faintly at Yitzhak, perhaps to apologize, perhaps to give him courage.

"The other day," the thin man went on, "one of the runners of my sleigh broke and I had to wait in an inn kept by Jews. I'll spare you a description of the terrible stench and the bawling children. . . . Sitting near me were two Jewish peddlers from Lublin. They paid no attention to me. I heard that they were talking about the Saint Andrew monastery near the Jewish cemetery of Grozyska."

He unhurriedly emptied his glass, well aware that he had aroused his listeners' interest. He took out a handkerchief, wiped his mustache with it, and put it back in his belt.

"One of the Jews was explaining to the other why the monastery is lower than the cemetery. The land, he said, once belonged to two brothers. One of them gave his part of it to the monks, who built a monastery on it, and the other gave his part to Jews who used it as a cemetery. The monks wanted to have all the land for themselves. They rang their bell each time the Jews buried someone. The Jews complained to the vaivode, and even to the king, but their complaints were ignored."

The thin man now held his listeners in the palm of his hand. Taking advantage of their rapt attention, Yitzhak discreetly left the center of the group and moved closer to Elena.

"One day, when the monks were again ringing their bell during the burial of a Jew, the lid of the coffin opened and the dead man sat up. He was a rabbi. He asked one of his pupils to go and bring him a book from his library. When the boy came back, the living-dead rabbi took the book and read a prayer that no one understood. And the more the bell rang, the faster the prayer became. Suddenly the monastery shook on its foundation and began sinking into the ground, a little farther with each word of the prayer."

The storyteller again took time to wipe his mustache.

"The green door," Elena whispered to Yitzhak as she slowly walked past him. "Come!"

"Then what happened?" a voice asked eagerly.

The storyteller smiled with satisfaction.

"Then, said the Jew, the monks stopped ringing the bell, ran to the cemetery, knelt in front of the open coffin, and begged the rabbi to forgive them. The rabbi gave the book back to his pupil and lay

470

down in his coffin. The monastery immediately stopped sinking, but it remained lower than the cemetery. And to this day, as you'll see if you ever go there . . ."

Yitzhak slipped out of the room.

Elena was sitting on a carved chest with her back against the tapestried wall, weeping softly in the shadows. Yitzhak went to her and took her hand.

"I'm ashamed," she said.

"You musn't be ashamed. It's just how things are, that's all."

"But why?"

He pulled her toward him. She stood up. They embraced and kissed, then clung to each other with their eyes closed, swaying gently like two trees in the wind.

The door was thrown open and slammed against the wall.

"Where are they?" thundered the formidable voice of Krzysztof Ostrowski. He saw them and rushed at them. "My daughter with a Jew! In my house!"

He was choking with rage. He put out his hand to seize Yitzhak but Elena stepped in front of him.

"No, father! It's my fault! Mine!"

He violently pushed her aside and she fell, gasping. With a kind of detachment, Yitzhak saw the broad, flushed face close in front of him and smelled the odor of mead. He thought of his parents and wondered if he should fight. He was certainly not as strong as Elena's father, but he was quicker and more agile. He was not afraid. He wanted to be rid of this man so that he could help Elena to her feet.

Jan came running into the room and placed himself between the two men. His father was breathing loudly.

"Take him away, Jan. Don't ever let me lay eyes on him again!"

Yitzhak saw that Elena, still on the floor, was watching the scene with a terrified expression. He tried to reach out his hand to her, but Krzysztof Ostrowski stopped him and bellowed, "Get out! You hear me? Get out, Jew! You're lucky that the Ostrowskis have never killed a guest in their house!"

Jan led Yitzhak to a back door and briefly squeezed his elbow. Yitzhak heard the door close behind him.

It was snowing and darkness was already falling. He did not know where to go. His fur-lined caftan was in the house; without it, he would freeze to death before morning if he stayed outside. Should he hide in one of the outbuildings? Go back and ask to be

471

forgiven? He walked toward the sleighs belonging to the guests and saw that some of them contained fur blankets. He quickly took two of them and asked forgiveness of the Almighty, blessed be He. After all, he was doing it to save a human life. He wrapped the blankets around him and set off in what he thought was the direction of Ostrow.

The wind rose, then the snow stopped and the sky cleared. In the cold starlight he saw a vast plain dotted with clumps of trees. He was hungry and cold. He repeated parts of the prayer for beginning a journey. "May it be Your holy will, O Lord our God and God of our fathers, that I make my journey in peace. . . . I trust in Your help, O Lord." To avoid becoming completely lost, he followed the frozen tracks left by the sleighs. He was at least sure that they would lead him somewhere, even if he did not know where it would be.

He seemed to see a dark mass in the distance. A village? A forest? His courage revived a little. "May it be Your holy will, O Lord our God. . . . I wonder what Elena is doing now. Maybe she left the house to go after me. . . . I trust in Your help, O Lord. . . . I never really believed that Elena and I could love each other. It's better for it to be ended now. . . . And God of our fathers, that I make my journey in peace. . . . Elena, I love you. Elena, I love you. Elena, I love you."

His words set the rhythm of his steps and filled the icy silence. Suddenly he stopped to listen. Wolves. The dark mass that stood out against the starry horizon was no longer very far away. He began running toward it. It was a forest. His chest was burning. He recognized the strong smell of birches, and another smell: smoke. There was a human presence in that wilderness. The wolves' howls were coming closer. He picked up a piece of broken branch that was big enough to use as a club.

It was darker in the forest; he lost the sleigh tracks but headed toward the smell of smoke. "Elena, I love you," he repeated, "Elena, I love you." It was like a magic incantation to keep the wolves away, or put off the time when he could no longer avoid fully, truly realizing that a Jewish printer could not love a nobleman's daughter.

Warned by a sudden sense of danger, he turned around. A dark shape was bounding toward him. He swung his club with all his strength and heard a cracking sound. The wolf fell dead, its skull broken. Yitzhak began running again but quickly realized that it made him more vulnerable to attack from the rear. He stopped and shouted into the night.

"Help! Wolves! Wolves!"

They had silently overtaken him and now surrounded him, watching him with boundless patience. He faced them with his back against a thick tree trunk. He thought of trying to climb a tree, but he had always heard that this was a fatal mistake: every spring the bodies of people who had escaped from wolves, only to die of cold, were found in trees.

Now and then he swung his club to keep the pack at a distance. Finally he heard a shout, from far away. He answered it at the top of his lungs. The wolves had also heard it. Evidently knowing that their time was limited, they came closer to Yitzhak and began moving around him. Then several of them attacked at once and he had to fight.

THERE WAS A CANDLE. It was the light of a candle. A yellow, incredibly motionless flame. Yitzhak closed his eyes. He was warm, he had a sense of well-being, and he did not feel like asking himself questions about a candle. He savored the blissful torpor of his body and sank back into sleep.

When he awoke, the candle was no longer burning. He tried to roll over but was stopped by a pain that made him moan.

"Praise the Almighty!" said a woman's voice.

"May He be praised forever, amen," replied a man's voice.

Yitzhak raised his head slowly and saw, beside the stove, a robust, red-bearded man and a blond woman with a very light complexion. As if everything had awakened at once, caged geese began cackling. Yitzhak tried to ask where he was, but no sound came from his lips.

"You're with friends," said the man. "We're good Jews, so you have nothing to fear!"

Just then the door opened, cold air whirled across the room, and a middle-aged woman wearing a man's smock came in. She set a bucket down on the floor, took off the smock, and shook the snow from it.

"Come and see, mama," said the young woman, "he's awake."

"If he's awake, that's a good sign. But I've already told you, Deborah, that looking at men is a sin. Instead of watching him, heat some milk for him. It will do him good."

Yitzhak moved to find out which part of his body was painful. His straw mattress rustled. He cleared his throat.

"Thank you," he said. "Thank you for your hospitality."

"Don't thank us, thank the Almighty," said the man. "In His mercy, He made me a light sleeper. I heard you shouting. My brother Shammai took his ax and I took my old companion." He pointed to a huge knotty club hanging beside the door by a leather thong. "We got to you just in time. You'd killed four of the wolves, but the others had already bitten you on your arms and legs. You lost a lot of blood."

The young woman came toward Yitzhak with a steaming cup in her hand.

"Where are you from?" asked the man.

Yitzhak did not answer. He had gone back to sleep.

HE WAS SO WEAK that for several days he was awake only a few minutes at a time. Then his strength began slowly returning. He saw that the wounds on his arms and legs had been dressed with leaves, and learned that he had been taken in by foresters who lived near Parczew. Mordecai, the man who had saved his life, was employed by a landowner he had not seen in ten years to keep watch on the forest that lay between the Tysmienica River and the Kalinka marshes. His brothers and cousins were all woodcutters, strong, simple men, he said, who knew trees better than the Scriptures. "But they're good Jews!" he added.

ONE MORNING Yitzhak was finally able to get up, purify his hands in a basin of water, and say the morning prayer. The time had come for him to leave.

It was Shammai who took him to Lublin. They had to go quickly, before the thaw. The horses and the sleigh were heavier than Jan Ostrowski's, and the furs were coarser; Yitzhak thought they must have come from either bears or wolves. Shammai was so taciturn that he spoke only twice during the whole journey. The first time was to offer Yitzhak a colorless liquid that, he said, would help him to bear the cold. Yitzhak took a drink of it and felt as if his mouth had burst into flames. The second time was to make a little speech that had obviously been prepared in advance.

"In the village," said Shammai, "we're all ignorant. We need an educated man, someone who can teach our children to read and write, and love the Torah." He kept looking straight ahead. Now and then a blinding flash of light broke through the mist. "If some-one came to teach our children, we could teach him, in return, how to recognize a tree by its voice. . . . Can a young man from Lu-blin understand that?"

The young man from Lublin no longer knew exactly who he was or what he wanted, or even what he was doing in that sleigh, with that Jew who never went anywhere without his ax and his jug. The print shop, Krzysztof Ostrowski, Elena, the Saint Andrew monas-tery—everything was mingled in a remote past, as though his nar-row escape from death had divided his life into two parts: before and after the wolves. He felt certain that his love for Elena be-longed to the first part.

ABRAHAM, Beatrice, and Jeremiah welcomed him with tears of joy. They had thought he was dead, especially since Jan Ostrowski had come several times to ask about him. Everyone who lived on the street stopped by the print shop to hear about Yitzhak's adven-tures.

Jan came again two days later.

"Tell your father," Yitzhak said to him, "that I hold nothing against him, and that I pray that God will protect him from him-self."

"And . . . Elena?"

Yitzhak suddenly felt like weeping, but as he would have wept for the sin of Adam and Eve in the garden of Eden.

"I loved her," he said.

Jan laughed.

"You talk like an old man!"

"I've aged."

"Aren't you going to ask me about her?"

"It is written, 'Sin is couching by the door; its desire is for you, but you must master it.' "

"But Yitzhak, my friend. . . . Don't you even want to see her?"

"It is written, 'The heart and the eyes are the procurers of sin. The eyes and the heart desires.' "

"Yitzhak!"

"Well, then," asked Yitzhak, "how is she?"

"I think she's unhappy. Our father is sending her to France."

"May God protect her."

"Is that all you have to say?"

"Tell her I was right: it's not that the Jews are sad, it's that love stories are sad. She'll understand."

IN THE SPRING, Mordecai the forester came to Lublin and paid a visit to the print shop: saving a man's life, he said, gave responsibilities. He had a private conversation with Abraham, in a closed room. When he came out, he was beaming. He lingered awhile beside Yitzhak, who was working on the press; then, after being introduced to Jeremiah, he blessed everyone and left the shop with a loud *"Shalom aleichem!"*

YITZHAK AND THE BLOND Deborah were married that summer in the Jewish woodcutters' village in the Parczew forest. Rabbi Meir ben Gedaliah, known as Maharam, came from Lublin to bless the young couple.

After the ceremony a rooster and a hen, symbols of fertility, were swung in circles above the bride and groom, and everyone stood while Abraham read aloud from the family book; those people of the forest, who knew trees eight hundred years old, were well able to understand the meaning of duration. Then there was dancing to the music of violins in the houses and barns, and outside in the clearing, by torchlight, far into the night—it is surely not true that all Jews and all love stories are sad.

In the opinion of everyone who had come to Parczew from Lublin with the rabbi, it was really a very fine wedding.

34

AMSTERDAM

The Excommunicated
Jew

YITZHAK'S YOUNGER brother Jeremiah went on working in
the print shop and married a gentle young woman named Rachel,
called Rochele. They had five children: Azariah, Ruth, Leah,
David, and Herschel. Azariah married an egg merchant's daughter
and, after his father-in-law died, took over the business and began
making the round of markets in the region. Ruth and Leah married
young and left home. Herschel replaced his grandfather Abraham
in the print shop. Jeremiah and Kalonymos's son Tzvi-Hirsch
managed the shop. Children were born, books were printed, and
the two families went on living as good Polish Jews, lively and
warm-hearted, stirred by all sorts of fears and hopes. When trouble
overwhelmed them, they prayed to the Almighty, blessed be He,
and consoled themselves with the old Hebrew saying, *"Yie tov"* [It
will turn out all right]; and if it actually did turn out all right, they
concluded, *"Sof tov, ha kol tov"* [All's well that ends well]. Those
simple people asked for nothing more than the simple lives they all
led. All, that is, except Herschel, Jeremiah's youngest son.

Adventure suited Herschel even less than the others, but he had
more than his share of it. He did not like to travel, but he spent a
good part of his life traveling. He wanted nothing so much as a
snug, restful home, with books, a cheerful wife, and quiet children,

but that was not what he got: he married a cold, domineering young woman and she quickly gave him three children who had teething pains only at night and would not stop crying till their father got up to soothe them.

Herschel's troubles came from the fact that he could not say no. Intelligent, sensitive, and imaginative, he was horrified at the thought of hurting someone's feelings. Whenever anything was proposed to him, he was perfectly capable of weighing the reasons for and against it, but he always ended by accepting it simply because he could not bring himself to inflict a refusal on anyone.

His great adventures began on the day when a distant cousin wrote to the print shop to ask if a member of the family could come to his wedding and read a few passages from the Book of Abraham. The letter was sent from Polonnoye, days and days away from Lublin. Jeremiah was busy printing a chapter from the Mishnah, the Treatise on Pure Things, and Azariah was waiting to set his hens at the time of the new moon; it was therefore only natural to ask Herschel to make the journey. As always, he agreed to do what was asked of him.

His wagon was loaded with books that he would try to sell along the way, and Jeremiah gave him one of the two remaining copies of the Book of Abraham; Yitzhak had taken the other copy with him when he went to live in his forest village. Herschel said good-bye to his wife and children as if he were going to return that evening.

He performed the fast of the ninth of Av, anniversary of the destruction of the Temple, in Radom, where he stayed with Rabbi Elhanan, nephew of Meir ben Gedaliah of Lublin. He spent part of the night rereading the Book of Abraham, which had come into being as a result of the destruction of the Temple.

The next day, he stopped at an inn kept by a one-eyed Jew. There he met two Cabalists from Prague who were on their way home after having traveled across Poland as far as the Volhynia region. They began expounding their theories to him and he listened patiently, not wanting to offend them by going off to bed, but when he left the next morning he still did not understand why "all union and all perfection culminate in the Mysterious Unknown, the object of all desires." He stopped in Ostrog to deliver some books to Rabbi Samson, and two days later he stopped at the *yeshiva* in Zaslaw, which had ordered three copies of the Talmud published by his grandfather Abraham and Tzvi-Hirsch Joffe.

After leaving Zaslaw, Herschel set off across the steppe, a flat, grassy, silent plain where a horseman or a camel could be seen from miles away, and where even the most insignificant sounds were strangely amplified and transformed into mournful cries. The solitude weighed heavily on him. To him, travel was interesting only because of the people it enabled him to meet. He liked people, all of them, good and bad; they were all different, yet all alike.

When he reached Polonnoye he found the town in turmoil. In the streets, people were hurriedly loading their possessions—furniture, pots and pans, furs—into wagons. The Cossacks, Herschel was told, had revolted, and their leader, a man named Pawlouk, was a bloodthirsty savage. Two hundred men, women, and children had been slaughtered in Biala-Cerkiew, and even more in Korsun. The governor of Polonnoye had just fled. For many people, this was a signal. "If lightning strikes the majestic fir," said one man, "what will become of the lowly ivy?"

Herschel did not have time to look for his cousin. He was caught up in the stream of wagons that flowed across the steppe, toward Zaslaw. He was afraid, like everyone else, but he remembered something his grandfather Abraham used to say: "Fear has big eyes but a small heart."

In the morning they were stopped by wagons coming from the opposite direction: the Cossacks had just burst into Zaslaw. Feeling that they were caught in an absurd but deadly trap, the fugitives shouted angrily, prayed, lamented, and finally began throwing out the humble treasures they had piled into their wagons: chests, household utensils, boxes of linen, cages of poultry . . . All that agitation in the middle of that wilderness struck Herschel as a bit ridiculous.

He saw two men coming toward him and recognized them as the Cabalists he had met at the inn, on his way to Polonnoye. They interrupted their endless discussion to ask him if he could take them into his wagon.

"Get in," he replied.

They wore fur hats despite the summer heat and seemed completely detached from everyone around them. After making room for themselves among the books in the wagon, they sat down with their bundles on their laps.

"Look," said one of them, "the dire prophecy made to our forefathers has come to pass!" With a long black fingernail at the end of a bony white finger, he pointed to the frantic activity in the wagons scattered over the steppe. "It is written, 'They cast their silver into the streets.' "

"I'm going back to Lublin," said Herschel.

"Lublin? You're mad! At this very moment, Zaslaw is occupied by the Cossack hordes—may the Almighty bring down His wrath upon them as He did upon Amalek! The roads to Lvov, Beresteczko, and Luck have surely been cut off by now."

"Then what shall we do?" asked Herschel.

"You have asked the right question, but you must not ask it of men. You must ask it of the Almighty, who knows and sees everything."

From the inside pocket of his caftan, the other Cabalist took out a book whose binding had been worn smooth.

"The Torah!" he said. "The Torah will tell us where to go!"

"How?" Herschel asked innocently.

The two Cabalists immediately leapt to their feet, raised their arms, pulled their beards, and denounced him with righteous anger.

"Blasphemer! Unbeliever! Infidel!"

After nearly tipping over the wagon, they sat down again and glared at Herschel like stern uncles confronting a misbehaving child.

"The Torah, young man," said one of them, "is a light that illuminates the world."

Just then Herschel saw three horsemen riding toward him at full speed. They were Jews, with faces marked by terror as well as fatigue. They stopped only long enough to shout a warning.

"Get away as fast as you can! The Cossacks are in Polonnoye!"

They spurred their panting horses and continued on toward Zaslaw, not knowing that the Cossacks were there too.

The two Cabalists seemed not to have heard anything. They were leaning over the Tanach.

"Here it is," said one of them.

The other read aloud: "Let me pass through your land; I will go only by the road, I will turn aside neither to the right nor to the left."

Then the other one read: "You shall sell me food for money, that I may eat, and give me water for money, that I may drink . . ."

". . . until I go over the Jordan."

Herschel looked at them in bewilderment. If what they were reading had not been so sacred, and if the situation had not been so

480

tragic, they would have reminded him of the men at the Lublin fair who put on little performances designed to catch the attention of passersby so that they could sell them medicines or separate them from their money in some other way.

They turned to Herschel.

"You see, young man, everything is clear."

"Clear as the water of a mountain stream."

"The road is the road from Proskurow to Kamienec-Podolski."

"And the Jordan is the Dniester."

"We therefore know the route we must follow: Transylvania, Hungary, Moravia, Bohemia."

"But I have nothing to do in those places!" Herschel protested. "I'm going to Lublin!"

"Lublin? Woe to you if you go there! Look around you: it's like a battlefield, and the Cossacks aren't even here yet! Nathan Praguer and I have seen how those barbarians flay men alive and throw their flesh to the dogs, how they cut open pregnant women and tear out their unborn babies. Believe me, young man, the Torah is never mistaken. It's better to be alive in Prague than dead in Lublin."

Herschel watched the three horsemen from Polonnoye disappearing over the horizon of the endless steppe. Crows circled overhead. He thought of the print shop, where his father Jeremiah must be worrying about him, and his brother Azariah the egg merchant, his two sisters, his wife, his children. . . . To reassure himself, he felt the Book of Abraham through the cloth bag that he always carried with him.

"May it be done according to Your holy will," he murmured, "O Lord our God and God of our fathers."

He clicked his tongue and the horses set the wagon in motion.

THEY REACHED Prague with the autumn rains of that year 5398 [1638] after the creation of the world by the Almighty, blessed be He. The two Cabalists exhibited Herschel in the ghetto as living proof that what they said could not be doubted; the Cossacks were overrunning Poland and the coming of the Messiah was imminent. The *parnasim* invited him to tell his story in the Jewish town hall, a dark building, surmounted by a tower, that resembled the Saint Eustachius Church in Lublin.

To make a living until he could go home, he went to work for the only Jewish printers in Prague, Joseph and Judah Bak. He found lodgings on Cervena Street, near the old synagogue. When he tried to leave the ghetto to explore the rest of the city, he was ordered at the gate to put on the distinctive signs by which Jews were recognized: a pointed yellow hat, a yellow badge over his chest, and a little ruff around his neck. Decked out in this way, he went to see one of the sights of Prague: the clock of the city hall. He joined the crowd already standing there, looking up to watch the ballet of the figurines. He saw Death appear, in the form of a skeleton ringing a little bell, then a Jew waving a purse. He was overwhelmed with sadness and decided to go back to Lublin, no matter what the risks might be.

When he returned to the print shop he met a visitor, a printer who had just come from Amsterdam after living there for several years. He told Herschel that he now wanted to live in Prague, where he had been born, and that he was looking for someone to replace him in Rabbi Manasseh ben Israel's print shop in Amsterdam. Only if another printer took his place, he said insistently, could he stay in Prague with his elderly parents and marry the young woman who had been waiting for him so long. Herschel thought of his family in Lublin. But once again, without having said either yes or no, he found himself committed to something he did not want.

As he set off for Amsterdam he thought ruefully, "When will I learn that I don't always have to do what's asked of me?"

HE DID NOT REGRET his journey. As soon as he arrived in Amsterdam he liked that prosperous commercial city, immense and yet compact, intersected by canals and narrow streets in the soft light of the low sky. The important Rabbi Manasseh ben Israel gave him an enthusiastic reception: most good Jewish printers, he said scornfully, preferred to work for *goyim* because they paid higher wages than he did. He had hired two Poles from Cracow, the brothers Jacob and Abraham ben Zevi, but they were only beginners and he needed someone to run the shop so that he could have time to fulfill his many obligations.

Manasseh ben Israel was the brilliant son of a Portuguese Marrano. The Amsterdam Jewish community had taken charge of his education and he had become a rabbi at the age of eighteen. He was the second assistant of Saul Levi Mortara, spiritual leader of the community, which had just been unified at the time when Herschel arrived. He worked for the tribunal and taught at the primary school. He spoke eight languages: Portuguese, Spanish, Hebrew, Latin, Greek, Dutch, Italian, and English. He knew all the Greek and Roman classics and was a writer himself; he had begun printing his "great work," *El Conciliador,* in 1632. He gave Hebrew lessons, carried on an extensive correspondence, helped Marranos to settle in Amsterdam, and received many non-Jewish friends in his home. His income was slender, and with all these activities he still found time to take a close interest in the East India Company. His brother Ephraim had just gone to Pernambuco, in Brazil, to keep watch on his business affairs. He was a strange, impetuous, truculent, sentimental little man. Everyone in Amsterdam recognized his plump figure as he hurried through the streets in his short cloak and pointed hat.

Herschel naturally accepted the terms offered to him by Rabbi Manasseh. He took charge of the print shop, and from then on the rabbi came there for only two hours a day, to read proofs or look over the accounts.

Herschel hoped to find comfortable lodgings for himself, but meanwhile he slept in the shop, on a thin straw mattress placed on a wooden platform that the proofreaders used as a bench during the day. The work was interesting and he found himself doing in Amsterdam what his father Jeremiah did in Lublin; with Rabbi Manasseh's permission, he even rearranged the shop and made it into an almost exact copy of the one in Lublin.

He had been there about two weeks when one night, shortly after the drum roll that was the signal for the guards to assemble, he heard someone knocking on the door. He lit a lantern, looked through the window, and saw only a vague shape in the winter mist.

"In the name of the Almighty, let me in!" a voice called out in Hebrew. "Don't be afraid!"

Herschel opened the door.

The man was tall and thin. His gray hair hung down below a soft, broad-brimmed hat and he wore a shabby purple tunic. He walked over to Herschel's makeshift bed and asked, "May I?" after he had sat down on it.

Herschel wondered how all those people managed to find him: he already knew that this feverish-eyed man was going to cost him a night's sleep. But what was he to do? He could not refuse to listen to him, send him away without even letting him tell why he had come.

"My name is Uriel Acosta," said the man. "Have you heard of me?"

"Maybe, but . . ."

"You see before you an excommunicated Jew, ostracized, proscribed, banished, cast out as if he were a leper."

It was despair, not madness, that shone in Acosta's eyes.

"What did you do?" asked Herschel.

"Nothing wrong. I only refused to be a monkey among monkeys."

"A monkey? What do you mean?"

"All those religious rites sin against reason, and I rejected them."

"But our rites *are* our religion!"

"If you only knew what I've suffered because of religion! First as a Marrano in Portugal, then as a Jew in Amsterdam. . . ."

"But why do you call yourself a Jew if you reject the religion of Israel?"

"I'm a Jew because I call myself a Jew! Don't misunderstand me: to me, the religion of Israel is not that wretched bondage to rites, gestures, prayers recited without faith. Judaism . . ." He took a deep breath and spread his arms wide, as though to embrace something immense. "Judaism is . . ."

Herschel was beginning to take a liking to this man.

"Have you ever danced around the scrolls of the Law, at feasts of rejoicing?" he asked. "That, too, is tradition. In our family we have a book in which we've been writing the names of our children and the important events of our lives, from generation to generation, for more than fifteen hundred years. . . . I don't know what you expect of me, but you'll never make me say anything different from this: Judaism is, first of all, memory and tradition."

Uriel Acosta looked at Herschel with gratitude.

"I understand what you're saying. But I don't understand the people who condemned me. If you knew how they've made me suffer, with their virtuous airs!" He stood up abruptly, as if he were already late for some important appointment. "Thank you for listening to me. You're the first one who's done it for a long time."

"But why don't you reconcile yourself with the synagogue?"

Acosta proudly drew himself erect and his face took on a fierce expression.

"The synagogue will have to reconcile itself with me, because I didn't desert it: it expelled me!" He took a few steps toward the door, then turned around. "I'll come back, if you're willing to see me again. God bless you!"

When he left, a cold, damp wind swept across the room.

In the nights that followed, Herschel waited in vain for Uriel Acosta. During this time he was setting type for an edition of *Shevet Yehudah,* a chronicle of Jewish martyrology, and another printer, Judah Leib Setzer, was doing the makeup. It was from Judah that he learned a little more about Uriel Acosta, a Portuguese Marrano from Oporto who had returned to Judaism when he came to Amsterdam.

"But," said Judah, "having imagined a faith of Israel that was not the faith of Israel, he felt he should try to transform the religion of Israel."

"And the community didn't appreciate his efforts?"

"Of course not. He then published a very belligerent work, *Examination of Pharisaic Traditions Compared with the Written Law.* The community excommunicated him and burned his books."

"Burned his books?"

"Yes. Most of the Jews in Amsterdam are Portuguese; they fled from the Inquisition, but they brought some of its spirit with them."

Herschel felt strangely fascinated by the excommunicated Jew of Amsterdam. He, too, had sometimes wondered to what extent the community necessarily expressed God's truth, but he had never allowed himself to carry his thoughts any further.

Although Uriel Acosta had said he would come back, the winter passed without his putting in another appearance at the print shop.

There were other visitors, however. Rabbi Manasseh ben Israel often came with customers, merchants or friends, such as the physician Ephraim Bueno. One day the rabbi and Ephraim Bueno brought to the shop a round little man with long red hair, wearing a plumed hat, a green velvet doublet, and brown breeches. Manasseh ben Israel began explaining the various phases of typesetting and printing. The man asked many questions but understood quickly. Suddenly he stopped in front of Herschel, who was busy with his composing stick.

"You're just the man I've been looking for!" he exclaimed. "I have a place for you: behind Samson, with the musicians."

Seeing Herschel's disconcerted expression, Manasseh ben Israel said to him, "Our friend Rembrandt van Rijn is a painter. He's

485

already done sketches for a portrait of Ephraim Bueno and his daughter."

The painter described the picture on which he was working. He demonstrated the postures of the people represented and proved himself to be an excellent actor.

"On the right, in a circle of light, sits Samson. Behind him stand four musicians, listening to him as he turns toward her. Delilah sits in the middle of the composition, impassive. Now, between the group of men, here, and Delilah, here, there's too much space. You see what I mean? That's why I want to add a fifth musician. I needed a face, and I've just found it."

He stepped back, drew himself erect, and looked at Herschel, squinting his eyes.

"Every face is a divine creation," he said, "a light in the darkness. The painter's privilege is to discover what is hidden behind appearance, as Job says. In a way, you also play with darkness and light: those dark lines that form the letters, and the white spaces around them." He stopped, frowned, and quoted: "The Infinite struck the void with the sound of the Word." He turned away as if he were about to leave, then turned back and said to Herschel, "Everything is in the Cabala!"

And with that, he walked out. Herschel, who had not had time to say a word, stared after him in bewilderment.

Judah Leib Setzer came over to him and said, "Pull yourself together, my friend, and don't worry about the fact that Jews are forbidden to depict the human face: you'll never be the fifth musician, your face won't be a spot of light in the darkness. Ten times a day, Rembrandt van Rijn finds 'just the man he's been looking for,' and quickly forgets him. That's how he is. . . ."

Herschel found a certain similarity between the painter and Uriel Acosta, even though everything seemed to set them apart from each other. This was probably what led him to speak of Acosta to Rabbi Manasseh a few days later.

"Don't mention that man to me!" the rabbi exclaimed indignantly. "Saying the name of someone who's been excommunicated sullies us as much as touching the flesh of a corpse, may the Almighty, blessed be He, preserve us from it!"

Herschel said nothing more about Acosta. It was nearly a year before he saw him again, but he did not forget him. During that year he had the surprise of seeing his wife Kaila arrive with their three children. Since he had written to Lublin without saying anything about returning, she had decided to come and live with him in Amsterdam. In a way, he was relieved: he no longer had any remorse; but Kaila's waspish character had not improved. They moved into a large house near the studio of painter Rembrandt van Rijn. Kaila went to Rabbi Manasseh and demanded that he raise her husband's salary.

One day when Kaila had gone out with the children, Uriel Acosta came to Herschel's house. He still wore his thin purple tunic, his eyes were as feverish as ever, and his cheeks seemed even more hollow.

"I had a hard time finding you," he said to Herschel. He tossed his hat onto a chest and sat down on a bench. "I wanted to tell you that I haven't forgotten you. I spent all that time writing the story of my life. It's a life that can serve as an example. . . . If men won't do me justice, at least the future will."

"And what's the title of your book?" Herschel asked, to ask something.

"Exemplar Humanae Vitae. What do you think of it?"

Herschel did not know what to say. He had mixed feelings: irritation, pity, and a certain admiration for Acosta's indomitable courage. And suddenly he became angry, violently and unexpectedly, in the manner of the weak.

"I've had enough of your complaints! No one is forcing you to behave that way! If you're a Jew, observe the laws of the Jews. Otherwise, become a Christian and live by the laws of the Christians!"

Acosta nodded sadly, as though to say that he was already familiar with that argument and that vehemence.

"You don't understand. . . . In my opinion, the Christians act as senselessly as the Jews. All our troubles come from not following reason and the law of nature."

"What are you talking about?"

Herschel had not regained his calm. Acosta had evidently touched something deep inside him.

"I mean that we must love our fellow man not because God commands it, but out of respect for his human dignity. Love is older than Moses. Love binds people together, whereas the Law of Moses separates them."

Herschel looked at him, horror-stricken. What he had just heard was nothing less than blasphemy. Yet the earth had not shaken and no storm of fire and brimstone had broken over Amsterdam. The

487

only explanation was that the Almighty, blessed be He, was putting him to the test and leaving him the responsibility of giving that excommunicated Jew the answer he deserved.

"Leave my house!" he said in a choked voice. "You're a blasphemer! Get out!"

To his great surprise, he saw Acosta wearily stand up, murmuring, "You don't understand, no one understands," and walk toward the door without even trying to justify himself.

As soon as he was gone, Herschel felt like running after him and apologizing, but he was unable to move. When his wife came back, he was weeping.

HERSCHEL DID NOT SEE Uriel Acosta again until several months later. It was during Succot, the Feast of Tabernacles. The streets and bridges of the Jewish quarter were decorated with branches, in accordance with tradition. Herschel was on his way to the Beth Yaacob synagogue, on the Oude Schans. As he was walking along the canal he recognized Acosta's tall figure on the opposite bank. Without thinking, he quickened his pace, crossed the next wooden bridge, and joined him. He could scarcely believe his eyes: Acosta seemed happy.

"You should have ignored me," said Acosta, briefly embracing Herschel. "It's not good for you to be seen with me. You'd better leave me now."

"I just wanted to know how you're doing."

"I'm doing very well, thank God." Acosta looked in all directions, as if he were afraid that someone might overhear the secret of his new joy. "I've met a woman who accepts me as I am. I think we're going to be married. And now, go!" But he was holding Herschel by the sleeve. "If you want to, you can meet me tomorrow evening in the red tavern at the end of Uilenburgstraat, on the Oude Schans. I'll be there."

All through the next day, Herschel was distressed at the thought that Acosta might wait for him in vain. He was afraid to tell his wife Kaila that he had an appointment in a disreputable tavern with an excommunicated Jew. When evening came, he suddenly said he had to go to the synagogue, took his prayer shawl, and walked out without giving Kaila time to ask any questions.

In the main room of the tavern, scratchy violins were playing and the air was so thick and foul that Herschel nearly suffocated when he came through the front door. Buxom women sat on benches along the walls, waiting for men to take them by the arm and push them into the throng of dancers that occupied the center of the floor. Struggling against an urge to turn back and run away, Herschel went down the three steps that led to the main room. To him, that place was like a foretaste of hell. He had hidden his prayer shawl under his doublet, against his chest, and he felt as if it were a shield.

Uriel Acosta was sitting at a little wooden table. His joy of the day before had vanished: he now seemed plunged in gloom. A bulky woman wearing an indecently low-cut bodice was stroking the back of his neck with her thick fingers. His fiancée? When he saw Herschel, he brusquely pushed her away.

"I'm not getting married," he announced, without greeting Herschel. "She doesn't want me anymore. The community sent its most virtuous women to tell her not to trust me. She's already left Amsterdam."

Taken aback, Herschel could only ask, "What was her name?"

"Ianthe."

"Maybe you should return to the synagogue," Herschel suggested quietly.

Acosta looked at him in surprise, as if he had just discovered his presence.

"Nothing good could come of that. The only result would be even greater sadness in my soul."

The woman came back with a stein of beer and sat down again beside Acosta. She seemed eager to comfort him but he paid no attention to her.

"If the synagogue is powerless to save the faithful," he said, "it can only drive them to despair. Salvation through immortality is a fraud if it replaces love with fear. We must free the mind from the fear that gives rise to superstition, we must—"

He stopped short, without finishing his sentence.

"Surely every man is a mere breath," said Herschel.

"What do you mean by that?"

"I was quoting from a psalm."

"Ah."

Herschel stood up to leave.

"Stay a little longer," said Acosta.

"I don't know what I can do for you, except to tell you that I don't despise you, even if I should."

Acosta took a swallow of beer from the woman's stein.

"I think I'm going to take your advice," he said.

"You'll return to the synagogue?"

"Yes. I'll go through the rituals as the others do, that's all. I'll be a monkey among monkeys."

"No," said Herschel, "you'll be a man among men."

The next day, Herschel spoke about Acosta to Rabbi Manasseh ben Israel, who agreed to meet with him. Acosta said that he was willing to undergo the shame of publicly confessing his sins and asking to be forgiven. It was decided that the ceremony would take place at the beginning of the year 5400 [1640] after the creation of the world by the Almighty, blessed be He.

It was snowing in Amsterdam that day and the Jews who went into the Portuguese synagogue, which was draped in black for the occasion, had white beards. The silence became oppressive when Uriel Acosta, dressed all in black, came in and was taken to the platform where the *parnasim* were waiting behind Saul Levi Mortara, the *chacham,* leader of the Amsterdam Jews. The *chazzan* lit a black candle and handed it to the penitent. Then the *chazzan* sang in his clear, strong voice and his words seemed to wind slowly around the massive marble pillars: "I will give thanks to the Lord with my whole heart. . . ." A kind of tremor ran through the two compact segments of the congregation: the men gathered around the platform, wearing white shawls with black stripes, and the women in the balcony.

"Arise, O Lord!" sang the *chazzan.* "Let man not prevail; let the nations be judged before Thee! Put them in fear, O Lord! Let the nations know that they are but men!"

"Let the nations know that they are but men!" the congregation repeated in unison.

Deeply moved, Herschel heard Rabbi Mortara summon Uriel Acosta to contrition. Acosta stood with the black candle in his hand and acknowledged his sins. Yes, he had broken the sabbath peace and violated the dietary laws. Yes, he had denied several articles of faith, notably the immortality of the soul. Yes, he had dissuaded several Portuguese Marranos from returning to the Jewish religion.

"Do you promise not to fall back into your errors?"

"I promise."

"Do you promise to live as a good Jew from this day forward?"

"I promise."

Acosta recited the thirteen articles of faith drawn up by Mai-

490

monides. "I believe with perfect faith that the Creator, may His name be praised, is the Creator and Master of all creatures, that He alone did, does, and will do all things. I believe. . . . I believe. . . ."

"Amen," replied the congregation when he had finished.

"Amen," Herschel said with all the others. He did not have the feeling of being a monkey among monkeys. He was part of a group of interdependent human beings, a body with a thousand heads, and he spoke with the same voice, and said the same words, and swayed to the same rhythm. Was that not miraculous? Was it not the union referred to by the two Cabalists from Prague when they spoke of "the Mysterious Unknown, the object of all desires"?

When everything had been said, it was time for the punishment. Acosta stripped to the waist. His thin body stood out sharply in the semidarkness and gave a vague impression of sickliness. He followed the *shammash* to a corner of the synagogue where two men tied him to a pillar, offering his bare back to the whip held by the *shammash*.

The first stroke of the whip drew a cry from the members of the congregation. At the second one, they began counting aloud. "Two. Three. Four." Herschel suffered in his own flesh and even in the depths of his soul. This ceremony was more than he could bear. "Twelve. Thirteen." The whip slashed the penitent's back. "Twenty-six. Twenty-seven." It was all Herschel could do to restrain himself from running out of the synagogue. The punishment was thirty-nine lashes, and Acosta underwent it without letting a sound escape from his lips.

When it was over, the *shammash* led him back to the platform. He put on his clothes, without seeming to be in pain. Rabbi Saul Levi Mortara loudly announced the end of Uriel Acosta's excommunication.

The *chazzan* solemnly sang a psalm: "Yet he, being compassionate, forgave their iniquity, and did not destroy them." Then the *shammash* accompanied Acosta to the door of the synagogue and made him lie down on the floor. The men took off their phylacteries, folded their prayer shawls, and left the synagogue, stepping over Acosta one by one; the most zealous among them kicked him as they passed. When it was Herschel's turn, he saw that Acosta had his eyes closed.

The next day, at the print shop, Herschel refused to talk about the expiation ceremony. For several days he lived with a taste of gall in his mouth.

SUMMER HAD NOT YET arrived when it was learned that Uriel Acosta had committed suicide, leaving behind, as a kind of revenge, only the autobiography he had mentioned to Herschel, for anyone who might try to understand.

35

AMSTERDAM-LUBLIN

The Deluge

"YOU'VE CHANGED," the painter Rembrandt van Rijn told Herschel a few days later. "Your face is less luminous. Have you been having troubles? Worries? Has someone died?"

"Yes," said Herschel.

"Someone close to you?"

"Yes."

"A friend?"

"Yes, a friend."

Rembrandt, who had been painting many portraits and selling them at the excellent price of five hundred florins each, suddenly seemed to discover something in Herschel's face: an angle, or a curve, or perhaps a shadow.

"Would you pose for me?" he asked as if his artistic career depended on it. "You're just the man I've been looking for. I have a place for you, behind the Virgin Mary, at the center, in a circle of light. . . ." He smiled. "It's said in the Zohar that when Jacob left this world, the moon shone and the sun felt desire for her. Since then, each time the sun disappears, another sun appears. And by her union with each sun, the moon shines."

Herschel also smiled.

"You see," said the painter, "your face is shining too! But let's come back to my painting. In a circle of light is a woman with an open book in her left hand. She's turned toward a child asleep in a wicker cradle. You see? Behind the woman, I'll place a man. Her husband. He's cutting a fresh branch. I see him exactly like you: light complexion, a beard . . . You *will* pose for me, won't you?"

At the rear of the print shop, Judah Leib was trying to hold back his laughter. It soon escaped from him and was echoed by the brothers Jacob and Abraham ben Zevi. Rembrandt turned around, surprised and on the verge of anger.

"What's so funny?" he asked.

Judah Leib was bent double with laughter so infectious that it spread to Herschel and even to Rembrandt himself. When he was finally able to explain to the painter that he had already wanted to use Herschel as his model for a musician behind Delilah, the laughter redoubled. But Rembrandt was delighted.

"I like being with you," he said a little later. "I'm tired of those self-important people I'm always meeting, with all their pretensions and honors. I enjoy feeling free and having my mind at ease."

But Herschel never posed for Rembrandt, unlike Ephraim Bueno, whose portrait Rembrandt painted a few years later, giving it the title of *The Jewish Physician*—though according to rumor he painted it only because Stella Bueno was one of his numerous mistresses.

Soon after that portrait was finished, reports of increasing persecution of Jews began reaching Amsterdam from many different places. Manasseh ben Israel, whose favorite son had just died, and who had been ruined by the bankruptcy of the East India Company, explained all those tribulations by the purification that had to precede the coming of the Messiah: the Zohar had announced it for the year 5408 [1648] after the creation of the world by the Almighty, blessed be He.

In Smyrna a man named Sabbatai Zevi, speaking to a group of disciples, had revealed himself as the Messiah by pronouncing the four letters of the sacred name of God, contrary to ancient custom and despite the prohibition in the Talmud. Then came news of a Cossack uprising in Poland, even bloodier than the one from which Herschel had fled.

The birth of a new era, it was said, had to be preceded by labor pains. But what pains! The Cossacks led by Bogdan Chmielnicki had allied themselves with the Tartars to invade and ravage the cities and towns east of the Dnieper. People who fell into the hands of the Cossacks were savagely massacred; the Tartars, however, took prisoners—and sold them as slaves in the Crimea and Turkey. In Amsterdam it was reported that the Cossacks had been stopped near Zamość and had therefore not reached Lublin.

For the moment, at least, there was evidently no need for Herschel to worry about his family's safety, but he was still tormented by anxiety. It seemed to him that the United Provinces were an island of peace in a sea of violence and chaos, and he could not help wondering how much longer it would be until that island was submerged. This did not prevent him from going to the print shop every morning and working as conscientiously as ever, following the advice of Yochanan ben Zakkai: "If you are planting an olive tree when you learn that the Messiah has come, finish planting the olive tree and then go to greet the Messiah."

In the autumn of that same year, 1648, a Jew from Constantinople, Jacob Amaraji, son of Rabbi Moses of Salonika, arrived in Amsterdam to ask the community for money with which to buy the freedom of Polish Jews who had been sold as slaves in the port of Galata. The Portuguese Jews of Amsterdam responded so generously that Herschel almost forgave them for Uriel Acosta's death. There was still the question of who would go to Constantinople with Jacob Amaraji to deliver the money that had been collected.

"You should volunteer to go," Herschel's wife Kaila said to him one evening. "You have relatives in Poland, you speak Polish, some of your ancestors lived in Constantinople. . . ."

"But . . ."

And so Herschel boarded a Venetian ship and left "the Jerusalem of the north" against his will, shortly after Yom Kippur of the year 5408 after the creation of the world by the Almighty, blessed be He. His wife and children went with him.

WHITE LIGHT, dust, flies, minarets, all sorts of domes, the color of the sea—how far they had come from the snows of Lublin and the mists of Amsterdam!

They waited on the wharf at Galata while a child ran off to bring Chief Rabbi Yom Tov ben Yaeche, who arrived with an air of haughty dignity but seemed to have been just awakened from his nap. He said a few words of welcome and thanks, and Herschel replied in the name of the Amsterdam community. Then they all took a boat to Balat, where the crowd was as tumultuous as the one they had left at Galata.

During the endless voyage to Galata, Herschel had told Jacob Amaraji about the printers among his ancestors. As soon as they reached Balat, Jacob Amaraji took him to the suburb of Fener to visit people who were presumably his distant relatives. A house surrounded by cypresses. Two dozen pairs of Turkish slippers lined up in front of the entrance. A bald, round-faced little man came out to greet them. His name was Sheshet Albrabez, he worked as a printer for Abraham Franco, and he had heard about the family book, though he had never seen it. Without much enthusiasm, he invited his newfound relatives to sleep in his house. They spent an uncomfortable night there, squeezed together on mats laid directly on the dusty floor, after the last guests—the circumcision of one of Sheshet's grandsons was being celebrated that evening—had left, loudly berating people who thought only of sleeping, when that was all they would have to do after they died.

While they were waiting for the time when they could ransom the prisoners, Herschel asked Sheshet to take him to the graves of his ancestors in the Egri Capu cemetery. Sheshet seemed surprised but granted his request without comment.

Burials in the cemetery had stopped long ago. Most of its visitors were Jews who, afflicted by some sort of calamity, came to ask for help from the souls of the holy rabbis buried there. Herschel found the graves of Meshulam, son of Abramo, and his son Abbahu, father of Abraham, the first member of the family to go to Poland. The inscriptions were barely legible; Herschel realized that what was carved in stone did not last as long as what was inscribed in memory. He recited the *kaddish* and read aloud from the Book of Abraham, mingling his story with the eternal song of the wind in the thistles and tall grass.

He would have liked to stay longer but Sheshet, sitting on a gravestone, was showing signs of impatience, and Kaila was probably expecting him to return.

A COMMITTEE had been formed to buy the freedom of the Jewish slaves. Its members went to Galata, where the ships containing the Polish prisoners were moored. Many other Constantinople Jews were already there, waiting to witness the liberation of the captives. They cited incredibly large figures, supposedly reported by Jacob Amaraji himself, concerning the money collected in Amsterdam. They spoke a mixture of Hebrew and Spanish that Herschel was scarcely able to understand. Wrapped in their *feredges,* with black hair and dark skin, they looked more like non-Jewish Turks than Polish Jews, yet Herschel sensed that in their souls they were his brothers.

Jacob Amaraji was notified that the Turkish official in charge of the operation had just arrived. He was a big, imposing man with an enormous mustache under his nose and a pair of impressive daggers in his belt. In his way, he was the Turkish empire in person.

"Peace be with you," Jacob Amaraji greeted him humbly.

"Peace and the mercy of Allah be with you," the official replied, eyeing him appraisingly, as if he were one of the slaves for sale.

They began a long, tortuous discussion over whether the committee would be allowed to board the two ships to count and identify the prisoners; the cargoes had already been bought by Turkish slave merchants, and it was with them that the committee would have to negotiate the total price.

Finally Jacob Amaraji held out a few coins to the Turkish official, who took them with an ugly smile on his thick, red lips. Only then were the members of the committee, including Herschel, permitted to board the ship.

First, the smell. Then the rattle of chains. Then the horrible sight of those starving people, tightly packed together, who had been soiled by their own excrement and vomit for weeks. Hands reached out toward Herschel and the men beside him. Feeble cries for help lacerated their hearts.

Scribes began writing names and places of origin. Herschel asked if there were any prisoners from Lublin. He was told that they were in the hold, with those from Zaslaw. He tried to go below but the stench was so powerful that he felt as if he was about to faint— not because of the smell itself, but because it made him fully realize the degradation of the men and women enclosed in that black hole. And so he waited on the deck, briefly answering those who thanked him as a representative of the Amsterdam community.

When the number of Jews chained on the deck had been established and the committee had paid the price demanded by the sellers, Turks with shaved heads came to break the chains with hammers and big tongs. As soon as the prisoners had been freed, they were taken away by members of the Constantinople community and assigned to families in the city. They were deathly pale, gasping, emaciated, filthy, and almost too weak to stand, but their eyes shone with joy at being enveloped in the warmth of those people who, like them, observed *shabbat* and prayed to the God of Israel.

Then the tarred hatch of the hold was opened. These prisoners, who had been cut off from fresh air and sunlight, were in even more pitiful condition than the others. Herschel examined those from Lublin—perhaps he would recognize one of them. Tragic faces, devastated bodies. One of the specters passing by him stopped and said, "I know you. You're the son of Jeremiah the printer, and brother of Azariah the egg merchant."

The man burst out sobbing. Herschel suddenly remembered.

"You're . . ." he began, then hesitated: ten years of separation, and the harsh conditions of his captivity, had changed the man so much that Herschel was not sure he had correctly identified him. "Are you Rabbi Elhanan of Rovno?" he asked. "The nephew of Meir ben Gedaliah of Lublin?"

"You recognized me!" the rabbi said with tears in his eyes. "I still have a human face. . . ." Then, abruptly: "Do you know that your father is here?"

"My father? My father?"

Herschel repeated the words as if he did not understand their meaning. Then he saw him, his father Jeremiah, a pallid phantom leaning on the arm of Azariah the egg merchant, his brother, now an old man with a ravaged face. He stepped forward and knelt before them.

JACOB AMARAJI TOOK THEM into his house. Herschel had also recovered his sister Ruth; her teeth were broken and she was half mad.

"Who's left in Lublin?" he asked.

"Your brother David, may long life be given to him," replied his father.

"Shall we say a prayer?" Herschel suggested. He saw infinite tenderness in his father's eyes and began reciting: "O You who have sustained me and kept me among the living . . ."

Before the end of the prayer Jeremiah had fallen asleep, as if it were at last permissible for him to rest.

Azariah told how they had been in Zaslaw, for cousin Nathan's wedding, when the Cossacks took the city.

"Ten years ago," said Herschel, "I barely escaped from them when I'd gone to Polonnoye for the wedding of our cousin there."

"It was the will of the Almighty."

Azariah had seen his wife and children die, but he said nothing about it. Their sister Leah had also died, as well as her husband Bunim. What were the survivors to do? Weep? Pray? Curse?

"Where was our God during all that time?" Herschel asked the next day when his father, in bed with a high fever, had told him about the atrocities he had witnessed: pregnant women disemboweled, children roasted, men cut in half.

"We mustn't blaspheme, my son," said Jeremiah the printer. "We must be grateful to the Creator for His mercy; thanks to Him, we're alive and together again."

Jeremiah talked a long time that day. He described how they had fled from the Cossacks, how Prince Wizniowiecki, a righteous man, had taken them in and protected them until Chmielnicki's hordes captured that fortress, between Zaslaw and Zytomir, and slaughtered more than two thousand people. They had the good fortune, relatively speaking, of being able to surrender to the Tartars. They had walked and walked. . . . The weight of their chains, the sound of their chains. . . .

That evening, Jeremiah seemed to have regained his peace of mind.

"Now," he said before falling asleep, "we can go back to Lublin. With the help of the Almighty, you, David, and I will put the print shop in working order again."

In the morning he was found dead in his bed. He had no doubt used up all his strength in surviving. Herschel and Azariah buried him in the Egri Capu cemetery, beside their ancestors Meshulam and Abbahu.

After thirty days of mourning they obeyed the last will of their father, may his soul rest in peace, and went back to Lublin.

HERSCHEL DID NOT RECOGNIZE Lublin. The Jewish quarter of Podzamsze, the houses, the synagogues—everything was still in place, but he knew that there was more to a city than its streets and buildings. The people had changed. They all wore mourning, walked slowly, and spoke in hushed voices. Even David, who had been a cheerful, high-spirited boy when Herschel left him, now seemed completely apathetic.

Azariah decided against becoming an egg merchant again and joined his two brothers in reopening the print shop. Herschel, Kaila, and their three children moved into Jeremiah's house, but their two sons, now sixteen and fifteen, did not like Lublin and said that they would go back to Amsterdam as soon as they were old enough.

"Lublin isn't good enough for you?" Herschel asked them.

"We'll only be following your example, father: you also left Lublin and went to Amsterdam."

Herschel soon realized that it was their mother who had planted that idea in their heads. From all sorts of signs, he could see that Kaila was bored in Poland. She demanded more and more money for household expenses, protested against the stinking refuse in the streets, angrily complained about the neighbors' constant lamentations. . . .

One day Herschel forgot to take a book that was needed at the print shop. When he remembered that he had left it in the bedroom, he came back to the house and opened the bedroom door. It was as if he had stepped into a nightmare: he saw Kaila, naked, in bed with a man. The man leapt to his feet and began frantically putting on his clothes. Only then did Herschel recognize him as their neighbor, Leibuch the pharmacist.

Herschel had become a solid mass of rage and pain.

"Get out!" he shouted.

Leibuch winced as if he had been struck in the face. Without a word, he ran out of the room and down the stairs.

Kaila had pulled the blanket up to her shoulders. She looked at Herschel defiantly, with no sign of shame or even embarrassment. He stepped toward her and slapped her. She turned pale.

"You have no right to do that! I'm not your slave!"

"You're my wife!"

"And because I'm your wife I have to waste my life in Lublin? The Jews here are savages! They've already forgotten the dead and think of nothing but business."

"Everyone has to make a living."

"Make a living? Do you know what the community center is like? A market!"

Realizing that Kaila was drawing him into an argument on her own terms, Herschel broke it off.

"I wonder if Lilith has taken possession of your soul," he said. "I don't understand what's happened to you."

She laughed bitterly.

"You're amiable and weak, you'll accept anything from anyone. Even finding me here with Leibuch! You always try to understand,

and you always fail." She paused, then said forcefully, "I want to go back to Amsterdam."

Herschel did not answer. He picked up the book he had come to get and returned to the print shop.

That evening, in the children's presence, they had dinner as usual. Later, when he and Kaila were in bed, Herschel wanted to talk, but he had that feeling that there was an impenetrable barrier between them in the darkness, and he said nothing. He knew she felt she had defeated him. But that, as least, did not matter to him: his life was not a battle.

The next day, he had no chance to discuss the Leibuch incident with her. It was the day before the Christian holiday of the Ascension and, as he did every year, the vaivode ordered the Jews of Lublin to gather in the marketplace at the upper end of the city to hear a sermon by the archpriest.

It was a kind of seasonal rite. The clergyman assigned to it always denounced the errors of the Jewish religion to a crowd of Jews with blank faces who waited for him to finish, then went home. This time the sermon was violent. The archpriest was one of those impassioned men who dreamed of bringing thousands of infidels to Christ, preferably by force. He spoke with fiery vehemence and was exasperated by the total lack of reaction in the assembly. Not one sound, gesture, or expression that could nourish his anger and zeal.

"How can you hear my words without trembling?" he cried out.

Nowhere in the assembly was there the slightest sign that anyone had heard the archpriest's provocations. He seemed ready to jump off the platform and into the front row of impassive Jews, to make them at least show surprise, if nothing else.

Then a very old man, wearing the clothes of a woodcutter, holding himself erect and brandishing a knotty cane, made his way through the crowd and climbed the three steps of the platform. Disconcerted, the archpriest sat down beneath his red silk canopy.

"Fellow Jews!" the old man said loudly.

The crowd responded with a quiver of anticipation. He calmly took possession of his listeners. He seemed both judicious and intransigent.

"Fellow Jews, I don't know if you'll allow me to speak in your name, but I'll at least speak in the name of my fathers, and in my own."

In perfect Polish, with occasional quotations in Hebrew, he be-

501

gan refuting the archpriest's arguments point by point. At first the Jews were so uneasy that they scarcely dared to look at each other, but soon they had to restrain themselves from applauding. The archpriest and the Polish dignitaries made no effort to silence the old man, not wanting to give the impression that they were troubled by what he said. When he had finished, he left the platform, again made his way through the crowd, and disappeared.

Some of the Christians who were present claimed that he was Satan. Some of the Jews believed that he might be the prophet Elijah, with the mission of announcing the coming of the Messiah.

Herschel, Azariah, and David left together. As they approached the print shop, they were astounded to see the old man sitting on the front steps with his knotty cane in his hands.

"Blessed be Adonai our God, Master of the world," he said.

"Amen," replied the three men.

"You don't know who I am?"

It was Azariah who recognized him.

"Uncle Yitzhak!"

He had not been seen in Lublin since the time when he went off to be married in the forest where he had nearly been killed by wolves. He told how, long ago, Jan Ostrowski's sleigh had caused crowds to gather on that same street, and he talked at length about what the woodcutters had taught him. Finally he told the reason for his visit: his oldest son had gone away, no one knew where, taking the last copy of the Book of Abraham in his possession, and he wondered if it would be possible to print a few more copies of it.

The printers set to work immediately. They used thinner paper and smaller type—which Tzvi-Hirsch had bought in Hanau, Germany—to reduce the size of the volume. The whole family helped with the work. "So that none will be forgotten on the day of forgiveness, I inscribe the names of my sons. . . ." They felt that those words were an intimate part of themselves.

A rumor soon began spreading that the strange old man who had publicly defied the archpriest and the vaivode was a mystical rabbi now engaged in secretly printing a book in which he would reveal the exact date of the coming of the Messiah. Jews gathered in front of the print shop, invaded the courtyard, and left only at nightfall, regretfully, because they wanted to be there when the first copy of the book appeared.

The day came when the typesetting and proofreading had been completed. Through the window, some of the people waiting outside saw that the press was being set in motion, and the news quickly traveled across the city. They now began waiting even at night. David's son Benjamin, a pale boy with feverish eyes, no longer dared to go out. When the printed sheets of paper had been folded and assembled, the crowd began reciting a psalm: "Sing to the Lord, bless His name; tell of His salvation from day to day. Declare His glory among the nations. . . ."

Old Yitzhak was greatly upset. Such strong expectations had been aroused that he was afraid of what might happen when they were disappointed. He took several unbound sections of the Book of Abraham and went out to prove to those impatient people that it contained no revelation. Carrying the sections in one hand and his knotty cane in the other, he walked into the courtyard, where a group of men in long, fluttering robes were dancing ecstatically in a circle with their arms raised and their eyes closed.

When Yitzhak appeared, holding himself erect as always, a great "Ah!" burst from the crowd. Those in front were pushed against the steps and broke through the wooden balustrade. Yitzhak struck a few vigorous blows with his cane.

"Jews!" he cried out. "Don't blaspheme! Don't follow pagan rites! Praise the Lord our God, who is worthy of all praise!"

"Praise be to the Lord our God!" replied those who had heard him.

He raised the Book of Abraham above his head.

"Jews! There's nothing mysterious about this book. It's only the story of my family. Listen."

He opened a section at random and read aloud: "Abraham begat Hanan, Miriam, Aurelia, and Solomon. Solomon begat Sarah, Ruth, and Jonathan. Sarah and Ruth were converted by force in the terrible year of 4295 after the creation of the world by the Almighty, blessed be He. May their memory remain in the family and in the House of Israel."

An old Jew in a brown robe, standing near Yitzhak, said in a grating voice, "He who understands only the literal meaning of words has a cursed mind!"

A murmur ran through the crowd.

"He's right!" shouted someone farther away. "It's a secret language!"

"And those names hide the name of the Messiah!" said someone else.

"And that date hides the date of his coming!"

The old man in the brown robe suddenly snatched the pages away from Yitzhak, who was taken by surprise. Others tried to seize them. There were scuffles that quickly turned into fights. The pages were scattered in the furious struggle for possession of them.

"Jews!" Yitzhak called out. "Jews!"

No one listened to him. He fell silent and watched the scene with pity. Men were running after scraps of paper that the wind playfully blew away from them. Azariah, who had come out to protect his uncle, heard him mutter, "The Talmud is right. Man is a walking latrine."

"You must try to understand them," said Azariah.

"The Cabala has made them lose their reason! May the Holy One, blessed be He, protect us from madness!"

YITZHAK WENT BACK to his forest as soon as the twelve copies they had decided to print were bound. He took three for himself, carefully wrapped them in a white cloth, and put them into his bag. With a chunk of bread and a piece of cheese in the pocket of his caftan, he set off along the road to Parczew, refusing to be taken in a wagon.

Herschel watched him walk away. Yitzhak's steps were firm and his iron-tipped cane tapped sharply on the pavement. Herschel felt like going with him.

But he stayed in Lublin, with his wife Kaila, who went on meeting with the pharmacist in secret while Herschel pretended not to know.

When their younger son was eighteen, he and his brother went to Amsterdam and wrote them an enthusiastic letter soon afterward. Their daughter married the cantor of the main synagogue. Life followed its course, with mingled desires and regrets, good and bad moments, good and bad memories. . . .

The Messiah had not come, as the Zohar predicted, in the year 5408 after the creation of the world by the Almighty, blessed be His name. Those who expected him had to begin waiting again, this time without counting the days.

SIX YEARS LATER, an eclipse of the sun was seen in Lublin. It was unanimously regarded as a bad omen. Rabbi Jacob ben Ezekiel of Platow declared that he had heard spirits of the dead weeping and moaning, and the *shammash* of the main synagogue said that he had seen a gathering of dead children beneath the Holy Ark. In the autumn of that same year, hundreds of people died in an epidemic.

Those who saw these events as premonitory signs were vindicated: before the year was over, the Cossacks led by the bloodthirsty Bogdan Chmielnicki reappeared. They first ravaged the Jewish communities in western Poland and Lithuania; the community of Vilna simply disappeared.

Winter had come early and children were already skating on the frozen water of the Bistryca and even the Czechowka, near the print shop. When the threat of the Cossacks began to take shape, the three brothers interrupted their work—they were printing an edition of the Tzeneh-Reneh, a Yiddish paraphrase of parts of the Bible, intended primarily for women—to discuss whether it would be wise to leave.

"We could go to Parczew," said Azariah. "Uncle Yitzhak may still be alive."

"Or Amsterdam," suggested Herschel. "It's a city where Jews are well treated. I know people there, and I speak the language."

But now, when for once he himself had proposed a journey, the others decided to wait awhile. The next day, the public criers announced that the prince and the vaivode had forbidden anyone to leave the city or send any property out of it. Two days later it was learned that Zamość had fallen. The Cossacks were coming. The following day, October 15, they were seen on the outskirts of Cracow.

A few Jews were able to take refuge with Christian friends or buy hiding places for themselves, then the Christian part of Lublin was closed and its defenses were reinforced. Only the Jewish quarter, which was outside the walls, remained at the mercy of the Cossacks. The Jews gathered in synagogues to wait for the outcome of the discussion that members of the city council were to have with the Russians, who this time were coming behind the Cossacks.

Azariah, Herschel, David, and their families—except for David's son Benjamin, who stayed at home because he had a fever—were in the little Saul-Wahl synagogue on Podzamsze Street. Suddenly Pessah the shoemaker came in with an air of self-importance, strode to the lectern, and stood facing the assembly. Silence immediately fell over the room, broken only by the rumble of the big stove.

505

"May the Almighty, blessed be He, come to our aid," said Pessah, "because I bring you bad news."

"What's happened?" a voice asked anxiously.

"Tell us!"

"Let him talk!"

Pessah took a deep breath.

"The emissaries of the city council accomplished nothing. Princes Borchinski and Poniatowski were arrested, and the Jesuit who went with them was pushed out into the cold, completely naked."

A murmur of despair rose from the crowd. It was all beginning again. . . . Old Rabbi Abraham ben Yehudah, leaning on the *shammash*'s arm, began reciting in a quavering voice: "How long, O Lord? Wilt Thou hide Thyself for ever?" A few other voices continued the psalm: "How long will Thy wrath burn like fire?" Finally everyone joined in: "Lord, where is Thy steadfast love of old, which by Thy faithfulness Thou didst swear to David? Remember, O Lord, how Thy servant is scorned. . . ."

When the psalm had ended, Pessah the shoemaker said, "The Russians are demanding that the city give them thirty thousand florins, several wagonloads of satin, silk, and brocade, a thousand rolls of English and Dutch cloth, all armaments, and all Jews."

"Woe is us!" someone cried out in an extraordinarily loud voice.

Rabbi Abraham ben Yehudah put his prayer shawl over his head, closed his eyes, and began the Shema Yisrael: "Hear, O Israel: The Lord our God is one Lord. . . ."

Dozens of heads covered with prayer shawls swayed back and forth to the same rhythm. The rabbi placed the ritual book on the lectern. Pessah the shoemaker kissed the curtain that concealed the Holy Ark, drew it aside, opened the Ark, took out the first scroll of the Torah, and kissed its dark blue velvet cover.

Just then the door of the synagogue was thrown open. Everyone looked around. It was Benjamin, David's son.

"The Cossacks are burning our houses!" he shouted.

David was one of the first to leave the synagogue. He ran to the print shop with Benjamin close behind him. Azariah and Herschel were caught in the crush of people all trying to force their way through the doorway at once.

"Jews!" cried the old rabbi. "Don't run away! Stay here and pray to the Almighty!"

All of Podzamsze was burning. David and his son Benjamin

hurried into the shop. The certainty of familiar things, the smell of ink. David nearly fell to his knees in horror at the thought that this was the end of everything, but he ran to the safe in which he kept his copies of the Book of Abraham, as well as the ancient scroll. He picked up a wooden box, emptied it of its contents, refilled it with the scroll, one copy of the book, and a complete set of type. Then he wrapped the box in the ink-stained rag and handed it to his son.

"You saw what I put into this box, didn't you, Benjamin?"

"Yes, father."

"Don't ever lose it."

They heard footsteps on the frozen ground of the courtyard, then men laughing.

"You can still escape through the back door, Benjamin. Try to go to Parczew. I'll join you there, if it's God's will." David put his hands on his son's head, blessed him, and said, "Amen, amen, amen. Run! And may God protect you!"

Just as Benjamin was slipping through the narrow opening that faced the hill, the front door was broken from its hinges.

HERSCHEL WAS STILL in the synagogue when it began burning. A roof beam fell on Pessah the shoemaker while he clutched the scroll of the Torah against his chest. Herschel went outside. Reddish reflections were dancing on the ice, dark figures were running in all directions. Herschel was seized by the cold and the smoke, and he realized that no one would escape. He called for his wife, in vain. He looked for his brother Azariah, whom he had just left, but could not find him. Hearing shouts behind him, he turned around. Men on horseback. He clearly saw iron-shod hooves making sprays of snow, then he felt a kind of burning sensation in his back. His sight dimmed and he fell. He thought of Rembrandt van Rijn, the painter, and what he had said about light. He again called for his wife but did not even hear the sound of his own voice. He wondered if he was already dead. He was not in pain.

His sight gradually came back to him. He had a quick glimpse of his father Jeremiah on the slave ship in Constantinople and tried to go to him. Then, through a milky mist, he saw Kaila, naked under the body of Leibuch the pharmacist. A moment later she was walking toward him, but a rider caught her with one hand and lifted her onto his horse. Leibuch, with his prayer shawl on his shoulders, took hold of the Cossack's horse and his head immediately rolled in the snow while his body collapsed a short distance away.

Herschel saw the Cossack throw Kaila to two other barbarians, on foot. They pulled her dress up over her head. A strange warmth filled Herschel's head and he heard her scream. One of the Cossacks held her down while the other took an enormous penis from his breeches. What was Leibuch doing?

"Lord, where is Thy steadfast love of old?" Herschel recited aloud, or believed he did. "Thy steadfast love . . . Thy steadfast love. . . ."

He summoned up all the life that still remained in him and raised himself on his elbows. He saw the face of the shouting horseman who was about to thrust his lance into his throat.

BEGINNING THAT DAY, two thousand seven hundred Jews were massacred in Lublin. "Some of them," says a chronicle, "were flayed alive and thrown to the dogs, others had their hands and feet cut off, and heavily loaded wagons were rolled over their mutilated bodies. Still others were bled to death or buried alive. The Cossacks slashed open the bodies of pregnant women, put furious cats inside them and sewed them closed; when the women tried to tear themselves open, their hands were cut off at the wrist. . . ."

Polish Jews refer to this episode in their history as the Deluge.

•   •   •

BENJAMIN ENDED UP IN Kamionka, a remote hamlet of the village of Lubartow. A little more than a dozen houses, a duck pond that was frozen six months of the year, a rabbi-schoolteacher, a population of about sixty, at least half of whom were Jews. Benjamin was taken in, half frozen, by a horse merchant named Nathan Peretz. A few years later he married Nathan's daughter, and then, when Nathan died, he became the richest man in Kamionka.

Benjamin made no effort to be loved by his wife or liked by his neighbors. He was a solitary, mistrustful, grasping man who scarcely talked to anyone but his horses. I tried to describe how he managed to get himself accepted into Nathan Peretz's home, and how arrogantly he behaved after he became rich. But I do not enjoy presenting "bad" characters any more than I enjoyed giving detailed accounts of the Jews' battles against the Roman Empire.

I am well aware that my ancestors, like those of everyone else, included disreputable, unjust, dishonest, demented, and violent peo-

ple. Is it really indispensable for me to exhibit them? I remember something Robert Laffont said to me during one of our many discussions about this book: "Be careful not to make all your characters good and nice." I understand his concern. But so many writers in so many generations have systematically depicted Jews as vile and depraved that my conscience is clear: my own depictions will not even restore the balance, much less tilt it in the opposite direction.

And then I love them so much, those Jews, my fathers and brothers, with their mobile faces and their anxious eyes fixed on centuries of misery. I believe I love them all; those of my childhood, of course, but also those I have happened to encounter at various crossroads of the world.

Images come to mind: that shy, red-haired shammash among his skittish red cats, glimpsed in the synagogue of the Ghetto Vecchio in Venice; those domino players insulting each other in Yiddish in a café on Corrientes Avenue in Buenos Aires; those Jewish gauchos strolling along the dusty streets of Mosesville in the Argentinian province of La Pampa. I love them, as I love those Jews dressed in rags who, in front of the ancient synagogue of Cairo, looked at me with a mixture of friendliness and apprehension while the guide told me with a straight face that Moses himself had come to pray there; and those young vegetarians of Sephardic origin eating gefilte fish in a New York restaurant to which I had been taken by Isaac Bashevis Singer; and those Yeshiva University students demonstrating in Central Park against the Vietnam war, wearing their skullcaps.

And that hunchbacked coppersmith in the mellah *of Rabat, Morocco, squatting at the low table on which he was hammering a sheet of copper, and looking as if he had been doing it since time immemorial.*

And that beggar on the island of Jerba, off the coast of Tunisia, dressed as an Arab and blessing me in Hebrew.

And those Chassidim, pious Jews always busy, hurrying across the Rue des Rosiers in Paris, with their beards and sidelocks blowing in the wind.

And that little thief who stole my wallet in Amsterdam.

And those newly rich people of dubious taste visiting Tel Aviv.

And all those I meet every day, in the street or in this book, recognizing them by gestures a little too nervous, eyes a little too intense, and a certain uneasiness that belongs to people whose memories are too vivid.

* * *

SOME OF THOSE JEWS are, like me, survivors of the greatest "deluge" in the history of the Jewish people, now symbolized by one name: Auschwitz. I look through Abraham Shulman's album of photographs, The Old Country. *They are all there, my Jews: water carriers in threadbare caftans; book peddlers with ironic eyes; pale-faced children leaning over sacred texts; women lighting the shabbat candles; a crowd dancing around scrolls of the Torah in the public square of a village; bearded workers, wearing square skullcaps, in front of a factory entrance; Jewish families seated around a Passover table.*

In Warsaw we always gathered for Pesach in the apartment of my grandfather Abraham on Nowolipie Street. Even though his daughter and two of his sons were absent—my aunt Regina was then in Buenos Aires, my uncle David in Paris, my uncle Samuel in Brussels —there were more than twenty of us: my parents, my aunt Topcia, her husband Moniek, and their children, and also cousins of my grandfather.

We arrived while he was still at the synagogue. When he came home, we had already been waiting for him a long time. He slowly climbed the stairs, coughing at each landing to announce that he was coming. We children stopped chasing each other in the apartment, our parents quickly straightened our clothes, and everyone sat down around the big table.

When he finally opened the door and saw his family gathered there, his face brightened. He took off his coat, sat down on the cushion reserved for him, and said "Goot yom tev!" [Good Holiday!] Passover then began.

Foggy memories, sketchy, superimposed images. My grandfather Abraham's face suddenly appears to me with perfect clarity, as though in a drawing. A tall figure, carefully combed white beard and sidelocks, eyes both cheerful and somber, a broad, high fore-head beneath a square skullcap. To me, he personifies all the rich-ness of that vanished world. Deeply religious, he was on close terms with the famous rabbi of Gur and often went to his home for schol-arly discussions. But he was also sympathetic to the Bund, the Jew-ish Socialist party. A mixture of authority and gentleness, of reserve and curiosity about others, he was equally in his place when he presided over the family table, read his prayer book in the syna-gogue, or paraded behind the red flag of the Bund on May Day.

He was a printer. I can still see him cleaning the print shop on

Friday evening, then covering the machines and typesetting tables with sheets of white paper before washing his hands and forearms and praying with the other workers, who were also bearded and pious. I scarcely ever left him. He had asked that I be given his father's name, Meir-Ikhiel.

Here I am with my grandfather in Warsaw when two and a half centuries still separate me from him. Perhaps it is because of impatience to reach the end of this project—though I already know I will miss it when it is finished. Or perhaps it is simply because of my distaste for that Benjamin who escaped from the burning ruins of Lublin and began leading another man's life in that isolated hamlet. He was harsh and unjust, as I have said; he mistreated his servant Yankel and Faivel the water carrier; he was contemptuous of Jacek the miller, indifferent to his wife Baile, brusque and tactless with his son Abraham, who preferred study to horsebreeding. The only person he was afraid to browbeat was Rabbi Lazard, a wise, even-tempered peasant who invariably replied with a quotation from Isaiah when someone complained to him about Benjamin: "Let the wicked forsake his way, and the unrighteous man his thoughts; let him return to the Lord, that He may have mercy on him, and to our God, for He will abundantly pardon."

When I think of that hamlet of Kamionka, and of life in countless shtetls, picturesque Jewish village communities that closely resembled each other and were perfectly organized for self-perpetuation, I have a pang in my heart, because the shtetls have vanished from the face of the earth as surely as prehistoric camps.

In France, as soon as I had begun earning a little money, my father, who unknowingly shared with many others the ideology of "returning to the land," urged me to buy a "place in the country." I must also have felt a need for it, since I bought what real-estate agencies call a "country cottage, to be restored, with exposed beams." It was near the highway, the neighbor had chickens and big, slow-moving cows, a brook flowed past the end of the garden. At night we listened to barking dogs and hooting owls. I soon realized, however, that my father and I saw that house in radically different ways: to me, it was only a country house; to him, it was a sign of our attachment to our new homeland. He was forgetting that although some of our ancestors had never left France, our roots in the Book had been enough to make us be rejected as "foreigners" at certain crucial times in history. And even now we are periodically asked to *choose between the Land and the Book, as if our presence here did not show that one can be faithful to both at once.*

IN BENJAMIN'S TIME—*the second half of the seventeenth century—the Jews of Kamionka, good and bad, lived in their own kind of eternity from day to day. The course of their lives was marked by the seasons, holidays, news of pogroms in more or less distant places, and announcements of the coming of the Messiah. In their prayers to the Almighty each morning they asked that their children be allowed to grow up in peace, for the joy of their parents and the whole people of Israel, amen.*

Abraham, son of Benjamin the horse merchant, took every chance to go away from Kamionka. One day he brought home a tall young man with blond hair and blue eyes, broad as a woodcutter, who wore a small white tallit next to his shirt, under his long gray jacket, as required by the Scriptures.

"Father," said Abraham, "I've met a cousin."

Since Yom Kippur was only a few days off, Abraham took this opportunity to fulfill his duty of charity by inviting the "cousin" to spend the night. The young man said he was the son of Ruth, sister of Azariah, Herschel, and David, the poor woman who had been half mad when she left the slave ship in Constantinople. After returning to Lublin and being raped by a Cossack, she found her way to Parczew, the village of woodcutters where her uncle Yitzhak lived, and gave birth to a blond son. She named him Abraham, but everyone soon began calling him Kosakl, "Little Cossack."

When he had heard Kosakl's story, Benjamin was suspicious. Thinking that this stranger might be trying to deceive him, he asked him to prove what he said. Kosakl reached into his shoulder bag and took out a book with a worn cover.

"This is the Book of Abraham, the history of our family," he said. "You must know about it."

Benjamin went to get the copy that his father David had given him when the Cossacks were about to break open the door of the print shop. His copy matched Kosakl's: they were two of the twelve that had been printed in Lublin.

Convinced that the Almighty had given him a sign, Benjamin spent Yom Kippur in prayer, asking forgiveness for all the evil acts he had committed and all the times when he had not committed good ones that were within his power. In this frame of mind, he could not refuse Kosakl's request for money with which to have

512

several more copies of the Book of Abraham printed. Kosakl would go to Zolkiew, where there was a print shop, and see to it that the new edition was brought up to date with a record of recent births and deaths and an account of the Lublin massacre.

Benjamin parted with the money, but sent his son to keep an eye on how it was spent. And so the two Abrahams—Kosakl and his cousin, who was then seventeen—left Kamionka.

36

ZOLKIEW

Braindl

ABRAHAM, KNOWN as Kosakl, was a good Jew. Having been brought up by the woodcutters of Parczew, he was not at all tormented by his paternal origin: his faith and the history in which he believed were much more important to him than the blood that flowed in his veins. His primary rule of conduct was inspired by the Chapters of the Fathers: "Where there are no men, strive to be a man." And when, as often happened, someone referred to the Cossacks in front of him, he simply said, "Don't judge others until you've been in their situation."

After Yitzhak's death in Parczew, Kosakl had discovered in his house a volume of Rashi's commentaries, from which he copied passages every day to teach himself to understand, and a copy of the Zohar, from which he learned to dream. In his childhood, his poor mother Ruth—who cried out in her sleep every night and confused the two massacres, six years apart, in which she had nearly died—had implanted in his mind the certainty that the bloody convulsions of history occurred in order to purify the earth for the coming of the Messiah. Otherwise, the very thought of them would have been too painful for her to bear. And there were Cabalists who used the Hebrew transcription of Chmielnicki's name to elaborate a conclusive acrostic: "The sufferings of the Messiah's birth will come upon the earth."

During this time there was again talk of Sabbatai Zevi, the man from Smyrna whom the eastern Jewish communities had believed to be the Messiah. News came to Parczew irregularly, in bits and pieces that often contradicted each other. Sabbatai Zevi, reported a traveler, had just affirmed his fidelity to the Torah before his assembled followers. No, said a passing merchant, what he had done before his followers was to marry a young Polish Jewish woman who had escaped from the massacres, and it was a very good omen for all Polish Jews. Then the people of Parczew learned that Sabbatai Zevi had been arrested by the grand vizier of Constantinople and imprisoned in Gallipoli. This made them sad all through a long winter, but it also gave them hope: if he really was the Messiah, he would free himself when the right time came. There was great jubilation in the spring, when his disciples went all over the known world to announce his release from prison. The good Jews of Poland were astounded to learn that he had decided to change the celebration of Tishah B'Av, commemorating the destruction of the Temple, into a feast of rejoicing. But that was nothing compared with what they felt when, shortly before Rosh Hashanah of the year 5426 [1666] after the creation of the world by the Almighty, blessed be He, they received the devastating news that the Messiah had converted to Islam!

Some Polish Jews saw this as confirmation of their doubts. Others simply refused to believe it. Fighting broke out in all the *shtetls* and all the Jewish quarters of cities and towns, and became so serious that King John had to issue a special decree forbidding Jews to disrupt public order with their demonstrations for or against Sabbatai Zevi. Kosakl, who was only ten at the time, swore that he would go to Turkey as soon as he was old enough to make such a long journey.

He left when he was eighteen, taking only three books with him: the Zohar, Rashi's commentaries, and the Book of Abraham that he had inherited from Yitzhak. After many adventures he reached Turkey. Traveling on the same ship with him was a Polish Jew named Nehemiah Cohen, who also claimed the title of Messiah and was going to challenge Sabbatai Zevi. Kosakl was able to witness their encounter. He was deeply perturbed by it.

Disenchanted but by no means in despair, he repeated to himself the lesson of the sages: "When God sees that the soul of Israel is deathly ill, He covers it with the abrasive sheet of poverty and misery, and plunges it into the sleep of forgetfulness so that it can bear its pain. But, lest the spirit expire completely, He awakens it from time to time with the false hope of a Messiah, then He again puts it to sleep until the night has passed and the time of the real Messiah has come."

Kosakl returned to Poland and taught in the Talmud Torah of Zolkiew, in Galicia, beyond Zamość. Then, after a period of wandering, he came to Lubartow, where he met Abraham, son of Benjamin the horse merchant of Kamionka.

NOW THAT THEY WERE traveling to Zolkiew together, Abraham was captivated by Kosakl. His way of swaying his powerful shoulders as he prayed, his broad cheekbones, his tranquil eyes, his *payesses* tied behind his head, his strange mixture of strength and submissiveness—everything about him was attractive to Abraham. But what he liked most were the answers Kosakl gave to strangers who approached him.

"Where are you coming from?" he would be asked, at an inn or on the road.

"From the forest," he would reply.

"And where are you going?"

"In search of light, like all blind men." If the stranger raised his eyebrows, Kosakl would add, "As it is written in Deuteronomy, 'And you shall grope at noonday as the blind grope in darkness.' "

"But why," he was sometimes asked, "do you spend so much time studying?"

He would calmly gaze at his questioner and answer, "Because the Holy One, blessed be He, hears the voices of those who study the Law, and from each of their discoveries a new heaven is created."

IN ZOLKIEW, Uri Faibuch the printer was in a bad temper: he had just learned that certain merchants "without honor" were ignoring an order by the Council of the Four Lands* stating that

---

* *Vaad Arbah Aratzot* in Hebrew. An organization that united the Jews of Great Poland, Little Poland, Galicia, and Volhynia from the first half of the sixteenth century until 1764. Recognized by the Polish authorities and enjoying a great degree of autonomy, it promulgated laws and regulations concerning the internal affairs of the Jewish communities, and was responsible for collecting taxes.

books printed in other countries were not to be sold in Poland. As evidence of this, he had been shown a Bible published in Amsterdam and a medical treatise published in Prague. He reacted by threatening to close his shop. It took all of Kosakl's persuasiveness to make him agree to reprint the Book of Abraham. Actually, he asked his son Chaim-David to do it, and accepted Abraham's offer to help him.

Kosakl and Abraham brought the book up to date with a concise account of events in Lublin and the names of those who had died or been born since the last printing. It was not without emotion that they added their own names to the list.

While the work in the print shop was being done, Kosakl spent most of his time in the big fortified synagogue of Zolkiew. Abraham learned the printing trade with passionate interest, as if he had inherited a taste for it from his grandfather David and his granduncles Herschel and Azariah, may they know eternal peace. When the typesetting was finished, they printed twelve copies of the book and had them bound in Lvov. Kosakl held one of the copies in his big hands and contemplated it, breathing in its good smell of leather, ink, and paper.

"It's like a baby in its mother's womb," he said. "It already exists and it's only waiting to become known."

He seemed happy, while young Abraham, for the first time in his life, felt the gnawing regret of an adventure that had come to an end.

Kosakl left the next day, with his six copies of the book in his shoulder bag.

"We'll see each other again," he said, "if it's the will of the Almighty, blessed be He. Don't forget to study the Torah, cousin, because it is written that those who show themselves worthy of the secrets of the Law become like a spring whose flow constantly increases."

The two cousins embraced.

"Before you go, Kosakl," said Abraham, "would you please give me one more quotation?"

Kosakl smiled as Abraham had never seen him smile before.

"According to Proverbs, 'To make an apt answer is a joy to a man, and a word in season, how good it is!' "

Kosakl turned and left, tall, broad, and strong, striding along as if he could cross the whole world without stopping, and Abraham thought that the Almighty, blessed be He, was walking beside him.

* * *

ABRAHAM DID NOT LEAVE Zolkiew: Uri Faibuch, who appreciated his willingness to work and his keen interest in the trade, offered to hire him. Abraham sent a letter to his father, with one of the new copies of the Book of Abraham. He wanted to go on learning the printing trade, he wrote, to carry on the family tradition, and he was sure his father would not object. He received no reply.

He took lodgings in the house of Rabbi Hillel ben Naphtali on the Jews' Street. The rabbi had two daughters: Zlata, fifteen, and Braindl, thirteen and a half. Their mother had died a few years earlier. They did the cooking, the washing, and all the other household work. Abraham, still seventeen, was troubled by the looks the two girls gave him, especially Zlata, who had an expressionless face but a provocative bosom. He wondered if he should marry her, but now that Kosakl was gone he did not know whom to ask for advice.

One night when he was cold in his attic room, he came down to the room on the first floor that was heated by a big stove. The rabbi was sleeping there, behind a screen. Abraham extended the wick of the oil lamp, sat down on the firewood box behind the stove, and read some rabbinical commentaries until he warmed up. Before long he fell asleep, lulled by Rabbi Hillel's rhythmic snoring. A noise awoke him. He opened his eyes: Zlata, in her nightgown, was putting wood into the stove.

Abraham thanked Providence for having sent her to him and watched her without moving. It was mainly her breasts that held his attention. Had she noticed that he was awake? He did not know. In any case, she bent down to pick up the book he had dropped when he fell asleep, and, no doubt prompted by the devil, he reached out his hand and touched the firm, heavy breast that had moved close to him. Zlata quickly straightened up, but without reproaching him in words or with her eyes. She went back to her room.

The next night, he came downstairs again as soon as Rabbi Hillel's snoring told him that the coast was clear. His heart was pounding wildly. He sat down behind the stove, as he had done the night before, and put his book on the floor. Time seemed as long to him as the Jews' exile. Finally Zlata came in, acting as if he were not there, or as if he were asleep. She poked the fire, then leaned down to pick up the book. This time Abraham's hand was able to

518

linger awhile before she straightened up. He heard her sigh, and then she walked away.

They both came back the following night, but he no longer pretended to be asleep. When she bent down to pick up the book of commentaries on the Talmud, their eyes met. Kneeling in front of him, she whispered, "Do you want to see them?"

His mouth was so dry that he could not answer.

"I've never shown them to anyone," she said.

She opened her purple nightgown and, looking him in the eyes, took out a dazzling breast, a treasure, a wonder, a sin. It was there in front of him, resting on her palm like an offering. Enraptured, he slowly moved his face toward it, as if his hands were unworthy of such splendor. He felt its soft warmth against his cheek and, to his great surprise, its dark nipple suddenly hardened. She stepped back.

"Do you want to see the other one?" she asked.

He nodded eagerly.

She smiled like a little girl pulling off a grasshopper's leg.

"The other one," she said, "is for tomorrow night."

He clutched her hand but she broke away from him and disappeared into the hall, with a rustling of cloth. Rabbi Hillel was still snoring.

It was not "for tomorrow night." One of Rabbi Hillel's sisters, a widow, came the next day to stay for two weeks, and she slept in the girls' room. At the end of the two weeks it was snowing and she had to prolong her stay. Abraham was distracted and nervous. Zlata's breasts haunted his days and nights.

One morning he made up his mind.

"Rabbi," he asked, "at what age should a man marry?"

Rabbi Hillel looked at him attentively.

"In Kiddushin it is written that the Holy One, blessed be He, wishes a man to marry by the age of twenty at the latest, and curses him if he does not do so by then. How old are you, Abraham?"

"I'll soon be eighteen, rabbi."

"Do you want to marry?"

"Yes, rabbi."

"Do you know a pious, hard-working girl?"

"Yes, rabbi."

"Do I know her too?"

"You must know her better than I do, rabbi."

519

"Does she live in this house?"

"She's lived here all her life."

"God be praised, Abraham! You've made a good choice. You couldn't have found a more pious and hard-working girl than my little Braindl."

"But, rabbi . . ."

Rabbi Hillel was already calling his sister to tell her the good news.

And so it was that, not of his own accord, Abraham married Braindl at the end of that winter. In the meantime he had learned that Zlata was engaged to a young man who was studying in Germany. Because of the snow, Abraham could not send word of his wedding to his parents, but he hoped they would come when his first child was born.

Braindl was not yet fourteen and her breasts were no match for her sister's. She was lively, cheerful, and probably as hard-working as her father said, but her breasts were no match for Zlata's. She looked at Abraham with fervent devotion and he could not have wished for a better wife, if only her breasts . . .

On their first night together he blew out the candle and they undressed in darkness. He waited till she was in bed, then cautiously lay down beside her. Listening to her light breathing, he wondered what she knew about "conjugal intimacy." He hesitated to approach that little girl who was now his wife. He remembered that, to avoid sin, it was proper to recite a passage from the Torah at the time of physical union, but as soon as he tried to think of a quotation Zlata's image came into his mind.

"Braindl?"

"Yes?"

"Are you asleep?"

"No."

She moved closer to him. When he felt the contact of her slender, warm body he put his hand on her hip and she nestled her head against his adolescent beard. They fell asleep that way, as chaste as children.

Zlata was over him, naked, kneeling with her breasts on her palms. "You see," she said, "I've brought you the other one." Suddenly it was as if he were being emptied of all the liquids in his body. He woke up, seized with anxiety. Braindl was still asleep. Feeling sullied, he got out of bed, groped his way to the basin, poured water into it, purified himself, and recited the prayer for the

520

occasion: "Master of the world, I did that unintentionally, but it was caused by bad thoughts. May it be Your will, O Lord my God and God of our fathers, to wipe away that sin, in Your great mercy. May You spare me bad thoughts and everything that resembles them, forever. Amen."

The following nights brought Abraham and Braindl no closer to consummating their marriage. He returned to his earlier habits: he went downstairs as soon as Braindl was asleep and the rabbi was snoring. He sat down on the firewood box and waited. Sometimes Zlata came, sometimes she did not. Sometimes she bared her breasts, sometimes she let him approach them, sometimes she asked him to kiss their hard tips. It was she who controlled the game, according to her own dreams and desires.

The inevitable finally happened. It was nearly dawn. Gray light was already coming through the window. Abraham and Zlata could not bring themselves to part. She had taken off her nightgown and was wearing only a kind of petticoat. Suddenly Rabbi Hillel's voice rang out.

"What are you doing here?"

Zlata leapt back, snatched up her nightgown, and ran away. Abraham hastily straightened his clothes. He was thunderstruck, yet at the same time he was not surprised that the Almighty had finally put an end to those episodes of depravity.

"What are you doing here?" the rabbi asked again, as if he knew no other question.

"Nothing . . . nothing wrong, rabbi," Abraham stammered. "We weren't doing anything wrong. . . ."

With his hair and beard disheveled, the rabbi raised his eyebrows, looking as though he could not believe his ears.

"What! Adultery isn't wrong? Bad Jew! Apostate!"

Abraham lowered his eyes. He seemed to hear the sound of a slap and felt a sharp pain on his left cheek.

"Demon!" the rabbi shouted, stamping his foot. "Get out! Get out of my house!"

Abraham dodged the second slap, bumped against the stove, and ran toward the door, taking his fur-lined coat. He still heard the rabbi's voice behind him when he had left the house.

"Bad Jew! Shame on you! Shame!"

Abraham walked along the awakening street. The fortified synagogue, looking like one of those red brick Polish citadels, was lighted inside.

521

"Good morning," people greeted him as he passed.

The Jews of Zolkiew were going to the synagogue for morning prayer.

"May the Almighty give us a good day," he replied.

"And may He give one to all of Israel."

"Amen."

He spent the day at the print shop without going home at noon, as he had sometimes done before when there was work that had to be finished quickly. But at the end of the day he did not know what to do. After what had happened, he was afraid to go back and confront Rabbi Hillel, his father-in-law.

He left the shop and began walking toward the upper part of the town. The evening was almost warm. This was the first time he had ever strolled aimlessly in Zolkiew, and everything seemed different to him. In the gathering dusk he noticed a church that he did not recall ever having seen before. He stepped aside to let sleighs pass and heard the laughter of women. Sounds of music came to him from far away. He crossed a public square and saw the castle. Its imposing mass was lighted by smoking torches.

He stopped, struck by the sight. On the front steps, in the reddish glow reflected by the snow, liveried servants were receiving guests who alighted from sleighs. An orchestra was playing and armed soldiers stood guard. Abraham came closer to see better. Near the wrought-iron gate surmounted by the royal escutcheon, noblemen on horseback were exchanging friendly insults and laughing loudly, probably already a little drunk. Abraham remembered what he had always been told about noblemen: "Be on your guard against them. If trouble doesn't start when they come, it starts when they leave."

Suddenly there was a drum roll and from the royal gardens came groups of men carrying torches, moving in Abraham's direction. He quickly stepped back into the shadows, and leaned against a fence. He heard a voice in the darkness.

"Come through the gate and sit here with me. The sight is worth seeing."

The voice, which spoke in Polish, was friendly and sounded as if it belonged to an old man. Abraham found the gate and climbed the front steps of a house.

"Have a seat," invited the voice.

Abraham felt a bench behind his knees and sat down on it. Sleighs were gliding past the house.

"Who are those people?" asked Abraham.

"You're not from here?"

"I'm from Kamionka."

"By the Black Virgin, that's one place I've never heard of!"

"It's near Lubartow."

"Well, it doesn't matter. . . . It's Prince Radziwill, the vaivode of Vilna, who's coming tonight. He's related to the king. When he goes somewhere, almost the whole Polish nobility goes with him! Watch carefully."

The crunching of footsteps in the snow, the smoky light of torches. Standard-bearers were passing. Beside Abraham, the voice commented on the spectacle.

"There's the infantry. . . . And here comes the cavalry. Behind them are the prince's personal guards. They're all ruined noblemen. Look at their clothes. No peasant would have imagined them like that, even in a dream. . . . Here's the band. . . . And the artillery on sleighs. . . ."

"Does that whole army belong to one prince?" asked Abraham.

"Wait, this is only the beginning: Prince Radziwill's army has more than ten thousand men! It's worth seeing! Look, there's the prince himself!"

Several sleighs full of standing soldiers went by, closely following each other. Then came another band, and finally a carriage on runners, drawn by six black horses.

"It's worth seeing," repeated the voice in the darkness.

"But who's seeing it?" asked Abraham.

"Who's seeing it? Everyone in the city is watching from windows! Or at least all the men are watching. The women . . ." The voice laughed unpleasantly. "Young man, if you have a wife somewhere in Zolkiew, you'd better hurry and hide her before it's too late! No woman is safe if the prince lays eyes on her, whether she's beautiful or ugly, fat or thin, clean or dirty. . . ."

Abraham felt a lump of anxiety rising in his throat. He had never seen a mob attacking Jews, but his mother Baile had taught him that groups of drunken men who went off looking for women often ended up looking for Jews.

"I thank you for your hospitality," he said, "but I think I'd better leave now."

"There's nothing really bad about the prince and his soldiers," the voice continued, "but you know how it is: they like to enjoy themselves once in a while, like all men. They drink, and then they . . ."

Abraham took a short cut between gardens and began running as fast as he could. He had nearly reached Rabbi Hillel's house when he abruptly turned and ran to the fortified synagogue, which was still lighted. Around one of the four thick pillars that held up the painted ceiling, three or four *minyanim* of Jews were praying. Abraham walked toward them.

"Sh!" someone hissed.

"Jews!" he called out softly.

No one moved.

"Jews!" he repeated.

Moshe the *chazzan* looked up.

"What's happening? Why are you disturbing us?"

"Prince Radziwill is crossing the town with ten thousand men."

"Who are you?"

"Abraham, son of Benjamin the horse merchant of Kamionka. I'm married to Rabbi Hillel's daughter."

When he said these words, he felt a pang in his heart.

"Don't worry, Abraham. The Almighty won't abandon His children. We have lookouts. We'll bar the doors in time, and, if we need them, we also have weapons. Go home and watch over your family."

As he was leaving the synagogue, Abraham saw men standing in the shadows, ready to close the heavy doors. Outside, he heard sleigh bells and the music of marching bands. He began running again and arrived at Rabbi Hillel's house just as the first of Radziwill's men appeared in the Jews' Street. Behind the garden gate he saw the shadowy figure of a woman. He leapt over the gate, seized her by the shoulders, threw her to the ground, and rolled in the snow with her.

"Abraham," she murmured. "Thank God! I was waiting for you!"

"Quiet!" he whispered.

Feeling her body slowly moving beneath his, he was filled with pleasant warmth.

By now some of the soldiers, cavalrymen, had come very close. They were making an infernal uproar, singing, swearing, calling for women, shouting that they were thirsty and wanted something to drink.

"Abraham," the woman murmured again.

524

Her voice was so soft, so tender, that Abraham was deeply stirred by it. And suddenly he knew who she was.

"My wife," he said.

They clung to each other with all their strength. In their embrace there was fear, desire, and perhaps already the love that was to unite them for the rest of their lives together.

When the last of the soldiers had passed, they saw the door of the house open. Rabbi Hillel appeared in the doorway.

"Braindl!" he called out. "Braindl!"

Shots were fired in the distance.

Abraham and Braindl stood up, shook off some of the snow that covered them, and walked toward Rabbi Hillel, hand in hand. The rabbi looked at them for a few moments, frowning. Then he must suddenly have forgotten what he had seen that morning, because he said, "Come in quickly and close the door, before the house gets cold."

That night Abraham knew Braindl his wife. Never again did he have any desire to go downstairs and warm himself by the stove on the first floor.

ABRAHAM WAS FIFTY-FIVE when Braindl died. Many of those close to him had already gone to meet the Almighty face to face: his father Benjamin, his mother Baile, Rabbi Hillel, Uri Faibuch, and even, despite his young age, Chaim-David Faibuch. But what he had felt then was nothing like what he felt now.

His heart was as heavy as the fortified synagogue of Zolkiew. With his clothes torn as a sign of mourning, he repeated to himself what the sages of the Talmud said: "When a man has lost his wife, for him the world has entered into darkness." May the Lord protect Braindl's pure soul.

37

ZOLKIEW

Sadness and Joy

DURING ABRAHAM'S lifetime, Zolkiew had been spared by the tides of history—Sweden had invaded Poland and occupied Warsaw; Lublin had been burned again; Jan Sobieski, the Polish king who had stopped the Turks at Vienna, had died, and King Louis XIV of France had tried to replace him with a prince whose name was scarcely known to anyone. As he grew older, Abraham had begun having gatherings of friends in his house every evening to discuss the news from all over the world and try to discern anything in it that might be "good for the Jews."

Braindl had taken an indulgent attitude toward those men's endless discussions of events that did not affect Zolkiew directly. Every day she thanked the Almighty for having been able to bring up her five children in peace. Her three daughters had married well. Her older son, Zalman, had become a peddler for the print shop, and the younger, Mendel, had used his share of the inheritance from his grandfather Benjamin to buy the right to keep an inn, or, more exactly, a combined inn and store where he not only took in guests but also sold grain, salt, mead, beer, brandy, and fodder. The steward of the nobleman who owned the inn and its environs came each month to collect his portion of the receipts, which was so large that, with what was left, Mendel could not afford to increase his stock of merchandise or even keep the inn in good repair.

Abraham did not feel sorry for him. He felt a certain resentment against him, in fact, for not having carried on the family tradition, and his hope was now that Mendel's son Joseph would do so. At thirteen, Joseph was already a real scholar. His intelligence and piety were known for miles around and there were often visits from rich merchants or moneylenders who wanted to give their daughters a learned husband. Mendel had always said no.

Then Berish, the steward from Vilna who came to collect money from Mendel each month, proposed a marriage between Joseph and his eleven-year-old daughter Shaine. Besides offering a large dowry, he promised to support the young couple for at least six years, provide them with a house, and rid Mendel of his debts. At another time Mendel might have refused, but this time he accepted. A contract was signed and the wedding took place three months after Joseph's *bar mitzvah*.

Joseph and Shaine spent their wedding night in Berish's house, an immense, damp, gloomy wooden structure in which even the furniture seemed to be bored. Joseph had obeyed his father without protest, but his marriage had little meaning for him: it was agreed that on the day after the wedding he would leave to go and study in Lvov for two years.

It was at this time that Zlata, now a childless widow, returned to Zolkiew. She asked Abraham to let her share the house in which she had grown up, in exchange for doing the housework. Her face was as expressionless as ever but her body had become thick and ponderous, and her breasts were no longer a threat of damnation to anyone. Abraham consulted his sons and daughters; they said they saw nothing wrong in letting Zlata share the house with him.

She moved in, and his life ceased to be peaceful. She began by rearranging the furniture, whitewashing the walls, and taking charge of all household purchases. Then she turned her attention to Abraham's friends who came to comment on the events of the day. After listening to them two or three times she declared that in a world where God decided who would rise and who would fall, such discussions had no other result than to dirty the table and the floor.

Two kings were then contending for the throne of Poland: Stanislas Leszczyński and Augustus of Saxony. It was unthinkable to let this situation pass without subjecting it to daily scrutiny, and so the little group, driven from the house by Zlata, began meeting in Mendel's inn. The buildings included a stable for two rows of horses, with a wide space in the middle where wagons and firewood were kept, with a hayloft above. Guests at the inn ate, drank, and slept in a single vast room, around a big stove. On weekdays Abraham and his friends always found a place where they could sit together, but on Sundays and Christian holidays, when the inn was crowded with people who came to drink and dance, they met in the synagogue.

Abraham spent as little time at home as possible. Zlata became bored and suggested that he bring back his friends, but he refused. He often thought sadly of his wife Braindl. His only joy was his grandson Joseph. He was going to ask Joseph to resume working in the print shop when he came back from Lvov.

STUDYING THE TALMUD with a rabbi to clear up the most obscure passages, spending hours in solitary reflection, reading the commentaries of the sages—Joseph was captivated by all this, as if it were an intricate mental game. But he was irritated by *pilpul,* the search for all possible combinations, even the most ridiculous, to interpret a text. The arguments among students of the *yeshiva,* and the absurdity of the explanations concocted to justify replacing one letter with another, exasperated him beyond endurance. When Rabbi Zaddok asked him the reason for his hostile attitude, he replied with a quotation from the Talmudic treatise Baba Metzia: "A man who has little knowledge makes more noise than a man who has much, just as a bottle with one coin in it makes more noise than a bottle full of coins."

To punish Joseph's arrogance, Rabbi Zaddok struck his fingers with the rod that he always kept close at hand and gave him several chapters of the Gemara to learn by heart. Joseph learned them willingly, not only because learning came easily to him but also because he was glad to have this painless way of freeing his conscience from the wrong he felt he had done. But he never set foot in Rabbi Zaddok's *yeshiva* again.

There were two *yeshivot* in Lvov at this time: the Russian one, where Rabbi Zaddok taught, and Rabbi Saul's German one. Joseph crossed the street and went to the German *yeshiva.* The teaching methods were almost the same, but Rabbi Saul's son, an apprentice to a cloth merchant who regularly went to Königsberg and spoke German, taught him the alphabet of the *goyim* and lent him several profane books.

What a revelation! The first two books he was able to read were treatises on optics and physics. He felt that, as in the Cabala, he was discovering the hidden reasons of things, but with an interest he had never known before: he learned what caused wind, where rain came from, how snow was formed. . . .

One day, in the course of a discussion with a visiting Talmudist, he said that the earth was round, like a ball, and that there were surely people on the other side of it, directly opposite Lvov. The Talmudist replied that it was impossible, since those people would fall into the void. Joseph explained to him, as he himself had just learned, that everything on the surface of the earth was attracted toward its center.

"And that's why we can't leave the earth," he concluded, "no matter where we are on its surface."

The Talmudist looked at him with a kind of fear, stammered a few confused words, and hurriedly left him.

It was not long before a rumor reached Zolkiew from Lvov: Joseph the young *illui,* grandson of Abraham the printer, was said to have taken up heretical theories. One of the servants in Mendel's inn went to Lvov and told Joseph that his father, his grandfather, and his father-in-law wanted him to come back to Zolkiew and explain himself.

At dawn, when the servant who was supposed to accompany him was still asleep, Joseph got up and set off in the opposite direction from Zolkiew. He went into a forest full of terrifying noises, finally came out of it, and sat down on a stump to rest. He realized that he was running away but he could see no other solution: he did not want to be confined in either his father's inn or the big, gloomy house where a wife he had not chosen was waiting for him.

He continued walking along the road without knowing where it was taking him. When his feet began to hurt, he sat down again. A peasant in a wagon stopped and invited him to get in. He was going to Rawa Ruska, he said, and could let him off at the edge of the village, at the Jew's Inn.

The Jew in question was named Mosheh-Yankel. He was a slovenly man of about fifty who spoke neither Hebrew nor Yiddish; the only language he spoke was a Russian dialect that Joseph could scarcely understand. He showed no interest in knowing who Joseph was or where he was going, but he told him that he had ten children, nine of whom were sons, and asked him to stay through the winter and teach them to read.

It was an unforgettable winter. The inn had only two rooms, one above the other. Because of the smoke that constantly hung below the ceiling like a thick cloud, the peasants who came there for a glass of brandy and a slice of sausage sat on the floor; and it was on the floor, behind the big square stove, that Joseph taught his pupils the rudiments of reading from an old Pentateuch that Mosheh-Yankel had turned up somewhere.

He sometimes felt like returning to Zolkiew, but the thought of facing his family always made him decide against it. In the spring he set off again and took the road that, he was told, would lead him to Belz. It passed through Uhnow, where he stopped in a little synagogue.

Passover was approaching and Joseph anxiously wondered where he could attend a *seder*. He prayed with all his might, like the child he still was—he was fifteen. As he was about to leave the synagogue, a Jew with powerful shoulders came up to him.

"My name is Baruch-Benjamin," he said. "I'm a blacksmith and my smithy is on the road to Laszczow. If you're away from your family and want to celebrate Passover in a friendly house, mine is open to you."

Joseph fervently thanked the Almighty, blessed be He, and accepted the invitation with relief.

In the few days before Passover, he helped the blacksmith and his two sons to whitewash the house, replace the old bricks in the oven, and search everywhere to make sure that all *chametz* was removed. On the day before the holiday he went with Baruch-Benjamin and his sons to the bath, then to the synagogue. In the evening, when it was time to recite the Haggadah, the blacksmith asked him to translate it and explain it to his family.

"You're a very learned young man," he remarked the next morning, after prayer. "Where is your journey taking you?"

"It doesn't matter," replied Joseph.

"I spoke without thinking," the blacksmith said apologetically. "Every man comes into the world to fulfill a mission and rectify something. That's why man travels from place to place."

Joseph looked at him with surprise and realized how much he liked him. He asked him if he could stay for a time after Passover and help him with his work.

530

"Only if you let me pay you," said the blacksmith.

During the few weeks he spent in the smithy, where he tried to make himself useful, Joseph observed Baruch-Benjamin. The blacksmith recited psalms as he worked at his anvil, he showed a kind of deference to the customers who brought him carts to repair or horses to shoe, and he always took time to talk with passing Jews and offer them a glass of cool water. Joseph asked him one day why he kept interrupting his work to listen to everyone's idle chatter. The strange blacksmith replied that "each thought is a complete step" and that "anyone who kills a thought is like a murderer."

"But where did you learn that?"

"I learned it by listening to people, Joseph."

"The people who stop by the smithy?"

"The sages say that it's possible to learn not only with the head, but also with the heart."

"Which sages say that?"

"The Chassidim."

"The disciples of Baal Shem Tov?"

In Lvov, the year before, a rabbi had come to bring the words of Rabbi Israel Baal Shem Tov, but the *yeshiva* students, caught up in their endless *pilpul,* had not even listened to him.

"I've heard that Rabbi Baal Shem Tov is like Sabbatai Zevi, that he takes himself for the Messiah," said Joseph.

Baruch-Benjamin laughed.

"Sabbatai Zevi claimed to be the Messiah himself, while the holy rabbi says that 'each son of Israel is a part of the Messiah, and each contributes his share to building the Messiah.' "

Baruch-Benjamin was so warm, so open, so radiant, that Joseph admitted to him that he had run away from Lvov to avoid going back to Zolkiew.

"And now?"

"Now I'm afraid to face my family."

"Did you intend to hurt them?"

"Why do you ask that?"

"Because it's the intention that counts, Joseph."

"It wasn't my intention to hurt anyone."

"Then go back to Zolkiew in peace!"

"But I'd be . . ."

The blacksmith put his hand on Joseph's shoulder.

"No, you won't be punished. The Almighty doesn't strike the

body, He only wants the soul. And yours is pure. Go back, ask your father and your wife to forgive you, and you'll be forgiven!"

Joseph left a few days later. Baruch-Benjamin embraced him as if he were his son.

"Don't forget: the soul and the intention," he said. "In this world, we Jews have the intention of building the Messiah!"

ZOLKIEW HAD CHANGED during Joseph's two-year absence. Shaine had almost become a woman and there was a new atmosphere in the town. Many Jews had begun doing manual work. They could be seen in gardens, on roofs, at forges, or in cabinet-makers' shops, doing things that they had formerly left to professional craftsmen. They seemed both contemplative and joyful, and would even begin dancing at the slightest occasion.

"The Jews are changing," Joseph's father Mendel told him, "thanks to the teachings of the holy Rabbi Baal Shem Tov."

"Are you a Chassid too, father?"

"The Chassid is someone who's sad because it's normal to be sad and because everyone has some reason for sadness, but he doesn't despair. The Chassid is saddened by the purity of joy and he rejoices in the purity of sorrow."

"Have you read the Cabala?" asked Joseph, surprised to hear his father speaking this way.

"No, my son. What I've just said has nothing to do with the Cabala. The Cabala makes the divine human, whereas for the Chassid it's the human that's divine."

Joseph had been joyously welcomed back by his family and he had asked them all to forgive him. He now realized how much he had underestimated them. He liked the inn, with its smell of horses and hay, and it even seemed to him that Berish's big house, where Shaine had been waiting for him, was no longer as damp as before. On the night of his return, he knew his wife for the first time.

A few days later a disciple of Baal Shem Tov came to Zolkiew. He was a rabbi with a wide beard and limpid eyes. He took lodgings at Mendel's inn. A throng of Jews quickly gathered there and sang, clapping their hands and stamping their feet, while they waited for him to speak.

Mendel introduced him as "Rabbi Isaac-Meir, who has come from Meziboz, where he saw the holy Rabbi Baal Shem Tov." He had come "to answer the questions of the Jews." The first one was soon asked:

"How can we best serve both the Creator and His children?"

The rabbi smiled.

"A good question, a good question. . . . It's not easy to serve both the Almighty, blessed be He, and His creatures. When someone finally learns to do it, it's because he's become a wise man."

"But how can we become wise?"

"He who wants to be wise must learn something from everyone, for it is written, 'I have become wise with the help of all those who have instructed me.'"

The gathering expressed approval. Faivel the water carrier asked, "Can everyone become wise and learn something from everyone?"

"A good question," the rabbi said again. "The holy Rabbi Israel Baal Shem Tov teaches that the light of God is the human soul." He looked at his listeners attentively. "Where there's light, there's shadow. Light can be compared to the soul, and shadow to the body. Baal Shem Tov says that when we're in the presence of a righteous man we feel that the influence emanating from him is like a spark that springs from his soul and kindles in us a desire to do good deeds." He lowered his voice. "We're also influenced by any relations we may have with sinners. They bring out the bad in us, and give us ideas that lead to evil."

"How true!" exclaimed someone.

"And so from the righteous man we learn to do good, while from the sinner we learn to turn away from evil."

The rabbi's listeners voiced their agreement and he concluded, "Thus we see the truth of the maxim 'He who wants to be wise must listen to everyone.'"

Joseph was strongly impressed. It seemed to him that although Rabbi Isaac-Meir's reasoning was a little simplistic, it had great emotional appeal and was well adapted to his audience. Through the teachings of Baal Shem Tov, those who were not educated and did not take part in directing the affairs of the community would still be able to express themselves.

"But," asked one of the stablemen of the inn, "if we really sin, can God's mercy help us? Wouldn't that mean that His mercy came before His justice?"

The questions and answers—about God, about man and his life —continued far into the night, in the heavy odor of the horses in the stable. Then the benches were pushed back and everyone danced to manifest the joy of placing one's life in the hands of the Almighty.

BERISH HAD HIS LEG crushed by a sleigh and could not keep his promise to support Joseph and Shaine for at least six years. Joseph had to end the innocent time of his studies and go to work, especially since his wife, now fourteen, was expecting a child.

Abraham gave him his place in the Faibuch print shop, which was now managed by Gershom and his son Wolf. The grandfather taught the grandson not only to practice the trade but also to love it. When it was well established that the family tradition would be carried out and when Joseph's son Berl had been born, Abraham died, satisfied that he had done his duty to his ancestors and his descendants, and sure that the family book, which he had given to his son Mendel, would continue on its way.

After Abraham's death, Joseph borrowed a wagon from his father and went to Baruch-Benjamin's smithy in Uhnow.

The blacksmith's beard had turned white but otherwise he did not seem to have changed. When he saw Joseph coming, he took off his thick leather apron, put down his hammer, quickly washed his hands, and embraced him.

"Baruch haba!"

"I haven't forgotten," Joseph said a little awkwardly.

"Baal Shem Tov says that exile comes from forgetfulness. . . ."

". . . but memory is the root of liberation," concluded Joseph.

They went into the house, arm in arm, and sat down before a jug of brandy. Joseph talked for a long time; it was as if he were relieving himself of the mysterious weight that presses down on man's shoulders and sometimes overwhelms him.

Hours later, when they had drunk a great deal and dawn was breaking, Baruch-Benjamin told how, in the synagogue, he had encouraged several young men to sing and dance, and how a group of pious and learned Jews had been so shocked that they accused them of showing disrespect for the Torah.

"Then what happened?" asked Joseph.

"They had a solemn debate," replied Baruch-Benjamin, "and finally decided that for ordinary workmen like me, such a way of celebrating God's love could be tolerated."

He laughed loudly, then admitted that—as Joseph already suspected—he was a rabbi.

When Baal Shem Tov asked his followers to settle in towns and

534

villages in Poland, Lithuania, and Byelorussia, Baruch-Benjamin had come to Uhnow and learned to be a blacksmith. He sincerely loved his work, which, like all manual work, made it possible to rise a step higher toward God. But the smithy was also one of the villagers' meeting places, and so he had been able to acquaint them with the teachings of Baal Shem Tov.

With his peace of mind restored, Joseph went home and resumed his work in the print shop. He never forgot the blacksmith-rabbi; whenever he was inclined toward sadness or revolt, he again saw Baruch-Benjamin's broad, open face and felt the light intoxication they had shared after Abraham's death.

He never joined the Chassidic movement, but each time the occasion arose he defended the Chassidim against the Mitnagdim, who accused them of turning Jews away from the Torah.

Baal Shem Tov died a few years later, in 1760 by the Christian calendar. He left the movement in the hands of his son Zevi, a man of great kindness, but far less intelligent than his father.

Not long afterward it was said that on the first anniversary of Baal Shem Tov's death he appeared to Zevi in a dream and asked him to yield leadership of the movement to Rabbi Dov Ber of Mezericz, saying, "Let Rabbi Ber take the place you now hold at the head of the table, while you take his." Rabbi Zevi did as his father asked. Witnesses reported that he took off his coat, gave it to Rabbi Ber, and warmly congratulated him. Having exchanged coats, they also exchanged places, and that was how Rabbi Ber became the guide of the Chassidim.

Joseph's son Berl was indignant when he heard this story.

"Those Chassidim are blasphemers!" he said. "How can they compare such childish stories to the Torah?"

"The Chassidim say that 'a story is a teaching of life,' and they're not wrong," replied Joseph. "And you're not wrong either, Berl, which proves that truth is not one, except for the truth of the Creator, blessed be He."

Berl accepted this, but did not change his opinion of the Chassidim's assertion that "the light of stories is as great as that of the Torah."

He reminded Joseph of the young man he himself had been: he learned easily; he was well advanced in knowledge of the Torah, the Talmud, and the rabbinic commentaries; he eagerly read all the new books from the Gentile world that reached Zolkiew—Rousseau, Voltaire, Leibnitz—but he lacked patience and indulgence.

Berl worked in the print shop. He had married Yente, a childhood friend, and at eighteen he was already the father of a son. He lived in a small but fairly comfortable wooden house that his father-in-law had given to the young couple as a wedding present. It was across the street from the inn that Joseph's brother Nathan had taken over after Mendel's death. If it had been located a little farther away, or if another building had separated it from the inn, the course of Berl's life would undoubtedly have been different.

WHILE KING STANISLAS II OF Poland was deciding to take measures against the Jews—abolition of the Council of the Four Lands, restrictions on the number of Jews allowed to live in cities —the Prussians, Austrians, and Russians took over part of Poland's territory.

Regiments of Russian soldiers went through Zolkiew in one direction, then regiments of Austrian soldiers went through it in the other. Then the Austrian army took up quarters in the environs. From then on Nathan's inn was always full. Day and night, he had to serve drunkards who threatened to throw torches into the hayloft and often left without paying.

Early one morning an Austrian officer, already drunk, forced open the door of Nathan's lodgings and demanded food. Nathan's wife Rivka quickly got up while he rekindled the fire in the fireplace. The officer had laid his saber on the table.

Rivka heated the chicken soup and served him a bowlful of it. He asked for bread and butter. Nathan brought some of the coarse black bread that he baked himself, but he brought no butter: it was unacceptable for a Jew to see meat and butter on the same table. The Austrian picked up his saber and struck a violent blow against the cabinet in which goblets and bowls were kept. Without a word, Nathan went to bring him some butter. The officer emptied his bowl, belched loudly, stood up, and walked toward the door. Nathan asked him to pay.

This enraged the Austrian. He shouted, swung his saber wildly, kicked over benches, and broke dishes. Then he seized Nathan's beard and slashed it in half with his saber. A moment later he brutally ripped open the front of Rivka's gray dress and, with a sudden, unforeseeable movement, cut off one of her breasts.

People who had been sleeping in the inn were awakened by the noise and came to see what was happening. Some of them ran away, others called for help, goading the Austrian into even greater fury with their cries. In the little house across the street, Yente woke up Berl. He quickly got dressed, ran to the inn, and saw his aunt Rivka lying in a pool of blood.

The Austrian officer had thrown Nathan's daughter Hana to the floor and was holding her down with one knee while he unbuckled his belt. Berl saw that he had laid his saber on the floor beside him. He leapt toward it, picked it up, swung it against the officer's skull with all his strength, and watched him slowly fall on his side. Hana screamed, and then there was silence.

Jews appeared in the doorway.

"*Oy, oy, oy,*" moaned the *shammash* of the fortified synagogue.

"Master of the world. . . ."

"If that officer is found," said Jacob Sandler the shoemaker, "we're all lost. Let's wrap him in sacks and get rid of him."

"We can throw him in the pond," suggested a voice.

"Let's bury him," said someone else.

Berl felt that he was on the verge of vomiting.

"You'd better leave Zolkiew," Jacob Sandler told him. "As long as the Austrians are here. . . ."

"Where can I go?" asked Berl.

A young man with dark, curly hair stepped forward.

"I'm Marcus Chelmer," he said. "I slept here last night. I saw what was happening but I was afraid to do anything. You were braver than I was. . . . I'm leaving this morning for Königsberg. If you want to, you can go with me."

38

KÖNIGSBERG-STRASBOURG

The Kaftanjude

MARCUS CHELMER was a Polish Jew who, as his name indicated, came from Chelm. His father, a prosperous grain merchant, had died and left him a small fortune. Instead of taking over the family business, Marcus decided to study. First he went to spend two years at the famous *yeshiva* in Vilna. Then, when he read Moses Mendelssohn's *Phaedo,* he admired him so much that he wanted to visit him.* "Your Mendelssohn lives in Berlin," he was told. He went to Berlin and learned that Moses Mendelssohn had left for Königsberg,† in East Prussia, only the day before. Marcus set off for Königsberg, but he was delayed by several incidents

---

* The German Jewish philosopher Moses Mendelssohn (1729–1786), spiritual father of the Haskalah (the Jewish Equivalent of the Enlightenment) and an advocate of Jewish political, intellectual, and moral reform, is regarded as the founder of Reform Judaism and one of the originators of Jewish emancipation. He wrote many books and translated the Bible into German. He was the grandfather of the composer Felix Mendelssohn.

He wrote his *Phaedo* (1767) on the model of the Platonic dialogue of the same name. In it he sets forth views close to those of Leibnitz on the immortality of the soul and the existence of an infinite number of monads in the universe.

† Now Kaliningrad, in the Soviet Union.

along the way. By the time he reached his destination, Mendelssohn had gone back to Berlin. It seemed obvious to him that fate was against him; he stayed in Königsberg and enrolled in the university there.

Berl found Marcus to be a charming, intelligent, and cultivated companion, though he could not help being a little suspicious of him because he had neither a beard nor *payesses* and wore a lace-trimmed shirt, a frock coat, velvet breeches, and buckled shoes.

Marcus tried to free Berl from the feeling of guilt that obsessed him.

"If you can't forget that you killed that officer," he said, "remember that the Almighty, blessed be He, chose you to carry out His justice."

"That man may have had a wife and children. . . ."

"If so, they're well rid of him! Believe me, Berl, no one in the world can reproach you for what you did."

"What will you do with me in Königsberg? I don't know anyone there, I have no money, and I don't know any trade except printing."

"Don't worry. We'll see. You only have to stay till it's safe for you to go home."

Königsberg was a city built around a high cathedral, near the Baltic Sea. Across the grayish-green water moved big, heavy ships flying English, Dutch, Danish, and Swedish flags. They brought metals and tropical commodities, Marcus explained, and left laden with natural products of Poland and Lithuania, such as grain and linen. Berl's first impression of Königsberg was good, but he changed his mind when, to enter the city, they had to go through a special gate for Jews and pay a special fee.

Marcus took Berl home with him. He lived with several other young Jews, university students like himself, in a half-timbered house on Brotbänkerstrasse. Its owner, the widow Gerlach, said Marcus, also owned the English House, where the philosopher Kant often went for lunch. Had Berl heard of Immanuel Kant?

Berl had read some of his works. He was excited at the thought of breathing the same air as such an important philosopher.

"Can we see Kant himself someday?"

WHEN BERL WENT INTO the house on Brotbänkerstrasse with Marcus, he saw students who were clean-shaven like Marcus and dressed in the same way, with one difference: unlike him, each of them wore a sword at his side. They laughed at the sight of Berl, who, with his black, threadbare caftan, his broad-brimmed hat, and his beard disheveled from his journey, struck them as belonging to another human species.

"A *Kaftanjude!*" [caftan Jew] said one of them.

"Where did you dig him up?" another asked Marcus.

"This is my friend Berl," Marcus said in German. "He's from Poland, as I am."

"Does he speak German?"

They turned to Berl. He felt like leaving but at the same time he wanted to stay and show them who he was.

"I've never spoken German," he replied in German, "but I can read it."

More laughter.

"What did he say?"

"What language was that?"

A short, plump, blond student with tears of laughter in his eyes held out a book to Berl.

"Here, read us a passage."

For Berl, a book was like a refuge. He took it. It was by Kant. He opened it at random and began reading aloud. He soon had to stop: the others were laughing so loudly that the windowpanes rattled.

"I didn't understand a word of it!" exclaimed the blond student.

"I understood everything," Berl said quietly.

"Prove it!"

Berl had an urge to attack the blond student but he told himself that it might be better simply to walk away. He looked at Marcus as though to ask him for advice. In his friend's eyes he saw more pity than anger. No, he must neither walk away nor lose his temper.

"Here's a challenge from the *Kaftanjude,*" he said. "I'll take a page of this German book and read it aloud in Hebrew, and I challenge each of you to do the same. Then we'll see who laughs."

He opened the book again and began translating a page of it from German into Hebrew, without hesitation, as if the structures of the two languages were exactly parallel. The others listened in silence. Those young Jews were capable of appreciating his performance. When he had finished he offered the book to the blond student, who refused it with a gesture.

"Bravo, *Kaftanjude,* that was brilliant!"

"Incredible!" exclaimed another student.

"My father knows much more than I do," Berl replied modestly.

"My friend Berl," Marcus said with a satisfied smile, "plans to be in Königsberg for some time. He has no money and no lodgings. I propose that we let him stay here, and take care of him while he looks for work. He's a printer. He can also give lessons—"

"But not in German!" Berl interrupted.

This time the laughter was on his side.

BERL WAS QUICKLY caught up in the hectic life of the students, a mixture of revelry, study, fights, and endless discussions. He could not enroll in the university because the limited number of places allotted to Jews were already taken, but he was able to earn a few talers a month as an assistant Hebrew teacher at the Friedricianum school.

He no longer wore his old black caftan. His friends had persuaded him to dress as they did, and had lent him the clothes that were then fashionable for students: a shirt with lace cuffs, a frock coat, velvet breeches, and buckled shoes. But he had refused to shave off his beard and wear a pigtail. He had become acquainted with the widow Gerlach and she had promised that she would arrange for him to meet Kant. One evening he had even gone to the theater, for Jews were allowed to attend it here, whereas in Poland it was forbidden to them. In Königsberg the company of an educated man was valued more highly than that of an ignoramus, even if the ignoramus was rich or noble. To be fully accepted, however, Jews had to forget that they were Jews.

Berl had almost stopped thinking about the Austrian officer collapsing into a pool of his own blood, and, to tell the truth, he thought even less about his wife Yente and their son Noah.

One evening his friends took him to a concert of chamber music in the house of Heinrich Friedländer, who was related to one of them. Berl found himself sitting among men in powdered wigs and women in low-cut gowns, wondering what he was doing there on that uncomfortable seat, trying to follow music that had no words and seemed meaningless to him.

At the end of the concert, the musicians were surrounded and complimented. Berl greeted a young woman he had met before: she was the sister of Mendel Bresselau, who often visited the little group in the Gerlach house.

"Do you like music?" she asked.

541

"I don't know if I like that kind of music or not," he answered honestly. "I'd never heard it before."

She laughed in a friendly, unaffected way. He saw her big, dark eyes, her sensuous lips, her bare shoulders, and he was suddenly embarrassed: he had never before had a private conversation with a foreign woman—and this one was not only foreign, but also half undressed.

"The music was composed by Händel," she said, "a German musician who lived in England."

"Oh."

"My brother has told me about you. Why do you still have your beard and *payesses?*"

"I want to keep a sign."

"A sign?"

"A sign that . . . I'm a Jew."

She laughed again, and he liked her laugh.

"But we're nearly all Jewish here," she said gaily. "My brother tells me you're from Poland. What's your name?"

"Berl."

"Berl what?"

In Königsberg, "enlightened" Jews, as they were called, used first and last names. Berl did not know what to answer. He thought of his friend Marcus, who had named himself after his village, and then he remembered the name attributed to the scribes of his family in Alsace.

"Berl Halter," he said with a touch of triumph in his voice, as if he had just found the answer to a riddle.

That was what he was called from then on. He saw the young woman several more times. Her name was Judith. Her brother Mendel belonged to a group of students organized by one of their friends who had inherited an abandoned print shop and conceived the idea of putting it back in working order for the purpose of publishing a Hebrew periodical devoted to current issues. The title of the periodical had already been chosen: *Ha-Meassef.** Since none of those students had the slightest knowledge of printing, they welcomed Berl as if he were the Messiah. He was able to give them some useful advice but, at eighteen, with his limited experi-

---

* *The Gatherer,* published by Maskilim (proponents of the Jewish Enlightenment) in Berlin and Königsberg at irregular intervals between 1783 and 1797.

542

ence in the trade, he felt incapable of setting up and operating the complex system of a print shop. He suggested asking his father, Joseph, to come and take charge of the project. They gave him a bill of exchange to pay Joseph's traveling expenses and enable him to buy type.

When he came back to the Gerlach house that day, Berl found a merchant from Lemberg, a fat, short-winded man, waiting for him. The merchant asked him twice if he was really Berl, son of Joseph the printer in Zolkiew; he was obviously surprised by the young man's appearance.

"I've come to tell you," he finally said, "that your wife wants you to bring her here to live with you, or come back to Zolkiew immediately, or give her a divorce."

Yente! Berl had almost forgotten what she looked like!

"Have you seen my father?" he asked the merchant.

"No. I met your wife in her parents' house. She seemed . . . uh . . . determined."

"Are the Austrians still in Zolkiew?"

"Yes, but your wife asked me to tell you that you're no longer in any danger."

Berl explained that he was in no position to bring his wife and child to Königsberg: he had only a small room that he shared with a student, and he was so poor that even his clothes were borrowed. As for going back to Zolkiew, it was out of the question, at least for the time being, because he had just been asked to set up a print shop in Königsberg.

The fat merchant nodded skeptically as he listened to all this. Berl asked him to wait a few minutes and wrote a letter to his father, telling him about the proposition of Mendel Bresselau and his friends. Then he took the merchant to a cheap inn in the village of Löbenicht and paid for his stay overnight.

He slowly walked back by way of the old part of the city, thinking about the message that the merchant had brought him. He suddenly felt a vague bitterness. Among the street stalls he saw bearded Jews in black caftans busily coming and going, an eternal little society of buyers and sellers. Was he one of them, when that evening he was going to a gathering where he would be with beardless "privileged Jews" who dressed like the Christians they invited to circumcisions, weddings, and the celebrations of Passover and Succot?

As though to rub salt in his wound, he approached one of those passing Jews, a man carrying two fish in a wicker basket. The man's face was lined by fatigue and he had a sad, kindly look in his eyes that was all too familiar.

"From where comes the Jew?" Berl asked him in Yiddish.

The man looked at him mistrustfully.

"From everywhere and nowhere," he answered. "And you?"

Other passersby had already stopped and begun to gather around them.

"From Zolkiew," replied Berl.

"Zolkiew, near Lemberg?"

"Yes."

The Jews examined him with obvious incredulity. One of them touched the lace of his cuffs. Then, as if obeying a signal, they all walked away from him in silence.

He remembered that only a few months earlier he had been laughingly called a *Kaftanjude*. What had happened to him since then? Had he betrayed something essential, denied a tradition? No, Judaism could not be identified with those dirty beards, those weary eyes, those shabby caftans. He persuaded himself that it was normal to be touched by those reminders of the past, but that he had to free himself from them to avoid missing the chances of the present and the future.

WHEN HE ARRIVED at his social gathering that evening, he was disappointed to learn that the philosopher Kant, who had been invited, had sent word that he would be unable to come. But Judith was there. Not daring to make open advances to her, Berl tried to impress her by shining in conversation. Someone referred to Kant, evidently the main topic of conversation at such gatherings in Königsberg, and Berl expressed surprise that a Christian philosopher should be able to speak Yiddish as if he had been born in a *shtetl*.

"We're not in Poland," Heinrich Friedländer replied to him. "The religious wars have brought people to reason and tolerance. Leibnitz, Wolf, Baumgarten, Locke—they all stress principles more than rites."

"What principles?" asked Berl.

"The existence of God, the immortality of the soul—principles common to all religions."

"Yet Kant regards Judaism not as a religion, but as a political community," remarked Berl. After a quick glance to make sure

544

that Judith was following the conversation, he continued. "Unlike Voltaire, who, being anticlerical, regarded Judaism as a religion."

"It comes to the same thing, doesn't it?" asked a tall, pimply-faced young man named Abraham Euchel who was standing close beside Judith.

"I suppose so," replied Berl, "except that, as far as I know, Voltaire didn't speak Yiddish!"

He was delighted to hear Judith laugh with the others. To Abraham Euchel, that laughter was like a slap. He turned to Berl with a hostile expression.

"Perhaps you can explain to us why you now wear city clothes but keep your beard as if you were in a *shtetl.*"

"I wear a beard," Berl said calmly, "as a reminder that people are all equal in their diversity. If the Christians refused to accept us unless we resembled them in every way, it would mean that they didn't consider us their equals. And if we tried to resemble them in every way, we'd be in danger of ceasing to be ourselves."

Mendel Bresselau intervened in a conciliatory tone.

"That's exactly what we'll try to say in our periodical. Maimonides, for example, was a man of progress who spoke Arabic and Greek, but he spared no effort to deepen and perpetuate Jewish tradition."

Berl recalled his thoughts that afternoon, among the *Kaftanjuden.* How hard it was to be oneself!

When they left, they were attacked by a group of Baltic students who had obviously been lying in wait for them to provoke one of their frequent fights against Jews, which sometimes ended in bloodshed. Both sides drew their swords and the night was soon filled with the sound of steel striking steel. Berl, having no sword, stayed with the young women. He took Judith's hand and squeezed it. With his heart pounding, he watched the battle as if it were a kind of unreal, faraway ballet. Passersby stopped and windows along the street were opened.

Suddenly a Jew fell. A shadowy figure rushed toward him, sword upraised. In a flash of memory, Berl saw the Austrian officer in Zolkiew, about to rape his cousin Hana. Again he did not hesitate. He leapt at the enemy student from behind and gripped him by the throat. They both fell, then got to their feet. The student had lost his sword. Berl saw it shining in the darkness and put his foot on it. The student ran away.

Berl leaned over the Jew lying on the pavement, recognized him

545

as Marcus, and helped him to stand up. Grimacing with pain from a wound in his thigh, Marcus was barely able to walk. Berl began leading him back toward Heinrich Friedländer's house, to have his wound treated. Marcus made a show of being unconcerned.

"Hurry!" Berl urged him. "You're bleeding!"

"I don't mind losing a little blood," said Marcus, "because I know I'll have my revenge." He leaned close to Berl's ear. "Leave me in Heinrich's house. The room will be all yours for the rest of the night. Invite Judith. . . ."

Berl invited Judith to come to the Gerlach house with him and she consented without having to be persuaded.

JOSEPH, BERL'S FATHER, came to Königsberg by stagecoach a month after Yom Kippur in the year 5543 [1783] after the creation of the world by the Almighty, blessed be He. He went straight to the Gerlach house and asked for directions to his son's room. The door of the room was open. When he stepped through the doorway, he saw a young man dressed like the *goyim* and a young woman wearing a tight bodice that revealed a large portion of her breasts. He stood there, speechless, with a bundle of clothes in one hand and a wicker basket in the other. Berl was also speechless for a moment, surprised by the sudden appearance of that Jew in a black hat and caftan, with *payesses* and a grayish-blond beard. Then he sprang to his feet.

"Father!"

After putting down his baggage and embracing his son, Joseph looked at the young woman suspiciously. Berl introduced her.

"This is Judith Bresselau. It was her brother Mendel who gave you the bill of exchange to buy type. He's also one of the founders of *Ha-Meassef.* When it begins to be published, it will be the start of a great battle for recognition of Jewish rights, and—"

Joseph interrupted him.

"Does she know that you're married and have a son?"

"We'll talk about that later, father," Berl said hurriedly. "Sit down and rest awhile."

Joseph turned his head to the left, then to the right.

"Are you looking for something, father?" asked Berl.

"Water, to purify my hands. I'd like to say the midday prayer."

JUDITH NEVER SAW Berl again. Joseph's arrival in the little group of students did not pass unnoticed. He refused to make any changes in his clothes, his habits, or his principles, and insisted on speaking only in Yiddish or Hebrew. He had bought several fonts of type in Zolkiew, and the day after his arrival he began bringing the abandoned print shop back to life. Jews were not allowed to set up print shops in Königsberg, but since this one was already in existence and had originally belonged to a Christian, there was no opposition from the authorities. Joseph resisted the young men's impatience; he tested each piece of equipment again and again, and refused to compose a single article until everything was ready. He justified himself with an old saying: "If the first letter is askew, the whole text will be worthless."

His stern pronouncements, his moralistic speeches, his quotations from the Talmud, his tendency to step back from events and draw lessons from them—all this, surprisingly, made him popular with those students who had rejected such ways when they stopped wearing caftans.

One evening when they had worked hard on a rough draft of their periodical, he showed them, as a reward, the copy of the Book of Abraham that he had brought with him. They were entranced by it.

"When do you read it?" asked Marcus.

"Whenever we're in difficulty, or when there's a birth or a death in the family, or during persecutions, when we must make an important decision. . . . As you know, Baal Shem Tov said that history is a teaching."

"But, for you, doesn't history come from heaven?" asked Mendel Bresselau.

"It's true that the Almighty gave us life and intelligence. He also gave us the Law, and with it He threw us into history."

The little group gathered more closely around Joseph. Berl looked at his father in astonishment.

"What do you mean?" asked Joel Loewe, a young man with a very pale face and a high forehead beneath his powdered wig.

"I mean that we must now act according to the Law, according to our interpretation of the Law, at the risk of accumulating interpretations."

"Isn't that at variance with the Talmud?"

Joseph smiled in his beard.

"No. The Talmud never states anything dogmatically. But have you read it? I have the impression that you all despise it a little. If so, you're wrong. I'm reminded of the dispute between Rabbis Eliezer and Joshua, in the Baba Metzia. . . ."

The students began listening with rapt attention: Joseph was going to tell one of his stories. Berl was proud of that adulation, but also a little irritated by it. Although his father had a wealth of tradition at his command, he could only repeat what he had learned.

Joseph slowly combed his beard with his fingers and told how Rabbi Joshua had once contested Rabbi Eliezer's interpretation of a certain rule. Rabbi Eliezer became angry and said, "If the rule is as I teach it, let this carob tree give us a sign," and the carob tree moved back a hundred cubits. But the sages pointed out that the comings and goings of a carob tree proved nothing. Rabbi Eliezer then said, "If the rule is as I teach it, let the water of this stream give us a sign," and the current of the stream reversed its direction. But the sages declared that the capricious behavior of a stream proved nothing either. Rabbi Eliezer said, "If the rule is as I teach it, let these walls give us a sign," and the walls of the house of study tilted until they were about to collapse. Then Rabbi Joshua stood up and furiously shouted at the walls, "When the sages discuss a rule among themselves, what concern is it of yours?" And out of respect for Rabbi Joshua, the walls did not collapse. But out of respect for Rabbi Eliezer, they did not straighten up either. Then a voice was heard from the sky: "Why are you badgering Rabbi Eliezer? The rule is still as he teaches it." Rabbi Joshua drew himself erect and answered, "It is not in the sky!"

Joseph paused, looked at those "enlightened" Jews who knew all books except the Talmud, and asked, "What do those words mean?"

None of them opened his mouth. Joseph answered his own question.

"They mean that the Law is no longer in heaven, that it was given to us on Mount Sinai once and for all, and that it is now too late to ask for a decision from heaven. Is it not written in the Law of Sinai that we shall abide by the opinion of the majority?"

The students applauded as if he had just performed a clever feat of mental agility, but he knew that no one ever sowed entirely in vain. He came back to the starting point of the discussion: the Book of Abraham. He put his prayer shawl over his shoulders and, swaying backward and forward, read a few passages from the book.

. . . we are still Your people. Our memory is the abode of Your Law. By the letter and the word, by prayer and fasting, we will maintain love and respect for Your commandments. . . . On this ninth day of the month of Av, a year after the fall of Jerusalem, I tear my garment as a sign of mourning. Until the stones of the Temple are rejoined, after being disjoined like the edges of this cloth, may the names that I have written on this scroll, and the names that others will write on it after me, be spoken aloud to rend the silence. Holy, holy, holy, You are the Almighty. Amen.

The first issue of *Ha-Meassef* was printed two weeks after the feast of Simchat Torah in the year 5543 after the creation of the world by the Almighty, blessed be He; that is, on October 21, 1783, by the Christian calendar.

Joseph took part in publishing the next three issues, then went back to Zolkiew as he had come, carrying a bundle of clothes in one hand and a wicker basket in the other. He would miss nothing, he said, except the company of Joseph Haltern, who had taught him French and translated Racine into Hebrew. Jewish life in Königsberg did not satisfy him: it lacked the fervor of *shabbat* and holidays, the happy excitement of Talmudic debates, the autonomy of behavior and thought that was found in the *shtetl;* to him, that autonomy was the continuity of Jerusalem, destroyed but still present, even in a foreign land.

His son Berl was now capable of composing and printing *Ha-Meassef* by himself. Joseph took leave of him without even mentioning his wife and son. He sensed that Berl would not return to Zolkiew before he had spent more time seeking he knew not what, "striving after wind," as Ecclesiastes said. He simply gave him the copy of the Book of Abraham that he had brought; it was his way of telling him that he had confidence in him.

BERL'S WIFE CAME TO Königsberg a year later, at the beginning of winter. Sheets of ice were slowly drifting down the Pregel. She brought their son Noah, a sluggish boy of four who, at the sight of his father, cried out in alarm and hid behind his mother's skirt. Yente was no longer the very young woman Berl had married. She was now twenty, like him, and she had not been spared by the difficult years she had lived. She had protruding light blue eyes, an abundant bosom, and the walk of a peasant in wooden

549

shoes, but the most striking thing about her was an impression of inflexible determination. Once she had taken something into her head. . . .

She did not question Berl about how he had been living and showed no interest in the city or *Ha-Meassef.* She only made a few acid remarks about those Jewish women who showed their hair in public, then demanded that he either take care of her or give her a divorce.

"It's not normal for a woman to be away from her husband so long," she said.

Berl no longer felt anything in common with that woman or that child. He was perfectly willing to give her a divorce but he did not know how he could get the money for it. It seemed to him that his life in Zolkiew had been reduced to childhood memories. In Königsberg, since Judith had left him, he had met other women and had brief affairs in which sentiment played no part. He had no intention of either living there with Yente or going back to Zolkiew with her.

For the time being, through the rabbi of the Löbenicht synagogue, he rented a room for her in the house of Jakobi the shoemaker. But Yente was a resolute woman: the next day, the rabbi came to the print shop with the mission of settling the divorce as quickly as possible. He had brought a copy of *Shulchan Aruch**; he opened it in front of Berl and the students in the shop and read aloud from it: "A vagabond who abandons his wife and does not send her enough money to provide for her needs must, if he is found, be forced by the *beth din* to grant her a divorce."

"I'm willing to divorce her," said Berl. "How much money does she want as compensation?"

"A hundred and twenty ducats."

Berl gasped.

"A hundred and . . ."

To him, it was a staggering sum.

"That seems unreasonable," said Mendel Bresselau. "I can lend you forty ducats, at most, and even that amount will keep you in debt for a long time."

The rabbi went off to ask Yente if she would settle for forty

---

* *The Set Table,* a summary of Jewish law and rabbinical jurisprudence written in the sixteenth century by Joseph Karo. By the seventeenth century it had been accepted as authoritative by all Jewish communities.

ducats and came back that evening to tell Berl that she refused to go below a hundred.

A week passed, a month, two months. Yente was still in Königsberg. She had become friendly with the rabbi's wife and spent her days chatting in the kitchen while she waited for her divorce settlement. Besides paying rent to Jakobi the shoemaker for the room in which Yente and Noah slept, and paying the rabbi's wife for their meals, Berl paid the municipal residence tax and obligatory contributions to the Chevra Kaddisha, a Jewish organization that, in Königsberg as in other places, provided medical services, conducted funerals, and even had its own infirmary. As a result of those payments, he was now in debt to all his friends.

Yente had been there four months when Berl received two letters, one a few days after the other, both addressed to him as the printer of *Ha-Meassef*. One had been sent from Metz by a man named Abraham Speyer, who was looking for printers to begin publishing a Yiddish magazine. The other was from a financier, Hirtz de Mendelsheim, chief syndic of the Jews of Alsace and Lorraine, who was preparing to set up a print shop in Strasbourg.

The solution to Berl's problem suddenly seemed obvious to him: since Yente refused to leave Königsberg, he would go away from her, so far away that, with a little luck, she would never find him.

He immediately wrote a reply to Hirtz de Mendelsheim in Strasbourg. He had chosen to go to Strasbourg because he knew from the Book of Abraham that his ancestors had lived there—it was there, in fact, that the scribes had become printers.

Hirtz de Mendelsheim hired him without delay. His letter arrived the day after Pesach. In it he wrote that he was glad he could count on the help of a skilled printer, descended from a man who had worked with Gutenberg himself, and he enclosed a bill of exchange for the large sum of five hundred talers to cover Berl's traveling expenses. Berl kept only half of it. He paid his debts with part of the other half, gave the rest of it to his friend Marcus, and asked him to give it to Yente after he was gone.

On the night before his departure, Heinrich Friedländer and Marcus Chelmer gave a party for him that lasted till dawn and, for once, was not disturbed by the band of Baltic students. When it was time for him to take the morning stagecoach he embraced his friends and his mistress of the moment, swearing that he would write to her as soon as he had found lodgings where she could come and live with him.

As the stagecoach was rolling away on the uneven pavement, he heard shouts behind him. He leaned out the window and saw swords glittering in the light of the rising sun. The Baltic students had finally arrived. Marcus was fighting fiercely and vehemently cursing in Yiddish. Berl smiled and leaned back against the seat. Soon the sea appeared.

WHAT A JOURNEY! Berl felt as if he were doomed to spend the rest of his life in that stagecoach. Bumpy roads, dust, relays, departures at dawn, indigestible food at inns . . . All this would have been easier to bear if some of the other passengers had been interesting and pleasant, but his luck was bad on that score. His first surprise came only toward the end of his journey: at Wissembourg, two days away from Strasbourg, a Jew in a caftan boarded the stagecoach. Berl greeted him and learned that he was Jacob Guggenheim, the rabbi of Haguenau. He spoke Yiddish with an accent different from Berl's. Though not very cultivated, he was a friendly, warm-hearted man, and Berl soon found himself telling him the story of his family in Alsace five or six centuries earlier.

"My last name, Halter, comes from them," he said.

The rabbi started.

"Halter? Halter? I think I've seen that name somewhere in Haguenau. Maybe in an old register, or on a gravestone. . . . You must visit the Jewish cemetery in Haguenau!"

Feeling that it would do no harm for him to delay his arrival in Strasbourg by one day, Berl left the stagecoach with the rabbi at Haguenau and they went to the cemetery together. A Star of David, now almost obliterated, was carved in each of the pillars on either side of the entrance. Pink sandstone slabs seemed to be sleeping in that garden of weeds. Time had rounded the edges of the stones. In the midst of fluttering butterflies, Berl savored the deep peace and poignant melancholy of the place. He tried to decipher some of the ancient inscriptions in Hebrew, but they were illegible.

"This sandstone doesn't resist time," remarked Rabbi Guggenheim.

Berl was awed at the thought that some of his ancestors might be buried there. He prayed in silence.

As they were leaving, the rabbi showed him a sign on the door of a small building: "In consideration of the recommendation of our lord the deputy magistrate, and to prove their friendship for him, the mayor and the council have allowed us to enlarge our cemetery. In return, we promise never to refuse burial in this cemetery to any Jews, from wherever they may be, and wherever they may have died." Berl read these words several times, feeling that across the centuries he was establishing a bond with all those ancestors whose names were recorded in the Book of Abraham: Nathan, Menachem, Mosselin, Ziporia, Gabriel . . .

"What are you going to do in Strasbourg?" the rabbi asked him.

Berl answered that he was going to work for the chief syndic of the Jews of Alsace and Lorraine, Hirtz de Mendelsheim.

"Ah, Cerf-Berr!" exclaimed the rabbi.

And he explained that this was the name commonly given to that important man, the only Jew who, thanks to the request of a royal minister, was allowed to live in the city of Strasbourg.

"His family and his servants," added the rabbi, smiling as if he were telling a good joke, "come to at least seventy people! For prayers, he has more than enough for three *minyanim!*"

THE NEXT DAY, in Strasbourg, Berl felt like a fish out of water. He asked directions to the Quai Finckwiller and was told to follow the Ill. It was not far away, near the Saint Thomas bridge.

Cerf-Berr's estate extended from the river to the Rue Sainte-Elisabeth and included several buildings besides the Ribeaupierre mansion itself. The gate was open and the portcullis was raised. In the courtyard were cages of poultry, two carriages whose drivers were talking with each other in Yiddish, and women in black ruffed capes. Berl stopped a moment to wonder about the turn his life was about to take, then went into the house.

Cerf-Berr received him immediately. He was being fitted by his tailor and his wigmaker. He could not spend much time with Berl today, he told him apologetically, because he was about to leave for Versailles to discuss the letters patent that the king was preparing to grant to the Jews of Alsace. He questioned Berl first about his journey, then about the sales of *Ha-Meassef.*

He was a rather stout man of about sixty, with a high, receding forehead and piercing eyes. When his wigmaker had adjusted his powdered wig, his tailor helped him to put on a plum-colored coat over his lace-trimmed shirt. The tailor then had him turn left and right, lift his arms singly and together, bend at the waist—all this while he continued talking with Berl.

He explained that he wanted to establish a typesetting workshop

553

while he waited for permission to publish. During his absence, his son, his son-in-law, and his secretary would help Berl to compose a commentary on the Avodah Zarah* by Shlomo ben Abraham Algazi, for which he, Cerf-Berr, would write a preface.

When the fitting was over and Cerf-Berr had left, Heym Wolff, the secretary, a young man of about the same age as Berl, introduced him to Samuel-Alexander, the son-in-law, and Marx, the son. Samuel-Alexander would be officially in charge of the print shop. Though he knew nothing about printing, he was greatly pleased with himself: any title, even an empty one, was enough to delight him.

Marx was a lively, vigorous, ruddy-faced young man who gave the impression that he did not spend his time in pious study of the Torah.

"How is emancipation going?" he asked.

"It's in great favor among the Jews," replied Berl. "If only it depended on them!"

Marx laughed. Just then a young maidservant with a shapely figure passed by. Marx noticed Berl following her with his eyes.

"Her name is Jeras," he said. "She's in my service. Pretty, isn't she? Unfortunately she thinks only of getting married. . . ."

Heym Wolff took Berl in a carriage to Bischheim, half a league outside of Strasbourg, where he would have his lodgings until Cerf-Berr obtained permission for him to live within the city. As he was about to leave him, Wolff gave him what he called a *breithaupt,* a kind of large felt hat that he would have to wear, like all other Jews in Alsace.

In Bischheim, Berl's lodgings were in the house of a fodder merchant named Meyer Bloch, whose four daughters always made visitors feel as if they had come into a birdcage. They were still too young to interest Berl; and furthermore he was preoccupied with trying to think of a way to become acquainted with Jeras, the pretty servant, who had made a strong impression on him.

BERL USUALLY TOOK THE public coach to Strasbourg in the morning and left the city before ten o'clock at night, as the law required. He and Marx Berr had quicky become friends. Marx occasionally took him to social gatherings or political meetings in the back rooms of fashionable suburban taverns. On those nights

---

* A Talmudic treatise dealing with idolatry.

Berl slept at the Raven Inn, where Marx sometimes carried on his love affairs, with the innkeeper's handsomely rewarded complicity.

Berl liked those nights at the inn. He did not always spend them alone; but whether he was alone or not, he always got up when he heard the old people from the poorhouse arrive with their handcarts, shovels, and brooms to clean the street. After saying the morning prayer, he went out to walk along the river. When the dawn was foggy, there were blurred halos around the lanterns of passing wagons. As he walked, he tried to achieve inner harmony, and he nearly always recalled the words of Acabaya ben Mahalel: "Reflect on three questions and you will avoid sin: From where do you come? Where are you going? By whom will you someday be called to account?" Berl felt that everything would become clear if he knew the answer to the second question.

One morning he decided to write to his father in Zolkiew and ask him to come and work with him in Strasbourg. Cerf-Berr had not been able to obtain an official authorization to open a print shop in his own name, but he had concluded a mutually advantageous agreement with a printer named Jonas Lorenz: in his shop, Berl composed books in Latin type for Lorenz, who in exchange printed Hebrew books that flattered Cerf-Berr's vanity. Lorenz, an excellent printer, had been complaining about the laziness and unreliability of the men who worked for him, and Berl was sure he would not regret hiring Joseph.

And one day, just as he had done in Königsberg, Joseph arrived with a bundle in one hand and a wicker basket in the other, as much a *Kaftanjude* as ever. But this time he was not alone: he had brought his wife Shaine, a frail, slender woman with a wrinkled face. She gazed at her son so lovingly that he felt tears come into his eyes.

"Where can I find some water?" asked Joseph. "I must purify myself before praying."

THREE YEARS WENT BY. Although he now had permission to live in Strasbourg, Berl went on living with his parents in Bischheim. Now and then he spent a night at the Raven Inn; his love life was centered around Jeras, Marx Berr's servant. She had given in to him when he promised to marry her, but first he would have to pay his wife Yente the hundred ducats she still demanded as compensation for a divorce.

His brief amorous interludes with Jeras left his body with the pleasure of reviving desire. He liked the mixture of pride and timidity in her eyes and the rare firmness of her flesh, but he knew he would not marry her and he was already wondering how he could tell her so.

Joseph and Shaine were perfectly content with their life in Bischheim. Jonas Lorenz had hired Joseph to work on the press. He printed few books in Hebrew—only three in three years—but he took great care in publishing *De la réforme politique des Juifs,* the French translation of a work by Christian Wilhelm Dohm* that had been published in Berlin a few years earlier, at Cerf-Berr's expense.

In the evening, after coming back to Bischheim, Joseph often went to visit Leo Kuppenheimer the schoolmaster or Rabbi David Sintzheim, Cerf-Berr's brother-in-law, to discuss a page of the Talmud. He did not yet know if he would settle permanently in Bischheim or return to Zolkiew, where his only grandson, Noah, now almost nine, was living after having been brought back from Königsberg by Yente. Joseph trusted the Almighty, blessed be He, to give him a sign when it was time for him to make a decision.

Meanwhile Berl's landlord, Meyer Bloch, had the unfortunate idea of asking him if he would be willing to marry one of his four daughters: he regarded Berl as a learned man and would have been proud to have him in the family. Berl detested those silly blond girls who still giggled and scuffled with each other as if they were five years old, but for some reason Meyer Bloch's proposition made him realize that their mother, Brintz, with her mature, voluptuous body, her full lips, and her dreamy gray eyes, aroused in him an excitement that he had been trying to repress while at the same time seeking out chances to experience it.

Did Brintz know how he felt? Did she feel the same way? One morning just after Shabuot in the year 5548 [1788] after the creation of the world by the Almighty, blessed be He, when her husband had gone to Metz, Brintz asked Berl to help her with some work she was doing in the house. By the time they finished, the public coach to Strasbourg had already left. She told him she

* A Prussian government official who was one of the precursors of Jewish emancipation. His book was translated into French in 1782 by the mathematician Jean Bernoulli, a member of the Berlin Academy of Science. It inspired Mirabeau's *Sur Moses Mendelssohn ou De la réforme politique des Juifs* (1787).

would take him there in her husband's wagon and he gladly accepted her offer.

On the way, they sat side by side while she held the reins. He sometimes looked at her profile and saw a vein throbbing in her neck. She kept her eyes fixed on the road and the horse, as if she felt that, with the thoughts that had taken possession of her mind, even looking at him would already be a sin. He wondered what color her hair was under the shawl that covered it.

"Since I've made you late," she said abruptly, "I'll take you all the way to Cerf-Berr's house."

"First I have to stop by the Raven Inn to get a book," he lied.

She did not answer. She had not looked at him since they left, but each was so sure of the other's desire that their anticipation was the strongest emotion they would ever share.

BRINTZ'S HAIR, spread over the white sheet, was black. Berl lovingly ran his fingers through it.

"Berl," she said softly. "I must go. . . ."

She had gray eyes, she had smooth, heavy breasts, she had vigorous, responsive legs, and he could not let her leave.

Suddenly they heard the door creaking on its hinges. It took Berl a moment to realize what was happening, then he turned his head. Jeras was standing in the doorway.

"Berl," she said, "you weren't at the print shop, so I thought . . ."

Just then she saw a naked woman beside Berl. Tumult followed: furious shrieks, stamping feet, shouted accusations and insults. Wallraff, the fat innkeeper, laboriously climbed the stairs, came into the room, and asked the three of them to leave. People were standing in the hall, curious to learn who was quarreling, and why. "The Jew was with two women!" a man with a pointed nose said when Berl, Brintz, and Jeras came out of the room. Jeras gave him a resounding slap.

As soon as they were outside, Jeras ran toward the Quai Finckwiller. When she had gone far enough to be sure that Berl could not catch her, she turned around and shouted, "You lied to me! I'll tell the rabbi! I'll tell everybody!"

Berl and Brintz walked to the wagon.

"It will be better if I go back to Bischheim alone," she said in a choked voice. "May God protect you!"

Berl watched the wagon move off toward the city gate. It was a hot day. He felt infinitely weary, as if he were a hundred years old, a man with a long past and little hope. As he was crossing the street in the direction of the river, he wondered if everyone really had his own special destiny and if he himself was fated to be always running away—for, overwhelmed and relieved at the same time, he did not see how he could avoid running away once again.

He wanted to tell Cerf-Berr good-bye and embrace his parents before leaving, he did not know for where.

Cerf-Berr was not at home and Berl regretted it. The last time they had seen each other, they had discussed a magazine that Cerf-Berr wanted to publish. His proposed title for it was *The Jewish Nation*. Berl had remarked that the expression "Jewish nation" seemed to imply that the Jews were unwilling to give up their particularism. Cerf-Berr had replied that they must struggle to obtain French citizenship, but without destroying the cohesion of the Jewish communities.

Though Berl did not find Cerf-Berr, he did find his son. Marx Berr looked at him with a stern expression that he had never seen on his face before.

"This time you've really stirred up a hornets' nest!" he said. "That little fool has told everyone in the community! She wants to take her case to the *beth din,* she's accused me of being a bad influence on you and leading you into debauchery. . . ." He suddenly became calmer and, with the look of a teacher disappointed in his pupil, asked, "But why the mother, Berl? Why the mother and not the daughters?"

Berl smiled sadly and shrugged his shoulders without answering.

"Did you really promise to marry her?"

"Well, I . . ."

"But you're already married!"

"I'm almost divorced."

Marx shook his head.

"You're lucky that the Jews don't kill sinners. Even so, you'd better be careful! Remember what's written in Proverbs: 'Wrath is cruel, anger is overwhelming; but who can stand before jealousy?' "

He suggested that Berl go to Metz and try to work for Abraham Speyer, the printer who had written to him while he was in Königsberg, then come back to Strasbourg when the scandal had been forgotten.

Berl left the garden of Cerf-Berr's estate and went to see his father at Jonas Lorenz's print shop. Joseph already knew about the scandal but he did not reproach Berl for it, because he had learned from Ecclesiastes that "a dream comes with much business, and a fool's voice with many words."

"I'll write to you," said Berl, "and I'd like you to send me my copy of the Book of Abraham. It's in Bischheim, with my other things."

He and Joseph embraced.

Berl made so many detours to avoid passing through places where he was known that he missed the stagecoach to Metz. Since another stagecoach was about to leave for Haguenau, he thought of Rabbi Jacob Guggenheim and decided to go and see him.

THE RABBI of Haguenau was a kindly man with gentle eyes and a sparse white beard that clung to his black caftan. His long gray hair was tied into a pigtail.

"God bless you!" he said to Berl when they had greeted each other. "Have you heard of the essay competition sponsored by the Metz Royal Society of the Arts and Sciences?"

"No," replied Berl, who was thinking of Brintz facing her husband and her four daughters.

"The essays had to be written on this question: 'Is there a way to make the Jews happier and more useful in France?' Here, look at this newspaper. You'll see the names of the winners."

He handed Berl a copy of the *Affiches des Evêchés et de Lorraine* dated August 28, 1788. The winners were Zalkind Hourvitz, a Polish Jew living in Paris; Baptiste-Henri Grégoire, a priest in Embermesnil; and Claude-Antoine Thiérry, a young lawyer in Nancy.

"I've met Zalkind Hourvitz and Baptiste-Henri Grégoire," said Rabbi Guggenheim. "If you should go to Paris, I'll give you Hourvitz's address. He's the most slovenly man I've ever known, but he has a brilliant mind. He lives in a little lodging house on the Rue Saint-Denis, called the Croix-de-Fer."

AND THAT WAS HOW Berl found himself in a stagecoach bound for Paris, with letters of recommendation from Rabbi Guggenheim.

•   •   •

PARIS. . . . I knew Paris before I went there—I had always known it, in fact. My guides had been Hugo, Dumas, Flaubert, Balzac, Eugène Sue. . . . Before I had ever left Warsaw, I could give detailed descriptions of Quasimodo's Notre-Dame; the Rue de Picpus and the Rue Plumet, in the Faubourg Saint-Germain, where Cosette lived; the Rue des Fossoyeurs, near the Luxembourg, where d'Artagnan had his lodgings; the Rue Langlade, where Esther Gobseck lived. I was used to going with Coralie from the Rue de Castellane to the Jardin des Tuileries; following Bouvard on his way to see Pécuchet, from the Rue de Béthune to the Rue Saint-Martin; visiting old Saül and his wife Bethsabée on the Rue Saint-François near the Rue Saint-Gervais, in Les Marais.

In 1945, after having escaped death in the Warsaw ghetto against all likelihood, and after having wandered between the plain of Moscow and the steppes of Kazakhstan, my parents and I found ourselves in Kokand, Uzbekistan. The city was in the grip of famine. My parents fell ill with typhoid fever. I had to get food for them but I did not know how to steal, so in exchange for a little rice I told about Paris to thieves my own age who did not know how to read. We would meet in vacant lots, and there I would evoke my favorite settings: the Place de la Bastille, the Place Royale for the duels of the Three Musketeers . . . I was nine years old.

Five years later I arrived in Paris on a train that stopped at the Gare de l'Est. This was in January 1950; it was cold, and Paris was no longer Paris. The Rue Langlade had given way to the Avenue de l'Opéra, the Rue de Castellane was occupied by a big hotel, and I never found the Rue Saint-François. I had been at home so long in my personal Paris that I felt completely foreign in the Paris that now lay before me, especially since Nazism and Stalinism had not prepared me to live in a free society.

I wandered on the boulevards, carried along by the crowd, looking without understanding at the sidewalk stalls, the nougat sellers, the displays of fruit and vegetables, the vendors of political newspapers, the lighted signs. My double feeling of strangeness—the West was not like the East, and this Paris was not like mine—disturbed me so much that I felt incapable of learning French.

Unable to communicate in words, I began painting. On a little street in Kokand I had come across a painter meticulously putting the finishing touches on a landscape, and that memory had left me with mixed feelings: I was filled with admiration, since the visible could be translated by another visible, but also with uncertainty,

560

since I saw that visible differently. That interplay of colors and forms had been a revelation to me. In Paris, it became my only means of expression.

To earn money for canvas and paint I worked at night in a Yiddish print shop—to my father's great satisfaction—on the Rue Elzévir. During the day I either painted or spent hours in front of Uccello's battle painting in the Louvre. Then I enrolled in the Ecole des Beaux-Arts and gradually drifted into another Paris: the Pont des Arts; Saint-Germain and its cafés, where I went to look at "Sartre's gang"; Montparnasse, the meeting place of painters; the Luxembourg . . . I was finally able to learn French, and it was in French that I again found Paris in the books of Hemingway, Sartre, Fitzgerald, and Proust.

My parents rented a little apartment at the Porte de La Chapelle and I missed none of the demonstrations that went from the Bastille to the République or from the République to the Bastille. Little by little, Paris ceased to be only the Paris of others, and I, the foreigner, finally settled into it, choosing my own reference points, habits, and sidewalks according to the state of things and my mood of the moment.

In preparation for writing about Berl Halter's arrival in Paris, I did some research and discovered that there has always been a Jewish Paris, strangely ignored by guidebooks. For example, the synagogue, described in 582 by Gregory of Tours, that stood on land now occupied by the square in front of Notre-Dame; and the "Court of Jewry," at the present site of the Gare de la Bastille: it was the quarter of the Jews of Paris before their expulsion by Philip Augustus in 1182. In the Middle Ages the Rue de la Harpe was called the Rue de la Harpe Juive [Street of the Jewish Harp], and it was there, during the reign of Louis IX, that Rabbi Yechiel had his famous yeshiva. In that time, the Jewish cemetery was in the area where the Boulevard Saint-Michel crosses the Boulevard Saint-Germain, and gravestones with Hebrew inscriptions were discovered there in the course of the reconstruction work that began in 1849. In the thirteenth century, when Abraham the scribe, son of Yochanan, came from Troyes and saw the Talmud burned at the Place de Grève, the great synagogue was on the Rue de la Cité, where the Sainte-Madeleine Church now stands; it was destroyed after the second expulsion of the Jews from Paris, this time by Philip the Fair, in 1306.

It is hard to retrace the past when all its imprints have been wiped away! I hoped to do better with the Paris of the eighteenth and

561

nineteenth centuries. Another disappointment. I knew from my reading that there had been a Jewish restaurant on the Rue Michelle-Comte; I went there and found only a Chinese restaurant, La Perle d'Orient. On the Rue des Bouchers I looked in vain for the synagogue I had read about, and on the Rue Saint-Denis I had no better luck in my search for the lodging house known as the Croix-de-Fer, where Zalkind Hourvitz had lived.

As if he were emptying his memory to make sure he kept nothing to himself that would be irretrievably lost, shortly before his death my father told me about our ancestor Berl Halter, who had come from Poland and worked in Jacob Simon's print shop on the Rue Montorgueil. Where did my father get that information? His father had given it to him. It did not interest me greatly then, but yesterday I went to the Rue Montorgueil for the first time in years.

My initial impression was that all the people who used to live on the street had moved away and been replaced by others. At number 24, a courtyard—big, uneven paving stones, a dilapidated old staircase—seemed to me a plausible setting for an eighteenth-century print shop. I went into it and looked around. The whole ground floor of the building was occupied by a repository for canned goods. An old woman came down the stairs and eyed me suspiciously.

"Are you looking for something?"

"Yes, a print shop."

"There's no print shop here."

"There used to be one on this street, and I thought it might have been here."

The old woman was perplexed.

"A print shop here? How long ago?"

"During the Revolution."

She seemed relieved: her memory was not playing tricks on her.

"In that case I can't tell you anything about it—I've only been here for sixty years!"

But when Berl Halter came to Paris, fleeing from his women, it was not Jacob Simon's print shop that formed the main setting of his new life: it was the Revolution.

39

PARIS

The Revolution

"LONG LIVE the king! Long live Monsieur Necker! Long live the king!"

The stagecoach had entered Paris through the Charenton Gate and stopped in front of the Hôpital des Enfants-Trouvés, where a public crier was announcing to the assembled crowd that Jacques Necker was returning to the government and that the king had induced the council to convene the parliament.

"Why are they shouting?" Berl asked the man sitting next to him.

"Probably because they think Necker's return will bring down the price of bread."

"It's the price of bread," Zalkind Hourvitz confirmed to Berl a little later, "that controls everything. It sets off public disturbances and makes governments fall. It's now fourteen and a half sous for four pounds. If it goes up one sou, just one sou. . . ." He raised a hand with dirty fingernails. "We'll have a revolution, and no one knows what will come out of it."

Berl had left the stagecoach at the Grand Châtelet, its last stop. Following directions given to him by one of the passengers, he had gone to the Rue Saint-Denis and found the Croix-de-Fer, the ramshackle lodging house where Zalkind Hourvitz lived. Hourvitz's room on the fourth floor was littered with piles of books, newspapers, and magazines surrounding a rickety armchair in which he evidently spent most of his time. He was even more slovenly than Rabbi Guggenheim had said, and probably looked much older than he really was.

After reading Rabbi Guggenheim's letter and examining Berl from head to foot, he asked, "Do you have any money?"

"A little."

"Then you'll invite me to dinner. Do you eat *kosher?*"

"Yes."

"Then we'll go to Meyer Lion's restaurant on the Rue Michel-le-Comte."

It was there, while they ate gefilte fish, that Hourvitz told how he had left Lublin and lived in Berlin—where he met Mendelssohn —Nancy, Metz, and Strasbourg, before coming to Paris three years earlier. His essay, *Apologia for the Jews,* had won a prize in Metz and now he was trying to raise money to have it printed.

In spite of his unprepossessing appearance, he was an interesting and likable man. His French was rich, aggressive, often defective, and spoken with a strong Yiddish accent, but it was in French that he described the current situation and expressed his fear that poverty would drive the common people into some sort of violent action with irreversible consequences. Sitting in Meyer Lion's restaurant, he stuffed himself as if he were eating for several days at once, and Berl realized that he lived on practically no money at all. He had applied for the post of curator of Oriental manuscripts at the Royal Library, but after several weeks he had still received no answer. He offered to share his room and his bed—a straw mattress on which he usually slept fully dressed, under a filthy blanket —with Berl until he found work and rented lodgings of his own.

He took Berl to several Jewish meeting places in Paris, including the Café de la Renommée on the Rue Saint-Martin, where the habitués played dominoes and worried about the health of the world. There Berl met Jacob Simon, a printer whose only employee had just been arrested for shouting "Death to the king!" Simon had to replace him as quickly as possible because orders for pamphlets, lampoons, and new gazettes were pouring in. He gave Berl a two-day trial, then hired him at forty sous a day. It was a rare stroke of luck: thousands of men were trying to find work at that time, and only specialists like Berl had any chance of succeeding. It happened not a moment too soon, because he and Zalkind Hourvitz had not eaten for three days.

Winter was cruel that year, so cold that ice floated in the Seine. The bakers of Paris evaded the parliamentary decree forbidding them to sell bread for more than the price set by the chief of police. All prices continued to rise and living conditions became more and more harsh. Thousands of unemployed men and women, hungry and dressed in rags, gathered outside of bakeries in the hope that a little stale bread would be thrown to them at closing time. When Berl had nothing to share with him, Zalkind went on *shabbat* to the little synagogue on the Rue des Bouchers, which gave food and clothing to those in greatest need. Hordes of grim-faced people, in such desperate straits that their appearance was frightening, came in from the provinces, forced their way past the guards at the gates, and wandered through the city, lighting big fires to warm themselves.

Jacob Simon the printer, who had just joined the Club of Friends of Liberty, said bitterly, "What are they waiting for? They beg in the streets and have to say 'thank you' for watery soup and crusts of bread, when they ought to *take* what they need!"

"Take it from where?" Berl asked naïvely.

"From the rich, of course, since they're the ones who have it!"

Zalkind was completely opposed to Jacob's views. The two men stopped speaking to each other until the convocation of the Estates-General was announced for April 27, with the stipulation that the third estate would have as many deputies as the nobility and the clergy combined. Jacob, satisfied, said it was the beginning of a revolution; and Zalkind, relieved, said it was good that things were going to be done legally.

Berl asked Jacob to increase his wages so that he could rent lodgings for himself. Jacob could not afford to pay him more, but instead he offered to let him live in an attic room above the print shop. Berl was glad to accept the offer, partly because Zalkind's company at night was becoming tiresome to him, and partly because he would now have a place where Marie, a young working woman whose parents lived near the shop, could visit him.

He had become used to his new life and it seemed to him that if he left Paris he would miss its smells, sounds, and colors. He made the best of poverty and hunger without thinking about it too much; he only prayed that he would not have to go without food for more than a day at a time. Jacob's imprecations against the rich and the nobility worried him a little. He began to wonder about the depth of the social problems he saw all around him when Marie's employer, who manufactured wallpaper with the trade name of Réveillon, spoke of reducing his workers' wages to fifteen sous a day. Berl could not decide whether the workers should take drastic action or try to negotiate.

Just then he received a letter from his father in Strasbourg: in his beautiful, serene handwriting, Joseph informed him that Yente and Noah had come there. The Zolkiew community had lent Yente money for the journey and she intended to repay it from the hundred ducats that Berl would give her as compensation for divorcing her. Joseph added that he was not sure he could prevent her from going to Paris.

This letter threw Berl into consternation. He read it to his friends Zalkind and Jacob. As far as Jacob was concerned, the decisions of rabbis had no value whatever, and Yente's claim against Berl was baseless.

"If she comes here to annoy you," he said, "just send her back to Poland!"

Zalkind laughed scornfully and quoted from the Talmud: "Every day I thank God for not having made me a *goy,* a slave, or a woman."

YENTE CAME to Berl's room above the print shop on the evening of April 26. He could not help feeling a kind of admiration for her tenacity. Then he recalled the maxim "Someone who gives in to pity when he ought to resist it will be cruel when he ought to be merciful." He steeled himself to hold firm.

Beside Yente was her son Noah, now ten years old and as tall as she was, wearing clothes too short for his frail arms and legs. As if the scene had been rehearsed in advance, he slowly put down the wicker basket that was their only baggage, then he and his mother stood looking at Berl in silence, like two angels of remorse. Berl had a powerful urge to run away from them, but they were blocking the doorway. Suddenly the silence became unbearable to him.

"Sit down," he said, "and rest. How was your journey?"

"Rest!" Yente spoke in a calm, hard voice that sent a chill up his spine. "Rest? In Zolkiew, we don't know that word. We're not princes. And as for sitting down, I won't do that till you've given me my money."

Noah nodded approvingly.

"Look at this room!" Berl said defensively. "You can see how I live! I have nothing but a bed and a basin, and I don't eat every day!"

"How do people live in this city where women walk around with their bosoms uncovered and give men indecent looks? Do they live on prayers? Promises?"

Yente's tone and accent reminded Berl of his childhood and he could not hide a half-smile. Outraged, she turned to her son.

"You see, Noah? He's smiling! He can't feed his wife and son, but he smiles! He's shameless!"

Something inside her abruptly seemed to relax. She went over to the bed and sat down on it.

"It's not very clean here," she said. "How are we going to sleep?"

Berl thought of Marie; luckily she was not coming that night. He considered going to Zalkind's room and asking him to let him stay there, but he gave up that idea: now that Yente had found him, she would stick to him like a leech. Finally, after sharing the piece of bread he had set aside for the next day, and the piece of dry cheese that Noah took from the wicker basket, the three of them lay down on the bed, with Noah between his parents. It was no doubt the best arrangement, since there was only one blanket.

That night Berl dreamed of the garden of Eden. He was lying under a big tree. Four rivers flowed past, one of milk, one of wine, one of balm, and one of honey, as in the description given by Rabbi Joshua ben Levi, and eight hundred varieties of roses and myrtles grew on their banks. The banquet of Leviathan was about to be served. Angels were preparing to sing in their melodious voices. Then Marie appeared.

"Let my beloved come to his garden, and eat its choicest fruits," she said.

Berl took her in his arms and intense warmth ran through his body. He answered like Solomon in the Song of Songs, "I come to my garden, my sister, my bride. . . ."

At the word *bride* he suddenly awoke. It was still dark. But that flesh, that odor, that grip holding him . . . He leapt out of bed, stood barefoot on the cold floor, looked at the two shapes under the blanket, and realized with horror that he had just made love with his wife! And in the same bed where their son was sleeping! He purified himself and, shivering, prayed till dawn.

When Yente awoke in the morning, she made no allusion to

567

what had happened; she only reproached him for having called out to a woman named Marie in his sleep. What duplicity! How could he have found himself lying beside her if she had not deliberately changed places with Noah?

She said nothing about either staying or leaving. He went downstairs while she and Noah remained in his room.

In the print shop, Jacob was in a state of feverish excitement.

"Come and see, Berl!" he said. "Come and see the Revolution on the march!"

Workers were passing in small groups, heading toward the Faubourg Saint-Antoine. Some of the women were shouting but the men were silent, heavy with their anger. Berl and Jacob went outside and, without consulting each other, began following the workers. Berl saw a clumsily written sign: DEATH TO RÉVEILLON.

"Look, Berl!" said Jacob. "The people are taking things into their own hands! The rich are about to get what's coming to them!"

Berl took him by the arm and they ran to the Réveillon factory. A few dozen soldiers had set up a barrier in front of it but, in spite of their guns, the crowd submerged them like an enormous wave. Almost immediately the windows of the factory opened and spewed out furniture, papers, and merchandise that the crowd seized and destroyed. Berl was frightened by that violence.

"Let's try to find Marie," he said to Jacob.

Then the crowd fell silent, listening to the approaching rumble of trotting horses: the army.

"Fire!" ordered a voice.

The bullets did not disperse the crowd: they only made gaps in it. Bodies lay on the pavement. The infuriated rioters began clinging to the necks of horses, pulling riders from the saddle, disarming them, and turning their own guns against them. They might have routed the soldiers if reinforcements—the Royal-Cravate regiment —had not arrived.

The police reported a hundred and thirty people killed and three hundred and fifty wounded that day. Berl and Jacob found Marie's body; her skull was shattered. Berl asked Jacob to help him carry her to her home, but Jacob said they had to leave her with the other victims from the Réveillon factory: their fellow workers were loading them into wagons, parading them through the streets, and calling out, "Here are the defenders of our country. Give money to have them buried."

Berl picked up Marie's body and, weeping and stumbling, carried her to her mother on the Rue Montorgueil. Then, without going up to his room, he went to Zalkind's.

THE NEXT DAY it was announced that all public gatherings were forbidden in Paris and its suburbs. A little later in the day it was also announced that the king had forbidden the printing and distribution of gazettes and pamphlets without his authorization.

After spending the night in Zalkind's room, Berl went home. He found Yente and Noah sitting on the bed with the wicker basket at their feet.

"We can do without anything except food," said Yente. "Your son and I are about to leave for Strasbourg. But we'll come back when times are better. Don't think I'm forgetting what you owe me, my husband."

It seemed to Berl that her voice was less harsh. Had she found out about Marie? Or was it because of what had happened the night before?

In any case, he was relieved when he saw Yente and Noah disappear at the end of the Rue Montorgueil. If they came back someday, he would then have more time and money to devote to that son who had not said a word to him.

The Estates-General were convened on May 5 at Versailles. Jacob went there, along with thousands of other Parisians, but heard nothing. Afterward, he could only describe the noblemen's whiteplumed hats and black coats adorned with gold cloth. Not until the news was being discussed in the streets did he learn that the two privileged estates had rejected the third estate's request that all three take part in the process of examining the validity of each deputy's election.

Every evening, when they had finished their work, Jacob and Berl went to the Palais-Royal. That was where news, true or false, first began circulating and was discussed most heatedly. What was said in the Café du Foy, the Café de Valois, and the Café de Correza quickly spread all over the city.

On one of those evenings Berl encountered Marx Berr, his friend from Strasbourg, who had come to meet with the deputies to the Estates-General from Alsace and Lorraine, because Jews in those provinces had been authorized to draw up lists of grievances. He threw his arms around Berl and pressed him against his broad chest.

"Our seducer!" he said. "How are you doing with Paris women?"

He spoke loudly. Berl was consumed with embarrassment. He excused himself, said he had to leave, and invited Marx to come and see Jacob Simon, on the Rue Montorgueil, if he had any lists or other texts that he needed to have printed. Marx said he would come, and eventually he did.

It was late June when he visited the print shop. By then, things were well advanced. The deputies of the third estate, considering that they represented ninety-three percent of the nation, had proclaimed themselves the National Assembly and sworn they would not disband until they had given France a constitution. It was said that Mirabeau had reduced the king to silence. In the streets, excitement was rising from day to day.

"What changes, my friends!" said Marx Berr, beaming, as he came into the shop.

He told how Abbé Grégoire had received him the day before and promised that he would soon present a motion in favor of the Jews to the new National Assembly.

"I know things are changing because I've heard deputies talk about us without animosity."

"That means our troubles are all over!" Jacob said sarcastically.

Marx turned to him, looking as if he had been insulted.

"Calm down, my friend. You don't understand anything about politics."

"Oh? And I suppose you—"

"I at least know that to have a motion adopted, a majority of the deputies must vote in favor of it. I also know that the Jews will have no guarantee of safety as long as most of the deputies are hostile to them."

"So says the very important son of the syndic of the Jews of Alsace. I'm only a printer, but I say that the Jews will never have any lasting guarantees except the ones they conquer for themselves."

"Conquer? What's needed is to persuade one people to respect another."

Convinced that Marx and Jacob were both right, each in his own way, Berl hoped that their discussion would not degenerate into a quarrel. But now that revolution was in the air, Jacob had no inclination to present his views with moderation.

"What are you talking about?" he said. "We don't want respect for a people, we want it for *everyone*, all human beings!" He pounded a tabletop with his ink-stained fist and thundered, "We demand respect because we're human!"

Marx gave Berl a look that seemed to ask how he was to cope with this wild fanatic.

"We'll talk about all that again," said Berl, "when the situation has become more stable. Meanwhile, how much longer will you stay in Paris?"

"I'm leaving tomorrow or the day after," replied Marx. "But I'll come back soon. This is where things happen."

"Please tell my father . . ." Berl hesitated. "Tell him . . . that I'm thinking of him."

ALL OVER PARIS there were endless comments on Necker's dismissal, the concentration of troops, and the formation of a ministry, headed by Marshal de Broglie, that was hostile to the revolutionary movement. The French army was harshly criticized. One day, when the Berchiny Hussars were confronted by a crowd that shouted insults at them and then began throwing stones and even firing pistols, the officer in command of the detached battalion lost his self-control and ordered a charge.

News of the clash quickly reached Jacob's print shop when Pierre Sombreil, a paper merchant who had witnessed it, came to make a delivery.

"Was anyone killed?" asked Jacob.

"I saw people fall."

"Then the Revolution is here!" Jacob untied his apron and announced that he was closing for the day. "Come," he said to Berl, "the Jews must be with the people!"

At the densely crowded Palais-Royal they came upon the poet Molina, who always knew about the latest developments, and Jonas Nathan the jeweler, one of those who were always concerned to know if what was happening was "good for the Jews." Molina led them to a young man in a black frock coat who was standing on a table and haranguing the crowd.

"Citizens," he cried, "the Swiss and German battalions are about to leave their camps and attack us! We must defend ourselves! To arms!"

"You're right!"

"Bravo!"

"Death to the Swiss!"

571

"How will we recognize each other?" asked a voice.

"We'll wear cockades," replied the young man in the black coat. "What color shall we choose? The green of hope? The blue of the American democracy?"

"Green!" shouted someone in the growing crowd, and others supported him.

"Yes, green!"

"We choose green!"

The young man took a green ribbon from his coat and attached it to his hat. Then he raised his arm, holding a pistol.

"Who is he?" Jacob asked Molina.

"His name is Desmoulins. He's a lawyer."

"I like him! He knows how to talk!"

Berl saw people taking out green handkerchiefs, ribbons, and scraps of cloth. Those who had nothing green with them took leaves from the linden trees. There was violence in the air, but also a kind of festive excitement.

It was July 12. That evening Berl went to see Zalkind, who had been appointed to the royal secretariat for Oriental languages; since then, he had been waiting to be given work—and money.

Neither the dilapidated staircase of Zalkind's lodging house nor the chaotic litter in his room had changed, and neither had Zalkind himself. He was huddled in his armchair with a blanket over his lap as if it were winter.

"I'm glad to see you," he said. "Do you have any money? Yes? Then take me to Meyer Lion's restaurant and tell me what's happening in the city."

When he came back to the Rue Montorgueil, Berl learned from Jacob that twelve hundred French Guards had surrendered, with their weapons.

"Who was in command of them?" asked Berl.

"No one, my friend, no one. That's how the Revolution is!"

"The Talmud says, 'Pray for the safety of the government, because if it were not for the fear it arouses, men would devour each other.'"

Jacob sneered.

"What an antiquated, idea! It will take a long time to clear such things out of the Jews' minds."

Next morning, Berl was awakened by the insistent ringing of the bells in all steeples. He took time to say the morning prayer; as the course of events became more and more disorderly, observing the ancient rule seemed even more important to him.

Jacob was in the courtyard with a group of excited neighbors. "The people are assembling at the city hall," he solemnly announced to Berl. "We're going there. Print the proclamations for the Club of Friends of Liberty and then join us."

Berl had almost finished his work when a traveler from Strasbourg came to the print shop with a letter for Berl Halter. Berl recognized his father's handwriting.

"Where's the Revolution?" asked the man.

"This morning," replied Berl, "it was at the city hall."

In his letter, Joseph said that Marx Berr had given him news of Berl and that he was glad to know he was doing well and still had work. He then said that Brintz had been forgiven and Jeras had married, so Berl could come back to Strasbourg whenever he chose. Yente and Noah were still living there. Joseph had taken Noah into the print shop to work with him: at ten, a Polish boy was almost a man.

There was something unusual in the tone of this letter and Berl was worried by it. He decided to go to Strasbourg as soon as possible.

He finished his work, left the shop, and nearly collided with Jacob, who was hurrying toward him in a state of great agitation, wearing a blue-and-red cockade.

"At last you're coming out into the street! You should have been there long ago!"

"What's happening?"

"The people have just formed a standing committee. Its chairman is Flesselles, the mayor. A bourgeois guard is going to be—" Jacob stopped short and stared at Berl. "You're not wearing a cockade! You'll be arrested!"

They worked until darkness forced them to stop: Jacob could not afford to buy candles or even oil for the lamps. Although he had many orders for posters, proclamations, lists, and programs, most of his customers were unable to pay and, in the name of the Revolution, he was bringing himself closer to total ruin every day.

Berl got up at dawn but Jacob had already gone. Customers soon began coming into the shop, one after another. They improvised texts to be printed on posters and signs, exchanged wild stories that they had gathered here and there, and sometimes sat down at the corner of a table to write a new proclamation on the basis of what they had just heard. Berl worked without interruption.

It seemed well established that the Hôtel des Invalides had been invaded and that the crowd had seized thousands of guns. Shots were heard now and then.

"They're at the Bastille!" shouted someone in the street. "Everyone to the Bastille!"

Jacob's wife came down to the shop and announced that she was going to the Bastille. It was not clear to Berl whether she intended to help take the fortress or wanted to bring back her husband. He went on working, feeling that in his own way he too was taking part in the Revolution.

He did not leave the shop until evening. He was so tired that his back ached and spots danced before his eyes. On the Rue Montorgueil, he was jostled by a band of urchins armed with sticks.

"Come with us, citizen!" one of them said to him. "The Bastille has fallen!"

The air smelled of gunpowder and smoke. Berl walked to the city hall, passing groups of men and women who carried bloody heads at the end of pikes and appeared to be going somewhere in a great hurry.

He was caught up in the crowd. There were shouts, the acrid smell of sweat, movements in all directions, and a kind of madness that seemed to be stimulated by the roll of drums. Orators were being either cheered or booed. Berl heard one of them say, "Your first thought is for revenge, when it ought to be for humanity!" He tried to see who was speaking, but he was swept away by a current in the crowd.

"If our friend Jonas were here," said a voice behind him, "he'd ask if all this is good for the Jews."

It was the poet Molina, wearing two cockades, one on his hat and the other over his chest.

"Have you seen Jacob Simon?" Berl asked him.

"He's making the Revolution! I saw him leave for the print shop with a list of men to be eliminated."

"Eliminated?"

Molina passed the edge of his hand across his throat.

"The whole upper nobility!"

As soon as he could escape from the throng pressing in on him from all sides, Berl walked to the boulevards, which were strangely calm. People were going about their business, cabs and wagons were carrying passengers and merchandise. It was as if he were in another city.

But when he reached the print shop he found more tumult. Armed men—he recognized several members of the Club of Friends of Liberty—were frenziedly arguing about the text of a poster, on the verge of fighting over commas.

"Ah, you've finally come back!" Jacob said when he saw Berl. "You're never there when the people need you!"

Berl felt like answering that he was not at the people's beck and call, but he said nothing and put on his apron.

That same evening a group of Jews held a meeting in the shop to decide if they would take action in the name of the community. Molina was there, along with representatives of the various Jewish associations in Paris. Zalkind, also present, declared that he represented only himself.

The most vehement was Jacob Goldsmidt, a frail, pallid man of Dutch origin.

"In this country," he said emphatically, "we've been given only duties—let's demand that we also be given some rights!"

"What rights shall we ask for, Monsieur Goldsmidt?" ventured a fat man with a blond beard.

"Not 'ask,' Monsieur Trenelle. Demand."

"We're not in a position to demand anything," said Abraham Lopez Lagouna, the representative of the Portuguese. "Who would listen to us?"

"I propose," replied Goldsmidt, "that we write a petition to the National Assembly in the name of all Jews living in Paris."

A committee was formed, with Goldsmidt as chairman and Abraham Lopez Lagouna as vice-chairman. Their first task would be to discuss the matter with the various Jewish communities in Paris and have them choose the members of a delegation that would take the petition to Versailles. Berl asked Zalkind to write a preliminary version of the text. Zalkind thanked his friend with a smile; it was perhaps the first time Berl had ever seen him smile. Toward midnight the men left the print shop, feeling that they had taken the first step toward accomplishing something of great importance.

But the Jews of Paris had their hopes badly shaken a few days later, when they learned that in Alsace the Jews had been the main targets of public disturbances. Elsewhere, anger was directed against noblemen, priests, and representatives of royal power, but in Alsace it was directed against the Jews: synagogues defiled, houses destroyed, proofs of debt burned. Hundreds of Jews fled to Basel, where, it was said, the authorities were taking up collections of money to help them.

Berl was filled with anxiety. He was wondering if he should go back to Strasbourg when Marx Berr, having come to Paris with a delegation of Alsatian Jews to ask for the king's protection, reassured him: his family was safe in Switzerland. Berl thought of his father and was relieved. Then he thought of his son and was unhappy.

THE FALL OF THE Bastille had dealt a hard blow to the monarchy. Necker was recalled. Bailly became the mayor of Paris and Lafayette took command of the National Guard. White was added to the blue and red of the cockade. But hunger remained. The men who came to the print shop sometimes joked about that terrible hunger, as a way of helping themselves to bear it.

In the streets, patrols arrested passersby on the slightest pretext. Jacob knew a baker who had nearly been hanged because his bread was not white enough. People who did menial work—water carriers, day laborers, porters, bootblacks—took revenge for their poverty. On August 5 there was exuberant rejoicing at the news that a law (proposed by a viscount) abolishing all privileges had been passed. All Frenchmen were now equal.

On August 22 Count de Castellane proposed a motion to the Assembly: "No one shall be molested because of his religious opinions." This was at last an opportunity to broach the subject of rights for Jews. The next day, Jacob got a copy of a speech by Rabaut-Saint-Etienne and printed part of it as a poster: "I therefore ask, gentlemen, for French Protestants and all other non-Catholics in the kingdom, what you ask for yourselves: freedom and equality of rights. I ask it for that people driven out of Asia, who for nearly eighteen centuries have been always wandering, always ostracized, always persecuted. If our laws made them an integral part of our society, they would adopt our ways and customs. We have no right to condemn their morality, because it is a product of our own barbarity and the humiliation to which we have unjustly subjected them."

"That was written by someone who wishes us well but doesn't know us!" Zalkind remarked when he had read the text.

"What's wrong with it?" Jacob asked as if he had been personally attacked.

"Our morality isn't a product of anyone's barbarity," answered Zalkind. "Barbarity has only reinforced our tendency to transgress our morality. But let's overlook that and be grateful to Rabaut-Saint-Etienne for his good intentions."

He was holding the Jews' petition to the National Assembly that he had been asked to write. He read it aloud to the two or three hundred people gathered in the print shop and the courtyard.

"We like to believe," he began, "and it is doubtless true, that your justice has no need to be solicited or influenced by our wishes." He spoke in a loud, firm voice, without hesitation, and his Yiddish accent seemed more pronounced than ever. "In restoring man to his original dignity and the enjoyment of his rights, you have intended to make no distinction between one man and another. That title belongs to us as it does to all other members of society. The rights that it implies also belong to us."

There was a sprinkling of applause, then a man named Joseph Pereyra Brandon proposed stressing the idea that the Jews belonged to the French nation.

"But that goes without saying!" exclaimed Jacob Goldsmidt.

"We must make sure we don't give the impression that we didn't consider ourselves French till now."

After a long discussion, the words suggested by Trenelle the elder were added: "We are French. There is a mistaken tendency among the people to regard us as foreign to the nation."

The petition was presented to the National Assembly three days later, on August 26, the day when the Declaration of the Rights of Man and Citizen was adopted.

The next day, Marx Berr came to the print shop once again, having just arrived from Strasbourg, and asked to see a copy of the petition. When he had read it and expressed approval, he told Berl that the situation of the Jews in Strasbourg had improved so much that his family had returned from Switzerland. Then he added, "Ah, yes, I was forgetting: your wife is pregnant. Congratulations! It's obvious that your mistresses aren't enough for you!"

He laughed heartily, as if Berl were the hero of a racy adventure.

40

STRASBOURG-PARIS

Leopoldine

IT TOOK time for news to reach Strasbourg from Paris, and the delay made it possible to take a calmer view of events and developments: the king compelled to return to Paris, nationalization of Church lands, division of the country into *départements,* the Civil Constitution of the Clergy, the flight of the king, the Champ-de-Mars massacre, the king's acceptance of the Constitution . . .

Two years had passed since the taking of the Bastille and the presentation of the Jews' petition to the National Assembly. Berl had gone back to Strasbourg as soon as he learned that Yente was pregnant. He was sure she had not made love with another man and that the child had been conceived during that night in his room on the Rue Montorgueil when he had dreamed of the garden of Eden. And so he went back, but without knowing exactly why—was he finally willing to accept his responsibilities, or did he only want to avoid having his father lose all respect for him? In any case, he had to face the fact that the woman he wanted to divorce was going to give him another child.

Joseph and Shaine, his parents, gave him a warm welcome; Yente, as usual, greeted him with complaints: he had taken a long time to come back, she said. She was living next door to Joseph and Shaine, in Bischheim, near the *yeshiva* and just across the street from Brintz's house. Cerf-Berr, who now seemed much older to Berl, agreed to let him work in the print shop again and live in one of the attic rooms, with the servants.

The child was born in the winter of the year 5550 [1790] after the creation of the world by the Almighty, blessed be He, and was named Lazare, after his maternal grandfather. Noah, already eleven, was working halfheartedly in the print shop. He kept asking to be told about Zolkiew and said he would go back there as soon as he was old enough.

Joseph had no intention of leaving France: things of crucial importance to the future of the whole human race were happening there. He kept newspaper clippings of speeches on the subject of the Jews, such as the one made by Robespierre to the Assembly, which he almost knew by heart: "You have been told things about the Jews that are enormously exaggerated and often contrary to history. How can they be reproached for the persecutions inflicted on them by various peoples? Those are national crimes, which we must expiate by giving them back the indefeasible human rights that no human power was entitled to abolish. Vices, prejudices, sectarianism, and a mercenary outlook are imputed to the Jews. Such imputations are exaggerated. But to what can those things be rightfully imputed, if not to our own injustices?"

Joseph tried to forget the hostile speeches, full of hatred, accusations, and suspicion. He was overjoyed when he learned that on September 27, 1791, the National Assembly had emancipated the Jews of Alsace, Lorraine, and Les Trois-Evêchés.

"Just think of it: I'm a citizen of a country!" he said to Berl and Shaine.

At the beginning of the next *shabbat*—Berl came to Bischheim every Friday—Joseph raised his glass to drink to life and to the Revolution. Yente then said, "But if the poor take everything from the rich, the rich will be poor, and it will all have to be done over again."

Joseph smiled in his beard and answered with a quotation from the Chapters of the Fathers: "There are four types of character among men. He who says, 'What is mine is mine and what is yours is yours.' He who says, 'What is mine is yours and what is yours is mine'; he is a boor. He who says, 'What is mine is yours and what is yours is yours'; he is a saint. He who says, 'What is yours is mine and what is mine is mine'; he is a scoundrel."

After a few moments of thoughtful silence, he asked Yente, "Do you believe that the Almighty will allow boors and scoundrels to triumph for very long?"

That autumn of 1791 was cold and foggy. Innkeepers and tavernkeepers hung lanterns above their doors. No one knew what the future would be like, but life went on.

Berl and Marx went to two or three meetings of the Society of Friends of the Constitution. At the end of one of those meetings, while the participants were slowly leaving, Berl saw Marx talking with two young men and a young woman. She was . . . Berl could not have described her, but the sight of her almost made his heart stop beating. And when he saw her walk away with the two men, he felt as if something had been torn from inside him.

The next day, trying to seem casual, he questioned Marx about the two men he had been talking with the night before.

"They were Junius Frey and his brother Emmanuel," replied Marx. "It's said that they're German gentlemen and that love of the Constitution has made them come to France to enjoy the rights of French citizens. That may be true, but I think it's also true that they're Jews. . . . Why do you . . . ?" He looked at Berl closely. "Berl, my friend, are you interested in the Frey brothers or in their sister?"

"Their sister?" Berl echoed.

Marx grinned broadly and slapped his thigh.

The Freys lived in a town house on the Rue des Serruriers, near the building where the Friends of the Constitution held their meetings. Berl began walking past it often, in the hope of seeing the young woman.

One day Marx brought Junius Frey and his sister to the print shop, showed them around it, and asked Berl to give them a demonstration of typesetting. Berl followed his usual practice of making souvenirs for visitors to the shop: he asked Junius Frey for the spelling of his name, took out the letters, placed them in his composing stick, secured the line of type in a galley, inked it, and put a sheet of paper over it. After brushing the paper, he picked it up and showed Junius Frey his name printed on it.

The young woman clapped her hands.

"Please print my name too!" she said.

Berl looked at her without moving.

"You don't want to do it?" she asked.

"I don't know your name."

"It's Leopoldine Frey."

580

For her, he chose an italic type that seemed to him more in keeping with her femininity. *Leopoldine Frey.* She was delighted and thanked him with a smile. His inner turmoil blurred his sight. Only when she and her brother were about to leave was he able to see her clearly: she was very young and had almond-shaped hazel eyes, a slender waist, and high breasts whose shape was molded by her close-fitting dress. She seemed to be part woman and part child, both innocent and sophisticated.

Berl did not put away the line of type that composed her name. That evening, when he was alone in the shop, he took the line *Leopoldine Frey,* inked it, and pressed it against the smooth skin on the inside of his wrist, under his sleeve. Then he opened his shirt and also printed the line over his heart. *Leopoldine Frey Leopoldine Frey Leopoldine Frey.* In the evening silence, it was as if he were calling out her name.

He continued going to the Rue des Serruriers every day. Once he saw her leaving her house. She came toward him.

"You're Marx Berr's printer, aren't you? I recognize you. Why are you here?"

"I come every day, hoping to see you."

She laughed briefly, then her face became serious.

"Are you in love with me?"

He answered with a fatalistic shrug.

Something new was happening to him. Leopoldine was sixteen, he was thirty-one—nearly twice her age—and there were vast social differences between them, yet he was confident that she would eventually share his love, and meanwhile he was not unhappy or even impatient. He went on walking past her house every day. If he saw her, he was elated; if he did not, he consoled himself with the thought that maybe tomorrow . . .

The following spring, 1792, when General Dumouriez had been placed at the head of a Girondist ministry and France had declared war on Austria, the city was shaken by the trial of Jean-Charles Laveaux, editor of the *Courrier de Strasbourg,* the organ of the local Jacobins. He was accused of having "defamed the constituted authorities" and of having "incited to murder and civil war" at a meeting of the Society of Friends of the Constitution.

Junius Frey was his most ardent defender. And when Laveaux was acquitted a month later, Frey gave the Jacobins of Strasbourg the handsome sum of sixteen and a half louis in gold and four hundred livres in assignats to have twenty medals struck for those who had supported his friend.

But so much hostility had been aroused on both sides that Laveaux decided to leave Strasbourg, and the Freys decided to go with him. Berl learned of it from a note that a stranger delivered to him at the print shop. He broke open the seal and saw childish handwriting that was unknown to him: "Dear Berl Halter, we are leaving for Paris this afternoon. I am curious to know that city, after having heard so much about it. If you come there, be sure to pass by my windows. I will be glad to see you. Leopoldine."

BERL ARRIVED IN PARIS on August 10. It had taken him more than two months to save up a little money, which he divided between his wife and the stagecoach. Yente had thanked him in her fashion: "Leaving your wife alone with *one* child wasn't enough for you, was it? Now you have to leave your wife alone with *two* children!"

"I'll come back to teach Lazare to read. And we'll celebrate Noah's *bar mitzvah.*"

Berl firmly believed in his promises, even though he had no idea what his stay in Paris would be like. But mainly he was counting on his father to keep an eye on things, help Yente, and teach the Torah to Noah.

After getting off the stagecoach in Paris, he began walking toward the Rue Montorgueil. It was a hot day. The insurrection seemed to have taken over the whole neighborhood. A woman wearing a red cap was brandishing a saber and demanding that everyone follow her. People were hurrying along the streets in groups, shouting vociferously.

"To the Tuileries!"

"Down with the tyrant!"

"Long live the nation!"

"Long live freedom!"

The crowd thinned out as Berl moved away from the Seine. The Rue Montorgueil was deserted. Jacob Simon laughed when he saw him.

"Just like a Pole! When a Pole says he'll be back in ten days, he may show up a year later!"

He wiped his hands and embraced Berl. He was thinner now, probably not only from hunger but also from overwork and lack of sleep.

"I'm happy to have you back," he said. "I need your help: I'm up to my ears in work."

"On my way here," said Berl, "I saw a big crowd that seemed to be heading for the Tuileries."

"The Tuileries? And we're standing here talking? Let's go!"

Jacob dashed out of the print shop and Berl followed him. They soon heard gunfire: there was fighting at the Tuileries.

"The palace is burning!"

"Long live the nation!"

Berl was separated from Jacob by the swirling crowd. He was about to turn back when he met the inevitable Molina. The poet was covered with dust and a tricolored cockade dangled precariously from his hat.

"You're back in Paris!" he exclaimed. Then, since a man in wooden shoes and a red cap was watching them, he shouted, "Long live Marat! Down with the tyrant!"

"I'm looking," said Berl, "for a man named Junius Frey who came here from Strasbourg a little more than two months ago. I think he's a Jew."

Molina led him a short distance away, reached into his coat pocket, and took out a rumpled cockade.

"Here, put this on and no one will bother us. . . . Junius Frey was born in Moravia. I've been told that he comes from a Jewish family who converted to Catholicism and were ennobled by the emperor."

"What's he doing in Paris?"

"The same as everyone else: he's making the Revolution."

"And where does he live?"

"Rue d'Anjou, Faubourg Honoré."

They were jostled by a dense troop of men and women.

"The king is at the Assembly! Everyone to the Assembly!"

"May the Almighty protect us," Molina said quietly. "I think the times are about to change."

BERL TOOK BACK HIS room above the print shop. The next morning he left his work for an hour to go to the Faubourg Honoré. New posters announced new laws: one authorized the arrest of presumed conspirators, another ordered the release of people imprisoned for slandering the king, the queen, and Lafayette. On the Rue d'Anjou, in answer to Berl's question, a woman pointed out the luxurious house that Junius Frey had rented. He went to it and identified himself to the servant at the door as "Berl Halter, Marx Berr's printer."

The servant left, came back a short time later, and said ceremoniously, "Citizen Junius Frey will be glad to receive you, citizen."

He led Berl through long halls decorated with busts of Lucius Junius Brutus and Cicero and paintings of Benjamin Franklin, Jean-Jacques Rousseau, and Voltaire. Finally they came to a big, sparsely furnished room where Leopoldine's brother sat at a table with a pen in his hand.

He stood up. He was dressed in revolutionary style: black dress coat with short lapels and flared tails, cassimere breeches, top boots, red cap. He was young and handsome but his piercing eyes made his visitor uneasy. Berl could not help thinking of an angel of death.

"Citizen Berl! Welcome! What brings you here?"

Outside the window, a tree was slowly stirring in the wind.

"I'd like to see Leopoldine."

"Leopoldine? Why?"

"Perhaps to marry her," Berl answered naïvely.

Junius Frey impatiently took a few steps.

"She's told me that in Strasbourg you walked past our house every day."

"That's not forbidden, is it?"

Berl vaguely sensed a kind of weakness in Frey. Weakness usually aroused his sympathy, but in this case he felt something close to repugnance.

"Leopoldine is engaged," Frey said curtly.

This news left Berl strangely calm.

"Is it true that your family was Jewish?" he asked.

"Yes. My name was originally Moses Dobruska. My family converted in Vienna. I was ennobled and I then became Franz Thomas von Schönfeld. Now I'm Junius Frey, a revolutionary."

"Why all those names?" asked Berl.

Frey turned toward the window. The tree moving in the wind seemed to bear witness to some sort of eternity.

"Moses," he said as though to himself, "the great Moses, our teacher, covered truth with a thick veil that has lasted into our own time. It's our duty, as free men, to tear away that veil." He turned back to Berl. "Promise me that you won't try to see Leopoldine again."

"I won't give you a promise that I couldn't keep."

584

"Then whatever happens will be your own fault!"

That evening Berl was arrested at the print shop, on the denunciation of a revolutionary committee. He was accused of carrying on an illicit correspondence with émigrés in Austria. Letters from his father, written in Yiddish, were found in his room, and they were taken as evidence in support of the accusation. As Berl was being led away, Jacob stood watching from the doorway of the print shop with his arms hanging at his sides, opening and closing his mouth like a fish out of water: he no longer felt at home in his Revolution.

In spite of everything that Jacob and Zalkind could do, Berl spent six months in Les Ecossais, the prison on the Rue des Fossés-Victor. Finally the citizen commissioner, a man named Teyssier, established that no criminal activity could be imputed to Citizen Berl Halter and that he evidently had a sincere wish to regenerate society; as for the letters found in his room, translation had revealed that they contained nothing contrary to the virtues of the Revolution. Berl was released on February 19, 1793.

During his imprisonment, he had learned of the proclamation of the Republic, the September massacres, the victories at Valmy and Jemmapes, and the execution of the king, and he had regarded those events as so many wrinkles in the face of history. He, too, had aged. He was thin, his hair had turned white at his temples, and he had almost stopped speaking. But he had never let himself become disheartened. Two flames had continued to burn inside him, making him want to go on living: his love for Leopoldine and his hatred of Junius.

After leaving Les Ecossais he wandered at random through the city. It was raining. He walked until he became tired, looking at the faces of the people he passed as if he were trying to read the future in them. Then he went to the print shop, where Jacob embraced him. They both wept.

"It was high time you came back, you sinner!" said Jacob. "We have work to do!"

SIX MONTHS LATER, after the creation of the Committee of Public Safety, the arrest of the Girondists, the referendum that ratified the Constitution of the Year I, and the compulsory loan, it became clear that the Revolution was far from being finished. Jacob and Berl spent most of their time at the shop, and they tried to distinguish the true from the false in everything they printed.

Junius Frey was now an important member of the Jacobin Club. He had published a book, *L'Antiféderaliste,* and become a close friend of Danton. Another of his friends was a former Capuchin monk named François Chabot, a fiery orator who was always ready for any kind of violence. In September, Chabot married Leopoldine.

Junius Frey's rapid rise had inevitably aroused hostility. Rumors had begun circulating: that Austrian was an enemy agent and he had bribed Chabot to work with him. . . . Berl was certain that Frey's downfall was only a matter of time.

On October 20, four days after the execution of the queen, he learned from the newspapers that Chabot had been censured by the Convention for having married a foreign woman.

"That's the end of him," Jacob told Berl. "And only a month ago he was regarded as 'the greatest Frenchman after Robespierre'!"

"You've changed too," remarked Berl.

Jacob bristled.

"I've changed? No, it's the Revolution that's changed! It used to inspire hope, and now it arouses only fear."

Each day the guillotine beheaded a new batch of suspects. The executioner's voluntary helpers threw the bodies into bloody carts and took them off to be buried in common graves.

"Why do you say it's the end of Chabot?" asked Berl.

"Because Robespierre won't miss a chance to get rid of Danton's friends. Nowadays, marrying an Austrian woman is a political mistake. Even for François Chabot."

A week later, Chabot was excluded from the Society of Friends of the Constitution. Berl followed the accelerating course of events with a chill in his heart.

When Chabot's trial began, it was said that the Freys had wanted him to marry into their family only so that they could use him to achieve their goal. The *Mercure universel* and the *Annales de la République française* published biographies of the Austrian brothers. An anonymous article accused Junius Frey of having been "employed for espionage by Emperor Joseph II, who knew that the children of Israel surpass all other nations in that trade."

At the beginning of November, those whom Robespierre accused of corruption, debauchery, or antirevolutionary subversion —Jacobins like himself—were arrested. Chabot was detained in the Luxembourg, Junius and Emmanuel Frey in the Fort-Libre prison. Leopoldine Chabot was taken to Les Anglaises, where Berl tried in vain to visit her. When she was released a month later, Berl hurried to her house on the Rue d'Anjou, but he was refused admittance. He wrote a letter and took it to the house the next morning. A week later he received a note in reply: "Thank you, Berl, for your kind and sympathetic words. My only desire is that my brothers and my husband be saved from execution. They are innocent. I hope that the Revolution will be as magnanimous to them as it is just and strong. Leopoldine." The note was not sealed and Berl preferred to believe that it was intended primarily to be read by the police.

On April 3, 1794, the "plotters"—Chabot, Frey, Danton, Camille Desmoulins, Fabre d'Eglantine, and their friends—were tried before the Convention. Two days later they were sentenced to death.

"HERE they are!"

In the Place de la Révolution, carts made their way through the enormous crowd that had gathered hours earlier to wait for the day's executions. The onlookers had been eating, drinking, and singing *"Ça ira"* and the "Marseillaise." They had struggled against each other to get the best places because they all wanted to have a good view of the spectacle, especially since the list of names announced that morning contained those of Danton, Chabot, Desmoulins, and Frey, names that were known to everyone and had once been spoken with fear.

Berl was too far away from the scaffold to see it well, but that did not matter to him. He did not know why he was there at all, in fact; he knew only that some dark force had made him come.

People were still pouring in from the Rue Honoré and the Rue Nationale. The crowd had become so compact that it seemed to be a single immense body, with one heart and one voice.

"Here they are!"

The carts passed near the place where Berl was standing. He recognized Danton, Camille Desmoulins, and Junius Frey. He closed his eyes.

A formidable cry burst from the entrails of the crowd.

"Long live the Republic!"

The procession had now reached the foot of the scaffold. Things began happening rapidly. A man stood on the platform, a kind of struggle took place, and the executioner raised his arm, holding a head by the hair.

"Hurrah for Samson!" someone shouted.

Samson was the executioner.

"And hurrah for Jacot!" shouted someone else.

Jacot was the sweeper, whose bloody broom was famous.

Each time the blade fell, the crowd was shaken by a spasm. Suddenly a voice beside Berl whispered in Hebrew, "And behold, the tears of the oppressed, and they had no one to comfort them! On the side of their oppressors there was power, and there was no one to comfort them." It was Molina, quoting from Ecclesiastes. When Junius Frey appeared on the scaffold, Berl had a taste of ashes in his mouth and he recited the *kaddish*, the prayer for the dead. "May His great name be magnified and sanctified in the world that He created according to His will. . . ."

He went back to his room on the Rue Montorgueil, picked up the Book of Abraham, and opened it. "May the names that I have written on this scroll, and the names that others will write on it after me, be spoken aloud to rend the silence. Holy, holy, holy, You are the Almighty. Amen."

Berl Halter, a French citizen, realized that his place was with his father and his sons. He said good-bye to Jacob, gave him a letter for Leopoldine, and went off to take the evening stagecoach to Strasbourg.

41

STRASBOURG-WARSAW

The Rights of the Jews

STRASBOURG ALSO knew the disappointment, suspicion, and terror in which the Revolution ended. When Cerf-Berr died, he had to be buried furtively at Rosenwiller. Marx Berr was thrown into prison. The Revolutionary Tribunal had daily sessions in a room of the city hall, formerly the Rohan palace. A guillotine had been erected in the Place d'Armes. Old Joseph was indignant at the closing of places of worship.

"They promised," he said, "that no one would be molested because of his religious opinions." He pointed menacingly at the city hall. "Anyone who profanes the name of God or His house will be punished!"

Afraid to go back to the room that Cerf-Berr had let him use during his last stay in Strasbourg, Berl went to Bischheim and settled into the house where his wife and sons lived. Yente accepted this without surprise, as if it had been destined to happen since the beginning of time. Noah, now fifteen and taller than Berl, looked at him with indifference and intimidated him. But Berl liked Lazare, a serious child with an active, curious mind. He was four—already! How was it possible?—and as blond as his brother was dark. He asked Berl if he was his father. Berl began teaching him to read that same day.

Berl found work in Jonas Lorenz's print shop on the Rue des Petites-Arcades. Joseph and Noah still worked in Marx Berr's shop, but it had been requisitioned by the Revolutionary Committee. The three of them went into Strasbourg each morning, by coach, and came back the same way at the end of the day. Far away from the frenzy of Paris, with his heart numb, Berl led a more or less peaceful life.

YEARS PASSED, bringing events and changes. The captive balloon, the velocipede, and the semaphore telegraph appeared. And Napoleon came. A new national adventure was beginning.

In Bischheim, Berl now lived alone with his son Lazare. Joseph and Shaine had died of old age, after cautioning Berl not to be taken in by Napoleon's dreams of grandeur. The intractable Yente had waited till Lazare celebrated his *bar mitzvah,* then gone back to Zolkiew with Noah, who had never stopped wanting to return there. Berl had asked her if she would ever come back to Bischheim. She had answered that she did not know, and that now it was his turn to live with the bitterness of waiting in uncertainty.

She had not come back and Berl did not miss her; his son was enough to fill his life. He remembered something that Joseph had once said to him: "The world's existence depends on schoolboys. We have no right to suspend their education, even to rebuild the Temple. A city where there are no schoolboys will be destroyed." He had tried to give Lazare a taste for study—and his own interest in it had revived—but it was Rabbi David Sintzheim, head of the nearby *yeshiva,* who had taught him, before going off to sit in the Paris Sanhedrin, a kind of administrative assembly of the Jewish nation that was one of Napoleon's innovations.

When Lazare was fourteen, Rabbi Guggenheim, visiting Bischheim from Haguenau, complimented him on the extent of his knowledge. Lazare modestly replied with a quotation: "If you have acquired great knowledge of the Torah, take no credit for it, because it is that for which you were created." He seemed to be directly inspired by the souls of Abraham, Isaac, and Jacob, and when Berl recalled the circumstances of his conception he could not believe that he had dreamed of the garden of Eden only by chance.

Lazare became a highly skilled printer and he could no doubt have become a renowned scholar of the Law. But in those years the emperor needed many men, more and more men, for his wars.

Young villagers shouted, "Long live the emperor!" as they went off to fight for him. Berl looked at his son and lived in fear. One evening he read to him a passage from Hosea: "And I will make for you a covenant on that day with the beasts of the field, and the birds of the air, and the creeping things on the ground; and I will abolish the bow, the sword, and war from the land; and I will make you lie down in safety."

Berl had never been as happy as he now was with his son. He tried to teach him whatever lessons could be drawn from his own aimless life, which had been shaped primarily by two Austrians: the one he had killed in Zolkiew and the one he had seen beheaded in Paris.

"No king, emperor, or idea," he said, "is worth killing or dying for."

"It is written," replied Lazare, "that 'he who saves one human being saves the whole world, and he who causes one death must be condemned as if he had destroyed the world.'"

Napoleon still needed new conscripts. In his edict of March 17, 1808, which became known as the "Infamous Decree," he had forbidden Jews to buy replacements for themselves. Berl urged Lazare to leave France and go to live in another country; America, for example, where it was said that Jews could become rich almost as soon as they arrived. But Lazare refused: France had given him citizenship, he said, and he had to take his chances in the conscription lottery, like everyone else. He drew a bad number and was assigned to the fifty-seventh regiment of the Grand Army.

On the day of Lazare's departure, Berl read passages from the Book of Abraham to him in a choked voice, then gave him his copy of it. It was the last one, since Joseph's copy had been given to Noah, who showed little interest in it. If Lazare dies on a battlefield, thought Berl, I'll never have any more names to write in this book and there will be no reason for me to keep it, but if anything can protect him from an ugly, senseless death, it will be this ancient record of our survival in spite of torments and disasters. He also gave him a *siddur* that had belonged to Joseph.

Berl followed his son's regiment as far as the Rhine and came back weeping. It was June 7, 1813, by the Christian calendar; that is, in the year 5573 after the creation of the world by the Almighty, blessed be He.

591

NAPOLEON WANTED TO AVENGE his humiliating retreat from Moscow, but Prussia, Austria, Russia, and Sweden had assembled nearly a million men to oppose him. The bulk of the French army had been immobilized for the winter near Leipzig, while part of it had been able to reach Dresden. A few regiments, including Lazare's, had advanced as far as Görlitz. Berl knew all this from the newspapers. But he was waiting for a letter to tell him if his son was cold or hungry, if he needed shoes or warm clothes. He waited so long for that letter, nearly seven months, that he was surprised when it finally arrived.

Do not blame me, father, but a man has died because of something I did. I had sworn to respect the commandment "You shall not kill," even at the cost of my own life, but the Almighty decided otherwise. We were in a forest. It was cold and the branches of trees were breaking from the weight of the ice on them. The Russians and the Prussians were coming toward us. Our officer deployed us and ordered us to charge. I will never forget those men's battle cries. We began running. Suddenly I found myself face to face with a young Prussian. He aimed his gun at me. Thinking I was about to die, I called out, *"Shema Yisrael!"* His expression changed and he answered with the same words: *"Shema Yisrael!"* The man beside me thought I was still in danger. He thrust his bayonet into the Prussian's heart. I saw him die, father. Blood came from his mouth and nose. The attack went on. I vomited. I had caused a man's death. Why did it have to be that he was also a Jew? I left the regiment and ran until I no longer heard the cannons and drums. I nearly died of cold during the night. In the morning I met a patrol from the Polish army; of all the emperor's allies, the Poles are the only ones who are still loyal to him. I said I had lost my way. They gave me food, took me with them across the frozen Nysa Luzycka River, and left me in a village named Zgorzelec. One of the Jews in the village told me I looked like his grandson, who was somewhere in the army, and invited me into his house. His name is Wolf and he is a saintly man. I do not know if I will stay here very long, because I am now a deserter, but I will write to you again. Meanwhile, I will pray to the Almighty every day and ask

Him to give you health and long life. Pray that He will forgive me. Your son forever, Lazare.

After Napoleon had abdicated and the Treaty of Paris had been signed on May 30, 1814, by King Louis XVIII, Czar Alexander, and the king of Prussia, Jewish merchants from Poland again began coming into Alsace. It was one of them who brought Berl a second letter from Lazare. He learned that Lazare had set out for Zolkiew and crossed Silesia, which had been devastated by the war. In the villages along his way he had usually been able to find Jews who would take him in for the night and, in spite of their great poverty, share an onion and a chunk of bread with him. He had arrived in Piotrków with the storks. In that half-Jewish market town, he had asked if there were any print shops where he might find work.

The Chassid I questioned took me into a dark courtyard where there was a *klaus,* a small synagogue in which the rabbi prayed and studied with his disciples.

The rabbi asked me where I came from and why I was looking for print shops. I told him that our family had been scribes, and then printers, since the time of Abraham the scribe, and I showed him the Book of Abraham. He looked at it, then embraced me and said, "Blessed be You, O Lord our God, King of the world, who have kept us alive and brought us to these times." Then he hurried home and came back with another copy of the Book of Abraham! That rabbi—can you believe it?—is the great-grandson of the man known as Kosakl, who, according to the Book, came to Zolkiew at the same time as your father's grandfather.

We talked all night. He called Napoleon a barbarian and said that "those who give nations false hopes are criminals, and the Almighty always punishes them." He had not forgiven Napoleon for having allowed the abolition of the civil rights of Jews in Poland. After the morning prayer, Rabbi Mosheh gave me a few zlotys and a letter of introduction to Zevi-Hirsch ben Nathan of Lutomirsk, a printer in Warsaw who had published one of Rabbi Mosheh's writings, a funeral oration for Rabbi Meir-Ikhiel of Ostrowiec. I am now in Warsaw, working for Zevi-Hirsch.

Warsaw is on the Vistula River. Several of its districts are inhabited only by Jews. The print shop is on the third floor of a house full of loud voices and strong smells. We have a great deal of work, thank God, and Zevi-Hirsch is willing to hire you too, father. Why should you not come here? It will soon be Rosh Hashanah of the year 5575 [1815] after the creation of the world by the Almighty, blessed be He, and I will pray that He will allow us to celebrate the new year together. Amen. Your son forever, Lazare.

Berl wrote to his son that he would be happy to join him in Warsaw and that he would leave in the spring.

LAZARE HALTER lived in a little room on the sixth and last floor of a house at the corner of Mila Street and Nalewki Street. His two small windows overlooked a maze of interconnected courtyards where workshops were lined up side by side, and where there were awnings under which a market was held each morning. Along the walls, sitting with drooping heads, like sleeping herons, motionless beggars chanted their mournful refrain, "Alms, Jews, alms," which formed a kind of accompaniment for the singing of workers in shops and the cries of peddlers.

The crowd was in constant motion all through the day, mingling Chassidim in caftans, porters dressed in Turkish style, organ grinders making their little monkeys dance. There was an atmosphere of expectancy, of impatient waiting for some unknown event. Lazare liked the spectacle of those bearded men dressed as everything except Poles, those students with guileless faces framed by heavy *payesses* under broad-brimmed hats, those pretty, dark-eyed young women whose brightly colored shawls failed to hide their tattered clothes. The whole scene smelled of leather, mildew, yeast, and pickled herring.

Every morning Lazare walked along Nalewki Street, lingering in blind alleys, exploring side streets where he found little synagogues and schools that he had never seen before. He knew all the shops on Kupiecka Street and Franciszkanska Street, the pavement of Swieto-Jerska Street was as familiar to him as the floor of his room, and he had counted the carved bars in the gate of the Krasinski Garden.

Zevi-Hirsch's print shop was on Tlomackie Street, next to a synagogue in which men wearing prayer shawls and shabby frock coats began gathering every Friday at noon. Some of them had

594

faces resembling those that Lazare attributed, in his imagination, to certain men in the Book of Abraham, and he gave them names: Gamaliel, Nomos the Red, Bonjusef, Meir-Ikhiel . . . To him, it was not so much a way of bringing his ancestors back to life as of marking the continuity of faces, destinies, and moral standards. Although he had been living in that quarter for less than a year, he felt as if he had known it all his life; and when he missed the warmth of a family, he opened the Book of Abraham. He had no wish for other horizons. In his daily walks, he had not yet gone even as far as the Vistula.

"I'm as strongly attached to this quarter as I am to my native village," he told Zevi-Hirsch one day.

The printer, a short man in a threadbare coat that gaped over his paunch, raised his finger and said sententiously, "In Ecclesiastes it is written, 'Better is the sight of the eyes than the wandering of desire.' "

Lazare smiled. Zevi-Hirsch sometimes reminded him of his grandfather.

As for his father, Berl, he would never know Warsaw. A letter from Rabbi Guggenheim of Haguenau informed Lazare that his father had died in the rabbi's house soon after he came there to tell him good-bye, intending to leave for Warsaw the next day. He had been buried in the old cemetery they had visited together forty years earlier, when he was on his way from Königsberg to Strasbourg. "His last words," wrote Rabbi Guggenheim, "were for his family. He asked all of you to forgive him and said that he wanted you, his younger son, to announce his death to your mother. May the Almighty have mercy on his soul. Amen."

Lazare immediately wrote to his mother Yente and his brother Noah, in Zolkiew. He had heard nothing from them for the last thirteen years, since they left Bischheim.

Several months went by. One day a visitor came to the print shop: a man with a bushy, graying beard, wearing a long black coat and a Polish cap with a lacquered visor. He looked at Lazare attentively, then asked, "Are you Lazare Halter, son of Berl?"

"Yes," replied Lazare.

The man held out his arms to him.

"I'm your brother Noah."

His wife and son were waiting outside, with a bundle and a wicker basket.

Noah told Lazare that their mother Yente had also died and that there was no longer any reason for him to stay in Zolkiew. He was a Chassid of the miraculous rabbi of Kotzk, who, confined to his room and devoting all his time to study of the Cabala, had not received any of his disciples for years, which did not prevent Noah from going regularly to stand outside his windows.

In Warsaw, Noah soon found work as a teacher in one of the many "street-corner schools," as they were called; they belonged to various Chassidic associations and one could attend them briefly at any time, long enough to learn a page of the Gemara. At Lazare's request, Zevi-Hirsch took Noah's son Yankel into the print shop as an apprentice. Yankel was a boy of twelve, with delicate features, big, limpid eyes, and long, dark lashes.

In October of that year, a few days after Succot, everyone in Warsaw began eagerly discussing the news that there was going to be a new constitution for the kingdom of Poland—or what was left of it after the Russians, Prussians, and Austrians had taken parts of its territory. The Jews hoped that, like the French Jews, they would be given the same rights as other citizens. They were disappointed. "No one who is not a citizen of the country can claim political rights," said the constitution promulgated in November, and since the Jews were not recognized as citizens, they could not claim the rights that went with citizenship. They were urged to convert to Christianity, however, and bands of impatient Poles began coming into the Jewish quarter to hasten the process of conversion.

One evening Lazare and his nephew Yankel were coming back from the print shop together. Light snow was falling, but the air was not yet cold. Yankel often questioned his uncle during these walks. This evening they were talking about the events that had preceded the destruction of the Temple of Jerusalem by Nebuchadnezzar in the year 3174 [586 B.C.] after the creation of the world by the Almighty, blessed be He.

"You remember that the first Temple was destroyed because of three transgressions," said Lazare. "Do you know what they were?"

Yankel, who was very studious and diligent, replied, "They were idolatry, licentiousness, and bloodshed, according to the Yoma."

"Exactly. And why was the second Temple destroyed at a time when the people were assiduously studying the Torah and faithfully performing their duties?"

"Because," said Yankel, "there was hatred without reason

among them, and that hatred alone produced the same effects as idolatry, licentiousness, and bloodshed."

Just then they heard shouts. Jews in caftans and flat caps who had been walking in front of them suddenly turned back and disappeared into side streets or doorways. Farther up the street, torches were flickering. Shopkeepers hurriedly took in their displays of merchandise and closed their wooden shutters. There were cries of warning: *"Polakn!"* [Poles].

Lazare and Yankel hid in a dark doorway and huddled against each other. Through the falling snowflakes, they saw an old cloth merchant struggling with a broken shutter. Lazare wondered if he should run across the street to help him, abandoning Yankel. It was clear that, left to himself, the old man had no chance of being able to close his shop in time.

"Wait for me here, Yankel," said Lazare. "Don't move. I'll come back."

Lazare dashed forward. The Poles were pouring down the street like a torrent. He snatched the shutter from the old man's hands, but too late.

"Convert, Jews!" he heard. "Abandon your dirty caftans and your impurities!"

Then he was struck on the back of the head and fell.

When he regained consciousness, he first saw Yankel's tearful face. He stood up. The old man was there too. His pale lips were quivering. A young woman stood beside him. Lazare had a throbbing pain in his head.

"Thank You, O Lord, Master of the world," he said, "thank You for giving me courage."

He looked around him. Pieces of cloth from the shop had been thrown into the street and snow was already beginning to cover them.

"Are they gone?" asked Lazare.

"Yes," said the old man. "Curses on them! Come in and rest."

The young woman's name was Deborah but she was called Deborele. The designs of the Almighty being impenetrable, Lazare married her three months later. They found a two-room apartment at the back of a courtyard on Muranow Square and had three children in three years, all boys: Solomon-Halevy, Jonah, and David. Lazare printed their names, and his wife's, in a new section that he glued at the end of the Book of Abraham. He had decided that when his children grew up, they would all print a new edition of the family book together.

IN THE YEAR 5590 [1830] after the creation of the world by the Almighty, blessed be He, Lazare was forty and his oldest son was sixteen. Yankel was now married and had children.

One Friday Zevi-Hirsch and Lazare closed the print shop at three o'clock in the afternoon, as they did every Friday. The street was emptying. A few peddlers were still trying to attract the attention of the last passersby, and were being sternly reprimanded: the hour of *shabbat* was sacred.

When he came home, Lazare kissed Deborele, washed his hands, and exchanged his rumpled cap for a velvet one with a rigid frame. He knew his sons were ready in the next room. He called them and the three of them came in, freshly washed, holding their ritual books. He embraced them one after another and once again thanked the Almighty for that blessing, for it was written, "Though the world can exist only with people of both sexes, happy is he whose children are sons."

Lazare sat down, and so did his sons. He opened his ritual book and, swaying backward and forward, began the Song of Songs: "O that you would kiss me with the kisses of your mouth! For your love is better than wine. . . ." Standing beside the alcove with her arms folded, Deborele watched the men initiating *shabbat*. When they fell silent, she lit the candles, recited the blessing, and said, "Good *shabbat*, children!"

Lazare stood up.

"Let's go to the synagogue."

There was nothing he liked more than walking along Nalewki Street with his three sons.

"Good *shabbat!*" people said to him. "Good *shabbat!*"

The street was filling again. Men in long satin coats and white stockings, and their beards carefully combed, were coming out of all the houses and courtyards, like brooks flowing into a river. Rapidly, but with dignity, each of them walked toward one of the many synagogues in the quarter.

In the synagogue, Lazare and his sons took out their prayer books. A voice recited, "Give thanks unto the Lord, for He is good." Other voices joined in, and soon there were only murmurs that rose and fell while the Jews swayed in prayer as though moved by waves that rolled in from the depths of time.

598

When the service was over, they all wished each other a good *shabbat* and returned home.

Yankel was waiting with two of his friends who wanted to talk with Lazare. Lazare had invited them all to the *shabbat* meal. Yankel, now thirty, had a long, thin face and a slanting forehead. He introduced his friends: Joseph Berkowicz, who was tall and had a square face with a big mustache and a small tuft of whiskers under his lower lip, and Chaim Szmulewicz, who was rather round and had a forked blond beard.

Lazare greeted them and said the prayer for returning from the synagogue: "Peace be with you, angels of the divine service, angels of the supreme God, of the King of Kings, of all kings, of the Holy One, blessed be He."

"Peace be with you," repeated the others.

Lazare poured wine for the *kiddush*.

Only when the meal was over, and the prayer of thanksgiving had been recited, did he turn to Yankel.

"Nu?"

That Yiddish word *nu,* which has all sorts of uses, meant this time, "All right, let's talk now. What's on your mind?"

"It's about the revolution, uncle Lazare."

The idea of revolution was being reborn. There were reports from Paris that printers had rebelled against the closing of print shops by the king, then looted armories and forced the king to take refuge in England. The movement seemed about to spread all over Europe: Belgium had revolted against the Netherlands, Italy against the pope and Austria . . .

"The revolution?" asked Lazare.

Yankel coughed nervously. The children looked at him as if he were going to take a gun from under his coat.

"Uncle Lazare," he said, "if there's an insurrection against the Russians in this country, we Jews must take part in it."

"Why? What could we gain?"

"Rights!"

"Is there anyone in Poland who cares about our rights?"

"Yes, the democrats. Joachim Lelewel, for example. He says that after victory over the czar, the Jews will have full rights in Poland and can even go to Eretz Israel if they want to, with the help of the Poles."

Lazare shook his head.

"I wonder if your democrats wouldn't rather have us in Palestine than in Poland."

Yankel seemed pained by his uncle's skepticism. He looked at his friend Joseph Berkowicz, who leaned closer to the table.

"We believe that the struggle against tyranny also concerns us," Berkowicz said in his harsh voice, "so we want to create Jewish units in the national guard. When the Poles confront the Russians, we'll be there, and no one will be able to accuse us of—"

"But," Lazare interrupted, "no Pole will accept armed Jewish units in Poland!"

"You're right, for the moment, but mainly because the leaders of the Jewish community are afraid, and haven't yet told the Poles that the Jews will stand beside them when the insurrection comes. If we're not going to seem like a group of fanatics, respectable and respected Jews must give us their support. That will be the signal for all Jews who are willing to fight for their rights, but don't want to take foolish risks, to commit themselves to the struggle."

"All the Jews in the community, including both the Chassidim and the Mitnagdim, appreciate your wisdom and respect you," Chaim Szmulewicz said to Lazare. "They know about the Book of Abraham and, through everything it represents, they feel as if they were related to you. They also know that you're on close terms with Rabbi Isaac-Meir Rothenberg, son of the venerated Israel, rabbi of Gur."

Chaim Szmulewicz said nothing more. Neither Yankel nor Joseph Berkowicz added anything.

"Have you already talked to other people?" asked Lazare.

"Joseph Joselewicz is with us—you know, the son of Berek Joselewicz, who fought in Kościuszko's rebellion. He was in the Polish hussars, he took part in Napoleon's campaign of 1812, and he won many honors."

Remembering his own campaign in the Grand Army, Lazare let the subject drop. He agreed with these young men: it was hard to live without elementary human rights. But how many of them would have to die before the survivors were given satisfaction—if they ever were?

He asked his son Solomon-Halevy to bring him the Book of Abraham. He put it down on the white tablecloth and solemnly opened it. Deborele put more oil into the lamp and moved it closer to him. He began reading silently, swaying backward and forward. He read one page, then another. Nothing moved in the room except his body, marking the rhythm of words that only he heard. No one ever knew what made him come to his decision, but finally he slowly closed the book, filled his glass with wine, wet his fingertips, and said, *"Lechaim!"*

"Lechaim!" replied the others, raising their glasses.

"To the revolution!" added Lazare.

"To the revolution!"

ON THE EVENING OF November 29, 1830, a group of insurgents took the palace of Grand Duke Constantine, the czar's representative in Poland. At the same time, units from the Polish military academy attacked the barracks of the Russian cavalry.

By the next morning, the center of Warsaw—the old city—was in the hands of the insurgents. The grand duke, who had been able to escape from the palace with a cavalry regiment, occupied the southern quarters.

It was said that many young Jews had taken part in the fighting, but the leaders of the rebellion still refused to have an armed Jewish unit among their troops. "They say they don't like us because we don't want to fight," people on Nalewki Street said indignantly, "but then, when we *ask* to fight, they still don't like us!" A few concluded that since no one wanted the Jews, they should simply watch the Poles and the Russians kill each other, but many still felt that the Jews should be among those fighting for freedom, which included rights for the Jews.

On December 5 Józef Chlopicki, a former general in Napoleon's army and a veteran of the campaigns in Italy, Spain, and Russia, took command of the rebellion. He drove the Russians out of Warsaw but allowed Grand Duke Constantine to leave Poland with his regiments and sent a negotiator to Saint Petersburg. But Czar Nicholas refused to negotiate with the rebels.

Meanwhile, in response to Lazare's urging, the famous Rabbi Isaac-Meir Rothenberg of Gur, one of the spiritual leaders of the Polish Chassidim, had organized a committee to support the Jewish volunteers. Shlomo Ajger, the chief rabbi of Warsaw, had joined it. A call for solidarity, written by the committee, was printed by Lazare and Zevi-Hirsch and sent to hundreds of Jewish communities all over the world. Encouragements, gifts, and even volunteers soon began coming in. The poet Heinrich Heine sent a long letter full of ardent feelings.

Chlopicki finally accepted the idea of a Jewish unit, but only on condition that it be composed entirely of "Polishized" Jews; that is, beardless ones. This condition aroused strong opposition, especially among the Chassidim: they had volunteered by the hundreds but they refused to shave off their beards. Protests, negotiations. Some Jews cared nothing about their beards; others, including Yankel, Berkowicz, and Szmulewicz, cared about them but were willing to sacrifice them to the revolution. Finally the leaders of the rebellion offered a compromise: beardless Jews would be taken into the national guard, while those who kept their beards would be assembled in a special unit that would constitute the municipal guard. It was stipulated that Jewish fighters and their families would automatically receive Polish citizenship.

The Jews accepted this compromise. Joseph Berkowicz wrote an appeal to Jewish youth in Yiddish and Polish, and Lazare printed it. More than a thousand volunteers came to the rabbinical school, where Yankel, Berkowicz, and Szmulewicz were waiting for them.

On March 12, 1831, at the corner of Franciszkanska Street and Nowiniarska Street, the first patrol of the first Jewish military unit was formed: the bearded Chassidim of the municipal guard. The unit composed of "Polishized" Jews was ordered to defend the two bridges over the Vistula that commanded the entrance to Warsaw.

They began waiting. They had learned that the Russians had put down the Lithuanian insurrection. It was said that Paskevich, commander of the czar's army, was approaching the Vistula at the head of several regiments. The waiting continued.

Passover was celebrated in that atmosphere of mingled uncertainty, hope, and fear. It was marked by a strange incident one *shabbat* evening at the Halters' house. In the last days of Passover, Noah came back from Kotzk, where he had spent several months ecstatically contemplating places that had been seen by the holy rabbi, his teacher. His hair and beard had turned completely white, but it was his eyes that had changed most strikingly: they seemed veiled and there was something frightening about them. He said that the Jews' war against the czar would be won not by weapons but by tears, because one tear, according to the holy rabbi of Kotzk, was deeper than the ocean of infinity. And when his son Yankel spoke of training Jewish units, Noah raised his long arms toward the soot-blackened ceiling and cried out, "I beseech you, Abraham, Isaac, and Jacob, to leave your golden seats in heaven and come to the aid of the children of the chosen people!"

His face went blank. Lazare suddenly recalled his father's description of the arrival of Yente and Noah in Paris during the Revolution. He raised his fist and violently struck the table with it, making the dishes rattle. Everyone looked at the two brothers.

"Why did you do that?" Noah asked in a hollow voice.

Lazare did not answer immediately. He seemed exhausted. Finally he said, "I only wanted to bring you back to earth."

Noah left the next day, to return to Kotzk. Yankel was sorry to see him leave, but he could not abandon the training of Jewish units to go off and look after his father. He promised himself that he would do it when the Russians had been driven back.

AT THE END OF summer the Russians came from the west and stopped in front of the outworks that defended the approaches to Warsaw. On September 6 they launched an assault. They had nearly eighty thousand soldiers and twice as much artillery as the Poles. The battle lasted two days. On the morning of the third day, the Polish regiments withdrew to Modlin. When the Russians came to the bridges over the Vistula, they found that the Jewish volunteers were the only obstacle preventing them from entering Warsaw.

Standing on a wagon between the two bridges, Yankel and Berkowicz were in command of the defending forces. Cannons on the other side of the river pounded their positions, smashing stones and men. Suddenly Russian horsemen appeared on one of the bridges.

"Fire!" Berkowicz ordered.

The cannon positioned to cover the whole length of the bridge fired a shot that killed two of the horsemen.

"Fire!" Berkowicz ordered again.

A little Chassid, whose long red *payesses* looked as if they were attached to either side of his high military cap, came up to Berkowicz and saluted him.

"Captain," he said, "we have only enough ammunition for a few more cannon shots."

Yankel saw a cannonball coming. He did not even have time to shout a warning. The ball struck the little Chassid in the back, hurled him far away, and left him sprawled on the ground, limp and lifeless.

"Fire!" Berkowicz ordered once again.

On the bridge, the Russians were falling back. The shooting on both sides was hellishly intense. Then a Russian cannonball killed three of the Jewish gunners whose cannon had been firing at the bridge. Panic-stricken, the others fled toward the center of the city. Yankel leapt down from the wagon and tried to stop them.

"Jews! Stay and fight!"

But they were running away as fast as they could. Yankel stopped beside the abandoned cannon. The Russians were coming across the bridge. He heard them shouting encouragement to each other. He thought, Why was the second Temple destroyed at a time when the people were assiduously studying the Torah and faithfully performing their duties? And, surprised to hear his voice in the uproar of war, he answered aloud as he had done in his childhood, "Because there was hatred without reason."

LAZARE WAS PRAYING in the synagogue when his oldest son Solomon-Halevy came for him.

"Father! Yankel has been wounded! But he's still alive! He fell near the bridge."

Lazare gripped his son by the shoulders.

"What were you doing there? I thought you were at home. Where are your brothers?"

"They're putting up a barricade at Zamkowy Square."

In the street, Jews were running wildly. "The Russians are coming!" The sound of shooting was growing louder. A runaway horse passed, dragging the wreckage of a wagon.

Opposite the palace, at the beginning of Boczna Street, boys were making a pile of furniture, stones, boards from fences, and doors that had been pulled from their hinges.

"Jonah! David!" called Lazare.

His two younger sons were carrying a big chest that they had found somewhere. They looked at him without saying anything.

"Thank God!" he murmured. "Hurry back to the house. I'll be there soon. You, Solomon-Halevy, you'll be responsible for your brothers."

He turned away from them and ran toward the river. Bodies lay in the street, dead or wounded. Suddenly he saw Rab Yudl the old-clothes dealer, with whom he had been on friendly terms before he disappeared from Warsaw a few years earlier.

"Rab Yudl!" he exclaimed. "What are you doing here? Come and help me. My nephew has been wounded, near the bridge."

The old-clothes dealer put his finger to his lips.

"Sh! I'm not Rab Yudl any more. My name is now Leon Rosenberg and I'm a British weapons merchant. . . . But let's not stay here."

They walked toward the bridge and saw Yankel lying in his own blood. The Russians had crossed the bridge and now had their backs to them as they tried to silence the other Jewish cannon. Lazare and Rab Yudl lifted Yankel by the arms and legs and began carrying him toward Zamkowy Square.

"As a British subject," said Rab Yudl, "I can easily cross borders, and weapons are always easy to sell: everyone needs them!" He heard Yankel moan. "Poor boy. . . . I remember when he first came to Warsaw. . . ."

YANKEL DIED three weeks later. By then, the Russians were firmly in control of Warsaw. Some Jews were in hiding, others had fled. Even Rabbi Isaac-Meir had left: he had gone back to his native village of Gur to let himself be forgotten for a time, and had changed his name to Alter. Fearing reprisals, Lazare entrusted his son Jonah to Rab Yudl and his son David to Joseph Berkowicz. Rab Yudl, traveling as Leon Rosenberg, left Jonah with a cousin of his who lived in Sampolna, near the German border. Berkowicz took David with him to London.

Unexpectedly, the Russians evidently did not want to take revenge on those who were still in Warsaw. They tried to win the sympathy of the Jewish community, in fact, by setting up a fund to pay compensation for losses suffered during the capture of the city. The Jewish quarter changed, however. The shops remained closed and selling was done in the streets. Each morning, narrow wagons loaded with merchandise were lined up in front of houses and merchants began hawking their wares. The Russians were good customers.

Several months later, in August 1832, the czar promulgated his first anti-Jewish law: it forbade Jews to live in houses at the intersection between a Jewish street and a Catholic street.

Polish Jews were still a long way from enjoying the rights of citizens.

42

WARSAW

A Very Old Man

TEN STRONG things have been created in this world, says the
Baba Batra: a mountain is strong, but iron can break it; iron is
strong, but fire can melt it; fire is strong, but water can extinguish
it; water is strong, but clouds can carry it away; clouds are strong,
but wind can dissipate them; wind is strong, but the body can
withstand it; the body is strong, but fear can overcome it; fear is
strong, but wine can drive it away; wine is strong, but sleep can
undo its effects; and death is strongest of all.

Lazare had seen death at work all his life. He was now ninety
and he had seen many people die since that day in a frozen forest
when a bayonet plunged into the heart of a young Jewish soldier
who had just called out, *"Shema Yisrael."* Yankel had died in that
insurrection. Zevi-Hirsch had died of consumption. Avigdor ben
Yoel, known as Lebenzon, the printer for whom he had worked
after Zevi-Hirsch's death, had also died. So had his sons Solomon-
Halevy and David, and his beloved wife Deborele, and even old
Meyer Amschel Rothschild, rich banker though he was.

Lazare was not tired of aging. Since the prolongation of life
depended on love of the Almighty and obedience to His voice, he
scrupulously observed all the Commandments. Not once in the last
fifty years had he failed to go to the synagogue, morning and eve-

ning. Those who knew him sometimes quoted a passage from the Chapters of the Fathers with regard to him: "A man whose acts of piety surpass his knowledge is like a tree that has few branches and many roots. If all the winds in the world blew against him, they could not shake him."

Even so, Lazare had nearly been killed in one of those demonstrations to which his son Solomon-Halevy had taken him, but he had forgotten if it was in 1848 or 1861; he sometimes confused the more recent events of his life. There had been clashes with soldiers and people had been killed, including a man walking beside him. He had then gone to the funeral for the victims. The Jews had assembled on Rimarska Street: guilds with their flags, students, rabbis . . . He had walked behind Rabbi Isaac-Meir Alter and Rabbi Meisels. The Jews had joined the Polish procession and Solomon-Halevy had said that it was a great moment, that from now on the Jews and the Poles would fight the Russians together. But Lazare felt that the Jews should not concern themselves with either the Poles or the Russians. They should simply fight against crime, because evil was the enemy of God.

He watched his city changing, and when he saw Jews who dressed like *goyim* and did things unknown to their forefathers— walking at night along streets lighted by burning gas, using a device for speaking over great distances, traveling in carriages that rolled on iron guides and were drawn either by horses or by machines that spat out smoke and cinders and whistled shrilly—he was afraid that Warsaw might meet the same fate as Sodom and Gomorrah.

While he was working in Lebenzon's print shop, Lebenzon had imported from England an enormous rotary press that turned out printed sheets with great speed and deafening noise. Each morning Lebenzon chose the strongest of the poor men who came to the shop to ask for work, and all day long they pedaled on a system that kept the press in motion through a series of gears and belts. Production was undoubtedly much greater than before, but what good did that do? Lazare thought of the question in Ecclesiastes: "What has a man from all the toil and strain with which he toils beneath the sun?"

The Almighty would not fail to exercise His justice at the time of His choosing, as could be seen every day. The revolution of 1848 had swept away all enemies of Israel and proclaimed equal rights for the Jews of Western Europe. And Czar Nicholas, cursed be his name, who had persecuted the Jews all through his reign, had died mysteriously the day before Purim, the holiday that recalled the punishment of another enemy of Israel, Haman, who had tried to exterminate the Jewish people in the hundred and twenty-seven provinces of the Persian Empire. "Whoever honors the Law," Rabbi Yoseh had said, "will himself be honored. Whoever profanes it will be dishonored."

At seventy Lazare had married a woman still in her thirties: Sarale, a relative of his beloved first wife Deborele. She had given him another son, Meir-Ikhiel, whom he had taught to be a printer in a little shop that he had set up at the request of Rabbi Isaac-Meir Alter. The shop had prospered and the rabbi had sold it to Mordecai Zisberg, an upright Jew, who had made it into one of the largest print shops in Warsaw. Meir-Ikhiel had just married Zisberg's daughter and, in accordance with the marriage contract, Zisberg had immediately made him his partner. Lazare was happy to know that again there was a Halter running his own print shop.

This son who had been born late in Lazare's life, later than some of his grandchildren, was a pious, scholarly man, though it sometimes seemed that there was also a vaguely irreverent side to his nature. In any case, he was a great comfort to Lazare in his old age.

Lazare occasionally received news of his grandsons. One of them, Jonah's son, had begun as a baker in Sampolna, then gone with his whole family to Liverpool, in England, and at last report was preparing to go either to Australia or to Winnipeg, in Canada. Meir-Ikhiel had shown Lazare a map and pointed out Canada to him, above the United States of America. Lazare did not understand why his grandson should want to go so far north, when a little farther south would have done just as well.

His other son, David, and Gershom, David's son, lived in London and wrote to him once a year. Gershom, a cantor in a synagogue, had sent him a photograph of himself, showing him as a handsome man with a trimmed beard, wearing a top hat and standing with his hands on the back of a chair. Lazare had looked at it for hours. A cantor in the family—who would ever have believed it?

He had never reprinted the Book of Abraham; for the last fifty years he had written records of births and deaths in the twelve-page section that he had added to his copy of the book. Why had he not reprinted it? He did not know. None of his children and grandchildren had shown any interest in having a copy of it. But it seemed to him that there should be at least one copy in that faraway America. Only the Almighty knew which of His seeds would yield fruit. As the guardian of the family memory, Lazare was the only rampart against oblivion. He bridged the gap between yesterday and tomorrow, he was the link between ancestors and descendants. As long as he was useful, he thought, the angel with the scythe would spare him.

ON THAT DAY in the year 5641 [1881] after the creation of the world by the Almighty, blessed be He, the Christians of Warsaw were celebrating Christmas. The Church of the Holy Cross was filled with worshipers. In the middle of the service, a voice shouted, "Fire!" The panic-stricken worshipers rushed toward the doors and twenty-nine of them were trampled to death. People unknown to the priest of the church accused the Jews: who else would have shouted "Fire!" except one of those Jews who had had Christ crucified? Torch-carrying fanatics headed for the Jewish streets. Shops were burned, the synagogue on Nalewki Street was devastated.

Lazare had gone to the synagogue to pray, as he did every evening. In the street, a group of Poles caught that very old man who could not run, and one of them hit him on the head with a club.

The snow exploded in Lazare's eyes. Blood flowed from his mouth. But he believed in life so much that he did not die immediately. Meir-Ikhiel found him and took him home. Lazare had time to give him the Book of Abraham before the angel with the scythe took him to the cherubim guarding the entrance of heaven.

43

WARSAW

Olga

ZLATA, MEIR-IKHIEL'S wife, urged him to be careful of those so-called literary circles that were said to be either places of debauchery or hotbeds of revolution—the czar's police had just arrested all the leaders of the Proletariat Socialist party at a meeting of a literary circle. But Meir-Ikhiel had been invited to one of those meetings by a publisher from Odessa who had come to visit the print shop, and he felt he had to go. Besides, the publisher, a man named Plotnitzki, did not look like either a libertine or a terrorist.

On Leszno Street, Meir-Ikhiel hesitated a moment before knocking. The door opened and an old woman greeted him in Russian. He asked for Mr. Plotnitzki. He waited in the anteroom till the publisher came in and stretched out his arms to him, smiling, with his little blond mustache arched above his mouth.

"At last!" he said.

He shook hands with Meir-Ikhiel and led him into a large room where a dozen people, in their twenties or early thirties, were sitting close together in one corner, on a sofa and several chairs. Meir-Ikhiel sat down on a stool. He was asked if he spoke Russian. He answered yes, and listened.

Nearly all those people were Litvaks, Jews from Lithuania, and they had probably come to Warsaw to look for work. They were discussing the need to organize study groups for workers and create libraries where books forbidden by government censorship could be obtained: Marx, Lassalle, Plekhanov, Herzen . . .

"Through study, the working class will become aware of its situation and its strength," said one man.

"But there are hardly any workers in Russia," remarked another. "Practically speaking, there are only peasants."

"But according to Plekhanov the number of workers is increasing!"

"Workers or peasants, we must go to the people!" said a third man.

Meir-Ikhiel felt uncomfortable. Why had Plotnitzki invited him there? Why were these people interested in the Russian workers? Two of them were women: besides the one who had opened the door when he arrived, there was a blue-eyed young woman whose blond hair was not covered by a shawl, which meant that she was not Jewish.

"What does our printer think of all this?" Plotnitzki asked abruptly.

"Hmm . . ." said Meir-Ikhiel. "I don't know very much about . . . When you say 'the people,' which people do you mean?"

"The Jewish workers," said the old woman.

Meir-Ikhiel was surprised. It seemed to him that the young woman was also surprised: she was looking at him as if she had just discovered his presence. He felt that no one had ever looked at him before.

"How will you talk to them?" he asked. "In what language?"

"Russian."

"Then you'll have no success with Polish Jews. For example, take those three hundred women who are now on strike at the Bonifraterska tobacco works—just try telling them about Marx and Plekhanov in Russian! Without Yiddish, you'll always be foreigners in Warsaw."

A well-groomed young man with a red scarf around his neck leaned forward.

"But there's no printed material in Yiddish that would be useful to us."

"In that case," replied Meir-Ikhiel, "the first thing to do is to print some."

"And you'll do the printing, won't you?" the well-groomed young man asked sarcastically.

Meir-Ikhiel stood up.

"I must go now. They're expecting me at home."

He walked out of the room. Plotnitzki caught up with him in the entrance hall.

"I'm very glad you could come. What you've said will make them think. They all have good intentions, but they're inexperienced." He put his hand on Meir-Ikhiel's shoulder. "What do you think of them?"

The question made Meir-Ikhiel uneasy.

"The Messiah won't be here anytime soon," he said.

"What do you mean?"

"The Talmud says that the Messiah will come during a generation that's either completely good or completely bad."

"And you think they're neither? You're mistaken, my friend. They're a magnificent generation—and furthermore they're *your* generation."

Meir-Ikhiel slowly walked home, wondering why he had spoken irritably. He actually knew it was because of the blond young woman, but he did not want to admit it to himself.

In the days that followed, he had to work twice as hard at the print shop because his father-in-law was sick, and he tried to forget.

Meir-Ikhiel liked his work, and especially the place where he did it. The hours he spent in the print shop were happy hours. The workers were all bearded Chassidim who wore hats over their skullcaps, and long coats held at the waist by scarves. They swayed over the type cases as if they were praying. Sometimes one of them would begin singing a Chassidic melody and the others would all join in. They worked skillfully and conscientiously, because they knew that "a blessing shines only over the work of man's hands." And during those days Meir-Ikhiel might have added, "for work makes us forget sin," as it is written in the Chapters of the Fathers.

Yet it was in the midst of his work that the blond young woman sought him out. She came into the shop one afternoon when the workers were singing. They suddenly fell silent, as if she had cut the thread of their Chassidic melody. Shocked by the appearance of a woman in their workplace, they turned away from her and acted as if she were not there. Meir-Ikhiel reluctantly went forward to meet her.

"Hello," she said. "I realize I'm interfering with your work."

"Well, you see . . ."

"What time do you leave?"

"Sometimes at six o'clock, sometimes not till seven."

"I'll wait for you in the street. I wanted to tell you that you were right the other night."

She walked out.

They worked late that day. When the machines had stopped, the printers washed their hands and forearms, opened their *siddurs,* and said the evening prayer together, as usual. Meir-Ikheil stayed till the others were gone, then he finally left.

She was waiting for him a short distance away. She walked toward him.

"Excuse me," he said, "but . . ."

"It doesn't matter, Meir, I wasn't bored. I like to watch the Jews living their lives. They do it in such a hurry! Do they have lost time to make up, or are they trying to make time go faster?"

"Both, probably. What's your name?"

"Olga. Or Vera. It depends."

"It depends?"

"Vera is the heroine of Chernyshevski's novel, *What Is to Be Done?* Have you read it?"

"No."

Standing still as they talked, they hindered the flow of people past them. They began walking toward the Krasinski Garden.

"Meir," she said, "my uncle has asked me to—"

"Your uncle?"

"Plotnitzki, the publisher. He's had some texts translated into Yiddish and he wants me to ask you if you'd be willing to print them. You're perfectly free to refuse, of course. They're what's called 'subversive writings.' Printing them might be dangerous for you. If you're at least willing to read them, I'll bring them to you tomorrow. If not, we'll drop the subject and never talk about it again."

Meir-Ikheil was a married man of thirty-seven, he and his father-in-law ran a large print shop, his wife Zlata had given him three children, he was intelligent and honest, he made decisions quickly, and he always tried to be fair. But with this woman, Olga, or Vera, who cut his name in half, asked him to risk going to prison, and walked around with her hair uncovered, he felt as if he were no longer anyone. He looked at her and sank into the deep water of her eyes. When he came back to his senses, she was telling him good-bye.

"I'll see you tomorrow, Meir. I'll be waiting in the same place."

The next day, it was Plotnitzki who brought the texts to the print shop. Meir-Ikhiel could not give him much time because he was busy with a bookseller who had come from Lublin to order a collection of prayers. Plotnitzki was leaving for Danzig that same day. He said he would come to see Meir-Ikhiel again as soon as he returned.

The afternoon stretched out endlessly. Absentminded, clumsy, scarcely able to work, Meir-Ikhiel mentally recited a passage from Psalms several times: "I keep the Lord always before me; because He is at my right hand, I shall not be moved." And, just before he left the shop: "Preserve me, O God, for in Thee I take refuge."

It was raining heavily. Meir-Ikhiel turned up the collar of his caftan and looked around for Olga. She was not there. Water trickled down his neck and his feet were wet. Furious with himself, he decided to go home. Just then he saw her, hurrying toward him through the curtain of rain, soaked to the skin.

"You're late," he grumbled.

She looked at him intently, as if she could see into the depths of his soul.

"Come," she said.

"Where?"

"It doesn't matter. To my room, if you like. . . . Don't look at me like that, Meir. We're not going to walk all night in the rain."

They started toward the Krasinski Garden, the way they had gone the night before. After a time they stopped; she pressed herself against him and he felt her light body through her wet clothes. Then they began walking again. At the corner of Tlomackie Street he hailed a cab.

Olga had a room in a hotel on Jerozolimska Street, beyond the Jewish quarter. The streets, sidewalks, and buildings seemed wider, newer, and better lighted here. The rain was the same, but its smell had changed. In front of the hotel, she took Meir-Ikhiel's arm. Two Russian policemen turned to look at them as they passed, but the man at the desk, occupied in pouring brandy into a chipped cup, paid no attention to them.

The room was so small that nearly all its space was taken up by a yellow bed, a chair, and a dresser. Olga drew the heavy yellow curtains, then disappeared behind the screen that cut off one corner of the room.

"Meir!" she called out.

"Yes?"

"Tell me about yourself."

"Well. . . ."

Olga reappeared, wearing a loose peasant dress, with a big red shawl over her shoulders. Meir-Ikhiel stood in the middle of the available space while water slowly dripped from his clothes.

"Meir, you'd better change clothes."

He felt himself blushing. This Russian woman's immodesty was boundless.

"I'd better leave instead," he said.

"Why?"

"Because staying would be a sin."

"But everyone sins, Meir! Your father must have sinned, and your grandfather, and your great-grandfather. . . ."

"My grandfather did. It's well known in the family."

"Tell me about it. And while you're talking, go behind the screen, take off your wet clothes, and put on this fur coat. It belongs to my uncle. I won't look at you."

Meir-Ikhiel told what he knew about Berl's adventures and how his wife from Zolkiew had pursued him to Strasbourg, Königsberg, and Paris. Olga was amused by his story.

When he came out from behind the screen, wearing the big black fur coat, she laughed and said, "I can't tell where the fur ends and your beard begins!" Then she stood up and put her arms around him. "You're trembling, Meir. Don't be afraid."

LYING SIDE BY SIDE, they heard a clock strike midnight. He sighed deeply and she put her hand on his bare chest as if she were soothing an unhappy child.

"I've always heard that Jews are good lovers," she said. "Now I can confirm it."

He was both embarrassed and flattered.

"Why should Jews be good lovers?"

"Because they recite psalms while they make love, I've been told, and that way they can make love all night."

His embarrassment redoubled.

"Do you believe in God, Meir?" she asked.

"Yes."

"You believe He created man?"

"Yes."

"And that He created him good?"

"If He had created all men good, the Messiah would already have come, and history would have been fulfilled long ago."

Olga sat up in bed.

"And did He create a remedy for evil?"

"Yes: His Law."

"Is it the same for everyone?"

"Of course. The Talmud says that God had everyone descend from the same man, Adam, so that no one could claim an advantage by saying he had a longer line of ancestors than someone else."

She laughed.

"Your God is against the czar! Now I understand why Plekhanov says that the Jews are the vanguard of the revolution. . . . Have you read the *Communist Manifesto,* by Marx and Engels?"

"No."

"But Marx was a Jew!"

"Being born a Jew is enough to make anti-Semites hate you, but it's not enough to make you a real Jew."

"What else does it take?"

"A Jew must respect the Law, love justice, and obey all the Commandments."

"But you just said that the Law is the same for everyone."

"Yes, but if a Russian violates it he's still a Russian, while a Jew who violates it ceases to be a Jew."

"And do you respect it, Meir?"

"Yes, I respect the Law. Unfortunately, though, I sometimes break a commandment or two."

"As you've done tonight?"

"Yes."

"Then have you ceased to be a Jew tonight?"

"No, but tonight I've become a bad Jew."

She nestled her naked body against him under the covers.

"Do you still desire me?"

"Don't talk like that!" he pleaded.

"Meir, you must help us. To make the Jews understand the meaning of our struggle, we must print and distribute leaflets in Yiddish—you've said so yourself. When the Jews move, everyone else will follow."

"Why should the Jews be the first ones to move?"

"Because they have more to gain than anyone else. They're doubly oppressed: as workers and as Jews. And furthermore . . ." She took his face between her hands, and despite the darkness he felt that she was again looking at him as if she could see into the depths of his soul. "And furthermore they defend the Law!"

MEIR-IKHIEL STILL HAD the Yiddish texts that Plotnitzki had brought. He printed them in the form of leaflets and posters. Two strangers came to take them, in the name of "Vera," and paid the bill for them: Meir-Ikhiel had to account for his hours of work and the paper he used, because his father-in-law checked the ledgers of the print shop every Friday.

Olga had come for him three more times after he finished his day's work, and three times they had spent the night together in her hotel room. When he came home in the morning, Zlata said nothing and it was worse than if she had wept and shouted so loudly that the whole neighborhood could hear her, as other deceived wives sometimes did. When the workers at the print shop began turning their backs on him and stopping their singing as soon as he approached them, he realized that the situation would not be bearable much longer, but he felt incapable of changing it.

Then one day she did not come. He waited till after nightfall. The next day he waited again, in vain. He went to the literary circle on Leszno Street but found no one there. The Litvaks must have been arrested, he thought. Then he went to see a cousin named Itzik, a thief and a police informer, the shame of the family —ordinarily he was seen only at Passover, and even then he was placed at the foot of the table and no one spoke to him.

"Meir-Ikhiel! Welcome!"

Itzik was a jovial little man with a shiny metal tooth. He lived with a tall, thin woman named Hadassah.

"What can I do for you?" he asked.

Meir-Ikhiel swallowed his pride and asked Itzik if he could use his police connections to find out if Olga Plotnitzki had been arrested. Hadassah was working in the kitchen with her back to them but she heard everything they said. Suddenly she turned around.

"Is she a whore?" she asked.

She was getting even for what the family had inflicted on her through the years. Meir-Ikhiel blushed violently.

"She's . . . she's a customer," he said.

And he quickly left.

Itzik came to the print shop the next day. Olga Plotnitzki, he said, was in the big barracks that had recently been made into a

617

prison, on Gesia Street. Under his arm he carried a silver-headed cane. Meir-Ikhiel looked at him and wondered how evil came into someone. Then he felt ashamed.

At the prison on Gesia Street, Meir-Ikhiel was received by a Russian police sergeant whose breath reeked of cheap brandy.

"What do you want, Jew?" the sergeant asked wearily from the metal cage in which he sat.

"I'm looking for a friend, Olga Plotnitzki."

The sergeant picked up a bundle of reports.

"Let's see. . . . What was your friend's name again?"

"Olga Plotnitzki."

"Plotnitzki. . . . Plotnitzki. . . ."

Looking through the bars of the cage, Meir-Ikhiel watched the sergeant's fingernail, yellowed by nicotine, moving down a list of names.

"And who are you?" asked the sergeant. "What's your name?"

"Halter."

"What do you do?"

"I'm a printer."

The sergeant looked up from his list.

"A printer? Write your name on this sheet of paper."

He slid it through the barred window. Meir-Ikhiel recognized it immediately. It was one of the Yiddish posters he had printed: *Appeal to the Jewish People*. He felt his cheeks burning and his heart pounding.

"Write your name and address," said the sergeant, pushing a pen and a bottle of ink toward him.

Meir-Ikhiel did as he was told. The sergeant took back the poster, looked at it with satisfaction, and said, "Your friend has been sent home, to Odessa. She'll spend a year in prison there, for subversive activities. Good-bye, Jew. From now on, be careful what you print!"

Two days later the police came for Meir-Ikhiel at the print shop. The poster on which he had written his name was used as evidence against him. He was convicted of an offense against public order and sentenced to five years of exile. This sentence staggered him— what a heavy price he would have to pay for his sins! But he could scarcely believe his ears when he heard the judge read off a list of cities where he could choose to spend his five years of exile: Kiev, Berdichev, Odessa. . . .

"Odessa!" he said with relief.

* * *

ZLATA WOULD NOT EVEN consider staying in her father's house in Warsaw with her three children. She would go with Meir-Ikhiel to Odessa, or even to Siberia if she had to. To her, it made no difference where they went: an exile was an exile. On her last evening in Warsaw she served a hot soup made of barley, mushrooms, and beans, the children's favorite meal.

"Eat as much of it as you can," she said, "because there's no telling when you'll be able to eat it again."

But Meir-Ikhiel ate only a few spoonfuls. When he had left the courtroom two days earlier, after being sentenced to exile, a beggar had clutched his sleeve and led him to a secluded place where a man was waiting for him. Meir-Ikhiel recognized him as the well-groomed young man he had met at the literary circle. After looking warily in all directions, he gave Meir-Ikhiel a package that was about the size of two books, but much heavier.

"This is for Plotnitzki," he said rapidly. "Someone will come for it in Odessa."

"But . . ."

"You won't be taking any risk. Long live the revolution!"

The young man hurried away. Meir-Ikhiel hid the package under his coat. When he came home he put it with his books, and the next day he packed it in a big trunk full of clothes and kitchen utensils, along with the Book of Abraham.

When it was time for Meir-Ikhiel and his family to leave, two policemen came to take them to the train station. They were preceded by a fat Jewish porter who carried the trunk on his back and cleared the way in front of him with brief shouts that sounded as if he were barking. All the neighbors were in the street, standing motionless with blank faces. Their disapproval was no doubt directed as much against the policemen as it was against Meir-Ikhiel, that sinner who had brought shame to his family, his wife's family, his neighbors, and perhaps the whole people of Israel.

On the station platform, policemen were prowling everywhere. Meir-Ikhiel's two guards took him and his family into a railroad car in which another policeman, a short blond man, had requisitioned two benches.

Meir-Ikhiel wondered when they were going to ask him to open the trunk. Why had he agreed to take that package to Odessa? To avoid seeming to back down? To see Olga again? Because he believed in that revolution? Probably for all those reasons together.

He told himself it was often that way when someone thought he was making a choice.

The policemen exchanged papers. Grunting, the fat porter put the trunk down next to the window.

Meir-Ikhiel was panic-stricken. He said the prayer for traveling: "May we travel in peace and arrive in peace, good health, and joy at the end of our journey."

"Amen," said Zlata and the children.

The policemen looked at the trunk, perhaps wondering if they had time to have it opened. Without thinking, Meir-Ikhiel said the first words that came into his mind: "May the names that I have written on this scroll, and the names that others will write on it after me, be spoken aloud to rend the silence. Holy, holy, holy, You are the Almighty."

"Amen," Zlata and the children said again.

Just then, a station employee walked past the car, shouting, "Passengers for Lublin, Chelm, and Kowel, all aboard! Passengers for Lublin, Chelm . . ."

The two policemen who had brought Meir-Ikhiel to the station left the train. The little blond policeman sized up the passengers he was supposed to deliver in Odessa. He sucked his teeth with an unpleasant sound, then recited, "If you make contact, or attempt to make contact, with any revolutionary elements during the journey, your five years of exile will be changed to a sentence of hard labor for life."

The children, terrified, looked at their father. He smiled at them to reassure them, then turned toward the window. Outside, the people on the platform were hidden by a cloud of steam. There was a sound of powerful panting and the train slowly got under way.

IT WAS GOING TO BE a long trip, more than six hundred miles, and they would change trains at Kowel. He looked at his family. His wife Zlata was reaching into the wicker basket in which she had brought food and drink. His two sons, Abraham and Yudl, were thirteen and ten; his daughter Leah was nine. He tried to reconstruct the chain of events that had brought them to that cold compartment of a train taking them into exile. And he suddenly realized with horror that what was in the trunk could have them all thrown into prison. Should he have refused to take it? What if the contents of that heavy package should help to advance the cause of justice in the world?

Abraham smiled at his father. Meir-Ikhiel was especially fond of Abraham, but precisely because of that he paid more attention to the two other children. He smiled back at him. Did Abraham know about Olga? The whole neighborhood had gossiped about it.

The train moved slowly and sometimes had to stop while snow-drifts were cleared from the track. The children slept. When Leah awoke, she complained of a sore throat. The Russian policeman took a flask from his coat pocket.

"Give some of this to your little girl," he said, handing the flask to Meir-Ikhiel. "It's brandy. It will make her throat feel better. Have a drink of it for yourself, too."

To avoid offending him, Meir-Ikhiel took a swallow of the brandy. It burned his stomach. Zlata held out a glass that she had taken from her basket.

"Here," she said curtly in Yiddish, "don't drink like a Pole!"

Meir-Ikhiel poured a little brandy into the glass and gave it to Leah. Her cautious sip made her shudder and grimace.

"It tastes terrible!" she exclaimed.

"You'll get used to it," the policeman said placidly.

Meir-Ikhiel's anxiety gradually died down, lulled by the steady motion of the train. It suddenly flared up again when the train stopped at Kowel. The narrow space between the benches became filled with passengers, boxes, bundles, and cages of poultry. Meir-Ikhiel went to find a porter but he had to wait for the passage to clear.

"You can go by yourself," said the policeman. "I'll stay with your family."

Meir-Ikhiel got off the train. On the platform he noticed a large number of soldiers who looked particularly vigilant. In the thick puffs of steam that came from the locomotive, people were looking for each other, calling out greetings, and embracing.

"Do you want a porter, sir?"

Meir-Ikhiel spun around. A short, stocky man was looking at him intently.

"Don't be afraid, sir," he said.

"Afraid?"

"I know how to recognize fear when I see it. But don't worry."

The man had the thick, powerful build of a bear and there was something reassuring about him.

"Are you Jewish?" Meir-Ikhiel asked him.

621

"Jewish? God forbid! I'm a Gypsy, and that's already more than enough for me!"

"I have a big trunk in that car."

"I'll carry it for you. Are you changing trains here?"

"Yes, for Odessa."

"Ah, Odessa!" exclaimed the porter. "What a city! I have a cousin there. He's also a porter, and his name is Vania. You'll recognize him when you see him in the station: you'll think you're seeing me again! Give him my best wishes. It's better to have a Gypsy with you than against you, sir."

"And what's *your* name?"

"It's also Vania. That makes it easy for you, sir: you only have to remember one name, instead of two."

With the porter carrying the trunk and the blond policeman keeping an eye on the procession, Meir-Ikhiel and his family boarded the train for Odessa. It seemed to be more comfortable than the other train. They sat down in a compartment where there was already one other passenger, a jovial fat lady. The porter waited till the policeman had turned away from him, then winked at Meir-Ikhiel and whispered, "Remember what I said, sir: don't worry."

Two officials of the Ochrana, the political police, were inspecting the train. They stopped in the compartment, exchanged papers with the young blond policeman, and looked at the trunk.

"What do you have in there?" asked one of them.

"Clothes," answered Meir-Ikhiel.

"And pots and pans," added Zlata. "When you go away for five years, you have to take things like that with you."

"Have they talked to anyone since leaving Warsaw?" one of the Ochrana men asked the blond policeman.

"No one except that porter. I stayed with them the whole time."

"Have a good trip."

Meir-Ikhiel's heart began beating again.

"ODESSA-ODESSA-ODESSA," the clattering wheels kept repeating. Leah was coughing. After a night on the train, Meir-Ikhiel felt as if his joints were frozen. The fat lady, who chuckled at the drop of a hat, stood up when the train began slowing down. She immediately fell onto the policeman's lap and burst out laughing.

"In a train, sooner or later you always find yourself on someone's lap!"

The train came to a stop. Meir-Ikhiel asked the policeman for permission to go and get some of the hot water that was provided in railroad stations.

"I'll go with you," said the policeman.

"I'll watch the trunk, father," said Abraham.

Zlata got off the train with Leah and Yudl: they had not had a chance to stretch their legs since changing trains at Kowel the day before.

A line had already formed in front of the hot-water tap. Men and women, their faces reddened by the cold, stamped their feet on the frozen ground. Meir-Ikhiel filled his teapot and went back to the compartment, where they all had a glass of hot tea; they even gave one to the policeman, since he had been nice enough to share his brandy.

The white plain gradually turned brown. The sky, which till now had been uniformly gray, began showing patches of blue.

THE ODESSA STATION was small but animated. The one-story building was now decorated with flags in honor of a delegation from Saint Petersburg. Meir-Ikhiel looked up and down the platform for Vania the Gypsy, but did not see him. The blond policeman called two of his colleagues, who picked up the trunk while Abraham relieved his mother of the food basket. They all went to the police office in the station, a small, overheated room where several men sat around a samovar. In exchange for a receipt, the blond policeman turned over his prisoners to the officer in command.

"Where do you intend to live?" asked the officer, a short man with a flat face.

"I don't know yet," answered Meir-Ikhiel. "I'll ask the Jewish community for help."

"And where will you work?"

"I don't know that either. I'm a printer. I'll look for work. I know Plotnitzki, the publisher."

"Open your trunk."

Meir-Ikhiel leaned over the lid of the trunk. "Master of the world . . ." he silently prayed. The lid creaked. He closed his eyes. When he opened them, he saw a policeman searching the trunk. The package had disappeared. "Praise be to You, O Master of the world, who comes to the aid of the oppressed in time of trouble." The policeman picked up the Book of Abraham and

623

handed it to the officer, who quickly looked through it and tossed it back into the trunk.

"It's a prayer book, you fool!"

Just then a dark-haired man wearing a fez appeared in the doorway. He was obviously the Vania in Odessa mentioned by the Vania in Kowel. He came in.

"Ah, here you are!" he said to Meir-Ikhiel. "I've been looking for you all over the station!" He turned to the officer. "I hope you haven't been making trouble for these people, sir. They're friends of my family."

He went over to the trunk, closed it, and picked it up on his back.

"Can I go now, sir?" he asked the officer.

"Yes, you can all go to hell!"

Meir-Ikhiel and his family walked toward the door.

"Don't forget: no contact with subversives!" the officer called after them. "We'll be watching you."

Outside, Vania walked toward the waiting cabs and put down the trunk.

"The sons of bitches!" he said, and spat on the ground.

"Your cousin in Kowel sends you his best wishes," Meir-Ikhiel told him. "But how did you know we were coming?"

"The telegraph," replied the Gypsy. "My cousin Vania told me you'd need . . . a good porter."

Meir-Ikhiel gave him two silver coins. The Gypsy bit one of them and smiled.

"Thank you, sir. If you need me again. . . ."

Vania the porter walked away with the rolling gait of a bear.

Meir-Ikhiel looked around. They were alone; the cab drivers could not hear them.

"Listen," he said to his family, "when we left Warsaw there was a package in this trunk, and it's not there now. Did someone . . . ?"

"I did, father," said Abraham. "I saw you were worried about the trunk, so when you all left the train to get hot water, I put the package at the bottom of mother's basket. And because I didn't want her to notice the extra weight, I carried the basket myself." He was smiling now, with a strong feeling of relief. "I was afraid in the police office, but luckily Vania came in."

Meir-Ikhiel looked at his son and was proud of him.

"WELCOME," said Plotnitzki the publisher, smiling under his blond mustache. "Did you have a good trip?"

"Yes," said Meir-Ikhiel, "except that my daughter Leah caught a cold."

• • •

THAT ABRAHAM, son of Meir-Ikhiel Halter, was my grandfather. I remember him. I recall his voice, the expression of his eyes; he used to take me on his lap to tell me stories, and at least once, probably in 1939, I asked him the four ritual questions on Passover. I believe he liked me. When I was born, he asked that I be given his father's name, Meir-Ikhiel, which a Polish clerk at the city hall translated as Marek. His arrival in this story intimidates me. Yet it was clear from the beginning that, as Rabbi Szteinzaltz had said in Jerusalem, I would "succeed in rejoining myself." From here on, this story will depend less on imagination than on reconstruction. File cards and documents will be replaced by family albums, the testimony of relatives and friends, and personal memories. How I regret not always having paid attention to what my parents told me! I was even surprised by their need to tell me those things!

THE PACKAGE that my grandfather Abraham saved from the police contained Hebrew type for printing leaflets and posters in Yiddish. In Russia at that time, it was forbidden to have such type without permission, and permission, of course, implied control. The first appeals by the Russian Social Democrats to the Jewish workers of Russia were printed with the type brought in by my grandfather.

MEIR-IKHIEL and his family were in Odessa when the twentieth century was born. I know that they had an apartment at the corner of Dolnitskaia Street and Balkhovskaia Street, on a courtyard where Jews and Christians lived. Meir-Ikhiel worked in Plotnitzki's print shop on Importation Square, in a building with a view of the sea.

AT THE END OF April 1903, news of the Kishinev pogrom reached Odessa: forty-nine killed, five hundred wounded, synagogues devastated. Jewish students came down Grechkaia Street, shouting, "Freedom!" History has not established exactly what happened that day. Shots were fired and the workers of the Shargorod bakery, armed with clubs and shovels, pursued the students. The hunt soon became general. Jewish shops and houses were broken into and pillaged.

Meir-Ikhiel was working in the print shop at that time. He tried to go home but was stopped by the crowd. A Jew named Krugliak, owner of a warehouse, was killed before his eyes, beaten to death with iron bars. When he was finally able to get back to his apartment, he found icons and a crucifix in the windows. The frenzied anti-Jewish mob had ravaged the apartments next door, but spared his, which was so obviously placed under the sign of the cross. Puzzled, he went in. Olga was there, in his apartment, with his wife Zlata. That camouflage had been her idea. The story has remained famous in my family; when we are afraid we may have some sort of undesirable visit, we will say, "Let's put icons in the windows."

Olga was unquestionably a remarkable woman. According to what my parents told me when I was old enough to hear about such things, at this point she broke off her affair with Meir-Ikhiel and replaced him in her heart and her bed with his son Abraham, who was then sixteen and more or less a man. This lasted until Olga, who had assumed responsibilities in her party, left Odessa to carry out propaganda missions elsewhere.

CONFRONTED WITH THE NEW WAVE of anti-Semitism that was breaking over Europe, the Jews were deeply divided. Some wanted to go to America, others to Palestine. And some were beginning to talk about self-defense; they were mostly socialists, and they, too, were divided. Those who belonged to the Bund—the Jewish Socialist party, founded at Vilna in October 1897, which rejected both national integration and cultural assimilation—supported the principle of revolutionary struggle, here and now, in collaboration with other national groups. The Zionist Socialists—composed of scattered groups that, under the leadership of the theoretician Ber Borochov, were to found the Poale Zion movement in February 1906 —accepted the idea of revolutionary struggle within Russia as long as Jews could not go to Eretz Israel, from which they were excluded by the Turkish rulers of Palestine. (Poale Zion, whose members later included David Ben-Gurion and Golda Meir, eventually developed into the Israeli Labor Party.) As for the nonsocialist Zionist parties, they had just rejected, at their sixth congress, any other solution for the Jewish people than a return to the land of their ancestors. Eighty years later they were joined in a governmental coalition headed by Menachem Begin.

Meir-Ikhiel was inclined to sympathize with Poale Zion.

THE FAMILY *finally went back to Warsaw, after five years of exile, in December 1904. My grandfather Abraham was nineteen. They all, including Meir-Ikhiel, had the feeling that the revolution announced by the Litvaks of the literary circle had cost them dearly. But, as my great-grandmother Zlata used to say, "If you like taking boat rides, you must expect that someday you'll have to row."*

44

WARSAW

Olga (Continued)

WHEN MEIR-IKHIEL returned from exile, Mordecai Zisberg, his father-in-law and partner, proposed that they form a partnership with a publisher named Eisenstein in order to expand their business. Meir-Ikhiel gave his consent. A new print shop was installed on Nalewki Street and the family moved into an apartment above it. Meir-Ikhiel's peccadilloes seemed to have been forgotten in the neighborhood; five years was a long time.

But the memory of Olga remained present between Meir-Ikhiel and his son. Abraham preferred to distance himself a little from his father. He went to work for the Hebrew newspaper *Hatsefira [The Epoch]*, which had just turned into a daily and needed someone to do makeup. He lived in a room not far from where he worked, on Nalewki Street, and his family hardly ever saw him except on *shabbat*.

Warsaw had changed. Whole quarters were inhabited entirely by Jews. There, the steady movement of wagons, carriages, and streetcars was stopped from Friday afternoon till Saturday evening and it was not unusual to see political or union parades, led by marchers carrying red flags, several times a day.

On January 23, 1905, Warsaw learned of the massacre committed the day before in front of the Winter Palace in Saint Petersburg. Abraham took part in the strike called by the two Polish Socialist parties and the Jewish Socialist party, the Bund. He also joined the committee that collected food for the strikers. And while patrols of torch-carrying Cossacks rode through the streets on horseback, Abraham and his friend David Pasirstein endlessly discussed that revolution on the march, at the end of which would begin the reign of justice announced by Isaiah.

When work resumed, the print shop of Meir-Ikhiel and his father-in-law received a new machine ordered from England by their partner Eisenstein: a linotype, the last word in printing technology, which cast whole lines of type. Abraham came to inspect it with his editor-in-chief, Nahum Sokolov, whom Meir-Ikhiel had invited.

The linotype, installed in a small room next to the print shop, was an impressive machine. At the top of it was the magazine containing the matrices. The operator worked at a keyboard like that of a typewriter. When he pushed down keys, matrices fell into a channel and were taken to the assembler in the proper order. As soon as a line of matrices had been assembled, it was moved to the mold, where a line of type, called a slug, was cast. After cooling, the slug went to the receiving galley, while the matrices used in casting it were taken to the distributor bar, sorted by means of their distinctive notches, and returned to their channels in the magazine.

Nahum Sokolov was enthusiastic.

"Time has passed since Gutenberg!" he said. "But what a contrast with the shop!"

In the shop next door, bearded men were working over type cases and composing tables, swaying as though at prayer. Now and then one of them would begin a song and the others would join in. There was something timeless about their clothes and their fervor.

"Those men will still be the same," said Meir-Ikhiel, "long after this machine has become obsolete."

Just then a broad-shouldered man with a graying mustache came in: the writer I. L. Peretz.

"Shalom aleichem, Rab Meir-Ikhiel," he said. "And here's Mr. Sokolov visiting his competitor! But who's this young man?"

"My son Abraham," replied Meir-Ikhiel.

"Is he a printer like his father?"

"Yes, and like my grandfather and my grandfather's father," said Abraham.

"A golden chain!" exclaimed I. L. Peretz. "I hope you'll tell me about it someday, and maybe I'll turn it into a novel. But I'm leaving for Vilna this evening. I've come to see if you have a few chapters of my book for me to proofread."

"We've been delayed by the strikes," said Meir-Ikhiel. "We should have some chapters ready for you by the time you come back."

"Then I'll go now, my carriage is waiting for me. Be healthy!"

"I'm leaving too," said Nahum Sokolov. "Thank you for letting me see the new machine." He took Meir-Ikhiel aside. "I'm very happy with your son. He's a good printer. And a good Jew!"

He put on his hat and walked out. Abraham, still awed at having met the great writer I. L. Peretz, was about to follow him when he suddenly stopped as if he had been turned to stone: Olga was standing in the doorway through which Nahum Sokolov had just disappeared.

"Father and son reunited!" she said playfully.

The two men had never talked about Olga, but each of them knew about the other's affair with her—and neither had forgotten her.

"I see you have a new print shop, Meir," she went on. "This one seems much bigger. I'm looking for my uncle. Have you seen him?"

Abraham took a step toward the door.

"I have to go now," he said.

THE FOLLOWING FRIDAY, Abraham came late for the *shabbat* meal. The family was already seated around the table and Mordecai Zisberg, Zlata's father, was also there. Abraham apologized for being late and washed his hands. Meir-Ikhiel blessed the bread and the wine. Zlata served the soup.

"I'm getting married," Abraham announced abruptly.

His brother Yudl nearly spat out a mouthful of soup.

"Mazel tov!" he managed to say. "Who are you marrying?"

"Rachel, the sister of my friend David Pasirstein."

Meir-Ikhiel raised his hand.

"Explain yourself," he said to Abraham.

"There's nothing to explain, father. I'm going to marry Rachel Pasirstein, that's all."

"I know the family," said Mordecai Zisberg. "They're good people. The father is a Chassid of the rabbi of Gur."

Meir-Ikhiel observed his son in silence, as though he were hoping to learn more from him. Then he raised his glass.

"Lechaim!"

The next day, Meir-Ikhiel had a talk with Rachel's father and they decided that the wedding would take place in May, a month later. But events decided otherwise.

At the end of April there was a rumor in Warsaw that the czarist authorities were going to proclaim a general mobilization in Poland: the Russian army was being driven back by the Japanese. The Jewish revolutionary parties launched a rallying cry: "Don't go to the slaughterhouse!" Many young men ran away. Meir-Ikhiel wanted Abraham and Yudl to go and stay with one of Zlata's cousins in Grodzisk, but Abraham refused: running away was no solution, he said; the police could find him in Grodzisk as well as in Warsaw. He preferred to join his friends who, whether they belonged to a political party or not, were organizing themselves into combat groups. They had no guns but they knew by heart the mechanism of a Browning, a Mauser, or a Nogant.

On May 1, 1905, the shops on Jewish streets lowered their shutters as though for Yom Kippur. But the people did not go to synagogues as they did on Yom Kippur. The streets became animated with joyous crowds on their way to Marszalkowska Street, where flags and streamers were displayed.

At the corner of Nalewki Street and Tlomackie Street, Abraham and his friend David Pasirstein met Mordecai Zisberg. Abraham greeted his grandfather, who angrily pounded the sidewalk with the tip of his cane.

"You too!" he said. "What are you going to do there?"

"Grandfather, have you ever seen so many hopes united?"

"It's only a desperate explosion of hopes, my boy!"

"Don't you realize that revolution is imminent? That the Jews are about to see the end of their persecution?"

Abraham thought this idea would appeal to his grandfather, but the old man sadly shook his head.

"I've never heard that the coming of the Messiah could be hastened with flags or guns. Remember: 'He who tries to determine the end of this world will have no luck in the next one.' "

"But grandfather . . ."

"You ought to reread the Book of Abraham one of these days," said old Mordecai Zisberg. "History has much to teach us, my boy." He put his brown-spotted hand on his grandson's arm.

"Meanwhile, be careful, and may the Almighty, blessed be He, protect you and your friend."

Abraham and David had not yet rejoined the procession when they heard the sound of shooting. Near Theater Square, the army had opened fire, killing several people.

A general strike was immediately decreed. In Łódź, Jewish spinning-mill workers put up barricades. In Warsaw, combat groups—including the one to which Abraham belonged—demonstrated in the streets. For four months there was a constant series of strikes and demonstrations.

In October a general strike paralyzed the whole empire. Rebellions broke out in Saint Petersburg and Moscow. Czar Nicholas II accepted a compromise: he announced the promulgation of a constitution and the convening of a parliament, the Duma.

For Abraham and his friends—who now spent most of their free time in the street, writing and handing out leaflets, taking part in the creation and training of self-defense groups, attending meetings of workers at the labor exchange—this decision by the czar represented a victory for them and the promise of an era of freedom. Their joy lasted several days, until another burst of gunfire, again near Theater Square, left several demonstrators lying on the pavement.

Abraham was puzzled. In Odessa, Olga had explained to him that the revolution would prevail because the people were invincible, yet innocent victims were still being killed. News of pogroms soon came from Russia: it seemed that there were massacres of Jews in every city, town, and village. Was Abraham's grandfather right, and was Olga wrong?

In Warsaw, however, freedom seemed to have triumphed. The workers held meetings at the labor exchange without interference from the police, called economic strikes when they considered it necessary, and freely distributed leaflets and newspapers published by the revolutionary parties. And so, when the first attacks against synagogues occurred, Abraham thought they must have been carried out by Russian provocateurs. Polish workers had been joining Jewish self-defense groups. In the courtyard on Pawia Street where the Pasirstein family lived, non-Jews even formed the majority. One of them, a medical student named Mietek, taught French to Abraham and David during nights when he was on duty.

But Polish anti-Semites, most of them belonging to the Polish National Democratic party, formed gangs that specialized in quick, violent actions; for example, they would run down a Jewish street, clubbing everyone they met, then disappear before the self-defense groups could intervene.

It was the period of Succot, the Feast of Tabernacles. At 7 Nalewki Street, Meir-Ikhiel built a large shelter of foliage combined with American Indian shawls sent from Canada by cousin Maurice, grandson of the baker of Sampolna. On the first day of the festival, the workers from the print shop came to drink brandy and Zlata gave them gefilte fish. But the celebration was only half-hearted. Where would the anti-Semites strike next?

"They won't come here," said Abraham. "The self-defense groups are on the lookout."

"But they've beaten Jews in the cemetery!"

"The dead can't defend themselves, but we can!"

"They've also beaten Jews in the Saxon Garden."

Mordecai Zisberg, Abraham's grandfather, was more somber than ever.

"If the Jews didn't defend themselves when they were beaten in the cemetery and the Saxon Garden," he said, "they won't defend themselves here either."

"Young Jews have changed," Abraham said forcefully.

"Maybe so, but our situation hasn't changed. We're a small band of castaways clinging to a raft afloat in a sea of hostility. Our only possible victory is to survive."

"Don't you think there are different ways of surviving, grandfather?"

"For us, there's only one: surviving while respecting the Law. It is written, 'Moses received the Law on Sinai and handed it on to Joshua. And Joshua handed it on to the Elders. The Elders handed it on to the Prophets. And the Prophets handed it on to the members of the Great Assembly, who taught three principles: be cautious in your judgments, train many disciples, and make a hedge around the Law.' "

"Here they come!" someone shouted at the entrance of the courtyard.

Everyone stood up. Some had fear in their eyes, others determination.

"Let them come!" Abraham said to his companions. "We'll show them what a self-defense group can do! Get your weapons and take up your positions!"

633

They armed themselves with spiked clubs, scythes, sabers, pitchforks, and cleavers.

Zlata held her son by the sleeve.

"You're not going to fight, are you, Abraham? Please, Abraham, please don't. . . ."

Meir-Ikhiel gently pushed her aside.

"Go upstairs and keep Leah with you, Zlata. Abraham is right. We can't let Jews be killed without fighting."

"All streams run to the sea, but the sea is not full," murmured old Mordecai Zisberg, quoting from Ecclesiastes.

The self-defense group stood in the entrance of the courtyard. Their faces were pale and drawn from the effects of tension, fear, and resolve. They were the faces of men before a battle, men about to confront the angel of death.

Abraham was holding a bayonet and Meir-Ikhiel had picked up a heavy club.

"They're killing Jews!" shrieked a woman's shrill voice from farther up the street.

"Let's go!" ordered Abraham.

His father followed him. It was the first time, Abraham thought briefly, that he had ever given his father an order. The workers from the print shop also followed him.

Several Chassidim ran past.

"Don't run away!" Abraham called out to them. "Defend yourselves!"

"They're coming after us," replied one of the Chassidim, his face twisted by terror.

Behind them, a bleeding man stumbled across the street and collapsed in front of the butcher's shop. Then about thirty men appeared, holding clubs, iron bars, pick handles, and shovels.

Abraham and Meir-Ikhiel walked side by side, with the others behind them. Then they all stopped and stood still, in a solid block, with strength in their hearts. Ahead of them, the Poles also stopped and waited.

Doors began opening, timidly at first, then boldly. Jews came out, armed with broomsticks, boards, or Succot branches, and joined the self-defense group.

Abraham and Meir-Ikhiel looked at each other. Yes, they had to go forward. They began walking again. The others followed them, pulling iron bars from shutters and throwing paving stones.

The Poles began an orderly withdrawal. But women and children on balconies threw flower pots, boiling water, and lumps of coal at them. The Jews in the street were seized with excitement that made them quicken their pace until they were running.

"Look out!" someone shouted. "Stop! They've got guns!"

At the corner of Stawki Street, a hundred Poles armed with rifles, shotguns, and pistols were putting up a makeshift barricade.

A woman stepped out from the shadow of a building and stood in the middle of the street, waving her arms as though to stop a train.

"Stop! Stop!"

Abraham saw her before his father did.

"Olga!" he cried.

"Olga!" cried his father.

"Stop!" Olga repeated. "Don't be stupid! They're going to shoot!"

But there was no stopping those Jews. They were charging the enemy, and this time they were beyond fear.

Abraham clearly saw the Poles take aim from behind the barricade. A moment later he heard a sound like the crack of a felled tree. Bullets whined past his ears.

Olga lay on the pavement. Her last image of the world she had tried to regenerate was of Meir-Ikhiel and Abraham leaning over her with tears in their eyes.

45

WARSAW

Long Live Free
Poland!

IT WOULD be hard to say exactly what Olga meant to Abraham, or what it was inside him that died with her that day: love, his revolutionary zeal, or his hope of freeing the Jewish people. In any case, he was transformed. He turned inward, stopped all his militant activities, began studying the Talmud again, and went to the village of Gura Kalwarja [Mount Calvary] to see the wondrous Rabbi Abraham-Mordecai Alter, great-grandson of Rabbi Isaac-Meir. The illustrious rabbi received him out of regard for his grandfather Lazare and spent several hours alone with him, to the detriment of dozens of disciples from all over Poland who had been waiting outside his door for days.

As soon as Abraham returned to Warsaw he went to Pawia Street to settle the terms of his marriage to Rachel. Aaron Pasirstein promised a large dowry. Abraham refused it, despite the insistence of his fiancée's family, whose honor was at stake. Meir-Ikhiel proposed a compromise: the Pasirsteins would provide the young couple with premises for a print shop, and Meir-Ikhiel would supply the necessary equipment.

And so Abraham opened his print shop at 29 Nowolipie Street on the day after his wedding. Unlike his father, who had just published the complete works of I. L. Peretz, Abraham decided to devote himself solely to printing. "I'm satisfied with printing and understanding what I print," he said. He hired only young Chassidim; they saw their trade as a continuation of the sacred work done by those ancient scribes who wore prayer shawls and washed their hands each time they had to write the holy name of the Almighty on a papyrus scroll.

Most of them were from Piotrków, Pilgorai, and Jozefowo and had come to Warsaw in search of both work and knowledge. As a result, Abraham was soon specializing in printing rabbinical texts as difficult as those of Rashi. With their *payesses* quivering and their hats awry, the Chassidim leaned over type boxes or punched the keys of the linotype machine, working with such fervor and animation that they reminded Abraham of "an assembly of young prophets standing on the volcano of inspiration."

A year later, Abraham's younger brother Yudl married the daughter of a sock manufacturer and went to work in his father-in-law's business. "You work for Jews' heads," he said to Abraham, "and I work for their feet!" Their sister Leah married Joseph Fainberg, a doctor from Vilna whom she had met in the hospital on Marszalkowska Street.

Zalta died of angina in 1913, just before Mendel Beilis, a Russian Jew accused of ritual murder by the czar's police, was tried in Kiev. The accusation set off a series of petitions, meetings, and demonstrations. The Jewish world seethed with indignation—ritual murder, as in the Middle Ages! Although Abraham had lost interest in politics and was indifferent to news about the dissolution of the first Duma, or the formation of the second and third ones, or conflicts between the two factions of Russian Marxism, the Bolsheviks and the Mensheviks, he was deeply affected by the Beilis trial. He understood why so many young Zionists were going to Palestine. "We can solve our problems," he said, "only in Eretz Israel, the land of our ancestors."

He himself would not go to Palestine. Warsaw was his city. But he withdrew more and more into his work, and into study of the Talmudic sages, especially the famous compiler Judah ha-Nasi, who maintained that "man should choose the way that honors him in his own eyes and earns him the esteem of others." And for a printer, what could be more estimable than reproducing the precepts of wisdom?

When he left the print shop in the evening, he often went to join a group of friends, all Chassidic disciples of the rabbi of Gur, in a small house of study at the back of a courtyard. He spent Saturdays with his family. Rachel had given him five children in five years, three boys and two girls. He would no doubt have gone on living this way through all the days allotted to him by the Almighty, blessed be He, if war had not disrupted millions of lives, including his.

During the night of August 4, 1914, the city changed. In the morning, columns of armed Russian soldiers invaded the streets. Waves of Jewish refugees, driven from outlying districts by order of the military commander in chief, Nikolai Nikolaevich, began arriving. While the Russian-French-British general staff installed itself in the Bristol Hotel, thousands of homeless people squeezed into courtyards, with the Jews from each village or community gathered around their rabbi.

It was said that because of the influx of Jewish refugees the Poles had demanded that the Russian authorities expel all Jews from Warsaw. The Poles were divided: some, with General Pilsudski, favored siding with the Germans and Austrians, hoping it would bring about Polish independence; others loudly proclaimed their loyalty to the czar. But, as Yudl said one day when he brought socks for his nephews and nieces, all Poles at least agreed on what should be done with the Jews.

In 1915 Polish anti-Semitic groups succeeded in having Yiddish banned, on the grounds that it was a German dialect and therefore a form of the enemy's language. The Russian administration prohibited the publication of Yiddish newspapers and books. Abraham and Meir-Ikhiel were forced to close their print shops.

Food was scarce and expensive. Abraham went to work doing makeup in a Polish print shop and his two older sons did what they could to help. One became an errand boy for a sausage merchant named Carlsberg, who paid him in kind; the other, Salomon, ten years old, also became an errand boy, for the print shop where Abraham worked. Every kopeck counted.

Finally, on the morning of August 5, 1915, two weeks after the battles of Tarnów and Görlitz, the defeated Russians began leaving Warsaw. All the streets that converged on the bridge over the Vistula were packed with men, trucks, and horse-drawn vehicles. Fleeing soldiers sold their equipment. Makeshift markets sprang up, where civilian clothes were traded for flour, groats, and lard.

The Germans came into Warsaw and the Jews regained hope:

the new authorities lifted the ban on publication of Yiddish newspapers and books.

The Jewish Socialists of the Bund set up a print shop at 7 Nowolipie Street to publish their weekly, *Lebensfragen* [Life Questions]. Abraham went to work there, and so did Salomon, as an apprentice. The father and son were happy to work together. "The apple doesn't fall far from the tree," said Abraham, smiling.

Salomon, who was now eleven and small for his age, proved to be attentive, gifted, and quick to learn. Within a year he was beginning to do typesetting for simple texts. He was one of the sights of the print shop when he worked standing on a crate, his hands moving from one type box to another with a deftness envied by many adults. And often, when he had nothing else to do, he would spend his time learning the linotype keyboard or developing his skills in other ways.

He worked so diligently at the shop that his parents were hardly surprised when, one day in August 1916, he did not come home at his usual time. But when he failed to come for dinner, they began looking for him. He was not at the print shop or in the courtyard. He did not come home to sleep. At dawn, he had still not been found.

His mother Rachel, who had a weak heart, had to take to her bed. The whole family—brothers, sisters, cousins—gathered in Abraham's apartment. The men prayed.

While Meir-Ikhiel went to notify the police, Abraham decided to ask for advice from the Jewish printers' union. At the office on Leszno Street he met Moshe Skliar, one of the union leaders. He could not explain his son's disappearance, he said; it seemed totally unlikely that he might have simply run away from home.

"Maybe he's been arrested," suggested Skliar.

"Arrested? For what?"

"Could he have had revolutionary leaflets in his possession?"

"He's never said anything to us about politics," replied Abraham.

"A father is the last to know what his son does," remarked an office worker who had been listening to their conversation.

Skliar stood up.

"Let's go and talk to a lawyer."

He and Abraham went to Krolewska Street to consult Jan Slonimski, a lawyer who sometimes handled cases for the union. Slonimski promised to do whatever he could to find Salomon.

The newspapers reported Salomon's disappearance. There were no developments for several days.

Finally, ten days before Rosh Hashanah, Moshe Skliar and Jan Slonimski came to tell Abraham that Salomon had been found, alive.

"Thank God! Where is he?"

"In the Mokotow prison."

Abraham went there immediately, with the lawyer. An iron gate, barred windows, dilapidated walls. They had to wait a long time before being allowed to speak with a German officer, who informed them that young Salomon Halter was in prison for having been caught with a copy of *Czervony Sztandar* [Red Flag], a collection of Polish revolutionary poems. The officer put on a monocle to look at a report on his desk.

"We suspect him of working at night in the clandestine print shop of *Tzum Kampf* [To Battle], the illicit Yiddish newspaper of the Jewish Communists."

"But that's impossible, sir!" said Abraham. "He's only a boy! I'm his father: I know very well that he was never away from home at night before he was arrested!"

"The report suggests otherwise."

The officer took off his monocle; it left a ring around his eye.

"I'm the young man's attorney," Jan Slonimski said in his most impressive voice. "May I see him?"

"Yes, you may. But not today."

Slonimski's arguments were futile. Salomon spent two more weeks in prison, and was released only after a vehement press campaign led by Wladimir Medem in the newspaper of the Bund, protesting every day against the imprisonment of a twelve-year-old boy.

When Salomon, looking thinner and even shorter, was brought home by Slonimski, all the friends and neighbors of the family came to see him and ask him if it was true that he had done this or that. He told them that he had been arrested with a collection of revolutionary poems in his possession. And when they asked him what he had done in prison, he answered, "I slept."

Rachel was in a state of nervous exhaustion. She died two weeks later and was buried in the Gesia cemetery. Abraham was left alone with his five children.

The war continued. Needing soldiers, the Germans conscripted young Poles and Jews, as the Russians had done before them.

Meir-Ikhiel received a letter from Canada; cousin Fred, brother of cousin Maurice, had written from a town named Kamsack, where he owned what he called a saloon. He had read in Canadian newspapers about the situation of the Jews in Poland. He asked if there was anything he could do to help, and in the meantime he enclosed two hundred dollars with his letter. According to him, the Americans would soon enter the war and quickly bring it to an end.

In February 1917, revolution broke out in Russia. The Polish newspapers gave contradictory accounts of it. A victory by the revolutionaries was reported one day and denied the next. In Warsaw, the revolutionaries' triumph was finally confirmed on March 11.

But the war on the Russian front continued until March 1918, when the Treaty of Brest-Litovsk was signed, enabling the Germans to strengthen their western front. Warsaw then became filled with deserters and wounded men. Israel, a shoemaker from the neighborhood who was not much older than Salomon, also came back, after two years of war. Abraham invited him to dinner. Israel was immediately bombarded with questions.

"Did you see the fall of the czar?"

"Tell us about the revolution."

"Did you see Trotsky?"

"Have you become a Bolshevik?"

"Where were you when the revolution started?"

"In a village near Voronezh."

"What happened?"

"The Germans ran away from the Red Army. I was hired as a steward by a Jewish family who had bought an estate after the Kerensky revolution."

"Why a steward?"

"Because they didn't need a shoemaker!"

"When did you realize that the revolution had succeeded?"

"When the Bolsheviks confiscated the estate. The peasants formed a soviet and shot several officers. Then came the Drozdov bandits, and finally the Austrians. I ran away, to another village. The region was occupied by Denikin's troops, then Makhno's, and then the Bolsheviks came back. I had no idea what was going on."

"What's it like with the Bolsheviks?"

"It's everyone against everyone else."

"Did you see the Petlyura pogrom?"

641

"Yes, but I'd rather not talk about it."

"Why don't you all stop asking Israel so many questions?" said Abraham.

He liked the young shoemaker, and he was glad later, when he realized that there were tender feelings between his daughter Regina and Israel. Although Israel practiced a modest trade, he had learned a great deal from clandestine seminars in which students explained Marx and Hegel, in the same way rabbis commented on the Gemara at street corners. But since coming back from the war, he seemed detached from everything. When Abraham tried to sound him out with regard to Regina, Israel evaded his questions.

"Don't be angry with me, Rab Abraham," he finally said one day. "As you know, it is written that 'man is the only unfinished animal on earth, and therefore each man must develop his own nature.' Mine hasn't taken shape yet. You wouldn't want your daughter to marry a man without a nature, would you? Give me a little more time. . . ."

He came to the house nearly every day. One evening he seemed tense and asked if he could stay overnight. A mattress was put on the floor for him. He left early the next morning, before even Abraham was awake. In the afternoon the newspapers reported that the head of the German military police in Warsaw had been assassinated. Salomon and his brother David wondered if Israel had been involved in the assassination, and they tried to find out from their sister Regina if he belonged to the military organization of the Socialist party, since, according to the newspapers, that was where the assassins were most likely to be found.

The killing of the head of the military police put the German army on the alert. The police made raids. The two linotypists who worked in the print shop of *Lebensfragen* were arrested. Salomon, who had learned to operate the machine on his own, offered to work in the shop and was accepted.

A few days later a neighbor who lived on the same floor as Abraham, and was the only one in the building who had a telephone, came to tell Regina that there was a call for her. It was Israel. He asked her to pack a few things and come to meet him at the railroad station.

Abraham had not come home by the time Regina finished packing. She wrote a short letter to him and left.

Dear father, I waited for you, but you were late. Israel is being hunted by the police. He is accused of taking part in the assassination of the head of the German military police. He cannot go on hiding indefinitely. He wants to leave the country and I think he is right. I am going with him. Knowing you as I do, I am sure you will understand.

Please forgive me, father, for the pain that my sudden departure may cause you, but I am sure we will see each other again soon. I pray that you will be given health and long life.

Your devoted daughter, Regina.

Abraham wondered if he would have time to get to the station before she took a train, but his sons persuaded him not to try.

He did not hear from Regina until shortly before Succot. She and Israel were in Danzig and were about to take a Swedish ship to France; from there, they would leave with other Jews for Argentina, "a new country where immigrants are not regarded as foreigners, no matter where they come from."

Meanwhile, in Warsaw, posters put on walls by unknown people were calling for a pogrom.

The abdication of the czar on March 15, 1917, and then the German defeat in November 1918, enabled Poland to proclaim its independence and establish its own institutions. Crowds in which Jews were mingled with non-Jews paraded through the streets, shouting, "Long live independent Poland! Long live free Poland!" General Pilsudski, head of the new Polish government, met with a delegation from the Zionist Organization to discuss the problems of the Jews in Poland. And the Jews in Poland began hoping again.

Meir-Ikhiel, now nearing sixty, was one of the few who showed skepticism.

"During the occupation," he said, "the Poles' hatred of the Jews was often pushed into the background. But now . . ."

"Grandfather," said Salomon, "it's not written anywhere that the Poles must hate us forever. My non-Jewish friends don't care whether I'm Jewish or not."

"I think Salomon is right, father," said Abraham. "Jews have been living in this country for centuries. They're part of the Polish nation's vital forces. General Pilsudski knows that if he excluded us, he couldn't build a free Poland."

"I hope with all my heart that you're both right," replied Meir-

Ikhiel. But his expression showed that he believed they were mistaken.

A few days after the proclamation of independence and the withdrawal of the German occupation forces from the last territories still under their control, a wave of anti-Semitism broke over the country. There were killings in Lvov, Cracow, Kielce, Lublin, Lida, Vilna, and all the villages of Galicia. At the Lapy station, policemen took Jews off the train for Bialystok and whipped them. Even in Warsaw, on Przejard Street in the heart of the city, Polish soldiers forced Jewish passersby to go into the barracks, where they were beaten and made to do humiliating work. In rural areas, Jews were again accused of ritual murders; in Warsaw, they were called Bolsheviks and accused of betraying Poland.

The most patient among them still tried to find excuses for the Poles. "These are labor pains," they said. "A new state is always born in disorder, but this violence will soon be forgotten and the Jews will become citizens like everyone else." But the government, by decree, gave them the status of a religious minority. Expressions of solidarity came in from all over the world. Every day *Lebensfragen* published lists of prestigious names—Anatole France, Henri Barbusse, Charles Seignobos, Ernest Lavisse—that warmed the Jews' hearts but did not change their situation.

Self-defense groups were again formed, and once again sons repeated their fathers' experience. Boys had discovered some guns in a former depot of the German army. Guns! The self-defense groups endlessly practiced taking them apart and putting them back together. That was all they could do: they had no ammunition.

At this time, only Salomon did not belong to the self-defense group formed by the families who lived around his courtyard, but his stay in prison had given him special status. Whenever he had some free time, he went off to talk music, painting, or revolution with a small circle of friends. The guiding spirit of the circle was Hinda, a tall, dark-haired young woman of eighteen. Like Salomon, she was a linotypist—the only woman linotypist in Warsaw. Despite the differences of height and age between them, he was madly in love with her. His rival was also his friend: Leibele Hechtman, a nervous young man who was said to be a Communist, though he worked in the print shop of the religious daily *Der Yid [The Jew]*. When Salomon and Leibele took Hinda to a concert, she stayed between them and each kept watch on the other to see if she had moved too close to him or was favoring him in any way.

For Salomon, who passionately loved music, those concerts were both exhausting and frustrating. His idol was the violinist Bronislaw Hubermann. Leibele, however, had little interest in Hubermann, and Salomon suspected him of going to the concerts only to keep him from being alone with Hinda.

"Your Bronimann Huberslaw plays a lot of notes, I'll grant you that," Leibele said one day when they had heard the Brahms concerto, "but when the anti-Semites come after you, you won't stop them with violins."

Salomon looked at him disdainfully and quoted from Zechariah: "Not by might, nor by power, but by my Spirit, says the Lord of hosts."

"It's easy to give a quotation when you don't have an answer!"

Meir-Ikhiel, who was present during the conversation, told himself it was true that there was nothing new under the sun.

"Hubermann uses his prestige to struggle for Jewish rights!" protested Salomon. "He has the support of famous people: Germans like Konrad Adenauer, Frenchmen like Romain Rolland, who won a Nobel prize a few years ago, and Aristide Briand . . ."

"Salomon, Salomon!" Meir-Ikhiel said with a sigh. "Romain Rolland is a fine writer, I've read him too, but our fate depends mainly on ourselves, on our own writers—that's why I published I. L. Peretz—and on our own values and traditions." He hesitated, then added, "And—why not?—on our own strength! On our faith too. You go to hear your violinist whenever you can, but have you seen those crowds that gather every Friday evening and Saturday morning in front of the synagogues on Tlomackie Street and Twarda Street, those thousands of Jews who wait for hours, even when it's raining or snowing, to hear the great *chazzans* Lewenson of Minsk and Moshe Kusowicki?"

Meir-Ikhiel regretted that his grandchildren did not pray more regularly. They and other members of their generation, brought up on revolutionary leaflets, posters, and manifestos, seemed almost foreign to him. He wondered how they would cope with affliction when it came, and if they would then return to the only valid truth: the truth of the Almighty, blessed be He.

HINDA BECAME PREGNANT. She announced it to her friends Leibele and Salomon one day at noon, while they were talking in the Saxon Garden. It was Sunday. The government did not require Jews to work on Friday afternoon and Saturday, but it did require them not to work on Sunday. Since many merchants could not make a living by working only four days a week, they surreptitiously sold their wares on Sunday, in the streets or the Saxon Garden. Hinda, Leibele, and Salomon watched them and were amused by their efforts to look as if they were only out for a stroll, while at the same time trying to catch the attention of the people they passed. Suddenly Hinda became serious, almost sullen. She told Leibele and Salomon that she was pregnant and that she wanted them to raise the money she would need for an abortion.

As soon as they were alone together, Salomon swore to Leibele that he could not be the father of Hinda's child, and Leibele swore the same to Salomon. They then went to see the fourth member of their little circle, the painter Janek Kobyla, who was said to paint only because it enabled him to lure women into his apartment on the pretext of wanting them to pose for him. But Janek had never gone to bed with Hinda either, though he admitted that it was not for lack of trying.

The three young men, united in their hatred of the unknown rival who had stolen Hinda from them, worked overtime, borrowed, and saved until they had the sum she needed.

The abortion went badly. Hinda hemorrhaged repeatedly and had to stay in bed several days. Salomon asked his uncle, Dr. Joseph Fainberg to treat her. When she was finally able to get up, she had changed. Her eyes had become harder.

SALOMON COULD NOT BEAR what had happened. He was sixteen and life was not giving him what he expected of it. He now did his work at the print shop only in order to draw his salary. The idea of going away came to him one day when he read a newspaper advertisement for a print shop in Danzig that had work for Yiddish linotypists. Applicants were asked to come to the Bristol Hotel.

He applied and was hired. He then went home and told his father that he was about to leave for Danzig.

Abraham was thunderstruck. First Regina, now Salomon. It seemed to him that if his children left home before they were married, it was because they did not feel happy there. But he did not ask Salomon any questions. He believed that a young man should be allowed to "walk in the ways of his heart and the sight of his eyes," as it was written in Ecclesiastes. He did, however, suggest to Salomon that as long as he had decided to leave Warsaw, it might be better to go to Eretz Israel: he could go there with his cousin Mordecai, who was about to leave with a group of young people known as *Chalutzim* [pioneers] to found one of the collective farms called *kibbutzim*. But Salomon had no desire to go to Palestine.

His father went to the station with him. There were soldiers everywhere. The Russo-Polish War was in full swing, and the advance of the Red Army had given rise to a real obsession with "Judeo-Bolsheviks." Two posters were displayed in the station. One showed Bolshevism as a red demon with Semitic features, sitting on a pile of skulls; the other showed soldiers of the Red Army waving white-and-blue flags bearing the Star of David. The names of the Bolshevik leaders appeared on the front pages of newspapers: Trotsky was "Trotsky-Bronstein," Zinoviev was "Zinoviev-Apfelbaum," Radek was "Radek-Sobelsohn."

"It's starting again," said Abraham.

"The bastards!" Salomon muttered under his breath.

As he was passing one of the posters, he tore off a corner of it. A short, timid-looking man immediately began shouting as if he were trying to stir up the whole population of Warsaw.

"He's tearing down the posters! He's a spy! A Bolshevik agent!"

"May God protect us!" said Abraham.

"Stay here, father. I can escape more easily by myself. You'll hear from me soon."

Salomon quickly kissed his father's hand and plunged into the crowd.

"This way! This way!" cried a fat lady.

A policeman who had been looking in the opposite direction turned around and, not knowing what was happening, grabbed the first man he saw.

"No, that's the wrong man!" shrieked the fat lady. "Go after the little Jew!"

She created enough confusion all by herself to enable the "little Jew" to disappear. Abraham watched the crowd open, then quickly close, like a clump of reeds through which a fox had passed. He heard a voice call out:

"Passengers for Gdansk, all aboard!"

The train creaked, groaned, and finally set off in a cloud of steam. The crowd slowly drained away from the platform. Salomon was not there. When Abraham passed the torn poster on his way out of the station, he murmured, "Praise be to You, O Lord our God, King of the world, who lift up the downtrodden."

46

WARSAW

Perl and Salomon

SALOMON DID not come back to Warsaw until springtime of the year 5688 after the creation of the world by the Almighty, blessed be He; that is, in March 1928. He was nearly twenty-three. The Jews were preparing to celebrate Passover and the Poles were preparing to celebrate the second anniversary of the *coup d'état* carried out by General Pilsudski, who had meanwhile made himself Marshal Pilsudski.

Abraham scarcely recognized his son: Salomon had grown taller, he now wore glasses, and he looked much more serious than before, though his beard was still as downy as an adolescent's.

Salomon looked at his father as though seeing him for the first time and discovered a man in his forties, tall but rather stooped, as many printers were, with calm eyes and a beard that had already turned gray. Abraham told him that Meir-Ikhiel had died two months earlier and that David and Samuel, Salomon's brothers, had left Warsaw. David, wanted by the police because of his union activities among the leather workers, had fled to France and was now living in Paris. Samuel, a great admirer of Dr. Zamenhof, was somewhere in Europe, propagating the new universal language, Esperanto.

Abraham was working in the print shop of *Der Moment [The*

Moment], the newspaper of the Jewish populists, and lived at 35 Nowolipie Street, not far from his former apartment. The new apartment was dark but more spacious than the old one. He lived there with his younger daughter Topcia and her family. After years of self-sacrifice during which she replaced the mother who had died and the older sister who had gone away, the good-hearted Topcia had finally married. She had two children who brightened Abraham's evenings and helped him to bear his regret at not having the rest of his family with him. It was Topcia who suggested that Salomon live in the apartment until he found work . . . and a wife.

On the day after his return, he spent hours strolling aimlessly. It was a beautiful day. On Nowolipie Street, in the Saxon Garden, and on Krolewska Street, he was amazed to see so many Jews. Nothing but Jews. With signs in Yiddish, and smells of pickles, onions, and fresh bread. He wondered what Palestine was like. Could Jews feel as much at home there as in Warsaw? In Grzybowski Square he stopped to watch a peddler selling potato pancakes, raisins, and hot chickpeas. What was the future of that picturesque, appealing little society? What was its place in the world? Did those questions ever come into the peddler's mind?

Salomon went to Twarda Street but learned that Hinda had moved away. He then went to see the painter Janek Kobyla. When he came into the apartment and saw a young woman putting on her clothes, he told himself that not everything in Warsaw had changed. Janek embraced him and took out a bottle of brandy. They drank to friendship and told each other what they had been doing. For Janek, things were going rather well.

"And how's Hinda doing?" asked Salomon. "And Leibele?"

Janek looked embarrassed.

"I don't see very much of them," he said. "They're not the same as they used to be. . . . A few months ago Leibele was wounded —a bullet in the chest. Someone knocked on his door and shot him as soon as he opened it. He said he didn't see who it was. I went to visit him in the hospital. I haven't seen him since then."

"A bullet in the chest!"

Salomon was astounded. He knew that people were shot every day, all over the world—but this was Leibele, his childhood friend!

"Tell me about Hinda," he said.

"She's married," replied Janek. "She's the secretary of the Jewish bureau of the Communist party. From what I hear, she's tough as nails. But I don't care about the Communists, or politics in general. People who claim to be struggling against oppression kill each other." He pointed to the paintings scattered at random in the studio, the easels, the tubes of paint, the rags, the big vase that held a bouquet of brushes. "Art is the only form of resistance I know. Painting is my politics. Tracking down beauty, fixing it on canvas, showing it to others . . ."

As he had done so often in the past, Salomon found a way to end the discussion.

"It's not the beautiful that pleases God; it's what pleases God that's beautiful."

"Now you sound like your old self, you little Jew! *Lechaim!*"

Salomon went to see Leibele Hechtman. They warmly shook hands. Leibele wore a velvet vest under his striped jacket, and a white scarf around his neck. His face had changed greatly: its bones had triumphed over its flesh.

"Come," he said, "let's take a walk. You'll see that this country is becoming more and more Jewish. If it goes on much longer, Yiddish will be the official language."

"Are you still a Communist?" Salomon asked when they were outside.

"Yes," Leibele answered with a bitter smile, "but being a Communist in Poland isn't very pleasant nowadays. We're harassed from all sides. People are afraid of us."

"Maybe because of the example of Russia."

Leibele stopped and turned to Salomon with a sigh, as if it tired him in advance to begin a conversation that he had already had countless times before.

"The fact remains that Russia is the only place where socialism has been established. And I'm not ashamed to defend a country that's come out of the Middle Ages and into the industrial era within a few years, a country that's given freedom and dignity to workers and peasants who only yesterday were slaves."

A Chassid wearing a fur hat approached the two friends.

"Jews," he said, "leave politics alone till after the holidays."

"Politics won't leave *us* alone, even on holidays!" retorted Leibele.

"Let's go," said Salomon, "before a crowd starts gathering."

At the corner of Karmelicka Street, Leibele stopped again.

"And what about you?" he asked Salomon. "What's on your mind these days?"

"I don't know. . . . The dangers that threaten us. . . ."

"You mean the counterrevolution?"

"Call it whatever you like. I'm talking about disorder, violence, maybe even war."

"You're a pessimist!"

"Have you read Barbusse?"

"Of course."

"Do you remember this passage in *Under Fire?* 'A serene flash between two masses of dark clouds . . .' "

" '. . . proves that the sun exists,' " Leibele concluded.

They slapped their right hands against each other, as they had done in their days of innocence. Then Salomon said, "I've heard that someone tried to kill you."

"Ah, so you know about that." Leibele frowned and looked down at his feet. "I opened my door and someone shot me. That's the whole story. I didn't see anything."

"Was it political?"

"It must have been someone like you, who didn't like Communists. Let's go and have a drink, to celebrate your return!"

FOR SALOMON'S FIRST PASSOVER at home after all those years, Abraham wanted the *seder* to be particularly impressive. Moniek, Topcia's husband, had enlarged the table, which now took up nearly all the space in the living room. Topcia set it as her mother—blessed be her memory—had done in the old days, when all the children were still at home.

On the white tablecloth, a plate covered with an embroidered cloth. On the plate, three pieces of unleavened bread represented the tribe of the Kohanim, the tribe of the Levites, and the rest of the people of Israel. Beside it, horseradish, whose bitter taste served to remind Jews of the time of slavery; a mixture of wine, ground nuts, and grated apples to represent the mortar used by their ancestors in building the Pyramids; a charred bone to evoke the sacrifice offered in the Temple on that day in ancient times; hard-boiled eggs in salty water to symbolize tears and mourning, in memory of the destruction of the Temple.

Salomon did not personally know everyone seated around the Passover table. Uncle Yudl's family, and aunt Leah's, and cousins with their own families. Yudl's son Fischel had brought his fiancée, Perl. Her father, Abraham Rotstein, owned a small sock factory, as Yudl did, and the two competitors had decided to form a partnership. There was also cousin Mordecai, who had gone to Palestine seven years earlier and was now back in Poland to help train young *chalutzim*. With him was a young woman named Droza, who had been born on a *kibbutz* in Galilee and, to everyone's amazement, spoke only Hebrew.

Abraham read the Hagaddah. He seemed happy. The light of the candles danced in his eyes. After the meal, he, Topcia, and Moniek sang several Chassidic melodies. Mordecai told about his life in "the land" and sang some songs of the pioneers. "We came to build the land and be rebuilt by it," said one of the songs, and Salomon was struck by that idea. But how, he wondered, do you go about rebuilding a Jew?

Then Abraham stood up and went to bring the family book. He and Meir-Ikhiel had added a printed section to the copy of it inherited from Lazare, giving the names, dates, and events of the family's life in Poland. Abraham regretted that he had not yet printed new copies of the book, so that each of his children and cousins could have one. He intended to devote his old age to that project. In the meantime, he devoutly read a few pages aloud. The last sentence mentioned Salomon's return from Danzig.

Salomon sensed that Perl, Fischel's fiancée, was looking at him. He turned toward her and she did not lower her eyes. He looked away from her, embarrassed because of Fischel.

At the end of the evening, when they were all standing and about to separate—"Good night." "Next year in Jerusalem!" she came up to him.

"Fischel tells me you love music."

"Yes, I do. I go to concerts whenever I can."

"Next time," she said, "think of me. . . . Good night."

"Good night," he answered in an unsteady voice.

SALOMON BEGAN LOOKING for work. He visited the print shops of newspapers and book publishers. There was nothing for the moment, he was told, but if he stopped by regularly and happened to be there at the right time. . . . He decided to go and see Hinda. Leibele had told him that she now lived on Chmielna Street, above a bakery near the central station.

Perhaps because he had been in love with her, he did not want to meet her husband or go into their apartment, so one morning he waited for her to come out. When he saw her, it seemed to him that she was less tall than he had remembered her. She wore her hair coiled over the back of her neck. Her grayish complexion and the dark rings around her eyes showed that she was one of those militants who spend night after night in smoke-filled rooms, discussing motions and composing slogans. Her dark-red wool dress danced around her calves to the rhythm of her steps.

"Hinda!" he called out softly.

She looked at him and stopped abruptly.

"Salomon! Little Salomon! You grew taller while you were away!"

He suddenly wished he were somewhere else. He had nothing to say to this woman. They kissed each other on the cheeks, brusquely, like two men.

"Leibele told me you were married. . . ."

"You've seen Leibele?"

She seemed upset.

"Yes, I've seen Leibele, and also Janek, and now I'm seeing you. I'm making a tour of my past."

"I have to hurry," she said. "Why don't you come with me?"

They began walking side by side.

"Do you have any children?" he asked.

She gave him a harsh look.

"I can't have children. But for a militant, it's probably better that way. . . . What about you? Do you have a wife and children?"

"Not yet."

He asked her what had happened to Leibele and she seemed infinitely weary.

"No one knows," she said. "But the party is going through a difficult phase. Sometimes violent means are used. . . . Comintern agents. . . . He didn't tell you anything?"

"No. He regards me as a dangerous counterrevolutionary."

For a moment he felt like asking her if she had ever been even a little in love with him, but he realized it no longer really mattered to him. He told her that he had to leave her because he had an appointment with someone who might give him work.

"Come and see us whenever you like," she said. "I'll introduce you to my husband, Tomasz. You'll like him."

When Salomon came back to the apartment on Nowolipie Street, his father told him that he had received two letters that morning. One of them was from Regina, in Argentina, announcing

653

the birth of a son named Marcos. The other was from his cousin Maurice, in Canada. Abraham handed this one to Salomon.

"Read it aloud," he said, "so that Topcia can hear."

Salomon unfolded the letter.

My dear uncle and cousins,

I have sad news: my brother Fred has died, may his memory be blessed. He was a hard worker and a man with a big heart. He did many different kinds of work before he was able to buy two modest stores, one at Saltcoats and the other at Stornoway, in Saskatchewan. Once he even kept a saloon at Kamsack, where he lived with his family. His partner at that time was a man named Sam Bronfman, who persuaded him to go into the business of making whisky. That same year, the American government made alcoholic beverages illegal. My brother always respected the law, as you know, so he refused to take part in his partner's plan to have their whisky smuggled into North Dakota. He and Bronfman split up, and Bronfman became one of the richest Jews in America! After that, Fred went into the fur business. He dealt with Indians who liked him and sold him mink and silver fox furs of a kind that you have never seen in Europe. They also supplied him with herbs and medicinal plants.

Fred was a good Jew. For him, a *shabbat* was a *shabbat*. He collected money for the Jews in Palestine and also contributed money from his own pocket. His house was always so full of passing strangers that it was called the "Halter Hotel."

He loved music and dancing. He was a very good dancer, and even won prizes in contests. And he died while dancing, with friends, one Sunday in a saloon.

I am telling you all this, my dear uncle and cousins, because I know how much you meant to my brother. He was proud of belonging to one of the oldest families of Jewish printers and he even told Indians about the family book that is in your keeping. He often regretted that he had never seen it. That reminds me: if you ever print more copies, I would appreciate your sending me one. It would make me feel less far away.

I hope that God will give me better news to announce in the future. I wish you a good Passover, if my letter arrives in time.

Your cousin,
Maurice

"YES, MAYBE WE SHOULD have reprinted the Book of Abraham," said Salomon. "Poor Fred!"

"I'm sorry I didn't reprint it," said Abraham, "when I had my own print shop and the best workers in Poland. But remember, Salomon: 'We wish that life were like the shadow cast by a wall or a tree, but it is like the shadow of a bird in flight.' By the way, my son, have you thought of marriage?"

SALOMON THOUGHT OF MARRIAGE a few days later. He had just been hired as a linotypist for a new Orthodox Jewish newspaper, *Dos Yiddishe Togeblat [The Yiddish Daily]*. Relieved at no longer having to be dependent on his father and his sister, he slowly walked back toward the apartment by way of Smocza Street, where several dozen people seemed to be on the verge of storming the entrance of the theater: the performance was about to begin. In front of the building next door, an old man was tapping on the sidewalk with his wooden leg and calling out, "Pistachio nuts! *Kosher* pistachio nuts from Palestine! Pistachio nuts!" The women stayed in front of the entrance while the men went over to the old peddler, handed him a coin, and held open one of their pockets to let him pour a measure of pistachio nuts into it. At the box office, the pale-faced ticket seller tirelessly repeated in the lilting Yiddish of Lithuania that only seats in the last row were still available.

"Salomon! What are you doing here?"

He had not seen Perl, his cousin Fischel's fiancée. Now that he did see her, he found her very elegant. She wore a light gray jacket and a matching skirt that fitted snugly over her hips.

"Perl!"

They looked at each other and there was a great silence between them. Then Perl asked, "Are you going into the theater?"

"Yes. . . . No. . . . Would you like . . . ?"

"Yes," she said. "What play are they doing?"

"I don't know. Does it matter?"

"No, it doesn't matter."

Salomon bought two of the last-row tickets. The theater was a former warehouse with whitewashed walls. Bare bulbs hanging from long wires swayed fitfully, casting fantastic shadows. A smell of sweat and perfume, the cracking of pistachio nuts, laughter, loud voices. Salomon and Perl found two seats at one end of a wooden bench. When the room was full, the spectators began impatiently clapping their hands, stamping their feet, and whistling. Then a bell rang three times, giving rise to an "ah!" of pleasure. The ceiling lights went off and a miraculous silence fell over the room. The curtain rose.

As if this were a signal, many of the spectators began fidgeting and murmuring. Some of them decided to change places and made their way along the rows, bumping against the knees of those who remained seated. Insults were exchanged near the prompter's box. On the stage, an actor and an actress, both wearing outrageously heavy makeup, waited for the hubbub to die down. Finally the actor stepped forward to the footlights. Beads of sweat glistened on his face.

"Will you please let me begin acting?" he asked. "I have two children, may they live a hundred and twenty years, and their mother is waiting for me to bring home my pay!"

Laughter, applause. People stood in front of Salomon and Perl, forcing them to look for other seats. After jostling and being jostled, they found themselves in the middle of a group of regular theatergoers who seemed to know the actors by name.

On the stage, now, a professional matchmaker was trying to bring a young man and a young woman into agreement.

The man sitting next to Salomon said to him, "Would you like some pistachio nuts? Here, reach into my pocket."

"No, thanks."

"Go ahead, take some! And take some for your wife, too!"

A woman sitting behind Salomon thrust her knees against his back.

"What's the matter with you two? Is this the first time you've ever been in a theater? Don't make so much noise!"

On stage, the two young people's parents were discussing the amount of the dowry, but the young people themselves were not sure they wanted to marry each other. Then the rabbi appeared and tried to have the engagement broken so that his own son could marry the young woman. His scheming scandalized the spectators. They loudly expressed their indignation and encouraged the matchmaker. A woman angrily berated a man who had stepped on her foot as he moved toward the aisle.

"This play is as long as the Jews' exile!" said a voice.

The exasperated actors gestured forcefully, trying to make the audience quiet down enough to let them continue.

"That matchmaker is a bungler!" said another voice.

"If you'd shut up, maybe I could do better," retorted the actor. More laughter, uproarious this time.

Salomon and Perl sat side by side, tightly pressed against each other. They never knew if the matchmaker in the theater on Smocza Street succeeded in bringing the two young people together. They were so isolated from everything around them that they heard nothing.

PERL BROKE HER ENGAGEMENT to Fischel, which caused a quarrel between Abraham and his brother Yudl and divided the family in two. Salomon and Perl became engaged.

Salomon was happier than he had ever been before. He read the poems that Perl wrote and became acquainted with the Rotstein family, who lived on Swietna-Jerska Street. Perl had two sisters and a brother, and another sister from her father's second marriage. The sock factory was next to their apartment. Salomon listened to the songs of the women who worked in it; they were sad, resigned songs, so different from the belligerent songs of the workers in print shops.

He went to tell his friend Leibele about his engagement. Leibele was delighted for his sake and congratulated him sincerely. Then, since the weather was fair, they decided to go out and walk through the streets, as they had liked to do in the past. They went toward the Vistula, along Franciszkanska Street. From the parapet they looked down at dozens and dozens of Jews wearing long robes and Chassidic hats, basking in the sunshine on a beach of gray sand. Boys with *payesses* played among the little waves that lapped the riverbank.

"I've seen Hinda," said Salomon.

"Did she say anything about me?"

"No."

Leibele sat on the parapet and looked around to make sure no one was near enough to overhear what he was about to say.

"Salomon, I'm having trouble with the party. I made the mistake of saying what I thought. . . ."

"About what?"

"About Stalin. Since Stalin took over, the party has changed. Anyone who doesn't agree with him is a Fascist. He recommends boycotting the elections of the Jewish writers' union and accuses it of fascism. Same for the congress of Yiddish primary schools. I

657

said that all of Jewish culture couldn't be called fascistic, and I was labeled a deviationist. That's how things still stand."

"But that can't be why someone tried to kill you! It's a debate, not a war!"

"When the Stalinists debate something, they use guns as their strongest argument. Ever since the party began regarding all Socialists as Fascists, there have been no more strikes in common with the unions of the Bund. And the central bureau decided to force all other unions to follow it. How? With guns if necessary!" Leibele was bitter and sad. He felt betrayed in what had been the combat of his life. His voice became harder: "Have you heard of Luxemburg, the baker?"

"I don't think so."

"Then listen to this. Our union and the Bund's were both trying to get a majority in a bakery. When I learned that our people wanted to resort to force, I went to the bakers' cell and urged them not to use guns. But no one would listen to me. And Luxemburg, a militant from our bakers' cell, shot a Bundist baker in broad daylight. The Bund sent its combat section after us. We came within a hairsbreadth of a bloodbath."

"And what happened to Luxemburg?"

"Our people hid him for two days. Then, to make sure the police wouldn't get him and make him talk, they decided to liquidate him. They were about to execute him when the police arrived. Luxemburg was arrested. His bones were broken and he was put through all kinds of torture. He didn't give one single name—but the party said he was a provocateur, and expelled him!"

"That's no better than the kind of injustice the party claims to be fighting against."

"Wait, there's more. Every Friday evening the Poale Zion Smol, the left-wing Zionists, hold a literary gathering at the workers' center on Karmelicka Street. We began going there to disrupt their gatherings. Two weeks ago, several people were seriously wounded. But when I protested to Pinye, one of the leaders of the attack group, here's what he said to me: 'You're worrying too much about a little Zionist blood!' "

"But why are they doing that kind of thing?"

"Orders from the Comintern. Stalin wants to take all Communist parties in hand, all over the world. He's sent two of his agents to Poland to control operations."

"What do you think of your Russian paradise now?"

"Stalin isn't the Soviet Union, you know that. He's a dictator who uses Communist ideology."

"Was it Stalin's two agents who tried to kill you?"

Leibele clenched his teeth for a moment, then said, "After so many years of fighting for the same cause, I never would have thought it was possible that any of my comrades would try to kill me. But that's what happened, Salomon. It's only by luck that I'm still alive."

At the edge of the Vistula the Chassidim's children were playfully splashing water on each other, with high-pitched cries that sounded like the chirping of birds.

"Let's go," said Leibele, hopping down from the parapet. "I've told you enough for today. Now it's your turn. Tell me about Perl."

THE WEDDING took place at the beginning of March 1932, on Lag B'Omer. The Rotsteins' apartment, emptied of all its furniture, was packed with cousins, aunts, and uncles who had come for the occasion from Grodzisk, Zyrardów, and the surrounding villages. The nuptial canopy was set up in the central room.

The rabbi arrived. Candles were lit and a glass was filled with wine. Salomon's sister Topcia and Perl's sister Zosia escorted the bride while she walked around the groom seven times. Then the rabbi said the blessing. When it was time to put the wedding ring on the bride's finger, Salomon was suddenly panic-stricken: he could not remember where he had put the ring to be sure of not losing it. Perl looked at him in dismay. He became so flustered that his mind almost stopped working altogether. Finally Abraham suggested that he look in the inside pocket of his coat. The ring was there, to everyone's great relief. (The family talked about the incident for a long time afterward.) Someone cried out, *"Mazel tov!"* and the others repeated it. After slipping the ring onto the forefinger of Perl's right hand, Salomon spoke the traditional words.

"See: with this ring you belong to me by the marriage oath, according to the Law of Moses and Israel."

The plan called for a table to be set in the apartment, but since it was a beautiful day someone had the idea of making a table with trestles and boards, covered with white tablecloths, in the courtyard. On it were placed candles, trays of pastry, baskets of fruit, and bottles of wine and brandy.

Abraham Rotstein sent the children to invite the neighbors to the celebration. They came, bringing still more pastry, fruit, and wine. The guests drank to the bride's health, then to the groom's. A violinist and an accordionist arrived, and the dancing went on till dawn. Perl never missed a dance; it was as if she had decided to dance with every man at the wedding. Salomon was a little jealous.

"You didn't invite Janek Kobyla?" Leibele asked him.

"Yes, I invited him, but he said that one *goy* among so many Jews would be indecent."

"What about the other way around?"

"One Jew among many *goyim?*"

"Yes."

"That would be tragic!"

They laughed. Perl came toward them. Night had fallen, a beautiful May night, and in her white gown she was like an apparition.

"You're not tired?" Salomon asked her.

"No. Getting married is something you don't do every day."

ABRAHAM ROTSTEIN GAVE the newlyweds an apartment in an attractive stone building on Smocza Street, opposite the Saint Augustine Church and not far from the theater where their future together had been decided. A week later, Perl invited her friends to a housewarming celebration.

Perl's friends were poets, writers, and journalists. They began coming to the apartment regularly to discuss current events. The outlook seemed bleak: Europe was in the grip of an unprecedented depression, with all the afflictions that went with it, including the inevitable resurgence of anti-Semitism. In Germany, Hitler was on his way to taking power and democrats had resigned themselves to it because he evidently intended to do it by legal means. The Comintern was pleased that the German Communists had fallen back without fighting: their forces were still intact. The Polish National Democratic party was encouraged by events in Germany. There was anti-Jewish violence in Michalin, Radom, Lublin, and Grodzisk. In Warsaw, armed bands attacked Jews in the streets. Combat groups from the Bund and the Poale Zion counterattacked in the vicinity of the Jewish quarter and several of their adversaries were sent to the hospital. Only then did the police intervene. The next day there was another assault against the Jews. This time two people were killed. Jewish shops were closed as a sign of protest.

There were public meetings to express solidarity in Geneva, Paris, London, Antwerp, and even Canada.

"A crisis doesn't show you who your real friends are," Abraham said to his family when they had gathered for *shabbat*.

"What do you mean?" asked Salomon.

"Imagine a man beating his slave. What would you do to help the slave? You'd stop the man from beating him, and then, satisfied with yourself, you'd go back to your usual occupations. But the slave would still be in slavery."

THE NEXT TWO YEARS, 1933 and 1934, were what historians call a "period of rising peril." The consequences of the Great Depression, and the increasingly harsh opposition between theorists of the "left" and those of the "right," might have seemed to indicate that major confrontations were imminent. But people had not forgotten the "great butchery" of 1914–1918 and they wanted to live a little.

In 1935 Henry Barbusse died. His book *Under Fire* had greatly influenced young people of Salomon's generation. Perl did not regard him as a great writer—she preferred Joyce, Thomas Mann, van Loon, Georg Brandes—but Salomon was deeply touched by his commitment to peace and what he had written about war. Salomon therefore decided to attend Barbusse's funeral, in Paris. It would also give him a chance to see his brother David.

He requested a visa. It was immediately denied to him, without explanation. He asked for help from old Slonimski, the union lawyer, who had connections in the Ministry of the Interior. But Slonimski failed to get either a visa or an explanation. Salomon Halter had probably been on file as a "dangerous element" ever since he was imprisoned at the age of twelve for having been found in possession of a collection of revolutionary poems.

He did not give up. He went to see a Communist printer he had known in Danzig, Joseph Majnemer, who now worked for the Jewish Polish-language newspaper *Nasz Przeglad*. Salomon had been told that he knew ways of leaving Poland clandestinely.

Majnemer gave him all the information and addresses he needed. Since Salomon would have to hike through rugged mountainous terrain to cross the border, it was out of the question for Perl to go with him. Besides, they had very little money and she preferred to wait till they could make a "real trip" to Paris.

Abraham disapproved of Salomon's plan, and told him so.

"Why take such risks when you don't have to?" he said. He hid his anxiety behind a smile. "And all that for the funeral of a man you don't even know!"

As he had done years earlier, he accompanied his son to the railroad station, this time with Perl. Leibele Hechtman also came. His face was even more gaunt and there were dark rings around his eyes. He took Salomon aside for a few moments.

"Salomon, I have to tell you. . . . I'm in danger again. If our group isn't thrown out of the party, they'll eliminate me. If we never see each other again, you'll know what happened."

"What shall I do?"

"Nothing. I just want you to know—and tell what you know when someone is willing to hear it." Leibele seemed on the verge of weeping. He took Salomon by the arm. "I also wanted to tell you. . . . Do you know who it was who shot me in cold blood, as if we'd never seen each other before? It was Hinda, Salomon. Hinda!" He sniffled and tears came into his eyes. "Our Hinda, you remember? Those concerts we went to, the three of us, to hear your violinist. . . ."

Salomon could not bear seeing his friend in tears.

"Go into hiding and stay there till I come back," he said. "Then we'll talk about what you should do next."

Leibele turned away to wipe his eyes.

"The train is about to leave!" Abraham called out to Salomon.

Perl was wearing the light gray skirt and jacket she had worn when she and Salomon went to the theater on Smocza Street. Since then, they had never been apart for a whole day. He felt a pang in his heart as he took her in his arms. The stationmaster blew his whistle. Abraham murmured the prayer for travel and blessed his son. Salomon made sure he still had his ticket for Zakopane, then kissed Perl one last time.

"Be careful," she said, "and hurry back!"

Only when he had sat down in his compartment was he able to think at leisure about what Leibele had told him. How could Hinda, "our Hinda," as Leibele had called her, have been willing to kill him? Was it because the party had ordered her to do it? Salomon wished he knew how it had come about: if she had been designated because she was the secretary of the party's bureau, if her name had been chosen at random, or if she had volunteered, to set an example. He would try to find out when he came back. He was deeply shocked at the idea that militant members of a political party had to wear an "armor of obedience," like medieval knights. It was incredible to him that anyone could accept such a morality, yet he knew that there were people, some of them quite intelligent, who did accept it. And Barbusse had imperturbably remained in Moscow despite purges, trials, police operations, and deportations. But how was a writer to be judged? By what he did? By what he did not do? Or simply by what he wrote? Barbusse was also the author of a long letter of friendship and devotion to the Jewish people. . . . But why judge?

IN ZAKOPANE, following Joseph Majnemer's instructions, Salomon went to see a man named Jaciek, who was to guide him to the Czech border. All day long he followed Jaciek up a mountainside, hardly seeing anything of him except the backs of his legs. They slept that night in a wooden shelter, then they started down the other side of the mountain at dawn and continued until they came to the border. Jaciek, who had not asked Salomon a single question, refused to take any payment. Salomon crossed the border without incident.

He took a boat on a misty river and landed an hour later at a Slovak village. Since it was Friday afternoon, he went to stay at a Jewish inn. On Sunday morning he took a train to Prague, where he took another train to Bratislava.

In Bratislava a "young Polish friend" put him on a night train to Vienna after giving him the papers he would need.

In Vienna he went to the address he had learned by heart and found a lively little man named Hans Fuchs, a history professor. Having been notified by Majnemer, Fuchs had prepared papers for Salomon and bought him a ticket to Paris by way of Basel. What a trip! Salomon finally arrived in Paris on the morning of September 6. His brother David, to whom he had sent a telegram from Vienna, was waiting for him at the station.

"Welcome to Paris, little brother!"

David had taken a day off from work and was wearing his best clothes: gray jacket, gray striped trousers, patent-leather shoes, bowler hat. Salomon was amazed by the subway ride they took. They stopped by David's apartment on the Rue des Pyrénées, where Salomon left his suitcase and met David's wife Hélène. Then they went off to do some sightseeing in Paris.

Everything Salomon saw made him feel that he had come into a different world: the dense traffic, the wide streets, the colorful and leisurely crowds on the boulevards, the richly stocked and decorated stores . . .

"It's not quite the same as Nowolipie Street, is it, little brother?" said David.

They sat down at one of the sidewalk tables of a big café in the Place de l'Opéra and Salomon had to answer all of David's questions about his father, his sister Topcia, and Perl, his new sister-in-law.

Although David, who made leather wallets and belts in a little workshop on the Rue de Lancry, seemed at ease and said he was happy in France, Salomon could not help thinking that he still missed Warsaw. It was normal to desire Paris, but could one forget Warsaw?

They went to the Rue Montorgueil, where their ancestor Berl had worked during the French Revolution, but they found no print shop there. Then they went to the Champs-Elysées, "the world's most beautiful avenue," and arrived in the Latin Quarter just in time to see a group of young men coming from the direction of the Panthéon and shouting, "France for the French! Death to aliens!" Armed with heavy canes and wearing black berets, the young men stopped in front of the Café Capoulade, repeated their truculent slogan several times, then went off along the Boulevard Saint-Michel.

"They're students who belong to Action Française and Jeunesses Patriotes," David told Salomon. "They hate foreigners and Jews. They've been encouraged by Hitler's coming to power in Germany."

"How do you defend yourselves?"

"A League Against Anti-Semitism has been organized. We're supported by leftist parties and antifascist groups."

"Is that scar from a fight against Fascists?"

David had a pale scar near his right ear. He ran his fingertips over it.

"It's a souvenir of a meeting. . . ."

"Tell me about it."

"Several hundred of us, members of the leather workers' union, were having a meeting when someone came to warn us that Fascists, supported by the police, were surrounding the building. Some of the workers panicked and headed for the door. A few of us stood in front of it to keep them from going outside and being beaten to a pulp. To make them stop, I told them they'd have to fight me to go out. . . ."

"Nu?"

"That's exactly what they did. I had to spend a week in the hospital."

THE VAST ESPLANADE OF La Villette was covered with people. Men and women with grave faces, red and tricolored flags, thousands of flowers placed around the coffin. Steady streams of more people, flags, and flowers were still flowing in from all the streets. Salomon had never seen such a crowd, or felt such contagious collective emotion. His chest swelled with pride. For the first time in his life, he realized that he belonged not only to a people, but to humanity.

The long, silent, solemn procession got under way at about eleven o'clock. The outer boulevards, the Rue de la Chapelle, the Rue Louis-Blanc, the Place du Combat, and finally the Père-Lachaise cemetery. There were men and women everywhere, on balconies, in doorways, clinging to the girders of the elevated railway. Many of them held red flags.

In the cemetery, David and Salomon were swept along by the crowd. David pointed out people unknown to Salomon and told him names he had never heard before: Victor Basch, Marcel Cachin, Francis Rolland. . . . André Malraux read a message from Romain Rolland. Salomon had read Romain Rolland—*Jean-Christophe, Above the Battle*—and regarded him as "one of the family."

After speeches whose words were scattered among the gravestones by the wind, the crowd filed past the coffin. When it was Salomon's turn, he reached into his coat pocket, took out the copy of *Under Fire* that he had owned since he was twelve, and piously put it down among the flowers.

ON HIS WAY TO work the next day, David took Salomon to the offices of *Parizer Haint* [Paris Day], a large Yiddish daily with a Zionist outlook. Salomon had to earn some money to go back to Poland. He had no identity card or work permit, but he was hired illegally to replace a linotypist who was going to be away for a week. During that week he earned four hundred and ten francs, which to him was a fortune. He sent two telegrams, one to Perl and the other to Abraham, for the Jewish New Year. Then he invited

David and his wife Hélène to dinner in a restaurant, and afterward they went to a cinema on one of the boulevards to see Raimu in *Tartarin de Tarascon*. Lifetime memories.

SALOMON'S WIFE AND father were waiting for him at the station in Warsaw. He got off the train and embraced them with the emotion of someone coming home after a trip around the world. On the next platform, a Jewish family was trying to board the train about to leave for Lódź, but Polish passengers were blocking the doors to keep them out. A woman carrying a baby shouted something in Yiddish. In the scuffle, her wig came off and fell. An elegantly dressed man picked it up with the tip of his cane and exhibited it in the midst of laughter. Salomon was livid. He clenched his fists. Abraham put his hand on his arm.

"Those *goyim* aren't worth your anger, my son. Thank the Almighty that in spite of their stupidity they're not killing us!"

Salomon continued to be angry for several days. He wandered through the city, exasperated by those Jews who looked as if they might have stepped out of the Rembrandt paintings he had seen in the Louvre, with their beards and fur hats. Agitated, uncertain, trying to hasten the coming of the Messiah by the intensity of their prayers and the depth of their learning, nearly all of them, whether they were rich or poor, pious or unbelieving, seemed to live apart from their time and accept its violence in advance. He felt like shaking them, making them pay attention to the dangers piling up above their scholarly heads, but what effect could he have on them? In the Diet, the Jewish parliamentary group was divided: some voted with the opposition, the others with the government; which meant that each faction more or less counterbalanced the other and their total influence was negligible.

Finally his anger and impatience gave way to understanding and affection. He rediscovered what his father had taught him long ago: that the attitude of the Polish Jews was the result of a choice, an act of will, a culture. When a prince struck a Jew with his riding crop as he rode through a *shtetl*, the Jew never rebelled. He merely looked at the prince with commiseration and said, "Poor man. . . ." And he was genuinely sorry for that prince who had to strike a poor Jew in order to assert his existence and his power.

And when Perl told Salomon that she was expecting a child, he promised himself that he would pass on to that new Jew what he had received from his parents, who had in turn received it from their parents: the certainty that the spirit always transcends violence.

The child, a boy, was born in January. Abraham asked that he be named Meir-Ikhiel, after his own father.

47

WARSAW

The Basement

IN JANUARY 1939, Perl invited her family and friends to a party for Meir-Ikhiel's third birthday. Dancing went on till about three in the morning, when Leibele Hechtman arrived with an unshaven man wearing a knapsack, a German refugee whom he could not take in because his apartment was being watched by the police.

The festive atmosphere abruptly vanished. Perl turned off the music. The few people who were still there surrounded the refugee and bombarded him with questions. His name was Hugo and he had just come from Berlin. He spoke Yiddish with a strong German accent.

"The Nazis will soon be in Warsaw," he said quietly. "You must get ready either to resist or to leave. There's not much time left."

The others listened to him attentively but remained skeptical. It would not be in Hitler's interest to invade Poland, since the agreement signed in Munich called for France and Britain to fight on Poland's side if war broke out. As for the situation of the Jews in Germany, Hugo was perhaps exaggerating. The persecutions they had suffered were more reminiscent of czarist pogroms than of the Spanish Inquisition, and Jews were used to pogroms. No, the Polish Jews did not feel threatened in the near future. They all agreed on one thing, however: it was urgent to collect money and food for the Jews in Germany.

Salomon and Perl let Hugo stay in their apartment on Smocza Street. After spending two nights there, he decided to go to the Soviet Union: that was the only border the Germans were not yet watching. When he had put on his knapsack and opened the front door, he gave his hosts one last warning.

"Leave Poland while there's still time! If you have enough money for it, take a ship to America. Believe me, you'd better go as far away from them as you can!"

Three months later, Hitler renounced his nonaggression pact with Poland and demanded the return of disputed Polish territory. This was a stunning blow to the Poles. Their confidence did not return until they learned of the joint Franco-British declaration of support for Poland.

The Jews began making preparations. On March 28, 1939, the central committee of the Zionist Organization in Poland stated, "Polish Jews are ready to shed their blood for the defense and integrity of the Polish state." Then it became known in Warsaw that a delegation from a federation of Polish Jews in the United States had informed the Polish ambassador that its members were willing to go back to Poland and fight to defend it. The Polish Jews in Palestine also said they were ready to return.

But in Warsaw a majority of the military mobilization commission voted to exclude Jews from the Polish army, in order, it was said, to prevent them from having access to military secrets. The Catholic newspaper *Maly Dziennik [Little Daily]* published an article maintaining that in his fight against the Jews, Hitler was doing the work of Providence.

On September 1, 1939, at dawn, the German army crossed the Polish border. It was the day before *shabbat,* three weeks from Yom Kippur.

Abraham had gone to spend several days at a hotel in Otwock, a health resort. Salomon was at work when the radio reported the first air raids and the first casualties. Two bombs, said the announcer, had fallen on Otwock, destroying a boarding school and a hotel. Salomon rushed to the telephone but learned that service to Otwock had been cut off. A train that went there was leaving in half an hour. He asked a friend to take over his work and tell Perl where he had gone, then he hurried to the station and caught the train when it was already in motion. It was packed with people, suitcases, and packages: an exodus from Warsaw was under way.

Otwock at last. Here, the situation was reversed: the station was full of Jews waiting for a train back to Warsaw. Some of them wore bandages. Salomon looked for his father in vain, then left the station. Heavy smoke lingered in the sky. The air smelled of soot and dust. The street on which Abraham's hotel had stood was lined with ruins. Buildings had been blasted open and three-sided rooms were exposed, as in a stage setting. At the site of the hotel, a signboard was swaying in front of a heap of rubble. Salomon walked toward the rescue team examining the wreckage. He was afraid to ask any questions. Sweat broke out on his forehead.

He was approached by a little Jew in a caftan that was too long for him and dragged on the ground. " 'Unless the Lord watches over the city, the watchman stays awake in vain,' " he quoted. "Are you looking for something, young man?"

"I'm looking for my father. He . . . he was staying in this hotel."

"Oy, oy, oy! May the Master of the world give him long life! If he's not at the station, maybe he's at the hospital, and if he's at neither the station nor the hospital . . . *Oy, oy, oy!"*

"Where's the hospital?"

Luckily the hospital had not been hit, and Salomon found his father there, acting as an interpreter between the chief surgeon and injured Jews who did not speak Polish. He had been praying, he told his son, when the first bomb fell. Everything had collapsed around him. He was not surprised at still being alive, because "he who studies the Torah for itself receives many rewards."

Since all his belongings had burned, he had no baggage when he and Salomon boarded the train.

Warsaw was plunged in darkness. Men wearing armbands were patrolling the streets. The buses and streetcars had stopped running. War had taken over the city in one day. Abraham and Salomon walked to Nowolipie Street. Just as they arrived, the air-raid sirens began howling. A savage, terrifying uproar. It was the first time. The street, the courtyard, and the staircase suddenly became animated. Shadows ran in the darkness. Here and there, spots of light appeared: the flame of a cigarette lighter, the furtive gleam of a lantern. There was a rush toward the entrances to basements and underground shelters.

Salomon and his father let the first wave pass, then started up the stairs. They nearly collided with Moniek, Topcia, and their children, who were coming down.

"Father!" cried Topcia. "Thank God! Come down to the basement with us!"

When the alert was over Salomon came out of the basement and went off to rejoin his wife and child in their apartment on Smocza Street. Abraham watched him disappear into the gray, sticky fog. At dawn he went up to his apartment and recited the morning prayer.

The next day, newspapers were published as usual and Abraham went to work. Long lines were forming in front of food stores and bakeries. People carried gas masks slung over their shoulders. The first refugees came into the city during the day, in trucks or in carts full of odds and ends. Many of them were Jews and, as always, they gathered around the rabbis of their respective villages. Abraham felt that he knew them and recognized them, with their bundles and their hopeless expressions. "What has been is what will be," says Ecclesiastes, "and what has been done is what will be done; and there is nothing new under the sun." These events, thought Abraham, were part of a long story that was in his keeping.

That evening, the family came to Abraham's apartment. Salomon with Perl and Meir-Ikhiel, several cousins, and even Yudl, who had finally become reconciled with his brother. Abraham blessed everyone and opened the family book. Even though Topcia had pasted blue paper over the windows, the electric lights were not turned on. It was by the glow of a candle that Abraham began reading aloud: "Praise be to You, O Lord our God, God of our fathers. You have turned away from us because of our sins. You have abandoned us. The world You made for us still exists, and we, for whom You made it, are disappearing. . . ."

Then came names: "Abraham, son of Solomon the Levite, lived in Jerusalem and the name of his wife was Judith. Elijah, his first son, became a scribe like his father. Gamaliel was the second son.

"Elijah begat Simon, Thermutorion, and Ezra. The name of his wife was Miriam. They lived in Alexandria, in exile.

"Gamaliel begat Theodoros, Judith, Rachel, and Absalom. The name of his wife was Sarah. They lived in Alexandria, in exile."

It suddenly seemed to Abraham that this chain was so resistant to time that there was no reason to believe it would ever stop. He regained confidence, closed the book, and asked Topcia to serve dinner. Moniek turned on the radio.

A voice announced a blockade of the North Sea by the British fleet, which was about to enter the Baltic. The French had bombed the Ruhr, but the Germans had destroyed a train carrying refugees near Kitno. The news was followed by appeals to the population: volunteers were needed to dig shelters and help in hospitals; lodgings, food, and clothing were needed for homeless people. . . .

On the afternoon of September 4 it was learned in Warsaw that the government had left the capital and gone to Lublin. This news was followed by several air raids and caused indescribable panic in the streets.

On September 5 there was another raid against the northern part of Warsaw, inhabited mainly by Jews. The Jewish hospital was filled to overflowing with victims of the raid. That evening, in spite of the alerts, Abraham went to the synagogue with his prayer book and shawl. He was by no means the only one who went there. The abnormal had become normal. All night long, Topcia, Moniek, Salomon, and Perl took turns standing in the line in front of the bakery so that they could get bread in the morning. Air raids sometimes forced them to go into shelters.

On September 18, five days before Yom Kippur, there was incredible news: the Soviet army had crossed the border to come to the rescue of Warsaw. Everyone was overjoyed. People danced in the streets and embraced each other. The celebration stopped when the radio announced that in accordance with the German-Soviet pact the Soviet army was going to occupy part of Poland, the remaining part being reserved for Germany. The air raids resumed.

On September 23, Yom Kippur, waves of Messerschmitts attacked the city for hours on end: Hitler had decided to "light a candle for the Jews of Warsaw." Explosions, fires. Buildings collapsed, whole neighborhoods burned. Pious Jews driven from flaming synagogues ran through streets in which victims of the bombs cried out for help. Abraham did not know what to do: help the injured, gather children who were looking for their parents, or hurry home. He hesitated a moment, then went home and found his family finishing the Yom Kippur ceremony. Without answering their questions, he went to his room and thanked the Almighty at length for having spared them.

The bombing lasted several more days, then stopped abruptly. The print shop in which Salomon worked had been burned. One morning he walked to the railroad station with Meir-Ikhiel. He carried a wooden box, his son a little shovel. The fronts of the buildings were blackened by fire and ruins were still smoking. They took a taxi that left them near the Vistula, in the open countryside. Salomon chose a thick chestnut tree on a hillside and dug a hole between two of its enormous roots. The boy watched him while he carefully filled in the hole again, after dropping the box into it. Then they walked away, hand in hand. Salomon looked back several times, as though to make sure he would not forget the ancient chestnut tree to which he had entrusted his treasure.

On October 1 the sun was again warm in Warsaw. The publishers of *Der Moment* had decided to resume putting out their newspaper, to give Jews news of the world. Abraham was on his way to the print shop, by way of Karmelicka Street, when he saw a silent crowd moving in the direction of Leszno Street. He followed it.

On Leszno Street, olive-green trucks full of helmeted soldiers were slowly rolling past. Abraham knew they were German soldiers, though he had never seen any before. He was surprised at his own serenity. But it was written, "It is not given to us to understand why the wicked prosper and the righteous suffer." He made his way through the crowd, left behind him the sound of caterpillar treads on the pavement of his city, and went to print the last issue of *Der Moment*.

THE GERMANS SEEMED TO have settled in for a long stay. Special brigades of the occupation army maintained around-the-clock patrols. Soldiers commandeered men to sweep the streets and sometimes amused themselves by setting fire to the beards of old Jews. Two of them would hold their victim while a third took out a lighter. When the old man's face was engulfed in flames, they would let go of him and go away. People who lived in the neighborhood would hurry to him but it would be too late. Only a swollen mass of burned flesh would be left of what had been a human face.

When the family gathered in Abraham's apartment one evening, he suggested that they leave Warsaw. It was still possible to escape to the part of Poland occupied by the Soviet Union. The people who organized such escapes charged a great deal of money, but they were efficient. Yudl's son Fischel, Perl's former fiancé, who had just come back from fighting Franco's forces in Spain, was in favor of leaving. But the women were reluctant. Yudl felt that the discussion was academic, since the war would soon be over.

Meanwhile, the Jewish Council had been ordered to give a list of Jews in Warsaw between the ages of sixteen and sixty. This seemed ominous; some Jews had already been conscripted to go and work in Germany.

It was agreed that since the men of the family were exposed to the greatest danger, they would leave as soon as possible and come back when the French and British had driven the Germans out of Warsaw.

Five men and Perl's sister Zosia left on the night of November 15: Salomon, Leibele, Majnemer, Fischel, and Perl's brother Felek. Those who stayed behind had an empty place in their hearts.

The next day it was learned that the Jews were going to be enclosed in a ghetto. A small ghetto, it was said at first, containing fifty-five streets of Warsaw and about a hundred and sixty thousand people. Then there was talk of a larger ghetto containing seventy streets. But nothing was certain yet, not even the rumor that Warsaw Jews would have to wear a distinctive sign, like the yellow stars worn by exiles in the Sierpc region.

Ghettos, yellow badges—Abraham's ancestors had known all that, and in a way it was encouraging, he thought, for if history repeated itself, the Jews would go on resisting. Enduring was the most human form of resistance.

"But to endure, we must be ready to fight," said cousin Mordecai, who had stayed in Poland with the groups of young pioneers he was training to go and live in Palestine. "We must make contact with the Poles and organize resistance—*armed* resistance."

"The Poles won't help us or have anything to do with us."

"Then we'll fight alone."

Abraham thought of the Germans, then of the Romans, the Zealots, and the destruction of the Temple, but he said nothing, not wanting to upset Mordecai.

A few weeks later, Fischel came back from the Soviet zone. The Russians were deporting many Jews to Siberia and Central Asia, and he had no desire to spend the rest of his life there, especially since he believed that the war would not last much longer.

Fischel reported that Salomon was working at a print shop in Bialystok, in the part of Poland occupied by the Soviet army. Every day he sent hundreds of copies of his newspaper into the zone occupied by the Nazis. Circulating news was also a way of resisting, he said.

THE GHETTO WAS NOT CREATED until a year later, just before the beginning of the year 5700 [October 2, 1940]. Jews living in other parts of Warsaw were ordered to move into the area marked off for the ghetto. The days between Rosh Hashanah and Yom Kippur were days of exodus. Men, women, and children, laden like beasts of burden with all sorts of household effects and personal belongings, lamented loudly and steadily as they crowded into synagogues, schools, and courtyards.

Abraham spent Yom Kippur in the little synagogue on Nowolipie Street where he usually went to pray. That evening the officiating rabbi, wearing his prayer shawl and ceremonial costume, was about to recite the concluding prayer of the *neilah,* the Yom Kippur service that symbolizes the closing of the gates of heaven, when a boy came in, his eyes widened by the gravity of the news he brought: the Germans were about to surround the ghetto with a barrier of barbed wire. The men moaned. Some, panic-stricken, ran out of the synagogue. The rabbi refused to say the prayer. How was it possible to pray, he asked, when the "gates of grace" were closing? Abraham was deeply troubled by the rabbi's refusal to conclude Yom Kippur.

When he came home, he sent one of Topcia's children to bring Mordecai, the "Palestinian" cousin. Mordecai soon arrived. He had lost weight and needed a shave.

"I'm glad to know that Droza and the children are on the *kibbutz!"* he said. "If the Jews had listened to us Zionists, they'd all be safe now, in Eretz Israel."

Abraham smiled.

"Would you like some tea? Or rather, would you like some hot water weakly flavored by a few tea leaves, without sugar?"

"You don't make it sound very tempting, but I'll still drink it!"

They sat down at the table, facing each other.

"Have you heard the news?" said Mordecai. "A group tried to escape to the Aryan part of the city; the Poles caught them and handed them over to the Germans."

"Yes, I know," Abraham said with a sigh. "When we jump out of the frying pan, we fall into the fire." He looked at Mordecai thoughtfully. "Mordecai, I think it's time . . . to act."

Mordecai frowned, as if he had not understood clearly.

"You, Rab Abraham? You want to use weapons?"

"Who said anything about weapons? Why should we use the same means as our enemy?"

"You said you thought it was time to act, so I assumed . . ."

Abraham waited till Topcia had served the tea, then he asked, "Why don't we put out a newspaper?"

"A newspaper? To rouse the Jews to revolt?"

"To inform them."

"How would you go about printing it? It would be dangerous, Rab Abraham."

"In the basement I still have some of the equipment from our old print shop. Mainly what I need is paper, and I know where I can get it: at the soup kitchen on Zamenhof Street. I've already talked with the people who run it. Before the war, they bought a big supply of paper to cover the tables. Now they don't need it: as long as there's something to eat, no one cares about the tables. I'd like you to mobilize your pioneers to bring the paper here and help me to set up the operation."

Mordecai pushed back his cup.

"You're an odd Jew, Rab Abraham!"

AT SUCCOT, sadness and poverty reigned in the overcrowded ghetto. Real poverty, the kind that arouses horror and disgust. In spite of the *Kommandantur*'s prohibition, a group of Chassidim decided to honor the Torah. In front of the soup kitchen on Zamenhof Street, they began dancing and whirling. They whirled faster and faster, sang more and more loudly, and soon reached such an ecstatic state, far beyond poverty and barbed wire, that they could no longer stop. It was an old Jewish woman in rags who brought them back to reality.

"Jews!" she said to them. "Saving one's own life is a commandment of the Torah. Nowadays, singing is dangerous. Stop!"

They stopped whirling and gradually fell silent, like a broken machine slowly running down. Unsteady on their feet, they again became aware of their human weight and the desolation of the street.

Mordecai's pioneers discreetly brought the paper to Abraham, cleaned the basement, set up the little hand press that had formerly been used for printing proofs, managed to get a supply of ink, and plugged in an old radio with which a red-haired boy named Nathan was able to bring in Radio London and Radio Moscow.

The first issue of *Yediess [News]*, in Yiddish, appeared on November 14. About three hundred copies of it were printed, and they were all snatched up immediately. That same day the Gestapo surrounded the neighborhood; they had probably been informed by the Jewish police, whose headquarters were at 13 Leszno Street, not far from Abraham's apartment. Several buildings on Nowolipie Street were searched, but to no avail. The young pioneers regarded this as a great victory and they openly expressed their admiration of Abraham, whom they called in Hebrew *ha-Zaken*, "the Old Man."

Three days later Abraham received a package and a letter from Argentina. The letter, written by Regina, had been opened; here and there, the censors had blacked out a word or a sentence. The package had been almost completely emptied: it now contained only a can of sardines and a chocolate bar, which Abraham divided among his grandchildren. He wrote an answer that day, just in time—that evening, November 17, 1940, the ghetto was walled in.

From then on, getting food became even more difficult. Exchanges were made over the wall: the family silverware for a few potatoes, furniture or furs for a loaf of bread or a little rice. And there was always danger from the three different police forces: Jewish, German, and Polish. Polish policemen were called "blues," from the color of their uniforms. It was cold; the price of a ton of coal rose from fifty zlotys to a thousand. Lice became common. When would the first epidemic begin?

The pioneers, who had spotted a gap in one wall of the basement, enlarged it and then made a passage that went from basement to basement and gave access to a building on Leszno Street and another on Ogrodowa Street. Finally, by way of sewers and tunnels, the passage ended at a building on the corner of Chlodna and Wronia Streets, in the Aryan section of the city, where the pioneers were able to buy food. They carried on a lively trade in pork, which Jews in the ghetto could now eat with special permission given by the rabbis in order to save human lives. They bought bacon for eleven zlotys a kilogram outside the ghetto and sold it for eighteen. With the profits they made in this way, they bought ink, paper, and, unknown to Abraham, several pistols.

Abraham scarcely ever left the basement: the apartment was tightly packed with relatives and it was too cold for him to spend much time in the street. Like the cave of Rabbi Simeon bar Yochai in the time of the Roman persecutions, Abraham's basement had

677

become a hiding place that provided ideal conditions for undisturbed thought. But would Abraham, like the famous rabbi, hear the voice of the prophet Elijah announcing the tyrant's death and the end of the persecutions?

Several basements that Jews had used as clandestine schools or for hiding mimeograph machines had been discovered by the Gestapo and either flooded or burned with flamethrowers. That was why Mordecai set about fortifying Abraham's basement. Heniek, a blond, broad-shouldered young man who could pass for an Aryan and was a mason by trade, devised a strong and simple closure: a sliding concrete slab with which the entrance could be quickly blocked. He then piped in water and installed a washbasin, and a few days later he even put in electrical wiring.

In the basement, Abraham wrote and printed *Yediess.* To lessen the Gestapo's chances of tracing it to its source, he brought it out at irregular intervals. He also wrote a little daily chronicle to be added to the Book of Abraham. And when he had time left over, he studied. He had begun delving into the Cabala. Like most other Jews in the ghetto, he felt an urgent need to try to understand the designs of the Almighty. On *shabbat,* the synagogues were full. So was the church on Leszno Street, the only church still functioning in the Jewish quarter. It was there that the children of Jews who had converted to Christianity, still regarded as Jews by the Nazis, and required to wear a yellow star sewn to their clothes, came to seek a ray of hope from a priest who also wore a yellow star.

The pioneers regularly came to the basement to talk with Abraham and bring him news.

"We've finally succeeded," Nathan the redhead told him one day. "Every political group is now putting out a newspaper!"

Mordecai laughed bitterly.

"The Jews are making progress," he said. "They've set up a center for aid to orphans, they've increased the number of soup kitchens, they've formed committees in buildings to take charge of the residents' finances, hygiene, food, and clothing. I've even heard of an organization that administers libraries and clandestine schools. A whole government! And to make sure everyone knows who we are, we all wear an identifying emblem." He pointed to the yellow star pinned over his chest. "We Jews are amazing—the Germans create a ghetto and we organize it!"

"And we organize it so well that the Germans come here on sightseeing expeditions," said Heniek the mason. "I saw some of

678

them this morning on Karmelicka Street. They had a guide and were taking pictures."

"The Jews are afraid," said a young woman with her dark hair in braids. "If they had weapons, they'd be less afraid."

Abraham took a deep breath.

"We have the weapon of words," he said. "It was by the word that the Almighty, blessed be His name, created the world. And Moses was not allowed to enter Canaan because, instead of speaking to the rock and telling it to provide water for his thirsty people, he struck it with his rod. If we—"

"You're wandering away from reality," Mordecai interrupted. "It's not a rock we're facing, it's the Nazis!"

"Even a murderer can be disarmed with words. Remember Balaam: he was supposed to curse the people of Israel and finally blessed them."

Suddenly they heard footsteps on the stone stairs that led down to the basement. Heniek and Mordecai turned off the lights and slid the concrete slab to block the doorway. They all listened for a long time; they heard men's voices but could not make out what they were saying. Who was it? Poor men looking for shelter? The Jewish police trying to track down clandestine print shops?

"May the Almighty protect us!" murmured Abraham.

The next day, three of Mordecai's pioneers who spoke German approached a group of German "tourists" and had a conversation with them on all sorts of topics, including even Nietzsche. They later reported that the Germans had seemed surprised.

"Father," Topcia said to Abraham, "you're sending those children to their death!"

Now it was Abraham who seemed surprised.

"But Topcia, who will redeem man's wrongdoing, if not man? Who will save both the world and God, if not man?"

Topcia gave her father such a harsh look that he scarcely recognized her.

"All I want is for my children to survive!"

In the days that followed, Jews often went up to Germans, opened conversations with them, questioned them, asked for explanations. When Abraham heard about this, he was proud of the Jews. He decided to go and see for himself, in spite of his painful arthritis.

The cold was fierce. Abraham took only shallow little breaths because the icy air burned his lungs. He felt dizzy. Families wearing only thin, ragged clothes were wandering in the streets, moaning, without even begging. Warmly dressed people walked past them with their eyes lowered. Abraham saw a cart, pushed by two men, coming toward him. It was full of corpses. Arms and legs, stiffened by cold and death, bristled on all sides of it. It was followed by a pitiful-looking and probably insane man who kept asking tirelessly, "Did they leave their bread cards? Did they leave their bread cards? Did they . . . ?"

Abraham went no farther. He returned to his basement, where Nathan was trying to tune in a news broadcast on the radio. Abraham sat down on the bed and, to Nathan's surprise, put his white-haired head between his cold-reddened hands and wept.

ON APRIL 1, 1941, Abraham was finally able to report some good news in *Yediess:* the revolt of the Yugoslavs, the British victories in Africa, the naval battles in which Italian ships had been sunk. Then he printed a story that, to him, represented a kind of victory, perhaps the first victory of the Jews over Nazism: Himmler had just issued a special decree forbidding Germans to visit the ghetto and carry on discussions with Jews.

But on April 9, the day before Passover, the Polish police arrested Heniek the mason with several kilograms of bacon in his possession and turned him over to the Gestapo. For any Jew found outside the ghetto, the punishment was death. Heniek was shot.

The next day, Topcia's husband Moniek was caught in a police roundup on Nalewki Street and taken to the relocation center at the corner of Niska and Stawski streets. From there, with several hundred men and women, he was taken to the railroad station. Topcia went to see the chief of the Jewish police, offered her silverware to a shady lawyer who was said to have contacts in the Polish police, and took Abraham to the president of the *Judenrat* [Jewish Council], an engineer named Czerniakow, whom he had known in the past. When he saw him, Abraham felt that he was looking at the haggard captain of a helplessly drifting ship. There was no hope. Topcia spent Passover night sobbing.

At dawn, when Topcia finally fell asleep, Abraham went back to his basement. Young people were sleeping on cots while one of their comrades kept watch.

Abraham lit a candle and began writing: "Passover of the year 5701 [1941] after the creation of the world by the Almighty, blessed be He. For the first *seder,* there was almost nothing to eat or drink; no *matzot,* no wine. The Jews are exhausted. Passover in the Warsaw ghetto will serve as an example, like Passover in Egypt, and will be celebrated by countless generations." It occurred to him that he was giving a very poor account of the reality around him, but he went on with his small handwriting: "I pray that before the Almighty makes us disappear, He will give us time to bear witness. Evil must not go unrecorded."

There was a knock on the door: once, twice, once. It was Mordecai. He was becoming thinner and thinner. He wore an old gray scarf around his neck, held by a big safety pin. He seemed in a bad humor.

"Who broke that tooth for you?" asked Nathan.

"A Jewish policeman. Don't worry, he'll pay for it!" Mordecai turned to Abraham. "What's the plan now?"

"The same. We must go on bearing witness, gathering documents and photographs, writing, reporting. . . ."

"Reporting what? That there's no more room in the cemeteries?"

Pained by Mordecai's bitterness, Abraham went up to the apartment to see if Topcia was awake. He said the morning prayer with some nephews and cousins of his wife Rachel, blessed be her memory. His eyes rested on a photograph of Jerusalem in a broken frame. Outside, a sunbeam shone like a searchlight on the broken pavement and the emaciated people who were slowly sifting through piles of trash. Abraham felt a surge of panic. That light, those people, that anxiety aroused by the spread of misery . . . He went back to the basement. He needed darkness.

On June 23, Abraham announced in *Yediess* that Germany was at war with the Soviet Union. The Jews in the ghetto hestitated to rejoice at this news, because everything that happened outside the ghetto set off increased violence inside it. The Germans' Polish-language broadcasts spoke of the coming defeat of the Soviet Union as if it were a matter of course.

Perl and her son Meir-Ikhiel came to live in Abraham's apartment on Nowolipie Street. Abraham was glad to have Salomon's son with him. He sometimes took him down into the basement, alone or with his mother, and read passages from the Book of Abraham, as though to give them hope.

One evening when the three of them were in the basement, they heard footsteps on the stairs. Abraham hurried to the concrete slab

681

but it was stuck: he could not move it in either direction. Perl came to help him, in vain. There was a knock on the door.

"Let me in!" said a voice in Polish.

Perl and Meir-Ikhiel huddled against Abraham.

"Let me in!" the voice repeated. "It's me, Janek Kobyla, the painter!"

"It's true," whispered Perl, "that's Janek's voice."

Meir-Ikhiel began crying.

"May the Almighty, blessed be He, protect us!" said Abraham, and he opened the door.

Janek was standing there, with two strangers.

"Janek!" said Perl. "What are you doing in the ghetto?"

"Salomon is waiting for you twelve miles from here, near Majden. I'll take you there. We have to hurry." He pointed to his two companions. "They'll guide us. This man is my cousin, the other one is a friend."

More footsteps on the stairs. This time it was Mordecai and the pioneers, armed with pistols. They had been told that three strangers had come into the building.

"We have to hurry!" Janek repeated.

He quickly explained to Mordecai that they had come by way of the sewer and that they were going to take Salomon's father, wife, and son out of the ghetto.

"You won't be able to leave," said Mordecai. "They're surrounding the neighborhood."

Two of the young pioneers succeeded in sliding the concrete slab in front of the door.

"Why are you sealing us in here?" asked Janek.

No one answered. A few moments later, Abraham broke the silence.

"There's a passage."

Mordecai reluctantly pushed aside one of the cots and pulled up several floorboards, uncovering a dark hole about two feet square. Colder air came into the basement. Janek stared at the hole incredulously. He was told that he could reach Wronia Street underground.

"I know the passage from Leszno Street to Wronia Street," confirmed his cousin.

Janek was puzzled.

"If you can leave, why are you still here?" he asked.

"Trying to escape would be useless," said Mordecai. "We're kept here not only by the German guards, but also by the Poles' hostility."

"Not all Poles are hostile to you," Janek said slowly. "You have proof of that now. . . . Hurry, Perl! Come, Mr. Halter!"

"No," said Abraham, "I'm staying. Take Perl and the boy. Embrace my son for me, and may God bless you!"

"We're going to walk through tunnels," Perl explained to Meir-Ikhiel. "You mustn't be afraid, or cry. Will you promise me not to? We're going to where Papa is. He's waiting for us."

Janek looked at Mordecai with a strange expression.

"If we all go," he said, "we'll be caught."

"We're staying, my friend," Mordecai answered with one of his bitter laughs. "Don't worry about us. We're staying . . . to bear witness, isn't that right, Rab Abraham?"

Abraham went to the table and picked up a sheet of paper on which he had printed the beginning of the Scroll of Abraham. He showed it to Meir-Ikhiel and leaned down toward him.

"Listen to me carefully. Do you remember what I read to you from the family book? Well, on this piece of paper is what our ancestor Abraham the scribe wrote for us. You know, the one who ran away from Jerusalem with his wife Judith and his sons Elijah and Gamaliel. Do you remember?"

He folded the paper and slipped it into Meir-Ikhiel's pocket, then he said the prayer for beginning a journey: "May it be Your holy will, O Lord our God and God of our fathers. . . ."

     •   •   •

I DO NOT remember leaving Warsaw through the sewer; I remember only that I was afraid. We were reunited with my father. Later, a Red Army patrol picked us up on the frozen plains of the Ukraine. First we were taken to Moscow, while it was being bombed, then we were sent to Kokand, in Uzbekistan.

In an atlas I found in the attic of the house we lived in, I read names of cities—Safad, Tiberias, Jericho, Jaffa—that were new to me, yet seemed more familiar than names I had already known, such as Tashkent, Samarkand, and Bukhara.

"Why not a Jewish republic in Palestine?" I asked a little later in an article published by the newspaper of the chalutzim *in Uzbekistan. The country was occupied by the British? The Jews had to struggle against that imperialist occupation. Another people also lived*

there? A binational Socialist state had to be created. The Jewish problem would then be solved, and socialism would be implanted in the Middle East. I did not realize that my Soviet education was making me reinvent Zionism.

My article was not received as well as I had hoped. The Soviet Union was not yet interested in the anticolonialist struggle of the Jews in Palestine, or in converting the Arabs to socialism. And the British were allies—they had, in fact, just routed Rommel's army. What was left of my theory? The idea that it was impossible for the Jews to solve their national problem within the framework of the Soviet Union. The editor of the newspaper was fired and my parents were ostracized.

When we returned to Poland after the war, our train was attacked by Polish peasants. They threw stones and insults at us. "Dirty Jews!" they shouted. "Get out! Go to Palestine!" Anti-Semitism did not surprise me; my memory was impregnated with it. But I was not resigned to it. The Jews in Eretz Israel were fighting for a Jewish state, and I felt I had to do what I could to help them. I became one of the leaders of Borochovist Youth, a left-wing Zionist organization. I was a grave child among other grave children.

One day, in collaboration with other Jewish groups, some Zionist and some not, we organized a march in Warsaw for the inauguration of a monument to the memory of those who had fought in the ghetto. Trains and special trucks brought in the remnants of the more than three million Jews who had lived in Poland: seventy-five thousand who had survived death camps and underground warfare—two and a half percent.

It was a beautiful day in May. The sun glittered playfully on the broken windowpanes of the few façades that were still standing. A passage had been cleared along the devastated streets. We walked in silence through the cemetery that Warsaw had become. I remember that silence, broken only by the sound of our footsteps and the flapping of flags—red flags, and white-and-blue flags. Poles who had come from the intact parts of the city watched us pass. They seemed surprised that we were not all dead. Some of them spat into the dust. "They're like rats," we heard someone say. "You keep killing them and they keep coming back." We clenched our fists. We were under orders not to answer. Silence.

I was in the group at the head of the march, carrying a big red flag that was too heavy for me. When I saw those people looking at us from the ruins of our houses—stairs, sections of walls, blackened chimneys—I felt like singing the song of the Jewish partisans:

> *From the land of palms*
> *And the land of white snow,*
> *We come with our misery,*
> *Our sufferings.*
> *Never say*
> *That you are on your last road.*
> *The leaden sky*
> *Hides the blue of the day.*
> *Our time will come,*
> *Our footsteps will resound.*
> *We are here.*

And our footsteps resounded, and we were there.

I was in bed with pneumonia when my friends from Borochovist Youth set off for the "Promised Land" aboard the *Exodus*, a ship overloaded with Jewish refugees. When the *Exodus* was stopped by the British navy, the refugees resisted, but they could not prevent the British from sending them back to another camp, in Germany.

I went to Israel for the first time in 1951. When, after five days at sea, we saw Mount Carmel and the city of Haifa appear in the distance, shimmering in the heat, I was so deeply moved that I wept. I traveled all over the country and worked on a kibbutz. The only reason I did not stay there was that I wanted to be a painter and felt it was impossible to paint anywhere but in Paris.

I became French, but that did not diminish my attachment to Israel. In 1967, when the country was encircled by large armies, I again felt I had to do what I could to help, as in 1948, during the war for independence. It seemed to me that I could best help in my own way, by working to achieve what I regarded as essential to Israel's survival: peace. I spent years pleading, trying to persuade, bringing Arabs and Israelis together, going to see powerful people in Cairo, Israel, and Beirut. For years I met with heads of state, and also terrorists. I do not know how many times I boarded planes that took me nowhere, arranged meetings that produced no results, made appointments that were kept only by me. I do not know how many hours I spent negotiating with people who rejected the very principle of negotiation, how many nights I spent writing without knowing who, if anyone, would read what I wrote.

Did all that do any good? Did I advance the cause of peace by even a single step? Everyone who, like me, has been involved in "trying to do something" has known my feeling of loneliness and sometimes bitterness.

The Temple and the sword were not able to preserve the Jewish people from exile in the time of Abraham the scribe, and I must recognize that the Book and the voice, exalted for centuries, failed to protect them from barbarity. There is probably no salvation if one of these triumphs to the exclusion of the other. But hope still remains. "Despair is not a solution," the Israelis said after the difficult Yom Kippur War of 1973. "Not for us."

48

WARSAW

Shema Yisrael

"MEIR-IKHIEL BEGAT Abraham, Leah, and Yudl.

"Abraham begat Salomon, Regina, David, Samuel, and Topcia.

"Salomon begat Meir-Ikhiel."

Abraham prayed for his daughter Regina, in Argentina, and for his son David, in Paris. What was happening to the Jews in Paris? He prayed for Samuel, now in Brussels. What was happening to the Jews in Brussels? He prayed for Salomon, Perl, and Meir-Ikhiel. Where were they now? He prayed that the Almighty would keep them alive, because the chain had to continue.

On the night of April 17, 1942, Abraham was awakened by Mordecai and several pioneers. The German police were making raids, trying to suppress the clandestine Jewish press once and for all. Mordecai had been warned by a man from the Bundist paper who had been able to escape.

For a week they never set foot outside the basement. They had little to eat. Whenever they had to relieve themselves, they went down to the sewer. They spent their time listening to radio broadcasts in English, French, Russian, and German. The news was ominous: Rommel was threatening Alexandria, Sebastopol had fallen, and all along the immense Russian front the Germans had launched an offensive that, according to Radio Berlin, would make Hitler victorious.

Mordecai and his friends were afraid. If the Suez Canal was threatened, so was Palestine. And if Tel Aviv was conquered, its builders and its children would be exiled or killed, and the destruction would then be complete—not only of a people, but also of its hope.

On April 24 the Germans invaded the building at 22 Nowolipie Street. They were heard running and shouting in the halls. In the evening they pounded their rifle butts against the concrete slab that blocked the entrance to the basement, but they soon stopped and went away, probably thinking it was a wall.

The next day, Mordecai went out to reconnoiter. The Germans, he said when he came back, had taken away all the men in the building. They had executed several dozen people and destroyed several clandestine print shops with flamethrowers.

It was then that Abraham decided, out of prudence, to suspend publication of *Yediess* for a week or two.

ABRAHAM'S DIARY

April 28, 1942. Year 5702 after the creation of the world by the Almighty, blessed be He. Since I now have nothing else to do, I am going to write about the experience of an old man in a basement, hoping that my account will serve as testimony, like the chronicle of another Abraham, son of Nomos, long ago in the faraway city of Hippo.

May 1. Mordecai, may he live a hundred and twenty years, has told me that the Jews in the ghetto are putting together clandestine archives intended for future generations. My poor old heart leapt up when I heard that, and I said, "At last they've understood!"

May 3. According to Proverbs, "Hope deferred makes the heart sick." My God, is it surprising that the Jews are nauseated? Yesterday we thought that Mussolini was dead. It turned out not to be true. It was also said that the *Judenrat* was going to hand out hundreds of visas for Palestine. Long lines immediately formed in front of the *Judenrat*'s building, and thousands of people spent the night there. The story about the visas also turned out not to be true.

May 6. It is now the time of Shabout, the Feast of the Giving of the Law. According to Mordecai it is also the Harvest Festival. He longs for Palestine and his *kibbutz,* where his wife is waiting for him. The Poles have been forbidden to enter the Saxon Garden. Who might see the hand of Providence in that?

May 7. I slept badly last night. I kow that Mordecai's *Chalutzim* do not tell me everything that happens in the ghetto, because they do not want to sadden me. But Baile, one of Nathan's cousins, told me how the Nazis burst into the ghetto cemetery, ordered the Jews to dance around a wagon filled with naked corpses, and filmed the scene. "Return, O Lord! How long? Have pity on Thy servants!"

May 30. Ezra, Topcia's first son, is sick. Typhus, perhaps. "Have pity on Thy servants!"

May 31. "Even if the sky were made of parchment and all reeds were pens," I could not record the horror I feel when I listen to young people telling me what they have seen. Death, over and over again. Sometimes I hear the victims' screams even here.

June 4. It seems that the forty thousand Jews of Lublin have perished. May the Almighty, blessed be His name, have mercy on their souls. Mordecai's friends now come to the basement every evening. Grief always shows in their faces. Outside: destruction. Inside: terror. "Help us, O God of our salvation."

June 17. Year 5702 after the creation of the world by the Almighty, blessed be He. A day of sorrow. Wailing in the morning, lamentations in the evening. "O that my head were waters, and my eyes a fountain of tears." Ezra, Topcia's first son, died at dawn. Moshe, her second son, died in the afternoon. Reward them according to their innocence, O Lord.

June 24. Year 5702 after the creation of the world by the Almighty, blessed be He. For a week, my daughter Topcia mourned for her husband and her children, moaning and bitterly lamenting. Then, at the end of *shiva,* she was seized with violent emotion. "Why?" she said. "Why? Why?" And she too died.

June 26. Year 5702 after the creation of the world by the Almighty, blessed be He. In the cemetery on Gesia Street, the gravediggers were exhausted and there were no rabbis. O Lord, why did You bring me out of my cave? Woe to these eyes that saw those bodies lying in the dust of the streets! Woe to these eyes dried by grief, as though by the wind of the desert! Enduring is our victory. Only that thought helps me to go on despite the weariness of my heart.

July 1, 1942. Year 5702 after the creation of the world by the Almighty, blessed be He. How much longer? "O my God, I cry by day, but Thou dost not answer; and by night, but find no rest." I no longer have much strength left. Each minute is like a thousand years, each day like an eternity. I know that I am nearing the time when the little flame of my soul will be extinguished.

Mordecai and his friends have made contact with some Poles to buy weapons from them. They do not tell me about everything they do. They are afraid I would disapprove. May the Almighty help us to face this new ordeal.

July 21. Year 5702 after the creation of the world by the Almighty, blessed be He. Yesterday was the ninth day of the month of Av, anniversary of the destruction of the Temple. No member of my family was here to listen to me read from the Book of Abraham. "Until the day when the stones of the Temple are rejoined, after being disjoined like the edges of this cloth, may the names that I have written on this scroll, and the names that others will write on it after me, be spoken aloud to rend the silence. Holy, holy, holy, You are the Almighty. Amen." Will there be anyone after me? Will I be the last? Alas!

July 22. Year 5702 after the creation of the world by the Almighty, blessed be He. "There were ten generations from Adam to Noah," it is written in the Chapters of the Fathers, "to show God's long patience as He saw how each of those generations continued to provoke Him, until He engulfed them all in the waters of the Flood." God's long patience: that is why the world can go on existing despite the presence of evil.

July 23. Year 5702 after the creation of the world by the Almighty, blessed be He. Czerniakow, the president of the *Judenrat,* has killed himself. I have often recalled the useless visit that Topica and I paid to him. "God knows everything in advance," said Rabbi Akiba, "but man is given free will." May God protect Czerniakow's soul.

August 11. Year 5702 after the creation of the world by the Almighty, blessed be He. Now we know: we are all going to die. After suspending publication of *Yediess* for too long, we have decided to begin again. Caution would be pointless now. Today we printed this as our headline: "Report by Salbe, a Jew who has come to Warsaw after escaping from Treblinka: a wooden building, five minutes, screams, silence, horribly swollen corpses."

September 10. Year 5702 after the creation of the world by the Almighty, blessed be He. Tomorrow will be Rosh Hashanah, first day of the year 5703. A gigantic police raid has nearly emptied the ghetto. Nathan, our Nathan, who had become like a son to me, was taken. He will not go to Palestine. My eyes have no more tears for weeping.

September 20. Year 5703 after the creation of the world by the Almighty, blessed be He. Yesterday was Yom Kippur. On that awesome day, little Baile was killed by the brutes. And now, O Lord of Hosts, Just Judge, please let me see Your vengeance against the tyrant, for I have entrusted my cause to You.

October 2. Year 5703 after the creation of the world by the Almighty, blessed be He. Mordecai and Hersch have gone to the Aryan section by way of the underground passage. They bought a seven-shot pistol for two thousand zlotys and four boxes of dynamite for five thousand zlotys. I gave them all my savings to buy weapons with, because time has now run out.

October 27. Year 5703 after the creation of the world by the Almighty, blessed be He. Mordecai and his friends spend most of their time on Mila Street, where the members of Mordecai Anielewicz's Jewish Fighting Organization are hiding. They are people of differing political opinions who have had narrow escapes from death and are now preparing to launch an uprising. Mordecai has given me a grenade and told me how to use it. "In Thee our fathers trusted; they trusted, and Thou didst deliver them." And why not us, Lord? Why not us?

January 16, 1943. Year 5703 after the creation of the world by the Almighty, blessed be He. How I regret not having printed a new edition of the Book of Abraham while there was still time! Each of my children would have had a copy, and my mind would now be more at ease.

I have just reread some of these notes and I do not recognize myself in them. Has affliction changed us so much?

January 17. Year 5703 after the creation of the world by the Almighty, blessed be He. The Jewish Fighting Organization has decided to go into action tomorrow. At Mordecai's request, I have printed a leaflet that will be distributed in the ghetto tonight: "Jews! The occupation forces have begun the second phase of our extermination. Do not passively accept death! Defend yourselves! Take up axes, iron bars, knives! Barricade yourselves in your houses! Fight!" I printed about a hundred copies by hand. We have almost no more paper and ink. O Lord, please grant that our persecutors will be punished, that those who kill us will go to hell. Amen.

January 18. Year 5703 after the creation of the world by the Almighty, blessed be He. Hersch, God bless him, has come to see if I needed anything. Mordecai and his friends are now at 58 Zamenhof Street. They are ready. Hersch has told me that the Germans have emptied the hospital. They shot some of the patients and dragged everyone else through the snow to the relocation center.

Gunfire, shouts, an explosion. O Lord!

Abraham came out of the basement in the hope of seeing his persecutors being shot down. He was so weak that his legs were unsteady. Before going into the street, he went up to his apartment to get the Scroll of Abraham, which he had not taken into the basement because he was afraid that the dampness there would damage the papyrus.

The apartment was empty. Doors had been broken open, furniture overturned; the family's belongings were scattered over the floor. Abraham went to the hiding place in the wall and took out the precious scroll wrapped in white cloth.

A sound of boots and voices came from the stairs. Abraham backed toward the French window, holding the Scroll and the Book of Abraham, and the grenade.

"Hands up!" a voice ordered in German. "Drop your packages!"

Abraham continued stepping back until he was on the balcony. Below him, a tank had stopped in front of the building.

"Hands up, Jew!"

Abraham turned sideways and took the pin out of the grenade as Mordecai had taught him to do. Then he said, *"Shema Yisrael. . . ."*

He did not recognize his own voice. He leapt off the balcony and fell toward the tank.

•   •   •

SO DIED ABRAHAM HALTER, my grandfather, a printer in Warsaw.

After the war, my parents and I came back to Poland and began living in Łódź. One day several men met in our house. They wanted to publish a Yiddish newspaper but did not have the type needed for printing it. The next day, my father and I went to Warsaw. A train, a taxi, the Vistula, the big chestnut tree with its roots clinging to time. My father dug into the ground with the short-handled shovel he had brought. When he took out the wooden box, we saw that it had begun to rot.

He opened it: it contained type. The first Yiddish newspaper published in Poland after the war was printed with that type. Our story continued.

My parents often talked to me about the Book of Abraham, the Narbonne millers, the Strasbourg scribes, the Soncino printers; but I hardly listened to them. To make a better world, we wanted to "wipe away the past and start over."

Then my parents died, and then I stopped believing that the better world was for here and now, and then I began painfully missing my family. My parents Perl and Salomon, of course, and my grandfather Abraham, but also the Soncino printers, the Strasbourg scribes, and the Narbonne millers. I wandered alone and in vain between the

693

two poles of my Jewish history: Auschwitz and Israel. I began gathering books and building up card files.

Since I had no children, writing this book was probably the only way I could have perpetuated the message that came to me, through all those generations of fathers and sons, from Abraham the scribe.

Glossary

Adar (Hebrew). Sixth month of the Jewish calendar. The holiday of Purin is celebrated in Adar.

aguna (Hebrew). If a woman's husband has disappeared and it cannot be determined whether he is alive or dead, she is known in Talmudic jurisprudence as an *aguna*. She can remarry only if her husband is found and grants her a divorce or if his death is established.

aleph-beth (Hebrew). When combined, *aleph* and *beth*, the names of the first two letters of the Hebrew alphabet, are used to designate the whole alphabet.

Amoraim (Aramaic). Jewish scholars in Palestine and Babylonia whose work was done in the period extending from the compilation of the Mishnah (about A.D. 200) to the completion of the Talmud (about A.D. 500).

Anusim (Hebrew). Jews who were converted to another religion by force. Many of them continued to practice Judaism in secret.

archisynagogos (Greek). The head of a Jewish congregation or community.

Ashkenazim (Hebrew; singular: *Ashkenazi).* The Jews of middle and northern Europe, as distinct from those of the Mediterranean region, who are known as Sephardim. (From *Ashkenaz*, the name used for Germany in medieval rabbinic writings.)

Av (Hebrew). Eleventh month of the Jewish calendar.

Baba Batra (Hebrew). A Talmudic treatise on property rights.

bar mitzvah (Hebrew). The ceremony that marks a Jewish boy's coming of age at thirteen. In the course of it, he is called upon to read a passage from the Torah to the congregation of the synagogue.

Baruch haba (Hebrew). An expression used for welcoming visitors. It can be freely translated simply as "Welcome."

Baruch ha-Shem (Hebrew). Literally, "Blessed be the Name." It can be used with about the same meaning as "Thank God."

Beezrat ha-Shem (Hebrew). With God's help.

beth din (Aramaic). A rabbinic tribunal.

beth ha-midrash (Hebrew). House of study, academy, rabbinic school.

breithaupt (Alemannic). A type of hat that Alsatian Jews were required to wear.

brit milah (Hebrew). The rite of circumcision.

Cabala (Hebrew). Literally, "tradition." A mystic current in Jewish thought that began in Spain and southern France with publication of the Zohar in the thirteenth century. The Cabala played an important part not only in the life of Jewish communities but also in humanist circles. It was developed to an extraordinary degree in the sixteenth century, largely because of the school founded in Safad by Isaac Luria.

cadi (Arabic). A Moslem religious judge.

chacham (Hebrew). Wise man. In some Sephardic communities, the word is used to designate the chief rabbi.

Chalutzim (Hebrew; singular: *Chalutz*). Literally, "pioneers." The first Zionist immigrants who came to Palestine to found Jewish agricultural settlements and *kibbutzim*.

chametz (Hebrew). Any bread or other baked food made with leaven. Its presence in a Jewish home during the eight days of Passover is strictly forbidden. *Bedikat chametz*, the traditional search for *chametz*, takes place on the evening before the first Passover night.

Chanukah (Hebrew). The Feast of Lights, which commemorates the victory of the Maccabees over the armies of Antiochus IV, the purification of the Temple of Jerusalem, and the return of religious freedom. During this feast it is customary to light one candle in a special candlestick *(chanukiah)* on the first evening, two on the second evening, and so on till the eighth evening.

Chassid (Hebrew; plural: *Chassidim).* Literally, "pious." After first appearing in the Rhineland during the Middle Ages, the mystic doctrine of Chassidism was developed in Poland from 1740 onward, under the authority of Baal Shem Tov (Master of the Good Name), known as the Besht. His followers, the Chassidim, give more importance to prayer than to study and are grouped around miraculous rabbis called *tzaddikim* (righteous men).

chazzan (Hebrew). Cantor.

cherem (Hebrew). Excommunication.

Chevra Kaddisha (Aramaic). Literally, "holy society." A mutual-aid organization that performed social, charitable, and religious functions in each Jewish community. It traditionally dealt primarily with everything relating to the funerals and burials of its members, but in some communities it also maintained poorhouses and hospitals.

Chumash (Hebrew). The Pentateuch.

chuppah (Hebrew). The canopy under which the bride and groom are married at a Jewish wedding. It symbolizes the home they will establish.

chutzpah (Aramaic). Audacity, brazenness, gall.

dhimmi (Arabic). A term applied to members of the religions of the Book who were allowed to live in Moslem countries on condition that they pay a special tax and obey certain prohibitions.

Elohim (Hebrew). One of the names of God.

Elul (Hebrew). Twelfth month of the Jewish calendar.

fattori (Italian). Official title of the three leaders of the Jewish community in Rome.

feredge (Turkish). In Turkey, a wide-sleeved coat worn over a dolman.

gaon (Hebrew; plural: *geonim).* An honorary title given to the heads of the Talmudic academies at Sura and Pumbedita, in Babylonia, from the end of the sixth century to the middle of the eleventh. Also an honorary title given in later times to certain rabbis renowned for their knowledge, such as the Gaon of Vilna in the eighteenth century.

Gemara (Aramaic). Literally, "completion." One of the divisions of the Talmud, namely, the commentaries on the Mishnah by the Amoraim. There is one Gemara for the Palestinian Talmud and another for the Babylonian Talmud.

Gerusia (Greek). A council of elders who, in Alexandria, administered the synagogue and regulated community life.

get (Hebrew). A writ of divorce and, by extension, divorce itself.

Goot yom tev! (Yiddish). "Good holiday!"

goy (Hebrew; plural: *goyim*). A non-Jew.

Haggadah (Hebrew). The story of the Exodus from Egypt, read at the Passover *seder*.

Halacha (Hebrew). Literally, "way." The whole body of religious law based on the Bible, the Talmud, and rabbinic interpretations.

Haskalah (Hebrew). The Jewish equivalent of the Enlightenment, founded by Moses Mendelssohn in eighteenth-century Germany. Its organ was the periodical *Ha-Meassef*. The movement later spread to Poland and Russia, where its proponents, the Maskilim, vigorously opposed the Chassidim.

hatzot (Hebrew). Prayer for the middle of the night.

Heshvan (Hebrew). Second month of the Jewish calendar.

illui (Hebrew). An intellectually gifted young person.

Iyar (Hebrew). Eighth month of the Jewish calendar.

kaddish (Aramaic). Literally, "sanctification." A prayer recited at the end of important passages in the liturgy. It is also recited after the death of a close relative, and has therefore come to be regarded as the prayer for the dead, even though it contains no mention of death. The Christian Lord's Prayer was inspired by the *kaddish*.

kahve (Turkish). Coffee.

kashrut (Hebrew). Fitness for use, according to Jewish religious law.

kehaya (Turkish). A government official in charge of collecting taxes.

ketubah (Hebrew). A marriage contract, written in Aramaic.

kibbutz (Hebrew; plural: *kibbutzim*). A collective farm in Israel, based on the principle of Socialist self-management.

kiddush (Hebrew). The blessing recited over wine at the beginning of *shabbat* and holidays.

Kiddushin (Aramaic). A Talmudic treatise dealing with marriage.

Marriage is called *kiddushin* ("sanctities") to stress its sacred nature.

Kislev (Hebrew). Third month of the Jewish calendar, in which Chanukah is celebrated.

klaus (Yiddish). A small Chassidic chapel.

kosher (Yiddish, from Hebrew *kasher*). Proper, ritually pure; applied to food that is permissible in accordance with Jewish dietary laws.

Lag B'Omer (Hebrew). A Jewish festival celebrated on the eighteenth of Iyar.

Lechaim! (Hebrew). To life!

maariv (Hebrew). Evening prayer.

machzor (Hebrew). Prayer book for religious holidays, as distinct from the *siddur*, the prayer book for other days.

malechet hakodesh (Hebrew). Sacred work. A scribe's work is regarded as *malechet hakodesh*.

marakib (Arabic). A type of ship used for transporting merchandise during the Middle Ages.

Maskilim (Hebrew; singular: *Maskil*). Proponents of the Haskalah, the Jewish Enlightenment.

matzot (Hebrew; singular: *matzah*). Thin cakes of unleavened bread eaten during Passover in memory of the "bread of affliction" eaten by the Hebrews at the time of the Exodus from Egypt.

Mazel tov! (Hebrew). Good luck! Congratulations!

medina (Arabic). The central part of a city.

Megillat Esther (Hebrew). The Scroll of Esther, read each year in the synagogue during Purim.

mellah (Arabic). Name given to a Jewish quarter—in Morocco, for example; the Moslem equivalent of a ghetto.

Messechtah Berachot (Hebrew). Treatise on Benedictions, the first treatise of the Talmud on the different benedictions and their meanings.

meturgan (Hebrew; plural: *meturganim*). Literally, "interpreter." An assistant who repeated loudly and intelligibly, for the public, the teachings given by the head of a Talmudic academy.

Midrash Tanchumah (Aramaic). A rabbinic commentary on the Pentateuch.

Midrashim (Hebrew). Jewish Biblical commentaries written between the fifth and thirteenth centuries.

minhah (Hebrew). The Jewish afternoon liturgy.

minyan (Hebrew; plural: *minyanim*). A group of at least ten Jewish men, required for public Jewish religious services.

Mishnah (Hebrew). The collection of Jewish Oral Law compiled by Judah ha-Nasi in about A.D. 200. The Mishnah is part of the Talmud.

Mitnagdim (Hebrew; singular: *Mitnaged*). Opponents of the Chassidic movement. They reproached Chassidism for its credulous piety, its disdain of study, and its worship of *tzaddikim*. They were particularly numerous in Lithuania.

mitzvah (Hebrew). Commandment, religious precept. The Bible contains six hundred and thirteen *mitzvot*.

mohel (Hebrew). A professional circumciser.

muezzin (from Arabic *mu'adhdhin*). A crier who summons the Moslem faithful to prayer from a minaret.

nasi (Hebrew). Prince; patriarch; exilarch.

neilah (Hebrew). The concluding religious service on Yom Kippur.

ner tamid (Hebrew). The lamp that burns constantly in front of the Holy Ark in a synagogue. Also, a light lit in honor of a dead person.

Nissan (Hebrew). Seventh month of the Jewish calendar, in which Passover occurs.

pan (Polish). A title of nobility.

parnas (Hebrew; plural: *parnasim*). Leader of a Jewish community.

payess (Yiddish). One of the side curls worn by pious Jewish males.

Pesach (Hebrew). Passover.

pilpul (Hebrew). Scholarly discussion; controversy; casuistry; a Talmudic method of reasoning that consists of elaborating many objections to an answer concerning a certain problem.

Pirke Abot (Hebrew). Chapters of the Fathers, a treatise in the Mishnah; it is a collection of sayings and maxims that have been incorporated into the Hebrew liturgy.

Purim (Aramaic). Also called the Feast of Lots. Celebrated during the month of Adar, it commemorates the downfall of Haman and the triumph of Esther and Mordecai. It is a joyous holiday that in some aspects (disguises, games) is similar to the Christian Carnival season. During Purim it is permissible to drink till one can no longer distinguish Haman's name from Mordecai's.

rayas (Turkish). The non-Moslem subjects of the Ottoman empire who had to pay a special head tax and were exempt from military service.

Rebono shel olam (Hebrew). Master of the world.

Rosh Hashanah (Hebrew). The Jewish New Year.

seder (Hebrew). Literally, "order." The Passover meal during which the story of the Exodus is read.

Sefer Chassidim (Hebrew). The Book of the Pious, a twelfth-century Jewish mystical work by Samuel ben Kalonymos, his son Judah ben Samuel, and his relative Eleazar ben Judah.

Sefer Minhagim (Hebrew). The Book of Customs, a compilation by the renowned Talmudic scholar Jacob ben Moses Halevi Mölln, known as Maharil. In this work, Maharil codified some of the ways and customs that were current in the German Judaism of his time.

Sephardim (Hebrew; singular: *Sephardi*). The word originally referred only to Spanish Jews, but later came to be used for Jews from anywhere in the Mediterranean region, as distinct from the Ashkenazim of middle and northern Europe.

shabbat (Hebrew). The Jewish sabbath, a day of rest. Various prohibitions (against making a fire, working, smoking, traveling, etc.) are connected with the observance of *shabbat*.

Shabuot (Hebrew). The Feast of Weeks, or Pentecost, celebrated on the sixth and seventh days of Sivan. Commemorates the giving of the Law to the people of Israel. One of the three pilgrimage festivals in ancient Israel, during which the first fruits of the summer harvest were brought to the Temple. For Shabuot, the Ten Commandments are read in the synagogue.

shaharith (Hebrew). Morning prayer.

Shalom aleichem (Hebrew). "Peace to you," a form of greeting.

shammash (Hebrew). The beadle or sexton of a synagogue.

Shechinah (Hebrew). God's Presence or Radiance.

Shema Yisrael (Hebrew). "Hear, Israel." Beginning of the essential prayer of Judaism: "Hear, Israel: the Lord is our God, the Lord is one."

sheol (Hebrew). The abode of the dead.

Sheva Enaim (Hebrew). *Seven Eyes* in English. It deals with seven important points in Judaism. Its author, a renowned physician and philosopher, was born in Portugal in 1436 and died in Con-

701

stantinople in 1487. This book is not listed by historians of printing in Soncino.

Shevat (Hebrew). Fifth month of the Jewish calendar.

Shevet Yehudah (Hebrew). *The Tribe of Judah,* a book written in about 1520 by the Spanish Jewish historian Solomon ibn-Verga. It describes the persecutions suffered by the Jews since the destruction of the second Temple.

shiva (Hebrew). Literally, "seven." The seven-day period of strict mourning observed after the death of a close relative. During that time, the mourners remain at home, abstain from their usual obligations, and pray.

shofar (Hebrew). The ram's horn that is blown during services for Rosh Hashanah and Yom Kippur. It is also blown during the ceremony of *cherem* (excommunication).

shormer (Alsatian Yiddish). Healer. The word comes from the French *charmer,* "to charm, to bewitch."

shtetl (Yiddish). One of the Jewish village communities that formerly existed in Eastern Europe.

shtramel (Yiddish). The fur hat traditionally worn by Chassidic men.

siddur (Hebrew). The prayer book for ordinary days, as distinct from the *machzor,* the prayer book for religious holidays.

Simchat Torah (Hebrew). Rejoicing in the Torah, a holiday celebrated at the end of Succot, when one annual cycle of reading from the Torah is completed and another is immediately begun. Part of the celebration consists in dancing while scrolls of the Torah are carried in processions inside the synagogue.

Sivan (Hebrew). Ninth month of the Jewish calendar, in which Shabuot occurs.

strea. A woman possessed by spirits of the dead.

Succot (Hebrew). The Feast of Tabernacles, during which it is customary to build booths with roofs of green boughs and eat meals in them, as a reminder of the tents in which the Jews lived while they wandered in the wilderness after leaving Egypt.

szlachcic (Polish). Nobleman.

takhanot (Hebrew). Ordinances enacted by Jewish communities to regulate the lives of their members.

tallit (Hebrew). The prayer shawl worn by Jewish men for morning prayer and holiday services.

Talmud (Hebrew). The compilation of Jewish Oral Law (as distinct from Written Law, or Scripture) begun in the second century and completed in about 500. There are two Talmuds: the Palestinian Talmud, also known as the Jerusalem Talmud, and the Babylonian Talmud. The latter is the authoritative work. The Talmud has two parts, the Mishnah and the Gemara, and is subdivided into Halacha (law) and Haggadah (a collection of such things as anecdotes, parables, legends, prayers, and wise sayings). It is written mainly in Aramaic.

Talmud Torah (Hebrew). An elementary Jewish school.

Tammuz (Hebrew). Tenth month of the Jewish calendar.

Tanach (Hebrew). A common name for the Hebrew Bible, formed from the beginnings of the words designating its main sections: *Torah* (the Pentateuch), *Neviim* (Prophets), and *Chetuvim* (Writings).

Tanaim (Aramaic). Jewish scholars who worked before the compilation of the Mishnah.

Tevet (Hebrew). Fourth month of the Jewish calendar.

Tishah B'Av (Hebrew). Ninth day of the month of Av. A fast is observed on the ninth in memory of the destruction of the first and second Temples of Jerusalem and the expulsion of the Jews from Spain in 1492—all of which took place on this day. According to a legend, the Messiah will come on the ninth of Av.

Tishri (Hebrew). First month of the Jewish calendar, in which Rosh Hashanah and Yom Kippur occur.

Torah (Hebrew). In the strict sense, this word refers to the Pentateuch; more generally, it refers to all of Jewish literature.

Tosaphists (from the Hebrew *tosafot*, "additions"). Disciples of Rashi who made additions to his commentaries.

tzaddik (Hebrew; plural: tzaddikim; feminine: *tzaddika).* A righteous man. In the Chassidic movement, a *tzaddik* is a highly venerated miraculous rabbi who intercedes between God and the faithful.

Tzeneh-Reneh (Yiddish). A Yiddish paraphrase of parts of the Bible, written in the late sixteenth century and intended primarily for women. It is one of the most widely read books in the Jewish world.

tzitzit (Hebrew). The fringes attached to the four corners of the prayer shawl and the *tallit katan* (a garment worn under outer clothing by pious Jewish males). They are intended to be a reminder of the divine commandments.

wali (Arabic). The governor of a city or a province.

Yad ha-Chazakah (Hebrew). The Strong Hand, also known as the Mishnah Torah. Its purpose is to codify the various aspects of Jewish law. It and *Guide for the Perplexed* are the two main works of the Spanish Jewish philosopher and theologian Moses ben Maimon (1135–1204), known as Maimonides, or Rambam, whose Neo-Aristotelian ideas gave rise to great controversy within the Jewish world.

yeshiva (Hebrew; plural: *yeshivot*). Originally, a Talmudic academy; the word is now applied to various types of Jewish religious schools.

Yiddish (from German *jüdisch*, "Jewish"). A Jewish language, written in Hebrew letters, that originated in the Rhineland in the eleventh century. It is derived mainly from High German dialects, with some words of Hebrew and Slavic origin. It was once commonly spoken by the Jews of Central and Eastern Europe and is still spoken by some Jews in the United States, the Soviet Union, Israel, and a number of other countries. It gave rise to a flourishing literature.

Yom Kippur (Hebrew). The Day of Atonement, which begins ten days after the Jewish New Year and is marked by a twenty-four-hour fast.

Yoma (Hebrew). A Talmudic treatise on Yom Kippur.

Zohar (Hebrew). A Cabalistic work published, and presumably written, by Moses of León in the thirteenth century, but ascribed to Simeon bar Yochai. It is the basic text of the Cabala.